Friedman

ONE BASKET

THIRTY-ONE
SHORT STORIES
BY

EDNA FERBER

1947

SIMON AND SCHUSTER, NEW YORK

Table of Contents

INTRODUCTION

୶ୠୖୣ୶

ୠୖ PERHAPS IT WAS THE VERY VASTNESS OF THIS LAND OF OURS THAT caused us to become, these past fifty years, a sort of capsule country in our tastes. We developed a craving for that which was quick and small. The drug-store lunch, the Ford car, the two-day excursion, the tabloid, the movie short, the one-act play. Somehow, in the minds of many Americans, the short story became involved in this quick-mix. That was a mistake.

There is nothing modern, there is nothing ephemeral, there is nothing contemptible in the well-written American short story. Or, for that matter, in the English, Russian, or French short story. All the way from Maugham and de Maupassant and Chekhov to Ring Lardner the short story has served to portray the characteristics, the habits, the manners, the morals, the emotions of a nation, a whole people.

Certainly I knew no such highfalutin arguments as these when first I began to write short stories. I wrote short stories for the same reason that a child has who begins to walk after he has learned to stand up and to balance himself. It was for me the next natural step following newspaper reporting. I still think it is one of the most exhilarating and the most difficult forms of the writing art. When a reader says, "Oh, only a short story!" he has me to fight.

There is something about the pace of the short story that catches the tempo of this country. If it is written with sincerity and skill it portrays a mood, a character, a background, or a situation. Sometimes it is not only typically American, it is universal in its feeling; sometimes its inherent truth is not a thing of the month, but of the years. When this is true, that short story is as genuinely a classic as any novel or play or piece of music.

At seventeen I was a newspaper reporter in the pleasant little tree-shaded town of Appleton, Wisconsin. As there never had been a female reporter in that town I was considered an odd specimen indeed. When, at eighteen, I went to Milwaukee to work on the Milwaukee *Journal* my home town put me down as definitely mad. When a girl of eighteen is put to work in a middle-size city (Milwaukee was about 400,000 then) covering police courts, juvenile courts, feature assignments, interviews, conventions, and flotsam and jetsam of all descriptions, she sees just about all the kinds of people that the human race can produce. Not only that, she sees them at close range, she must make them talk—often against their will—and she must translate them and their story into daily newspaper terms. Mine happened to be a bulletin afternoon paper whose city editor used to shout up and down the city room, "Boil it! Keep it down! Whaddyou think this is—a weekly!" It taught us reporters to jam our story into a single paragraph, to search our very innards for the single right word that would contain the meaning of ten words.

So then, when I left newspaper reporting behind me and began to write fiction it was the short story form that came as the natural step. That first short story was entitled *The Homely Heroine,* and I'm not ashamed of it today. It was the story of a lonely, homely, warmhearted fat girl who never had been kissed, and for years after it was published in the old *Everybody's Magazine* no fat girl in Appleton, Wisconsin, would speak to me. It isn't included in this volume of short stories, but I still insist that it isn't really dated. Just young. That is a fault which I now have overcome. In fact, overdone.

It is difficult to write a really good short story because it must be a complete and finished reflection of life with only a few words to use as tools. There isn't time for bad writing in a short story. In a novel one can be dull for pages and still get away with it. It is, to me, an interesting and baffling fact that today, more than thirty years after *The Homely Heroine* was written, it still is as difficult for me to write a short story (or anything, for that matter) as it was when first I began. A single short story may take a month, six weeks, two months to write. Usually, the easier they are to read the harder they are to write. Often a short story theme may take a year of conscious and subconscious thinking before it is ripe for writing. Sometimes a possible short story seems too tough to be worth the fight. But it stays around, taunting you, daring you to come on, and finally you write it to be rid of it. This might be said of stories, for example only, such as

The Gay Old Dog, Old Man Minick, Trees Die at the Top. There
are many stories of which I am fond but which are not included in this
collection because they aren't good enough, or are too dated, or because
they follow too closely, perhaps, the pattern of another included story. In
some cases the reader may feel, after reading a short story, approximately
the sensation he has experienced after having too hastily eaten a heavy
meal. He has treated a dinner as a snack and his digestion rebels. Some of
these short stories should have been novels. I shan't, here at least, run the
risk attendant on pointing them out.

In these past three decades (and what a three decades they have been,
covering as they have a century of change!) I have followed a certain unconsciously established work-rhythm. A novel, a play, a group of short
stories, and repeat. At this moment I feel impelled to do all three at once.
This may be a bad or a good sign. But good or bad, this act of collecting
more than thirty of my favorite short stories and seeing them snugly en-
cased in book jackets gives me a reassuring, though temporary, feeling of
solidity in a frighteningly fluid world.

During World War I and World War II, I wrote few short stories. I
wrote, in fact, little of anything other than propaganda, and for ordered
propaganda writing I have scant ability. Thousands of fictional so-called
war stories were written. Few possessed the slightest value. The best, in
my opinion, were those published in *The New Yorker* during World War
II. Some of these were brilliant, courageous, and carried a terrific impact.

All my writing life I have written to please first myself. Never, except in
wartime, have I written to order on a theme or subject definitely requested
or suggested. But war, to me, is not life at all. It is an excrescence, a cancer
on the body of civilization. Of the short stories written during World
War I only two or three are included in this book. It is depressing and
actually frightening to realize that today, though more than a quarter of a
century has gone by, the pattern of these old stories could have been applied to today's situations. Of the period covering World War II only two
stories are included here. One is *No Room at the Inn;* the other,
Grandma Isn't Playing. The first was written because I wanted to write
it out of my own indignation and burning sense of injustice. The second

was requested as propaganda and it is printed here purely as an example. In it everything turns out just lovely. This sometimes happens in life, but infrequently.

Here is an interesting point—to me, at least. With the exception of the covered-wagon half of *Trees Die at the Top,* the thirty-one short stories in this book treat of modern life. This, too, is the background of the seven plays which I have written for the theater, in collaboration.

Early in my short-story career I hit upon the character of a traveling saleswoman named Mrs. Emma McChesney. I never had met or seen a traveling saleswoman and I don't know why I named her Emma McChesney, but she became enormously popular and very nearly turned out to be my undoing. The first story, entitled *Representing T. A. Buck,* was published in the *American Magazine* in 1911. I hadn't meant to write a series, but at the urging of the editors I tried a second, called *Roast Beef Medium.* Well, that did it. The American businesswoman, inexplicably enough, had not been presented in fiction. This now seems incredible, but it was so. The magazine-reading public took Emma to its heart. Up and down the land she went, brave as anything, selling her product, which was Featherloom Petticoats, and wrestling with male competitors, hotel accommodations, love, train schedules, and her son, Jock McChesney, as offensive a young whelp as you'd meet in a year's subscription to the *American* or any other magazine. Emma was hearty, salty, good as gold (better), and oh, so courageous. She was fine in her day, but this is not it; she is as dated as the Featherloom Petticoats she sold, and no Emma McChesney story— there were thirty or more—is included in this volume.

Many of the stories contained in this book I have not seen or thought of during these past ten—twenty—twenty-five years. This is not extraordinary. The writer given to rereading his or her past work is a writer in danger. Once you begin to mumble among your souvenirs you're through. Any writer who is properly a writer is working as long as he is alive or awake. It is virtually impossible for a writer to ride in the subway or on a bus, walk on the street or down a country road, telephone, read a book, talk, listen, breathe, without consciously or unconsciously sustaining the act of writing, in his mind at least. The analytical creative mind goes click-click-click while it is awake—and sometimes while it is asleep. It makes the writer's life interesting but somewhat feverish. Frequently one wishes it were possible to turn off the machinery that is eternally registering, collecting, discarding, filing. Writers are a tired lot, for the most part; and no wonder.

It would be pleasant to know that these stories, some born long ago, others still young, have the strength and vitality to make new friends and even to renew old friendships. The writer herself is fond of them, or they would not be here. But the feeling is much that of a parent whose sons and daughters have married and gone off into the world. There they are, on their own at last, sink or swim, live or die. The author is finished with them, everything she can do for them has been done. And a new infant, not yet strong enough to walk alone, waits to be shown a way of life.

EDNA FERBER

Stepney, Connecticut
November, 1946

ONE BASKET

The Woman Who Tried to Be Good
[1913]

Thirty-three years ago, American magazine editors considered this story too daring. It went the rounds and was rejected until The Saturday Evening Post *said they would take it at a very bargain price only. Since the* Post *was a weekly of conventional pattern, I had not considered it as a possibility; but I wanted it published, and they published it. It may seem rather quaint today, with its upper-case Very Young Husband and Very Young Wife, but it has appeared in a number of anthologies and it isn't so dated after all, if you happen to know your small town.*

   BEFORE SHE TRIED TO BE A GOOD WOMAN SHE HAD BEEN A VERY BAD woman—so bad that she could trail her wonderful apparel up and down Main Street, from the Elm Tree Bakery to the railroad tracks, without once having a man doff his hat to her or a woman bow. You passed her on the street with a surreptitious glance, though she was well worth looking at— in her furs and laces and plumes. She had the only full-length mink coat in our town, and Ganz's shoe store sent to Chicago for her shoes. Hers were the miraculously small feet you frequently see in stout women.

Usually she walked alone; but on rare occasions, especially round Christmastime, she might have been seen accompanied by some silent, dull-eyed, stupid-looking girl, who would follow her dumbly in and out of stores, stopping now and then to admire a cheap comb or a chain set with flashy imitation stones—or, queerly enough, a doll with yellow hair and blue eyes and very pink cheeks. But, alone or in company, her appearance in the stores of our town was the signal for a sudden jump in the cost of living. The storekeepers mulcted her; and she knew it and paid in silence, for she was of the class that has no redress. She owned the House with the Closed Shutters, near the freight depot—did Blanche Devine.

In a larger town than ours she would have passed unnoticed. She did not look like a bad woman. Of course she used too much make-up, and as she passed you caught the oversweet breath of a certain heavy scent. Then, too, her diamond eardrops would have made any woman's features look hard; but her plump face, in spite of its heaviness, wore an expression of good-humored intelligence, and her eyeglasses gave her somehow a look of respectability. We do not associate vice with eyeglasses. So in a large city she would have passed for a well-dressed, prosperous, comfortable wife and mother who was in danger of losing her figure from an overabundance of good living; but with us she was a town character, like Old Man Givins, the drunkard, or the weak-minded Binns girl. When she passed the drug-store corner there would be a sniggering among the vacant-eyed loafers idling there, and they would leer at each other and jest in undertones.

So, knowing Blanche Devine as we did, there was something resembling a riot in one of our most respectable neighborhoods when it was learned that she had given up her interest in the house near the freight depot and was going to settle down in the white cottage on the corner and be good. All the husbands in the block, urged on by righteously indignant wives, dropped in on Alderman Mooney after supper to see if the thing could not be stopped. The fourth of the protesting husbands to arrive was the Very Young Husband who lived next door to the corner cottage that Blanche Devine had bought. The Very Young Husband had a Very Young Wife, and they were the joint owners of Snooky. Snooky was three-going-on-four, and looked something like an angel—only healthier and with grimier hands. The whole neighborhood borrowed her and tried to spoil her; but Snooky would not spoil.

Alderman Mooney was down in the cellar, fooling with the furnace. He was in his furnace overalls; a short black pipe in his mouth. Three protesting husbands had just left. As the Very Young Husband, following Mrs. Mooney's directions, descended the cellar stairs, Alderman Mooney looked up from his tinkering. He peered through a haze of pipe smoke.

"Hello!" he called, and waved the haze away with his open palm. "Come on down! Been tinkering with this blamed furnace since supper. She don't draw like she ought. 'Long toward spring a furnace always gets balky. How many tons you used this winter?"

"Oh—five," said the Very Young Husband shortly. Alderman Mooney considered it thoughtfully. The Young Husband leaned up against the side of the water tank, his hands in his pockets. "Say, Mooney, is that right about Blanche Devine's having bought the house on the corner?"

"You're the fourth man that's been in to ask me that this evening. I'm expecting the rest of the block before bedtime. She bought it all right."

The Young Husband flushed and kicked at a piece of coal with the toe of his boot.

"Well, it's a darned shame!" he began hotly. "Jen was ready to cry at supper. This'll be a fine neighborhood for Snooky to grow up in! What's a woman like that want to come into a respectable street for, anyway? I own my home and pay my taxes——"

Alderman Mooney looked up.

"So does she," he interrupted. "She's going to improve the place—paint it, and put in a cellar and a furnace, and build a porch, and lay a cement walk all round."

The Young Husband took his hands out of his pockets in order to emphasize his remarks with gestures.

"What's that got to do with it? I don't care if she puts in diamonds for windows and sets out Italian gardens and a terrace with peacocks on it. You're the alderman of this ward, aren't you? Well, it was up to you to keep her out of this block! You could have fixed it with an injunction or something. I'm going to get up a petition—that's what I'm going——"

Alderman Mooney closed the furnace door with a bang that drowned the rest of the threat. He turned the draft in a pipe overhead and brushed his sooty palms briskly together like one who would put an end to a profitless conversation.

"She's bought the house," he said mildly, "and paid for it. And it's hers. She's got a right to live in this neighborhood as long as she acts respectable."

The Very Young Husband laughed.

"She won't last! They never do."

Alderman Mooney had taken his pipe out of his mouth and was rubbing his thumb over the smooth bowl, looking down at it with unseeing eyes. On his face was a queer look—the look of one who is embarrassed because he is about to say something honest.

"Look here! I want to tell you something: I happened to be up in the mayor's office the day Blanche signed for the place. She had to go through a lot of red tape before she got it—had quite a time of it, she did! And say, kid, that woman ain't so—bad."

The Very Young Husband exclaimed impatiently:

"Oh, don't give me any of that, Mooney! Blanche Devine's a town character. Even the kids know what she is. If she's got religion or something, and wants to quit and be decent, why doesn't she go to another town—Chicago or someplace—where nobody knows her?"

That motion of Alderman Mooney's thumb against the smooth pipe bowl stopped. He looked up slowly.

"That's what I said—the mayor too. But Blanche Devine said she wanted to try it here. She said this was home to her. Funny—ain't it? Said she wouldn't be fooling anybody here. They know her. And if she moved away, she said, it'd leak out some way sooner or later. It does, she said. Always! Seems she wants to live like—well, like other women. She put it like this: she says she hasn't got religion, or any of that. She says she's no different than she was when she was twenty. She says that for the last ten years the ambition of her life has been to be able to go into a grocery store and ask the price of, say, celery; and, if the clerk charged her ten when it ought to be seven, to be able to sass him with a regular piece of her mind—and then sail out and trade somewhere else until he saw that she didn't have to stand anything from storekeepers, any more than any other woman that did her own marketing. She's a smart woman, Blanche is! God knows I ain't taking her part—exactly; but she talked a little, and the mayor and me got a little of her history."

A sneer appeared on the face of the Very Young Husband. He had been known before he met Jen as a rather industrious sower of wild oats. He knew a thing or two, did the Very Young Husband, in spite of his youth! He always fussed when Jen wore even a V-necked summer gown on the street.

"Oh, she wasn't playing for sympathy," went on Alderman Mooney in answer to the sneer. "She said she'd always paid her way and always expected to. Seems her husband left her without a cent when she was eighteen—with a baby. She worked for four dollars a week in a cheap eating house. The two of 'em couldn't live on that. Then the baby——"

"Good night!" said the Very Young Husband. "I suppose Mrs. Mooney's going to call?"

"Minnie! It was her scolding all through supper that drove me down to monkey with the furnace. She's wild—Minnie is." He peeled off his overalls and hung them on a nail. The Young Husband started to ascend the cellar stairs. Alderman Mooney laid a detaining finger on his sleeve. "Don't say anything in front of Minnie! She's boiling! Minnie and the kids are going to visit her folks out West this summer; so I wouldn't so much as dare to say 'Good morning!' to the Devine woman. Anyway, a person wouldn't talk to her, I suppose. But I kind of thought I'd tell you about her."

"Thanks!" said the Very Young Husband dryly.

In the early spring, before Blanche Devine moved in, there came stonemasons, who began to build something. It was a great stone fireplace that rose in massive incongruity at the side of the little white cottage. Blanche Devine was trying to make a home for herself.

Blanche Devine used to come and watch them now and then as the work progressed. She had a way of walking round and round the house, looking up at it and poking at plaster and paint with her umbrella or finger tip. One day she brought with her a man with a spade. He spaded up a neat square of ground at the side of the cottage and a long ridge near the fence that separated her yard from that of the Very Young Couple next door. The ridge spelled sweet peas and nasturtiums to our small-town eyes.

On the day that Blanche Devine moved in there was wild agitation among the white-ruffed bedroom curtains of the neighborhood. Later on certain odors, as of burning dinners, pervaded the atmosphere. Blanche Devine, flushed and excited, her hair slightly askew, her diamond eardrops flashing, directed the moving, wrapped in her great fur coat; but on the third morning we gasped when she appeared out-of-doors, carrying a little household ladder, a pail of steaming water, and sundry voluminous white cloths. She reared the little ladder against the side of the house, mounted it cautiously, and began to wash windows with housewifely thoroughness. Her stout figure was swathed in a gray sweater and on her head was a battered felt hat—the sort of window-washing costume that has been worn by women from time immemorial. We noticed that she used plenty of hot water and clean rags, and that she rubbed the glass until it sparkled, leaning perilously sideways on the ladder to detect elusive streaks. Our keenest housekeeping eye could find no fault with the way Blanche Devine washed windows.

By May, Blanche Devine had left off her diamond eardrops—perhaps it was their absence that gave her face a new expression. When she went downtown we noticed that her hats were more like the hats the other women in our town wore; but she still affected extravagant footgear, as is right and proper for a stout woman who has cause to be vain of her feet. We noticed that her trips downtown were rare that spring and summer. She used to come home laden with little bundles; and before supper she would change her street clothes for a neat, washable housedress, as is our thrifty custom. Through her bright windows we could see her moving briskly about from kitchen to sitting room; and from the smells that floated out from her kitchen door, she seemed to be preparing for her solitary supper the same homely viands that were frying or stewing or baking in our kitchens. Sometimes you could detect the delectable scent of browning, hot tea biscuit. It takes a determined woman to make tea biscuit for no one but herself.

Blanche Devine joined the church. On the first Sunday morning she came to the service there was a little flurry among the ushers at the vestibule door. They seated her well in the rear. The second Sunday morning a dreadful thing happened. The woman next to whom they seated her turned, regarded her stonily for a moment, then rose agitatedly and moved to a pew across the aisle. Blanche Devine's face went a dull red beneath her white powder. She never came again—though we saw the minister visit her once or twice. She always accompanied him to the door pleasantly, holding it well open until he was down the little flight of steps and on the sidewalk. The minister's wife did not call.

She rose early, like the rest of us; and as summer came on we used to see her moving about in her little garden patch in the dewy, golden morning. She wore absurd pale-blue negligees that made her stout figure loom immense against the greenery of garden and apple tree. The neighborhood women viewed these negligees with Puritan disapproval as they smoothed down their own prim, starched gingham skirts. They said it was disgusting —and perhaps it was; but the habit of years is not easily overcome. Blanche Devine—snipping her sweet peas, peering anxiously at the Virginia creeper that clung with such fragile fingers to the trellis, watering the flower baskets that hung from her porch—was blissfully unconscious of the disapproving eyes. I wish one of us had just stopped to call good morning to her over the fence, and to say in our neighborly, small-town way: "My, ain't this a scorcher! So early too! It'll be fierce by noon!" But we did not.

I think perhaps the evenings must have been the loneliest for her. The summer evenings in our little town are filled with intimate, human, neighborly sounds. After the heat of the day it is pleasant to relax in the cool comfort of the front porch, with the life of the town eddying about us. We sew and read out there until it grows dusk. We call across lots to our next-door neighbor. The men water the lawns and the flower boxes and get together in little, quiet groups to discuss the new street paving. I have even known Mrs. Hines to bring her cherries out there when she had canning to do, and pit them there on the front porch partially shielded by her porch vine, but not so effectually that she was deprived of the sights and sounds about her. The kettle in her lap and the dishpan full of great ripe cherries on the porch floor by her chair, she would pit and chat and peer out through the vines, the red juice staining her plump bare arms.

I have wondered since what Blanche Devine thought of us those lonesome evenings—those evenings filled with friendly sights and sounds. It must have been difficult for her, who had dwelt behind closed shutters so long, to seat herself on the new front porch for all the world to stare at; but she did sit there—resolutely—watching us in silence.

She seized hungrily upon the stray crumbs of conversation that fell to her. The milkman and the iceman and the butcher boy used to hold daily conversation with her. They—sociable gentlemen—would stand on her doorstep, one grimy hand resting against the white of her doorpost, exchanging the time of day with Blanche in the doorway—a tea towel in one hand, perhaps, and a plate in the other. Her little house was a miracle of cleanliness. It was no uncommon sight to see her down on her knees on the kitchen floor, wielding her brush and rag like the rest of us. In canning and preserving time there floated out from her kitchen the pungent scent of pickled crab apples; the mouth-watering smell that meant sweet pickles; or the cloying, divinely sticky odor that meant raspberry jam. Snooky, from her side of the fence, often used to peer through the pickets, gazing in the direction of the enticing smells next door.

Early one September morning there floated out from Blanche Devine's kitchen that fragrant, sweet scent of fresh-baked cookies—cookies with butter in them, and spice, and with nuts on top. Just by the smell of them your mind's eye pictured them coming from the oven—crisp brown circlets, crumbly, delectable. Snooky, in her scarlet sweater and cap, sniffed them from afar and straightway deserted her sand pile to take her stand at the fence. She peered through the restraining bars, standing on tiptoe. Blanche Devine, glancing up from her board and rolling pin, saw the eager golden head. And Snooky, with guile in her heart, raised one fat, dimpled hand above the fence and waved it friendlily. Blanche Devine waved back. Thus encouraged, Snooky's two hands wigwagged frantically above the pickets. Blanche Devine hesitated a moment, her floury hand on her hip. Then she went to the pantry shelf and took out a clean white saucer. She selected from the brown jar on the table three of the brownest, crumbliest, most perfect cookies, with a walnut meat perched atop of each, placed them temptingly on the saucer and, descending the steps, came swiftly across the grass to the triumphant Snooky. Blanche Devine held out the saucer, her lips smiling, her eyes tender. Snooky reached up with one plump white arm.

"Snooky!" shrilled a high voice. "Snooky!" A voice of horror and of wrath. "Come here to me this minute! And don't you dare to touch those!" Snooky hesitated rebelliously, one pink finger in her pouting mouth. "Snooky! Do you hear me?"

And the Very Young Wife began to descend the steps of her back porch. Snooky, regretful eyes on the toothsome dainties, turned away aggrieved. The Very Young Wife, her lips set, her eyes flashing, advanced and seized the shrieking Snooky by one arm and dragged her away toward home and safety.

Blanche Devine stood there at the fence, holding the saucer in her hand. The saucer tipped slowly, and the three cookies slipped off and fell to the grass. Blanche Devine stood staring at them a moment. Then she turned quickly, went into the house, and shut the door.

It was about this time we noticed that Blanche Devine was away much of the time. The little white cottage would be empty for weeks. We knew she was out of town because the expressman would come for her trunk. We used to lift our eyebrows significantly. The newspapers and handbills would accumulate in a dusty little heap on the porch; but when she returned there was always a grand cleaning, with the windows open, and

Blanche—her head bound turbanwise in a towel—appearing at a window every few minutes to shake out a dustcloth. She seemed to put an enormous amount of energy into those cleanings—as if they were a sort of safety valve.

As winter came on she used to sit up before her grate fire long, long after we were asleep in our beds. When she neglected to pull down the shades we could see the flames of her cosy fire dancing gnomelike on the wall.

There came a night of sleet and snow, and wind and rattling hail—one of those blustering, wild nights that are followed by morning-paper reports of trains stalled in drifts, mail delayed, telephone and telegraph wires down. It must have been midnight or past when there came a hammering at Blanche Devine's door—a persistent, clamorous rapping. Blanche Devine, sitting before her dying fire half asleep, started and cringed when she heard it, then jumped to her feet, her hand at her breast—her eyes darting this way and that, as though seeking escape.

She had heard a rapping like that before. It had meant bluecoats swarming up the stairway, and frightened cries and pleadings, and wild confusion. So she started forward now, quivering. And then she remembered, being wholly awake now—she remembered, and threw up her head and smiled a little bitterly and walked toward the door. The hammering continued, louder than ever. Blanche Devine flicked on the porch light and opened the door. The half-clad figure of the Very Young Wife next door staggered into the room. She seized Blanche Devine's arm with both her frenzied hands and shook her, the wind and snow beating in upon both of them.

"The baby!" she screamed in a high, hysterical voice. "The baby! The baby——!"

Blanche Devine shut the door and shook the Young Wife smartly by the shoulders.

"Stop screaming," she said quietly. "Is she sick?"

The Young Wife told her, her teeth chattering:

"Come quick! She's dying! Will's out of town. I tried to get the doctor. The telephone wouldn't—— I saw your light! For God's sake——"

Blanche Devine grasped the Young Wife's arm, opened the door, and together they sped across the little space that separated the two houses. Blanche Devine was a big woman, but she took the stairs like a girl and found the right bedroom by some miraculous woman instinct. A dreadful choking, rattling sound was coming from Snooky's bed.

"Croup," said Blanche Devine, and began her fight.

It was a good fight. She marshaled her inadequate forces, made up of the half-fainting Young Wife and the terrified and awkward hired girl.

"Get the hot water on—lots of it!" Blanche Devine pinned up her sleeves. "Hot cloths! Tear up a sheet—or anything! Got an oilstove? I want a tea-kettle boiling in the room. She's got to have the steam. If that don't do it we'll raise an umbrella over her and throw a sheet over, and hold the kettle under till the steam gets to her that way. Got any ipecac?"

The Young Wife obeyed orders, white-faced and shaking. Once Blanche Devine glanced up at her sharply.

"Don't you dare faint!" she commanded.

And the fight went on. Gradually the breathing that had been so frightful became softer, easier. Blanche Devine did not relax. It was not until the little figure breathed gently in sleep that Blanche Devine sat back, satisfied. Then she tucked a cover at the side of the bed, took a last satisfied look at the face on the pillow, and turned to look at the wan, disheveled Young Wife.

"She's all right now. We can get the doctor when morning comes—though I don't know's you'll need him."

The Young Wife came round to Blanche Devine's side of the bed and stood looking up at her.

"My baby died," said Blanche Devine simply. The Young Wife gave a little inarticulate cry, put her two hands on Blanche Devine's broad shoulders, and laid her tired head on her breast.

"I guess I'd better be going," said Blanche Devine.

The Young Wife raised her head. Her eyes were round with fright.

"Going! Oh, please stay! I'm so afraid. Suppose she should take sick again! That awful—breathing——"

"I'll stay if you want me to."

"Oh, please! I'll make up your bed and you can rest——"

"I'm not sleepy. I'm not much of a hand to sleep anyway. I'll sit up here in the hall, where there's a light. You get to bed. I'll watch and see that everything's all right. Have you got something I can read out here—something kind of lively—with a love story in it?"

So the night went by. Snooky slept in her white bed. The Very Young Wife half dozed in her bed, so near the little one. In the hall, her stout figure looming grotesque in wall shadows, sat Blanche Devine, pretending to read. Now and then she rose and tiptoed into the bedroom with miraculous quiet, and stooped over the little bed and listened and looked—and tiptoed away again, satisfied.

The Young Husband came home from his business trip next day with tales of snowdrifts and stalled engines. Blanche Devine breathed a sigh of relief when she saw him from her kitchen window. She watched the house now with a sort of proprietary eye. She wondered about Snooky; but she knew better than to ask. So she waited. The Young Wife next door had told her husband all about that awful night—had told him with tears and sobs. The Very Young Husband had been very, very angry with her—angry, he said, and astonished! Snooky could not have been so sick! Look at her now! As well as ever. And to have called such a woman! Well, he did not want to be harsh; but she must understand that she must never speak to the woman again. Never!

So the next day the Very Young Wife happened to go by with the Young Husband. Blanche Devine spied them from her sitting-room window, and she made the excuse of looking in her mailbox in order to go to the door. She stood in the doorway and the Very Young Wife went by on the arm of her husband. She went by—rather white-faced—without a look or a word or a sign!

And then this happened! There came into Blanche Devine's face a look that made slits of her eyes, and drew her mouth down into an ugly, narrow line, and that made the muscles of her jaw tense and hard. It was the ugliest look you can imagine. Then she smiled—if having one's lips curl away from one's teeth can be called smiling.

Two days later there was great news of the white cottage on the corner. The curtains were down; the furniture was packed; the rugs were rolled. The wagons came and backed up to the house and took those things that had made a home for Blanche Devine. And when we heard that she had bought back her interest in the House with the Closed Shutters, near the freight depot, we sniffed.

"I knew she wouldn't last!" we said.

"They never do!" said we.

The Gay Old Dog

[1917]

This should, of course, have been a novel. For years I packed full-length book material into short stories. It was like stuffing a trunkful of clothes into a suitcase. I jammed it down, sat on the lid, and if a bit of sleeve or coat collar protruded I snipped it off. This is the life story of the middle-aged, unmarried brother of three selfish sisters. Written about thirty years ago, it is a rather good example of condensation. I hadn't read it in years, but now, when I came to the description of the parade, I wept a little—which was gratifying.

✒ THOSE OF YOU WHO HAVE DWELT—OR EVEN LINGERED—IN CHICAGO, Illinois, are familiar with the region known as the Loop. For those others of you to whom Chicago is a transfer point between New York and California there is presented this brief explanation:

The Loop is a clamorous, smoke-infested district embraced by the iron arms of the elevated tracks. In a city boasting fewer millions, it would be known familiarly as downtown. From Congress to Lake Street, from Wabash almost to the river, those thunderous tracks make a complete circle, or loop. Within it lie the retail shops, the commercial hotels, the theaters, the restaurants. It is the Fifth Avenue and the Broadway of Chicago. And he who frequents it by night in search of amusement and cheer is known, vulgarly, as a Loop-hound.

Jo Hertz was a Loop-hound. On the occasion of those sparse first nights granted the metropolis of the Middle West he was always present, third row, aisle, left. When a new Loop café was opened, Jo's table always commanded an unobstructed view of anything worth viewing. On entering he was wont to say, "Hello, Gus," with careless cordiality to the headwaiter, the while his eye roved expertly from table to table as he removed his gloves. He ordered things under glass, so that his table, at midnight or thereabouts, resembled a hotbed that favors the bell system. The waiters fought for him. He was the kind of man who mixes his own salad dressing. He liked to call for a bowl, some cracked ice, lemon, garlic, paprika, salt, pepper, vinegar, and oil and make a rite of it. People at near-by tables would lay down their knives and forks to watch, fascinated. The secret of it seemed to lie in using all the oil in sight and calling for more.

That was Jo—a plump and lonely bachelor of fifty. A plethoric, roving-eyed, and kindly man, clutching vainly at the garments of a youth that

11

had long slipped past him. Jo Hertz, in one of those pinch-waist suits and a belted coat and a little green hat, walking up Michigan Avenue of a bright winter's afternoon, trying to take the curb with a jaunty youthfulness against which every one of his fat-encased muscles rebelled, was a sight for mirth or pity, depending on one's vision.

The gay-dog business was a late phase in the life of Jo Hertz. He had been a quite different sort of canine. The staid and harassed brother of three unwed and selfish sisters is an underdog.

At twenty-seven Jo had been the dutiful, hard-working son (in the wholesale harness business) of a widowed and gummidging mother, who called him Joey. Now and then a double wrinkle would appear between Jo's eyes—a wrinkle that had no business there at twenty-seven. Then Jo's mother died, leaving him handicapped by a deathbed promise, the three sisters, and a three-story-and-basement house on Calumet Avenue. Jo's wrinkle became a fixture.

"Joey," his mother had said, in her high, thin voice, "take care of the girls."

"I will, Ma," Jo had choked.

"Joey," and the voice was weaker, "promise me you won't marry till the girls are all provided for." Then as Jo had hesitated, appalled: "Joey, it's my dying wish. Promise!"

"I promise, Ma," he had said.

Whereupon his mother had died, comfortably, leaving him with a completely ruined life.

They were not bad-looking girls, and they had a certain style, too. That is, Stell and Eva had. Carrie, the middle one, taught school over on the West Side. In those days it took her almost two hours each way. She said the kind of costume she required should have been corrugated steel. But all three knew what was being worn, and they wore it—or fairly faithful copies of it. Eva, the housekeeping sister, had a needle knack. She could skim the State Street windows and come away with a mental photograph of every separate tuck, hem, yoke, and ribbon. Heads of departments showed her the things they kept in drawers, and she went home and reproduced them with the aid of a seamstress by the day. Stell, the youngest, was the beauty. They called her Babe.

Twenty-three years ago one's sisters did not strain at the household leash, nor crave a career. Carrie taught school, and hated it. Eva kept house expertly and complainingly. Babe's profession was being the family beauty, and it took all her spare time. Eva always let her sleep until ten.

This was Jo's household, and he was the nominal head of it. But it was an empty title. The three women dominated his life. They weren't consciously selfish. If you had called them cruel they would have put you down as mad. When you are the lone brother of three sisters, it means that you must constantly be calling for, escorting, or dropping one of them somewhere. Most men of Jo's age were standing before their mirror of a Saturday night, whistling blithely and abstractedly while they discarded a blue polka-dot for a maroon tie, whipped off the maroon for a shot-silk, and at the last moment decided against the shot-silk in favor of a plain black-and-white because she had once said she preferred quiet ties. Jo, when he should have been preening his feathers for conquest, was saying:

"Well, my God, I *am* hurrying! Give a man time, can't you? I just got home. You girls been laying around the house all day. No wonder you're ready."

He took a certain pride in seeing his sisters well dressed, at a time when he should have been reveling in fancy waistcoats and brilliant-hued socks, according to the style of that day and the inalienable right of any unwed male under thirty, in any day. On those rare occasions when his business necessitated an out-of-town trip, he would spend half a day floundering about the shops selecting handkerchiefs, or stockings, or feathers, or gloves for the girls. They always turned out to be the wrong kind, judging by their reception.

From Carrie, "What in the world do I want of long white gloves!"

"I thought you didn't have any," Jo would say.

"I haven't. I never wear evening clothes."

Jo would pass a futile hand over the top of his head, as was his way when disturbed. "I just thought you'd like them. I thought every girl liked long white gloves. Just," feebly, "just to—to have."

"Oh, for pity's sake!"

And from Eva or Babe, "I've *got* silk stockings, Jo." Or, "You brought me handkerchiefs the last time."

There was something selfish in his giving, as there always is in any gift freely and joyfully made. They never suspected the exquisite pleasure it gave him to select these things, these fine, soft, silken things. There were many things about this slow-going, amiable brother of theirs that they never suspected. If you had told them he was a dreamer of dreams, for example, they would have been amused. Sometimes, dead-tired by nine o'clock after a hard day downtown, he would doze over the evening paper. At intervals he would wake, red-eyed, to a snatch of conversation such as, "Yes, but if you get a blue you can wear it anywhere. It's dressy, and at the same time it's quiet, too." Eva, the expert, wrestling with Carrie over the problem of the new spring dress. They never guessed that the commonplace man in the frayed old smoking jacket had banished them all from the room long ago; had banished himself, for that matter. In his place was a tall, debonair, and rather dangerously handsome man to whom six o'clock spelled evening clothes. The kind of man who can lean up against a mantel, or propose a toast, or give an order to a manservant, or whisper a gallant speech in a lady's ear with equal ease. The shabby old house on Calumet Avenue was transformed into a brocaded and chandeliered rendezvous for the brilliance of the city. Beauty was here, and wit. But none so beautiful and witty as She. Mrs.—er—Jo Hertz. There was wine, of course; but no vulgar display. There was music; the soft sheen of satin; laughter. And he, the gracious, tactful host, king of his own domain——

"Jo, for heaven's sake, if you're going to snore, go to bed!"

"Why—did I fall asleep?"

"You haven't been doing anything else all evening. A person would think you were fifty instead of thirty."

And Jo Hertz was again just the dull, gray, commonplace brother of three well-meaning sisters.

Babe used to say petulantly, "Jo, why don't you ever bring home any of your men friends? A girl might as well not have any brother, all the good you do."

Jo, conscience-stricken, did his best to make amends. But a man who has been petticoat-ridden for years loses the knack, somehow, of comradeship with men.

One Sunday in May Jo came home from a late-Sunday-afternoon walk to find company for supper. Carrie often had in one of her schoolteacher friends, or Babe one of her frivolous intimates, or even Eva a staid guest of the old-girl type. There was always a Sunday-night supper of potato salad, and cold meat, and coffee, and perhaps a fresh cake. Jo rather enjoyed it, being a hospitable soul. But he regarded the guests with the undazzled eyes of a man to whom they were just so many petticoats, timid of the night streets and requiring escort home. If you had suggested to him that some of his sisters' popularity was due to his own presence, or if you had hinted that the more kittenish of these visitors were probably making eyes at him, he would have stared in amazement and unbelief.

This Sunday night it turned out to be one of Carrie's friends.

"Emily," said Carrie, "this is my brother, Jo."

Jo had learned what to expect in Carrie's friends. Drab-looking women in the late thirties, whose facial lines all slanted downward.

"Happy to meet you," said Jo, and looked down at a different sort altogether. A most surprisingly different sort, for one of Carrie's friends. This

Emily person was very small, and fluffy, and blue-eyed, and crinkly looking. The corners of her mouth when she smiled, and her eyes when she looked up at you, and her hair, which was brown, but had the miraculous effect, somehow, of looking golden.

Jo shook hands with her. Her hand was incredibly small, and soft, so that you were afraid of crushing it, until you discovered she had a firm little grip all her own. It surprised and amused you, that grip, as does a baby's unexpected clutch on your patronizing forefinger. As Jo felt it in his own big clasp, the strangest thing happened to him. Something inside Jo Hertz stopped working for a moment, then lurched sickeningly, then thumped like mad. It was his heart. He stood staring down at her, and she up at him, until the others laughed. Then their hands fell apart, lingeringly.

"Are you a schoolteacher, Emily?" he said.

"Kindergarten. It's my first year. And don't call me Emily, please."

"Why not? It's your name. I think it's the prettiest name in the world." Which he hadn't meant to say at all. In fact, he was perfectly aghast to find himself saying it. But he meant it.

At supper he passed her things, and stared, until everybody laughed again, and Eva said acidly, "Why don't you feed her?"

It wasn't that Emily had an air of helplessness. She just made him feel he wanted her to be helpless, so that he could help her.

Jo took her home, and from that Sunday night he began to strain at the leash. He took his sisters out, dutifully, but he would suggest, with a carelessness that deceived no one, "Don't you want one of your girl friends to come along? That little What's-her-name—Emily, or something. So long's I've got three of you, I might as well have a full squad."

For a long time he didn't know what was the matter with him. He only knew he was miserable, and yet happy. Sometimes his heart seemed to ache with an actual physical ache. He realized that he wanted to do things for Emily. He wanted to buy things for Emily—useless, pretty, expensive things that he couldn't afford. He wanted to buy everything that Emily needed, and everything that Emily desired. He wanted to marry Emily. That was it. He discovered that one day, with a shock, in the midst of a transaction in the harness business. He stared at the man with whom he was dealing until that startled person grew uncomfortable.

"What's the matter, Hertz?"

"Matter?"

"You look as if you'd seen a ghost or found a gold mine. I don't know which."

"Gold mine," said Jo. And then, "No. Ghost."

For he remembered that high, thin voice, and his promise. And the harness business was slithering downhill with dreadful rapidity, as the automobile business began its amazing climb. Jo tried to stop it. But he was not that kind of businessman. It never occurred to him to jump out of the down-going vehicle and catch the up-going one. He stayed on, vainly applying brakes that refused to work.

"You know, Emily, I couldn't support two households now. Not the way things are. But if you'll wait. If you'll only wait. The girls might—that is, Babe and Carrie——"

She was a sensible little thing, Emily. "Of course I'll wait. But we mustn't just sit back and let the years go by. We've got to help."

She went about it as if she were already a little matchmaking matron. She corralled all the men she had ever known and introduced them to Babe, Carrie, and Eva separately, in pairs, and en masse. She got up picnics. She stayed home while Jo took the three about. When she was present she tried to look as plain and obscure as possible, so that the sisters should show up to advantage. She schemed, and planned, and contrived, and hoped; and smiled into Jo's despairing eyes.

And three years went by. Three precious years. Carrie still taught school, and hated it. Eva kept house more and more complainingly as prices advanced and allowance retreated. Stell was still Babe, the family beauty. Emily's hair, somehow, lost its glint and began to look just plain brown. Her crinkliness began to iron out.

"Now, look here!" Jo argued, desperately, one night. "We could be happy, anyway. There's plenty of room at the house. Lots of people begin that way. Of course, I couldn't give you all I'd like to, at first. But maybe, after a while——"

No dreams of salons, and brocade, and velvet-footed servitors, and satin damask now. Just two rooms, all their own, all alone, and Emily to work for. That was his dream. But it seemed less possible than that other absurd one had been.

Emily was as practical a little thing as she looked fluffy. She knew women. Especially did she know Eva, and Carrie, and Babe. She tried to imagine herself taking the household affairs and the housekeeping pocketbook out of Eva's expert hands. So then she tried to picture herself allowing the reins of Jo's house to remain in Eva's hands. And everything feminine and normal in her rebelled. Emily knew she'd want to put away her own freshly laundered linen, and smooth it, and pat it. She was that kind of woman. She knew she'd want to do her own delightful haggling with butcher and grocer. She knew she'd want to muss Jo's hair, and sit on his knee, and even quarrel with him, if necessary, without the awareness of three ever-present pairs of maiden eyes and ears.

"No! No! We'd only be miserable. I know. Even if they didn't object. And they would, Jo. Wouldn't they?"

His silence was miserable assent. Then, "But you do love me, don't you, Emily?"

"I do, Jo. I love you—and love you—and love you. But, Jo, I—can't."

"I know it, dear. I knew it all the time, really. I just thought, maybe, somehow——"

The two sat staring for a moment into space, their hands clasped. Then they both shut their eyes with a little shudder, as though what they saw was terrible to look upon. Emily's hand, the tiny hand that was so unexpectedly firm, tightened its hold on his, and his crushed the absurd fingers until she winced with pain.

That was the beginning of the end, and they knew it.

Emily wasn't the kind of girl who would be left to pine. There are too many Jos in the world whose hearts are prone to lurch and then thump at the feel of a soft, fluttering, incredibly small hand in their grip. One year later Emily was married to a young man whose father owned a large, pie-shaped slice of the prosperous state of Michigan.

That being safely accomplished, there was something grimly humorous in the trend taken by affairs in the old house on Calumet. For Eva married. Married well, too, though he was a great deal older than she. She went off in a hat she had copied from a French model at Field's, and a suit she had contrived with a home dressmaker, aided by pressing on the part of the little tailor in the basement over on Thirty-first Street. It was the last of that, though. The next time they saw her, she had on a hat that even she would have despaired of copying, and a suit that sort of melted into your gaze. She moved to the North Side (trust Eva for that), and Babe assumed the management of the household on Calumet Avenue. It was rather a pinched little household now, for the harness business shrank and shrank.

"I don't see how you can expect me to keep house decently on this!" Babe would say contemptuously. Babe's nose, always a little inclined to sharpness, had whittled down to a point of late. "If you knew what Ben gives Eva."

"It's the best I can do, Sis. Business is something rotten."

"Ben says if you had the least bit of——" Ben was Eva's husband, and quotable, as are all successful men.

"I don't care what Ben says," shouted Jo, goaded into rage. "I'm sick of your everlasting Ben. Go and get a Ben of your own, why don't you, if you're so stuck on the way he does things."

And Babe did. She made a last desperate drive, aided by Eva, and she captured a rather surprised young man in the brokerage way, who had made up his mind not to marry for years and years. Eva wanted to give her her wedding things, but at that Jo broke into sudden rebellion.

"No, sir! No Ben is going to buy my sister's wedding clothes, understand? I guess I'm not broke—yet. I'll furnish the money for her things, and there'll be enough of them, too."

Babe had as useless a trousseau, and as filled with extravagant pink-and-blue and lacy and frilly things, as any daughter of doting parents. Jo seemed to find a grim pleasure in providing them. But it left him pretty well pinched. After Babe's marriage (she insisted that they call her Estelle now) Jo sold the house on Calumet. He and Carrie took one of those little flats that were springing up, seemingly overnight, all through Chicago's South Side.

There was nothing domestic about Carrie. She had given up teaching two years before, and had gone into social-service work on the West Side. She had what is known as a legal mind—hard, clear, orderly—and she made a great success of it. Her dream was to live at the Settlement House and give all her time to the work. Upon the little household she bestowed a certain amount of grim, capable attention. It was the same kind of attention she would have given a piece of machinery whose oiling and running had been entrusted to her care. She hated it, and didn't hesitate to say so.

Jo took to prowling about department-store basements, and household-goods sections. He was always sending home a bargain in a ham, or a sack of potatoes, or fifty pounds of sugar, or a window clamp, or a new kind of paring knife. He was forever doing odd jobs that the janitor should have done. It was the domestic in him claiming its own.

Then, one night, Carrie came home with a dull glow in her leathery cheeks, and her eyes alight with resolve. They had what she called a plain talk.

"Listen, Jo. They've offered me the job of first assistant resident worker. And I'm going to take it. Take it! I know fifty other girls who'd give their ears for it. I go in next month."

They were at dinner. Jo looked up from his plate, dully. Then he glanced around the little dining room, with its ugly tan walls and its heavy, dark furniture (the Calumet Avenue pieces fitted cumbersomely into the five-room flat).

"Away? Away from here, you mean—to live?"

Carrie laid down her fork. "Well, really, Jo! After all that explanation.'

"But to go over there to live! Why, that neighborhood's full of dirt, and disease, and crime, and the Lord knows what all. I can't let you do that, Carrie."

Carrie's chin came up. She laughed a short little laugh. "Let me! That's eighteenth-century talk, Jo. My life's my own to live. I'm going."

And she went.

Jo stayed on in the apartment until the lease was up. Then he sold what furniture he could, stored or gave away the rest, and took a room on Michigan Avenue in one of the old stone mansions whose decayed splendor was being put to such purpose.

Jo Hertz was his own master. Free to marry. Free to come and go. And he found he didn't even think of marrying. He didn't even want to come or go, particularly. A rather frumpy old bachelor, with thinning hair and a thickening neck.

Every Thursday evening he took dinner at Eva's, and on Sunday noon at Stell's. He tucked his napkin under his chin and openly enjoyed the homemade soup and the well-cooked meats. After dinner he tried to talk business with Eva's husband, or Stell's. His business talks were the old-fashioned kind, beginning:

"Well, now, looka here. Take, f'rinstance, your raw hides and leathers."

But Ben and George didn't want to take, f'rinstance, your raw hides and leathers. They wanted, when they took anything at all, to take golf, or politics, or stocks. They were the modern type of businessman who prefers to leave his work out of his play. Business, with them, was a profession—a finely graded and balanced thing, differing from Jo's clumsy, downhill style as completely as does the method of a great criminal detective differ from that of a village constable. They would listen, restively, and say, "Uh-uh," at intervals, and at the first chance they would sort of fade out of the room, with a meaning glance at their wives. Eva had two children now. Girls. They treated Uncle Jo with good-natured tolerance. Stell had no children. Uncle Jo degenerated, by almost imperceptible degrees, from the position of honored guest, who is served with white meat, to that of one who is content with a leg and one of those obscure and bony sections which, after much turning with a bewildered and investigating knife and fork, leave one baffled and unsatisfied.

Eva and Stell got together and decided that Jo ought to marry.

"It isn't natural," Eva told him. "I never saw a man who took so little interest in women."

"Me!" protested Jo, almost shyly. "Women!"

"Yes. Of course. You act like a frightened schoolboy."

So they had in for dinner certain friends and acquaintances of fitting age. They spoke of them as "splendid girls." Between thirty-six and forty. They talked awfully well, in a firm, clear way, about civics, and classes, and politics, and economics, and boards. They rather terrified Jo. He didn't understand much that they talked about, and he felt humbly inferior, and yet a little resentful, as if something had passed him by. He escorted them home, dutifully, though they told him not to bother, and they evidently meant it. They seemed capable not only of going home quite unattended but of delivering a pointed lecture to any highwayman or brawler who might molest them.

The following Thursday Eva would say, "How did you like her, Jo?"

"Like who?" Joe would spar feebly.

"Miss Matthews."

"Who's she?"

"Now, don't be funny, Jo. You know very well I mean the girl who was here for dinner. The one who talked so well on the emigration question."

"Oh, her! Why, I liked her all right. Seems to be a smart woman."

"Smart! She's a perfectly splendid girl."

"Sure," Jo would agree cheerfully.

"But didn't you like her?"

"I can't say I did, Eve. And I can't say I didn't. She made me think a lot of a teacher I had in the fifth reader. Name of Himes. As I recall her, she must have been a fine woman. But I never thought of Himes as a woman at all. She was just Teacher."

"You make me tired," snapped Eva impatiently. "A man of your age. You don't expect to marry a girl, do you? A child!"

"I don't expect to marry anybody," Jo had answered.

And that was the truth, lonely though he often was.

The following spring Eva moved to Winnetka. Anyone who got the meaning of the Loop knows the significance of a move to a North Shore suburb, and a house. Eva's daughter, Ethel, was growing up, and her mother had an eye on society.

That did away with Jo's Thursday dinners. Then Stell's husband bought a car. They went out into the country every Sunday. Stell said it was getting so that maids objected to Sunday dinners, anyway. Besides, they were unhealthful, old-fashioned things. They always meant to ask Jo to come along, but by the time their friends were placed, and the lunch, and the boxes, and sweaters, and George's camera, and everything, there seemed to be no room for a man of Jo's bulk. So that eliminated the Sunday dinners.

"Just drop in any time during the week," Stell said, "for dinner. Except Wednesday—that's our bridge night—and Saturday. And, of course, Thursday. Cook is out that night. Don't wait for me to phone."

And so Jo drifted into that sad-eyed, dyspeptic family made up of those you see dining in second-rate restaurants, their paper propped up against the bowl of oyster crackers, munching solemnly and with indifference to the stare of the passer-by surveying them through the brazen plate-glass window.

And then came the war. The war that spelled death and destruction to millions. The war that brought a fortune to Jo Hertz, and transformed him, overnight, from a baggy-kneed old bachelor whose business was a failure to a prosperous manufacturer whose only trouble was the shortage in hides for the making of his product. Leather! The armies of Europe called for it. Harnesses! More harnesses! Straps! Millions of straps. More! More!

The musty old harness business over on Lake Street was magically changed from a dust-covered, dead-alive concern to an orderly hive that hummed and glittered with success. Orders poured in. Jo Hertz had inside information on the war. He knew about troops and horses. He talked with French and English and Italian buyers commissioned by their countries to get American-made supplies. And now, when he said to Ben or George, "Take, f'rinstance, your raw hides and leathers," they listened with respectful attention.

And then began the gay-dog business in the life of Jo Hertz. He developed into a Loop-hound, ever keen on the scent of fresh pleasure. That side of Jo Hertz which had been repressed and crushed and ignored began to bloom, unhealthily. At first he spent money on his rather contemptuous nieces. He sent them gorgeous furs, and watch bracelets, and bags. He took two expensive rooms at a downtown hotel, and there was something more tear-compelling than grotesque about the way he gloated over the luxury of a separate ice-water tap in the bathroom. He explained it.

"Just turn it on. Any hour of the day or night. Ice water!"

He bought a car. Naturally. A glittering affair; in color a bright blue, with pale-blue leather straps and a great deal of gold fittings, and special tires. Eva said it was the kind of thing a chorus girl would use, rather than an elderly businessman. You saw him driving about in it, red-faced and rather awkward at the wheel. You saw him, too, in the Pompeian Room at the Congress Hotel of a Saturday afternoon when roving-eyed matrons in mink coats are wont to congregate to sip pale-amber drinks. Actors grew to recognize the semibald head and the shining, round, good-natured face looming out at them from the dim well of the theater, and sometimes, in a musical show, they directed a quip at him, and he liked it. He could pick out the critics as they came down the aisle, and even had a nodding acquaintance with two of them.

"Kelly, of the *Herald*," he would say carelessly. "Bean, of the *Trib*. They're all afraid of him."

So he frolicked, ponderously. In New York he might have been called a Man About Town

And he was lonesome. He was very lonesome. So he searched about in his mind and brought from the dim past the memory of the luxuriously furnished establishment of which he used to dream in the evenings when he dozed over his paper in the old house on Calumet. So he rented an apartment, many-roomed and expensive, with a manservant in charge, and furnished it in styles and periods ranging through all the Louis. The living room was mostly rose color. It was like an unhealthy and bloated boudoir. And yet there was nothing sybaritic or uncleanly in the sight of this paunchy, middle-aged man sinking into the rosy-cushioned luxury of his ridiculous home. It was a frank and naïve indulgence of long-starved senses, and there was in it a great resemblance to the rolling-eyed ecstasy of a schoolboy smacking his lips over an all-day sucker.

The war went on, and on, and on. And the money continued to roll in— a flood of it. Then, one afternoon, Eva, in town on shopping bent, entered a small, exclusive, and expensive shop on Michigan Avenue. Eva's weakness was hats. She was seeking a hat now. She described what she sought with a languid conciseness, and stood looking about her after the saleswoman had vanished in quest of it. The room was becomingly rose-illumined and somewhat dim, so that some minutes had passed before she realized that a man seated on a raspberry brocade settee not five feet away— a man with a walking stick, and yellow gloves, and tan spats, and a check suit—was her brother Jo. From him Eva's wild-eyed glance leaped to the woman who was trying on hats before one of the many long mirrors. She was seated, and a saleswoman was exclaiming discreetly at her elbow.

Eva turned sharply and encountered her own saleswoman returning, hat-laden. "Not today," she gasped. "I'm feeling ill. Suddenly." And almost ran from the room.

That evening she told Stell, relating her news in that telephone pidgin English devised by every family of married sisters as protection against the neighbors. Translated, it ran thus:

"He looked straight at me. My dear, I thought I'd die! But at least he had sense enough not to speak. She was one of those limp, willowy creatures with the greediest eyes that she tried to keep softened to a baby stare, and couldn't, she was so crazy to get her hands on those hats. I saw it all in one awful minute. You know the way I do. I suppose some people would call her pretty. I don't. And her color. Well! And the most expensive-looking hats. Not one of them under seventy-five. Isn't it disgusting! At his age! Suppose Ethel had been with me!"

The next time it was Stell who saw them. In a restaurant. She said it spoiled her evening. And the third time it was Ethel. She was one of the guests at a theater party given by Nicky Overton II. The North Shore Overtons. Lake Forest. They came in late, and occupied the entire third row at the opening performance of *Believe Me!* And Ethel was Nicky's partner. She was glowing like a rose. When the lights went up after the first act Ethel saw that her uncle Jo was seated just ahead of her with what she afterward described as a blonde. Then her uncle had turned around, and seeing her, had been surprised into a smile that spread genially all over his plump and rubicund face. Then he had turned to face forward again, quickly.

"Who's the old bird?" Nicky had asked. Ethel had pretended not to hear, so he had asked again.

"My uncle," Ethel answered, and flushed all over her delicate face, and down to her throat. Nicky had looked at the blonde, and his eyebrows had gone up ever so slightly.

It spoiled Ethel's evening. More than that, as she told her mother of it later, weeping, she declared it had spoiled her life.

Eva talked it over with her husband in that intimate hour that precedes bedtime. She gesticulated heatedly with her hairbrush.

"It's disgusting, that's what it is. Perfectly disgusting. There's no fool like an old fool. Imagine! A creature like that. At his time of life."

"Well, I don't know," Ben said, and even grinned a little. "I suppose a boy's got to sow his wild oats sometime."

"Don't be any more vulgar than you can help," Eva retorted. "And I think you know, as well as I, what it means to have that Overton boy interested in Ethel."

"If he's interested in her," Ben blundered, "I guess the fact that Ethel's uncle went to the theater with someone who isn't Ethel's aunt won't cause a shudder to run up and down his frail young frame, will it?"

"All right," Eva had retorted. "If you're not man enough to stop it, I'll have to, that's all. I'm going up there with Stell this week."

They did not notify Jo of their coming. Eva telephoned his apartment when she knew he would be out, and asked his man if he expected his master home to dinner that evening. The man had said yes. Eva arranged to meet Stell in town. They would drive to Jo's apartment together, and wait for him there.

When she reached the city Eva found turmoil there. The first of the American troops to be sent to France were leaving. Michigan Boulevard was a billowing, surging mass: flags, pennants, banners, crowds. All the elements that make for demonstration. And over the whole—quiet. No holiday crowd, this. A solid, determined mass of people waiting patient hours

to see the khaki-clads go by. Three years had brought them to a clear
knowledge of what these boys were going to.

"Isn't it dreadful!" Stell gasped.

"Nicky Overton's too young, thank goodness."

Their car was caught in the jam. When they moved at all, it was by
inches. When at last they reached Jo's apartment they were flushed, nervous, apprehensive. But he had not yet come in. So they waited.

No, they were not staying to dinner with their brother, they told the
relieved houseman.

Stell and Eva, sunk in rose-colored cushions, viewed the place with disgust and some mirth. They rather avoided each other's eyes.

"Carrie ought to be here," Eva said. They both smiled at the thought of
the austere Carrie in the midst of those rosy cushions, and hangings, and
lamps. Stell rose and began to walk about restlessly. She picked up a vase
and laid it down; straightened a picture. Eva got up, too, and wandered
into the hall. She stood there a moment, listening. Then she turned and
passed into Jo's bedroom, Stell following. And there you knew Jo for what
he was.

This room was as bare as the other had been ornate. It was Jo, the
clean-minded and simplehearted, in revolt against the cloying luxury with
which he had surrounded himself. The bedroom, of all rooms in any house,
reflects the personality of its occupant. True, the actual furniture was paneled, cupid-surmounted, and ridiculous. It had been the fruit of Jo's first
orgy of the senses. But now it stood out in that stark little room with an air
as incongruous and ashamed as that of a pink tarlatan danseuse who finds
herself in a monk's cell. None of those wall pictures with which bachelor
bedrooms are reputed to be hung. No satin slippers. No scented notes.
Two plain-backed military brushes on the chiffonier (and he so nearly
hairless!). A little orderly stack of books on the table near the bed. Eva
fingered their titles and gave a little gasp. One of them was on gardening.

"Well, of all things!" exclaimed Stell. A book on the war, by an Englishman. A detective story of the lurid type that lulls us to sleep. His shoes
ranged in a careful row in the closet, with a shoe tree in every one of them.
There was something speaking about them. They looked so human. Eva
shut the door on them quickly. Some bottles on the dresser. A jar of
pomade. An ointment such as a man uses who is growing bald and is panic-
stricken too late. An insurance calendar on the wall. Some rhubarb-and-
soda mixture on the shelf in the bathroom, and a little box of pepsin tablets.

"Eats all kinds of things at all hours of the night," Eva said, and wandered out into the rose-colored front room again with the air of one who is

chagrined at her failure to find what she has sought. Stell followed her furtively.

"Where do you suppose he can be?" she demanded. "It's"—she glanced at her wrist—"why, it's after six!"

And then there was a little click. The two women sat up, tense. The door opened. Jo came in. He blinked a little. The two women in the rosy room stood up.

"Why—Eve! Why, Babe! Well! Why didn't you let me know?"

"We were just about to leave. We thought you weren't coming home." Jo came in slowly.

"I was in the jam on Michigan, watching the boys go by." He sat down, heavily. The light from the window fell on him. And you saw that his eyes were red.

He had found himself one of the thousands in the jam on Michigan Avenue, as he said. He had a place near the curb, where his big frame shut off the view of the unfortunates behind him. He waited with the placid interest of one who has subscribed to all the funds and societies to which a prosperous, middle-aged businessman is called upon to subscribe in wartime. Then, just as he was about to leave, impatient at the delay, the crowd had cried, with a queer, dramatic, exultant note in its voice, "Here they come! Here come the boys!"

Just at that moment two little, futile, frenzied fists began to beat a mad tattoo on Jo Hertz's broad back. Jo tried to turn in the crowd, all indignant resentment. "Say, looka here!"

The little fists kept up their frantic beating and pushing. And a voice—a choked, high little voice—cried, "Let me by! I can't see! You *man,* you! You big fat man! My boy's going by—to war—and I can't see! Let me by!"

Jo scrooged around, still keeping his place. He looked down. And upturned to him in agonized appeal was the face of Emily. They stared at each other for what seemed a long, long time. It was really only the fraction of a second. Then Jo put one great arm firmly around Emily's waist and swung her around in front of him. His great bulk protected her. Emily was clinging to his hand. She was breathing rapidly, as if she had been running. Her eyes were straining up the street.

"Why, Emily, how in the world——!"

"I ran away. Fred didn't want me to come. He said it would excite me too much."

"Fred?"

"My husband. He made me promise to say good-by to Jo at home."

"Jo?"

"Jo's my boy. And he's going to war. So I ran away. I had to see him. I had to see him go."

She was dry-eyed. Her gaze was straining up the street.

"Why, sure," said Jo. "Of course you want to see him." And then the crowd gave a great roar. There came over Jo a feeling of weakness. He was trembling. The boys went marching by.

"There he is," Emily shrilled, above the din. "There he is! There he is! There he——" And waved a futile little hand. It wasn't so much a wave as a clutching. A clutching after something beyond her reach.

"Which one? Which one, Emily?"

"The handsome one. The handsome one." Her voice quavered and died.

Jo put a steady hand on her shoulder. "Point him out," he commanded. "Show me." And the next instant, "Never mind. I see him."

Somehow, miraculously, he had picked him from among the hundreds. Had picked him as surely as his own father might have. It was Emily's boy. He was marching by, rather stiffly. He was nineteen, and fun-loving, and he had a girl, and he didn't particularly want to go to France and—to go to France. But more than he had hated going, he had hated not to go. So he marched by, looking straight ahead, his jaw set so that his chin stuck out just a little. Emily's boy.

Jo looked at him, and his face flushed purple. His eyes, the hard-boiled eyes of a Loop-hound, took on the look of a sad old man. And suddenly he was no longer Jo, the sport; old J. Hertz, the gay dog. He was Jo Hertz, thirty, in love with life, in love with Emily, and with the stinging blood of young manhood coursing through his veins.

Another minute and the boy had passed on up the broad street—the fine, flag-bedecked street—just one of a hundred service hats bobbing in rhythmic motion like sandy waves lapping a shore and flowing on.

Then he disappeared altogether.

Emily was clinging to Jo. She was mumbling something, over and over. "I can't. I can't. Don't ask me to. I can't let him go. Like that. I can't."

Jo said a queer thing.

"Why, Emily! We wouldn't have him stay home, would we? We wouldn't want him to do anything different, would we? Not our boy. I'm glad he enlisted. I'm proud of him. So are you glad."

Little by little he quieted her. He took her to the car that was waiting, a worried chauffeur in charge. They said good-by, awkwardly. Emily's face was a red, swollen mass.

So it was that when Jo entered his own hallway half an hour later he blinked, dazedly, and when the light from the window fell on him you saw that his eyes were red.

Eva was not one to beat about the bush. She sat forward in her chair, clutching her bag rather nervously.

"Now, look here, Jo. Stell and I are here for a reason. We're here to tell you that this thing's going to stop."

"Thing? Stop?"

"You know very well what I mean. You saw me at the milliner's that day. And night before last, Ethel. We're all disgusted. If you must go about with people like that, please have some sense of decency."

Something gathering in Jo's face should have warned her. But he was slumped down in his chair in such a huddle, and he looked so old and fat that she did not heed it. She went on. "You've got us to consider. Your sisters. And your nieces. Not to speak of your own——"

But he got to his feet then, shaking, and at what she saw in his face even Eva faltered and stopped. It wasn't at all the face of a fat, middle-aged sport. It was a face Jovian, terrible.

"You!" he began, low-voiced, ominous. "You!" He raised a great fist high. "You two murderers! You didn't consider me, twenty years ago. You come to me with talk like that. Where's my boy! You killed him, you two, twenty years ago. And now he belongs to somebody else. Where's my son that should have gone marching by today?" He flung his arms out in a great gesture of longing. The red veins stood out on his forehead. "Where's my son! Answer me that, you two selfish, miserable women. Where's my son!" Then, as they huddled together, frightened, wild-eyed. "Out of my house! Out of my house! Before I hurt you!"

They fled, terrified. The door banged behind them.

Jo stood, shaking, in the center of the room. Then he reached for a chair, gropingly, and sat down. He passed one moist, flabby hand over his forehead and it came away wet. The telephone rang. He sat still. It sounded far away and unimportant, like something forgotten. But it rang and rang insistently. Jo liked to answer his telephone when he was at home.

"Hello!" He knew instantly the voice at the other end.

"That you, Jo?" it said.

"Yes."

"How's my boy?"

"I'm—all right."

"Listen, Jo. The crowd's coming over tonight. I've fixed up a little poker game for you. Just eight of us."

"I can't come tonight, Gert."

"Can't! Why not?"

"I'm not feeling so good."

"You just said you were all right."

"I *am* all right. Just kind of tired."

The voice took on a cooing note. "Is my Joey tired? Then he shall be all comfy on the sofa, and he doesn't need to play if he don't want to. No, sir."

Jo stood staring at the black mouthpiece of the telephone. He was seeing a procession go marching by. Boys, hundreds of boys, in khaki.

"Hello! Hello!" The voice took on an anxious note. "Are you there?"

"Yes," wearily.

"Jo, there's something the matter. You're sick. I'm coming right over."

"No!"

"Why not? You sound as if you'd been sleeping. Look here——"

"Leave me alone!" cried Jo, suddenly, and the receiver clacked onto the hook. "Leave me alone. Leave me alone." Long after the connection had been broken.

He stood staring at the instrument with unseeing eyes. Then he turned and walked into the front room. All the light had gone out of it. Dusk had come on. All the light had gone out of everything. The zest had gone out of life. The game was over—the game he had been playing against loneliness and disappointment. And he was just a tired old man. A lonely, tired old man in a ridiculous rose-colored room that had grown, all of a sudden, drab.

That's Marriage

[1917]

The divorce courts call it incompatibility. So often it is just the way in which he eats his egg or she sneezes.
"I wish you wouldn't do that!"
"Do what?"
A nerve snaps.

❧ THERESA PLATT (SHE HAD BEEN TERRY SHEEHAN) WATCHED HER HUSband across the breakfast table with eyes that smoldered. But Orville Platt was quite unaware of any smoldering in progress. He was occupied with his eggs. How could he know that these very eggs were feeding the dull red menace in Terry Platt's eyes?

When Orville Platt ate a soft-boiled egg he concentrated on it. He treated it as a great adventure. Which, after all, it is. Few adjuncts of our daily life contain the element of chance that is to be found in a three-minute breakfast egg.

This was Orville Platt's method of attack: first, he chipped off the top, neatly. Then he bent forward and subjected it to a passionate and relentless scrutiny. Straightening—preparatory to plunging his spoon therein—he flapped his right elbow. It wasn't exactly a flap; it was a pass between a hitch and a flap, and presented external evidence of a mental state. Orville Platt always gave that little preliminary jerk when he was contemplating a serious step, or when he was moved, or argumentative. It was a trick as innocent as it was maddening.

Terry Platt had learned to look for that flap—they had been married four years—to look for it, and to hate it with a morbid, unreasoning hate. That flap of the elbow was tearing Terry Platt's nerves into raw, bleeding fragments.

Her fingers were clenched tightly under the table, now. She was breathing unevenly. "If he does that again," she told herself, "if he flaps again when he opens the second egg, I'll scream. I'll scream. I'll scream! I'll sc——"

He had scooped the first egg into his cup. Now he picked up the second, chipped it, concentrated, straightened, then—up went the elbow, and down, with the accustomed little flap.

The tortured nerves snapped. Through the early-morning quiet of

Wetona, Wisconsin, hurtled the shrill, piercing shriek of Terry Platt's hysteria.

"Terry! For God's sake! What's the matter!"

Orville Platt dropped the second egg, and his spoon. The egg yolk trickled down his plate. The spoon made a clatter and flung a gay spot of yellow on the cloth. He started toward her.

Terry, wild-eyed, pointed a shaking finger at him. She was laughing, now, uncontrollably. "Your elbow! Your elbow!"

"Elbow?" He looked down at it, bewildered, then up, fright in his face. "What's the matter with it?"

She mopped her eyes. Sobs shook her. "You f-f-flapped it."

"F-f-f——" The bewilderment in Orville Platt's face gave way to anger. "Do you mean to tell me that you screeched like that because my—because I moved my elbow?"

"Yes."

His anger deepened and reddened to fury. He choked. He had started from his chair with his napkin in his hand. He still clutched it. Now he crumpled it into a wad and hurled it to the center of the table, where it struck a sugar bowl, dropped back, and uncrumpled slowly, reprovingly. "You—you——" Then bewilderment closed down again like a fog over his countenance. "But why? I can't see——"

"Because it—because I can't stand it any longer. Flapping. This is what you do. Like this."

And she did it. Did it with insulting fidelity, being a clever mimic.

"Well, all I can say is you're crazy, yelling like that, for nothing."

"It isn't nothing."

"Isn't, huh? If that isn't nothing, what is?" They were growing incoherent. "What d'you mean, screeching like a maniac? Like a wild woman? The neighbors'll think I've killed you. What d'you mean, anyway!"

"I mean I'm tired of watching it, that's what. Sick and tired."

"Y'are, huh? Well, young lady, just let me tell *you* something——"

He told her. There followed one of those incredible quarrels, as sickening as they are human, which can take place only between two people who love each other; who love each other so well, that each knows with cruel certainty the surest way to wound the other; and who stab, and tear, and claw at these vulnerable spots in exact proportion to their love.

Ugly words. Bitter words. Words that neither knew they knew flew between them like sparks between steel striking steel.

From him: "Trouble with you is you haven't got enough to do. That's the trouble with half you women. Just lay around the house, rotting. I'm a fool, slaving on the road to keep a good-for-nothing——"

"I suppose you call sitting around hotel lobbies slaving! I suppose the house runs itself! How about my evenings? Sitting here alone, night after night, when you're on the road."

Finally, "Well, if you don't like it," he snarled, and lifted his chair by the back and slammed it down, savagely, "if you don't like it, why don't you get out, hm? Why don't you get out?"

And from her, her eyes narrowed to two slits, her cheeks scarlet: "Why, thanks. I guess I will."

Ten minutes later he had flung out of the house to catch the 8:19 for Manitowoc. He marched down the street, his shoulders swinging rhythmically to the weight of the burden he carried—his black leather handbag and the shiny tan sample case, battle-scarred, both, from many encounters with ruthless porters and busmen and bellboys. For four years, as he left for his semi-monthly trip, he and Terry had observed a certain little ceremony (as had the neighbors). She would stand in the doorway, watching him down the street, the heavier sample case banging occasionally at his shin. The depot was only three blocks away. Terry watched him with fond but un-illusioned eyes, which proves that she really loved him. He was a dapper, well-dressed fat man, with a weakness for pronounced patterns in suitings, and addicted to derbies. One week on the road, one week at home. That was his routine. The wholesale grocery trade liked Platt, and he had for his customers the fondness that a traveling salesman has who is successful in his territory. Before his marriage to Terry Sheehan his little red address book had been overwhelming proof against the theory that nobody loves a fat man.

Terry, standing in the doorway, always knew that when he reached the corner just where Schroeder's house threatened to hide him from view, he would stop, drop the sample case, wave his hand just once, pick up the sample case and go on, proceeding backward for a step or two until Schroeder's house made good its threat. It was a comic scene in the eyes of the onlooker, perhaps because a chubby Romeo offends the sense of fitness. The neighbors, lurking behind their parlor curtains, had laughed at first. But after a while they learned to look for that little scene, and to take it unto themselves, as if it were a personal thing. Fifteen-year wives whose husbands had long since abandoned flowery farewells used to get a vicarious thrill out of it, and to eye Terry with a sort of envy.

This morning Orville Platt did not even falter when he reached Schroeder's corner. He marched straight on, looking steadily ahead, the heavy bags swinging from either hand. Even if he had stopped—though she knew he wouldn't—Terry Platt would not have seen him. She remained seated at the disordered breakfast table, a dreadfully still figure, and sinister; a figure

of stone and fire, of ice and flame. Over and over in her mind she was mill-
ing the things she might have said to him, and had not. She brewed a hundred vitriolic cruelties that she might have flung in his face. She would
concoct one biting brutality, and dismiss it for a second, and abandon that
for a third. She was too angry to cry—a dangerous state in a woman. She
was what is known as cold mad, so that her mind was working clearly and
with amazing swiftness, and yet as though it were a thing detached; a
thing that was no part of her.

She sat thus for the better part of an hour, motionless except for one
forefinger that was, quite unconsciously, tapping out a popular and cheap
little air that she had been strumming at the piano the evening before,
having bought it downtown that same afternoon. It had struck Orville's
fancy, and she had played it over and over for him. Her right forefinger
was playing the entire tune, and something in the back of her head was
following it accurately, though the separate thinking process was going on
just the same. Her eyes were bright, and wide, and hot. Suddenly she became conscious of the musical antics of her finger. She folded it in with its
mates, so that her hand became a fist. She stood up and stared down at the
clutter of the breakfast table. The egg—that fateful second egg—had congealed to a mottled mess of yellow and white. The spoon lay on the cloth.
His coffee, only half consumed, showed tan with a cold gray film over it.
A slice of toast at the left of his plate seemed to grin at her with the semi-
circular wedge that he had bitten out of it.

Terry stared down at these congealing remnants. Then she laughed, a
hard high little laugh, pushed a plate away contemptuously with her
hand, and walked into the sitting room. On the piano was the piece of
music (Bennie Gottschalk's great song hit, "Hicky Boola") which she had
been playing the night before. She picked it up, tore it straight across,
once, placed the pieces back to back, and tore it across again. Then she
dropped the pieces to the floor.

"You bet I'm going," she said, as though concluding a train of thought.
"You just bet I'm going. Right now!"

And Terry went. She went for much the same reason as that given by
the ladye of high degree in the old English song—she who had left her
lord and bed and board to go with the raggle-taggle gipsies-O! The thing
that was sending Terry Platt away was much more than a conjugal quarrel
precipitated by a soft-boiled egg and a flap of the arm. It went so deep that
it is necessary to delve back to the days when Theresa Platt was Terry
Sheehan to get the real significance of it, and of the things she did after
she went.

When Mrs. Orville Platt had been Terry Sheehan, she had played the piano, afternoons and evenings, in the orchestra of the Bijou Theater, on Cass Street, Wetona, Wisconsin. Anyone with a name like Terry Sheehan would, perforce, do well anything she might set out to do. There was nothing of genius in Terry, but there was something of fire, and much that was Irish. Which meant that the Watson Team, Eccentric Song and Dance Artists, never needed a rehearsal when they played the Bijou. Ruby Watson used merely to approach Terry before the Monday performance, sheet music in hand, and say, "Listen, dearie. We've got some new business I want to wise you to. Right here it goes '*Tum* dee-dee *dum* dee-dee *tum dum dum.*' See? Like that. And then Jim vamps. Get me?"

Terry, at the piano, would pucker her pretty brow a moment. Then, "Like this, you mean?"

"That's it! You've got it."

"All right. I'll tell the drum."

She could play any tune by ear, once heard. She got the spirit of a thing, and transmitted it. When Terry played a martial number you tapped the floor with your foot, and unconsciously straightened your shoulders. When she played a home-and-mother song you hoped that the man next to you didn't know you were crying (which he probably didn't, because he was weeping, too).

At that time motion pictures had not attained their present virulence. Vaudeville, polite or otherwise, had not yet been crowded out by the ubiquitous film. The Bijou offered entertainment of the cigar-box-tramp variety, interspersed with trick bicyclists, soubrettes in slightly soiled pink, trained seals, and Family Fours with lumpy legs who tossed each other about and struck Goldbergian attitudes.

Contact with these gave Terry Sheehan a semiprofessional tone. The more conservative of her townspeople looked at her askance. There never had been an evil thing about Terry, but Wetona considered her rather fly. Terry's hair was very black, and she had a fondness for those little, close-fitting scarlet turbans. Terry's mother had died when the girl was eight, and Terry's father had been what is known as easygoing. A good-natured, lovable, shiftless chap in the contracting business. He drove around Wetona in a sagging, one-seated cart and never made any money because he did honest work and charged as little for it as men who did not. His mortar stuck, and his bricks did not crumble, and his lumber did not crack. Riches are not acquired in the contracting business in that way. Ed Sheehan and his daughter were great friends. When he died (she was nineteen) they say she screamed once, like a banshee, and dropped to the floor.

After they had straightened out the muddle of books in Ed Sheehan's gritty, dusty little office Terry turned her piano-playing talent to practical

account. At twenty-one she was still playing at the Bijou, and into her face
was creeping the first hint of that look of sophistication which comes from
daily contact with the artificial world of the footlights.

There are, in a small Midwest town like Wetona, just two kinds of
girls. Those who go downtown Saturday nights, and those who don't.
Terry, if she had not been busy with her job at the Bijou, would have
come in the first group. She craved excitement. There was little chance to
satisfy such craving in Wetona, but she managed to find certain means.
The traveling men from the Burke House just across the street used to
drop in at the Bijou for an evening's entertainment. They usually sat well
toward the front, and Terry's expert playing, and the gloss of her black
hair, and her piquant profile as she sometimes looked up toward the stage
for a signal from one of the performers caught their fancy, and held it.

She found herself, at the end of a year or two, with a rather large acquaintance among these peripatetic gentlemen. You occasionally saw one
of them strolling home with her. Sometimes she went driving with one of
them of a Sunday afternoon. And she rather enjoyed taking Sunday dinner at the Burke Hotel with a favored friend. She thought those small-
town hotel Sunday dinners the last word in elegance. The roast course was
always accompanied by an aqueous, semifrozen concoction which the bill
of fare revealed as Roman Punch. It added a royal touch to the repast,
even when served with roast pork.

Terry was twenty-two when Orville Platt, making his initial Wisconsin trip for the wholesale grocery house he represented, first beheld her
piquant Irish profile, and heard her deft manipulation of the keys. Orville
had the fat man's sense of rhythm and love of music. He had a buttery
tenor voice, too, of which he was rather proud.

He spent three days in Wetona that first trip, and every evening saw
him at the Bijou, first row, center. He stayed through two shows each
time, and before he had been there fifteen minutes Terry was conscious of
him through the back of her head. Orville Platt paid no more heed to the
stage, and what was occurring thereon, than if it had not been. He sat
looking at Terry, and waggling his head in time to the music. Not that
Terry was a beauty. But she was one of those immaculately clean types.
That look of fragrant cleanliness was her chief charm. Her clear, smooth
skin contributed to it, and the natural penciling of her eyebrows. But the
thing that accented it, and gave it a last touch, was the way in which her
black hair came down in a little point just in the center of her forehead,
where hair meets brow. It grew to form what is known as a cowlick. (A
prettier name for it is widow's peak.) Your eye lighted on it, pleased, and
from it traveled its gratified way down her white temples, past her little

ears, to the smooth black coil at the nape of her neck. It was a trip that rested you.

At the end of the last performance on the night of his second visit to the Bijou, Orville waited until the audience had begun to file out. Then he leaned forward over the rail that separated orchestra from audience.

"Could you," he said, his tones dulcet, "could you oblige me with the name of that last piece you played?"

Terry was stacking her music. "George!" she called to the drum. "Gentleman wants to know the name of that last piece." And prepared to leave.

" 'My Georgia Crackerjack,' " said the laconic drum.

Orville Platt took a hasty side step in the direction of the door toward which Terry was headed. "It's a pretty thing," he said fervently. "An awful pretty thing. Thanks. It's beautiful."

Terry flung a last insult at him over her shoulder: "Don't thank *me* for it. I didn't write it."

Orville Platt did not go across the street to the hotel. He wandered up Cass Street, and into the ten-o'clock quiet of Main Street, and down as far as the park and back. "Pretty as a pink! And play! . . . And good, too. Good."

A fat man in love.

At the end of six months they were married. Terry was surprised into it. Not that she was not fond of him. She was; and grateful to him, as well. For, pretty as she was, no man had ever before asked Terry to be his wife. They had made love to her. They had paid court to her. They had sent her large boxes of stale drugstore chocolates, and called her endearing names as they made cautious declarations such as:

"I've known a lot of girls, but you've got something different. I don't know. You've got so much sense. A fellow can chum around with you. Little pal."

Wetona would be their home. They rented a comfortable, seven-room house in a comfortable, middle-class neighborhood, and Terry dropped the red velvet turbans and went in for picture hats. Orville bought her a piano whose tone was so good that to her ear, accustomed to the metallic discords of the Bijou instrument, it sounded out of tune. She played a great deal at first, but unconsciously she missed the sharp spat of applause that used to follow her public performance. She would play a piece, brilliantly, and then her hands would drop to her lap. And the silence of her own sitting room would fall flat on her ears. It was better on the evenings when Orville was home. He sang, in his throaty, fat man's tenor, to Terry's expert accompaniment.

"This is better than playing for those ham actors, isn't it, hon?" And he would pinch her ear.

"Sure"—listlessly.

But after the first year she became accustomed to what she termed private life. She joined an afternoon sewing club, and was active in the ladies' branch of the U.C.T. She developed a knack at cooking, too, and Orville, after a week or ten days of hotel fare in small Wisconsin towns, would come home to sea-foam biscuits, and real soup, and honest pies and cake. Sometimes, in the midst of an appetizing meal he would lay down his knife and fork and lean back in his chair, and regard the cool and unruffled Terry with a sort of reverence in his eyes. Then he would get up, and come around to the other side of the table, and tip her pretty face up to his.

"I'll bet I'll wake up, someday, and find out it's all a dream. You know this kind of thing doesn't really happen—not to a dub like me."

One year; two; three; four. Routine. A little boredom. Some impatience. She began to find fault with the very things she had liked in him: his superneatness; his fondness for dashing suit patterns; his throaty tenor; his worship of her. And the flap. Oh, above all, that flap! That little, innocent, meaningless mannerism that made her tremble with nervousness. She hated it so that she could not trust herself to speak of it to him. That was the trouble. Had she spoken of it, laughingly or in earnest, before it became an obsession with her, that hideous breakfast quarrel, with its taunts, and revilings, and open hate, might never have come to pass.

Terry Platt herself didn't know what was the matter with her. She would have denied that anything was wrong. She didn't even throw her hands above her head and shriek: "I want to live! I want to live! I want to live!" like a lady in a play. She only knew she was sick of sewing at the Wetona West End Red Cross shop; sick of marketing, of home comforts, of Orville, of the flap.

Orville, you may remember, left at 8:19. The 11:23 bore Terry Chicagoward. She had left the house as it was—beds unmade, rooms unswept, breakfast table uncleared. She intended never to come back.

Now and then a picture of the chaos she had left behind would flash across her order-loving mind. The spoon on the tablecloth. Orville's pajamas dangling over the bathroom chair. The coffeepot on the gas stove.

"Pooh! What do I care?"

In her pocketbook she had a tidy sum saved out of the housekeeping money. She was naturally thrifty, and Orville had never been niggardly. Her meals when Orville was on the road had been those sketchy, haphazard affairs with which women content themselves when their household is manless. At noon she went into the dining car and ordered a flaunting little repast of chicken salad and asparagus and Neapolitan ice cream. The men in the dining car eyed her speculatively and with appreciation. Then their glance dropped to the third finger of her left hand, and wandered away. She had meant to remove it. In fact, she had taken it off and dropped it into her bag. But her hand felt so queer, so unaccustomed, so naked, that she had found herself slipping the narrow band on again, and her thumb groped for it, gratefully.

It was almost five o'clock when she reached Chicago. She felt no uncertainty or bewilderment. She had been in Chicago three or four times since her marriage. She went to a downtown hotel. It was too late, she told herself, to look for a less expensive room that night. When she had tidied herself she went out. The things she did were the childish, aimless things that one does who finds herself in possession of sudden liberty. She walked up State Street, and stared in the windows; came back, turned into Madison, passed a bright little shop in the window of which taffy—white and gold—was being wound endlessly and fascinatingly about a double-jointed machine. She went in and bought a sackful, and wandered on down the street, munching.

She had supper at one of those white-tiled sarcophagi that emblazon Chicago's downtown side streets. It had been her original intention to dine in state in the rose-and-gold dining room of her hotel. She had even thought daringly of lobster. But at the last moment she recoiled from the idea of dining alone in that wilderness of tables so obviously meant for two.

After her supper she went to a picture show. She was amazed to find there, instead of the accustomed orchestra, a pipe organ that panted and throbbed and rumbled over lugubrious classics. The picture was about a faithless wife. Terry left in the middle of it.

She awoke next morning at seven, as usual, started up wildly, looked around, and dropped back. Nothing to get up for. The knowledge did not fill her with a rush of relief. She would have her breakfast in bed. She telephoned for it, languidly. But when it came she got up and ate it from the table, after all.

That morning she found a fairly comfortable room, more within her means, on the North Side in the boardinghouse district. She unpacked and hung up her clothes and drifted downtown again, idly. It was noon when she came to the corner of State and Madison Streets. It was a maelstrom that caught her up, and buffeted her about, and tossed her helplessly this way and that.

The thousands jostled Terry, and knocked her hat awry, and dug her with unheeding elbows, and stepped on her feet.

"Say, look here!" she said once futilely. They did not stop to listen. State and Madison has no time for Terrys from Wetona. It goes its way, pell-mell. If it saw Terry at all it saw her only as a prettyish person, in the wrong kind of suit and hat, with a bewildered, resentful look on her face. Terry drifted on down the west side of State Street, with the hurrying crowd. State and Monroe. A sound came to Terry's ears. A sound familiar, beloved. To her ear, harassed with the roar and crash, with the shrill scream of the whistle of the policeman at the crossing, with the hiss of feet shuffling on cement, it was a celestial strain. She looked up, toward the sound. A great second-story window opened wide to the street. In it a girl at a piano, and a man, red-faced, singing through a megaphone. And on a flaring red and green sign:

BERNIE GOTTSCHALK'S MUSIC HOUSE!

COME IN! HEAR BERNIE GOTTSCHALK'S LATEST HIT! THE HEART-THROB SONG THAT HAS GOT 'EM ALL! THE SONG THAT MADE THE SQUAREHEADS CRAWL!

"I COME FROM PARIS, ILLINOIS, BUT OH! YOU PARIS, FRANCE!
I USED TO WEAR BLUE OVERALLS BUT NOW IT'S KHAKI PANTS."
COME IN!   COME IN!

Terry accepted.

She followed the sound of the music. Around the corner. Up a little flight of stairs. She entered the realm of Euterpe; Euterpe with her hair frizzed; Euterpe with her flowing white robe replaced by soiled white shoes; Euterpe abandoning her flute for jazz. She sat at the piano, a red-haired young lady whose familiarity with the piano had bred contempt. Nothing else could have accounted for her treatment of it. Her fingers, tipped with sharp-pointed and glistening nails, clawed the keys with a dreadful mechanical motion. There were stacks of music sheets on counters and shelves and dangling from overhead wires. The girl at the piano never ceased playing. She played mostly by request. A prospective purchaser would mumble something in the ear of one of the clerks. The fat man with the megaphone would bawl out, "Hicky Boola, Miss Ryan!" And Miss Ryan would oblige. She made a hideous rattle and crash and clatter of sound.

Terry joined the crowds about the counter. The girl at the piano was not looking at the keys. Her head was screwed around over her left shoulder and as she played she was holding forth animatedly to a girl friend who had evidently dropped in from some store or office during the lunch hour. Now and again the fat man paused in his vocal efforts to reprimand her for her slackness. She paid no heed. There was something gruesome, uncanny, about the way her fingers went their own way over the defenseless keys. Her conversation with the frowzy little girl went on

"Wha'd he say?" (Over her shoulder.)

"Oh, he laffed."

"Well, didja go?"

"Me! Well, whutya think I yam, anyway?"

"I woulda took a chanst."

The fat man rebelled.

"Look here! Get busy! What are you paid for? Talkin' or playin'? Huh?"

The person at the piano, openly reproved thus before her friend, lifted her uninspired hands from the keys and spake. When she had finished she rose.

"But you can't leave now," the megaphone man argued. "Right in the rush hour."

"I'm gone," said the girl. The fat man looked about, helplessly. He gazed at the abandoned piano, as though it must go on of its own accord. Then at the crowd. "Where's Miss Schwimmer?" he demanded of a clerk.

"Out to lunch."

Terry pushed her way to the edge of the counter and leaned over. "I can play for you," she said.

The man looked at her. "Sight?"

"Yes."

"Come on."

Terry went around to the other side of the counter, took off her hat and coat, rubbed her hands together briskly, sat down, and began to play. The crowd edged closer.

It is a curious study, this noonday crowd that gathers to sate its music hunger on the scraps vouchsafed it by Bernie Gottschalk's Music House. Loose-lipped, slope-shouldered young men with bad complexions and slender hands. Girls whose clothes are an unconscious satire on present-day fashions. On their faces, as they listen to the music, is a look of peace and dreaming. They stand about, smiling a wistful half smile. The music seems to satisfy a something within them. Faces dull, eyes lusterless, they listen in a sort of trance.

Terry played on. She played as Terry Sheehan used to play. She played as no music hack at Bernie Gottschalk's had ever played before. The crowd swayed a little to the sound of it. Some kept time with little jerks of the shoulder—the little hitching movement of the dancer whose blood is filled with the fever of syncopation. Even the crowd flowing down State Street must have caught the rhythm of it, for the room soon filled.

At two o'clock the crowd began to thin. Business would be slack, now, until five, when it would again pick up until closing time at six.

The fat vocalist put down his megaphone, wiped his forehead, and regarded Terry with a warm blue eye. He had just finished singing "I've Wandered Far from Dear Old Mother's Knee." (Bernie Gottschalk Inc., Chicago. New York. You can't get bit with a Gottschalk hit. 15 cents each.)

"Girlie," he said, emphatically, "you sure—can—play!" He came over to her at the piano and put a stubby hand on her shoulder. "Yessir! Those little fingers——"

Terry just turned her head to look down her nose at the moist hand resting on her shoulder. "Those little fingers are going to meet your face if you don't move on."

"Who gave you your job?" demanded the fat man.

"Nobody. I picked it myself. You can have it if you want it."

"Can't you take a joke?"

"Label yours."

As the crowd dwindled she played less feverishly, but there was nothing slipshod about her performance. The chubby songster found time to proffer brief explanations in asides. "They want the patriotic stuff. It used to be all that Hawaiian dope, and Wild Irish Rose stuff, and songs about wanting to go back to every place from Dixie to Duluth. But now seems it's all these here flag wavers. Honestly, I'm so sick of 'em I got a notion to enlist to get away from it."

Terry eyed him with withering briefness. "A little training wouldn't ruin your figure."

She had never objected to Orville's *embonpoint*. But then, Orville was a different sort of fat man; pink-cheeked, springy, immaculate.

At four o'clock, as she was in the chorus of "Isn't There Another Joan of Arc?" a melting masculine voice from the other side of the counter said, "Pardon me. What's that you're playing?"

Terry told him. She did not look up.

"I wouldn't have known it. Played like that—a second 'Marseillaise.' If the words—— What are the words? Let me see a——"

"Show the gentleman a 'Joan,'" Terry commanded briefly, over her shoulder. The fat man laughed a wheezy laugh. Terry glanced around, still playing, and encountered the gaze of two melting masculine eyes that matched the melting masculine voice. The songster waved a hand uniting Terry and the eyes in informal introduction.

"Mr. Leon Sammett, the gentleman who sings the Gottschalk songs wherever songs are heard. And Mrs.—that is—and Mrs. Sammett——"

Terry turned. A sleek, swarthy world-old young man with the fashionable concave torso, and alarmingly convex bone-rimmed glasses. Through them his darkly luminous gaze glowed upon Terry. To escape their warmth she sent her own gaze past him to encounter the arctic stare of the large blonde who had been included so lamely in the introduction. And at that the frigidity of that stare softened, melted, dissolved.

"Why, Terry Sheehan! What in the world!"

Terry's eyes bored beneath the layers of flabby fat. "It's—why, it's Ruby Watson, isn't it? Eccentric Song and Dance——"

She glanced at the concave young man and faltered. He was not Jim, of the Bijou days. From him her eyes leaped back to the fur-bedecked splendor of the woman. The plump face went so painfully red that the make-up stood out on it, a distinct layer, like thin ice covering flowing water. As she surveyed that bulk Terry realized that while Ruby might still claim eccentricity, her song-and-dance days were over. "That's ancient history, m' dear. I haven't been working for three years. What're you doing in this joint? I'd heard you'd done well for yourself. That you were married."

"I am. That is I—well, I am. I——"

At that the dark young man leaned over and patted Terry's hand that lay on the counter. He smiled. His own hand was incredibly slender, long, and tapering.

"That's all right," he assured her, and smiled. "You two girls can have a reunion later. What I want to know is can you play by ear?"

"Yes, but——"

He leaned far over the counter. "I knew it the minute I heard you play. You've got the touch. Now listen. See if you can get this, and fake the bass."

He fixed his somber and hypnotic eyes on Terry. His mouth screwed up into a whistle. The tune—a tawdry but haunting little melody—came through his lips. Terry turned back to the piano. "Of course you know you flatted every note," she said.

This time it was the blonde who laughed, and the man who flushed. Terry cocked her head just a little to one side, like a knowing bird, looked up into space beyond the piano top, and played the lilting little melody with charm and fidelity. The dark young man followed her with a wagging of the head and little jerks of both outspread hands. His expression was beatific, enraptured. He hummed a little under his breath and anyone who was music-wise would have known that he was just a half beat behind her all the way.

When she had finished he sighed deeply, ecstatically. He bent his lean frame over the counter and, despite his swart coloring, seemed to glitter upon her—his eyes, his teeth, his very fingernails.

"Something led me here. I never come up on Tuesdays. But something——"

"You was going to complain," put in his lady, heavily, "about that Teddy Sykes at the Palace Gardens singing the same songs this week that you been boosting at the Inn."

He put up a vibrant, peremptory hand. "Bah! What does that matter now! What does anything matter now! Listen Miss—ah—Miss——?"

"Pl—Sheehan. Terry Sheehan."

He gazed off a moment into space. "Hm. 'Leon Sammett in Songs. Miss Terry Sheehan at the Piano.' That doesn't sound bad. Now listen, Miss Sheehan. I'm singing down at the University Inn. The Gottschalk song hits. I guess you know my work. But I want to talk to you, private. It's something to your interest. I go on down at the Inn at six. Will you come and have a little something with Ruby and me? Now?"

"Now?" faltered Terry, somewhat helplessly. Things seemed to be moving rather swiftly for her, accustomed as she was to the peaceful routine of the past four years.

"Get your hat. It's your life chance. Wait till you see your name in two-foot electrics over the front of every big-time house in the country. You've got music in you. Tie to me and you're made." He turned to the woman beside him. "Isn't that so, Rube?"

"Sure. Look at *me!*" One would not have thought there could be so much subtle vindictiveness in a fat blonde.

Sammett whipped out a watch. "Just three quarters of an hour. Come on, girlie."

His conversation had been conducted in an urgent undertone, with side glances at the fat man with the megaphone. Terry approached him now.

"I'm leaving now," she said.

"Oh, no, you're not. Six o'clock is your quitting time."

In which he touched the Irish in Terry. "Any time I quit is my quitting time." She went in quest of hat and coat much as the girl had done whose place she had taken early in the day. The fat man followed her, protesting. Terry, putting on her hat, tried to ignore him. But he laid one plump hand on her arm and kept it there, though she tried to shake him off.

"Now, listen to me. That boy wouldn't mind grinding his heel on your face if he thought it would bring him up a step. I know'm. See that walking stick he's carrying? Well, compared to the yellow stripe that's in him, that cane is a lead pencil. He's a song tout, that's all he is." Then, more feverishly, as Terry tried to pull away: "Wait a minute. You're a decent girl. I want to—— Why, he can't even sing a note without you give it to him first. He can put a song over, yes. But how? By flashing that toothy grin of his and talking every word of it. Don't you——"

But Terry freed herself with a final jerk and whipped around the counter. The two, who had been talking together in an undertone, turned to welcome her. "We've got a half-hour. Come on. It's just over to Clark and up a block or so."

The University Inn, that gloriously intercollegiate institution which welcomes any graduate of any school of experience, was situated in the basement, down a flight of stairs. Into the unwonted quiet that reigns during the hour of low potentiality, between five and six, the three went, and seated themselves at a table in an obscure corner. A waiter brought them things in little glasses, though no order had been given. The woman who had been Ruby Watson was so silent as to be almost wordless. But the man talked rapidly. He talked well, too. The same quality that enabled him, voiceless though he was, to boost a song to success was making his plea sound plausible in Terry's ears now.

"I've got to go and make up in a few minutes. So get this. I'm not going to stick down in this basement eating house forever. I've got too much talent. If I only had a voice—I mean a singing voice. But I haven't. But then, neither had Georgie Cohan, and I can't see that it wrecked his life any. Now listen. I've got a song. It's my own. That bit you played for me up at Gottschalk's is part of the chorus. But it's the words that'll go big. They're great. It's an aviation song, see? Airplane stuff. They're yelling that it's the airyoplanes that're going to win this war. Well, I'll help 'em. This song is going to put the aviator where he belongs. It's going to be the big song of the war. It's going to make 'Tipperary' sound like a Moody and Sankey hymn. It's the——"

Ruby lifted her heavy-lidded eyes and sent him a meaning look. "Get down to business, Leon. I'll tell her how good you are while you're making up."

He shot her a malignant glance, but took her advice. "Now what I've been looking for for years is somebody who has got the music knack to give me the accompaniment just a quarter of a jump ahead of my voice, see? I can follow like a lamb, but I've got to have that feeler first. It's more than a knack. It's a gift. And you've got it. I know it when I see it. I want to get away from this night-club thing. There's nothing in it for a man of my talent. I'm gunning for bigger game. But they won't sign me without a try-out. And when they hear my voice they—— Well, if me and you work together we can fool 'em. The song's great. And my make-up's one of these av-iation costumes to go with the song, see? Pants tight in the knee and baggy on the hips. And a coat with one of those full-skirt whaddyoucall-'ems——"

"Peplums," put in Ruby, placidly.

"Sure. And the girls'll be wild about it. And the words!" He began to sing, gratingly off key:

> *Put on your sky clothes,*
> *Put on your fly clothes,*
> *And take a trip with me.*
> *We'll sail so high*
> *Up in the sky*
> *We'll drop a bomb from Mercury.*

"Why, that's awfully cute!" exclaimed Terry. Until now her opinion of Mr. Sammett's talents had not been on a level with his.

"Yeah, but wait till you hear the second verse. That's only part of the chorus. You see, he's supposed to be talking to a French girl. He says:

> *I'll parlez-vous in Français plain,*
> *You'll answer, "Cher Américain,"*
> *We'll both . . .'* "

The six-o'clock lights blazed up suddenly. A sad-looking group of men trailed in and made for a corner where certain bulky, shapeless bundles were soon revealed as those glittering and tortuous instruments which go to make a jazz band.

"You better go, Lee. The crowd comes in awful early now, with all these buyers in town."

Both hands on the table, he half rose, reluctantly, still talking. "I've got three other songs. They make Gottschalk's stuff look sick. All I want's a chance. What I want you to do is accompaniment. On the stage, see? Grand piano. And a swell set. I haven't quite made up my mind to it. But a kind of an army camp room, see? And maybe you dressed as Liberty. Anyway, it'll be new, and a knockout. If only we can get away with the voice thing. Say, if Eddie Foy, all those years never had a——"

The band opened with a terrifying clash of cymbal and thump of drum. "Back at the end of my first turn," he said as he fled. Terry followed his lithe, electric figure. She turned to meet the heavy-lidded gaze of the woman seated opposite. She relaxed, then, and sat back with a little sigh. "Well! If he talks that way to the managers I don't see——"

Ruby laughed a mirthless little laugh. "Talk doesn't get it over with the managers, honey. You've got to deliver."

"Well, but he's—that song *is* a good one. I don't say it's as good as he thinks it is, but it's good."

"Yes," admitted the woman, grudgingly, "it's good."

"Well, then?"

The woman beckoned a waiter; he nodded and vanished, and reappeared with a glass that was twin to the one she had just emptied. "Does he look like he knew French? Or could make a rhyme?"

"But didn't he? Doesn't he?"

"The words were written by a little French girl who used to skate down here last winter, when the craze was on. She was stuck on a Chicago kid who went over to fly for the French."

"But the music?"

"There was a Russian girl who used to dance in the cabaret and she——"

Terry's head came up with a characteristic little jerk. "I don't believe it!"

"Better." She gazed at Terry with the drowsy look that was so different from the quick, clear glance of the Ruby Watson who used to dance so nimbly in the old Bijou days. "What'd you and your husband quarrel about, Terry?"

Terry was furious to feel herself flushing. "Oh, nothing. He just—I—it was—— Say, how did you know we'd quarreled?"

And suddenly all the fat woman's apathy dropped from her like a garment and some of the old sparkle and animation illumined her heavy face. She pushed her glass aside and leaned forward on her folded arms, so that her face was close to Terry's.

"Terry Sheehan, I know you've quarreled, and I know just what it was about. Oh, I don't mean the very thing it was about; but the kind of thing. I'm going to do something for you, Terry, that I wouldn't take the trouble to do for most women. But I guess I ain't had all the softness knocked out of me yet, though it's a wonder. And I guess I remember too plain the decent kid you was in the old days. What was the name of that little small-time house me and Jim used to play? Bijou, that's it; Bijou."

The band struck up a new tune. Leon Sammett—slim, sleek, lithe in his evening clothes—appeared with a little fair girl in pink chiffon. The woman reached across the table and put one pudgy, jeweled hand on Terry's arm. "He'll be through in ten minutes. Now listen to me. I left Jim four years ago, and there hasn't been a minute since then, day or night, when I wouldn't have crawled back to him on my hands and knees if I could.

But I couldn't. He wouldn't have me now. How could he? How do I know you've quarreled? I can see it in your eyes. They look just the way mine have felt for four years, that's how. I met up with this boy, and there wasn't anybody to do the turn for me that I'm trying to do for you. Now get this. I left Jim because when he ate corn on the cob he always closed his eyes and it drove me wild. Don't laugh."

"I'm not laughing," said Terry.

"Women are like that. One night—we was playing Fond du Lac; I remember just as plain—we was eating supper before the show and Jim reached for one of those big yellow ears, and buttered and salted it, and me kind of hanging on to the edge of the table with my nails. Seemed to me if he shut his eyes when he put his teeth into that ear of corn I'd scream. And he did. And I screamed. And that's all."

Terry sat staring at her with a wide-eyed stare, like a sleepwalker. Then she wet her lips slowly. "But that's almost the very——"

"Kid, go on back home. I don't know whether it's too late or not, but go anyway. If you've lost him I suppose it ain't any more than you deserve, but I hope to God you don't get your deserts this time. He's almost through. If he sees you going he can't quit in the middle of his song to stop you. He'll know I put you wise, and he'll prob'ly half kill me for it. But it's worth it. You get."

And Terry—dazed, shaking, but grateful—fled. Down the noisy aisle, up the stairs, to the street. Back to her rooming house. Out again, with her suitcase, and into the right railroad station somehow, at last. Not another Wetona train until midnight. She shrank into a remote corner of the waiting room and there she huddled until midnight, watching the entrances like a child who is fearful of ghosts in the night.

The hands of the station clock seemed fixed and immovable. The hour between eleven and twelve was endless. She was on the train. It was almost morning. It was morning. Dawn was breaking. She was home! She had the house key clutched tightly in her hand long before she turned Schroeder's corner. Suppose he had come home! Suppose he had jumped a town and come home ahead of his schedule. They had quarreled once before, and he had done that.

Up the front steps. Into the house. Not a sound. She stood there a moment in the early-morning half-light. She peered into the dining room. The table, with its breakfast debris, was as she had left it. In the kitchen the coffeepot stood on the gas stove. She was home. She was safe. She ran up the stairs, got out of her clothes and into gingham morning things. She flung open windows everywhere. Downstairs once more she plunged into an orgy of cleaning. Dishes, table, stove, floor, rugs. She washed, scoured, swabbed, polished. By eight o'clock she had done the work that would ordinarily have taken until noon. The house was shining, orderly, and redolent of soapsuds.

During all this time she had been listening, listening, with her subconscious ear. Listening for something she had refused to name definitely in her mind, but listening, just the same; waiting.

And then, at eight o'clock, it came. The rattle of a key in the lock. The boom of the front door. Firm footsteps.

He did not go to meet her, and she did not go to meet him. They came together and were in each other's arms. She was weeping.

"Now, now, old girl. What's there to cry about? Don't, honey; don't. It's all right."

She raised her head then, to look at him. How fresh and rosy and big he seemed, after that little sallow restaurant rat.

"How did you get here? How did you happen——?"

"Jumped all the way from Ashland. Couldn't get a sleeper, so I sat up all night. I had to come back and square things with you, Terry. My mind just wasn't on my work. I kept thinking how I'd talked—how I'd talked——"

"Oh, Orville, don't! I can't bear—— Have you had your breakfast?"

"Why, no. The train was an hour late. You know that Ashland train."

But she was out of his arms and making for the kitchen. "You go and clean up. I'll have hot biscuits and everything in no time. You poor boy. No breakfast!"

She made good her promise. It could not have been more than half an hour later when he was buttering his third feathery, golden-brown biscuit. But she had eaten nothing. She watched him, and listened, and again her eyes were somber, but for a different reason. He broke open his egg. His elbow came up just a fraction of an inch. Then he remembered, and flushed like a schoolboy, and brought it down again, carefully. And at that she gave a tremulous cry, and rushed around the table to him.

"Oh, Orville!" She took the offending elbow in her two arms, and bent and kissed the rough coat sleeve.

"Why, Terry! Don't, honey. Don't!"

"Oh, Orville, listen——"

"Yes."

"Listen, Orville——"

"I'm listening, Terry."

"I've got something to tell you. There's something you've got to know."

"Yes, I know it, Terry. I knew you'd out with it, pretty soon, if I just waited."

She lifted an amazed face from his shoulder then, and stared at him. "But how could you know? You couldn't! How could you?"

He patted her shoulder then, gently. "I can always tell. When you have something on your mind you always take up a spoon of coffee, and look at it, and kind of joggle it back and forth in the spoon, and then dribble it back into the cup again, without once tasting it. It used to get me nervous, when we were first married, watching you. But now I know it just means you're worried about something, and I wait, and pretty soon——"

"Oh, Orville!" she cried then. "Oh, Orville!"

"Now, Terry. Just spill it, hon. Just spill it to Daddy. And you'll feel better."

Farmer in the Dell
[1919]

If I hadn't happened to write this short story, I never should have written the novel So Big. A quarter of a century ago (how the days do fly! just yesterday it was Thursday), wandering about Chicago's gritty streets or driving through the outlying districts that sprawled all over the Illinois prairies, I sometimes saw vaguely familiar, shambling figures that resembled the farmers I had known in my Appleton, Wisconsin, days. One saw them sitting on the front porches of bungalows that lined the streets of Chicago's far South Side. Their gnarled brown hands lay inert on their knees, palms up. They stared vacantly across the prairie at nothing. I imagined one of these going down to the South Water Street market, perhaps, early in the morning, for solace, when the avalanches of food for a great city are poured into the market. So I went down myself at dawn, and there I saw a little wrenlike woman in a blue suit and sailor hat. She had great pansy eyes and a delicate face, and she was vying with the hoarse-voiced, red-faced market men. I did not speak with her, I never again saw her, but in her the character of Selina in So Big was born, and out of that early-morning visit to the market came the idea for So Big, written five years later.

⌐§ OLD BEN WESTERVELD WAS TAKING IT EASY. EVERY MUSCLE TAUT, every nerve tense, his keen eyes vainly straining to pierce the blackness of the stuffy room—there lay Ben Westerveld in bed, taking it easy. And it was hard. Hard. He wanted to get up. He wanted so intensely to get up that the mere effort of lying there made him ache all over. His toes were curled with the effort. His fingers were clenched with it. His breath came short, and his thighs felt cramped. Nerves. But old Ben Westerveld didn't know that. What should a retired and well-to-do farmer of fifty-eight know of nerves, especially when he has moved to the city and is taking it easy?

If only he knew what time it was. Here in Chicago you couldn't tell whether it was four o'clock or seven unless you looked at your watch. To do that it was necessary to turn on the light. And to turn on the light meant that he would turn on, too, a flood of querulous protest from his wife, Bella, who lay asleep beside him.

When for forty-five years of your life you have risen at four-thirty daily, it is difficult to learn to loll. To do it successfully, you must be a natural-born loller to begin with and revert. Bella Westerveld was and had. So there she lay, asleep. Old Ben wasn't and hadn't. So there he lay, terribly wide-

49

awake, wondering what made his heart thump so fast when he was lying so still. If it had been light, you could have seen the lines of strained resignation in the sagging muscles of his patient face.

They had lived in the city for almost a year, but it was the same every morning. He would open his eyes, start up with one hand already reaching for the limp, drab work-worn garments that used to drape the chair by his bed. Then he would remember and sink back while a great wave of depression swept over him. Nothing to get up for. Store clothes on the chair by the bed. He was taking it easy.

Back home on the farm in southern Illinois he had known the hour the instant his eyes opened. Here the flat next door was so close that the bedroom was in twilight even at midday. On the farm he could tell by the feeling—an intangible thing, but infallible. He could gauge the very quality of the blackness that comes just before dawn. The crowing of the cocks, the stamping of the cattle, the twittering of the birds in the old elm whose branches were etched eerily against his window in the ghostly light —these things he had never needed. He had known. But here in the unsylvan section of Chicago which bears the bosky name of Englewood, the very darkness had a strange quality. A hundred unfamiliar noises misled him. There were no cocks, no cattle, no elm. Above all, there was no instinctive feeling. Once, when they first came to the city, he had risen at twelve-thirty, thinking it was morning, and had gone clumping about the flat, waking up everyone and loosing from his wife's lips a stream of acid vituperation that seared even his case-hardened sensibilities. The people sleeping in the bedroom of the flat next door must have heard her.

"You big rube! Getting up in the middle of the night and stomping around like cattle. You'd better build a shed in the back yard and sleep there if you're so dumb you can't tell night from day."

Even after thirty-three years of marriage he had never ceased to be appalled at the coarseness of her mind and speech—she who had seemed so mild and fragile and exquisite when he married her. He had crept back to bed shamefacedly. He could hear the couple in the bedroom of the flat just across the little court grumbling and then laughing a little, grudgingly, and yet with appreciation. That bedroom, too, had still the power to appall him. Its nearness, its forced intimacy, were daily shocks to him whose most immediate neighbor, back on the farm, had been a quarter of a mile away. The sound of a shoe dropped on the hardwood floor, the rush of water in the bathroom, the murmur of nocturnal confidences, the fretful cry of a child in the night, all startled and distressed him whose ear had found music in the roar of the thresher and had been soothed by the rattle of the tractor and the hoarse hoot of the steamboat whistle at the landing. His farm's edge had been marked by the Mississippi rolling grandly by.

Since they had moved into town, he had found only one city sound that he really welcomed—the rattle and clink that marked the milkman's matutinal visit. The milkman came at six, and he was the good fairy who released Ben Westerveld from durance vile—or had until the winter months made his coming later and later, so that he became worse than useless as a timepiece. But now it was late March, and mild. The milkman's coming would soon again mark old Ben's rising hour. Before he had begun to take it easy, six o'clock had seen the entire mechanism of his busy little world humming smoothly and sweetly, the whole set in motion by his own big work-callused hands. Those hands puzzled him now. He often looked at them curiously and in a detached sort of way, as if they belonged to someone else. So white they were, and smooth and soft, with long, pliant nails that never broke off from rough work as they used to. Of late there were little splotches of brown on the backs of his hands and around the thumbs.

"Guess it's my liver," he decided, rubbing the spots thoughtfully. "She gets kind of sluggish from me not doing anything. Maybe a little spring tonic wouldn't go bad. Tone me up."

He got a little bottle of reddish-brown mixture from the druggist on Halsted Street near Sixty-third. A genial gentleman, the druggist, white-coated and dapper, stepping affably about the fragrant-smelling store. The reddish-brown mixture had toned old Ben up surprisingly—while it lasted. He had two bottles of it. But on discontinuing it he slumped back into his old apathy.

Ben Westerveld, in his store clothes, his clean blue shirt, his incongruous hat, ambling aimlessly about Chicago's teeming, gritty streets, was a tragedy. Those big, capable hands, now dangling so limply from inert wrists, had wrested a living from the soil; those strangely unfaded blue eyes had the keenness of vision which comes from scanning great stretches of earth and sky; the stocky, square-shouldered body suggested power unutilized. All these spelled tragedy. Worse than tragedy—waste.

For almost half a century this man had combated the elements, head set, eyes wary, shoulders squared. He had fought wind and sun, rain and drought, scourge and flood. He had risen before dawn and slept before sunset. In the process he had taken on something of the color and the rugged immutability of the fields and hills and trees among which he toiled. Something of their dignity, too, though your town dweller might fail to see it beneath the drab exterior. He had about him none of the highlights and sharp points of the city man. He seemed to blend in with the background of nature so as to be almost undistinguishable from it, as were the furred and feathered creatures. This farmer differed from the city man as a hillock differs from an artificial golf bunker, though form and substance are the same.

Ben Westerveld didn't know he was a tragedy. Your farmer is not given to introspection. For that matter, anyone knows that a farmer in town is a comedy. Vaudeville, burlesque, the Sunday supplement, the comic papers, have marked him a fair target for ridicule. Perhaps one should know him in his overalled, stubble-bearded days, with the rich black loam of the Mississippi bottomlands clinging to his boots.

At twenty-five, given a tasseled cap, doublet and hose, and a long, slim pipe, Ben Westerveld would have been the prototype of one of those rollicking, lusty young mynheers that laugh out at you from a Frans Hals canvas. A roguish fellow with a merry eye; red-cheeked, vigorous. A serious mouth, though, and great sweetness of expression. As he grew older, the seriousness crept up and up and almost entirely obliterated the roguishness. By the time the life of ease claimed him, even the ghost of that ruddy wight of boyhood had vanished.

The Westerveld ancestry was as Dutch as the name. It had been hundreds of years since the first Westervelds came to America, and they had married and intermarried until the original Holland strain had almost entirely disappeared. They had drifted to southern Illinois by one of those slow processes of migration and had settled in Calhoun County, then almost a wilderness, but magnificent with its rolling hills, majestic rivers, and gold-and-purple distances. But to the practical Westerveld mind, hills and rivers and purple haze existed only in their relation to crops and weather. Ben, though, had a way of turning his face up to the sky sometimes, and it was not to scan the heavens for clouds. You saw him leaning on the plow handle to watch the whirring flight of a partridge across the meadow. He liked farming. Even the drudgery of it never made him grumble. He was a natural farmer as men are natural mechanics or musicians or salesmen. Things grew for him. He seemed instinctively to know facts about the kinship of soil and seed that other men had to learn from books or experience. It grew to be a saying in that section that "Ben Westerveld could grow a crop on rock."

At picnics and neighborhood frolics Ben could throw farther and run faster and pull harder than any of the other farmer boys who took part in the rough games. And he could pick up a girl with one hand and hold her at arm's length while she shrieked with pretended fear and real ecstasy. The girls all liked Ben. There was that almost primitive strength which appealed to the untamed in them as his gentleness appealed to their softer side. He liked the girls, too, and could have had his pick of them. He teased them all, took them buggy riding, beaued them about to neighborhood parties. But by the time he was twenty-five the thing had narrowed down to the Byers girl on the farm adjoining Westerveld's. There was what the neighbors called an understanding, though perhaps he had never actually asked the Byers girl to marry him. You saw him going down the road toward the Byers place four nights out of the seven. He had a quick, light step at variance with his sturdy build, and very different from the heavy, slouching gait of the work-weary farmer. He had a habit of carrying in his hand a little twig or switch cut from a tree. This he would twirl blithely as he walked along. The switch and the twirl represented just so much energy and animal spirits. He never so much as flicked a dandelion head with it.

An inarticulate sort of thing, that courtship.

"Hello, Emma."

"How do, Ben."

"Thought you might like to walk a piece down the road. They got a calf at Aug Tietjens' with five legs."

"I heard. I'd just as lief walk a little piece. I'm kind of beat, though. We've got the threshers day after tomorrow. We've been cooking up."

Beneath Ben's bonhomie and roguishness there was much shyness. The two would plod along the road together in a sort of blissful agony of embarrassment. The neighbors were right in their surmise that there was no definite understanding between them. But the thing was settled in the minds of both. Once Ben had said: "Pop says I can have the north eighty on easy payments if—when——"

Emma Byers had flushed up brightly, but had answered equably: "That's a fine piece. Your pop is an awful good man."

The stolid exteriors of these two hid much that was fine and forceful. Emma Byers' thoughtful forehead and intelligent eyes would have revealed that in her. Her mother was dead. She kept house for her father and brother. She was known as "that smart Byers girl." Her butter and eggs and garden stuff brought higher prices at Commercial, twelve miles away, than did any other's in the district. She was not a pretty girl, according to the local standards, but there was about her, even at twenty-two, a clearheadedness and a restful serenity that promised well for Ben Westerveld's future happiness.

But Ben Westerveld's future was not to lie in Emma Byers' capable hands. He knew that as soon as he saw Bella Huckins. Bella Huckins was the daughter of old "Red Front" Huckins, who ran the saloon of that cheerful name in Commercial. Bella had elected to teach school, not from any bent toward learning but because teaching appealed to her as being a rather elegant occupation. The Huckins family was not elegant. In that day a year or two of teaching in a country school took the place of the present-day normal-school diploma. Bella had an eye on St. Louis, forty miles from the town of Commercial. So she used the country school as a step toward her ultimate goal, though she hated the country and dreaded her apprenticeship.

"I'll get a beau," she said, "who'll take me driving and around. And Saturdays and Sundays I can come to town."

The first time Ben Westerveld saw her she was coming down the road toward him in her tight-fitting black alpaca dress. The sunset was behind her. Her hair was very golden. In a day of tiny waists hers could have been spanned by Ben Westerveld's two hands. He discovered that later. Just now he thought he had never seen anything so fairylike and dainty, though he did not put it that way. Ben was not glib of thought or speech.

He knew at once this was the new schoolteacher. He had heard of her coming, though at the time the conversation had interested him not at all. Bella knew who he was, too. She had learned the name and history of every eligible young man in the district two days after her arrival. That was due partly to her own bold curiosity and partly to the fact that she was boarding with the Widow Becker, the most notorious gossip in the county. In Bella's mental list of the neighborhood swains Ben Westerveld already occupied a position at the top of the column.

He felt his face redden as they approached each other. To hide his embarrassment he swung his little hickory switch gaily and called to his dog Dunder, who was nosing about by the roadside. Dunder bounded forward, spied the newcomer, and leaped toward her playfully and with natural canine curiosity.

Bella screamed. She screamed and ran to Ben and clung to him, clasping her hands about his arm. Ben lifted the hickory switch in his free hand and struck Dunder a sharp cut with it. It was the first time in his life that he had done such a thing. If he had had a sane moment from that time until the day he married Bella Huckins, he never would have forgotten the dumb hurt in Dunder's stricken eyes and shrinking, quivering body.

Bella screamed again, still clinging to him. Ben was saying: "He won't hurt you. He won't hurt you," meanwhile patting her shoulder reassuringly. He looked down at her pale face. She was so slight, so childlike, so apparently different from the sturdy country girls. From—well, from the girls he knew. Her helplessness, her utter femininity, appealed to all that was masculine in him. Bella, the experienced, clinging to him, felt herself swept from head to foot by a queer electric tingling that was very pleasant but that still had in it something of the sensation of a wholesale bumping of one's crazy bone. If she had been anything but a stupid little flirt, she would have realized that here was a specimen of the virile male with which she could not trifle. She glanced up at him now, smiling faintly. "My, I was scared!" She stepped away from him a little—very little.

"Aw, he wouldn't hurt a flea."

But Bella looked over her shoulder fearfully to where Dunder stood by the roadside, regarding Ben with a look of uncertainty. He still thought that perhaps this was a new game. Not a game that he cared for, but still one to be played if his master fancied it. Ben stooped, picked up a stone, and threw it at Dunder, striking him in the flank.

"Go on home!" he commanded sternly. "Go home!" He started toward the dog with a well-feigned gesture of menace. Dunder, with a low howl, put his tail between his legs and loped off home, a disillusioned dog.

Bella stood looking up at Ben. Ben looked down at her.

"You're the new teacher, ain't you?"

"Yes. I guess you must think I'm a fool, going on like a baby about that dog."

"Most girls would be scared of him if they didn't know he wouldn't hurt nobody. He's pretty big."

He paused a moment, awkwardly. "My name's Ben Westerveld."

"Pleased to meet you," said Bella.

"Which way was you going? There's a dog down at Tietjens' that's enough to scare anybody. He looks like a pony, he's so big."

"I forgot something at the school this afternoon, and I was walking over to get it." Which was a lie. "I hope it won't get dark before I get there. You were going the other way, weren't you?"

"Oh, I wasn't going no place in particular. I'll be pleased to keep you company down to the school and back." He was surprised at his own sudden masterfulness.

They set off together, chatting as freely as if they had known one another for years. Ben had been on his way to the Byers farm, as usual. The Byers farm and Emma Byers passed out of his mind as completely as if they had been whisked away on a magic rug.

Bella Huckins had never meant to marry him. She hated farm life. She was contemptuous of farmer folk. She loathed cooking and drudgery. The Huckinses lived above the saloon in Commercial and Mrs. Huckins was always boiling ham and tongue and cooking pigs' feet and shredding cabbage for slaw, all these edibles being destined for the free-lunch counter downstairs. Bella had early made up her mind that there should be no boiling and stewing and frying in her life. Whenever she could find an excuse she loitered about the saloon. There she found life and talk and color. Old Red Front Huckins used to chase her away, but she always turned up again, somehow, with a dish for the lunch counter or with an armful of clean towels.

Ben Westerveld never said clearly to himself, "I want to marry Bella." He never dared meet the thought. He intended honestly to marry Emma Byers. But this thing was too strong for him. As for Bella, she laughed at him, but she was scared, too. They both fought the thing, she selfishly, he unselfishly, for the Byers girl, with her clear, calm eyes and her dependable ways, was heavy on his heart. Ben's appeal for Bella was merely that of the magnetic male. She never once thought of his finer qualities. Her appeal for him was that of the frail and alluring woman. But in the end they married. The neighborhood was rocked with surprise.

Usually in a courtship it is the male who assumes the bright colors of pretense in order to attract a mate. But Ben Westerveld had been too honest to be anything but himself. He was so honest and fundamentally truthful that he refused at first to allow himself to believe that this slovenly shrew was the fragile and exquisite creature he had married. He had the habit of personal cleanliness, had Ben, in a day when tubbing was a ceremony in an environment that made bodily nicety difficult. He discovered that Bella almost never washed and that her appearance of fragrant immaculateness, when dressed, was due to a natural clearness of skin and eye, and to the way her blond hair swept away in a clean line from her forehead. For the rest, she was a slattern, with a vocabulary of invective that would have been a credit to any of the habitués of old Red Front Huckins' bar.

They had three children, a girl and two boys. Ben Westerveld prospered in spite of his wife. As the years went on he added eighty acres here, eighty acres there, until his land swept down to the very banks of the Mississippi. There is no doubt that she hindered him greatly, but he was too expert a farmer to fail. At threshing time the crew looked forward to working for Ben, the farmer, and dreaded the meals prepared by Bella, his wife. She was notoriously the worst cook and housekeeper in the county. And all through the years, in trouble and in happiness, her plaint was the same: "If I'd thought I was going to stick down on a farm all my life, slavin' for a pack of menfolks day and night, I'd rather have died. Might as well be dead as rottin' here."

Her schoolteacher English had early reverted. Her speech was as slovenly as her dress. She grew stout, too, and unwieldy, and her skin coarsened from lack of care and from overeating. And in her children's ears she continually dinned a hatred of farm life and farming. "You can get away from it," she counseled her daughter, Minnie. "Don't you be a rube like your pa," she cautioned John, the older boy. And they profited by her advice. Minnie went to work in Commercial when she was seventeen, an overdeveloped girl with an inordinate love of cheap finery. At twenty, she married an artisan, a surly fellow with roving tendencies. They moved from town to town. He never stuck long at one job. John, the older boy, was as much his mother's son as Minnie was her mother's daughter. Restless, dissatisfied, emptyheaded, he was the despair of his father. He drove the farm horses as if they were racers, lashing them up hill and down dale. He was forever lounging off to the village or wheedling his mother for money to take him to Commercial. It was before the day of the ubiquitous automobile. Given one of those present adjuncts to farm life, John would have ended his career much earlier. As it was, they found him lying by the roadside at dawn one morning after the horses had trotted into the yard with the wreck of the buggy bumping the road behind them. He had stolen the horses out of the barn after the help was asleep, had led them stealthily down the road, and then had whirled off to a rendezvous of his own in town. The fall from the buggy might not have hurt him, but evidently he had been dragged almost a mile before his battered body became somehow disentangled from the splintered wood and the reins.

That horror might have served to bring Ben Westerveld and his wife together, but it did not. It only increased her bitterness and her hatred of the locality and the life.

"I hope you're good an' satisfied now," she repeated in endless reproach. "I hope you're good an' satisfied. You was bound you'd make a farmer out of him, an' now you finished the job. You better try your hand at Dike now for a change."

Dike was young Ben, sixteen; and old Ben had no need to try his hand at him. Young Ben was a born farmer, as was his father. He had come honestly by his nickname. In face, figure, expression, and manner he was a five-hundred-year throwback to his Holland ancestors. Apple-cheeked, stocky, merry of eye, and somewhat phlegmatic. When, at school, they had come to the story of the Dutch boy who saved his town from flood by thrusting his finger into the hole in the dike and holding it there until help came, the class, after one look at the accompanying picture in the reader, dubbed young Ben "Dike" Westerveld. And Dike he remained.

Between Dike and his father there was a strong but unspoken feeling. The boy was cropwise, as his father had been at his age. On Sundays you might see the two walking about the farm, looking at the pigs—great black fellows worth almost their weight in silver; eying the stock; speculating on the winter wheat showing dark green in April, with rich patches that were almost black. Young Dike smoked a solemn and judicious pipe, spat expertly, and voiced the opinion that the winter wheat was a fine prospect.

Ben Westerveld, listening tolerantly to the boy's opinions, felt a great surge of joy that he did not show. Here, at last, was compensation for all the misery and sordidness and bitter disappointment of his married life.

That married life had endured now for more than thirty years. Ben Westerveld still walked with a light, quick step—for his years. The stocky, broad-shouldered figure was a little shrunken. He was as neat and clean at fifty-five as he had been at twenty-five—a habit that, on a farm, is fraught with difficulties. The community knew and respected him. He was a man of standing. When he drove into town on a bright winter morning, in his big sheepskin coat and his shaggy cap and his great boots, and entered the First National Bank, even Shumway, the cashier, would look up from his desk to say:

"Hello, Westerveld! Hello! Well, how goes it?"

When Shumway greeted a farmer in that way you knew that there were no unpaid notes to his discredit.

All about Ben Westerveld stretched the fruit of his toil; the work of his hands. Orchards, fields, cattle, barns, silos. All these things were dependent on him for their future well-being—on him and on Dike after him. His days were full and running over. Much of the work was drudgery; most of it was backbreaking and laborious. But it was his place. It was his reason for being. And he felt that the reason was good, though he never put that thought into words, mental or spoken. He only knew that he was part of the great scheme of things and that he was functioning ably. If he had expressed himself at all, he might have said:

"Well, I got my work cut out for me, and I do it, and do it right."

There was a tractor, now, of course; and a sturdy, middle-class automobile in which Bella lolled red-faced when they drove into town.

As Ben Westerveld had prospered, his shrewish wife had reaped her benefits. Ben was not the selfish type of farmer who insists on twentieth-century farm implements and medieval household equipment. He had added a bedroom here, a cool summer kitchen there, an icehouse, a commodious porch, a washing machine, even a bathroom. But Bella remained unplacated. Her face was set toward the city. And slowly, surely, the effect of thirty years of nagging was beginning to tell on Ben Westerveld. He was the finer metal, but she was the heavier, the coarser. She beat him and molded him as iron beats upon gold.

Minnie was living in Chicago now—a good-natured creature, but slack, like her mother. Her surly husband was still talking of his rights and crying down with the rich. They had two children. Minnie wrote of them, and of the delights of city life. Movies every night. Halsted Street just around the corner. The big stores. State Street. The el took you downtown in no time. Something going on all the while. Bella Westerveld, after one of those letters, was more than a chronic shrew; she became a terrible termagant.

When Ben Westerveld decided to concentrate on hogs and wheat he didn't dream that a world would be clamoring for hogs and wheat for four long years. When the time came, he had them, and sold them fabulously. But wheat and hogs and markets became negligible things on the day that Dike, with seven other farm boys from the district, left for the nearest training camp that was to fit them for France and war.

Bella made the real fuss, wailing and mouthing and going into hysterics. Old Ben took it like a stoic. He drove the boy to town that day. When the train pulled out, you might have seen, if you had looked close, how the veins and cords swelled in the lean brown neck above the clean blue shirt. But that was all. As the weeks went on, the quick, light step began to lag a little. He had lost more than a son; his right-hand helper was gone. There were no farm helpers to be had. Old Ben couldn't do it all. A touch of rheumatism that winter half crippled him for eight weeks. Bella's voice seemed never to stop its plaint.

"There ain't no sense in you trying to make out alone. Next thing you'll die on me, and then I'll have the whole shebang on my hands." At that he eyed her dumbly from his chair by the stove. His resistance was wearing down. He knew it. He wasn't dying. He knew that, too. But something in him was. Something that had resisted her all these years. Something that had made him master and superior in spite of everything.

In those days of illness, as he sat by the stove, the memory of Emma Byers came to him often. She had left that district twenty-eight years ago, and had married, and lived in Chicago somewhere, he had heard, and was prosperous. He wasted no time in idle regrets. He had been a fool, and he paid the price of fools. Bella, slamming noisily about the room, never suspected the presence in the untidy place of a third person—a sturdy girl of twenty-two or -three, very wholesome to look at, and with honest, intelligent eyes and a serene brow.

"It'll get worse an' worse all the time," Bella's whine went on. "Everybody says the war'll last prob'ly for years an' years. You can't make out alone. Everything's goin' to rack and ruin. You could rent out the farm for a year, on trial. The Burdickers'd take it, and glad. They got those three strappin' louts that's all flat-footed or slab-sided or cross-eyed or somethin', and no good for the army. Let them run it on shares. Maybe they'll even buy, if things turn out. Maybe Dike'll never come b——"

But at the look on his face then, and at the low growl of unaccustomed rage that broke from him, even she ceased her clatter.

They moved to Chicago in the early spring. The look that had been on Ben Westerveld's face when he drove Dike to the train that carried him to camp was stamped there again—indelibly this time, it seemed. Calhoun County in the spring has much the beauty of California. There is a peculiar golden light about it, and the hills are a purplish haze. Ben Westerveld, walking down his path to the gate, was more poignantly dramatic than any figure in a rural play. He did not turn to look back, though, as they do in a play. He dared not.

They rented a flat in Englewood, Chicago, a block from Minnie's. Bella was almost amiable these days. She took to city life as though the past thirty years had never been. White kid shoes, delicatessen stores, the movies, the haggling with peddlers, the crowds, the crashing noise, the cramped, unnatural mode of living—necessitated by a four-room flat—all these urban adjuncts seemed as natural to her as though she had been bred in the midst of them.

She and Minnie used to spend whole days in useless shopping. Theirs was a respectable neighborhood of well-paid artisans, bookkeepers, and small shopkeepers. The women did their own housework in drab garments and soiled boudoir caps that hid a multitude of unkempt heads. They seemed to find a great deal of time for amiable, empty gabbling. From seven to four you might see a pair of boudoir caps leaning from opposite bedroom windows, conversing across back porches, pausing in the task of sweeping front steps, standing at a street corner, laden with grocery bundles. Minnie wasted hours in what she called "running over to Ma's for a minute." The two quarreled a great deal, being so nearly of a nature. But the very qualities that combated each other seemed, by some strange chemical process, to bring them together as well.

"I'm going downtown today to do a little shopping," Minnie would say. "Do you want to come along, Ma?"

"What you got to get?"

"Oh, I thought I'd look at a couple little dresses for Pearlie."

"When I was your age I made every stitch you wore."

"Yeh, I bet they looked like it, too. This ain't the farm. I got all I can do to tend to the house, without sewing."

"I did it. I did the housework and the sewin' and cookin', an' besides——"

"A swell lot of housekeepin' you did. You don't need to tell me."

The bickering grew to a quarrel. But in the end they took the downtown el together. You saw them, flushed of face, with twitching fingers, indulging in a sort of orgy of dime spending in the five-and-ten-cent store on the wrong side of State Street. They pawed over bolts of cheap lace and bits of stuff in the stifling air of the crowded place. They would buy a sack of salted peanuts from the great mound in the glass case, or a bag of the greasy pink candy piled in profusion on the counter, and this they would munch as they went.

They came home late, fagged and irritable, and supplemented their hurried dinner with hastily bought food from the near-by delicatessen.

Thus ran the life of ease for Ben Westerveld, retired farmer. And so now he lay impatiently in bed, rubbing a nervous forefinger over the edge of the sheet and saying to himself that, well, here was another day. What day was it? L'see now. Yesterday was—yesterday. A little feeling of panic came over him. He couldn't remember what yesterday had been. He counted back laboriously and decided that today must be Thursday. Not that it made any difference.

They had lived in the city almost a year now. But the city had not digested Ben. He was a leathery morsel that could not be assimilated. There he stuck in Chicago's crop, contributing nothing, gaining nothing. A rube in a comic collar ambling aimlessly about Halsted Street or State downtown. You saw him conversing hungrily with the gritty and taciturn Swede who was janitor for the block of red-brick flats. Ben used to follow him around pathetically, engaging him in the talk of the day. Ben knew no men except the surly Gus, Minnie's husband. Gus, the firebrand, thought Ben hardly worthy of his contempt. If Ben thought, sometimes, of the respect with which he had always been greeted when he clumped down the main street of Commercial—if he thought of how the farmers for miles around had come to him for expert advice and opinion—he said nothing.

Sometimes the janitor graciously allowed Ben to attend to the furnace of the building in which he lived. He took out ashes, shoveled coal. He tinkered and rattled and shook things. You heard him shoveling and scraping down there, and smelled the acrid odor of his pipe. It gave him something to do. He would emerge sooty and almost happy.

"You been monkeying with that furnace again!" Bella would scold. "If you want something to do, why don't you plant a garden in the back yard and grow something? You was crazy about it on the farm."

His face flushed a slow, dull red at that. He could not explain to her that he lost no dignity in his own eyes in fussing about an inadequate little furnace, but that self-respect would not allow him to stoop to gardening— he who had reigned over six hundred acres of bountiful soil.

On winter afternoons you saw him sometimes at the movies, whiling away one of his many idle hours in the dim, close-smelling atmosphere of the place. Tokyo and Rome and Gallipoli came to him. He saw beautiful tiger-women twining fair, false arms about the stalwart but yielding forms of young men with cleft chins. He was only mildly interested. He talked to anyone who would talk to him, though he was naturally a shy man. He talked to the barber, the grocer, the druggist, the streetcar conductor, the milkman, the iceman. But the price of wheat did not interest these gentlemen. They did not know that the price of wheat was the most vital topic of conversation in the world.

"Well, now," he would say, "you take this year's wheat crop, with about 917,000,000 bushels of wheat harvested, why, that's what's going to win the war! Yes, sirree! No wheat, no winning, that's what I say."

"Ya-as, it is!" the city men would scoff. But the queer part of it is that Farmer Ben was right.

Minnie got into the habit of using him as a sort of nursemaid. It gave her many hours of freedom for gadding and gossiping.

"Pa, will you look after Pearlie for a little while this morning? I got to run downtown to match something and she gets so tired and mean-acting if I take her along. Ma's going with me."

He loved the feel of Pearlie's small, velvet-soft hand in his big fist. He called her "little feller," and fed her forbidden dainties. His big brown fingers were miraculously deft at buttoning and unbuttoning her tiny garments, and wiping her soft lips, and performing a hundred tender offices. He was playing a sort of game with himself, pretending this was Dike become a baby again. Once the pair managed to get over to Lincoln Park, where they spent a glorious day looking at the animals, eating popcorn, and riding on the miniature railway.

They returned, tired, dusty, and happy, to a double tirade.

Bella engaged in a great deal of what she called worrying about Dike. Ben spoke of him seldom, but the boy was always present in his thoughts. They had written him of their move, but he had not seemed to get the impression of its permanence. His letters indicated that he thought they were visiting Minnie, or taking a vacation in the city. Dike's letters were few. Ben treasured them, and read and reread them. When the Armistice news came, and with it the possibility of Dike's return, Ben tried to fancy him fitting into the life of the city. And his whole being revolted at the thought.

He saw the pimply-faced, sallow youths standing at the corner of Halsted and Sixty-third, spitting languidly and handling their limp cigarettes with an amazing labial dexterity. Their conversation was low-voiced, sinister, and terse, and their eyes narrowed as they watched the overdressed, scarlet-lipped girls go by. A great fear clutched at Ben Westerveld's heart.

The lack of exercise and manual labor began to tell on Ben. He did not grow fat from idleness. Instead his skin seemed to sag and hang on his frame, like a garment grown too large for him. He walked a great deal. Perhaps that had something to do with it. He tramped miles of city pavements. He was a very lonely man. And then, one day, quite by accident, he came upon South Water Street. Came upon it, stared at it as a water-crazed traveler in a desert gazes upon the spring in the oasis, and drank from it, thirstily, gratefully.

South Water Street feeds Chicago. Into that close-packed thoroughfare come daily the fruits and vegetables that will supply a million tables. Ben had heard of it, vaguely, but had never attempted to find it. Now he stumbled upon it and, standing there, felt at home in Chicago for the first time in more than a year. He saw ruddy men walking about in overalls and carrying whips in their hands—wagon whips, actually. He hadn't seen men like that since he had left the farm. The sight of them sent a great pang of homesickness through him. His hand reached out and he ran an accustomed finger over the potatoes in a barrel on the walk. His fingers lingered and gripped them, and passed over them lovingly.

At the contact something within him that had been tight and hungry seemed to relax, satisfied. It was his nerves, feeding on those familiar things for which they had been starving.

He walked up one side and down the other. Crates of lettuce, bins of onions, barrels of apples. Such vegetables! The radishes were scarlet globes. Each carrot was a spear of pure orange. The green and purple of fancy asparagus held his expert eye. The cauliflower was like a great bouquet, fit for a bride; the cabbages glowed like jade.

And the men! He hadn't dreamed there were men like that in this big, shiny-shod, stiffly laundered, white-collared city. Here were rufous men in overalls—worn, shabby, easy-looking overalls and old blue shirts, and mashed hats worn at a careless angle. Men, jovial, good-natured, with clear eyes, and having about them some of the revivifying freshness and wholesomeness of the products they handled.

Ben Westerveld breathed in the strong, pungent smell of onions and garlic and of the earth that seemed to cling to the vegetables, washed clean though they were. He breathed deeply, gratefully, and felt strangely at peace.

It was a busy street. A hundred times he had to step quickly to avoid a hand truck, or dray, or laden wagon. And yet the busy men found time to greet him friendlily. "H'are you!" they said genially. "H'are you this morning!"

He was marketwise enough to know that some of these busy people were commission men, and some grocers, and some buyers, stewards, clerks. It was a womanless thoroughfare. At the busiest business corner, though, in front of the largest commission house on the street, he saw a woman. Evidently she was transacting business, too, for he saw the men bringing boxes of berries and vegetables for her inspection. A woman in a plain blue skirt and a small black hat.

A funny job for a woman. What weren't they mixing into nowadays! He turned sidewise in the narrow, crowded space in order to pass her little group. And one of the men—a red-cheeked, merry-looking young fellow in a white apron—laughed and said: "Well, Emma, you win. When it comes to driving a bargain with you, I quit. It can't be did!"

Even then he didn't know her. He did not dream that this straight, slim, tailored, white-haired woman, bargaining so shrewdly with these men, was the Emma Byers of the old days. But he stopped there a moment, in frank curiosity, and the woman looked up. She looked up, and he knew those intelligent eyes and that serene brow. He had carried the picture of them in his mind for more than thirty years, so it was not so surprising.

He did not hesitate. He might have if he had thought a moment, but he acted automatically. He stood before her. "You're Emma Byers, ain't you?"

She did not know him at first. Small blame to her, so completely had the roguish, vigorous boy vanished in this sallow, sad-eyed old man. Then: "Why, Ben!" she said quietly. And there was pity in her voice, though she did not mean to have it there. She put out one hand—that capable, reassuring hand—and gripped his and held it a moment. It was queer and significant that it should be his hand that lay within hers.

"Well, what in all get-out are you doing around here, Emma?" He tried to be jovial and easy. She turned to the aproned man with whom she had been dealing and smiled.

"What am I doing here, Joe?"

Joe grinned, waggishly. "Nothin'; only beatin' every man on the street at his own game, and makin' so much money that——"

But she stopped him there. "I guess I'll do my own explaining." She turned to Ben again. "And what are you doing here in Chicago?"

Ben passed a faltering hand across his chin.

"Me? Well, I'm—we're living here, I s'pose. Livin' here."

She glanced at him sharply. "Left the farm, Ben?"

"Yes."

"Wait a minute." She concluded her business with Joe; finished it briskly and to her own satisfaction. With her bright brown eyes and her alert manner and her quick little movements she made you think of a wren—a businesslike little wren—a very early wren that is highly versed in the worm-catching way.

At her next utterance he was startled but game.

"Have you had your lunch?"

"Why, no; I——"

"I've been down here since seven, and I'm starved. Let's go and have a bite at the little Greek restaurant around the corner. A cup of coffee and a sandwich, anyway."

Seated at the bare little table, she surveyed him with those intelligent, understanding, kindly eyes, and he felt the years slip from him. They were walking down the country road together, and she was listening quietly and advising him.

She interrogated him gently. But something of his old masterfulness came back to him. "No, I want to know about you first. I can't get the rights of it, you being here on South Water, tradin' and all."

So she told him briefly. She was in the commission business. Successful. She bought, too, for such hotels as the Blackstone and the Congress, and for half a dozen big restaurants. She gave him bare facts, but he was shrewd enough and sufficiently versed in business to know that here was a woman of established commercial position.

"But how does it happen you're keepin' it up, Emma, all this time? Why, you must be anyway—it ain't that you look it—but——" He floundered, stopped.

She laughed. "That's all right, Ben. I couldn't fool you on that. And I'm working because it keeps me happy. I want to work till I die. My children keep telling me to stop, but I know better than that. I'm not going to rust out. I want to wear out." Then, at an unspoken question in his eyes: "He's dead. These twenty years. It was hard at first, when the children were small. But I knew garden stuff if I didn't know anything else. It came natural to me. That's all."

So then she got his story from him bit by bit. He spoke of the farm and of Dike, and there was a great pride in his voice. He spoke of Bella, and the son who had been killed, and of Minnie. And the words came falteringly. He was trying to hide something, and he was not made for deception. When he had finished:

"Now, listen, Ben. You go back to your farm."

"I can't. She—I can't."

She leaned forward, earnestly. "You go back to the farm."

He turned up his palms with a little gesture of defeat. "I can't."

"You can't stay here. It's killing you. It's poisoning you. Did you ever hear of toxins? That means poisons, and you're poisoning yourself. You'll die of it. You've got another twenty years of work in you. What's ailing you? You go back to your wheat and your apples and your hogs. There isn't a bigger job in the world than that."

For a moment his face took on a glow from the warmth of her own inspiring personality. But it died again. When they rose to go, his shoulders drooped again, his muscles sagged. At the doorway he paused a moment, awkward in farewell. He blushed a little, stammered.

"Emma—I always wanted to tell you. God knows it was luck for you the way it turned out—but I always wanted to——"

She took his hand again in her firm grip at that, and her kindly, bright brown eyes were on him. "I never held it against you, Ben. I had to live a long time to understand it. But I never held a grudge. It just wasn't to be, I suppose. But listen to me, Ben. You do as I tell you. You go back to your wheat and your apples and your hogs. There isn't a bigger man-size job in the world. It's where you belong."

Unconsciously his shoulders straightened again. Again they sagged. And so they parted, the two.

He must have walked almost all the long way home, through miles and miles of city streets. He must have lost his way, too, for when he looked up at a corner street sign it was an unfamiliar one.

So he floundered about, asked his way, was misdirected. He took the right streetcar at last and got off at his own corner at seven o'clock, or later. He was in for a scolding, he knew.

But when he came to his own doorway he knew that even his tardiness could not justify the bedlam of sound that came from within. High-pitched voices. Bella's above all the rest, of course, but there was Minnie's too, and Gus's growl, and Pearlie's treble, and the boy Ed's and——

At the other voice his hand trembled so that the knob rattled in the door, and he could not turn it. But finally he did turn it, and stumbled in, breathing hard. And that other voice was Dike's.

He must have just arrived. The flurry of explanation was still in progress. Dike's knapsack was still on his back, and his canteen at his hip, his helmet slung over his shoulder. A brown, hard, glowing Dike, strangely tall and handsome and older, too. Older.

All this Ben saw in less than one electric second. Then he had the boy's two shoulders in his hands, and Dike was saying, "Hello, Pop."

Of the roomful, Dike and old Ben were the only quiet ones. The others were taking up the explanation and going over it again and again, and marveling, and asking questions.

"He come in to—what's that place, Dike?—Hoboken—yesterday only. An' he sent a dispatch to the farm. Can't you read our letters, Dike, that you didn't know we was here now? And then he's only got an hour more. They got to go to Camp Grant to be, now, demobilized. He came out to Minnie's on a chance. Ain't he big!"

But Dike and his father were looking at each other quietly. Then Dike spoke. His speech was not phlegmatic, as of old. He had a new clipped way of uttering his words:

"Say, Pop, you ought to see the way the Frenchies farm! They got about an acre each, and, say, they use every inch of it. If they's a little dirt blows into the crotch of a tree, they plant a crop in there. I never seen nothin' like it. Say, we waste enough stuff over here to keep that whole country in food for a hundred years. Yessir. And tools! Outta the ark, believe me. If they ever saw our tractor, they'd think it was the Germans comin' back. But they're smart at that. I picked up a lot of new ideas over there. And you ought to see the old birds—womenfolks and men about eighty years old—runnin' everything on the farm. They had to. I learned somethin' off them about farmin'."

"Forget the farm," said Minnie.

"Yeh," echoed Gus, "forget the farm stuff. I can get you a job here out at the works for four-fifty a day, and six when you learn it right."

Dike looked from one to the other, alarm and unbelief on his face. "What d'you mean, a job? Who wants a job! What you all——"

Bella laughed jovially. "F'r heaven's sakes, Dike, wake up! We're livin' here. This is our place. We ain't rubes no more."

Dike turned to his father. A little stunned look crept into his face. A stricken, pitiful look. There was something about it that suddenly made old Ben think of Pearlie when she had been slapped by her quick-tempered mother.

"But I been countin' on the farm," he said miserably. "I just been livin' on the idea of comin' back to it. Why, I—— The streets here, they're all narrow and choked up. I been countin' on the farm. I want to go back and be a farmer. I want——"

And then Ben Westerveld spoke. A new Ben Westerveld—the old Ben Westerveld. Ben Westerveld, the farmer, the monarch over six hundred acres of bounteous bottomland.

"That's all right, Dike," he said. "You're going back. So'm I. I've got another twenty years of work in me. We're going back to the farm."

Bella turned on him, a wildcat. "We ain't! Not me! We ain't! I'm not agoin' back to the farm."

But Ben Westerveld was master again in his own house. "You're goin' back, Bella," he said quietly, "an' things are goin' to be different. You're goin' to run the house the way I say, or I'll know why. If you can't do it, I'll get them in that can. An' me and Dike, we're goin' back to our wheat and our apples and our hogs. Yessir! There ain't a bigger man-size job in the world."

Un Morso doo Pang

[1919]

In 1941, as in 1917, they went to England to California to Texas to France to Florida to Germany—millions and millions of young men of the United States. It was terrible, it was fantastic, to see the pattern repeated This time, hundreds of thousands of girls and women went too, but the millions were left behind. In the faces of these women and in their voices were the same fears. There was not only the fundamental fear that death or injury might strike the far-off lover or husband; there was the fear of his coming back changed, superior in life's experience, traveled, world-wise. Often the women kept step with the marching world. Sometimes they faltered and fell behind.

&§ WHEN YOU ARE TWENTY YOU DO NOT PATRONIZE SUNSETS UNLESS you are unhappy, in love, or both. Tessie Golden was both. Six months ago a sunset had wrung from her only a casual tribute, such as: "My! Look how red the sky is!" delivered as unemotionally as a weather bulletin.

Tessie Golden sat on the top step of the back porch now, a slim, inert heap in a cotton house coat and scuffed slippers. Her head was propped wearily against the porch post. Her hands were limp in her lap. Her face was turned toward the west, where shone that mingling of orange and rose known as salmon pink. But no answering radiance in the girl's face met the glow in the Wisconsin sky.

Saturday night, after supper in Chippewa, Wisconsin, Tessie Golden of the presunset era would have been calling from her bedroom to the kitchen: "Ma, what'd you do with my pink blouse?"

And from the kitchen: "It's in your second bureau drawer. The collar was kind of mussed from Wednesday night, and I give it a little pressing while my iron was on."

At seven-thirty Tessie would have emerged from her bedroom in the pink blouse that might have been considered alarmingly frank as to texture and precariously low as to neck had Tessie herself not been so reassuringly unopulent; a black taffeta skirt, very brief; a hat with a good deal of French blue about it; fragile high-heeled pumps with bows.

As she passed through the sitting room on her way out, her mother would appear in the doorway, dishtowel in hand. Her pride in this slim

68

young thing and her love of her she concealed with a thin layer of carping criticism.

"Runnin' downtown again, I s'pose." A keen eye on the swishing skirt hem.

Tessie, the quick-tongued, would toss the wave of shining hair that lay against either glowing cheek. "Oh, my, no! I just thought I'd dress up in case Angie Hatton drove past in her auto and picked me up for a little ride. So's not to keep her waiting."

Angie Hatton was Old Man Hatton's daughter. Anyone in the Fox River Valley could have told you who Old Man Hatton was. You saw his name at the top of every letterhead of any importance in Chippewa, from the Pulp and Paper Mill to the First National Bank, and including the watch factory, the canning works, and the Mid-Western Land Company. Knowing this, you were able to appreciate Tessie's sarcasm. Angie Hatton was as unaware of Tessie's existence as only a young woman could be whose family residence was in Chippewa, Wisconsin, but who wintered in Italy, summered in the mountains, and bought (so the town said) her very hairpins in New York. When Angie Hatton came home from the East the town used to stroll past on Mondays to view the washing on the Hatton line. Angie's underwear, flirting so audaciously with the sunshine and zephyrs, was of silk and crepe de Chine and satin—materials that we had always thought of heretofore as intended exclusively for party dresses and wedding gowns. Of course, two years later they were showing practically the same thing at Megan's dry-goods store. But that was always the way with Angie Hatton. Even those of us who went to Chicago to shop never quite caught up with her.

Delivered of this ironic thrust, Tessie would walk toward the screen door with a little flaunting sway of the hips. Her mother's eyes, following the slim figure, had a sort of grudging love in them. A spare, caustic, wiry little woman, Tessie's mother. Tessie resembled her as a water color may resemble a blurred charcoal sketch. Tessie's wide mouth curved into humor lines. She was the cutup of the escapement department at the watch factory; the older woman's lips sagged at the corners. Tessie was buoyant and colorful with youth. The other was shrunken and faded with years and labor. As the girl minced across the room in her absurdly high-heeled shoes, the older woman thought: My, but she's pretty! But she said aloud: "I should think you'd stay home once in a while and not be runnin' the streets every night."

"Time enough to be sittin' home when I'm old like you."

And yet between these two there was love, and even understanding. But in families such as Tessie's, demonstration is a thing to be ashamed of;

affection a thing to conceal. Tessie's father was janitor of the Chippewa
High School. A powerful man, slightly crippled by rheumatism, loquacious, lively, fond of his family, proud of his neat gray frame house and
his new cement sidewalk and his carefully tended yard and garden patch.
In all her life Tessie had never seen a caress exchanged between her
parents.

Nowadays Ma Golden had little occasion for finding fault with Tessie's
evening diversion. She no longer had cause to say, "Always gaddin' downtown, or over to Cora's or somewhere, like you didn't have a home to stay
in. You ain't been in a evening this week, only when you washed your
hair."

Tessie had developed a fondness for sunsets viewed from the back porch
—she who had thought nothing of dancing until three and rising at half-
past six to go to work.

Stepping about in the kitchen after supper, her mother would eye the
limp, relaxed figure on the back porch with a little pang at her heart. She
would come to the screen door, or even out to the porch on some errand or
other—to empty the coffee grounds, to turn the row of half-ripe tomatoes
reddening on the porch railing, to flap and hang up a damp tea towel.

"Ain't you goin' out, Tess?"

"No."

"What you want to lop around here for? Such a grand evening. Why
don't you put on your things and run downtown, or over to Cora's or somewhere, hm?"

"What for?"—listlessly.

"What for! What does anybody go out for!"

"I don't know."

If they could have talked it over together, these two, the girl might have
found relief. But the family shyness of their class was too strong upon
them. Once Mrs. Golden had said, in an effort at sympathy, "Person'd
think Chuck Mory was the only one who'd gone to war an' the last fella
left in the world."

A grim flash of the old humor lifted the corners of the wide mouth. "He
is. Who's there left? Stumpy Gans, up at the railroad crossing? Or maybe
Fatty Weiman, driving the garbage. Guess I'll doll up this evening and see
if I can't make a hit with one of them."

She relapsed into bitter silence. The bottom had dropped out of Tessie
Golden's world.

In order to understand the Tessie of today one would have to know the
Tessie of six months ago—Tessie the impudent, the life-loving. Tessie

Golden could say things to the escapement-room foreman that anyone else would have been fired for. Her wide mouth was capable of glorious insolences. Whenever you heard shrieks of laughter from the girls' washroom at noon you knew that Tessie was holding forth to an admiring group. She was a born mimic; audacious, agile, and with the gift of burlesque. The autumn that Angie Hatton came home from Europe wearing the first tight skirt that Chippewa had ever seen, Tessie gave an imitation of that advanced young woman's progress down Grand Avenue in this restricting garment. The thing was cruel in its fidelity, though containing just enough exaggeration to make it artistic. She followed it up by imitating the stricken look on the face of Mattie Haynes, cloak-and-suit buyer at Megan's, who, having just returned from the East with what she considered the most fashionable of the new fall styles, now beheld Angie Hatton in the garb that was the last echo of the last cry in Paris modes—and no model in Mattie's newly selected stock bore even the remotest resemblance to it.

You would know from this that Tessie was not a particularly deft worker. Her big-knuckled fingers were cleverer at turning out a blouse or retrimming a hat. Hers were what are known as handy hands, but not sensitive. It takes a light and facile set of fingers to fit pallet and arbor and fork together: close work and tedious. Seated on low benches along the tables, their chins almost level with the table top, the girls worked with pincers and flame, screwing together the three tiny parts of the watch's anatomy that were their particular specialty. Each wore a jeweler's glass in one eye. Tessie had worked at the watch factory for three years, and the pressure of the glass on the eye socket had given her the slightly hollow-eyed appearance peculiar to experienced watchmakers. It was not unbecoming, though, and lent her, somehow, a spiritual look which made her impudence all the more piquant.

Tessie wasn't always witty, really. But she had achieved a reputation for wit which insured applause for even her feebler efforts. Nap Ballou, the foreman, never left the escapement room without a little shiver of nervous apprehension—a feeling justified by the ripple of suppressed laughter that went up and down the long tables. He knew that Tessie Golden, like a naughty schoolgirl when teacher's back is turned, had directed one of her sure shafts at him.

Ballou, his face darkling, could easily have punished her. Tessie knew it. But he never did, or would. She knew that, too. Her very insolence and audacity saved her.

"Someday," Ballou would warn her, "you'll get too gay, and then you'll find yourself looking for a job."

"Go on—fire me," retorted Tessie, "and I'll meet you in Lancaster"—a form of wit appreciated only by watchmakers. For there is a certain type of watch hand who is as peripatetic as the old-time printer. Restless, ne'er-do-well, spendthrift, he wanders from factory to factory through the chain of watchmaking towns: Springfield, Trenton, Waltham, Lancaster, Waterbury, Chippewa. Usually expert, always unreliable, certainly fond of drink, Nap Ballou was typical of his kind. The steady worker had a mingled admiration and contempt for him. He, in turn, regarded the other as a stick-in-the-mud. Nap wore his cap on one side of his curly head, and drank so evenly and steadily as never to be quite drunk and never strictly sober. He had slender, sensitive fingers like an artist's or a woman's, and he knew the parts of that intricate mechanism known as a watch from the jewel to the finishing room. It was said he had a wife or two. He was forty-six, good-looking in a dissolute sort of way, possessing the charm of the wanderer, generous with his money. It was known that Tessie's barbs were permitted to prick him without retaliation because Tessie herself appealed to his errant fancy.

When the other girls teased her about this obvious state of affairs, something fine and contemptuous welled up in her. "Him! Why, say, he ought to work in a pickle factory instead of a watchworks. All he needs is a little dill and a handful of grape leaves to make him good eatin' as a relish."

And she thought of Chuck Mory, perched on the high seat of the American Express truck, hatless, sunburned, stockily muscular, clattering down Winnebago Street on his way to the depot and the 7:50 train.

Something about the clear simplicity and uprightness of the firm little figure appealed to Nap Ballou. He used to regard her curiously with a long, hard gaze before which she would grow uncomfortable. "Think you'll know me next time you see me?" But there was an uneasy feeling beneath her flip exterior. Not that there was anything of the beautiful, persecuted factory girl and villainous foreman about the situation. Tessie worked at watchmaking because it was light, pleasant, and well paid. She could have found another job for the asking. Her money went for shoes and blouses and lingerie and silk stockings. She was forever buying a vivid necktie for her father and dressing up her protesting mother in gay colors that went ill with the drab, wrinkled face. "If it wasn't for me, you'd go round looking like one of those Polack women down by the tracks," Tessie would scold. "It's a wonder you don't wear a shawl!"

That was the Tessie of six months ago, gay, carefree, holding the reins of her life in her own two capable hands. Three nights a week, and Sunday, she saw Chuck Mory. When she went downtown on Saturday night it was frankly to meet Chuck, who was waiting for her on Schroeder's drugstore corner. He knew it, and she knew it. Yet they always went through a little ceremony. She and Cora, turning into Grand from Winnebago Street, would make for the post office. Then down the length of Grand with a leaping glance at Schroeder's corner before they reached it. Yes, there they were, very clean-shaven, clean-shirted, slick-looking. Tessie would have known Chuck's blond head among a thousand. An air of studied hauteur and indifference as they approached the corner. Heads turned the other way. A low whistle from the boys.

"Oh, how do!"

"Good evening!"

Both greetings done with careful surprise. Then on down the street. On the way back you took the inside of the walk, and your hauteur was now stony to the point of insult. Schroeder's corner simply did not exist. On as far as Megan's, which you entered and inspected, up one brightly lighted aisle and down the next. At the dress-goods counter there was a neat little stack of pamphlets entitled "In the World of Fashion." You took one and sauntered out leisurely. Down Winnebago Street now, homeward bound, talking animatedly and seemingly unconscious of quick footsteps sounding nearer and nearer. Just past the Burke House, where the residential district began, and where the trees cast their kindly shadows: "Can I see you home?" A hand slipped through her arm; a little tingling thrill.

"Oh, why, how do, Chuck! Hello, Scotty. Sure, if you're going our way."

At every turn Chuck left her side and dashed around behind her in order to place himself at her right again, according to the rigid rule of Chippewa etiquette. He took her arm only at street crossings until they reached the tracks, which perilous spot seemed to justify him in retaining his hold throughout the remainder of the stroll. Usually they lost Cora and Scotty without having been conscious of their loss.

Their talk? The girls and boys that each knew; the day's happenings at factory and express office; next Wednesday night's dance up in the Chute; and always the possibility of Chuck's leaving the truck and assuming the managership of the office.

"Don't let this go any further, see? But I heard it straight that old Benke is going to be transferred to Fond du Lac. And if he is, why, I step in, see? Benke's got a girl in Fondy, and he's been pluggin' to get there. Gee, maybe I won't be glad when he does!" A little silence. "Will you be glad, Tess? Hm?"

Tess felt herself glowing and shivering as the big hand closed more tightly on her arm. "Me? Why, sure I'll be pleased to see you get a job that's coming to you by rights, and that'll get you better pay, and all."

But she knew what he meant, and he knew she knew.

No more of that now. Chuck—gone. Scotty—gone. All the boys at the watchworks, all the fellows in the neighborhood—gone. At first she hadn't minded. It was exciting. You kidded them at first: "Well, believe me, Chuck, if you shoot the way you play ball, you're a gone goon already."

"All you got to do, Scotty, is to stick that face of yours up over the top of the trench and the Germans'll die of fright and save you wasting bullets."

There was a great knitting of socks and sweaters and caps. Tessie's big-knuckled, capable fingers made you dizzy, they flew so fast. Chuck was outfitted as for a polar expedition. Tess took half a day off to bid him good-by. They marched down Grand Avenue, that first lot of them, in their everyday suits and hats, with their shiny yellow suitcases and their paste-board boxes in their hands, sheepish, red-faced, awkward. In their eyes, though, a certain look. And so off for Camp Sherman, their young heads sticking out of the car windows in clusters—black, yellow, brown, red. But for each woman on the depot platform there was just one head. Tessie saw a blurred blond one with a misty halo around it. A great shouting and wav-ing of handkerchiefs:

"Good-by! Good-by! Write, now! Be sure! Mebbe you can get off in a week, for a visit. Good-by! Good——"

They were gone. Their voices came back to the crowd on the depot plat-form—high, clear young voices; almost like the voices of children, shouting.

Well, you wrote letters—fat, bulging letters—and in turn you received equally plump envelopes with a red emblem in one corner. You sent boxes of homemade fudge (nut variety) and cookies and the more durable forms of cake.

Then, unaccountably, Chuck was whisked all the way to California. He was furious at parting with his mates, and his indignation was expressed in his letters to Tessie. She sympathized with him in her replies. She tried to make light of it, but there was a little clutch of terror in it, too. California! Might as well send a person to the end of the world while they were about it. Two months of that. Then, inexplicably again, Chuck's letters bore the astounding postmark of New York. She thought, in a panic, that he was Franceward bound, but it turned out not to be so. Not yet. Chuck's letters were taking on a cosmopolitan tone. "Well," he wrote, "I guess the little old town is as dead as ever. It seems funny you being right there all this time and I've traveled from the Atlantic to the Pacific. Everybody treats me swell. You ought to seen some of those California houses. They make Hat-ton's place look like a dump."

The girls, Cora and Tess and the rest, laughed and joked among them-selves and assured one another, with a toss of the head, that they could have a good time without the fellas. They didn't need boys around.

They gave parties, and they were not a success. There was one of the type known as a stag. "Some hen party!" they all said. They danced, and sang "Over There." They had ice cream and chocolate layer cake and went home in great hilarity, with their hands on each other's shoulders, still singing.

But the thing was a failure, and they knew it. Next day, at the lunch hour and in the washroom, there was a little desultory talk about the stag. But the meat of such an aftergathering is contained in phrases such as "I says to him" and "He says to me." They wasted little conversation on the stag. It was much more exciting to exhibit letters on blue-lined paper with the red emblem at the top. Chuck's last letter had contained the news of his sergeancy.

Angie Hatton, home from the East, was writing letters, too. Everyone in Chippewa knew that. She wrote on that new art paper with the gnawed-looking edges and stiff as a newly laundered cuff. But the letters which she awaited so eagerly were written on the same sort of paper as were those Tessie had from Chuck—blue-lined, cheap in quality. A New York fellow, Chippewa learned; an aviator. They knew, too, that young Hatton was an infantry lieutenant somewhere in the East. These letters were not from him.

Ever since her home-coming, Angie had been sewing at the Red Cross shop on Grand Avenue. Chippewa boasted two Red Cross shops. The Grand Avenue shop was the society shop. The East End crowd sewed there, capped, veiled, aproned—and unapproachable. Were your fingers ever so deft, your knowledge of seams and basting mathematical, your skill with that complicated garment known as a pneumonia jacket uncanny; if you did not belong to the East End set, you did not sew at the Grand Avenue shop. No matter how grossly red the blood which the Grand Avenue bandages and pads were ultimately to stanch, the liquid in the fingers that rolled and folded them was pure cerulean.

Tessie and her crowd had never thought of giving any such service to their country. They spoke of the Grand Avenue workers as "that stinkin' bunch." Yet each one of the girls was capable of starting a blouse in an emergency on Saturday night and finishing it in time for a Sunday picnic, buttonholes and all. Their help might have been invaluable. It never was asked.

Without warning, Chuck came home on three days' furlough. It meant that he was bound for France right enough this time. But Tessie didn't care.

"I don't care where you're goin'," she said exultantly, her eyes lingering on the stocky, straight, powerful figure in its rather ill-fitting khaki. "You're here now. That's enough. Ain't you tickled to be home, Chuck? Gee!"

"I'll say," responded Chuck. But even he seemed to detect some lack in his tone and words. He elaborated somewhat shamefacedly: "Sure. It's swell to be home. But I don't know. After you've traveled around, and come back, things look so kind of little to you. I don't know—kind of——" He floundered about, at a loss for expression. Then tried again: "Now, take Hatton's place, for example. I always used to think it was a regular palace, but, gosh, you ought to see places where I was asked to in San Francisco and around there. Why, they was—were—enough to make the Hatton house look like a shack. Swimmin' pools of white marble, and acres of yard like a park, and the help always bringing you something to eat or drink. And the folks themselves—why, say! Here we are scraping and bowing to Hattons and that bunch. They're pikers to what some people are that invited me to their houses in New York and Berkeley, and treated me and the other guys like kings or something. Take Megan's store, too"—he was warming to his subject, so that he failed to notice the darkening of Tessie's face—"it's a joke compared to New York and San Francisco stores. Reg'lar hick joint."

Tessie stiffened. Her teeth were set, her eyes sparkled. She tossed her head. "Well, I'm sure, Mr. Mory, it's good enough for me. Too bad you had to come home at all now you're so elegant and swell, and everything. You better go call on Angie Hatton instead of wasting time on me. She'd probably be tickled to see you."

He stumbled to his feet, then, awkwardly. "Aw, say, Tessie, I didn't mean—why, say—you don't suppose—why, believe me, I pretty near busted out cryin' when I saw the Junction eatin' house when my train came in. And I been thinking of you every minute. There wasn't a day——"

"Tell that to your swell New York friends. I may be a hick but I ain't a fool." She was near to tears.

"Why, say, Tess, listen! Listen! If you knew—if you knew—— A guy's got to—he's got no right to——"

And presently Tessie was mollified, but only on the surface. She smiled and glanced and teased and sparkled. And beneath was terror. He talked differently. He walked differently. It wasn't his clothes or the army. It was something else—an ease of manner, a new leisureliness of glance, an air. Once Tessie had gone to Milwaukee over Labor Day. It was the extent of her experience as a traveler. She remembered how superior she had felt for at least two days after. But Chuck! California! New York! It wasn't the distance that terrified her. It was his new knowledge, the broadening of his vision, though she did not know it and certainly could not have put it into words.

They went walking down by the river to Oneida Springs, and drank some of the sulphur water that tasted like rotten eggs. Tessie drank it with little shrieks and shudders and puckered her face up into an expression indicative of extreme disgust.

"It's good for you," Chuck said, and drank three cups of it, manfully. "That taste is the mineral qualities the water contains—sulphur and iron and so forth."

"I don't care," snapped Tessie irritably. "I hate it!" They had often walked along the river and tasted of the spring water, but Chuck had never before waxed scientific. They took a boat at Baumann's boathouse and drifted down the lovely Fox River.

"Want to row?" Chuck asked. "I'll get an extra pair of oars if you do."

"I don't know how. Besides, it's too much work. I guess I'll let you do it."

Chuck was fitting his oars in the oarlocks. She stood on the landing, looking down at him. His hat was off. His hair seemed blonder than ever against the rich tan of his face. His neck muscles swelled a little as he bent. Tessie felt a great longing to bury her face in the warm red skin. He straightened with a sigh and smiled at her. "I'll be ready in a minute." He took off his coat and turned his khaki shirt in at the throat, so that you saw the white line of his untanned chest in strange contrast to his sun-burned throat. A feeling of giddy faintness surged over Tessie. She stepped blindly into the boat and would have fallen if Chuck's hard, firm grip had not steadied her. "Whoa, there! Don't you know how to step into a boat? There. Walk along the middle."

She sat down and smiled up at him. "I don't know how I come to do that. I never did before."

Chuck braced his feet, rolled up his sleeves, and took an oar in each brown hand, bending rhythmically to his task. He looked about him, then at the girl, and drew a deep breath, feathering his oars. "I guess I must have dreamed about this more'n a million times."

"Have you, Chuck?"

They drifted on in silence. "Say, Tess, you ought to learn to row. It's good exercise. Those girls in California and New York, they play tennis and row and swim as good as the boys. Honest, some of 'em are wonders!"

"Oh, I'm sick of your swell New York friends! Can't you talk about something else?"

He saw that he had blundered without in the least understanding how or why. "All right. What'll we talk about?" In itself a fatal admission.

"About—you." Tessie made it a caress.

"Me? Nothin' to tell about me. I just been drillin' and studyin' and marchin' and readin' some—— Oh, say, what d'you think?"

"What?"

"They been learnin' us—teachin' us, I mean—Frencʰ. It's the darnedest language! Bread is pain. Can you beat that? If you want to ask for a piece of bread, you say like this: *Donnay ma un morso doo pang.* See?"

"My!" breathed Tessie.

And within her something was screaming: Oh, my God! Oh, my God! He knows French. And those girls that can row and swim and everything. And me, I don't know anything. Oh, God, what'll I do?

It was as though she could see him slipping away from her, out of her grasp, out of her sight. She had no fear of what might come to him in France. Bullets and bayonets would never hurt Chuck. He'd make it, just as he always made the 7:50 when it seemed as if he was going to miss it sure. He'd make it there and back, all right. But he'd be a different Chuck, while she stayed the same Tessie. Books, travel, French, girls, swell folks——

And all the while she was smiling and dimpling and trailing her hand in the water. "Bet you can't guess what I got in that lunch box."

"Chocolate cake."

"Well, of course I've got chocolate cake. I baked it myself this morning."

"Yes, you did!"

"Why, Chuck Mory, I did so! I guess you think I can't do anything, the way you talk."

"Oh, don't I! I guess you know what I think."

"Well, it isn't the cake I mean. It's something else."

"Fried chicken!"

"Oh, now you've gone and guessed it." She pouted prettily.

"You asked me to, didn't you?"

Then they laughed together, as at something exquisitely witty.

Down the river, drifting, rowing. Tessie pointed to a house half hidden among the trees on the farther shore: "There's Hatton's camp. They say they have grand times there with their swell crowd some Saturdays and Sundays. If I had a house like that, I'd live in it all the time, not just a couple of days out of the whole year." She hesitated a moment. "I suppose it looks like a shanty to you now."

Chuck surveyed it, patronizingly. "No, it's a nice little place."

They beached their boat, and built a little fire, and had supper on the riverbank, and Tessie picked out the choice bits for him—the breast of the chicken, beautifully golden brown; the ripest tomato; the firmest, juiciest pickle; the corner of the little cake which would give him a double share of icing.

From Chuck, between mouthfuls: "I guess you don't know how good this tastes. Camp grub's all right, but after you've had a few months of it you get so you don't believe there *is* such a thing as real fried chicken and homemade chocolate cake."

"I'm glad you like it, Chuck. Here, take this drumstick. You ain't eating a thing!" His fourth piece of chicken.

Down the river as far as the danger line just above the dam, with Tessie pretending fear just for the joy of having Chuck reassure her. Then back again in the dusk, Chuck bending to the task now against the current. And so up the hill, homeward bound. They walked very slowly, Chuck's hand on her arm. They were dumb with the tragic, eloquent dumbness of their kind. If she could have spoken the words that were churning in her mind, they would have been something like this:

"Oh, Chuck, I wish I was married to you. I wouldn't care if only I had you. I wouldn't mind babies or anything. I'd be glad. I want our house, with a dining-room set, and a mahogany bed, and one of those overstuffed sets in the living room, and all the housework to do. I'm scared. I'm scared I won't get it. What'll I do if I don't?"

And he, wordlessly: "Will you wait for me, Tessie, and keep on thinking about me? And will you keep yourself like you are so that if I come back——"

Aloud, she said: "I guess you'll get stuck on one of those French girls. I should worry! They say wages at the watch factory are going to be raised, workers are so scarce. I'll probably be as rich as Angie Hatton time you get back."

And he, miserably: "Little old Chippewa girls are good enough for Chuck. I ain't counting on taking up with those Frenchies. I don't like their jabber, from what I know of it. I saw some pictures of 'em, last week, a fellow in camp had who'd been over there. Their hair is all funny, and fixed up with combs and stuff, and they look real dark like foreigners."

It had been reassuring enough at the time. But that was six months ago. And now here was the Tessie who sat on the back porch, evenings, surveying the sunset. A listless, lackadaisical, brooding Tessie. Little point to going downtown Saturday nights now. There was no familiar, beloved figure to follow you swiftly as you turned off Elm Street, homeward bound. If she went downtown now, she saw only those Saturday-night family groups which are familiar to every small town. The husband, very damp as to hair and clean as to shirt, guarding the gocart outside while the woman accomplished her Saturday-night trading at Ding's or Halpin's. Sometimes there were as many as half a dozen gocarts outside Halpin's, each containing a sleeping burden, relaxed, chubby, fat-cheeked. The waiting men smoked their pipes and conversed largely. "Hello, Ed. The woman's inside, buyin' the store out, I guess."

"That so? Mine, too. Well, how's everything?"

Tessie knew that presently the woman would come out, bundle laden, and that she would stow these lesser bundles in every corner left available by the more important sleeping bundle—two yards of oilcloth; a spool of 100, white; a banana for the baby; a new stewpan at the five-and-ten.

There had been a time when Tessie, if she thought of these women at all, felt sorry for them—worn, drab, lacking in style and figure. Now she envied them.

There were weeks upon weeks when no letter came from Chuck. In his last letter there had been some talk of his being sent to Russia. Tessie's eyes, large enough now in her thin face, distended with a great fear. Russia! His letter spoke, too, of French villages and châteaux. He and a bunch of fellows had been introduced to a princess or a countess or something—it was all one to Tessie—and what do you think? She had kissed them all on both cheeks! Seems that's the way they did in France.

The morning after the receipt of this letter the girls at the watch factory might have remarked her pallor had they not been so occupied with a new and more absorbing topic.

"Tess, did you hear about Angie Hatton?"

"What about her?"

"She's going to France. It's in the Milwaukee paper, all about her being Chippewa's fairest daughter, and a picture of the house, and her being the belle of the Fox River Valley, and she's giving up her palatial home and all to go to work in a canteen for her country and bleeding France."

"Ya-as she is!" sneered Tessie, and a dull red flush, so deep as to be painful, swept over her face from throat to brow. "Ya-as she is, the doll-faced simp! Why, say, she never wiped up a floor in her life, or baked a cake, or stood on them feet of hers. She couldn't cut up a loaf of bread decent. Bleeding France! Ha! That's rich, that is." She thrust her chin out brutally, and her eyes narrowed to slits. "She's going over there after that fella of hers. She's chasing him. It's now or never, and she knows it and she's scared, same's the rest of us. On'y we got to set home and make the best of it. Or take what's left." She turned her head slowly to where Nap Ballou stood over a table at the far end of the room. She laughed a grim, unlovely little laugh. "I guess when you can't go after what you want, like Angie, why you gotta take second choice."

All that day, at the bench, she was the reckless, insolent, audacious Tessie of six months ago. Nap Ballou was always standing over her, pretending to inspect some bit of work or other, his shoulder brushing hers. She laughed up at him so that her face was not more than two inches from his. He flushed, but she did not. She laughed a reckless little laugh.

"Thanks for helping teach me my trade, Mr. Ballou. 'Course I only been at it over three years now, so I ain't got the hang of it yet."

He straightened up slowly, and as he did so he rested a hand on her shoulder for a brief moment. She did not shrug it off.

That night, after supper, Tessie put on her hat and strolled down to Park Avenue. It wasn't for the walk. Tessie had never been told to exercise systematically for her body's good, or her mind's. She went in a spirit of unwholesome brooding curiosity and a bitter resentment. Going to France, was she? Lots of good she'd do there. Better stay home and—and what? Tessie cast about in her mind for a fitting job for Angie. Guess she might's well go, after all. Nobody'd miss her, unless it was her father, and he didn't see her but about a third of the time. But in Tessie's heart was a great envy of this girl who could bridge the hideous waste of ocean that separated her from her man. Bleeding France. Yeh! Joke!

The Hatton place, built and landscaped twenty years before, occupied a square block in solitary grandeur, the show place of Chippewa. In architectural style it was an impartial mixture of Norman castle, French château, and Rhenish schloss, with a dash of Coney Island about its façade. It represented Old Man Hatton's realized dream of landed magnificence.

Tessie, walking slowly past it, and peering through the high iron fence, could not help noting an air of unwonted excitement about the place, usually so aloof, so coldly serene. Automobiles standing out in front. People going up and down. They didn't look very cheerful. Just as if it mattered whether anything happened to her or not!

Tessie walked around the block and stood a moment, uncertainly. Then she struck off down Grand Avenue and past Donovan's pool shack. A little group of after-supper idlers stood outside, smoking and gossiping, as she knew there would be. As she turned the corner she saw Nap Ballou among them. She had known that, too. As she passed she looked straight ahead, without bowing. But just past the Burke House he caught up with her. No half-shy "Can I walk home with you?" from Nap Ballou. No. Instead: "Hello, sweetheart!"

"Hello, yourself."

"Somebody's looking mighty pretty this evening, all dolled up in pink."

"Think so?"

She tried to be pertly indifferent, but it was good to have someone following, someone walking home with you. What if he was old enough to be her father, with graying hair? Lots of the movie heroes had graying hair at the sides.

They walked for an hour. Tessie left him at the corner. She had once heard her father designate Ballou as "that drunken skunk." When she entered the sitting room her cheeks held an unwonted pink. Her eyes were brighter than they had been in months. Her mother looked up quickly, peering at her over a pair of steel-rimmed spectacles, very much askew.

"Where you been, Tessie?"

"Oh, walkin'."

"Who with?"

"Cora."

"Why, she was here, callin' for you, not more'n an hour ago."

Tessie, taking off her hat on her way upstairs, met this coolly. "Yeh, I ran into her comin' back."

Upstairs, lying fully dressed on her hard little bed, she stared up into the darkness, thinking, her hands limp at her sides. Oh, well, what's the diff? You had to make the best of it. Everybody makin' a fuss about the soldiers—feeding 'em, and asking 'em to their houses, and sending 'em things, and giving dances and picnics and parties so they wouldn't be lonesome. Chuck had told her all about it. The other boys told the same. They could just pick and choose their good times. Tessie's mind groped about, sensing a certain injustice. How about the girls? She didn't put it thus squarely. Hers was not a logical mind. Easy enough to paw over the menfolks and get silly over brass buttons and a uniform. She put it that way. She thought of the refrain of a popular song: "What Are You Going to Do to Help the Boys?" Tessie, smiling a crooked little smile up there in the darkness, parodied the words deftly: "What're you going to do to help the girls?" she demanded. "What're you going to do——" She rolled over on one side and buried her head in her arms.

There was news again next morning at the watch factory. Tessie of the old days had never needed to depend on the other girls for the latest bit of gossip. Her alert eye and quick ear had always caught it first. But of late she had led a cloistered existence, indifferent to the world about her. The Chippewa *Courier* went into the newpaper pile behind the kitchen door without a glance from Tessie's incurious eye.

She was late this morning. As she sat down at the bench and fitted her glass in her eye, the chatter of the others, pitched in the high key of unusual excitement, penetrated even her listlessness.

"And they say she never screeched or fainted or anything. She stood there, kind of quiet, looking straight ahead, and then all of a sudden she ran to her pa——"

"I feel sorry for her. She never did anything to me. She——"

Tessie spoke, her voice penetrating the staccato fragments all about her and gathering them into a whole. "Say, who's the heroine of this picture? I come in in the middle of the film, I guess."

They turned on her with the unlovely eagerness of those who have ugly news to tell. They all spoke at once, in short sentences, their voices high with the note of hysteria.

"Angie Hatton's beau was killed——"

"They say his airyoplane fell ten thousand feet——"

"The news come only last evening about eight——"

"She won't see nobody but her pa——"

Eight! At eight Tessie had been standing outside Hatton's house, envying Angie and hating her. So that explained the people, and the automobiles, and the excitement. Tessie was not receiving the news with the dramatic reaction which its purveyors felt it deserved. Tessie, turning from one to the other quietly, had said nothing. She was pitying Angie. Oh, the luxury of it! Nap Ballou, coming in swiftly to still the unwonted commotion in work hours, found Tessie the only one quietly occupied in that chatter-filled room. She was smiling as she worked. Nap Ballou, bending over her on some pretense that deceived no one, spoke low-voiced in her ear. But she veiled her eyes insolently and did not glance up. She hummed contentedly all the morning at her tedious work.

She had promised Nap Ballou to go picknicking with him Sunday. Down the river, boating, with supper on shore. The small, still voice within her had said, "Don't go! Don't go!" But the harsh, high-pitched, reckless overtone said, "Go on! Have a good time. Take all you can get."

She would have to lie at home and she did it. Some fabrication about the girls at the watchworks did the trick. Fried chicken, chocolate cake. She packed them deftly and daintily. High-heeled shoes, flimsy blouse, rustling skirt. Nap Ballou was waiting for her over in the city park. She saw him before he espied her. He was leaning against a tree, idly, staring straight ahead with queer, lackluster eyes. Silhouetted there against the tender green of the pretty square, he looked very old, somehow, and different—much older than he looked in his shop clothes, issuing orders. Tessie noticed that he sagged where he should have stuck out, and protruded where he should have been flat. There flashed across her mind a vividly clear picture of Chuck as she had last seen him—brown, fit, high of chest, flat of stomach, slim of flank.

Ballou saw her. He straightened and came toward her swiftly. "Somebody looks mighty sweet this afternoon."

Tessie plumped the heavy lunch box into his arms. "When you get a line you like you stick to it, don't you?"

Down at the boathouse even Tessie, who had confessed ignorance of boats and oars, knew that Ballou was fumbling clumsily. He stooped to adjust the oars to the oarlocks. His hat was off. His hair looked very gray in the cruel spring sunshine. He straightened and smiled up at her.

"Ready in a minute, sweetheart," he said. He took off his collar and turned in the neckband of his shirt. His skin was very white. Tessie felt a little shudder of disgust sweep over her, so that she stumbled a little as she stepped into the boat.

The river was very lovely. Tessie trailed her fingers in the water and told herself that she was having a grand time. She told Nap the same when he asked her.

"Having a good time, little beauty?" he said. He was puffing a little with the unwonted exercise.

Tessie tried some of her old-time pertness of speech. "Oh, good enough, considering the company."

He laughed admiringly at that and said she was a sketch.

When the early evening came on they made a clumsy landing and had supper. This time Nap fed her the tidbits, though she protested. "White meat for you," he said, "with your skin like milk."

"You must of read that in a book," scoffed Tessie. She glanced around her at the deepening shaadows. "We haven't got much time. It gets dark so early."

"No hurry," Nap assured her. He went on eating in a leisurely, finicking sort of way, though he consumed very little food, actually.

"You're not eating much," Tessie said once, halfheartedly. She decided that she wasn't having such a very grand time, after all, and that she hated his teeth, which were very bad. Now, Chuck's strong, white, double row——

"Well," she said, "let's be going."

"No hurry," again.

Tessie looked up at that with the instinctive fear of her kind. "What d'you mean, no hurry! 'Spect to stay here till dark?" She laughed at her own joke.

"Yes."

She got up then, the blood in her face. "Well, *I* don't."

He rose, too. "Why not?"

"Because I don't, that's why." She stooped and began picking up the remnants of the lunch, placing spoons and glass bottles swiftly and thriftily into the lunch box. Nap stepped around behind her.

"Let me help," he said. And then his arm was about her and his face was close to hers, and Tessie did not like it. He kissed her after a little wordless struggle. And then she knew. She had been kissed before. But not like this. Not like this! She struck at him furiously. Across her mind flashed the memory of a girl who had worked in the finishing room. A nice girl, too. But that hadn't helped her. Nap Ballou was laughing a little as he clasped her.

At that she heard herself saying: "I'll get Chuck Mory after you—you drunken bum, you! He'll lick you black and blue. He'll——"

The face, with the ugly, broken brown teeth, was coming close again. With all the young strength that was in her she freed one hand and clawed at that face from eyes to chin. A howl of pain rewarded her. His hold loosened. Like a flash she was off. She ran. It seemed to her that her feet did not touch the earth. Over brush, through bushes, crashing against trees, on and on. She heard him following her, but the broken-down engine that was his heart refused to do the work. She ran on, though her fear was as great as before. Fear of what might have happened—to her, Tessie Golden, that nobody could even talk fresh to. She gave a sob of fury and fatigue. She was stumbling now. It was growing dark. She ran on again, in fear of the overtaking darkness. It was easier now. Not so many trees and bushes. She came to a fence, climbed over it, lurched as she landed, leaned against it weakly for support, one hand on her aching heart. Before her was the Hatton summer cottage, dimly outlined in the twilight among the trees. A warm, flickering light danced in the window.

Tessie stood a moment, breathing painfully, sobbingly. Then, with an instinctive gesture, she patted her hair, tidied her blouse, and walked uncertainly toward the house, up the steps to the door. She stood there a moment, swaying slightly. Somebody'd be there. The light. The woman who cooked for them or the man who took care of the place. Somebody'd——

She knocked at the door feebly. She'd tell 'em she had lost her way and got scared when it began to get dark. She knocked again, louder now. Footsteps. She braced herself and even arranged a crooked smile. The door opened wide. Old Man Hatton!

She looked up at him, terror and relief in her face. He peered over his glasses at her. "Who is it?" Tessie had not known, somehow, that his face was so kindly.

Tessie's carefully planned story crumbled into nothingness. "It's me!" she whimpered. "It's me!"

He reached out and put a hand on her arm and drew her inside.

"Angie! Angie! Here's a poor little kid——"

Tessie clutched frantically at the last crumbs of her pride. She tried to straighten, to smile with her old bravado. What was that story she had planned to tell?

"Who is it, Dad? Who——?" Angie Hatton came into the hallway. She stared at Tessie. Then: "Why, my dear!" she said. "My dear! Come in here."

Angie Hatton! Tessie began to cry weakly, her face buried in Angie Hatton's expensive shoulder. Tessie remembered later that she had felt no surprise at the act.

"There, there!" Angie Hatton was saying. "Just poke up the fire, Dad. And get something from the dining room. Oh, I don't know. To drink, you know. Something——"

Then Old Man Hatton stood over her, holding a small glass to her lips. Tessie drank it obediently, made a wry little face, coughed, wiped her eyes, and sat up. She looked from one to the other, like a trapped little animal. She put a hand to her tousled head.

"That's all right," Angie Hatton assured her. "You can fix it after a while."

There they were, the three of them: Old Man Hatton with his back to the fire, looking benignly down upon her; Angie seated, with some knitting in her hands, as if entertaining bedraggled, tear-stained young ladies at dusk were an everyday occurrence; Tessie, twisting her handkerchief in a torment of embarrassment. But they asked no questions, these two. They evinced no curiosity about this disheveled creature who had flung herself in upon their decent solitude.

Tessie stared at the fire. She looked up at Old Man Hatton's face and opened her lips. She looked down and shut them again. Then she flashed a quick look at Angie, to see if she could detect there some suspicion, some disdain. None. Angie Hatton looked—well, Tessie put it to herself, thus: "She looks like she'd cried till she couldn't cry no more—only inside."

And then, surprisingly, Tessie began to talk. "I wouldn't never have gone with this fella, only Chuck, he was gone. All the boys're gone. It's fierce. You get scared, sitting home, waiting, and they're in France and everywhere, learning French and everything, and meeting grand people and having a fuss made over 'em. So I got mad and said I didn't care, I wasn't going to squat home all my life, waiting——"

Angie Hatton had stopped knitting now. Old Man Hatton was looking down at her very kindly. And so Tessie went on. The pent-up emotions and thoughts of these past months were finding an outlet at last. These things which she had never been able to discuss with her mother she now was laying bare to Angie Hatton and Old Man Hatton! They asked no questions. They seemed to understand. Once Old Man Hatton interrupted with: "So that's the kind of fellow they've got as escapement-room fore-man, eh?"

Tessie, whose mind was working very clearly now, put out a quick hand. "Say, it wasn't his fault. He's a bum, all right, but I knew it, didn't I? It was me. I didn't care. Seemed to me it didn't make no difference who I went with, but it does." She looked down at her hands clasped so tightly in her lap.

"Yes, it makes a whole lot of difference," Angie agreed, and looked up at her father.

At that Tessie blurted her last desperate problem: "He's learning all kind of new things. Me, I ain't learning anything. When Chuck comes home he'll just think I'm dumb, that's all. He——"

"What kind of thing would you like to learn, Tessie, so that when Chuck comes home——"

Tessie looked up then, her wide mouth quivering with eagerness. "I'd like to learn to swim—and row a boat—and play tennis—like the rich girls—like the girls that's making such a fuss over the soldiers."

Angie Hatton was not laughing. So, after a moment's hesitation, Tessie brought out the worst of it. "And French. I'd like to learn to talk French."

Old Man Hatton had been surveying his shoes, his mouth grim. He looked at Angie now and smiled a little. "Well, Angie, it looks as if you'd found your job right here at home, doesn't it? This young lady's just one of hundreds, I suppose. Thousands. You can have the whole house for them, if you want it, Angie, and the grounds, and all the money you need. I guess we've kind of overlooked the girls. Hm, Angie? What d'you say?"

But Tessie was not listening. She had scarcely heard. Her face was white with earnestness.

"Can you speak French?"

"Yes," Angie answered.

"Well," said Tessie, and gulped once, "well, how do you say in French: 'Give me a piece of bread'? That's what I want to learn first."

Angie Hatton said it correctly.

"That's it! Wait a minute! Say it again, will you?"

Angie said it again.

Tessie wet her lips. Her cheeks were smeared with tears and dirt. Her hair was wild and her blouse awry. *"Donnay-ma-un-morso-doo-pang,"* she articulated painfully. And in that moment, as she put her hand in that of Chuck Mory, across the ocean, her face was very beautiful with contentment.

Long Distance

[1919]

It is a great pity that this story, written in 1918, is not a museum piece belonging to a past Dark Age. Shockingly enough, it is part of our own present Dark Age. And a replica of the boy of this story, multiplied by thousands and thousands, can now be found, almost thirty years later, still sitting in a hospital ward or garden, painting that wooden chicken yellow and waiting for the light to break.

CHET BALL WAS PAINTING A WOODEN CHICKEN YELLOW. THE WOODEN chicken was mounted on a six-by-twelve board. The board was mounted on four tiny wheels. The whole would eventually be pulled on a string guided by the plump, moist hand of some blissful five-year-old.

You got the incongruity of it the instant your eye fell upon Chet Ball. Chet's shoulders alone would have loomed large in contrast with any wooden toy ever devised, including the Trojan horse. Everything about him, from the big, blunt-fingered hands that held the ridiculous chick to the great muscular pillar of his neck, was in direct opposition to his task, his surroundings, and his attitude.

Chet's proper milieu was Chicago, Illinois (the West Side); his job that of lineman for the Gas, Light & Power Company; his normal working position astride the top of a telegraph pole, supported in his perilous perch by a lineman's leather belt and the kindly fates, both of which are likely to trick you in an emergency.

Yet now he lolled back among his pillows, dabbing complacently at the absurd yellow toy. A description of his surroundings would sound like pages 3 to 17 of a novel by Mrs. Humphry Ward. The place was all greensward, and terraces, and sundials, and beeches, and even those rhododendrons without which no English novel or country estate is complete. The presence of Chet Ball among his pillows and some hundreds similarly disposed revealed to you at once the fact that this particular English estate was now transformed into Reconstruction Hospital No. 9.

The painting of the chicken quite finished (including two beady black paint eyes), Chet was momentarily at a loss. Miss Kate had not told him to stop painting when the chicken was completed. Miss Kate was at the other end of the sunny garden walk, bending over a wheel chair. So Chet went on painting, placidly. One by one, with meticulous nicety, he painted all his fingernails a bright and cheery yellow. Then he did the whole of his left thumb and was starting on the second joint of the index finger when Miss Kate came up behind him and took the brush gently from his strong hands.

"You shouldn't have painted your fingers," she said.

Chet surveyed them with pride. "They look swell."

Miss Kate did not argue the point. She put the freshly painted wooden chicken on the table to dry in the sun. Her eyes fell upon a letter bearing an American postmark and addressed to Sergeant Chester Ball, with a lot of cryptic figures and letters strung out after it, such as A.E.F. and Co. 11.

"Here's a letter for you!" She infused a lot of Glad into her voice. But Chet only cast a languid eye upon it and said, "Yeh?"

"I'll read it to you, shall I? It's a nice fat one."

Chet sat back, indifferent, negatively acquiescent. And Miss Kate began to read in her clear young voice, there in the sunshine and scent of the centuries-old English garden.

It marked an epoch in Chet's life—that letter. It reached out across the Atlantic Ocean from the Chester Ball of his Chicago days, before he had even heard of English gardens.

Your true lineman has a daredevil way with the women, as have all men whose calling is a hazardous one. Chet was a crack workman. He could shinny up a pole, strap his emergency belt, open his tool kit, wield his pliers with expert deftness, and climb down again in record time. It was his pleasure—and seemingly the pleasure and privilege of all lineman's gangs the world over—to whistle blithely and to call impudently to any passing petticoat that caught his fancy.

Perched three feet from the top of the high pole he would cling protected, seemingly, by some force working in direct defiance of the law of gravity. And now and then, by way of brightening the tedium of their job, he and his gang would call to a girl passing in the street below, "Hoo-hoo! Hello, sweetheart!"

There was nothing vicious in it. Chet would have come to the aid of beauty in distress as quickly as Don Quixote. Any man with a blue shirt as clean and a shave as smooth and a haircut as round as Chet Ball's has no meanness in him. A certain daredeviltry went hand in hand with his work—a calling in which a careless load dispatcher, a cut wire, or a faulty strap may mean instant death. Usually the girls laughed and called back to them or went on more quickly, the color in their cheeks a little higher.

But not Anastasia Rourke. Early the first morning of a two-week job on the new plant of the Western Castings Company, Chet Ball, glancing down from his dizzy perch atop an electric-light pole, espied Miss Anastasia Rourke going to work. He didn't know her name or anything about her, except that she was pretty. You could see that from a distance even more remote than Chet's. But you couldn't know that Stasia was a lady not to be trifled with. We know her name was Rourke, but he didn't.

So then: "Hoo-hoo!" he had called. "Hello, sweetheart! Wait for me and I'll be down."

Stasia Rourke had lifted her face to where he perched so high above the streets. Her cheeks were five shades pinker than was their wont, which would make them border on the red.

"You big ape, you!" she called, in her clear, crisp voice. "If you had your foot on the ground you wouldn't dast call to a decent girl like that. If you were down here I'd slap the face of you. You know you're safe up there."

The words were scarcely out of her mouth before Chet Ball's sturdy legs were twinkling down the pole. His spurred heels dug into the soft pine of the pole with little ripe, tearing sounds. He walked up to Stasia and stood squarely in front of her, six feet of brawn and brazen nerve. One ruddy cheek he presented to her astonished gaze. "Hello, sweetheart," he said. And waited. The Rourke girl hesitated just a second. All the Irish heart in her was melting at the boyish impudence of the man before her. Then she lifted one hand and slapped his smooth cheek. It was a ringing slap. You saw the four marks of her fingers upon his face. Chet straightened, his blue eyes bluer. Stasia looked up at him, her eyes wide. Then down at her own hand, as if it belonged to somebody else. Her hand came up to her own face. She burst into tears, turned, and ran. And as she ran, and as she wept, she saw that Chet was still standing there, looking after her.

Next morning, when Stasia Rourke went by to work, Chet Ball was standing at the foot of the pole, waiting.

They were to have been married that next June. But that next June Chet Ball, perched perilously on the branch of a tree in a small woodsy spot somewhere in France, was one reason why the American artillery in that same woodsy spot was getting such a deadly range on the enemy. Chet's costume was so devised that even through field glasses (made in Germany) you couldn't tell where tree left off and Chet began.

Then, quite suddenly, the Germans got the range. The tree in which Chet was hidden came down with a crash, and Chet lay there, more than ever indiscernible among its tender foliage.

Which brings us back to the English garden, the yellow chicken, Miss Kate, and the letter.

His shattered leg was mended by one of those miracles of modern war surgery, though he never again would dig his spurred heels into the pine of a G. L. & P. Company pole. But the other thing—they put it down under the broad general head of shock. In the lovely English garden they set him to weaving and painting as a means of soothing the shattered nerves. He had made everything from pottery jars to bead chains, from baskets to rugs. Slowly the tortured nerves healed. But the doctors, when they stopped at Chet's cot or chair, talked always of "the memory center." Chet seemed satisfied to go on placidly painting toys or weaving chains with his great, square-tipped fingers—the fingers that had wielded the pliers so cleverly in his pole-climbing days.

"It's just something that only luck or an accident can mend," said the nerve specialist. "Time may do it—but I doubt it. Sometimes just a word—the right word—will set the thing in motion again. Does he get any letters?"

"His girl writes to him. Fine letters. But she doesn't know yet about—about this. I've written his letters for him. She knows now that his leg is healed and she wonders——"

That had been a month ago. Today Miss Kate slit the envelope post-marked Chicago. Chet was fingering the yellow wooden chicken, pride in his eyes. In Miss Kate's eyes there was a troubled, baffled look as she began to read:

Chet, dear, it's raining in Chicago. And you know when it rains in Chicago it's wetter, and muddier, and rainier than any place in the world. Except maybe this Flanders we're reading so much about. They say for rain and mud that place takes the prize.

I don't know what I'm going on about rain and mud for, Chet darling, when it's you I'm thinking of. Nothing else and nobody else. Chet, I got a funny feeling there's something you're keeping back from me. You're hurt worse than just the leg. Boy, dear, don't you know it won't make any difference with me how you look, or feel, or anything? I don't care how bad you're smashed up. I'd rather have you without any features at all than any other man with two sets. Whatever's happened to the out-side of you, they can't change your insides. And you're the same man that called out to me that day, "Hoo-hoo! Hello, sweetheart!" and when I gave you a piece of my mind, climbed down off the pole, and put your face up to be slapped, God bless the boy in you——

A sharp little sound from him. Miss Kate looked up, quickly. Chet Ball was staring at the beady-eyed yellow chicken in his hand.

"What's this thing?" he demanded in a strange voice.

Miss Kate answered him very quietly, trying to keep her own voice easy and natural. "That's a toy chicken, cut out of wood."

"What'm I doin' with it?"

"You've just finished painting it."

Chet Ball held it in his great hand and stared at it for a brief moment, struggling between anger and amusement. And between anger and amusement he put it down on the table none too gently and stood up, yawning a little.

"That's a hell of a job for a he-man!" Then in utter contrition: "Oh, beggin' your pardon! That was fierce! I didn't——"

But there was nothing shocked about the expression on Miss Kate's face. She was registering joy—pure joy.

The Maternal Feminine
[*1919*]

All spinsters, myself included, think they have a finer, deeper understanding of the younger generation than have their married relatives and friends. Sometimes, in their efforts to prove this, their roguish offhand conversation with nieces and nephews is as unconvincing as that of the Reverend Smith when he's down at the docks, just one of the boys as he talks to the longshoremen. But frequently the unwed do have a kind of special insight. Perhaps this is compensatory. Perhaps they themselves have retained a trace of infantilism, and this gives them an understanding of and a sympathy with young people.

CALLED UPON TO DESCRIBE AUNT SOPHY, YOU WOULD HAVE TO COIN a term or fall back on the dictionary definition of a spinster. "An unmarried woman," states that worthy work, baldly, "especially when no longer young." That, to the world, was Sophy Decker. Unmarried, certainly. And most certainly no longer young. In figure, she was, at fifty, what is known in the corset ads as a "stylish stout." Well dressed in dark suits, with broad-toed health shoes and a small, astute hat. The suit was practical common sense. The health shoes were comfort. The hat was strictly business. Sophy Decker made and sold hats, both astute and ingenuous, to the female population of Chippewa, Wisconsin. Chippewa's East End set bought the knowing type of hat, and the mill hands and hired girls bought the naïve ones. But whether lumpy or possessed of that thing known as line, Sophy Decker's hats were honest hats.

The world is full of Aunt Sophys, unsung. Plump, ruddy, capable women of middle age. Unwed, and rather looked down upon by a family of married sisters and tolerant, good-humored brothers-in-law, and careless nieces and nephews.

"Poor Aunt Soph," with a significant half smile. "She's such a good old thing. And she's had so little in life, really."

She was, undoubtedly, a good old thing—Aunt Soph. Forever sending a model hat to this pert little niece in Seattle; or taking Adele, Sister Flora's daughter, to Chicago or New York as a treat on one of her buying trips.

Burdening herself, on her business visits to these cities, with a dozen foolish shopping commissions for the idle womenfolk of her family. Hearing without partisanship her sisters' complaints about their husbands, and her sisters' husbands' complaints about their wives. It was always the same.

94

"I'm telling you this, Sophy. I wouldn't breathe it to another living soul. But I honestly think, sometimes, that if it weren't for the children——"

There is no knowing why they confided these things to Sophy instead of to each other, these wedded sisters of hers. Perhaps they held for each other an unuttered distrust or jealousy. Perhaps, in making a confidante of Sophy, there was something of the satisfaction that comes of dropping a surreptitious stone down a deep well and hearing it plunk, safe in the knowledge that it has struck no one and that it cannot rebound, lying there in the soft darkness. Sometimes they would end by saying, "But you don't know what it is, Sophy. You can't. I'm sure I don't know why I'm telling you all this."

But when Sophy answered, sagely, "I know; I know," they paid little heed, once having unburdened themselves. The curious part of it is that she did know. She knew as a woman of fifty must know who, all her life, has given and given and in return has received nothing. Sophy Decker had never used the word inhibition in her life. She may not have known what it meant. She only knew (without in the least knowing she knew) that in giving of her goods, of her affections, of her time, of her energy, she found a certain relief. Her own people would have been shocked if you had told them that there was about this old-maid aunt something rather splendidly Rabelaisian. Without being what is known as a masculine woman, she had, somehow, acquired the man's viewpoint, his shrewd value sense. She ate a good deal, and enjoyed her food. She did not care for those queer little stories that married women sometimes tell, with narrowed eyes, but she was strangely tolerant of what is known as sin. So simple and direct she was that you wondered how she prospered in a line so subtle as the millinery business.

You might have got a fairly true characterization of Sophy Decker from one of fifty people: from a salesman in a New York or Chicago whole-sale millinery house; from Otis Cowan, cashier of the First National Bank of Chippewa; from Julia Gold, her head milliner and trimmer; from almost anyone, in fact, except a member of her own family. They knew her least of all. Her three married sisters—Grace in Seattle, Ella in Chicago, and Flora in Chippewa—regarded her with a rather affectionate disapproval from the snug safety of their own conjugal inglenooks.

"I don't know. There's something—well—common about Sophy," Flora confided to Ella. Flora, on shopping bent, and Sophy, seeking hats, had made the five-hour run from Chippewa to Chicago together. "She talks to everybody. You should have heard her with the porter on our train. Chums! And when the conductor took our tickets it was a social occasion. You know how packed the seven-fifty-two is. Every seat in the parlor car taken. And Sophy asking the colored porter about how his wife was getting along—she called him William—and if they were going to send her West, and all about her. I wish she wouldn't."

Aunt Sophy undeniably had a habit of regarding people as human beings. You found her talking to chambermaids and delivery boys, and elevator starters, and gas collectors, and hotel clerks—all that aloof, unapproachable, superior crew. Under her benign volubility they bloomed and spread and took on color as do those tight little paper water flowers when you cast them into a bowl. It wasn't idle curiosity in her. She was interested. You found yourself confiding to her your innermost longings, your secret tribulations, under the encouragement of her sympathetic, "You don't say!" Perhaps it was as well that Sister Flora was in ignorance of the fact that the millinery salesmen at Danowitz & Danowitz, Importers, always called Miss Decker Aunt Soph, as, with one arm flung about her plump shoulder, they revealed to her the picture of their girl in the back flap of their billfold.

Flora, with a firm grip on Chippewa society, as represented by the East End set, did not find her position enhanced by a sister in the millinery business in Elm Street.

"Of course it's wonderful that she's self-supporting and successful and all," she told her husband. "But it's not so pleasant for Adele, now that she's growing up, having all the girls she knows buying their hats of her aunt. Not that I—but you know how it is."

H. Charnsworth Baldwin said yes, he knew.

When the Decker girls were young, the Deckers had lived in a sagging old frame house (from which the original paint had long ago peeled in great scrofulous patches) on an unimportant street in Chippewa. There was a worm-eaten, russet-apple tree in the yard, an untidy tangle of wild-cucumber vine over the front porch, and an uncut brush of sunburned grass and weeds all about. From May until September you never passed the Decker place without hearing the plunkety-plink of a mandolin from somewhere behind the vines, laughter, and the creak-creak of the hard-worked and protesting hammock hooks.

Flora, Ella, and Grace Decker had had more beaux and fewer clothes than any other girls in Chippewa. In a town full of pretty young things, they were, undoubtedly, the prettiest; and in a family of pretty sisters (Sophy always excepted) Flora was the acknowledged beauty. She was the kind of girl whose nose never turns red on a frosty morning. A little, white, exquisite nose, purest example of the degree of perfection which may be attained by that vulgarest of features. Under her great gray eyes were faint violet shadows which gave her a look of almost poignant wistfulness. Her slow, sweet smile give the beholder an actual physical pang. Only her family knew she was lazy as a behemoth, untidy about her person, and as sentimental as a hungry shark. The strange and cruel part of it was that, in some grotesque, exaggerated way, as a cartoon may be like a photograph, Sophy resembled Flora. It was as though nature, in prankish mood, had given a cabbage the color and texture of a rose, with none of its fragile reticence and grace.

It was a manless household. Mrs. Decker, vague, garrulous, referred to her dead husband, in frequent reminiscence, as poor Mr. Decker. Mrs. Decker dragged one leg as she walked—rheumatism, or a spinal affection. Small wonder, then, that Sophy, the plain, with a gift for hatmaking, a knack at eggless cake baking, and a genius for turning a sleeve so that last year's style met this year's without a struggle, contributed nothing to the sag in the center of the old twine hammock on the front porch.

That the three girls should marry well, and Sophy not at all, was as inevitable as the sequence of the seasons. Ella and Grace did not manage badly, considering that they had only their girlish prettiness and the twine hammock to work with. But Flora, with her beauty, captured H. Charnsworth Baldwin. Chippewa gasped. H. Charnsworth Baldwin drove a skittish mare to a high-wheeled yellow runabout; had his clothes made at Proctor Brothers in Milwaukee; and talked about a game called golf. It was he who advocated laying out a section of land for what he called links, and erecting a clubhouse thereon.

"The section of the bluff overlooking the river," he explained, "is full of natural hazards, besides having a really fine view."

Chippewa—or that comfortable, middle-class section of it which got its exercise walking home to dinner from the store at noon, and cutting the grass evenings after supper—laughed as it read this interview in the *Chippewa Eagle.*

"A golf course," they repeated to one another, grinning. "Conklin's cow pasture, up the river. It's full of natural—wait a minute—what was?—oh, yeh, here it is—hazards. Full of natural hazards. Say, couldn't you die!"

For H. Charnsworth Baldwin had been little Henry Baldwin before he went East to college. Ten years later H. Charnsworth, in knickerbockers and gay-topped stockings, was winning the cup in the men's tournament played on the Chippewa golf-club course, overlooking the river. And his name, in stout gold letters, blinked at you from the plate-glass windows of the office at the corner of Elm and Winnebago:

NORTHERN LUMBER AND LAND COMPANY
H. Charnsworth Baldwin, Pres.

Two blocks farther down Elm Street was another sign, not so glittering, which read:

Miss Sophy Decker
Millinery

Sophy's hatmaking, in the beginning, had been done at home. She had always made her sisters' hats, and her own, of course, and an occasional hat for a girl friend. After her sisters had married, Sophy found herself in possession of a rather bewildering amount of spare time. The hat trade grew so that sometimes there were six rather botchy little bonnets all done up in yellow paper pyramids with a pin at the top, awaiting their future wearers. After her mother's death Sophy still stayed on in the old house. She took a course in millinery in Milwaukee, came home, stuck up a home-made sign in the parlor window (the untidy cucumber vines came down), and began her hatmaking in earnest. In five years she had opened a shop on a side street near Elm, had painted the old house, installed new plumbing, built a warty stucco porch, and transformed the weedy, grass-tangled yard into an orderly stretch of green lawn and bright flower beds. In ten years she was in Elm Street, and the *Chippewa Eagle* ran a half column twice a year describing her spring and fall openings. On these occasions Aunt Sophy, in black satin and marcel wave and her most relentless corsets, was, in all the superficial things, not a pleat or fold or line or wave behind her city colleagues. She had all the catch phrases:

"This is awfully good this year."

"Here's a sweet thing. A Mornet model."

". . . Well, but, my dear, it's the style—the line—you're paying for, not the material."

"No, that hat doesn't do a thing for you."

"I've got it. I had you in mind when I bought it. Now don't say you can't wear henna. Wait till you see it on."

When she stood behind you as you sat, uncrowned and expectant before the mirror, she would poise the hat four inches above your head, holding it in the tips of her fingers, a precious, fragile thing. Your fascinated eyes were held by it, and your breath as well. Then down it descended, slowly, slowly. A quick pressure. Her fingers firm against your temples. A little sigh of relieved suspense.

"That's wonderful on you! . . . You don't! Oh, my dear! But that's

because you're not used to it. You know how you said, for years, you had
to have a brim, and couldn't possibly wear a turban, with your nose, until
I proved to you that if the head size was only big . . . Well, perhaps this
needs just a lit-tle lift here. Ju-u-ust a nip. There! That does it."

And that did it. Not that Sophy Decker ever tried to sell you a hat
against your judgment, taste, or will. She was too wise a psychologist and
too shrewd a businesswoman for that. She preferred that you go out of her
shop hatless rather than with an unbecoming hat. But whether you bought
or not you took with you out of Sophy Decker's shop something more
precious than any hatbox ever contained. Just to hear her admonishing a
customer, her good-natured face all aglow:

"My dear, always put on your hat before you get into your dress. I do.
You can get your arms above your head, and set it right. I put on my hat
and veil as soon's I get my hair combed."

In your mind's eye you saw her, a stout, well-stayed figure in tight bras-
sière and scant slip, bare-armed and bare-bosomed, in smart hat and veil,
attired as though for the street from the neck up and for the bedroom from
the shoulders down.

The East End set bought Sophy Decker's hats because they were modish
and expensive hats. But she managed, miraculously, to gain a large and
lucrative following among the paper-mill girls and factory hands as well.
You would have thought that any attempt to hold both these opposites
would cause her to lose one or the other. Aunt Sophy said, frankly, that of
the two, she would have preferred to lose her smart trade.

"The mill girls come in with their money in their hands, you might say.
They get good wages and they want to spend them. I wouldn't try to sell
them one of those little plain model hats. They wouldn't understand 'em or
like them. And if I told them the price they'd think I was trying to cheat
them. They want a hat with something good and solid on it. Their fathers
wouldn't prefer caviar to pork roast, would they? It's the same idea."

Her shopwindows reflected her business acumen. One was chastely,
severely elegant, holding a single hat poised on a slender stick. In the other
were a dozen honest arrangements of velvet and satin and plumes.

At the spring opening she always displayed one of those little toques
completely covered with violets. That violet-covered toque was a symbol.

"I don't expect 'em to buy it," Sophy Decker explained. "But everybody
feels there should be a hat like that at a spring opening. It's like a fruit
centerpiece at a family dinner. Nobody ever eats it, but it has to be there."

The two Baldwin children—Adele and Eugene—found Aunt Sophy's
shop a treasure trove. Adele, during her doll days, possessed such boxes of
satin and velvet scraps, and bits of lace and ribbon and jet as to make her

the envy of all her playmates. She used to crawl about the floor of the shop workroom and under the table and chairs like a little scavenger.

"What in the world do you do with all that truck, child?" asked Aunt Sophy. "You must have barrels of it."

Adele stuffed another wisp of tulle into the pocket of her pinafore. "I keep it," she said.

When she was ten Adele had said to her mother, "Why do you always say 'Poor Sophy'?"

"Because Aunt Sophy's had so little in life. She never has married, and has always worked."

Adele considered that. "If you don't get married do they say you're poor?"

"Well—yes——"

"Then I'll get married," announced Adele. A small, dark, eerie child, skinny and rather foreign-looking.

The boy, Eugene, had the beauty which should have been the girl's. Very tall, very blond, with the straight nose and wistful eyes of the Flora of twenty years ago. "If only Adele could have had his looks," his mother used to say. "They're wasted on a man. He doesn't need them, but a girl does. Adele will have to be well dressed and interesting. And that's such hard work."

Flora said she worshiped her children. And she actually sometimes still coquetted heavily with her husband. At twenty she had been addicted to baby talk when endeavoring to coax something out of someone. Her admirers had found it irresistible. At forty it was awful. Her selfishness was colossal. She affected a semi-invalidism and for fifteen years had spent one day a week in bed. She took no exercise and a great deal of soda bicarbonate and tried to fight her fat with baths. Fifteen or twenty years had worked a startling change in the two sisters, Flora the beautiful and Sophy the plain. It was more than a mere physical change. It was a spiritual thing, though neither knew nor marked it. Each had taken on weight, the one, solidly, comfortably; the other, flabbily, unhealthily. With the encroaching fat, Flora's small, delicate features seemed, somehow, to disappear in her face, so that you saw it as a large white surface bearing indentations, ridges, and hollows like one of those enlarged photographs of the moon's surface as seen through a telescope. A self-centered face, and misleadingly placid. Aunt Sophy's large, plain features, plumply padded now, impressed you as indicating strength, courage, and a great human understanding.

From her husband and her children, Flora exacted service that would have chafed a galley slave into rebellion. She loved to lie in bed, in an orchid bed jacket with ribbons, and be read to by Adele, or Eugene, or her husband. They all hated it.

"She just wants to be waited on, and petted, and admired," Adele had stormed one day, in open rebellion, to her Aunt Sophy. "She uses it as an excuse for everything and has, ever since Gene and I were children. She's as strong as an ox." Not a daughterly speech, but true.

Years before, a generous but misguided woman friend, coming in to call, had been ushered in to where Mrs. Baldwin lay propped up in a nest of pillows.

"Well, I don't blame you," the caller had gushed. "If I looked the way you do in bed I'd stay there forever. Don't tell me you're sick, with all that lovely color!"

Flora Baldwin had rolled her eyes ceilingward.

"Nobody ever gives me credit for all my suffering and ill-health. And just because all my blood is in my cheeks."

Flora was ambitious, socially, but too lazy to make the effort necessary for success in that direction.

"I love my family," she would say. "They fill my life. After all, that's a profession in itself—being a wife and mother."

She showed her devotion by taking no interest whatever in her husband's land schemes; by forbidding Eugene to play football at school for fear he might be injured; by impressing Adele with the necessity for vivacity and modishness because of what she called her unfortunate lack of beauty.

"I don't understand it," she used to say in the child's presence. "Her father's handsome enough, goodness knows; and I wasn't such a fright when I was a girl. And look at her! Little dark skinny thing."

The boy, Eugene, grew up a very silent, handsome, shy young fellow. The girl, dark, voluble, and rather interesting. The husband, more and more immersed in his business, was absent from home for long periods; irritable after some of these home-comings; boisterously high-spirited following other trips. Now growling about household expenses and unpaid bills; now urging the purchase of some almost prohibitive luxury. Anyone but a nagging, self-absorbed, and vain woman such as Flora would have marked these unmistakable signs. But Flora was a taker, not a giver. She thought herself affectionate because she craved affection unduly. She thought herself a fond mother because she insisted on having her children with her, under her thumb, marking their devotion as a prisoner marks time with his feet, stupidly, shufflingly, advancing not a step.

Sometimes Sophy, the clear-eyed, seeing this state of affairs, tried to stop it.

"You expect too much of your husband and children," she said one day, bluntly, to her sister.

"I!" Flora's dimpled hand had flown to her breast like a wounded thing. "I! You're crazy! There isn't a more devoted wife and mother in the world. That's the trouble. I love them too much."

"Well, then," grimly, "stop it for a change. That's half Eugene's nervousness—your fussing over him. He's eighteen. Give him a chance. You're weakening him. And stop dinning that society stuff into Adele's ears. She's got brains, that child. Why, just yesterday, in the workroom, she got hold of some satin and a shape and turned out a little turban that Angie Hatton——"

"Do you mean to tell me that Angie Hatton saw my Adele working in your shop! Now, look here, Sophy. You're earning your living, and it's to your credit. You're my sister. But I won't have Adele associated in the minds of my friends with your hat store, understand? I won't have it. That isn't what I sent her away to an expensive school for. To have her come back and sit around a millinery workshop with a lot of little, cheap, shoddy sewing girls! Now, understand, I won't have it! You don't know what it is to be a mother. You don't know what it is to have suffered. If you had brought two children into the world——"

So, then, it had come about during the years between their childhood and their youth that Aunt Sophy received the burden of their confidences, their griefs, their perplexities. She seemed, somehow, to understand in some miraculous way, and to make the burden a welcome one.

"Well, now, you tell Aunt Sophy all about it. Stop crying, Della. How can I hear when you're crying! That's my baby. Now, then."

This when they were children. But with the years the habit clung and became fixed. There was something about Aunt Sophy's house—the old frame house with the warty stucco porch. For that matter, there was something about the very shop downtown, with its workroom in the rear, that had a cozy, homelike quality never possessed by the big Baldwin house. H. Charnsworth Baldwin had built a large brick mansion, in the Tudor style, on a bluff overlooking the Fox River, in the best residential section of Chippewa. It was expensively furnished. The hall console alone was enough to strike a preliminary chill to your heart.

The millinery workroom, winter days, was always bright and warm and snug. The air was a little close, perhaps, and heavy, but with a not unpleasant smell of dyes and stuffs and velvet and glue and steam and flatiron and a certain racy scent that Julia Gold, the head trimmer, always used. There was a sociable cat, white with a dark-gray patch on his throat and a swipe of it across one flank that spoiled him for style and beauty but made him a comfortable-looking cat to have around. Sometimes, on very cold days, or in the rush season, the girls would not go home to dinner, but would bring their lunches and cook coffee over a little gas heater in the corner. Julia Gold, especially, drank quantities of coffee. Aunt Sophy had hired her from Chicago. She had been with her for five years. She said Julia was the best trimmer she had ever had. Aunt Sophy often took her to New York or Chicago on her buying trips. Julia had not much genius for original design, or she never would have been content to be head milliner in a small-town shop. But she could copy a fifty-dollar model from memory down to the last detail of crown and brim. It was a gift that made her invaluable.

The boy, Eugene, used to like to look at Julia Gold. Her hair was very black and her face was very white, and her eyebrows met in a thick dark line. Her face as she bent over her work was sullen and brooding, but when she lifted her head suddenly, in conversation, you were startled by a vivid flash of teeth and eyes and smile. Her voice was deep and low. She made you a little uncomfortable. Her eyes seemed always to be asking something. Around the worktable, mornings, she used to relate the dream she had had the night before. In these dreams she was always being pursued by a lover. "And then I woke up, screaming." Neither she nor the sewing girls knew what she was revealing in these confidences of hers. But Aunt Sophy, the shrewd, somehow sensed it.

"You're alone too much, evenings. That's what comes of living in a boardinghouse. You come over to me for a week. The change will do you good, and it'll be nice for me, too, having somebody to keep me company."

Julia often came for a week or ten days at a time. Julia, about the house after supper, was given to those vivid splashy negligees with big flower patterns strewn over them. They made her hair look blacker and her skin whiter by contrast. Sometimes Eugene or Adele or both would drop in and the four would play bridge. Aunt Sophy played a shrewd and canny game, Adele a rather brilliant one, Julia a wild and disastrous hand, always, and Eugene so badly that only Julia would take him on as a partner. Mrs. Baldwin never knew about these evenings.

It was on one of these occasions that Aunt Sophy, coming unexpectedly into the living room from the kitchen, where she and Adele were foraging for refreshments after the game, beheld Julia Gold and Eugene, arms clasped about each other, cheek to cheek. They started up as she came in and faced her, the woman defiantly, the boy bravely. Julia Gold was thirty (with reservations) at that time, and the boy not quite twenty-one.

"How long?" said Aunt Sophy, quietly. She had a mayonnaise spoon and a leaf of lettuce in her hand then, and still she did not look comic.

"I'm crazy about her," said Eugene. "We're crazy about each other. We're going to be married."

Aunt Sophy listened for the reassuring sound of Adele's spoons and plates in the kitchen. She came forward. "Now, listen——" she began.

"I love him," said Julia Gold, dramatically. "I love him!"

Except that it was very white and, somehow, old-looking, Aunt Sophy's face was as benign as always. "Now, look here, Julia, my girl. That isn't love, and you know it. I'm an old maid, but I know what love is when I see it. I'm ashamed of you, Julia. Sensible woman like you, hugging and kissing a boy like that, and old enough to be his mother."

"Now, look here, Aunt Sophy! If you're going to talk that way—— Why, she's wonderful. She's taught me what it means to really——"

"Oh, my land!" Aunt Sophy sat down, looking suddenly very ill.

And then, from the kitchen, Adele's clear young voice: "Heh! What's the idea! I'm not going to do all the work. Where's everybody?"

Aunt Sophy started up again. She came up to them and put a hand—a capable, firm, steadying hand—on the arm of each. The woman drew back, but the boy did not.

"Will you promise me not to do anything for a week? Just a week! Will you promise me? Will you?"

"Are you going to tell Father?"

"Not for a week, if you'll promise not to see each other in that week. No, I don't want to send you away, Julia, I don't want to. . . . You're not a bad girl. It's just—he's never had—at home they never gave him a chance. Just a week, Julia. Just a week, Eugene. We can talk things over then."

Adele's footsteps coming from the kitchen.

"Quick!"

"I promise," said Eugene. Julia said nothing.

"Well, really," said Adele, from the doorway, "you're a nervy lot, sitting around while I slave in the kitchen. Gene, see if you can open the olives with this fool can opener. I tried."

There is no knowing what she expected to do in that week, Aunt Sophy; what miracle she meant to perform. She had no plan in her mind. Just hope. She looked strangely shrunken and old, suddenly. But when, three days later, the news came that America was to go into the war she had her answer.

Flora was beside herself. "Eugene won't have to go. He isn't old enough, thank God! And by the time he is it will be over. Surely." She was almost hysterical.

Eugene was in the room. Aunt Sophy looked at him and he looked at Aunt Sophy. In her eyes was a question. In his was the answer. They said nothing. The next day Eugene enlisted. In three days he was gone. Flora took to her bed. Next day Adele, a faint, unwonted color marking her cheeks, walked into her mother's bedroom and stood at the side of the recumbent figure. Her father, his hands clasped behind him, was pacing up and down, now and then kicking a cushion that had fallen to the floor. He was chewing a dead cigar, one side of his face twisted curiously over the cylinder in his mouth so that he had a sinister and crafty look.

"Charnsworth, won't you please stop ramping up and down like that! My nerves are killing me. I can't help it if the war has done something or other to your business. I'm sure no wife could have been more economical than I have. Nothing matters but Eugene, anyway. How could he do such a thing! I've given my whole life to my children——"

H. Charnsworth kicked the cushion again so that it struck the wall at the opposite side of the room. Flora drew her breath in between her teeth as though a knife had entered her heart.

Adele still stood at the side of the bed, looking at her mother. Her hands were clasped behind her, too. In that moment, as she stood there, she resembled her mother and her father so startlingly and simultaneously that the two, had they been less absorbed in their own affairs, must have marked it.

The girl's head came up stiffly. "Listen. I'm going to marry Daniel Oakley."

Daniel Oakley was fifty, and a friend of her father's. For years he had been coming to the house and for years she had ridiculed him. She and Eugene had called him Sturdy Oak because he was always talking about his strength and endurance, his walks, his rugged health; pounding his chest meanwhile and planting his feet far apart. He and Baldwin had had business relations as well as friendly ones.

At this announcement Flora screamed and sat up in bed. H. Charnsworth stopped short in his pacing and regarded his daughter with a queer look; a concentrated look, as though what she had said had set in motion a whole mass of mental machinery within his brain.

"When did he ask you?"

"He's asked me a dozen times. But it's different now. All the men will be going to war. There won't be any left. Look at England and France. I'm not going to be left." She turned squarely toward her father, her young face set and hard. "You know what I mean. You know what I mean."

Flora, sitting up in bed, was sobbing. "I think you might have told your mother, Adele. What are children coming to! You stand there and say,

'I'm going to marry Daniel Oakley.' Oh, I am so faint . . . all of a sudden . . . Get the spirits of ammonia."

Adele turned and walked out of the room. She was married six weeks later. They had a regular prewar wedding—veil, flowers, dinner, and all. Aunt Sophy arranged the folds of her gown and draped her veil. The girl stood looking at herself in the mirror, a curious half smile twisting her lips. She seemed slighter and darker than ever.

"In all this white, and my veil, I look just like a fly in a quart of milk," she said, with a laugh. Then, suddenly, she turned to her aunt, who stood behind her, and clung to her, holding her tight, tight. "I can't!" she gasped. "I can't! I can't!"

Aunt Sophy held her off and looked at her, her eyes searching the girl.

"What do you mean, Della? Are you just nervous or do you mean you don't want to marry him? Do you mean that? Then what are you marrying for? Tell me! Tell your Aunt Sophy."

But Adele was straightening herself and pulling out the crushed folds of her veil. "To pay the mortgage on the old homestead, of course. Just like the girl in the play." She laughed a little. But Aunt Sophy did not.

"Now look here, Della. If you're——"

But there was a knock at the door. Adele caught up her flowers. "It's all right," she said.

Aunt Sophy stood with her back against the door. "If it's money," she said. "It is! It is, isn't it! I've got money saved. It was for you children. I've always been afraid. I knew he was sailing pretty close, with his speculations and all, since the war. He can have it all. It isn't too late yet. Adele! Della, my baby."

"Don't, Aunt Sophy. It wouldn't be enough, anyway. Daniel has been wonderful, really. Dad's been stealing money for years. Dan's. Don't look like that. I'd have hated being poor, anyway. Never could have got used to it. It is ridiculous, though, isn't it? Like something in the movies. I don't mind. I'm lucky, really, when you come to think of it. A plain little black thing like me."

"But your mother——"

"Mother doesn't know a thing."

Flora wept mistily all through the ceremony, but Adele was composed enough for two.

When, scarcely a month later, Baldwin came to Sophy Decker, his face drawn and queer, Sophy knew.

"How much?" she said.

"Thirty thousand will cover it. If you've got more than that——"

"I thought Oakley—— Adele said——"

"He did, but he won't any more, and this thing's got to be met. It's this damned war that's done it. I'd have been all right. People got scared. They wanted their money. They wanted it in cash."

"Speculating with it, were you?"

"Oh, well, a woman doesn't understand these business deals."

"No, naturally," said Aunt Sophy, "a butterfly like me."

"Sophy, for God's sake don't joke now. I tell you this will cover it, and everything will be all right. If I had anybody else to go to for the money I wouldn't ask you. But you'll get it back. You know that."

Aunt Sophy got up, heavily, and went over to her desk. "It was for the children, anyway. They won't need it now."

He looked up at that. Something in her voice. "Who won't? Why won't they?"

"I don't know what made me say that. I had a dream."

"Eugene?"

"Yes."

"Oh, well, we're all nervous. Flora has dreams every night and presentiments every fifteen minutes. Now, look here, Sophy. About this money. You'll never know how grateful I am. Flora doesn't understand these things, but I can talk to you. It's like this——"

"I might as well be honest about it," Sophy interrupted. "I'm doing it, not for you, but for Flora, and Della—and Eugene. Flora has lived such a sheltered life. I sometimes wonder if she ever really knew any of you. Her husband, or her children. I sometimes have the feeling that Della and Eugene are my children—were my children."

When he came home that night Baldwin told his wife that old Soph was getting queer. "She talks about the children being hers," he said.

"Oh, well, she's awfully fond of them," Flora explained. "And she's lived her little, narrow life, with nothing to bother her but her hats and her house. She doesn't know what it means to suffer as a mother suffers —poor Sophy."

"Um," Baldwin grunted.

When the official notification of Eugene's death came from the War Department, Aunt Sophy was so calm it might have appeared that Flora had been right. She took to her bed now in earnest, did Flora. Sophy neglected everything to give comfort to the stricken two.

"How can you sit there like that!" Flora would rail. "How can you sit there like that! Even if you weren't his mother, surely you must feel something."

"It's the way he died that comforts me," said Aunt Sophy.

"What difference does that make!"

AMERICAN RED CROSS
(Croix Rouge Américaine)

MY DEAR MRS. BALDWIN:

I am sure you must have been officially notified by the U.S. War Dept. of the death of your son, Lieut. Eugene H. Baldwin. But I want to write you what I can of his last hours. I was with him much of that time as his nurse. I'm sure it must mean much to a mother to hear from a woman who was privileged to be with her boy at the last.

Your son was brought to our hospital one night badly gassed from the fighting in the Argonne Forest. Ordinarily we do not receive gassed patients, as they are sent to a special hospital near here. But two nights before, the Germans wrecked that hospital, so many gassed patients have come to us.

Your son was put in the officers' ward, where the doctors who examined him told me there was absolutely no hope for him, as he had inhaled so much gas that it was only a matter of a few hours. I could scarcely believe that a man so big and strong as he was could not pull through.

The first bad attack he had, losing his breath and nearly choking, rather frightened him, although the doctor and I were both with him. He held my hand tightly in his, begging me not to leave him, and repeating, over and over, that it was good to have a woman near. He was propped high in bed and put his head on my shoulder while I fanned him until he breathed more easily. I stayed with him all that night, though I was not on duty. You see, his eyes also were badly burned. But before he died he was able to see very well. I stayed with him every minute of that night and have never seen a finer character than he showed during all that fight for life.

He had several bad attacks that night and came through each one simply because of his great will power and fighting spirit. After each attack he would grip my hand and say, "Well, we made it that time, didn't we, nurse?" Toward morning he asked me if he was going to die. I could not tell him the truth. He needed all his strength. I told him he had one chance in a thousand. He seemed to become very strong then, and sitting bolt upright in bed, he said: "Then I'll fight for it!" We kept him alive for three days, and actually thought we had won when on the third day . . .

But even in your sorrow you must be very proud to have been the mother of such a son. . . .

I am a Wisconsin girl—Madison. When this is over and I come home, will you let me see you so that I may tell you more than I can possibly write?

MARIAN KING

It was in March, six months later, that Marian King came. They had hoped for it, but never expected it. And she came. Four people were waiting in the living room of the big Baldwin house overlooking the river. Flora and her husband, Adele and Aunt Sophy. They sat, waiting. Now and then Adele would rise, nervously, and go to the window that faced the street. Flora was weeping with audible sniffs. Baldwin sat in his chair, frowning a little, a dead cigar in one corner of his mouth. Only Aunt Sophy sat quietly, waiting.

There was little conversation. None in the last five minutes. Flora broke the silence, dabbing at her face with her handkerchief as she spoke.

"Sophy, how can you sit there like that? Not that I don't envy you. I do. I remember I used to feel sorry for you. I used to say 'Poor Sophy.' But you unmarried ones are the happiest, after all. It's the married woman who drinks the cup to the last, bitter drop. There you sit, Sophy, fifty years old, and life hasn't even touched you. You don't know how cruel life can be to a mother."

Suddenly, "There!" said Adele. The other three in the room stood up and faced the door. The sound of a motor stopping outside. Daniel Oakley's hearty voice: "Well, it only took us five minutes from the station. Pretty good."

Footsteps down the hall. Marian King stood in the doorway. They faced her, the four—Baldwin and Adele and Flora and Sophy. Marian King stood a moment, uncertainly, her eyes upon them. She looked at the two older women with swift, appraising glances. Then she came into the room, quickly, and put her two hands on Aunt Soph's shoulders and looked into her eyes straight and sure.

"You must be a very proud woman," she said. "You ought to be a very proud woman."

Old Man Minick

[1922]

They used to sit on the benches in Washington Park, Chicago—the old men. They talked, they argued, they stared uncertainly at the world slipping by. There was a difference in the groups. Some were rather spruce and cocky. They were the free ones, living in glorious independence at the Old Men's Home. Others were spotty of coat lapel, unassertive, turning toward home with reluctant feet when the afternoon shadows began to lengthen. These old ones were living with married sons or daughters.

George Kaufman and I made a play of this short story which I had written about these oldsters almost a quarter of a century ago. Minick, we called it. But somehow the quavery hero lost dimensions in the process of being transferred from the printed page to the stage. No one knows why. Just a pretty good play.

HIS WIFE HAD ALWAYS SPOILED HIM OUTRAGEOUSLY. NO DOUBT OF that. Take, for example, the mere matter of the pillows. Old Man Minick slept high. That is, he thought he slept high. He liked two pillows on his side of the great, wide, old-fashioned cherry bed. He would sink into them with a vast grunting and sighing and puffing expressive of nerves and muscles relaxed and gratified. But in the morning there always was one pillow on the floor. He had thrown it there. Always, in the morning, there it lay, its plump white cheek turned reproachfully up at him from the side of the bed. Ma Minick knew this, naturally, after forty years of the cherry bed. But she never begrudged him that extra pillow. Each morning, when she arose, she picked it up on her way to shut the window. Each morning the bed was made up with two pillows on his side of it, as usual.

Then there was the window. Ma Minick liked it open wide. Old Man Minick, who rather prided himself on his modernism (he called it being up to date), was distrustful of the night air. In the folds of its sable mantle lurked a swarm of dread things—colds, clammy miasmas, fevers.

"Night air's just like any other air," Ma Minick would say, with some asperity. Ma Minick was no worm; and as modern as her husband. So when they went to bed the window would be open wide. They would lie there, the two old ones, talking comfortably about commonplace things. The kind of talk that goes on between a man and a woman who have lived together in wholesome peace (spiced with occasional wholesome bickerings) for more than forty years.

"Remind me to see Gerson tomorrow about that lock on the basement door. The paper's full of burglars."

"If I think of it." She never failed to.

"George and Nettie haven't been over in a week now."

"Oh, well, young folks. . . . Did you stop in and pay that Koritz the fifty cents for pressing your suit?"

"By golly, I forgot again! First thing in the morning."

A sniff. "Just smell the Yards." It was Chicago.

"Wind must be from the west."

Sleep came with reluctant feet, but they wooed her patiently. And presently she settled down between them and they slept lightly. Usually, sometime during the night, he awoke, slid cautiously and with infinite stealth from beneath the covers, and closed the wide-flung window to within a bare two inches of the sill. Almost invariably she heard him; but she was a wise old woman, a philosopher of parts. She knew better than to allow a window to shatter the peace of their marital felicity. As she lay there, smiling a little grimly in the dark and giving no sign of being awake, she thought, Oh, well, I guess a closed window won't kill me either.

Still, sometimes, just to punish him a little, and to prove that she was nobody's fool, she would wait until he had dropped off to sleep again and then she, too, would achieve a stealthy trip to the window and would raise it slowly, carefully, inch by inch.

"How did that window come to be open?" he would say in the morning, being a poor dissembler.

"Window? Why, it's just the way it was when we went to bed." And she would stoop to pick up the pillow that lay on the floor.

There was little or no talk of death between this comfortable, active, sound-appearing man of almost seventy and this plump, capable woman of sixty-six. But as always between husband and wife, it was understood wordlessly (and without reason) that Old Man Minick would go first. Not that either of them had the slightest intention of going. In fact, when it happened, they were planning to spend the winter in California and perhaps live there indefinitely if they liked it and didn't get too lonesome for George and Nettie, and the Chicago smoke, and Chicago noise, and Chicago smells and rush and dirt. Still, the solid sum paid yearly in insurance premiums showed clearly that he meant to leave her in comfort and security. Besides, the world is full of widows. Everyone sees that. But how many widowers? Few. Widows there are by the thousands; living alone, living in hotels, living with married daughters and sons-in-law or married sons and daughters-in-law. But of widowers in a like situation there are bewilderingly few. And why this should be no one knows.

So, then. The California trip never materialized. And the year that followed never was quite clear in Old Man Minick's dazed mind. In the first place, it was the year in which stocks tumbled and broke their backs. Gilt-edged securities showed themselves to be tinsel. Old Man Minick had retired from active business just one year before, meaning to live comfortably on the fruit of a half century's toil. He now saw that fruit rotting all about him. There was in it hardly enough nourishment to sustain them. Then came the day when Ma Minick went downtown to see Matthews about that pain right here and came home looking shriveled, talking shrilly about nothing, and evading Pa's eyes. Followed months that were just a jumble of agony, X-rays, hope, despair, morphia, nothingness.

After it was all over: "But I was going first," Old Man Minick said dazedly.

The old house on Ellis near Thirty-ninth was sold for what it would bring. George, who knew Chicago real estate if anyone did, said they might as well get what they could. Things would only go lower. You'll see. And nobody's going to have any money for years. Besides, look at the neighborhood!

Old Man Minick said George was right. He said everybody was right. You would hardly have recognized in this shrunken figure and wattled face the spruce and dressy old man whom Ma Minick used to spoil so delightfully. "You know best, George. You know best." He who used to stand up to George until Ma Minick was moved to say, "Now, Pa, you don't know everything."

After Matthews' bills, and the hospital, and the nurses and the medicines and the thousand and one things were paid, there was left exactly five hundred dollars a year.

"You're going to make your home with us, Father," George and Nettie said. Alma, too, said this would be the best. Alma, the married daughter, lived in Seattle. "Though you know Fred and I would be only too glad to have you."

Seattle! The ends of the earth. Oh, no. No! he protested, every fiber of his old frame clinging to the accustomed. Seattle, at seventy! He turned piteous eyes on his son, George, and his daugther-in-law, Nettie. "You're going to make your home with us, Father," they reassured him. He clung to them gratefully. After it was over Alma went home to her husband and their children.

So now he lived with George and Nettie in the five-room flat on South

Park Avenue, just across from Washington Park. And there was no extra pillow on the floor.

Nettie hadn't said he couldn't have the extra pillow. He had told her he used two and she had given him two the first week. But every morning she had found a pillow on the floor.

"I thought you used two pillows, Father."

"I do."

"But there's always one on the floor when I make the bed in the morning. You always throw one on the floor. You only sleep on one pillow, really."

"I use two pillows."

But the second week there was one pillow. He tossed and turned a good deal there in his bedroom off the kitchen. But he got used to it in time. Not used to it, exactly, but—well——

The bedroom off the kitchen wasn't as menial as it sounds. It was really rather cozy. The five-room flat held living room, front bedroom, dining room, kitchen, and maid's room. The room off the kitchen was intended as a maid's room, but Nettie had no maid. George's business had suffered with the rest. George and Nettie had said, "I wish there was a front room for you, Father. You could have ours and we'd move back here, only this room's too small for twin beds and the dressing table and the chest of drawers." They had meant it—or meant to mean it.

"This is fine," Old Man Minick had said. "This is good enough for anybody." There were a narrow white enamel bed and a tiny dresser and a table. Nettie had made gay cretonne covers and spreads and put a little reading lamp on the table and arranged his things. Ma Minick's picture on the dresser with her mouth sort of pursed to make it look small. It wasn't a recent picture. Nettie and George had had it framed for him as a surprise. They had often urged her to have a picture taken, but she had dreaded it. Old Man Minick didn't think much of that photograph, though he never said so. He needed no photograph of Ma Minick. He had a dozen of them; a gallery of them; thousands of them. Lying on his one pillow, he could take them out and look at them one by one as they passed in review, smiling, serious, chiding, praising, there in the dark. He needed no picture on his dresser.

A handsome girl, Nettie, and a good girl. He thought of her as a girl, though she was well past thirty. George and Nettie had married late. This was only the third year of their marriage. Alma, the daughter, had married young, but George had stayed on, unwed, in the old house on Ellis until he was thirty-six and all Ma Minick's friends' daughters had

had a try at him in vain. The old people had urged him to marry, but it had been wonderful to have him around the house, just the same. Somebody young around the house. Not that George had stayed around very much. But when he was there you knew he was there. He whistled while dressing. He sang in the bath. He roared down the stairway, "Ma, where're my clean shirts?" The telephone rang for him. Ma Minick prepared special dishes for him. The servant girl said, "Oh, now, Mr. George, look what you've done! Gone and spilled the grease all over my clean kitchen floor!" and wiped it up adoringly while George laughed and gobbled his bit of food filched from pot or frying pan.

They had been a little surprised about Nettie. George was in the bond business and she worked for the same firm. A plump handsome eye-glassed woman with fine fresh coloring, a clear skin that Old Man Minick called appetizing, and a great coil of smooth dark hair. She wore plain tailored things and understood the bond business in a way that might have led you to think hers a masculine mind if she hadn't been so feminine, too, in her manner. Old Man Minick had liked her better than Ma Minick had.

Nettie had called him Pop and joked with him and almost flirted with him in a daughterly sort of way. He liked to squeeze her plump arm and pinch her soft cheek between thumb and forefinger. She would laugh up at him and pat his shoulder and that shoulder would straighten spryly and he would waggle his head doggishly.

"Look out there, George!" the others in the room would say. "Your dad'll cut you out. First thing you know you'll lose your girl, that's all."

Nettie would smile. Her teeth were white and strong and even. Old Man Minick would laugh and wink, immensely pleased and flattered. "We understand each other, don't we, Pop?" Nettie would say.

During the first years of their married life Nettie stayed home. She fussed happily about her little flat, gave parties, went to parties, played bridge. She seemed to love the ease, the relaxation, the small luxuries. She and George were very much in love. Before her marriage she had lived in a boardinghouse on Michigan Avenue. At mention of it now she puckered up her face. She did not attempt to conceal her fondness for these five rooms of hers, so neat, so quiet, so bright, so cozy. Overstuffed velvet in the living room, with silk lamp shades, and small tables holding books and magazines, and little boxes containing cigarettes or hard candies. Very modern. A gate-legged table in the dining room. Caramel-colored walnut in the bedroom, rich and dark and smooth. She loved it. An orderly woman. Everything in its place. Before eleven o'clock the little apartment was shining, spotless; cushions plumped, crumbs brushed, vegetables in cold water. The telephone. "Hello! . . . Oh, hello, Bess! . . . Oh, hours ago. . . . Not a thing. . . . Well, if George is willing. . . . I'll call him up and ask him. We haven't seen a show in two weeks. I'll call you back within the next half-hour. . . . No, I haven't done my marketing yet. . . . Yes, and have dinner downtown. Meet at seven."

Into this orderly, smooth-running mechanism was catapulted a bewildered old man. She no longer called him Pop. He never dreamed of squeezing the plump arm or pinching the smooth cheek. She called him Father. Sometimes George's father. Sometimes, when she was telephoning, there came to him: "George's father's living with us now, you know. I can't."

They were very kind to him, Nettie and George. "Now just you sit right down here, Father. What do you want to go poking off into your own room for?"

He remembered that in the last year Nettie had said something about going back to work. There wasn't enough to do around the house to keep her busy. She was sick of afternoon parties. Sew and eat, that's all, and gossip, or play bridge. Besides, look at the money. Business was awful. The two old people had resented this idea as much as George had—more, in fact. They were scandalized.

"Young folks nowadays!" shaking their heads. "Young folks nowadays. What are they thinking of! In my day when you got married you had babies."

George and Nettie had had no babies. At first Nettie had said, "I'm so happy. I just want a chance to rest. I've been working since I was seventeen. I just want to rest, first." One year. Two years. Three. And now Pa Minick.

Ma Minick, in the old house on Ellis Avenue, had kept a loose sort of larder; not lavish, but plentiful. They both ate a great deal, as old people are likely to do. Old Man Minick, especially, had liked to nibble. A handful of raisins from the box on the shelf. A couple of nuts from the dish on the sideboard. A bit of candy, rolled beneath the tongue. At dinner (sometimes, toward the last, even at noontime) a plate of steaming soup, hot, revivifying. Plenty of this and plenty of that. "What's the matter, Jo? You're not eating." But he was, amply. Ma Minick had liked to see him eat too much. She was wrong, of course.

But at Nettie's things were different. Hers was a sufficient but stern ménage. So many mouths to feed; just so many lamb chops. Nettie knew about calories and vitamins and mysterious things like that, and talked about them. So many calories in this. So many calories in that. He never was quite clear in his mind about these things said to be lurking in his food. He had always thought of spinach as spinach, chops as chops. But to Nettie they were calories. They lunched together, these two. George was, of course, downtown. For herself Nettie would have one of those feminine pickup lunches; a dab of applesauce, a cup of tea, and a slice of cold toast left from breakfast. This she would eat while Old Man Minick guiltily supped up his cup of warmed-over broth, or his coddled egg. She always pressed upon him any bit of cold meat that was left from the night before, or any remnants of vegetable or spaghetti. Often there was quite a little fleet of saucers and sauce plates grouped about his main plate. Into these he dipped and swooped uncomfortably, and yet with a relish. Sometimes, when he had finished, he would look about, furtively.

"What'll you have, Father? Can I get you something?"

"Nothing, Nettie, nothing. I'm doing fine." She had finished the last of her wooden toast and was waiting for him, kindly.

Still, this balanced and scientific fare seemed to agree with him. As the winter went on he seemed actually to have regained most of his former hardiness and vigor. A handsome old boy he was, ruddy, hale, with the zest of a juicy old apple, slightly withered but still sappy. It should be mentioned that he had a dimple in his cheek which flashed unexpectedly when he smiled. It gave him a roguish—almost boyish—effect, most appealing to the beholder. Especially the female beholder. Much of his spoiling at the hands of Ma Minick had doubtless been due to this mere depression of the skin.

Spring was to bring a new and welcome source of enrichment into his life. But these first six months of his residence with George and Nettie were hard. No spoiling there. He missed being made much of. He got kindness, but he needed love. Then, too, he was rather a gabby old man. He liked to hold forth. In the old house on Ellis there had been visiting back and forth between men and women of his own age, and Ma's. At these gatherings he had waxed oratorical or argumentative, and they had heard him, some in agreement, some in disagreement, but always respectfully, whether he prated of real estate or social depravity, Prohibition or European exchange.

"Let me tell you, here and now, something's got to be done before you can get a country back on a sound financial basis. Why, take Russia alone, why . . ." Or: "Young people nowadays! They don't know what respect means. I tell you there's got to be a change and there will be, and it's the older generation that's got to bring it about. What do they know of hardship! What do they know about work—real work. Most of 'em's never done a real day's work in their life. All they think of is dancing and running around and drinking. Look at the way they dress! Look at . . ."

Ad lib.

"That's so," the others would agree. "I was saying only yesterday . . ."

Then, too, until a year or two before, he had taken active part in business. He had retired only at the urging of Ma and the children. They said he ought to rest and play and enjoy himself.

Now, as his strength and good spirits gradually returned he began to go downtown, mornings. He would dress, carefully, though a little shakily. He had always shaved himself and he kept this up. All in all, during the day, he occupied the bathroom literally for hours, and this annoyed Nettie to the point of frenzy, though she said nothing. He liked the white cheerfulness of the little tiled room. He puddled about in the water endlessly. Snorted and splashed and puffed and snuffled and blew. He was one of those audible washers who emerge dripping and whose ablutions are distributed impartially over ceiling, walls, and floor.

Nettie, at the closed door: "Father, are you all right?"

Splash! Prrf! "Yes. Sure. I'm all right."

"Well, I didn't know. You've been in there so long."

He was a neat old man, but there was likely to be a spot or so on his vest or his coat lapel, or his tie. Ma used to remove these, on or off him as the occasion demanded, rubbing carefully and scolding a little, making a chiding sound between tongue and teeth indicative of great impatience of his carelessness. He had rather enjoyed these sounds, and this rubbing and scratching on the cloth with the fingernail and a moistened rag. They indicated that someone cared. Cared about the way he looked. Had pride in him. Loved him. Nettie never removed spots. Though infrequently she said, "Father, just leave that suit out, will you? I'll send it to the cleaner's with George's. The man's coming tomorrow morning." He would look down at himself, hastily, and attack a spot here and there with a futile fingernail.

His morning toilette completed, he would make for the Fifty-first Street el. Seated in the train, he would assume an air of importance and testy haste; glance out of the window; look at his watch. You got the impression of a handsome and well-preserved old gentleman on his way downtown to consummate a shrewd business deal. He had been familiar with Chicago's downtown for fifty years and he could remember when State Street was a tree-shaded cottage district. The noise and rush and clangor of the Loop had long been familiar to him. But now he seemed to find the downtown trip arduous, even hazardous. The roar of the elevated trains, the hoarse toots of the motor horns, the clang of the streetcars, the bedlam that is Chicago's downtown district bewildered him, frightened him almost. He would skip across the street like a harried hare, just missing a motor truck's nose and all unconscious of the stream of invective directed at him by its charioteer. "Heh! Whatcha! . . . Look!" Sometimes a policeman came to his aid, or attempted to, but he resented this proffered help.

"Say, look here, my lad," he would say to the tall, tired, and not at all burly policeman, "I've been coming downtown since long before you were born. You don't need to help me. I'm no jay from the country."

He visited the Stock Exchange. This depressed him. Stocks were lower than ever and still going down. His five hundred a year was safe, but the rest seemed doomed for his lifetime, at least. He would drop in at George's office. George's office was pleasantly filled with dapper, neat young men and (surprisingly enough) dapper, slim young women, seated at desks in the big light-flooded room. At one corner of each desk stood a polished metal placard bearing the name of the desk's occupant. Mr. Owens. Mr. Satterlee. Mr. James. Miss Rauch. Mr. Minick.

"Hello, Father," Mr. Minick would say, looking annoyed. "What's bringing you down?"

"Oh, nothing. Nothing. Just had a little business to tend to over at the Exchange. Thought I'd drop in. How's business?"

"Rotten."

"I should think it was!" Old Man Minick would agree. "I—should—think—it—was! Hm."

George wished he wouldn't. He couldn't have it, that's all. Old Man Minick would stroll over to the desk marked Satterlee, or Owens, or James. These brisk young men would toss an upward glance at him and concentrate again on the sheets and files before them. Old Man Minick would stand, balancing from heel to toe and blowing out his breath a little. He looked a bit yellow and granulated and wavering, there in the cruel morning light of the big plate-glass windows. Or perhaps it was the contrast he presented with these slim, slick young salesmen.

"Well, h'are you today, Mr.—uh—Satterlee? What's the good word?"

Mr. Satterlee would not glance up this time. "I'm pretty well. Can't complain."

"Good. Good."

"Anything I can do for you?"

"No-o-o. Not a thing. Just dropped in to see my son a minute."

"I see." Not unkindly. Then, as Old Man Minick still stood there, balancing, Mr. Satterlee would glance up again, frowning a little. "Your son's desk is over there, I believe. Yes."

George and Nettie had a bedtime conference about these visits and Nettie told him, gently, that the bond-house head objected to friends and relatives dropping in. It was against office rules. It had been so when she was employed there. Strictly business. She herself had gone there only once since her marriage.

Well, that was all right. Business was like that nowadays. Rush and grab and no time for anything.

The winter was a hard one, with a record snowfall and intense cold. He stayed indoors for days together. A woman of his own age in like position could have occupied herself usefully and happily. She could have hemmed a sash curtain; knitted or crocheted; tidied a room; taken a hand in the cooking or preparing of food; ripped an old gown; made over a new one; indulged in an occasional afternoon festivity with women of her own years. But for Old Man Minick there were no small tasks. There was nothing he could do to make his place in the household justifiable. He wasn't even particularly good at those small jobs of hammering, or painting, or general "fixing." Nettie could drive a nail more swiftly, more surely than he. "Now, Father, don't you bother. I'll do it. Just you go and sit down. Isn't it time for your afternoon nap?"

He waxed a little surly. "Nap! I just got up. I don't want to sleep my life away."

George and Nettie frequently had guests in the evening. They played bridge, or poker, or talked.

"Come in, Father," George would say. "Come in. You all know Dad, don't you, folks?" He would sit down, uncertainly. At first he had attempted to expound, as had been his wont in the old house on Ellis. "I want to say, here and now, that this country's got to . . ." But they went on, heedless of him. They interrupted or refused, politely, to listen. So he sat in the room, yet no part of it. The young people's talk swirled and eddied all about him. He was utterly lost in it. Now and then Nettie or George would turn to him and with raised voice (he was not at all deaf and prided himself on it) would shout, "It's about this or that, Father. He was saying . . ."

When the group roared with laughter at a sally from one of them he would smile uncertainly but amiably, glancing from one to the other in complete ignorance of what had passed, but not resenting it. He took to sitting more and more in his kitchen bedroom, smoking a comforting pipe and reading and rereading the evening paper. During that winter he and Canary, the Negro washwoman, became quite good friends. She washed down in the basement once a week but came up to the kitchen for her massive lunch. A walrus-waisted black woman, with a rich, throaty voice, a rolling eye, and a kindly heart. He actually waited for her appearance above the laundry stairs.

"Weh, how's Mist' Minick today! Ah nev' did see a gennelman spry's you ah for yo' age. No, suh! nev' did."

At this rare praise he would straighten his shoulders and waggle his head. "I'm worth any ten of these young sprats today." Canary would throw back her head in a loud and companionable guffaw.

Nettie would appear at the kitchen swinging door. "Canary's having her lunch, Father. Don't you want to come into the front room with me? We'll have our lunch in another half-hour."

He followed her obediently enough. Nettie thought of him as a troublesome and rather pathetic child—a child who would never grow up. If she attributed any thoughts to that fine old head they were ambling thoughts, bordering, perhaps, on senility. Little did she know how expertly this old one surveyed her and how ruthlessly he passed judgment. She never suspected the thoughts that formed in that active brain.

He knew about women. He had married a woman. He had had children by her. He looked at this woman—his son's wife—moving about her little five-room flat. She had theories about children. He had heard her expound them. You didn't have them except under such and such circumstances. It wasn't fair otherwise. Plenty of money for their education. Well. He and his wife had had three children. Paul, the second, had died at thirteen. A blow, that had been. They had not always planned for the coming of the three, but they always had found a way, afterward. You managed, somehow, once the little wrinkled red ball had fought its way into the world. You managed. You managed. Look at George! Yet when he was born, thirty-nine years ago, Pa and Ma Minick had been hard put to it.

Sitting there, while Nettie dismissed him as negligible, he saw her clearly, grimly. He looked at her. She was plump, but not too short, with a generous width between the hips; a broad full bosom, but firm; round arms and quick slim legs; a fine sturdy throat. The curve between arm and breast made a graceful gracious line. . . . Working in a bond office . . . Working in a bond office . . . There was nothing in the Bible about working in a bond office. Here was a woman built for childbearing.

She thought him senile, negligible.

In March Nettie had in a sewing woman for a week. She had her two or three times a year. A hawk-faced woman of about forty-nine, with a blue-bottle figure and a rapacious eye. She sewed in the dining room and there was a pleasant hum of machine and snip of scissors and murmur of conversation and rustle of silky stuff; and hot, savory dishes for lunch. She and Old Man Minick became great friends. She even let him take out bastings. This when Nettie had gone out from two to four, between fittings.

He chuckled and waggled his head. "I expect to be paid regular assistant's wages for this," he said.

"I guess you don't need any wages, Mr. Minick," the woman said. "I guess you're pretty well fixed."

"Oh, well, I can't complain." (Five hundred a year.)

"Complain! I should say not! If I was to complain it'd be different. Work all day to keep myself; and nobody to come home to at night."

"Widow, ma'am?"

"Since I was twenty. Work, work, that's all I've had. And lonesome! I suppose you don't know what lonesome is." .

"Oh, don't I!" slipped from him. He had dropped the bastings.

The sewing woman flashed a look at him from the cold hard eye. "Well, maybe you do. I suppose living here like this, with sons and daughters, ain't so grand, for all your money. Now me, I've always managed to keep my own little place that I could call home to come back to. It's only two rooms, and nothing to rave about, but it's home. Evenings I just cook and fuss around. Nobody to fuss for, but I fuss, anyway. Cooking, that's what I love to do. Plenty of good food, that's what folks need to keep their strength up." Nettie's lunch that day had been rather scant.

She was there a week. In Nettie's absence, she talked against her. He protested, but weakly. Did she give him eggnogs? Milk? Hot toddy? Soup? Plenty of good, rich gravy and meat and puddings? Well! That's what folks needed when they weren't so young any more. Not that he looked old. My, no. Spryer than many young boys, and handsomer than his own son, if she did say so.

He fed on it, hungrily. The third day she was flashing meaning glances at him across the luncheon table. The fourth she pressed his foot beneath the table. The fifth, during Nettie's afternoon absence, she got up, ostensibly to look for a bit of cloth which she needed for sewing, and, passing him, laid a caressing hand on his shoulder. Laid it there and pressed his shoulder ever so little. He looked up, startled. The glances across the luncheon had largely passed over his head; the foot beneath the table might have been an accident. But this—this was unmistakable. He stood up, a little shakily. She caught his hand. The hawklike face was close to his.

"You need somebody to love you," she said. "Somebody to do for you, and love you." The hawk face came nearer. He leaned a little toward it. But between it and his face was Ma Minick's face, plump, patient, quizzical. His head came back sharply. He threw the woman's hot hand from him.

"Woman!" he cried. "Jezebel!"

The front door slammed. Nettie. The woman flew to her sewing. Old Man Minick, shaking, went into his kitchen bedroom.

"Well," said Nettie, depositing her bundles on the dining-room table, "did you finish that faggoting? Why, you haven't done so very much, have you!"

"I ain't feeling so good," said the woman. "That lunch didn't agree with me."

"Why, it was a good plain lunch. I don't see——"

"Oh, it was plain enough, all right."

Next day she did not come to finish her work. Sick, she telephoned. Nettie called it an outrage. She finished the sewing herself, though she hated sewing. Pa Minick said nothing, but there was a light in his eye. Now and then he chuckled, to Nettie's infinite annoyance, though she said nothing.

"Wanted to marry me!" he said to himself, chuckling. "Wanted to marry me! The old rip!"

At the end of April, Pa Minick discovered Washington Park, and the Club, and his whole life was from that day transformed.

He had taken advantage of the early spring sunshine to take a walk, at Nettie's suggestion.

"Why don't you go into the park, Father? It's really warm out. And the sun's lovely. Do you good."

He had put on his heaviest shirt, and a muffler, and George's old red sweater with the great white C on its front, emblem of George's athletic prowess at the University of Chicago; and over all, his greatcoat. He had taken warm mittens and his cane with the greyhound's-head handle, carved. So equipped, he had ambled uninterestedly over to the park across the way. And there he had found new life.

New life in old life. For the park was full of old men. Old men like himself, with greyhound's-head canes, and mufflers, and somebody's sweater worn beneath their greatcoats. They wore arctics, though the weather was fine. The skin of their hands and cheekbones was glazed and had a tight look, though it lay in fine little folds. There were splotches of brown on the backs of their hands, and on the temples and forehead. Their heavy gray or brown socks made comfortable pleats above their ankles. From that April morning until winter drew on, the park saw Old Man Minick daily. Not only daily, but by the day. Except for his meals, and a brief hour for his after-luncheon nap, he spent all his time there.

For in the park Old Man Minick and all the old men gathered there found a forum—a safety valve, a means of expression. It did not take him long to discover that the park was divided into two distinct sets of old men.

There were the old men who lived with their married sons and daughters-in-law or married daughters and sons-in-law. Then there were the old men who lived in the Grant Home for Aged Gentlemen. You saw its fine red-brick façade through the trees at the edge of the park.

And the slogan of these first was:

"My son and my da'ter, they wouldn't want me to live in any public home. No, sirree! They want me right there with them. In their own home. That's the kind of son and da'ter I've got!"

The slogan of the second was:

"I wouldn't live with any son or daughter. Independent. That's me. My own boss. Nobody to tell me what I can do and what I can't. Treat you like a child. I'm my own boss. Pay my own good money and get my keep for it!"

The first group, strangely enough, was likely to be spotted of vest and a little frayed as to collar. You saw them going on errands for their daughters-in-law. A loaf of bread. Spool of white No. 100. They took their small grandchildren to the duck pond, and between the two toddlers hand in hand—the old and infirm and the infantile and infirm—it was hard to tell which led which.

The second group was shiny as to shoes, spotless as to linen, dapper as to clothes. They had no small errands. Theirs was a magnificent leisure. And theirs was magnificent conversation. The questions they discussed and settled there in the park—these old men—were not international merely. They were cosmic in scope.

The war? Peace? Disarmament? China? Mere conversational bubbles to be tossed in the air and disposed of in a burst of foam. Strong meat for Old Man Minick, who had so long been fed on pap. But he soon got used to it. Between four and five in the afternoon, in a spot known as Under the Willows, the meeting took the form of a club—an open forum. A certain group made up of Socialists, freethinkers, parlor rebels, had for years drifted there for talk. Old Man Minick learned high-sounding phrases. "The Masters . . . democracy . . . toil of the many for the good of the few . . . the ruling class . . . free speech . . . the People. . . ."

The strong-minded ones held forth. The weaker ones drifted about on the outskirts, sometimes clinging to the moist and sticky paw of a round-eyed grandchild. Earlier in the day—at eleven o'clock, say—the talk was not so general nor so inclusive. The old men were likely to drift into groups of two or three or four. They sat on sun-bathed benches, and their conversation was likely to be rather smutty at times, for all that they looked so mild and patriarchal and desiccated. They paid scant heed to the white-haired old women who, like themselves, were sunning in the park. They watched the young women switch by, with appreciative glances at their trim figures and slim ankles. The day of the short skirt was a grand time for them. They chuckled among themselves and made wicked comment. One saw only white-haired, placid, tremulous old men, but their minds still worked with belated masculinity. They were like naughty small boys talking behind the barn.

Old Man Minick early achieved a certain leadership in the common talk. He had always liked to hold forth. This last year had been one of almost unendurable bottling up. At first he had timidly sought the less assertive ones of his kind. Mild old men who sat in rockers in the pavilion, waiting for lunchtime. Their conversation irritated him. They remarked everything that passed before their eyes.

"There's a boat. Fella with a boat."

A silence. Then, heavily: "Yeh."

Five minutes.

"Look at those people laying on the grass. Shouldn't think it was warm enough for that. . . . Now they're getting up."

A group of equestrians passed along the bridle path on the opposite side of the lagoon. They made a frieze against the delicate spring greenery. The coats of the women were scarlet, vivid green, arresting.

"Riders."

"Yes."

"Good weather for riding."

A man was fishing near by. "Good weather for fishing."

"Yes."

"Wonder what time it is, anyway." From a pocket, deep-buried, came forth a great gold blob of a watch. "I've got one minute to eleven."

Old Man Minick dragged forth a heavy globe. "Mm. I've got eleven."

"Little fast, I guess."

Old Man Minick shook off this conversation impatiently. This wasn't conversation. This was oral death, though he did not put it thus. He joined the other men. They were discussing spiritualism. He listened, ventured an opinion, was heard respectfully and then combated mercilessly. He rose to the verbal fight, and won it.

"Let's see," said one of the old men. "You've not living at the Grant Home, are you?"

"No," Old Man Minick made reply, proudly. "I live with my son and his wife. They wouldn't have it any other way."

"Hm. Like to be independent myself."

"Lonesome, ain't it? Over there?"

"Lonesome! Say, Mr.—what'd you say your name was? Minick? Mine's

Hughes—I never was lonesome in my life, 'cept for six months when I lived with my daughter and her husband and their five children. Yes, sir. That's what I call lonesome."

George and Nettie said, "It's doing you good, Father, being out in the air so much." His eyes were brighter, his figure was straighter, his color better. It was that day he had held forth so eloquently on the emigration question. He had to read a lot—papers and magazines and one thing and another—to keep up. He devoured all the books and pamphlets about bond issues and national finances brought home by George. In the park he was considered an authority on bonds and banking. He and a retired real-estate man named Mowry sometimes debated a single question for weeks. George and Nettie, relieved, thought he ambled to the park and spent senile hours with his drooling old friends discussing nothing amiably and witlessly. This while he was eating strong meat, drinking strong drink.

Summer sped. Was past. Autumn held a new dread for Old Man Minick. When winter came where should he go? Where should he go? Not back to the five-room flat all day, and the little back bedroom, and nothingness. In his mind there rang a childish old song they used to sing at school. A silly song:

> *Where do all the birdies go?*
> *I know. I know.*

But he didn't know. He was terror-stricken. October came and went. With the first of November the park became impossible, even at noon, and with two overcoats and the sweater. The first frost was a black frost for him. He scanned the heavens daily for rain or snow. There was a cigar store and billiard room on the corner across the boulevard and there he sometimes went, with a few of his park cronies, to stand behind the players' chairs and watch them at pinochle or rum. But this was a dull business. Besides, the Grant men never came there. They had card rooms of their own.

He turned away from this smoky little den on a drab November day, sick at heart. The winter. He tried to face it, and at what he saw he shrank and was afraid.

He reached the apartment and went around to the rear, dutifully. His rubbers were wet and muddy and Nettie's living-room carpet was a fashionable gray. The back door was unlocked. It was Canary's day downstairs, he remembered. He took off his rubbers in the kitchen and passed into the dining room. Voices. Nettie had company. Some friends, probably, for tea. He turned to go to his room, but stopped at hearing his own name. Father Minick. Father Minick. Nettie's voice.

"Of course, if it weren't for Father Minick I would have. But how can we as long as he lives with us? There isn't room. And we can't afford a bigger place now, with rents what they are. This way it wouldn't be fair to the child. We've talked it over, George and I. Don't you suppose? But not as long as Father Minick is with us. I don't mean we'd use the maid's room for a—for the—if we had a baby. But I'd have to have someone in to help, then, and we'd have to have that extra room."

He stood there in the dining room, quiet. Quiet. His body felt queerly remote and numb, but his mind was working frenziedly. Clearly, too, in spite of the frenzy. Death. That was the first thought. Death. It would be easy. But he didn't want to die. Strange, but he didn't want to die. He liked life. The park, the trees, the Club, the talk, the whole show. . . . Nettie was a good girl. . . . The old must make way for the young. They had the right to be born. . . . Maybe it was just another excuse. Almost four years married. Why not three years ago? . . . The right to live. The right to live. . . .

He turned, stealthily, stealthily, and went back into the kitchen, put on his rubbers, stole out into the darkening November afternoon.

In an hour he was back. He entered at the front door this time, ringing the bell. He had never had a key. As if he were a child, they would not trust him with one. Nettie's women friends were just leaving. In the air you smelled a mingling of perfume and tea and cakes and powder. He sniffed it, sensitively.

"How do you do, Mr. Minick!" they said. "How are you! Well, you certainly look it. And how do you manage these gloomy days?"

He smiled genially, taking off his greatcoat and revealing the red sweater with the big white *C* on it. "I manage. I manage." He puffed out his cheeks. "I'm busy moving."

"Moving!" Nettie's startled eyes flew to his, held them. "Moving, Father?"

"Old folks must make way for the young," he said gaily. "That's the law of life. Yes, sir! New ones. New ones."

Nettie's face was scarlet. "Father, what in the world——"

"I signed over at the Grant Home today. Move in next week." The women looked at her, smiling. Old Man Minick came over to her and patted her plump arm. Then he pinched her smooth cheek with a quizzical thumb and forefinger. Pinched it and shook it ever so little.

"I don't know what you mean," said Nettie, out of breath.

"Yes, you do," said Old Man Minick, and while his tone was light and jesting there was in his old face something stern, something menacing. "Yes, you do."

When he entered the Grant Home a group of them was seated about the fireplace in the main hall. A neat, ruddy, septuagenarian circle. They greeted him casually, with delicacy of feeling, as if he were merely approaching them at their bench in the park.

"Say, Minick, look here. Mowry here says China ought to have been included in the four-power treaty. He says——"

Old Man Minick cleared his throat. "You take China, now," he said, "with her vast and practically, you might say, virgin resources, why——"

An apple-cheeked maid in a black dress and a white apron stopped before him. He paused.

"Housekeeper says for me to tell you your room's all ready, if you'd like to look at it now."

"Minute. Minute, my child." He waved her aside with the air of one who pays five hundred a year for independence and freedom. The girl turned to go. "Uh—young lady! Young lady!" She looked at him. "Tell the housekeeper two pillows, please. Two pillows on my bed. Be sure."

"Yes, sir. Two pillows. Yes, sir. I'll be sure."

The Afternoon of a Faun

[1921]

*Just why this story of a garage mechanic on his afternoon off should have
appeared in so many short-story anthologies in the past twenty-five years is
a baffling question. William Allen White and I were strolling along Fifty-
seventh Street one brilliant New York spring afternoon. We had just heard
the New York Symphony Orchestra at Carnegie Hall play* The Afternoon
of a Faun.

*"Might make a nice short story," I said, still under the spell of the sensu-
ous music. "Tough young kid with his girl in the park on a hot summer's
afternoon."*

"Write it," said Bill.

So I did.

◆§ THOUGH HE RARELY HEEDED ITS SUMMONS—CAGEY BOY THAT HE WAS
—the telephone rang oftenest for Nick. Because of the many native noises
of the place, the telephone had a special bell that was a combination buzz
and ring. It sounded above the roar of outgoing cars, the splash of the hose,
the sputter and hum of the electric battery in the rear. Nick heard it, unheeding. A voice—Smitty's or Mike's or Elmer's—answering its call. Then,
echoing through the gray, vaulted spaces of the big garage: "Nick! Oh,
Ni-ick!"

From the other side of the great cement-floored enclosure, or in muf-
fled tones from beneath a car: "Whatcha want?"

"Dame on the wire."

"I ain't in."

The obliging voice again, dutifully repeating the message: "He ain't in.
. . . Well, it's hard to say. He might be in in a couple hours and then again
he might not be back till late. I guess he's went to Hammond on a job——"
(Warming to his task now.) "Say, won't I do? . . . Who's fresh! Aw, say,
lady!"

You'd think, after repeated rebuffs of this sort, she could not possibly be
so lacking in decent pride as to leave her name for Smitty or Mike or
Elmer to bandy about. But she invariably did, baffled by Nick's elusive-
ness. She was likely to be any one of a number. "Miss Bauers phoned. Will
you tell him, please?" (A nasal voice, and haughty, with the hauteur that
seeks to conceal secret fright.) "Tell him it's important." "Miss Ahearn

128

phoned. Will you tell him, please? Just say Miss Ahearn, A-h-e-a-r-n." Miss Olson. Just Gertie. But oftenest Miss Bauers.

Cupid's messenger, wearing grease-grimed overalls and the fatuous grin of the dalliant male, would transmit his communication to the uneager Nick.

" 'S wonder you wouldn't answer the phone oncet yourself. Says you was to call Miss Bauers any time you come in between one and six at Hyde Park—wait a min't'—yeh—Hyde Park 6079, and any time after six at——"

"Wha'd she want?"

"Well, how the hell should I know! Says call Miss Bauers any time between one and six at Hyde Park 6——"

"Swell chanst. *Swell* chanst!"

Which explains why the calls came oftenest for Nick. He was so indifferent to them. You pictured the patient and persistent Miss Bauers, or the oxlike Miss Olson, or Miss Ahearn, or Just Gertie hovering within hearing distance of the telephone, listening, listening—while one o'clock deepened to six—for the call that never came; plucking up fresh courage at six until six o'clock dragged on to bedtime. When next they met: "I bet you was there all the time. Pity you wouldn't answer a call when a person leaves their name. You could of give me a ring. I bet you was there all the time."

"Well, maybe I was."

Bewildered, she tried to retaliate with the boomerang of vituperation.

How could she know? How could she know that this slim, slick young garage mechanic was a woodland creature in disguise—a satyr in store clothes—a wild thing who perversely preferred to do his own pursuing? How could Miss Bauers know—she who cashiered in the Green Front Grocery and Market on Fifty-third Street? Or Miss Olson, at the Rialto ticket window? Or the Celtic, emotional Miss Ahearn, the manicure? Or Gertie the goof? They knew nothing of mythology; of pointed ears and pug noses and goats' feet. Nick's ears, to their fond gaze, presented an honest red surface protruding from either side of his head. His feet, in tan laced shoes, were ordinary feet, a little more than ordinarily expert, perhaps, in the convolutions of the dance at Englewood Masonic Hall, which is part of Chicago's vast South Side. No; a faun, to Miss Bauers, Miss Olson, Miss Ahearn, and Just Gertie, was one of those things in the Lincoln Park Zoo.

Perhaps, sometimes, they realized, vaguely, that Nick was different. When, for example, they tried—and failed—to picture him looking interestedly at one of those three-piece bedroom sets glistening like pulled taffy in the window of the installment furniture store, while they, shy yet proprietary, clung to his arm and eyed the price ticket: Now $98.50. You couldn't see Nick interested in bedroom sets, in price tickets, in any of those settled, fixed, everyday things. He was fluid, evasive, like quicksilver, though they did not put it thus.

Miss Bauers, goaded to revolt, would say pettishly: "You're like a mosquito, that's what. Person never knows from one minute to the other where you're at."

"Yeah," Nick would retort. "When you know where a mosquito's at, what do you do to him? Plenty. I ain't looking to be squashed."

Miss Ahearn, whose public position (the Hygienic Barber Shop. Gent's manicure, 50¢.) offered unlimited social opportunities, would assume a gay indifference. "They's plenty boys begging to take me out every hour in the day. Swell lads, too. I ain't waiting round for any greasy mechanic like you. Don't think it. Say, lookit your nails! They'd queer you with me, let alone what else all is wrong with you."

In answer Nick would put one hand—one broad, brown, steel-strong hand with its broken, discolored nails—on Miss Ahearn's arm, in its flimsy georgette sleeve. Miss Ahearn's eyelids would flutter and close, and a little shiver would run with icy-hot feet all over Miss Ahearn.

Nick was like that.

Nick's real name wasn't Nick at all—or scarcely at all. His last name was Nicholas, and his parents, long before they became his parents, traced their origin to some obscure Central European province—long before we became so glib with our Central Europe. His first name was Pershing—knowing which, you automatically know the date of his birth. It was a patriotic but unfortunate choice on the part of his parents. The name did not fit him; was too mealy; not debonair enough. Nick. Nicky in tenderer moments (Miss Bauers, Miss Olson, Miss Ahearn, Just Gertie, *et al.*).

His method with women was firm and somewhat stern, but never brutal. He never waited for them if they were late. Any girl who assumed that her value was enhanced in direct proportion to her tardiness found herself standing disconsolate on the corner of Fifty-third and Lake, trying to look as if she were merely waiting for the Lake Park car and not peering wistfully up and down the street in search of a slim, graceful, hurrying figure that never came.

It is difficult to convey in words the charm that Nick possessed. Seeing him, you beheld merely a medium-sized young mechanic in reasonably grimed garage clothes when working; and in modish male habiliments when at leisure. A rather pallid skin due to the nature of his work. Large deft hands, a good deal like the hands of a surgeon, square, blunt-fingered, spatulate. Indeed, as you saw him at work, a wire-netted electric bulb held in one hand, the other plunged deep into the vitals of the car on which he was engaged, you thought of a surgeon performing a major operation. He wore one of those round skullcaps characteristic of his craft (the brimless crown of an old felt hat). He would deftly remove the transmission case and plunge his hand deep into the car's guts, feeling expertly about with his engine-wise fingers as a surgeon feels for liver, stomach, gall bladder, intestines, appendix. When he brought up his hand, all dripping with grease (which is the warm blood of the car), he invariably had put his finger on the sore spot.

All this, of course, could not serve to endear him to the girls. On the contrary, you would have thought that his hands alone, from which he could never quite free the grease and grit, would have caused some feeling of repugnance among the lily-fingered. But they, somehow, seemed always to be finding an excuse to touch him: his tie, his hair, his coat·sleeve. They seemed even to derive a vicarious thrill from holding his hat or cap when on an outing. They brushed imaginary bits of lint from his coat lapel. They tried on his seal ring, crying: "Oo, lookit, how big it is for me, even my thumb!" He called this "pawing a guy over"; and the lint ladies he designated as "thread pickers."

No; it can't be classified, this powerful draw he had for them. His conversation furnished no clue. It was commonplace conversation, limited, even dull. When astonished, or impressed, or horrified, or amused, he said: "Whaddy yuh know!" When emphatic or confirmatory, he said: *"I'll* say!"

It wasn't his car and the opportunities it furnished for drives, both country and city. That motley piece of mechanism represented such an assemblage of unrelated parts as could only have been made to co-ordinate under Nick's expert guidance. It was out of commission more than half the time, and could never be relied upon to furnish a holiday. Both Miss Bauers and Miss Ahearn had sixteen-cylinder opportunities that should have rendered them forever unfit for travel in Nick's one-lung vehicle of locomotion.

It wasn't money. Though he was generous enough with what he had, Nick couldn't be generous with what he hadn't. And his wage at the garage was forty-five dollars a week. Miss Ahearn's silk stockings cost one-fifty.

His unconcern should have infuriated them, but it served to pique. He wasn't actually as unconcerned as he appeared, but he had early learned that effort in their direction was unnecessary. Nick had little imagination, a gorgeous selfishness, a tolerantly contemptuous liking for the sex. Naturally, however, his attitude toward them had been somewhat embittered by being obliged to watch their method of driving a car in and out·of the Ideal Garage doorway. His own manipulation of the wheel was nothing short of wizardry.

He played the harmonica.

Each Thursday afternoon was Nick's half day off. From twelve until seven-thirty he was free to range the bosky highways of Chicago. When his car—he called it "the bus"—was agreeable, he went awheel in search of amusement. The bus being indisposed, he went afoot. He rarely made plans in advance; usually was accompanied by some successful telephonee. He rather liked to have a silken skirt beside him fluttering and flirting in the breeze as he broke the speed regulations.

On this Thursday afternoon in July he had timed his morning job to a miraculous nicety so that at the stroke of twelve his workaday garments dropped from him magically, as though he were a male (and reversed) Cinderella. There was a washroom and a rough sort of sleeping room containing two cots situated in the second story of the Ideal Garage. Here Nick shed the loose garments of labor for the fashionably tight habiliments of leisure. Private chauffeurs whose employers housed their cars in the Ideal Garage used this nook for a lounge and smoker. Smitty, Mike, Elmer, and Nick snatched stolen siestas there in the rare absences of the manager. Sometimes Nick spent the night there when forced to work overtime. His home life, at best, was a sketchy affair. Here, chauffeurs, mechanics, washers lolled at ease, exchanging soft-spoken gossip, motor chat, speculation, comment, and occasional verbal obscenity. Each possessed a formidable knowledge of that neighborhood section of Chicago known as Hyde Park. This knowledge was not confined to car costs and such impersonal items, but included meals, scandals, relationships, finances, love affairs, quarrels, peccadilloes. Here Nick often played his harmonica, his lips sweeping the metal length of it in throbbing rendition of sure-fire song sentimentality while the others talked, joked, kept time with tapping feet or wagging heads.

Today the hot little room was empty except for Nick, shaving before the cracked mirror on the wall, and old Elmer, reading a scrap of yesterday's newspaper as he lounged his noon hour away. Old Elmer was thirty-seven, and Nicky regarded him as an octogenarian. Also, old Elmer's conversation bored Nick to the point of almost sullen resentment. Old Elmer was a family man. His talk was all of his family—his wife, the kids, the flat. A garrulous person, lank, pasty, dish-faced, and amiable. His half day off was invariably spent tinkering about his stuffy little flat—painting, nailing up shelves, mending a broken window shade, puttying a window, playing with his pasty little boy, aged sixteen months, and his pasty little girl, aged three years. Next day he regaled his fellow workers with elaborate recitals of his holiday hours.

"Believe me, that kid's a caution. Sixteen months old, and what does he do yesterday? He unfastens the ketch on the back-porch gate. We got a gate on the back porch, see." (This frequent "see" which interlarded Elmer's verbiage was not used in an interrogatory way, but as a period, and by way of emphasis. His voice did not take the rising inflection as he uttered it.) "What does he do, he opens it. I come home, and the wife says to me: 'Say, you better get busy and fix a new ketch on that gate to the back porch. Little Elmer, first thing I know, he got it open today and was crawling out almost.' Say, can you beat that for a kid sixteen months——"

Nick had finished shaving, had donned his clean white soft shirt. His soft collar fitted to a miracle about his strong throat. Nick's sartorial effects were a triumph—on forty-five a week. "Say, can't you talk about nothing but that kid of yours? I bet he's a bum specimen at that. Runt, like his pa."

Elmer flung down his newspaper in honest indignation as Nick had wickedly meant he should. "Is that so! Why, he was wrastling round—me and him, see—last night on the floor, and what does he do, he raises his mitt and hands me a wallop in the stomick it like to knock the wind out of me. That's all. Sixteen months——"

"Yeh. I suppose this time next year he'll be boxing for money."

Elmer resumed his paper. "What do *you* know." His tone mingled pity with contempt.

Nick took a last critical survey of the cracked mirror's reflection and found it good. "Nothing, only this: you make me sick with your kids and your missus and your place. Say, don't you never have no fun?"

"Fun! Why, say, last Sunday we was out to the beach, and the kid swum out first thing you know——"

"Oh, shut up!" He was dressed now. He slapped his pockets. Harmonica. Cigarettes. Matches. Money. He was off, his hat pulled jauntily over his eyes.

Elmer, bearing no rancor, flung a last idle query: "Where you going?"

"How should I know? Bus is outa commission, and I'm outa luck."

He clattered down the stairs, whistling.

Next door for a shine at the Greek bootblack's. Enthroned on the dais, a minion at his feet, he was momentarily monarchial. How's the boy? Good? Same here. Down, his brief reign ended. Out into the bright noonday glare of Fifty-third Street.

A fried-egg sandwich. Two blocks down and into the white-tiled lunchroom. He took his place in the row perched on stools in front of the white slab, his feet on the railing, his elbows on the counter. Four white-aproned vestals with blotchy skins performed rites over the steaming nickel urns, slid dishes deftly along the slick surface of the white slab, mopped up moisture with a sly gray rag. No nonsense about them. This was the rush hour. Hungry men from the shops and offices and garages of the district were bent on food, not badinage. They ate silently, making a dull business of it. Coffee? What kinda pie do you want? No fooling here. "Hello, Jessie."

As she mopped the slab in front of him you noticed a slight softening of her features, intent so grimly on her task. "What's yours?"

"Bacon-and-egg sandwich. Glass of milk. Piece of pie. Blueberry."

Ordinarily she would not have bothered. But with him: "The blueberry ain't so good today. I noticed. Try the peach?"

"All right." He looked at her. She smiled. Incredibly, the dishes ordered seemed to leap out at her from nowhere. She crashed them down on the glazed white surface in front of him. The bacon-and-egg sandwich was served open-faced, an elaborate confection. Two slices of white bread, side by side. On one reposed a fried egg, hard, golden, delectable, indigestible. On the other three crisp curls of bacon. The ordinary order held two curls only. A dish so rich in calories as to make it food sufficient for a day. Jessie knew nothing of calories, nor did Nick. She placed a double order of butter before him—two yellow pats, moisture-beaded. As she scooped up his milk from the can, you saw that the glass was but three quarters filled. From a deep crock she ladled a smaller scoop and filled the glass to the top. The deep crock held cream. Nick glanced up at her again. Again Jessie smiled. A plain damsel, Jessie, and capable. She went on about her business. What's yours? Coffee with? White or rye? No nonsense about her. And yet: "Pie all right?"

"Yeh. It's good."

She actually blushed.

He finished, swung himself off the stool, nodded to Jessie. She stacked his dishes with one lean, capable hand, mopped the slab with the other, but as she made for the kitchen she flung a glance at him over her shoulder.

"Day off?"

"Yeh."

"Some folks has all the luck."

He grinned. His teeth were strong and white and even. He walked toward the door with his light quick step, paused for a toothpick as he paid his check, was out again into the July sunlight. Her face became dull again.

Well, not one o'clock. Guessed he'd shoot a little pool. He dropped into Moriarty's cigar store. It was called a cigar store because it dealt in magazines, newspapers, soft drinks, golf balls, cigarettes, pool, billiards, chocolates, chewing gum, and cigars. In the rear of the store were four green-topped tables, three for pool and one for billiards. He hung about aimlessly, watching the game at the one occupied table. The players were slim young men like himself, their clothes replicas of his own, their faces lean and somewhat hard. Two of them dropped out. Nick took a cue from the rack, shed his tight coat. They played under a glaring electric light in the heat of the day, yet they seemed cool, aloof, immune from bodily discomfort. It was a strangely silent game and as mirthless as that of the elfin bowlers in Rip Van Winkle. The slim-waisted, shirted figures bent plastically over the table in the graceful postures of the game. You heard only the click of the balls, an occasional low-voiced exclamation. A solemn crew, and unemotional.

Now and then: "What's all the shootin' fur?"

"In she goes."

Nick, winner, tired· of it in less than an hour. He bought a bottle of some acidulous drink just off the ice and refreshed himself with it, drinking from the bottle's mouth. He was vaguely restless, dissatisfied. Out again into the glare of two o'clock Fifty-third Street. He strolled up a block toward Lake Park Avenue. It was hot. He wished the bus wasn't sick. Might go in swimming, though. He considered this idly. Hurried steps behind him. A familiar perfume wafted to his senses. A voice nasal yet cooing. Miss Bauers. Miss Bauers on pleasure bent, palpably, being attired in the briefest of silks, white pumps, silk stockings, scarlet hat. The Green Front Grocerv and Market closed for a half day each Thursday afternoon during July and August. Nicky had not availed himself of the knowledge.

"Well, if it ain't Nicky! I just seen you come out of Moriarty's as I was passing." (She had seen him go in an hour before and had waited a patient hour in the drugstore across the street.) "What you doing around loose this hour the day, anyway?"

"I'm off 'safternoon."

"Are yuh? So'm I." Nicky said nothing. Miss Bauers shifted from one plump silken leg to the other. "What you doing?"

"Oh, nothing much."

"So'm I. Let's do it together." Miss Bauers employed the direct method.

"Well," said Nick vaguely. He didn't object particularly. And yet he was conscious of some formless program forming mistily in his mind—a program that did not include the berouged, bepowdered, plump, and silken Miss Bauers.

"I phoned you this morning, Nicky. Twice."

"Yeh?"

"They said you wasn't in."

"Yeh?"

A hard young woman, Miss Bauers, yet simple: powerfully drawn toward this magnetic and careless boy; powerless to forge chains strong enough to hold him. "Well, how about Riverview? I ain't been this summer."

"Oh, that's so darn far. Take all day getting there, pretty near."

"Not driving, it wouldn't."

"I ain't got the bus. Busted."

His apathy was getting on her nerves. "How about a movie, then?" Her feet hurt. It was hot.

His glance went up the street toward the Harper, down the street toward the Hyde Park. The sign above the Harper offered *Mother o' Mine*. The lettering above the Hyde Park announced *Love Crazy*.

"Gawd, no," he made decisive answer.

Miss Bauers' frazzled nerves snapped. "You make me sick! Standing there. Nothing don't suit you. Say, I ain't so crazy to go round with you. Cheap guy! Prob'ly you'd like to go over to Wooded Island or something, in Jackson Park, and set on the grass and feed the squirrels. That'd be a treat for me, that would." She laughed a high, scornful tear-near laugh.

"Why, say——" Nick stared at her, and yet she felt he did not see her. A sudden peace came into his face—the peace of a longing fulfilled. He turned his head. A Lake Park Avenue bus was roaring its way toward them. He took a step toward the roadway. "I got to be going."

Fear flashed its flame into Miss Bauers' pale-blue eyes. "Going! How do you mean, going? Going where?"

"I got to be going." The bus had stopped opposite them. His young face was stern, implacable. Miss Bauers knew she was beaten, but she clung to hope tenaciously, piteously. "I got to see a party, see?"

"You never said anything about it in the first place. Pity you wouldn't say so in the first place. Who you got to see, anyway?" She knew it was useless to ask. She knew she was beating her fists against a stone wall, but she must needs ask notwithstanding: "Who you got to see?"

"I got to see a party. I forgot." He made the bus step in two long strides; had swung himself up. "So long!" The door slammed after him. Miss Bauers, in her unavailing silks, stood disconsolate on the hot street corner.

He swayed in the aisle until Sixty-third Street was reached. There he alighted and stood a moment at the curb, surveying idly the populous corner. He purchased a paper bag of hot peanuts from a vender's glittering scarlet and nickel stand, and crossed the street into the pathway that led to Jackson Park, munching as he went. In an open space reserved for games some boys were playing baseball with much hoarse hooting and frenzied action. He drew near to watch. The ball, misdirected, sailed suddenly toward him. He ran backward at its swift approach, leaped high, caught it, and with a long curving swing, so easy as to appear almost effortless, sent it hurtling back. The lad on the pitcher's mound made as if to catch it, changed his mind, dodged, started after it.

The boy at bat called to Nick: "Heh, you! Wanna come on and pitch?"

Nick shook his head and went on.

He wandered leisurely along the gravel path that led to the park golf shelter. The wide porch was crowded with golfers and idlers. A foursome was teed up at the first tee. Nick leaned against a porch pillar, waiting for them to drive. That old boy had pretty good practice swing. . . . Stiff, though. . . . Lookit that dame. Jeez! I bet she takes fifteen shots before she ever gets on to the green. . . . There, that kid had pretty good drive. Must of been hunderd and fifty, anyway. Pretty good for a kid.

Nick, in the course of his kaleidoscopic career, had been a caddie at thirteen in torn shirt and flapping knickers. He had played the smooth, expert, scornful game of the caddie, with a natural swing from the lithe waist and a follow-through that was the envy of the muscle-bound men who watched him. He hadn't played in years. The game no longer interested him. He entered the shelter lunchroom. The counters were lined with lean, brown, hungry men and lean, brown, hungry women. They were eating incredible dishes considering that the hour was 3 P.M. and the day a hot one. Corned-beef hash with a poached egg on top; wieners and potato salad; meat pies; hot roast-beef sandwiches; steaming cups of coffee in thick white ware; watermelon. Nick slid a leg over a stool as he had done earlier in the afternoon. Here, too, the Hebes were of stern stuff, as they needs must be to serve these ravenous hordes of club swingers who swarmed upon them from dawn to dusk. Their task it was to wait upon the golfing male, which is man at his simplest—reduced to the least common denominator and shorn of all attraction for the female eye and heart. They represented merely hungry mouths, weary muscles, reaching fists. The waitresses served them as a capable attendant serves another woman's child—efficiently and without emotion.

"Blueberry pie à la mode," said Nick, "with strawberry ice cream."

Inured as she was to the horrors of gastronomic miscegenation, the waitress—an old girl—recoiled at this.

"Say, I don't think you'd like that. They don't mix so very good. Why don't you try the peach pie instead with the strawberry ice cream—if you want strawberry?" He looked so young and cool and fresh.

"Blueberry," repeated Nick sternly, and looked her in the eye. The old waitress laughed a little and was surprised to find herself laughing. " 'S for you to say." She brought him the monstrous mixture, and he devoured it to the last chromatic crumb.

"Nothing the matter with that," he remarked as she passed, dish-laden.

She laughed again tolerantly, almost tenderly. "Good thing you're young." Her busy glance lingered a brief moment on his face. He sauntered out.

Now he took the path to the right of the shelter, crossed the road, struck the path again, came to a rustic bridge that humped high in the middle, spanning a cool green stream, willow-bordered. The cool green stream was an emerald chain that threaded its way in a complete circlet about the sylvan spot known as Wooded Island, relic of World's Fair days.

The little island lay, like a thing under enchantment, silent, fragrant, golden, green, exquisite. Squirrels and blackbirds, rabbits and pigeons, mingled in Aesopian accord. The air was warm and still, held by the encircling trees and shrubbery. There was not a soul to be seen. At the far north end the two Japanese model houses, survivors of the Exposition, gleamed white among the trees.

Nick stood a moment. His eyelids closed, languorously. He stretched his arms out and up deliciously, bringing his stomach in and his chest out. He took off his hat and stuffed it into his pocket. He strolled across the thick cool nap of the grass, deserting the pebble path. At the west edge of the island a sign said: NO ONE ALLOWED IN THE SHRUBBERY. Ignoring it, Nick parted the branches, stooped and crept, reached the bank that sloped down to the cool green stream, took off his coat, and lay relaxed upon the ground. Above him the tree branches made a pattern against the sky. Little ripples lipped the shore. Scampering velvet-footed things, feathered things, winged things made pleasant stir among the leaves. Nick slept.

He awoke in half an hour, refreshed. He lay there, thinking of nothing—a charming gift. He found a stray peanut in his pocket and fed it to a friendly squirrel. His hand encountered the cool metal of his harmonica. He drew out the instrument, placed his coat, folded, under his head, crossed his knees, one leg swinging idly, and began to play rapturously. He was perfectly happy. He played "Gimme Love," whose measures are stolen from Mendelssohn's "Spring Song." He did not know this. The leaves rustled. He did not turn his head.

"Hello, Pan," said a voice. A girl came down the slope and seated herself beside him. She was not smiling.

Nick removed the harmonica from his lips and wiped his mouth with the back of his hand. "Hello who?"

"Hello, Pan."

"Wrong number, lady," Nick said, and again applied his lips to the mouth organ. The girl laughed then, throwing back her head. Her throat was long and slim and brown. She clasped her knees with her arms and looked at Nick amusedly. Nick thought she was a kind of homely little thing.

"Pan," she explained, "was a pagan deity. He played pipes in the woods."

"It's O.K. with me," Nick ventured, bewildered but amiable. He wished she'd go away. But she didn't. She began to take off her shoes and stockings. She went down to the water's edge, then, and paddled her feet. Nick sat up, outraged. "Say, you can't do that."

She glanced back at him over her shoulder. "Oh, yes, I can. It's so hot." She wriggled her toes ecstatically.

The leaves rustled again, briskly, unmistakably this time. A heavy tread. A rough voice. "Say, looka here! Get out of there, you! What the——" A policeman, red-faced, wroth. "You can't do that! Get outa here!"

It was like a movie, Nick thought.

The girl turned her head. "Oh, now, Mr. Elwood," she said.

"Oh, it's you, miss," said the policeman. You would not have believed it could be the same policeman. He even giggled. "Thought you was away."

"I was. In fact, I am, really. I just got sick of it and ran away for a day. Drove. Alone. The family'll be wild."

"All the way?" said the policeman, incredulously. "Say, I thought that looked like your car standing out there by the road; but I says no, she ain't in town." He looked sharply at Nick, whose face had an Indian composure, though his feelings were mixed. "Who's this?"

"He's a friend of mine. His name's Pan." She was drying her feet with an inadequate rose-colored handkerchief. She crept crabwise up the bank, and put on her stockings and slippers.

"Why'n't you come out and set on a bench?" suggested the policeman, worriedly.

The girl shook her head. "In Arcadia we don't sit on benches. I should think you'd know that. Go on away, there's a dear. I want to talk to this— to Pan."

He persisted. "What'd your pa say, I'd like to know!" The girl shrugged her shoulders. Nick made as though to rise. He was worried. A nut, that's what. She pressed him down again with a hard brown hand.

"Now, it's all right. He's going. Old Fuss!" The policeman stood a brief moment longer. Then the foliage rustled again. He was gone. The girl sighed, happily. "Play that thing some more, will you? You're a wiz at it, aren't you?"

"I'm pretty good," said Nick modestly. Then the outrageousness of her conduct struck him afresh. "Say, who're you, anyway?"

"My name's Berry—short for Bernice. . . . What's yours, Pan?"

"Nick—that is—Nick."

"Ugh, terrible! I'll stick to Pan. What d'you do ,when you're not Pan-ning?" Then, at the bewilderment in his face: "What's your job?"

"I work in the Ideal Garage. Say, you're pretty nosy, ain't you?"

"Yes, pretty. . . . That accounts for your nails, hm?" She looked at her own brown paws. " 'Bout as bad as mine. I drove two hundred and fifty miles today."

"Ya-as, you did!"

"I did! Started at six. And I'll probably drive back tonight."

"You're crazy!"

"I know it," she agreed, "and it's wonderful. . . . Can you play 'Truck Line'?"

"Yeh. It's kind of hard, though, where the runs are. I don't get the runs so very good." He played it. She kept time with head and feet. When he had finished he wiped his lips.

"Elegant!" she said. She took the harmonica from him, wiped it brazenly on the much-abused, rose-colored handkerchief and began to play, her cheeks puffed out, her eyes round with effort. She played "Truck Line," and her runs were perfect. Nick's chagrin was swallowed by his admira-tion and envy.

"Say, kid, you got more wind than a sax player. Who learned you to play?"

She struck her chest with a hard brown fist. "Tennis. . . . Tim taught me."

"Who's Tim?"

"The—a chauffeur."

Nick leaned closer. "Say, do you ever go to the dances at Englewood Masonic Hall?"

"I never have."

" 'Jah like to go sometime?"

"I'd love it." She grinned up at him, her teeth flashing white in her brown face.

"It's swell here," he said dreamily. "Like the woods?"

"Yes."

"Winter, when it's cold and dirty, I think about how it's here summers. It's like you could take it out of your head and look at it whenever you wanted to."

"Endymion."

"Huh?"

"A man said practically the same thing the other day. Name of Keats."

"Yeh?"

"He said: 'A thing of beauty is a joy forever.' "

"That's one way putting it," he agreed graciously.

Unsmilingly she reached over with one slim forefinger, as if compelled, and touched the blond hairs on Nick's wrist. Just touched them. Nick remained motionless. The girl shivered a little, deliciously. She glanced at him shyly. Her lips were provocative. Thoughtlessly, blindly, Nick suddenly flung an arm about her, kissed her. He kissed her as he had never kissed Miss Bauers—as he had never kissed Miss Ahearn, Miss Olson, or Just Gertie. The girl did not scream, or push him away, or slap him, or protest, or giggle as the above-mentioned young ladies would have. She sat breathing rather fast, a tinge of scarlet showing beneath the tan.

"Well, Pan," she said, low voiced, 'you're running true to form, anyway." She eyed him appraisingly. 'Your appeal is in your virility, I suppose. Yes."

"My what?"

She rose. "I've got to go."

Panic seized him. "Say, don't drive back tonight, huh? Wherever it is you've got to go. You ain't driving back tonight?"

She made no answer; parted the bushes, was out on the gravel path in the sunlight, a slim, short-skirted, almost childish figure. He followed. They crossed the bridge, left the island, reached the roadway in silence. At the side of the road was a roadster. Its hood was the kind that conceals power. Its lamps were two giant eyes rimmed in precious metal. Its line spelled strength. Its body was vast. Nick's engine-wise eyes saw these things at a glance.

"That your car?"

"Yes."

"Gosh!"

She unlocked it, threw in the clutch, shifted, moved. "Say!" was wrung from Nick helplessly. She waved at him. "Good-by, Pan." He stared, stricken. She was off swiftly, silently; flashed around a corner; was hidden by the trees and shrubs.

He stood a moment. He felt bereaved, cheated. Then a little wave of exaltation shook him. He wanted to talk to someone. "Gosh!" he said again. He glanced at his wrist. Five-thirty. He guessed he'd go home. He guessed he'd go home and get one of Ma's dinners. One of Ma's dinners and talk to Ma. He could make it and back in plenty time.

Nick lived in that section of Chicago known as Englewood, which is not so sylvan as it sounds, but appropriate enough for a faun. Not only that; he lived in S. Green Street, Englewood. S. Green Street, near Seventieth, is almost rural with its great elms and poplars, its frame cottages, its back gardens. A neighborhood of thrifty, foreign-born fathers and mothers, **many** children, tree-lined streets badly paved. Nick turned in at a two-story brown frame cottage. He went around to the back. Ma was in the kitchen.

Nick's presence at the evening meal was an uncertain thing. Sometimes he did not eat at home for a week, excepting only his hurried early breakfast. He rarely spent an evening at home, and when he did used the opportunity for making up lost sleep. Pa never got home from work until after six. Nick liked his dinner early and hot. On his rare visits his mother welcomed him like one of the Gracchi. Mother and son understood each other wordlessly, having much in common. You would not have thought it of her (forty-six bust, forty waist, measureless hips), but Ma was a nymph at heart. Hence Nick.

"Hello, Ma!" She was slamming expertly about the kitchen.

"Hello, yourself," said Ma. Ma had a line of slang gleaned from her numerous brood. It fell strangely from her lips. Ma had never quite lost a tinge of foreign accent, though she had come to America when a girl. A hearty, zestful woman, savoring life with gusto, undiminished by childbearing and hard work. "Eating home, Pershing?" She alone used his given name.

"Yeh, but I gotta be back by seven-thirty. Got anything ready?"

"Dinner ain't, but I'll get you something. Plenty. Platter ham and eggs and a quick fry. Cherry cobbler's done. I'll fix you some."

He ate enormously at the kitchen table, she hovering over him.

"What's the news?"

"Ain't none." He ate in silence. Then: "How old was you when you married Pa?"

"Me? Say, I wasn't no more'n a kid. I gotta laugh when I think of it."

"What was Pa earning?"

She laughed a great hearty laugh, dipping a piece of bread sociably in the ham fat on the platter as she stood by the table, just to bear him company.

"Say, earn! If he'd of earned what you was earning now, we'd of thought we was millionaires. Time Etty was born he was pulling down fifteen a week, and we saved on it." She looked at him suddenly, sharply. "Why?"

"Oh, I was just wondering."

"Look what good money he's getting now! If I was you, I wouldn't stick around no old garage for what they give you. You could get a good job in the works with Pa; first thing you know you'd be pulling down big money. You're smart like that with engines. . . . Takes a lot of money nowadays for fellers to get married."

"*I'll* say!" agreed Nick. He looked up at her, having finished eating. His glance was almost tender. "How'd you come to marry Pa, anyway? You and him's so different."

The nymph in Ma leaped to the surface and stayed there a moment, sparkling, laughing, dimpling. "Oh, I dunno. I kept running away and he kept running after. Like that."

He looked up again quickly at that. "Yeh. That's it. Fella don't like to have no girl chasing him all the time. Say, he likes to do the chasing himself. Ain't that the truth?"

"*I'll* say!" agreed Ma. A great jovial laugh shook her. Heavy-footed now, but light of heart.

Suddenly: "I'm thinking of going to night school. Learn something. I don't know nothing."

"You do, too, Pershing!"

"Aw, wha'd I know? I never had enough schooling. Wished I had."

"Who's doings was it? You wouldn't stay. Wouldn't go no more than sixth reader and quit. Nothing wouldn't get you to go."

He agreed gloomily. "I know it. I don't know what nothing is. Uh—Arcadia—or Pan or—now—vitality or nothing."

"Oh, that comes easy," she encouraged him, "when you begin once."

He reached for her hand gratefully. "You're a swell cook, Ma." He had a sudden burst of generosity, of tenderness. "Soon's the bus is fixed I'll take you riding over to the lake."

Ma always wore a hat of draggled flowers and ribbon for motoring. Nick almost never offered her a ride. She did not expect him to.

She pushed him playfully. "Go on! You got plenty young girls to take riding, not your ma."

"Oh, girls!" he said scornfully. Then in another tone: "Girls."

He was off. It was almost seven. Pa was late. He caught a bus back to Fifty-third Street. Elmer was lounging in the cool doorway of the garage. Nick, in sheer exuberance of spirits, squared off, doubled his fists, and danced about Elmer in a semicircle, working his arms as a prize fighter does, warily. He jabbed at Elmer's jaw playfully.

"What you been doing," inquired that long-suffering gentleman, "makes you feel so good? Where you been?"

"Oh, nowheres. Just around. Park."

He turned in the direction of the stairway. Elmer lounged after him. "Oh, say, dame's been calling you for the last hour and a half. Like to busted the phone. Makes me sick."

"Aw, Bauers."

"No, that wasn't the name. Name's Mary or Berry, or something like that. A dozen times, I betcha. Says you was to call her as soon as you come in. Drexel 47—— Wait a min't'—yeh, that's right, Drexel 473——"

"Swell chanst," said Nick. Suddenly his buoyancy was gone. His shoulders drooped. His cigarette dangled limp. Disappointment curved his lips, burdened his eyes. "*Swell* chanst!"

Old Lady Mandle
[1920]

Old people always have interested me as short-story material even when I, myself, was still in my twenties. Theirs is the final, the inescapable, tragedy. Life seems to me to have managed this matter rather badly. Born at, say, eighty, we really could begin to enjoy life's flavor at seventy, partaking of it with increasing vigor and winding up between the age of ten and infancy with no regrets and no gnarled and baffled old age to contemplate. Old age, the philosophers say, has its compensations. Name two.

◆§ OLD LADY MANDLE WAS A QUEEN. HER DEMESNE, UNDISPUTED, WAS A six-room flat on South Park Avenue, Chicago. Her faithful servitress was Anna, an ancient person of Polish nativity, bad teeth, and a cunning hand at cookery. Not so cunning, however, but that old lady Mandle's was more artful still in such matters as meat soups, broad noodles, fish with egg sauce, and the like. As ladies in waiting, flattering yet jealous, admiring though resentful, she had Mrs. Lamb, Mrs. Brunswick, and Mrs. Wormser, themselves old ladies and erstwhile queens, now deposed. And the crown jewel in Old Lady Mandle's diadem was "my son Hugo."

Mrs. Mandle was not only a queen but a spoiled old lady. And not only a spoiled old lady but a confessedly spoiled old lady. Bridling and wagging her white head, she admitted her pampered state. It was less an admission than a boast. Her son Hugo had spoiled her. This, too, she acknowledged. "My son Hugo spoils me," she would say, and there was no proper humbleness in her voice. Though he was her only son, she never spoke of him merely as "Hugo," or "My son," but always as "My son Hugo." She rolled the three words on her tongue as though they were delicious morsels from which she would extract all possible savor and sweetness. And when she did this you could almost hear the click of the stiffening spines of Mrs. Lamb, Mrs. Brunswick, and Mrs. Wormser. For they envied her her son Hugo, and resented him as only three old ladies could who were living, tolerated and dependent, with their married sons and their sons' wives.

Any pleasant summer afternoon at four o'clock you might have seen Mrs. Mandle holding court. The four old women sat, a decent black silk row, on a shady bench in Washington Park (near the refectory and afternoon coffee). Three of them complained about their daughters-in-law. One of them bragged about her son. Adjective crowding adjective, pride in her voice, majesty in her mien, she bragged about my son Hugo.

145

My son Hugo had no wife. Not only that, Hugo Mandle, at forty, had
no thought of marrying. Not that there was anything austere or saturnine
about Hugo. He made you think, somehow, of a cherubic, jovial monk. It
may have been his rosy rotundity, or, perhaps, the way in which his thinning hair vanished altogether at the top of his head, so as to form a tonsure.
Hugo Mandle, kindly, generous, shrewd, spoiled his old mother in the way
in which women of seventy, whose middle life had been hard, like to be
spoiled. First of all, of course, she reigned unchecked over the South Park
Avenue flat. She quarreled wholesomely and regularly with Polish Anna.
Alternately she threatened Anna with dismissal and Anna threatened Ma
Mandle with impending departure. This had been going on, comfortably,
for fifteen years. Ma Mandle held the purse and her son filled it. Hugo
paid everything from the rent to the iceman, and this without once making his mother feel a beneficiary. She possessed an infinitesimal income of
her own, left out of the ruins of her dead husband's money, but this Hugo
always waved aside did she essay to pay for her own movie ticket or ice-cream
soda. "Now, now! None of that, Ma. Your money's no good tonight."

When he returned from a New York business trip he usually brought
her two gifts, one practical, the other absurd. She kissed him for the first
and scolded him for the second, but it was the absurdity, fashioned of lace,
or silk, or fragile stuff, that she pridefully displayed to her friends.

"Look what my son Hugo brought me. I should wear a thing like that in
my old days. But it's beautiful anyway, hm? He's got taste, my son Hugo."

In the cool of the evening you saw them taking a slow and solemn walk
together, his hand on her arm. He surprised her with matinee tickets in
pairs, telling her to treat one of her friends. On Anna's absent Thursdays
he always offered to take dinner downtown. He brought her pound boxes
of candy tied with sly loops and bands of gay satin ribbon, which she carefully rolled and tucked away in a drawer. He praised her cooking, and
teased her with elephantine playfulness, and told her that she looked like
a chicken in that hat. Oh, yes, indeed! Mrs. Mandle was a spoiled old lady.

At half-past one she always prepared to take her nap in the quiet of her
neat flat. She would select a plump, after-lunch chocolate from the box in
her left-hand bureau drawer, take off her shoes, and settle her old frame in
comfort. No noisy grandchildren to disturb her rest. No faultfinding
daughter- in-law to bustle her out of the way. The sounds that Anna made,
moving about in the kitchen at the far end of the long hall, were the subdued homely swishings and brushings that lulled and soothed rather than
irritated. At half-past two she rose, refreshed, and dressed herself in her
crepe with its trimming of val, or in black silk, modish both. She was, in
fact, a modish old lady, as were her three friends. They were not the ultra-

modern type of old lady who at sixty apes sixteen. They were neat and rather tart-tongued septuagenarians, guiltless of artifice. Their soft white hair was dressed neatly and craftily so as to conceal the thinning spots that revealed the pink scalp beneath. Their corsets and their stomachs were too high, perhaps, for fashion, and their heavy brooches and chains and rings appeared clumsy when compared to the hoarfrost tracery of the platinum-smith's exquisite art. But their skirts had pleats when pleated skirts were worn, and their sleeves were snug when snug sleeves were decreed. They were inclined to cling overlong to a favorite leather reticule, scuffed and shapeless as an old shoe, but they could hold their own at bridge on a rainy afternoon. In matters of material and cut Mrs. Mandle triumphed. Her lace was likely to be real where that of the other three was imitation.

So there they sat on a park bench in the pleasant afternoon air, filling their lives with emptiness. They had married, and brought children into the world; sacrificed for them, managed a household, been widowed. They represented magnificent achievement, those four old women, though they themselves did not know it. They had come up the long hill, reached its apex, and come down. Their journey was over and yet they sat by the road-side. They knew that which could have helped younger travelers over the next hill, but those fleet-footed ones pressed on, wanting none of their wisdom. Ma Mandle alone still moved. She still queened it over her own household; she alone still had the delightful task of making a man comfortable. If the world passed them by as they sat there, it did not pass unscathed. Their shrewd old eyes regarded the panorama, undeceived. They did not try to keep up with the procession, but they derived a sly amusement and entertainment from their observation of the modes and manners of this amazing day and age.

Their talk, stray as it might, always came back to two subjects. They seemed never to tire of them. Three talked of their daughters-in-law, and bitterness rasped their throats. One talked of her son, and her voice was unctuous with pride.

"My son's wife——" one of the three would begin. There was something terribly significant in the mock respect with which she uttered the title.

"If I had ever thought," Mrs. Brunswick would say, shaking her head, "if I had ever thought that I would live to see the day when I had to depend on strangers for my comfort, I would have wished myself dead."

"You wouldn't call your son a stranger, Mrs. Brunswick!" in shocked tones from Mrs. Mandle.

"A stranger has got more consideration. I count for nothing. Less than nothing. I'm in the way. I don't interfere in that household. I see enough, and I hear enough, but I say nothing. My son's wife, she says it all."

A silence, thoughtful, brooding. Then, from Mrs. Wormser: "What good do you have of your children? They grow up, and what do you have of them?"

More shaking of heads, and a dark murmur about the advisability of an Old People's Home as a refuge. Then:

"My son Hugo said only yesterday, 'Ma,' he said, 'when it comes to housekeeping you could teach them all something, believe me. Why,' he says, 'if I was to try and get a cup of coffee like this in a restaurant—well, you couldn't get it in a restaurant, that's all. You couldn't get it in any hotel, Michigan Avenue or I don't care where.'"

Goaded, Mrs. Lamb would look up from her knitting. "Mark my words, he'll marry yet." She was a sallow, lively woman, her hair still markedly streaked with black. Her rheumatism-twisted fingers were always grotesquely busy with some handiwork, and the finished product was a marvel of perfection.

Mrs. Wormser, plump, placid, agreed. "That's the kind always marries late. And they get it the worst. Say, my son was no spring chicken either when he married. And you would think the sun rises and sets in his wife. Well, I suppose it's only natural. But you wait."

"Some girl is going to have a snap." Mrs. Brunswick, eager, peering, a trifle vindictive, offered final opinion. "The girls aren't going to let a boy like your Hugo get away. Not nowadays, the way they run after them like crazy. All they think about is dress and a good time."

The three smiled grimly. Ma Mandle smiled, too, a little nervously, her fingers creasing and uncreasing a fold of her black silk skirt as she made airy answer: "If I've said once I've said a million times to my son Hugo, 'Hugo, why don't you pick out some nice girl and settle down? I won't be here always.' And he says, 'Getting tired of me, are you, Ma? I guess maybe you're looking for a younger fellow.' Only last night I said, at the table, 'Hugo, when are you going to get married?' And he laughed. 'When I find somebody that can cook dumplings like these. Pass me another, Ma.'"

"That's all very well," said Mrs. Wormser. "But when the right one comes along he won't know dumplings from mud."

"Oh, a man of forty isn't such a——"

"He's just like a man of twenty-five—only worse."

Mrs. Mandle would rise abruptly. "Well, I guess you all know my son Hugo better than his own mother. How about a cup of coffee, ladies?"

They would proceed solemnly and eagerly to the columned coolness of the park refectory, where they would drink their thick, creamy coffee. They never knew, perhaps, how keenly they counted on that cup of coffee, or how hungrily they drank it. Their minds, unconsciously, were definitely fixed on the four-o'clock drink that stimulated the old nerves.

Life had not always been so plumply upholstered for Old Lady Mandle. She had known its sharp corners and cruel edges. At twenty-three, a strong, healthy, fun-loving girl, she had married Herman Mandle, a dour man twenty-two years her senior. In their twenty-five years of married life together Hattie Mandle never had had a five-cent piece that she could call her own. Her husband was reputed to be wealthy, and probably was, according to the standards of that day. There were three children: Etta, the oldest; a second child, a girl, who died; and Hugo. Her husband's miserliness, and the grind of the planning, scheming, and contriving necessary to clothe and feed her two children would have crushed the spirit of many women. But hard and glum as her old husband was, he never quite succeeded in subduing her courage or her love of fun. The habit of heartbreaking economy clung to her, however, even when days of plenty became hers. It showed in little hoarding ways; in the saving of burned matches, of bits of ribbon, of scraps of material, of the very furniture and linen, as though, when these were gone, no more would follow.

Ten years after her marriage her husband retired from active business. He busied himself now with his real estate, with mysterious papers, documents, agents. He was forever poking around the house at hours when a household should be manless, grumbling about the waste where there was none, peering into breadboxes, prying into corners never meant for masculine eyes. Etta, the girl, was like him, sharp-nosed, ferret-faced, stingy. The mother and the boy turned to each other. In a wordless way they grew silently close, those two. It was as if they were silently matched against the father and daughter.

It was a queer household, brooding, sinister, like something created in a Brontë brain. The two children were twenty-four and twenty-two when the financial avalanche of '93 thundered across the continent, sweeping Herman Mandle, a mere speck, into the debris. Stocks and bonds and real estate became paper, with paper value. He clawed about with frantic, clutching fingers, but his voice was lost in the shrieks of thousands more hopelessly hurt. You saw him sitting for hours together with a black tin box in front of him, pawing over papers, scribbling down figures, muttering. The bleak future that confronted them had little of terror for Hattie Mandle. It presented no contrast with the bleakness of the past. On the day that she came upon him, his head fallen at a curious angle against the black tin box, his hands, asprawl, clutching the papers that strewed the table, she was appalled, not at what she found, but at the leap her heart gave at what she found. Herman Mandle's sudden death was one of the least of the tragedies that trailed in the wake of the devastating panic.

Thus it was that Hugo Mandle, at twenty-three, became the head of a household. He did not need to seek work. From the time he was seventeen he had been employed in a large china-importing house, starting as a stock boy. Brought up under the harsh circumstances of Hugo's youth, a boy becomes food for the reformatory or takes on the seriousness and responsibility of middle age. In Hugo's case the second was true. From his father he had inherited a mathematical mind and a sense of material values. From his mother, a certain patience and courage, though he never attained her iron indomitability.

It had been a terrific struggle. His salary at twenty-three was modest, but he was getting on. He intended to be a buyer, someday, and take trips abroad to the great Austrian and French and English china houses.

The day after the funeral he said to his mother, "Well, now we've got to get Etta married. But married well. Some boy who'll take care of her."

"You're a good son, Hugo," Mrs. Mandle had said.

Hugo shook his head. "It isn't that. If she's comfortable and happy—or as happy as she knows how to be—she'll never come back. That's what I want. There's debts to pay, too. But I guess we'll get along."

They did get along, but at snail's pace. There followed five years of economy so rigid as to make the past seem profligate. Etta, the acid-tongued, the ferret-faced, was not the sort to go off without the impetus of a dowry. The man for Etta, the shrew, must be kindly, long-suffering, subdued—and in need of a start. He was. They managed a very decent trousseau and the miracle of five thousand dollars in cash. Every stitch in the trousseau and every penny in the dowry represented incredible sacrifice and self-denial on the part of mother and brother. Etta went off to her new home in Pittsburgh with her husband. She had expressed thanks for nothing and had bickered with her mother to the last, but even Hugo knew that her suit and hat and gloves and shoes were right. She was almost handsome in them, the unwonted flush of excitement coloring her cheeks, brightening her eyes.

The next day Hugo came home with a new hat for his mother, a four-pound steak, and the announcement that he was going to take music lessons. A new era had begun in the life of Ma Mandle.

Two people, no matter how far apart in years or tastes, cannot struggle side by side, like that, in a common cause, without forging between them a bond indissoluble. Hugo, at twenty-eight, had the serious mien of a man of forty. At forty he was to revert to his slighted twenty-eight, but he did not know that then. His music lessons were his one protest against a beauty-starved youth. He played rather surprisingly well the cheap music of the day, waggling his head (already threatening baldness) in a professional vaudeville manner and squinting up through his cigar smoke, happily. His mother, seated in the room, sewing, would say, "Play that again, Hugo. That's beautiful. What's the name of that?" He would tell her, for the dozenth time, and play it over, she humming, off key, in his wake. The relation between them was more than that of mother and son. It was a complex thing that had in it something conjugal. When Hugo kissed his mother with a resounding smack and assured her that she looked like a kid she would push him away with little futile shoves, pat her hair into place, and pretend annoyance. "Go away, you big, rough thing!" she would cry. But all unconsciously she got from it a thrill that her husband's withered kisses had never given her.

Twelve years had passed since Etta's marriage. Hugo's salary was a comfortable thing now, even in these days of soaring prices. The habit of economy, so long a necessity, had become almost a vice in Old Lady Mandle. Hugo, with the elasticity of younger years, learned to spend freely, but his mother's thrift and shrewdness automatically swelled his savings. When he was on the road, as he sometimes was for weeks at a time, she spent only a tithe of the generous sum he left with her. She and Anna ate those sketchy meals that obtain in a manless household. When Hugo was home the table was abundant and even choice, though Ma Mandle often went blocks out of her way to save three cents on a bunch of new carrots. So strong is usage. She would no more have wasted his money than she would have knifed him in the back. She ran the household capably, but her way was the old-fashioned way. Sometimes Hugo used to protest, aghast at some petty act of parsimony.

"But, Ma, what do you want to scrimp like that for! You're the worst tightwad I ever saw. Here, take this ten and blow it. You're worse than the squirrels in the park, darned if you ain't!"

She couldn't resist the ten. Neither could she resist showing it, next day, to Mrs. Brunswick, Mrs. Lamb, and Mrs. Wormser. "How my son Hugo spoils me! He takes out a ten-dollar bill, and he stuffs it into my hand and says, 'Ma, you're the worst tightwad I ever saw.'" She laughed contentedly. But she did not blow the ten. As she grew older Hugo regularly lied to her about the price of theater tickets, dainties, articles of dress, railway fares, luxuries. Her credulity increased with age, shrewd though she naturally was.

It was a second blooming for Ma Mandle. When he surprised her with an evening at the theater she would fuss before her mirror for a full hour. "Some gal!" Hugo would shout when finally she emerged. "Everybody'll be asking who the old man is you're out with. First thing I know I'll have a cop after me for going around with a babe."

"Don't talk foolishness." But she would flush like a bride. She liked musical comedy with a lot of girls in it and a good-looking tenor. Next day you would hear her humming the hit song in an airy falsetto. Sometimes she wondered about him. She was, after all, a rather wise old lady, and she knew something of men. She had a secret horror of his becoming what she called fast.

"Why don't you take out some nice young girl instead of an old woman like me, Hugo? Any girl would be only too glad." But in her heart was a dread. She thought of Mrs. Lamb, Mrs. Wormser, and Mrs. Brunswick.

So they had gone on, year after year, in the comfortable flat on South Park Avenue. A pleasant thing, life.

And then Hugo married, suddenly, breathlessly, as a man of forty does.

Afterward, Ma Mandle could recall almost nothing from which she might have taken warning. That was because he had said so little. She remembered that he had come home to dinner one evening and had spoken admiringly of a woman buyer from Omaha. He did not often speak of business.

"She buys like a man," he had said at dinner. "I never saw anything like it. Knew what she wanted and got it. She bought all my best numbers at rock bottom. I sold her a four-figure bill in half an hour. And no fuss. Everything right to the point and when I asked her out to dinner she turned me down. Good-looking, too. She's coming in again tomorrow for novelties."

Ma Mandle didn't even recall hearing her name until the knife descended. Hugo played the piano a great deal all that week, after dinner. Sentimental things, with a minor wail in the chorus. Smoked a good deal, too. Twice he spent a full hour in dressing, whistling absent-mindedly during the process and leaving his necktie rack looking like a nest of angry pythons when he went out, without saying where he was going. The following week he didn't touch the piano and took long walks in Washington Park, alone, after ten. He seemed uninterested in his meals. Usually he praised this dish, or that.

"How do you like the blueberry pie, Hugo?"

" 'S all right." And declined a second piece.

The third week he went West on business. When he came home he dropped his bag in the hall, strode into his mother's bedroom, and stood before her like a schoolboy. "Lil and I are going to be married," he said.

Ma Mandle had looked up at him, her face a blank. "Lil?"

"Sure. I told you all about her." He hadn't. He had merely thought about her, for three weeks, to the exclusion of everything else. "Ma, you'll love her. She knows all about you. She's the grandest girl in the world.

Say, I don't know why she ever fell for a mug like me. Well, don't look so stunned. I guess you kind of suspicioned, huh?"

"But who——?"

"I never thought she'd look at me. Earned her own good salary, and strictly business, but she's a real woman. Says she wants her own home and—'n' everything. Says every normal woman does. Says——"

Ad lib.

They were married the following month.

Hugo subleased the flat on South Park and took an eight-room apartment farther east. Ma Mandle's red and green plush parlor pieces, and her mahogany rockers, and her rubber plant, and the fern, and the can of grapefruit pits that she and Anna had planted and that had come up, miraculously, in the form of shiny, little green leaves, all were swept away in the upheaval that followed. Gone, too, was Polish Anna with her damp calico and her ubiquitous pail and dripping rag and her gutturals. In her place was a trim Swede who wore white kid slippers in the afternoon and gray dresses and cobweb aprons. The sight of the neat Swede sitting in her room at two-thirty in the afternoon, tatting, never failed to fill Ma Mandle with fury. Anna had been an all-day scrubber.

But Lil. Hugo thought her very beautiful, which she was not. A plump, voluble, full-bosomed woman, exquisitely neat, with a clear, firm skin, bright brown eyes, an unerring instinct for clothes, and a shrewd business head. Hugo's devotion amounted to worship.

He used to watch her at her toilette in their rose and mahogany front bedroom. Her plump white shoulders gleamed from pink satin straps. She smelled pleasantly of sachet and a certain heady scent she affected. Seated before the mirror, she stared steadily at herself with a concentration such as an artist bestows upon a work that depends for its perfection upon nuances of light and shade. Everything about her shone and glittered. Her pink nails were like polished coral. Her hair gleamed in smooth undulations, not a strand out of place. Her skin was clear and smooth as a baby's. Her hands were plump and white. She was always getting what she called a facial, from which process she would emerge looking pinker and creamier than ever. The contents of her scented bureau drawers needed only a dab of whipped cream on top to look as if they might have been eaten as something souffléed.

"How do I look in it, Hugo? Do you like it?" was a question that rose daily to her lips. A new hat, or frock, or negligee. Not that she was unduly extravagant. She knew values, and profited by her knowledge.

"Le's see. Turn around. It looks great on you. Yep. That's all right."

He liked to fancy himself a connoisseur in women's clothes and to prove

it he sometimes brought home an article of feminine apparel glimpsed in a
shopwindow or showcase, but Lil soon put a stop to that. She had her own
ideas on clothes. He turned to jewelry. On Lil's silken bosom reposed a
diamond-and-platinum clip the size and general contour of a fish knife.
She had a ring that crowded the second knuckle, and on her plump wrist
sparkled an oblong so encrusted with diamonds that its utilitarian dial was
almost lost.

It wasn't a one-sided devotion, however. Lil knew much about men,
and she had an instinct for making them comfortable. She had a way of
laying his clean things out on the bed—fresh linen, clean white socks
(Hugo was addicted to white socks and tan, low-cut shoes), shirt, immaculate handkerchief. When he came in at the end of a hard day downtown—
hot, fagged, sticky—she saw to it that the bathroom was his own for an
hour so that he could bathe, shave, powder, dress, and emerge refreshed to
eat his good dinner in comfort. Lil was always waiting for him, cool, interested, sweet-smelling.

When she said, "How's business, lover?" she really wanted to know.
More than that, when he told her she understood, having herself been so
long a business woman. She gave him shrewd advice, too, so shrewdly ad-
ministered that he never realized he had been advised, and so, manlike,
could never resent it.

Ma Mandle's reign was over.

To Mrs. Lamb, Mrs. Brunswick, and Mrs. Wormser, Ma Mandle lied
magnificently. Their eager, merciless questions pierced her like knives, but
she made placid answer: "Young folks are young folks. They do things
different. I got my way. My son's wife has got hers." Their quick ears
caught the familiar phrase.

"It's hard, just the same," Mrs. Wormser insisted, "after you've been boss
all these years to have somebody else step in and shove you out of the way.
Don't I know!"

"I'm glad to have a little rest. Marketing and housekeeping nowadays is
no snap, with the prices what they are. Anybody that wants the pleasure
is welcome."

But they knew, the three. There was, in Ma Mandle's tone, a hollow
pretense that deceived no one. They knew, and she knew that they knew.
She was, even as they were, a drinker of the hemlock cup, an eater of
ashes.

Hugo Mandle was happier and more comfortable than he had ever been
in his life. It wasn't merely his love for Lil, and her love for him that made
him happy. Lil set a good table, though perhaps it was not as bounteous as
his mother's had been. His food, somehow, seemed to agree with him better

than it used to. It was because Lil selected her provisions with an eye to their building value, and to Hugo's figure. She told him he was getting too fat, and showed him where, and Hugo agreed with her and took off twenty-five burdensome pounds, but Ma Mandle fought every ounce of it.

"You'll weaken yourself, Hugo! Eat! How can a man work and not eat? I never heard of such a thing. Fads!"

But these were purely physical things. It was a certain mental relaxation that Hugo enjoyed, though he did not definitely know it. He only knew that Lil seemed, somehow, to understand. For years his mother had trailed after him, putting away things that he wanted left out, tidying that which he preferred left in seeming disorder. Lil seemed miraculously to understand about those things. He liked, for example, a certain grimy, gritty old rag with which he was wont to polish his golf clubs. It was caked with dirt, and most disreputable, but it was of just the right material, or weight, or size, or something, and he had for it the unreasoning affection that a child has for a tattered rag doll among a whole family of golden-haired, blue-eyed beauties. Ma Mandle, tidying up, used to throw away that rag in horror. Sometimes he would rescue it, crusted as it was with sand and mud and scouring dust. Sometimes he would have to train in a new rag, and it was never as good as the old. Lil understood about that rag, and approved of it. For that matter, she had a rag of her own which she used to remove cold cream from her face and throat. It was a clean enough bit of soft cloth to start with, but she clung to it until it was smeared with the pink of makeup and the black of Chicago soot. She used to search remote corners of it for an inch of unused, unsmeared space. Lil knew about not talking when you wanted to read the paper, too. Ma Mandle, at breakfast, had always had a long and intricate story to tell about the milkman or the strawberries that she had got the day before and that had spoiled overnight in the icebox. Sometimes he had wanted to say, "Let me read my paper in peace, won't you!" But he never had. Now it was Lil who listened patiently to Ma Mandle's small grievances, and Hugo was left free to peruse the headlines.

If you had told Ma Mandle that she was doing her best to ruin the life of the one person she loved best in all the world she would have told you that you were insane. If you had told her that she was jealous she would have denied it, furiously. But both were true.

When Hugo brought his wife a gift he brought one for his mother as well.

"You don't need to think you have to bring your old mother anything," she would say, unreasonably.

"Didn't I always bring you something, Ma?"

If seventy can be said to sulk, Ma Mandle sulked.

Lil, on her way to market in the morning, was a pleasant sight, trim, well-shod, immaculate. Ma, whose marketing costume had always been neat but sketchy, would eye her disapprovingly. "Are you going out?"

"Just to market. I thought I'd start early, before everything was picked over."

"Oh—to market! I thought you were going to a party, you're so dressy."

In the beginning Lil had offered to allow Ma Mandle to continue with the marketing, but Mrs. Mandle had declined, acidly. "Oh, no," she had said. "This is your household now."

But she never failed to inspect the groceries as they lay on the kitchen table after delivery. She would press a wise and disdainful thumb into a head of lettuce; poke a pot roast with disapproving finger; turn a plump chicken over and thump it down with a look that was pregnant with meaning.

Ma Mandle disapproved of many things. Of Lil's silken, lacy lingerie; of her social activities; of what she termed her wastefulness. Lil wore the fewest possible undergarments, according to the fashion of the day, and she worried, good-naturedly, about additional plumpness that was the result of leisure and of rich food. She was addicted to afternoon parties at the homes of married women of her own age and station—pretty, well-dressed, overindulged women who regularly ate too much. They served a mayonnaise chicken salad, and little hot, buttery biscuits, and strong coffee with sugar and cream, and there were dishes of salted almonds, and great, shining, oily, black ripe olives, and a heavy, rich dessert. When she came home she ate nothing.

"I couldn't eat a bite of dinner," she would say. "Let me tell you what we had." She would come to the table in one of her silken, lace-bedecked negligees and talk animatedly to Hugo while he ate his dinner and eyed her appreciatively as she sat there, leaning one elbow on the cloth, the sleeve fallen back so that you saw her plump white forearm. She kept her clear, rosy skin in spite of the pastry and sweets and the indolent life, and even the layers of powder with which she was forever dabbing her skin had not coarsened its texture.

Hugo, manlike, was unconscious of the undercurrent of animosity between the two women. He was very happy. He only knew that Lil understood about cigar ashes; that she didn't mind if a pillow wasn't plumped and patted after his Sunday nap on the davenport; that she never complained to him about the shortcomings of the little Swede, as Ma Mandle had about Polish Anna. Even at house-cleaning time, which Ma Mandle had always treated as a scourge, things were as smooth-running and peaceful as at ordinary times. Just a little bare, perhaps, as to floors, and smelling of cleanliness. Lil applied businesslike methods to the conduct of her house, and they were successful in spite of Ma Mandle's steady efforts to block them. Old Lady Mandle did not mean to be cruel. She only thought that she was protecting her son's interests. She did not know that the wise men had a definite name for the mental processes which caused her, perversely, to do just the thing which she knew she should not do.

Hugo and Lil went out a great deal in the evening. They liked the theater, restaurant life, gaiety. Hugo learned to dance and became marvelously expert at it, as does your fat man.

"Come on and go out with us this evening, Mother," Lil would say.

"Sure!" Hugo would agree heartily. "Come along, Ma. We'll show you some night life."

"I don't want to go," Ma Mandle would mutter. "I'm better off at home. You enjoy yourself better without an old woman dragging along."

That being true, they vowed it was not, and renewed their urging. In the end she went, grudgingly. But her old eyes would droop; the late supper would disagree with her; the noise, the music, the laughter, and shrill talk bewildered her. She did not understand the banter, and resented it. Next day, in the park, she would boast of her life of gaiety to the vaguely suspicious three.

Later she refused to go out with them. She stayed in her room a good deal, fussing about, arranging bureau drawers already geometrically precise, winding endless old ribbons, ripping the trimming off hats long passé and retrimming them with odds and ends and scraps of feathers and flowers. Hugo and Lil used to ask her to go with them to the movies, but they liked the second show at nine while she preferred the earlier one at seven. She grew sleepy early, though she often lay awake for hours after composing herself for sleep. She would watch the picture absorbedly, but when she stepped, blinking, into the bright glare of Fifty-third Street, she always had a sense of letdown, of depression.

A wise old lady of seventy, who could not apply her wisdom for her own good. A rather lonely old lady, with hardening arteries and a dilating heart. An increasingly faultfinding old lady. Even Hugo began to notice it. She would wait for him to come home and then, motioning him mysteriously into her own room, would pour a tale of fancied insult into his ear.

"I ran a household and brought up a family before she was born. I don't have to be told what's what. I may be an old woman but I'm not so old that I can sit and let my own son be made a fool of. One girl isn't enough, she's got to have a washwoman. And now a washwoman isn't enough, she's got to have a woman to clean one day a week."

An hour later, from the front bedroom, where Hugo was dressing, would come the low murmur of conversation. Lil had reached the complaining point, goaded by much repetition.

The attitude of the two women distressed and bewildered Hugo. He was a simple soul, and this was a complex situation. His mind leaped from mother to wife, and back again joltingly.

"What's got into you womenfolks!" he would say. "Always quarreling. Why can't you get along!"

One night after dinner Lil said, quite innocently, "Mother, we haven't a decent picture of you. Why don't you have one taken? In your black lace."

Old Lady Mandle broke into sudden fury. "I guess you think I'm going to die! A picture to put on the piano after I'm gone, huh? 'That's my dear mother that's gone.' Well, I don't have any picture taken. You can think of me the way I was when I was alive."

The thing grew and swelled and took on bitterness as it progressed. Lil's face grew strangely flushed and little veins stood out on her temples. All the pent-up bitterness that had been seething in Ma Mandle's mind broke bounds now, and welled to her lips. Accusation, denial; vituperation, retort.

"You'll be happy when I'm gone."

"If I am it's your fault."

"It's the ones that are used to nothing that always want the most. They don't know where to stop. When you were working in Omaha——"

"The salary I gave up to marry your son was more money than you ever saw."

And through it all, like a leitmotif, ran Hugo's attempt at pacification: "Now, Ma! Don't, Lil. You'll only excite yourself. What's got into you two women?"

It was after dinner. In the end, Ma Mandle slammed out of the house, hatless. Her old legs were trembling. Her hands shook. It was a hot June night. She felt as if she were burning up. In her frantic mind there was even thought of self-destruction. There were thousands of motorcars streaming by. The glare of their lamps and the smell of the gasoline blinded and stifled her. Once, at a crossing, she almost stumbled in front of an onrushing car. The curses of the startled driver sounded in her terrified ears after she had made the opposite curb in a frantic bound. She walked on and on for what seemed to her to be a long time, with plodding, heavy step. She was not conscious of being tired. She came to a park bench and sat down, feeling very abused, and lonely, and agonized. This was what she had come to in her old days. It was for this you bore children, and brought them up, and sacrificed for them. How right they were—Mrs.

Lamb, Mrs. Brunswick, and Mrs. Wormser. Useless. Unconsidered. In the way. By degrees she grew calmer. Her brain cooled as her fevered old body lost the heat of anger. Lil had looked kind of sick. Perhaps . . . And how worried Hugo had looked! . . .

Feeling suddenly impelled, she got up from the bench and started toward home. Her walk, which had seemed interminable, had really lasted scarcely more than half an hour. She had sat in the park scarcely fifteen minutes. Altogether her flight had been, perhaps, an hour in duration.

She had her latchkey in her pocket. She opened the door softly. The place was in darkness. Voices from the front bedroom, and the sound of someone sobbing, as though spent. Old Lady Mandle's face hardened again. The door of the front bedroom was closed. Plotting against her! She crouched there in the hall, listening. Lil's voice, hoarse with sobs.

"I've tried and tried. But she hates me. Nothing I do suits her. If it wasn't for the baby coming sometimes I think I'd——"

"You're just nervous and excited, Lil. It'll come out all right. She's an old lady——"

"I know it. I know it. I've said that a million times in the last year and a half. But that doesn't excuse everything, does it? Is that any reason why she should spoil our lives? It isn't fair. It isn't fair!"

"Sh! Don't cry like that, dear. Don't! You'll only make yourself sick."

Her sobs again, racking, choking, and the gentle murmur of his soothing endearments. Then, unexpectedly, a little, high-pitched laugh through the tears.

"No, I'm not hysterical. I—it just struck me funny. I was just wondering if I might be like that. When I grow old, and my son marries, maybe I'll think everything his wife does is wrong. I suppose if we love them too much we really harm them. I suppose——"

"Oh, it's going to be a son, is it?"

"Yes."

Another silence. Then: "Come, dear. Bathe your poor eyes. You're all worn out from crying. Why, sweetheart, I don't believe I ever saw you cry before."

"I know it. I feel better now. I wish crying could make it all right. I'm sorry. She's so old, dear. That's the trouble. They live in the past and they expect us to live in the past with them. You were a good son to her, Hughie. That's why you make such a wonderful husband. Too good, maybe. You've spoiled us both, and now we both want all of you."

Hugo was silent a moment. He was not a quick-thinking man. "A husband belongs to his wife," he said then, simply. "He's his mother's son by accident of birth. But he's his wife's husband by choice, and deliberately."

But she laughed again at that. "It isn't as easy as that, sweetheart. If it were there'd be no jokes in the funny papers. My poor boy! And just now, too, when you're so worried about business."

"Business'll be all right, Lil. Trade'll open up next winter. It's got to. We've kept going on the domestic stuff. But if the French and Austrian factories start running we'll have a whirlwind year. If it hadn't been for you this last year I don't know how I'd have stood the strain. No importing, and the business just keeping its head above water. But you were right, honey. We've weathered the worst of it now."

"I'm glad you didn't tell Mother about it. She'd have worried herself sick. If she had known we both put every cent we had into the business——"

"We'll get it back ten times over. You'll see."

The sound of footsteps. "I wonder where she went. She oughtn't to be out alone. I'm kind of worried about her, Hugo. Don't you think you'd better——"

Ma Mandle opened the front door and then slammed it, ostentatiously, as though she had just come in.

"That you, Ma?" called Hugo.

He turned on the hall light. She stood there, blinking, a bent, pathetic little figure. Her eyes were averted. "Are you all right, Ma? We began to worry about you."

"I'm all right. I'm going to bed."

He made a clumsy, masculine pretense at heartiness. "Lil and I are going over to the drugstore for a soda, it's so hot. Come on along, Ma."

Lil joined him in the doorway of the bedroom. Her eyes were red-rimmed behind the powder that she had hastily dabbed on, but she smiled.

"Come on, Mother," she said. "It'll cool you off."

But Ma Mandle shook her head. "I'm better off at home. You run along, you two."

That was all. But the two standing there caught something in her tone. Something new, something gentle, something wise.

She went on down the hall to her room. She took off her clothes, and hung them away neatly. But once in her nightgown she did not get into bed. She sat there, in the chair by the window. Old Lady Mandle had lived to be seventy and had acquired much wisdom. One cannot live to be seventy without having experienced almost everything in life. But to crystallize that experience of a long lifetime into terms that would express the meaning of life—this she had never tried to do. She could not do it now, for that matter. But she groped around, painfully, in her mind. There had been herself and Hugo. And now Hugo's wife and the child to be. They were the ones that counted, now. That was the law of life. She did not put it into words. But something of this she thought as she sat there in her plain white nightgown, her scant white locks pinned in a neat knob at the top of her head. Selfishness. That was it. They called it love, but it was selfishness. She must tell them about it tomorrow—Mrs. Lamb, Mrs. Brunswick, and Mrs. Wormser. Only yesterday Mrs. Brunswick had waxed bitter because her daughter-in-law had let a moth get into her husband's winter suit.

"I never had a moth in my house!" Mrs. Brunswick had declared. "Never. But nowadays housekeeping is nothing. A suit is ruined. What does my son's wife care! I never had a moth in my house."

Ma Mandle chuckled to herself there in the darkness. "I bet she did. She forgets. We all forget."

It was very hot tonight. Now and then there was a wisp of breeze from the lake, but not often.

. . . How red Lil's eyes had been . . . poor girl. Moved by a sudden impulse, Ma Mandle thudded down the hall in her bare feet, found a scrap of paper in the writing-desk drawer, scribbled a line on it, turned out the light, and went into the empty front bedroom. With a pin from the tray on the dresser she fastened the note to Lil's pillow, high up, where she must see it the instant she turned on the light. Then she scuttled down the hall to her room again.

She felt the heat terribly. She would sit by the window again. All the blood in her body seemed to be pounding in her head . . . pounding in her head . . . pounding . . .

At ten Hugo and Lil came in, softly. Hugo tiptoed down the hall, as was his wont, and listened. The room was in darkness. "Sleeping, Ma?" he whispered. He could not see the white-gowned figure sitting peacefully by the window, and there was no answer. He tiptoed with painful awkwardness up the hall again.

"She's asleep, all right. I didn't think she'd get to sleep so early on a scorcher like this."

Lil turned on the light in her room. "It's too hot to sleep," she said. She began to disrobe languidly. Her eye fell on the scrap of paper pinned to her pillow. She went over to it, curiously, leaned over, read it.

"Oh, look, Hugo!" She gave a little tremulous laugh that was more than half sob. He came over to her and read it, his arm around her shoulder.

"My son Hugo and my daughter Lil they are the best son and daughter in the world."

A sudden, hot haze before his eyes blotted out the words as he finished reading them.

Gigolo

[1922]

*When this story was written, the word "gigolo" had not crept into the
American language. The lost boys of postwar Europe dancing their weary
jig of death were to be seen everywhere on the Continent, but their like
was unknown in the vital and thriving United States. To see them in
Vienna, Paris, Rome, Berlin, Lake Como, Karlsbad, dancing by day, by
night, was a grisly sight. Impressed and saddened by this by-product of
war, I tried to set down something of the picture as I traveled about the
doomed cities of Europe in 1921.*

A GIGOLO, GENERALLY SPEAKING, IS A MAN WHO LIVES OFF WOMEN'S
money. In the mad year of 1922 A.W., a gigolo, definitely speaking,
designated one of those incredible and pathetic male creatures, born of the
war, who, for ten francs or more or even less, would dance with any
woman wishing to dance on the crowded floors of public tearooms, dinner
or supper rooms in the cafés, hotels, and restaurants of Europe. Lean, sallow, handsome, expert, one saw them everywhere, their slim waists and
sleek heads in juxtaposition to plump, respectable American matrons and
slender, respectable American flappers. For that matter, female respectability of almost every nationality (except the French) yielded itself to the
skillful guidance of the genus gigolo in the tango or fox trot. Naturally,
no decent French girl would have been allowed for a single moment to
dance with a gigolo. But America, touring Europe like mad after years of
enforced absence, outnumbered ten to one all other nations atravel.

By no feat of fancy could one imagine Gideon Gory, of the Winnebago,
Wisconsin, Gorys, employed daily and nightly as a gigolo in the gilt and
marble restaurants that try to outsparkle the Mediterranean along the
Promenade des Anglais in Nice. Why, anyone knows that the Gorys were
to Winnebago what the Romanovs were to Russia—royal, remote, omnip-
otent. Yet the Romanovs went in the cataclysm, and so, too, did the Gorys.
To appreciate the depths to which the boy Gideon had fallen one must
have known the Gorys in their glory. It happened something like this:

The Gorys lived for years in the great, ugly, sprawling, luxurious old
frame house on Cass Street. It was high up on the bluff overlooking the
Fox River and, incidentally, the huge pulp and paper mills across the river
in which the Gory money had been made. The Gorys were so rich and
influential (for Winnebago, Wisconsin) that they didn't bother to tear

down the old frame house and build a stone one, or to cover its faded front with cosmetics of stucco. In most things, the Gorys led where Winnebago could not follow. They disdained to follow where Winnebago led. The Gorys had an automobile when those vehicles were entered from the rear and when Winnebago roads were a wallow of mud in the spring and fall and a snow-lined trench in the winter. The family was of the town, and yet apart from it. The Gorys knew about golf, and played it in far, foreign playgrounds when the rest of us thought of it, if we thought of it at all, as something vaguely Scotch, like haggis. They had Oriental rugs and hard-wood floors when the town still stepped on carpets; and by the time the rest of the town had caught up on rugs, the Gorys had gone back to carpets, neutral-tinted. They had fireplaces in bedrooms, and used them, like characters in an English novel. Old Madame Gory had a slim patent-leather foot, with a buckle, and carried a sunshade when she visited the flowers in the garden. Old Gideon was rumored to have wine with his dinner. Gideon Junior (father of Giddy) smoked cigarettes with his monogram on them. Schroeder's grocery ordered endive for them, all blanched and delicate in a wicker basket from France or Belgium, when we had just become accustomed to head lettuce.

Every prosperous small American town has its Gory family. Every small-town newspaper relishes the savory tidbits that fall from the rich table of the family life. Thus you saw that Mr. and Mrs. Gideon Gory, Jr., have returned from California, where Mr. Gory had gone for the polo. Mr. and Mrs. Gideon Gory, Jr., announce the birth, in New York, of a son, Gideon III (our, in a manner of speaking, hero). Mr. and Mrs. Gideon Gory, Jr., and son Gideon III, left today for England and the Continent. It is understood that Gideon III will be placed at school in England. Mr. and Mrs. Gideon Gory, accompanied by Madame Gory, have gone to Chicago for a week of the grand opera.

Born of all this, young Giddy, you would have thought, would grow up a somewhat objectionable young man; and so, in fact, he did, though not nearly so objectionable as he might well have been, considering things in general and his mother in particular. At sixteen, for example, Giddy was driving his own car—a car so exaggerated and low-slung and with such a long predatory and glittering nose that one marveled at the expertness with which he swung its slim length around the corners of the narrow, tree-shaded streets. He was a real Gory, was Giddy, with his thick, waving black hair (which he tried for vain years to train into docility), his lean, swart face, and his slightly hooked Gory nose. In appearance, Winnebago pronounced him foreign-looking—an attribute which he later turned into a doubtful asset at Nice. On the rare occasions whereby Giddy graced Winnebago with his presence, you were likely to find him pursuing the pleasures that occupied other Winnebago boys of his age, if not station. In some miraculous way he had escaped being a snob. Still, training and travel combined to lead him into many innocent errors. When he dropped into Fetzer's pool shack, carrying a Malacca cane, for example. He had carried a cane every day for six months in Paris, whence he had just returned. Now it was as much a part of his street attire as his hat—more, to be exact, for the hatless head had just then become the street mode. There was a good game of Kelly in progress. Giddy, leaning slightly on his stick, stood watching it. Suddenly he was aware that all about the dim smoky little room players and loungers were standing in attitudes of exaggerated elegance. Each was leaning on a cue, his elbow crooked in as near an imitation of Giddy's position as the stick's length would permit. The figure was curved so that it stuck out behind and before; the expression on each face was as asinine as its owner's knowledge of the comic-weekly swell could make it; the little finger of the free hand was extravagantly bent. The players themselves walked with a mincing step about the table. And: "My deah fellah, what a pretty play. Mean to say, neat, don't you know," came incongruously from the lips of Reddy Lennigan, whose father ran the Lennigan House on Outagamie Street. He spatted his large hands delicately together in further expression of approval.

"Think so?" giggled his opponent, Mr. Dutchy Meisenberg. "*Aw*-fly sweet of you to say so, old thing." He tucked his unspeakable handkerchief up his cuff and coughed behind his palm. He turned to Giddy. "Excuse my not having my coat on, deah boy."

Just here Giddy might have done a number of things, all wrong. The game was ended. He walked to the table, and, using the offending stick as a cue, made a rather pretty shot that he had learned from Benoît in London. Then he ranged the cane neatly on the rack with the cues. He even grinned a little boyishly. "You win," he said. "My treat. What'll you have?"

Which was pretty sporting for a boy whose American training had been what Giddy's had been.

Giddy's father, on the death of old Gideon, proved himself much more expert at dispensing the paper-mill money than at accumulating it. After old Madame Gory's death just one year following that of her husband, Winnebago saw less and less of the three remaining members of the royal family. The frame house on the river bluff would be closed for a year or more at a time. Giddy's father rather liked Winnebago and would have been content to spend six months of the year in the old Gory house, but

Giddy's mother, who had been a Leyden, of New York, put that idea out of his head pretty effectively.

"Don't talk to me," she said, "about your duty toward the town that gave you your money and all that kind of feudal rot, because you know you don't mean it. It bores you worse than it does me, really, but you like to think that the villagers are pulling a forelock when you walk down Normal Avenue. As a matter of fact, they're not doing anything of the kind. They've got their thumbs to their noses, more likely."

Her husband protested rather weakly. "I don't care. I like the old shack. I know the heating apparatus is bum and that we get the smoke from the paper mills, but—I don't know—last year, when we had that punk pink palace at Cannes I kept thinking——"

Mrs. Gideon Gory raised the Leyden eyebrow. "Don't get sentimental, Gid, for God's sake! It's a shanty, and you know it. And you know that it needs everything from plumbing to linen. I don't see any sense in sinking thousands in making it livable when we don't want to live in it."

"But I do want to live in it—once in a while. I'm used to it. I was brought up in it. So was the kid. He likes it, too. Don't you, Giddy?" The boy was present, as usual, at this particular scene.

The boy worshiped his mother. But, also, he was honest. So, "Yeh, I like the ol' barn all right," he confessed.

Encouraged, his father went on: "Yesterday the kid was standing out there on the bluff edge, breathing like a whale, weren't you, Giddy? And when I asked him what he was puffing about he said he liked the smell of the sulphur and chemicals and stuff from the paper mills, didn't you, kid?"

Shamefacedly, "Yeh," said Giddy.

Betrayed thus by husband and adored son, the Leyden did battle. "You can both stay here, then," she retorted with more spleen than elegance, "and sniff sulphur until you're black in the face. I'm going to London in May."

They, too, went to London in May, of course, as she had known they would. She had not known, though, that in leading her husband to England in May she was leading him to his death as well.

"All Winnebago will be shocked and grieved to learn," said the Winnebago *Courier* to the extent of two columns and a cut, "of the sudden and violent death in England of her foremost citizen, Gideon Gory. Death was due to his being thrown from his horse while hunting."

". . . to being thrown from his horse while hunting." Shocked and grieved though it might or might not be, Winnebago still had the fortitude to savor this with relish. Winnebago had died deaths natural and unnatural. It had been run over by automobiles, and had its skull fractured at football, and been drowned in Lake Winnebago, and struck by lightning, and poisoned by mushrooms, and shot by burglars. But never had Winnebago citizen had the distinction of meeting death by being thrown from his horse while hunting. While hunting. Scarlet coats. Hounds in full cry. Baronial halls. Hunt breakfasts. *Vogue. Vanity Fair.*

Well! Winnebago was almost grateful for this final and most picturesque gesture of Gideon Gory II.

The widowed Leyden did not even take the trouble personally to superintend the selling of the Gory place on the river bluff. It was sold by an agent while she and Giddy were in Italy, and if she was ever aware that the papers in the transaction stated that the house had been bought by Orson J. Hubbell, she soon forgot the fact and the name. Giddy, leaning over her shoulder while she handled the papers and signed on the line indicated by a legal forefinger, may have remarked:

"Hubbell. That's old Hubbell, the drayman. Must be money in the draying line."

Which was pretty stupid of him, because he should have known that the draying business was now developed into the motor-truck business, with great vans roaring their way between Winnebago and Kaukauna, Winnebago and Oshkosh. He learned that later.

Just now Giddy wasn't learning much of anything, and, to do him credit, the fact distressed him not a little. His mother insisted that she needed him, and developed a bad heart whenever he rebelled and threatened to sever the apron strings. They lived abroad entirely now. Mrs. Gory showed a talent for spending the Gory gold that must have set old Gideon whirling in his Winnebago grave. Her spending of it was foolish enough, but her handling of it was criminal. She loved Europe. America bored her. She wanted to identify herself with foreigners, with foreign life. Against advice, she sold her large and lucrative interest in the Winnebago paper mills and invested great sums in French stocks, in Russian enterprises, in German shares.

She liked to be mistaken for a Frenchwoman.

She and Gideon spoke the language like natives—or nearly.

She was vain of Gideon's un-American looks, and cross with him when, on their rare and brief visits to New York, he insisted that he liked American tailoring and American-made shoes. Once or twice, soon after his father's death, he had said, casually, "You didn't like Winnebago, did you? Living in it, I mean."

"*Like* it!"

"Well, these English, I mean, and French—they sort of grow up in a place, and stay with it and belong to it, see what I mean? And it gives you a kind of permanent feeling. Not patriotic, exactly, but solid and native-heathy and Scots-wha-hae-wi'-Wallace and all that kind of slop."

"Giddy darling, don't be silly."

Occasionally, too, he said, "Look here, Julia"—she liked this modern method of address—"look here, Julia, I ought to be getting busy. Doing something. Here I am, nineteen, and I can't do a thing except dance pretty well, but not as well as that South American eel we met last week; mix a cocktail pretty well, but not as good a one as Benny the bartender turns out at Voyot's; ride pretty well, but not as well as the English chaps; drive a car——"

She interrupted him there. "Drive a car better than even an Italian chauffeur. Had you there, Giddy darling."

She undoubtedly had Giddy darling there. His driving was little short of miraculous, and his feeling for the intricate inside of a motor engine was as delicate and unerring as that of a professional pianist for his pet pianoforte. They motored a good deal, with France as a permanent background and all Europe as a playground. They flitted about the Continent, a whirl of glittering blue-and-cream enamel, tan leather coating, fur robes, air cushions, gold-topped flasks, and petrol. Giddy knew Como and Villa d'Este as the place where that pretty Hungarian widow had borrowed a thousand lire from him at the Casino roulette table and never paid him back; London as a pleasing potpourri of brier pipes, smart leather gloves, music-hall revues, and night clubs; Berlin as a rather stuffy hole where they tried to ape Paris and failed, but you had to hand it to them when it came to the skating at the Eis Palast. A pleasing existence, but unprofitable. No one saw the cloud gathering because of cloud there was none, even of the man's-hand size so often discerned as a portent.

When the storm broke, Giddy promptly went into the Lafayette Escadrille. Later he learned never to mention this to an American because the American was so likely to say, "There must have been about eleven million scrappers in that outfit. Every fella you meet's been in the Lafayette Escadrille. If all the guys were in it that say they were they could have licked the Germans the first day out. That outfit's worse than the old *Floradora* Sextette."

Mrs. Gory was tremendously proud of him, and not as worried as she should have been. She thought it all a rather smart game, and not at all serious. She wasn't even properly alarmed about her European money, at first. Giddy looked thrillingly distinguished and handsome in his aviation uniform. When she walked in the Paris streets with him she glowed like a girl with her lover. But after the first six months of it, Mrs. Gory, grown rather drawn and haggard, didn't think the whole affair quite so delightful. She scarcely ever saw Giddy. She never heard the drum of an airplane without getting a sick, gone feeling at the pit of her stomach. She knew, now, that there was more to the air service than a becoming uniform. She was doing some war work herself in an incompetent, frenzied sort of way. With Giddy soaring high and her foreign stocks and bonds falling low, she might well be excused for the panic that shook her from the time she opened her eyes in the morning until she tardily closed them at night.

"Let's go home, Giddy darling," like a scared child.

"Where's that?"

"Don't be cruel. America's the only safe place now."

"Too darned safe!" This was 1915.

By 1917 she was actually in need of money. But Giddy did not know much about this because Giddy had, roughly speaking, got his. He had the habit of soaring up into the sunset and sitting around in a large pink cloud like a kid bouncing on a feather bed. Then, one day, he soared higher and farther than he knew, having, perhaps, grown careless through over-confidence. He heard nothing above the roar of his own engine, and the two planes were upon him almost before he knew it. They were not French, or English, or American planes. He got one of them and would have got clean away if the other had not caught him in the arm. The right arm. His mechanic lay limp. Even then he might have managed a landing, but the pursuing plane got in a final shot. There followed a period of time that seemed to cover, say, six years but that was actually only a matter of seconds. At the end of that period Giddy, together with a tangle of wire, silk, wood, and something that had been the mechanic, lay inside the German lines, and you would hardly have thought him worth the disentangling.

They did disentangle him, though, and even patched him up pretty expertly, but not so expertly, perhaps, as they might have, being enemy surgeons and rather busy with the patching of their own injured. The bone, for example, in the lower right arm knitted promptly and properly, being a young and healthy bone, but they rather overlooked the matter of arm nerves and muscles, so that later, thought it looked a perfectly proper arm, it couldn't lift three pounds. His head had emerged slowly, month by month, from swathings of gauze. What had been quite a crevasse in his skull became only a scarlet scar that his hair pretty well hid when he brushed it over the bad place. But the surgeon, perhaps being overly busy, or having no real way of knowing that Giddy's nose had been a distinguished and aristocratically hooked Gory nose, had remolded that wrecked feature into a pure Greek line at first sight of which Giddy stood staring

weakly into the mirror; reeling a little with surprise and horror and unbelief and general misery. "Can this be I?" he thought, feeling like the old
woman of the bramble bush in the Mother Goose rhyme. A well-made and
becoming nose, but not so fine-looking as the original feature had been, as
worn by Giddy.

"Look here!" he protested to the surgeon, months too late. "Look here,
this isn't my nose."

"Be glad," replied that practical Prussian person, "that you have any."

With his knowledge of French and English and German, Giddy acted as
interpreter during the months of his invalidism and later internment, and
things were not so bad with him. He had no news of his mother, though,
and no way of knowing whether she had news of him. With 1918, and the
Armistice and his release, he hurried to Paris and there got the full impact
of the past year's events.

Julia Gory was dead and the Gory money nonexistent.

Out of the ruins—a jewel or two and some paper not quite worthless—
he managed a few thousand francs and went to Nice. There he walked in
the sunshine, and sat in the sunshine, and even danced in the sunshine,
a dazed young thing together with hundreds of other dazed young things,
not thinking, not planning, not hoping. Existing only in a state of semi-
consciousness like one recovering from a blinding blow. The francs dribbled away. Sometimes he played baccarat and won; oftener he played
baccarat and lost. He moved in a sort of trance, feeling nothing. Vaguely
he knew that there was a sort of conference going on in Paris. Sometimes
he thought of Winnebago, recalling it remotely, dimly, as one is occasionally conscious of a former unknown existence. Twice he went to Paris
for periods of some months, but he was unhappy there and even strangely
bewildered, like a child. He was still sick in mind and body, though he did
not know it. Driftwood, like thousands of others, tossed up on the shore
after the storm; lying there bleached and useless and battered.

Then, one day in Nice, there was no money. Not a franc. Not a centime.
He knew hunger. He knew terror. He knew desperation. It was out of this
period that there emerged Giddy, the gigolo. Now, though, the name
bristled with accent marks, thus: Gédéon Goré.

This Gédéon Goré, of the Nice dansants, did not even remotely resemble
Gideon Gory of Winnebago, Wisconsin. This Gédéon Goré wore French
clothes of the kind that Giddy Gory had always despised. A slim, sallow,
sleek, sad-eyed gigolo in tight French garments, the pants rather flappy at
the ankle; effeminate French shoes with fawn-colored uppers and patent-
leather eyelets and vamps, most despicable; a slim cane; hair with a magnificent natural wave that looked artificially marcelled and that was worn

with a strip growing down from the temples on either side in the sort of cut used only by French dandies and English stage butlers. No, this was not Giddy Gory. The real Giddy Gory lay in a smart but battered suitcase under the narrow bed in his lodgings. The suitcase contained:

Item: one pair Russian-calf oxfords of American make.

Item: one French aviation uniform with leather coat, helmet, and gloves all bearing stiff and curious splotches of brown or rust color which you might not recognize as dried bloodstains.

Item: one handful assorted medals, ribbons, orders, etc.

All Europe was dancing. It seemed a death dance, grotesque, convulsive, hideous. Paris, Nice, Berlin, Budapest, Rome, Vienna, London writhed and twisted and turned and jiggled. Saint Vitus himself never imagined contortions such as these. In the narrow side-street dance rooms of Florence and in the great avenue restaurants of Paris they were performing exactly the same gyrations—wiggle, squirm, shake. And over all, the American jazz music boomed and whanged its syncopations. On the music racks of violinists who had meant to be Elmans or Kreislers were sheets entitled "Jazz Baby Fox Trot." Drums, horns, cymbals, castanets, sandpaper. So the mannequins and marionettes of Europe tried to whirl themselves into forgetfulness.

The Americans thought Giddy was a Frenchman. The French knew him for an American, dress as he would. Dancing became with him a profession—no, a trade. He danced flawlessly, holding and guiding his partner impersonally, firmly, expertly in spite of the weak right arm—it served well enough. Gideon Gory had always been a naturally rhythmic dancer. Then, too, he had been fond of dancing. Years of practice had perfected him. He adopted now the manner and position of the professional. As he danced he held his head rather stiffly to one side, and a little down, the chin jutting out just a trifle. The effect was at the same time stiff and chic. His footwork was infallible. The intricate and imbecilic steps of the day he performed in flawless sequence. Under his masterly guidance the feet of the least rhythmic were suddenly endowed with deftness and grace. One swayed with him as naturally as with an elemental force. He danced politely and almost wordlessly unless first addressed, according to the code of his kind. His touch was firm, yet remote. The dance concluded, he conducted his partner to her seat, bowed stiffly from the waist, heels together, and departed. For these services he was handed ten francs, twenty francs, thirty francs, or more, if lucky, depending on the number of times he was called upon to dance with a partner during the evening. Thus was dancing, the most spontaneous and unartificial of the Muses, vulgarized, commercialized, prostituted. Lower than Gideon Gory, of Winnebago, Wisconsin, had fallen, could no man fall.

Sometimes he danced in Paris. During the high season he danced in Nice. Afternoon and evening found him busy in the hot, perfumed, over-crowded dance salons. The Negresco, the Ruhl, Maxim's, Belle Meunière, the Casino Municipale. He learned to make his face go a perfect blank— pale, cryptic, expressionless. Between himself and the other boys of his ilk there was little or no professional comradeship. A weird lot they were, young, though their faces were strangely lacking in the look of youth. All of them had been in the war. Most of them had been injured. There was Aubin, the Frenchman. The right side of Aubin's face was rather star-tlingly handsome in its Greek perfection. It was like a profile chiseled. The left side was another face—the same, and yet not the same. It was as though you saw the left side out of drawing, or blurred, or out of focus. It puzzled you—shocked you. The left side of Aubin's face had been done over by an army surgeon who, though deft and scientific, had not had a hand as expert as that of the Original Sculptor. Then there was Mazzetti, the Roman. He parted his hair on the wrong side, and under the black wing of it was a deep groove into which you could lay a forefinger. A piece of shell had plowed it neatly. The Russian boy who called himself Orloff had the look in his eyes of one who has seen things upon which eyes never should have looked. He smoked constantly and ate, apparently, not at all. Among these three existed a certain unwritten code and certain unwritten signals.

You did not take away the paying partner of a fellow gigolo. If in too great demand, you turned your surplus partners over to gigolos unem-ployed. You did not accept less than ten francs (they all broke this rule). Sometimes Gédéon Goré made ten francs a day, sometimes twenty, some-times fifty, infrequently a hundred. Sometimes not enough to pay for his one decent meal a day. At first he tried to keep fit by walking a certain number of miles daily along the ocean front. But usually he was too weary to persist in this. He did not think at all. He felt nothing. Sometimes, down deep, deep in a long-forgotten part of his being a voice called feebly, plain-tively, to the man who had been Giddy Gory. But he shut his ears and mind and consciousness and would not listen.

The American girls were best, the gigolos all agreed, and they paid well, though they talked too much. Gédéon Goré was a favorite among them. They thought he was so foreign-looking, and kind of sad and stern and everything. His French, fluent, colloquial, and bewildering, awed them. They would attempt to speak to him in halting and hackneyed phrases acquired during three years at Miss Pence's Select School at Hastings-on-the-Hudson. At the cost of about a thousand dollars a word they would enunciate, painfully:

"*Je pense que*—um—*que Nice est le plus belle*—uh—*ville de France.*"

Giddy, listening courteously, his head inclined as though unwilling to miss one conversational pearl falling from the pretty American's lips, would appear to consider this gravely. Then, sometimes in an unexpected burst of pure mischief, he would answer:

"You said something! *Some* burg, I'm telling the world."

The girl, startled, would almost leap back from the confines of his arms only to find his face stern, immobile, his eyes somber and reflective.

"Why! Where did you pick that up?"

His eyebrows would go up. His face would express complete lack of comprehension. "*Pardon?*"

Afterward, at home, in Toledo or Kansas City or Los Angeles, the girl would tell about it. "I suppose some American girl taught it to him, just for fun. It sounded too queer—because his French was so wonderful. He danced divinely. A Frenchman, and so aristocratic! Think of his being a professional partner. They have them over there, you know. Everybody's dancing in Europe. And gay! Why, you'd never know there'd been a war."

Mary Hubbell, of the Winnebago Hubbells, did not find it so altogether gay. Mary Hubbell, with her father, Orson J. Hubbell, and her mother, Bee Hubbell, together with what appeared to be practically the entire white population of the United States, came to Europe early in 1922, there to travel, to play, to rest, to behold, and to turn their good hard American dollars into cordwood-size bundles of German marks, Austrian kronen, Italian lire, and French francs. Most of the men regarded Europe as a wine list. In their mental geography, Rheims, Rhine, Moselle, Bordeaux, Champagne, or Würzburg were not localities but libations. The women, for the most part, went in for tortoise-shell combs, fringed silk shawls, jade earrings, beaded bags, and coral neck chains. Up and down the famous thoroughfares of Europe went the absurd pale-blue tweed *tailleurs* and the lavender tweed cape suits of America's wives and daughters. Usually, after the first month or two, they shed these respectable, middle-class habiliments for what they fondly believed to be smart Paris costumes; and you could almost invariably tell a good, moral, church-going matron of the Middle West by the fact that she was got up like a demimondaine of the second class, in the naïve belief that she looked French and chic.

The three Hubbells were thoroughly nice people. Mary Hubbell was more than thoroughly nice. She had done a completely good job during the 1918–1919 period, including the expert driving of a wild and unbroken Ford up and down the shell-torn roads of France. One of those small-town girls with a big-town outlook, a well-trained mind, a slim, boyish body, a good clear skin, and a steady eye that saw. Mary Hubbell wasn't a beauty by a good many measurements, but she had her points, as witness the number of bouquets, bundles, books, and bonbons piled in her cabin when she sailed.

The well-trained mind and the steady, seeing eye enabled Mary Hubbell to discover that Europe wasn't so gay as it seemed to the blind; and she didn't write home to the effect that you'd never know there'd been war.

The Hubbells had the best that Europe could afford. Orson J. Hubbell, a mild-mannered, gray-haired man with a nice flat waistline and a good, keen eye (hence Mary's), adored his womenfolk and spoiled them. During the first years of his married life he had been Hubbell the drayman, as Giddy Gory had said. He had driven one of his three drays himself, standing sturdily in the front of the red-painted wooden two-horse wagon as it rattled up and down the main business thoroughfare of Winnebago. But the war and the soaring freight rates had dealt generously with Orson Hubbell. As railroad and shipping difficulties increased, the Hubbell draying business waxed prosperous. Factories, warehouses, and wholesale business firms could be assured that their goods would arrive promptly, safely, and cheaply when conveyed by a Hubbell van. So now the three red-painted, wooden, horse-driven drays were magically transformed into a great fleet of monster motor vans that plied up and down the state of Wisconsin and even into Michigan and Illinois and Indiana. "The Orson J. Hubbell Transportation Company," you read. And below, in yellow lettering on the red background:

Have HUBBELL Do Your HAULING

There was actually a million in it, and more to come. The buying of the old Gory house on the river bluff had been one of the least of Orson's feats. And now that house was honeycombed with sleeping porches and linen closets and enamel fittings and bathrooms white and glittering as an operating auditorium. And there were shower baths, and blue rugs, and great, soft, fuzzy bath towels and little, white, innocent guest towels embroidered with curly *H*'s whose tails writhed at you from all corners.

Orson J. and Mrs. Hubbell had never been in Europe before, and they enjoyed themselves enormously. That is to say, Mrs. Orson J. did, and Orson, seeing her happy, enjoyed himself vicariously. His hand slid in and out of his inexhaustible pocket almost automatically now. And "How much?" was his favorite locution. They went everywhere, did everything. Mary boasted a pretty fair French. Mrs. Hubbell conversed in the various languages of Europe by speaking pidgin English very loud, and omitting all verbs, articles, adverbs, and other cumbersome superfluities. Thus, to the *fille de chambre:*

"Me out now you beds." The red-cheeked one from the provinces understood, in some miraculous way, that Mrs. Hubbell was now going out and the beds could be made and the rooms tidied.

They reached Nice in February and plunged into its gaieties. "Just think!" exclaimed Mrs. Hubbell rapturously, "only three francs for a facial or a manicure and two for a marcel. It's like finding them."

"If the Mediterranean gets any bluer," said Mary, "I don't think I can stand it."

Mrs. Hubbell, at tea, expressed a desire to dance. Mary, at tea, desired to dance but didn't express it. Orson J. loathed tea; and the early draying business had somewhat unfitted his sturdy legs for the lighter movements of the dance. But he wanted only their happiness. So he looked about a bit, and asked some questions, and came back.

"Seems there's a lot of young fellas who make a business of dancing with the womenfolks who haven't dancing men along. Hotel hires 'em. Funny to us, but I guess it's all right, and quite the thing around here. You pay 'em so much a dance, or so much an afternoon. You girls want to try it?"

"I do," said Mrs. Orson J. Hubbell. "It doesn't sound respectable. Then that's what all those thin little chaps are who've been dancing with those pretty American girls. They're sort of ratty-looking, aren't they? What do you call 'em? That's a nice-looking one, over there—no, no!—dancing with the girl in gray, I mean. Good land, what would the Winnebago ladies say! What do they call 'em, I wonder."

Mary had been gazing very intently at the nice-looking one over there who was dancing with the girl in gray. She answered her mother's question, still gazing at him. "They call them gigolos," she said, slowly. Then, "Get that one, Dad, will you, if you can? You dance with him first, Mother, and then I'll——"

"I can get two," volunteered Orson J.

"No," said Mary Hubbell, sharply.

The nice-looking gigolo seemed to be in great demand, but Orson J. succeeded in capturing him after the third dance. It turned out to be a tango, and though Mrs. Hubbell, pretty well scared, declared that she didn't know it and couldn't dance it, the nice-looking gigolo assured her, through the medium of Mary's interpretation, that Mrs. Hubbell had only to follow his guidance. It was quite simple. He did not seem to look directly at Mary, or at Orson J., or at Mrs. Hubbell, as he spoke. The dance concluded, Mrs. Hubbell came back breathless, but enchanted.

"He has beautiful manners," she said, aloud, in English. "And dance! You feel like a swan when you're dancing with him. Try him, Mary." The gigolo's face, as he bowed before her, was impassive, inscrutable.

But, "Sh!" said Mary.

"Nonsense! Doesn't understand a word."

Mary danced the next dance with him. They danced wordlessly until the dance was half over. Then, abruptly, Mary said in English, "What's your name?"

Close against him she felt a sudden little sharp contraction of the gigolo's diaphragm—the contraction that reacts to surprise or alarm. But he said, in French, *"Pardon?"*

So, "What's your name?" said Mary, in French this time.

The gigolo with the beautiful manners hesitated longer than really beautiful manners should permit. But finally, *"Je m'appelle Gédéon Goré."* He pronounced it in his most nasal, perfect, Paris French. It didn't sound even remotely like Gideon Gory.

"My name's Hubbell," said Mary, in her pretty fair French. "Mary Hubbell. I come from a little town called Winnebago."

The Goré eyebrow expressed polite disinterestedness.

"That's in Wisconsin," continued Mary, "and I love it."

"Naturellement," agreed the gigolo, stiffly.

They finished the dance without further conversation. Mrs. Hubbell had the next dance. Mary the next. They spent the afternoon dancing, until dinnertime. Orson J.'s fee, as he handed it to the gigolo, was the kind that mounted grandly into dollars instead of mere francs. The gigolo's face, as he took it, was not more inscrutable than Mary's as she watched him take it.

From that afternoon, throughout the next two weeks, if any girl as thoroughly fine as Mary Hubbell could be said to run after any man, Mary ran after that gigolo. At the same time one could almost have said that he tried to avoid her. Mary took a course of tango lessons, and urged her mother to do the same. Even Orson J. noticed it.

"Look here," he said, in kindly protest. "Aren't you getting pretty thick with this jigger?"

"Sociological study, Dad. I'm all right."

"Yeh, you're all right. But how about him?"

"He's all right, too."

The gigolo resisted Mary's unmaidenly advances, and yet, when he was with her, he seemed sometimes to forget to look somber and blank and remote. They seemed to have a lot to say to each other. Mary talked about

America a good deal. About her home town . . . "and big elms and maples and oaks in the yard . . . the Fox River Valley . . . Middle West . . . Normal Avenue . . . Cass Street . . . Fox River paper mills. . . ."

She talked in French and English. The gigolo confessed, one day, to understanding some English, though he seemed to speak none. After that Mary, when very much in earnest, or when enthusiastic, spoke in her native tongue altogether. She claimed an intense interest in European after-war conditions, in reconstruction, in the attitude toward life of those millions of young men who had actually participated in the conflict. She asked questions that might have been considered impertinent, not to say nervy.

"Now you," she said brutally, "are a person of some education, refinement, and background. Yet you are content to dance around in these—these —well, back home a man might wash dishes in a cheap restaurant or run an elevator in an East Side New York loft building, but he'd never——"

A very faint, dull red crept suddenly over the pallor of the gigolo's face. They were sitting out on a bench on the promenade, facing the ocean. Mary Hubbell had said rather brusque things before. But now, for the first time, the young man defended himself faintly.

"For us," he replied in his exquisite French, "it is finished. For us there is nothing. This generation, it is no good. I am no good. They are no good." He waved a hand in a gesture that included the promenaders, the musicians in the cafés, the dancers, the crowds eating and drinking at the little tables lining the walk.

"What rot!" said Mary Hubbell, briskly. "They probably said exactly the same thing in Asia after Alexander had got through with 'em. I suppose there was such dancing and general devilment in Macedonia that everyone said the younger generation had gone to the dogs since the war, and the world would never amount to anything again. But it seemed to pick up, didn't it?"

The boy turned and looked at her squarely for the first time, his eyes meeting hers. Mary looked at him. She even swayed toward him a little, her lips parted. There was about her a breathlessness, an expectancy. So they sat for a moment, and between them the air was electric, vibrant. Then, slowly, he relaxed, sat back, slumped a little on the bench. Over his face, that for a moment had been alight with something vital, there crept again the look of defeat, of somber indifference. At sight of that look Mary Hubbell's jaw set. She leaned forward. She clasped her fine large hands tight. She did not look at the gigolo, but out, across the blue Mediterranean, and beyond it. Her voice was low and a little tremulous and she spoke in English only.

"It isn't finished here—here in Europe. But it's sick. Back home, in America, though, it's alive. Alive! And growing. I wish I could make you understand what it's like there. It's all new, and crude, maybe, and ugly, but it's so darned healthy and sort of clean. I love it. I love every bit of it. I know I sound like a flag waver, but I don't care. I mean it. And I know it's sentimental, but I'm proud of it. The kind of thing Mencken sneers at. You don't know who Mencken is. He's a critic who pretends to despise everything because he's really a sentimentalist and afraid somebody'll find it out. I don't say I don't appreciate the beauty of all this Italy and France and England and Germany. But it doesn't get me the way just the mention of a name will get me back home. This trip, for example. Why, last summer four of us—three other girls and I—motored from Wisconsin to California, and we drove every inch of the way ourselves. The Santa Fe Trail! The Ocean-to-Ocean Highway! The Lincoln Highway! The Dixie Highway! The Yellowstone Trail! The very sound of those words gives me a sort of prickly feeling. They mean something big and vital and new. I get a thrill out of them that I haven't had once over here. Why, even this," she threw out a hand that included and dismissed the whole sparkling panorama before her, "this doesn't begin to give the jolt that I got out of Walla Walla, and Butte, and Missoula, and Spokane, and Seattle, and Albuquerque. We drove all day, and ate ham and eggs at some little hotel or lunch counter at night, and outside the hotel the drummers would be sitting, talking and smoking; and there were Western men, very tanned and tall and lean, in those big two-gallon hats and khaki pants and puttees. And there were sunsets, and sand, and cactus and mountains, and campers and Fords. I can smell the Kansas cornfields and I can see the Iowa farms and the ugly little raw American towns, and the big thin American men, and the grain elevators near the railroad stations, and I know those towns weren't the way towns ought to look. They were ugly and crude and new. Maybe it wasn't all beautiful, but gosh! it was real, and growing, and big, and alive! Alive!"

Mary Hubbell was crying. There, on the bench along the promenade in the sunshine at Nice, she was crying.

The boy beside her suddenly rose, uttered a little inarticulate sound, and left her there on the bench in the sunshine. Vanished, completely, in the crowd.

For three days the Orson J. Hubbells did not see their favorite gigolo. If Mary was disturbed she did not look it, though her eye was alert in the throng. During the three days of their gigolo's absence, Mrs. Hubbell and Mary availed themselves of the professional services of the Italian gigolo, Mazzetti. Mrs. Hubbell said she thought his dancing was, if anything, more nearly perfect than that What's-his-name's, but his manner wasn't so nice and she didn't like his eyes. Sort of sneaky. Mary said she thought so, too.

Nevertheless, she was undoubtedly affable toward him, and talked (in French) and laughed and even walked with him, apparently in complete ignorance of the fact that these things were not done. Mazzetti spoke frequently of his colleague, Goré, and always in terms of disparagement. A low fellow. A clumsy dancer. One unworthy of Mary's swanlike grace. Unfit to receive Orson J. Hubbell's generous fees.

Late one evening, during the midweek after-dinner dance, Goré appeared suddenly in the doorway. It was ten o'clock. The Hubbells were dallying with their after-dinner coffee at one of the small tables about the dance floor.

Mary, keen-eyed, saw him first. She beckoned Mazzetti, who stood in attendance beside Mrs. Hubbell's chair. She snatched up the wrap that lay at hand and rose. "It's stifling in here. I'm going out on the Promenade for a breath of air. Come on." She plucked Mazzetti's sleeve and actually propelled him through the crowd and out of the room. She saw Goré's startled eyes follow them.

She even saw him crossing swiftly to where her mother and father sat. Then she vanished into the darkness with Mazzetti. And the Mazzettis put but one interpretation upon a young woman who strolls into the soft darkness of the Promenade with a gigolo.

And Mary Hubbell knew this.

Gédéon Goré stood before Mr. and Mrs. Orson J. Hubbell. "Where is your daughter?" he demanded, in French.

"Oh, howdy-do," chirped Mrs. Hubbell. "Well, it's Mr. Goré! We missed you. I hope you haven't been sick."

"Where is your daughter?" demanded Gédéon Goré, in French. "Where is Mary?"

Mrs. Hubbell caught the word Mary. "Oh, Mary. Why, she's gone out for a walk with Mr. Mazzetti."

"Good God!" said Gédéon Goré, in perfectly plain English. And vanished.

Orson J. Hubbell sat a moment, thinking. Then, "Why, say, he talked English. That young French fella talked English."

The young French fella, hatless, was skimming down the Promenade des Anglais, looking intently ahead, and behind, and to the side, and all around in the darkness. He seemed to be following a certain trail, however. At one side of the great wide walk, facing the ocean, was a canopied bandstand. In its dim shadow, he discerned a wisp of white. He made for it, swiftly, silently. Mazzetti's voice low, eager, insistent. Mazzetti's voice hoarse, ugly, importunate. The figure in white rose. Goré stood before the two. The girl took a step toward him, but Mazzetti took two steps and snarled like a villain in a movie.

"Get out of here!" said Mazzetti, in French, to Goré. "You pig! To intrude when I talk with a lady. You are finished."

"The hell I am!" said Giddy Gory in perfectly plain American and swung for Mazzetti with his bad right arm. Mazzetti, after the fashion of his kind, let fly in most unsportsmanlike fashion with his feet, kicking at Giddy's stomach and trying to bite with his small, sharp yellow teeth. And then Giddy's left, that had learned some neat tricks of boxing in the days of the Gory greatness, landed fairly on the Mazzetti nose. And with a howl of pain and rage and terror the Mazzetti, a hand clapped to the bleeding feature, fled in the darkness.

And, "Oh, Giddy!" said Mary, "I thought you'd never come."

"Mary. Mary Hubbell. You think I'm a bum, don't you? Don't you?"

Her hand on his shoulder. "Giddy, I've been stuck on you since I was nine years old, in Winnebago. I kept track of you all through the war, though I never once saw you. Then I lost you. Giddy, when I was a kid I used to look at you from the sidewalk through the hedge of the house on Cass. Honestly. Honestly, Giddy."

"But look at me now. Why, Mary, I'm—I'm no good. Why, I don't see how you ever knew——"

"It takes more than a new Greek nose and French clothes and a busted arm to fool me, Gid. Do you know, there were a lot of photographs of you left up in the attic of the Cass Street house when we bought it. I know them all by heart, Giddy. By heart. . . . Come on home, Giddy. Let's go home."

Home Girl

[1922]

Home Girls are to be found not only on Wilson Avenue, Chicago, but on Broadway and on Park Avenue, New York, and for that matter in every city in the world—or what used to be the world. They are really married mistresses without the sense of decent obligation usually found in their less legal sisters, and should be sent to do a stretch in the salt mines.

In this twenty-four-year-old story there are certain statements about home-building and maid-shortage which strike an all-too-familiar note of timeliness.

꿍 WILSON AVENUE, CHICAGO, IS NOT MERELY AN AVENUE BUT A DIS-trict; not only a district but a state of mind; not a state of mind alone but a condition of morals. For that matter, it is none of these things so much as a mode of existence. If you know your Chicago you are aware that, long ago, Wilson Avenue proper crept slyly around the corner and achieved a clandestine alliance with big, glittering Sheridan Road—which escapade changed the demure thoroughfare into Wilson Avenue improper.

When one says, "A Wilson Avenue girl," the mind—that is, the Chicago mind—pictures immediately a slim, daring, scented, exotic creature dressed in next week's fashions; wise-eyed, doll-faced; rapacious. Wilson Avenue's hosiery is but a film over the flesh. Mink coats are its winter uniform. A feverish district this, all plate-glass windows and delicatessen dinners and one-room-and-kitchenette apartments, where light housekeepers take their housekeeping all too lightly.

At six o'clock you are likely to see Wilson Avenue scurrying about in its mink coat and its high heels and its crepe frock, assembling its hap-hazard dinner. Wilson Avenue food, as displayed in the ready-cooked shops, resembles in a startling degree the Wilson Avenue ladies them-selves; highly colored, artificial, chemically treated, tempting to the eye, but unnutritious. In and out of the food emporiums these dart, buying dabs of this and bits of that. Chromatic viands. Vivid scarlet, orange, yellow, green. A strip of pimento here. A mound of mayonnaise there. A green pepper stuffed with such burden of deceit as no honest green pepper ever was meant to hold. Two eggs. A quarter pound of your best creamery butter. An infinitesimal bottle of cream. "*And* what else?" says the plump woman in the white bib-apron, behind the counter. "*And* what else?" Nothing. I guess that'll be all. Mink coats prefer to dine out.

As a cripple displays his wounds and sores, proudly, so Wilson Avenue throws open its one-room front door with a grandiloquent gesture as it boasts, "Two hundred and fifty a month!"

It took Raymond and Cora Atwater twelve years to reach this Wilson Avenue, though they carried it with them all the way. They had begun their married life in this locality before it had become a definite district. Twelve years ago the neighborhood had shown no signs of mushrooming into its present opulence. Twelve years ago Raymond, twenty-eight, and Cora, twenty-four, had taken a six-room flat at Racine and Sunnyside. Six rooms. Modern. Light. Rental, $28.50 per month.

"But I guess I can manage it, all right," Raymond had said. "That isn't so terrible—for six rooms."

Cora's full under lip had drawn itself into a surprisingly thin straight line. Later, Raymond came to recognize the meaning of that labial warning. "We don't need all those rooms. It's just that much more work."

"I don't want you doing your own work. Not unless you want to. At first, maybe, it'd be sort of fun for you. But after a while you'll want a girl to help. That'll take the maid's room off the kitchen."

"Well, supposing? That leaves an extra room, anyway."

A look came into Raymond's face. "Maybe we'll need that, too—later. Later on." He actually could have been said to blush, then, like a boy. There was much of the boy in Raymond at twenty-eight.

Cora did not blush.

Raymond had married Cora because he loved her; and because she was what is known as a "home girl." From the first, business girls—those alert, pert, confident little sparrows of office and shop and the street at lunch hour—rather terrified him. They gave you as good as you sent. They were always ready with their own nickel for carfare. You never knew whether they were laughing at you or not. There was a little girl named Calhoun in the binoculars (Raymond's first Chicago job was with the Erwin H. Nagel Optical Company on Wabash). The Calhoun girl was smart. She wore those plain white waists. Tailored, Raymond thought they called them. They made her skin look fresh and clear and sort of downy, like the peaches that grew back home in his own Michigan. Or perhaps only girls with clear fresh skins could wear those plain white waist things. Raymond had heard that girls thought and schemed about things that were becoming to them, and then stuck to those things. He wondered how the Calhoun girl might look in a fluffy waist. But she never wore one down to work. When business was dull in the motor and sun glasses (which was where he held forth) Raymond would stroll over to Laura Calhoun's counter and talk. He would talk about the Invention. He had no one else to talk to about it. No one he could trust, or who understood.

The Calhoun girl, polishing the great black eyes of a pair of field glasses, would look up brightly to say, "Well, how's the Invention coming on?" Then he would tell her.

The Invention had to do with spectacles. Not only that, if you are a wearer of spectacles of any kind, it had to do with you. For now, twelve years later, you could not well do without it. The little contraption that keeps the side piece from biting into your ears—that's Raymond's.

Knowing, as we do, that Raymond's wife is named Cora, we know that the Calhoun girl of the fresh, clear skin, the tailored white shirtwaists, and the friendly interest in the Invention, lost out. The reason for that was Raymond's youth, and Raymond's vanity, and Raymond's unsophistication, together with Laura Calhoun's own honesty and efficiency.

Of course, when Raymond talked to her about the Invention she should have looked adoringly into his eyes and said, "How perfectly *wonderful!* I don't see how you think of such things."

What she said, after studying its detail thoughtfully for a moment, was: "Yeh, but look. If this little tiny wire had a spring underneath—just a little bit of spring—it'd take all the pressure off when you wear a hat. Women's hats are worn so much lower over their ears, d'you see? That'd keep it from pressing. Men's hats, too, for that matter."

She was right. Grudgingly, slowly, he admitted it. Not only that; he carried out her idea and perfected the spectacle contrivance as you know it today. Without her suggestion it would have had a serious flaw. He knew he ought to be grateful. He told himself that he was grateful. But in reality he was resentful. She was a smart girl, but—well—a fella didn't feel comfortable going with a girl that knew more than he did. He took her to the theater. She enjoyed it. So did he. Perhaps they might have repeated the little festivity and the white shirtwaist might have triumphed in the end. But that same week Raymond met Cora.

Though he had come to Chicago from Michigan almost a year before, he knew few people. The Erwin H. Nagel Company kept him busy by day. The Invention occupied him at night. He read, too—books on optometry. He was naturally somewhat shy, and further handicapped by an unusually tall lean frame which he handled awkwardly. If you had a good look at his eyes you forgot his shyness, his leanness, his awkwardness, his height. They were the keynote of his gentle, studious, kindly, humorous nature. But Chicago, Illinois, is too busy looking, to see anything. Eyes are something you see with, not into.

Two of the boys at Nagel's had an engagement for the evening with two girls who were friends. On the afternoon of that day, one of the boys went home at four with a well-developed case of grippe. The other approached Raymond with his plea.

"Say, Atwater, help me out, will you? I can't reach my girl because she's downtown somewheres for the afternoon with Cora. That's her girl friend. And me and Harvey was to meet 'em for dinner, see? And a show. I'm in a jam. Help me out, will you? Go along and date Cora. She's a nice girl. Pretty, too, Cora is. Will you, Ray? Huh?"

Ray went. By nine-thirty that evening he had told Cora about the Invention. And Cora had turned sidewise in her seat next to him at the theater and had looked up at him adoringly, awe-struck. "Why, how perfectly *wonderful!* I don't see how you think of such things."

"Oh, that's nothing. I got a lot of ideas. Things I'm going to work out. Say, I won't always be plugging down at Nagel's, believe me. I got a lot of ideas."

"Really! Why, you're an inventor, aren't you! Like Edison and those. My, it must be wonderful to think of things out of your head. Things that nobody's ever thought of before."

Ray glowed. He felt comfortable, and soothed, and relaxed, and stimulated. And too large for his clothes. "Oh, I don't know. I just think of things. That's all there is to it. That's nothing."

"Oh, isn't it! No, I guess not. I've never been out with a real inventor before. . . . I bet you think I'm a silly little thing."

He protested, stoutly. "I should say not." A thought struck him. "Do you do anything? Work downtown somewheres, or anything?"

She shook her head. Her lips pouted. Her eyebrows made pained twin crescents. "No. I don't do anything. I was afraid you'd ask that." She looked down at her hands—her white, soft hands with little dimples at the finger bases. "I'm just a home girl. That's all. A home girl. Now you *will* think I'm a silly, stupid thing." She flashed a glance at him, liquid-eyed, appealing.

He was surprised to find his hand closed tight and hard over her soft, dimpled one. He was terror-stricken to hear his voice saying, "I think you're wonderful. I think you're the most wonderful girl I ever saw, that's what." He crushed her hand and she winced a little. "Home girl."

Cora's name suited her to a marvel. Her hair was black and her coloring a natural pink and white, which she abetted expertly. Cora did not wear plain white tailored waists. She wore thin, fluffy, transparent things that drew your eyes and fired your imagination. Raymond began to call her Coral in his thoughts. Then, one evening, it slipped out. Coral. She liked it. He denied himself all luxuries and most necessities and bought her a strand of beads of that name, presenting them to her stammeringly, clumsily, tenderly. Tender pink and cream, they were, like her cheeks, he thought.

"Oh, Ray, for me! How darling! You naughty boy! . . . But I'd rather have had those clear white ones, without any coloring. They're more stylish. Do you mind?"

When he told Laura Calhoun she said, "I hope you'll be very happy. She's a lucky girl. Tell me about her, will you?"

Would he! His home girl!

When he had finished she said, quietly, "Oh, yes."

And so Raymond and Cora were married and went to live in six-room elegance at Sunnyside and Racine. The flat was furnished sumptuously in mission and those red and brown soft leather cushions with Indian heads stamped on them. There was a wooden rack on the wall with six monks' heads in colored plaster, very lifelike, stuck on it. This was a pipe rack, though Raymond did not smoke a pipe. He liked a mild cigar. Then there was a print of Gustave Richter's *Queen Louise* coming down that broad marble stair, one hand at her breast, her great, girlish eyes looking out at you from the misty folds of her scarf. What a lot of the world she has seen from her stairway! The shelf that ran around the dining-room wall on a level with your head was filled with steins in such shapes and colors as would have curdled their contents—if they had ever had any contents.

They planned to read a good deal, evenings. Improve their minds. It was Ray's idea, but Cora seconded it heartily. This was before their marriage.

"Now, take history alone," Ray argued. "American history. Why, you can read a year and hardly know the half of it. That's the trouble. People don't know the history of their own country. And it's interesting, too, let me tell you. Darned interesting. Better'n novels, if folks only knew it."

"My, yes," Cora agreed. "And French. We could take up French, evenings. I've always wanted to study French. They say if you know French you can travel anywhere. It's all in the accent; and goodness knows I'm quick at picking up things like that."

"Yeh," Ray had said, a little hollowly, "yeh, French. Sure."

But, somehow, these literary evenings never did materialize. It may have been a matter of getting the books. You could borrow them from the public library, but that made you feel so hurried. History was something you wanted to take your time over. Then, too, the books you wanted never were in. You could buy them. But buying books like that! Cora showed her first real display of temper. Why, they came in sets and cost as much as twelve or fifteen dollars. Just for books! The literary evenings degenerated into Ray's thorough scanning of the evening paper, followed by Cora's skimming of the crumpled sheets that carried the department-store ads, the society column, and the theatrical news. Raymond began to use the sixth room—the unused bedroom—as a workshop. He had perfected the spectacle contrivance and had made the mistake of selling his rights to it. He got a good sum for it.

"But I'll never do that again," he said grimly. "Somebody'll make a fortune on that thing." He had unwisely told Cora of this transaction. She never forgave him for it. On the day he received the money for it he brought her home a fur set of baum marten. He thought the stripe in it beautiful. There was a neckpiece known as a stole, and a large muff.

"Oh, honey!" Cora had cried. "Aren't you *fun*-ny!" She often said that, always with the same accent. "Aren't you *fun*-ny!"

"What's the matter?"

"Why didn't you let me pick it out? They're wearing Persian lamb."

"Oh. Well, maybe the feller'll change it. It's all paid for, but maybe he'll change it."

"Do you mind? It may cost a little bit more. You don't mind my changing it, though, do you?"

"No. No-o-o-o! Not a bit."

They had never furnished the unused bedroom as a bedroom. When they moved out of the flat at Racine and Sunnyside into one of those new four-room apartments on Glengyle, the movers found only a long rough worktable and a green-shaded lamp in that sixth room. Ray's delicate tools and implements were hard put to it to find a resting place in the new four-room apartment. Sometimes Ray worked in the bathroom. He grew rather to like the white-tiled place, with its look of a laboratory. But then, he didn't have as much time to work at home as he had formerly had. They went out more evenings.

The new four-room flat rented at sixty dollars. "Seems the less room you have the more you pay," Ray observed.

"There's no comparison. Look at the neighborhood! And the living room's twice as big."

It didn't seem to be. Perhaps this was due to its furnishings. The mission pieces had gone to the secondhand dealer. Ray was assistant manager of the optical department at Nagel's now and he was getting royalties on a new smoked-glass device. There were large overstuffed chairs in the new living room, and a seven-foot davenport, and Oriental rugs, and lamps and lamps and lamps. The silk-lamp-shade conflagration had just begun to smolder in the American household. The dining room had one of those built-in Chicago buffets. There was a large punch bowl in the center, in which Cora usually kept receipts, old bills, moth balls, buttons, and the tarnished silver top to a sirup jug that she always meant to have repaired.

Queen Louise was banished to the bedroom, where she surveyed a world of cretonne.

Cora was a splendid cook. She had almost a genius for flavoring. Roast or cheese soufflé or green apple pie—your sense of taste never experienced that disappointment which comes of too little salt, too much sugar, a lack of shortening. Expert as she was at it, Cora didn't like to cook. That is, she didn't like to cook day after day. She rather liked doing an occasional meal and producing it in a sort of red-cheeked triumph. When she did this it was an epicurean thing, savory, hot, satisfying. But as a day-after-day program Cora would not hear of it. She had refused a maid. Four rooms could not accommodate her. A woman came in twice a week to wash and iron and clean. Often Cora did not get up for breakfast and Ray got his at one of the little lunchrooms that were springing up all over that section of the North Side. Eleven o'clock usually found Cora at the manicurist's, or the dressmaker's, or shopping, or telephoning luncheon arrangements with one of the Crowd. Ray and Cora were going out a good deal with the Crowd. Young married people like themselves, living royally just a little beyond their income. The women were well dressed, vivacious, somewhat shrill. They liked stories that were a little off-color. "Blue," one of the men called these stories. He was in the theatrical business. The men were, for the most part, a rather drab-looking lot. Colorless, good-natured, open-handed. Almost imperceptibly, the Crowd began to use Ray as a target for a certain raillery. It wasn't particularly ill-natured, and Ray did not resent it.

"Oh, come on, Ray! Don't be a wet blanket. . . . Lookit him! I bet he's thinking about those smoked glasses again. Eh, Atwater? He's in a daze about that new rim that won't show on the glasses. Come out of it! First thing you know you'll lose your little Cora!"

There was little danger of that. Though Cora flirted mildly with the husbands of the other girls in the Crowd (they all did), she was true to Ray.

Ray was always talking of building a little place of their own. People were beginning to move farther and farther north, into the suburbs.

"Little place of your own," Ray would say, "that's the only way to live. Then you're not paying it all out in rent to the other feller. Little place of your own. That's the right idear."

But as the years went by, and Ray earned more and more money, he and Cora seemed to be getting farther and farther away from the right idear. In the $28.50 apartment Cora's morning marketing had been an orderly daily proceeding. Meat, vegetables, fruit, dry groceries. But now the maid-less four-room apartment took on, in spite of its cumbersome furnishings, a certain air of impermanence.

"Ray, honey, I haven't a scrap in the house. I didn't get home until almost six. Do you mind going over to Bauer's to eat? I won't go, because Myrtle served a regular spread at four. I couldn't eat a thing. D'you mind?"

"Why, no." He would get into his coat again and go out into the bleak November wind-swept street to Bauer's restaurant.

Cora was always home when Raymond got there at six. She prided herself on this. She would say, primly, to her friends, "I make a point of being there when Ray gets home. Even if I have to cut bridge. If a woman can't be there when a man gets home from work, I'd like to know what she's good for, anyway."

The girls in the Crowd said she was spoiling Raymond. She told Ray this. "They think I'm old-fashioned. Well, maybe I am. But I guess I never pretended to be anything but a home girl."

"That's right," Ray would answer. "Say, that's the way you caught me. With that home-girl stuff."

"Caught you!" The thin straight line of the mouth. "If you think for one minute——"

"Oh, now, dear. You know what I mean, sweetheart. Why, say, I never could see any girl until I met you. You know that."

He was as honestly in love with her as he had been nine years before. Perhaps he did not feel now, as then, that she had conferred a favor upon him in marrying him. Or, if he did, he must have known that he had made fair return for such favor.

Cora had a broadtail coat now, with a great fur collar. Her vivid face bloomed rosily in this soft frame. Cora was getting a little heavier. Not stout, but heavier, somehow. She tried, futilely, to reduce. She would starve herself at home for days, only to gain back the vanished pounds at one afternoon's orgy of chicken salad and coffee and sweets at the apartment of some girl in the Crowd. Dancing had come in and the Crowd had taken it up vociferously. Raymond was not very good at it. He had not filled out with the years. He still was lean and tall and awkward. The girls in the crowd tried to avoid dancing with him. That often left Cora partnerless unless she wanted to dance again and again with Raymond.

"How can you expect the boys to ask me to dance when you don't dance with their wives! Good heavens, if they can learn, you can. And for pity's sake *don't count!* You're so *fun*-ny!"

He tried painstakingly to heed her advice, but his long legs made a sorry business of it. He heard one of the girls refer to him as "that giraffe." He had put his foot through an absurd wisp of tulle.

They were spending a good deal of money now, but Ray jousted the landlord, the victualer, the furrier, the milliner, and the hosiery maker valiantly and still came off the victor. He did not have as much time as he would have liked to work on the new invention. The invisible rim. It was calculated so to blend with the glass of the lens as to be, in appearance, one with it, while it still protected the eyeglass from breakage. "Fortune in it, girlie," he would say, happily, to Cora. "Million dollars, that's all."

He had been working on the invisible rim for five years. Familiarity with it had bred contempt in Cora. Once, in a temper, "Invisible is right," she had said.

They had occupied the four-room apartment for five years. Cora declared it was getting beyond her. "You can't get any decent help. The washwoman acts as if she was doing me a favor coming from eight to four, for four dollars and eighty-five cents. And yesterday she said she couldn't come to clean any more on Saturdays. I'm sick and tired of it."

Raymond shook a sympathetic head. "Same way down at the store. Seems everything's that way now. You can't get help and you can't get goods. You ought to hear our customers. Yesterday I thought I'd go clear out of my nut, trying to pacify them."

Cora inserted the entering wedge, deftly. "Goodness knows I love my home. But the way things are now . . ."

"Yeh," Ray said, absently. When he spoke like that Cora knew that the invisible rim was revolving in his mind. In another moment he would be off into the little cabinet in the bathroom where he kept his tools and instruments.

She widened the opening. "I noticed as I passed today that those new one-room kitchenette apartments on Sheridan will be ready for occupancy October first." He was going toward the door. "They say they're wonderful."

"Who wants to live in one room, anyway?"

"It's really two rooms—and the kitchenette. There's the living room—perfectly darling—and a sort of combination breakfast room and kitchen. The breakfast room is partitioned off with sort of cupboards so that it's really another room. And so handy!"

"How'd you know?"

"I went in—just to look at them—with one of the girls."

Until then he had been unconscious of her guile. But now, suddenly, struck by a hideous suspicion: "Say, looka here. If you think——"

"Well, it doesn't hurt to look at 'em, does it!"

A week later. "Those kitchenette apartments on Sheridan are almost all gone. One of the girls was looking at one on the sixth floor. There's a view of the lake. The kitchen's the sweetest thing. All white enamel. And the breakfast-room thing is done in Italian."

"What d'you mean—done in Italian?"

"Why—uh—Italian period furniture, you know. Dark and rich. The living room's the same. Desk, and table, and lamps."

"Oh, they're furnished?"

"Complete. Down to the kettle covers and the linen and all. The work there would just be play. All the comforts of a home, with none of the terrible aggravations."

"Say, look here, Coral, we don't want to go to work and live in any one room. You wouldn't be happy. Why, we'd feel cooped up. No room to stretch. . . . Why, say, how about the beds? If there isn't a bedroom, how about the beds? Don't people sleep in those places?"

"There are Murphy beds, silly."

"Murphy? Who's he?"

"Oh, goodness, I don't know! The man who invented 'em, I suppose. Murphy."

Raymond grinned in anticipation of his own forthcoming joke. "I should think they'd call 'em Morphy beds." Then, at her blank stare, "You know —short for Morpheus, god of sleep. Learned about him at high school."

Cora still looked blank. Cora hardly ever understood Ray's jokes, or laughed at them. He would turn, chuckling, to find her face a blank. Not even bewildered, or puzzled, or questioning. Blank. Unheeding. Uninterested as a slate.

Three days later Cora developed an acute pain in her side. She said it was nothing. Just worn out with the work, and the worry, and the aggravation, that's all. It'll be all right.

Ray went with her to look at the Sheridan Road apartment. It was one hundred and fifty dollars. "Phew!"

"But look at what you save! Gas. Light. Maid service. Laundry. It's really cheaper in the end."

Cora was amazingly familiar with all the advantages and features of the sixth-floor apartment. "The sun all morning." She had all the agent's patter. "Harvey-Dickson ventilated double-spring mattresses. Dressing room off the bathroom. No, it isn't a closet. Here's the closet. Range, refrigerator, combination sink and laundry tub. Living room's all paneled in ivory. Shower in the bathroom. Buffet kitchen. Breakfast room has folding-leaf Italian table. Look at the chairs. Aren't they darlings! Built-in bookshelves——"

"Bookshelves?"

"Oh, well, we can use them for fancy china and ornaments. Or—oh, look!—you could keep your stuff there. Tools and all. Then the bathroom wouldn't be mussy all the time."

"Bed?"

"Right here. Isn't that wonderful. Would you ever know it was there?
You can work it with one hand. Look."

"Do you really like it, Coral?"

"I love it. It's heavenly."

He stood in the center of the absurd living room, a tall, lank, awkward
figure, a little stooped now. His face was beginning to be furrowed with
lines—deep lines that yet were softening and not unlovely. He made you
think, somehow, as he stood there, one hand on his own coat lapel, of
Saint-Gaudens' figure of Lincoln, there in the park, facing the Drive.
Kindly, thoughtful, harried.

They moved in October first.

The overstuffed furniture of the four-room apartment was sold. Cora
kept a few of her own things—a rug or two, some china, silver, bric-a-brac,
lamps. Queen Louise was now permanently dethroned. Cora said her own
things—"pieces"—would spoil the effect of the living room. All Italian.

"No wonder the Italians sit outdoors all the time, on the steps and in the
street"—more of Ray's dull humor. He surveyed the heavy, gloomy pieces,
so out of place in the tiny room. One of the chairs was black velvet. It was
the only really comfortable chair in the room, but Ray never sat in it. It
reminded him, vaguely, of a coffin. The corridors of the apartment house
were long, narrow, and white-walled. You traversed these like a convict,
speaking to no one, and entered your own cubicle. A toy dwelling for toy
people. But Ray was a man-size man. When he was working downtown
his mind did not take temporary refuge in the thought of the feverish little
apartment to which he was to return at night. It wasn't a place to come
back to, except for sleep. A roost. Bedding for the night. As permanent-
seeming as a haymow.

Cora, too, gave him a strange feeling of impermanence. He realized one
day, with a shock, that he hardly ever saw her with her hat off. When he
came in at six or six-thirty Cora would be busy at the tiny sink, or the toy
stove, her hat on, a cigarette dangling limply from her mouth. Ray did not
object to women smoking. That is, he had no moral objection. But he
didn't think it became them. But Cora said a cigarette rested and stimulated her. "Doctors say all nervous women should smoke," she said. "Soothes
them." But Cora, cooking in the little kitchen, squinting into a kettle's
depths through a film of cigarette smoke, outraged his sense of fitness. It
was incongruous, offensive. The time, and occupation, and environment,
together with the limply dangling cigarette, gave her an incredibly rowdy
look.

When they ate at home they had steak or chops, and, perhaps, a chocolate éclair for dessert, and a salad. Raymond began to eat mental meals. He would catch himself thinking of breaded veal chops, done slowly, simmeringly, in butter, so that they came out a golden brown on a parsley-decked platter. With this, mashed potatoes with brown butter and onions that have just escaped burning; creamed spinach with egg grated over the top; a rice pudding, baked in the oven, and served with a tart crown of grape jelly. He sometimes would order these things in a restaurant at noon, or on the frequent evenings when they dined out. But they never tasted as he had thought they would.

They dined out more and more as spring drew on and the warm weather set in. The neighborhood now was aglitter with eating places of all sorts and degrees, from the humble Automat to the proud plush of the Sheridan Plaza dining room. There were tearooms, cafeterias, Hungarian cafés, chop-suey restaurants. At the table-d'hôte places you got a soup, followed by a lukewarm plateful of meat, vegetables, salad. The meat tasted of the vegetables, the vegetables tasted of the meat, and the salad tasted of both. Before ordering, Ray would sit down and peer about at the food on the near-by tables as one does in a dining car when the digestive fluids have dried in your mouth at the first whiff through the doorway. It was on one of these evenings that he noticed Cora's hat.

"What do you wear a hat for all the time?" he asked, testily.

"Hat?"

"Seems to me I haven't seen you without a hat in a month. Gone bald, or something?" He was often cross like this lately. Grumpy, Cora called it. Hats were one of Cora's weaknesses. She had a great variety of them. These added to Ray's feeling of restlessness and impermanence. Sometimes she wore a hat that came down over her head, covering her forehead and her eyes, almost. The hair he used to love to touch was concealed. Sometimes he dined with an ingénue in a poke bonnet; sometimes with a señorita in black turban and black lace veil, mysterious and provocative; sometimes with a demure miss in a wistful little turned-down brim. It was like living with a stranger who was always about to leave.

When they ate at home, which was rarely, Ray tried, at first, to dawdle over his coffee and his mild cigar, as he liked to do. But you couldn't dawdle at a small, inadequate table that folded its flaps and shrank into a corner the minute you left it. Everything in the apartment folded, or flapped, or doubled, or shot in, or shot out, or concealed something else, or pretended to be something it was not. It was irritating. Ray took his cigar and his evening paper and wandered uneasily into the Italian living room, doubling his lean length into one of the queer, angular, hard chairs.

Cora would appear in the doorway, hatted. "Ready?"

"Huh? Where you going?"

"Oh, Ray, aren't you *fun*-ny! You know this is the Crowd's poker night at Lil's."

The Crowd began to say that old Ray was going queer. Honestly, didja hear him last week? Talking about the instability of the home, and the home being the foundation of the state, and the country crumbling? Cora's face was a sight! I wouldn't have wanted to be in his boots when she got him home. What's got into him, anyway?

Cora was a Wilson Avenue girl now. You saw her in and out of the shops of the district, expensively dressed. She was almost thirty-six. Her legs, beneath the absurdly short skirt of the day, were slim and shapely in their chiffon hose, but her upper figure was now a little prominent. The scant, brief skirt foreshortened her, gave her a storklike appearance—a combination of girlishness and matronliness not pleasing.

There were times when Ray rebelled. A peace-loving man, and gentle. But a man. "I don't want to go out to eat. My God, I'm tired! I want to eat at home."

"Honey, dear, I haven't a thing in the house. Not a scrap."

"I'll go out and get something, then. What d'you want?"

"Get whatever looks good to you. I don't want a thing. We had tea after the matinee. That's what made me so late. I'm always nagging the girls to go home. It's getting so they tease me about it."

He would go foraging amongst the delicatessen shops of the neighborhood. He saw other men, like himself, scurrying about with moist paper packets and bags and bundles, in and out of Leviton's, in and out of the Sunlight Bakery. A bit of ham. Some cabbage salad in a wooden boat. A tiny broiler, lying on its back, its feet neatly trussed, its skin crackly and tempting-looking, its white meat showing beneath the brown. But when he cut into it at home it tasted like sawdust and gutta-percha. "*And* what else?" said the plump woman in the white bib-apron behind the counter. "*And* what else?"

In the new apartment you rather prided yourself on not knowing your next-door neighbors. The paper-thin walls permitted you to hear them living the most intimate details of their lives. You heard them laughing, talking, weeping, singing, scolding, caressing. You didn't know them. You did not even see them. When you met in the halls or elevators you did not speak. Then, after they had lived in the new apartment about a year, Cora met the woman in 618 and Raymond met the woman in 620, within the same week. The Atwaters lived in 619.

There was some confusion in the delivery of a package. The woman in

618 pressed the Atwaters' electric button for the first time in their year's residence there.

A plump woman, 618; blond; in black. You felt that her flesh was expertly restrained in tight, pink satin brassières and long-hipped corsets and many straps.

"I hate to trouble you, but did you get a package for Mrs. Hoyt? It's from Field's."

It was five-thirty. Cora had her hat on. She did not ask the woman to come in. "I'll see. I ordered some things from Field's today, too. I haven't opened them yet. Perhaps yours . . . I'll look."

The package with Mrs. Hoyt's name on it was there. "Well, thanks so much. It's some georgette crepe. I'm making myself one of those new two-tone, slipover negligees. Field's had a sale. Only one-sixty-nine a yard."

Cora was interested. She sewed rather well when she was in the mood. "Are they hard to make?"

"Oh, land, no! No trick to it at all. They just hang from the shoulder, see? Like a slipover. And then your cord comes round—"

She stepped in. She undid the box and shook out the folds of the filmy stuff, vivid green and lavender. "You wouldn't think they'd go well together, but they do. Makes a perfectly stunning negligee."

Cora fingered the stuff. "I'd get some. Only I don't know if I could cut the——"

"I'll show you. Glad to." She was very friendly. Cora noticed she used expensive perfume. Her hair was beautifully waved. The woman folded up the material and was off, smiling. "Just let me know when you get it. I've got a lemon cream pie in the oven and I've got to run." She called back over her shoulder. "Mrs. Hoyt."

Cora nodded and smiled. "Mine's Atwater." She saw that the woman's simple-seeming black dress was one she had seen in a Michigan Avenue shop, and had coveted. Its price had been beyond her purse.

Cora mentioned the meeting to Ray when he came home. "She seems real nice. She's going to show me how to cut out a new negligee."

"What'd you say her name was?" She told him. He shrugged. "Well, I'll say this: she must be some swell cook. Whenever I go by that door at dinnertime my mouth just waters. One night last week there was something must have been baked spareribs and sauerkraut. I almost broke in the door."

The woman in 618 did seem to cook a great deal. That is, when she cooked. She explained that Mr. Hoyt was on the road a lot of the time and when he was home she liked to fuss for him. This when she was helping Cora cut out the georgette negligee.

"I'd get coral color if I was you, honey. With your hair and all," Mrs. Hoyt had advised her.

"Why, that's my name! That is, it's what Ray calls me. My name's really Cora." They were quite good friends now.

It was that same week that Raymond met the woman in 620. He had left the apartment half an hour later than usual (he had a heavy cold, and had not slept) and encountered the man and woman just coming out of 620.

"And guess who it was!" he exclaimed to Cora that evening. "It was a girl who used to work at Nagel's, in the binoculars, years ago, when I started there. Calhoun, her name was. Laura Calhoun. Smart little girl, she was. She's married now. And guess what! She gets a big salary fitting glasses for women at the Bazaar. She learned to be an optician. Smart girl."

Cora bridled, virtuously. "Well, I think she'd better stay home and take care of that child of hers. I should think she'd let her husband earn the living. That child is all soul alone when she comes home from school. I hear her practicing. I asked Mrs. Hoyt about her. She says she's seen her. A spindling, scrawny, little thing, about ten years old. She leaves her alone all day."

Ray encountered the Calhoun girl again, shortly after that, in the way encounters repeat themselves, once they have started.

"She didn't say much, but I guess her husband is a nit-wit. Funny how a smart girl like that always marries one of these sapheads that can't earn a living. She said she was working because she wanted her child to have the advantages she'd missed. That's the way she put it."

One heard the long-legged, melancholy child next door practicing at the piano daily at four. Cora said it drove her crazy. But then, Cora was rarely home at four. "Well," she said now, virtuously, "I don't know what she calls advantages. The way she neglects that kid. Look at her! I guess if she had a little more mother and a little less education it'd be better for her."

"Guess that's right," Ray agreed.

It was in September that Cora began to talk about the mink coat. A combination anniversary and Christmas gift. December would mark their twelfth anniversary. A mink coat.

Raymond remembered that his mother had had a mink coat, back there in Michigan, years ago. She always had taken it out in November and put it away in moth balls and tar paper in March. She had done this for years and years. It was a cheerful yellow mink, with a slightly darker marking running through it, and there had been little mink tails all around the bottom edge of it. It had spread comfortably at the waist. Women had had hips in those days. With it his mother had carried a mink muff; a small yellow-brown cylinder just big enough for her two hands. It had been her outdoor uniform, winter after winter, for as many years as he could remember of his boyhood. When she had died the mink coat had gone to his sister Carrie, he remembered.

A mink coat. The very words called up in his mind sharp winter days; the pungent moth-bally smell of his mother's fur-coated bosom when she had kissed him good-by that day he left for Chicago; comfort; womanliness. A mink coat.

"How much could you get one for? A mink coat."

Cora hesitated a moment. "Oh—I guess you could get a pretty good one for three thousand."

"You're crazy," said Ray unemotionally. He was not angry. He was amused.

But Cora was persistent. Her coat was a sight. She had to have something. She never had had a real fur coat.

"How about your seal?"

"Hudson seal! Did you ever see any seals in the Hudson! Fake fur. I've never had a really decent piece of fur in my life. Always some mangy make-believe. All the girls in the Crowd are getting new coats this year. The woman next door—Mrs. Hoyt—is talking of getting one. She says Mr. Hoyt——"

"Say, who are these Hoyts, anyway?"

Ray came home early one day to find the door to 618 open. He glanced in, involuntarily. A man sat in the living room—a large, rather red-faced man in his shirt sleeves, relaxed, comfortable, at ease. From the open door came the most tantalizing and appetizing smells of candied sweet potatoes, a browning roast, steaming vegetables.

Mrs. Hoyt had run in to bring a slice of fresh-baked chocolate cake to Cora. She often brought in dishes of exquisitely prepared food thus, but Raymond had never before encountered her. Cora introduced them. Mrs. Hoyt smiled, nervously, and said she must run away and tend to her dinner. And went. Ray looked after her. He strode into the kitchenette, where Cora stood, hatted, at the sink.

"Say, looka here, Cora. You got to quit seeing that woman, see?"

"What woman?"

"One calls herself Mrs. Hoyt. That woman. Mrs. Hoyt! Ha!"

"Why, Ray, what in the world are you talking about! Aren't you *fun*-ny!"

"Yeh; well, you cut her out. I won't have you running around with a woman like that. Mrs. Hoyt! Mrs. Hell."

They had a really serious quarrel about it. When the smoke of battle cleared away Raymond had paid the first installment on a three-thousand-dollar mink coat. And, "If we could sublease," Cora said, "I think it would be wonderful to move to the Shoreham. Lil and Harry are going there in January. You know yourself this place isn't half respectable."

Raymond had stared. "Shoreham! Why, it's a hotel. Regular hotel."

"Yes," placidly. "That's what's so nice about it. No messing around in a miserable little kitchenette. You can have your meals sent up. Or you can go down to the dining room. Lil says it's wonderful. And if you order for one up in your room the portions are big enough for two. It's really economy, in the end."

"Nix," said Ray. "No hotel in mine. A little house of our own. That's the right idear. Build."

"But nobody's building now. Materials are so high. It'll cost you ten times as much as it would if you waited a few—a little while. And no help. No maids coming over, hardly. I think you might consider me a little. We could live at the Shoreham awhile, anyway. By that time things will be better, and we'd have money saved up and then we might talk of building. Goodness knows I love my home as well as any woman——"

They looked at the Shoreham rooms on the afternoon of their anniversary. They were having the Crowd to dinner, downtown, that evening. Cora thought the Shoreham rooms beautiful, though she took care not to let the room clerk know she thought so. Ray, always a silent, inarticulate man, was so wordless that Cora took him to task for it in a sibilant aside.

"Ray, for heaven's sake say something. You stand there! I don't know what the man'll think."

"A hell of a lot I care what he thinks." Ray was looking about the garish room—plush chairs, heavy carpets, brocade hangings, shining table top, absurd desk.

"Two hundred and seventy-five a month," the clerk was saying. "With the yearly lease, of course. Otherwise it's three-twenty-five." He seemed quite indifferent.

Ray said nothing. "We'll let you know," said Cora.

The man walked to the door. "I can't hold it for you, you know. Our apartments are practically gone. I've a party who practically has closed for this suite already. I'd have to know."

Cora looked at Ray. He said nothing. He seemed not to have heard. His face was gaunt and haggard. "We'll let you know—tomorrow," Cora said. Her full under lip made a straight thin line.

When they came out it was snowing. A sudden flurry. It was already dark. "Oh, dear," said Cora. "My hat!" Ray summoned one of the hotel taxis. He helped Cora into it. He put money into the driver's hand.

"You go on, Cora. I'm going to walk."

"Walk! Why! But it's snowing. And you'll have to dress for dinner."

"I've got a headache. I thought I'd walk. I'll be home. I'll be home."

He slammed the door then, and turned away. He began to walk in the opposite direction from that which led toward the apartment house. The snow felt cool and grateful on his face. It stung his cheeks. Hard and swift and white it came, blinding him. A blizzard off the lake. He plunged through it, head down, hands jammed into his pockets.

So. A home girl. Home girl. God, it was funny. She was a selfish, idle, silly, vicious woman. She was nothing. Nothing. It came over him in a sudden blinding crashing blaze of light. The woman in 618 who wasn't married to her man, and who cooked and planned to make him comfortable; the woman in 620 who blindly left her home and her child every day in order to give that child the thing she called advantages—either of these was better than his woman. Honester. Helping someone. Trying to, anyway. Doing a better job than she was.

He plunged across the street, blindly, choking a little with the bitterness that had him by the throat. "Hey! Watcha!"—a shout rising to a scream. A bump. Numbness. Silence. Nothingness.

"Well, anyway, Cora," said the girls in the Crowd, "you certainly were a wonderful wife to him. You can always comfort yourself with that thought. My! the way you always ran home so's to be there before he got in."

"I know it," said Cora, mournfully. "I always was a home girl. Why, we always had planned we should have a little home of our own someday. He always said that was the right idear—idea."

Lil wiped her eyes. "What are you going to do about your new mink coat, Cora?"

Cora brushed her hair away from her forehead with a slow, sad gesture. "Oh, I don't know. I've hardly thought of such trifling things. The woman next door said she might buy it. Hoyt, her name is. Of course I couldn't get what we paid for it, though I've hardly had it on. But money'll count with me now. Ray never did finish that invisible rim he was working on all those years. Wasting his time. Poor Ray. . . . I thought, though, I might keep it. You can wear mink with black, it's considered mourning. I feel that Ray would want me to wear it. After all, he was the one wanted me to have it. I wouldn't hurt Ray for the world."

The Sudden Sixties

[1922]

The old sob song used to say, "She's somebody's mother." Hannah Winter is practically anybody's mother.

✑ HANNAH WINTER WAS SIXTY ALL OF A SUDDEN, AS WOMEN OF SIXTY are. Just yesterday—or the day before, at most—she had been a bride of twenty in a wine-colored silk wedding gown, very stiff and rich. And now here she was, all of a sudden, sixty.

The actual anniversary that marked her threescore had had nothing to do with it. She had passed that day painlessly enough—happily, in fact. But now, here she was, all of a sudden, consciously, bewilderingly, sixty. This is the way it happened.

She was rushing along Peacock Alley to meet her daughter Marcia. Anyone who knows Chicago knows that smoke-blackened pile, the Congress Hotel; and anyone who knows the Congress Hotel has walked down that glittering white marble crypt called Peacock Alley. It is neither so glittering nor so white, nor, for that matter, so prone to preen itself as it was in the hotel's palmy nineties. But it still serves as a convenient short cut on a day when Chicago's lake wind makes Michigan Boulevard a hazard, and thus Hannah Winter was using it. She was to have met Marcia at the Michigan Boulevard entrance at two, sharp. And here it was 2:07. When Marcia said two, there she was at two, waiting, lips slightly compressed. When you came clattering up, breathless, at 2:07, she said nothing in reproach. But within the following half-hour bits of her conversation, if pieced together, would have summed up something like this:

"I had to get the children off in time and give them their lunch first because it's wash day and Lutie's busy with the woman and won't do a single extra thing; and all my marketing for today and tomorrow because tomorrow's Memorial Day and they close at noon; and stop at the real-estate agent's on Fifty-third to see them about the wallpaper before I came down. I didn't even have time to swallow a cup of tea. And yet I was here at two. You haven't a thing to do. Not a blessed thing, living at a hotel. It does seem to me . . ."

So then here it was 2:07, and Hannah Winter, rather panicky, was rushing along Peacock Alley, dodging loungers, and bellboys, and traveling salesmen, and visiting provincials, and the inevitable red-faced delegates with satin badges. In her hurry and nervous apprehension she looked, as she scuttled down the narrow passage, very much like the Rabbit who was late for the Duchess's dinner. Her rubber-heeled oxfords were pounding down hard on the white marble pavement. Suddenly she saw coming swiftly toward her a woman who seemed strangely familiar—a well-dressed woman, harassed-looking, a tense frown between her eyes, and her eyes staring so that they protruded a little, as one who runs ahead of herself in her haste. Hannah had just time to note, in a flash, that the woman's smart hat was slightly askew and that, though she walked very fast, her trim ankles showed the inflexibility of age, when she saw that the woman was not going to get out of her way. Hannah Winter swerved quickly to avoid a collision. So did the other woman. Next instant Hannah Winter brought up with a crash against her own image in that long and tricky mirror which forms a broad full-length panel set in the marble wall at the north end of Peacock Alley. Passers-by and the loungers on near-by red plush seats came running, but she was unhurt except for a forehead bump that remained black-and-blue for two weeks or more. The bump did not bother her, nor did the slightly amused concern of those who had come to her assistance. She stood there, her hat still askew, staring at this woman—this woman with her stiff ankles, her slightly protruding eyes, her nervous frown, her hat a little sideways—this stranger—this murderess who had just slain, ruthlessly and forever, a sallow, lively, high-spirited girl of twenty in a wine-colored silk wedding gown.

Don't think that Hannah Winter, at sixty, had tried to ape sixteen. She was not one of those grisly sexagenarians who think that, by wearing pink, they can combat the ocher of age. Not at all. In dress, conduct, mode of living she was as an intelligent and modern woman of sixty should be. The youth of her was in that intangible thing called, sentimentally, the spirit. It had survived forty years of buffeting and disappointment and sacrifice and hard work. Inside this woman who wore well-tailored black and small close hats and clean white wash gloves (even in Chicago) was the girl, Hannah Winter, still curious about this adventure known as living; still capable of bearing its disappointments or enjoying its surprises. Still capable, even, of being surprised. This all unsuspected by the Marcias until the Marcias are, themselves, suddenly sixty. When it is too late to say to the Hannah Winters, "Now I understand."

We know that Hannah Winter had been married in wine-colored silk, very stiff and grand. So stiff and rich that the dress would have stood alone if Hannah had ever thought of subjecting her wedding gown to such indignity. It was the sort of silk of which it is said that they don't make such silk now. It was cut square at the neck and trimmed with passementerie and fringe brought crosswise from breast to skirt hem. It's in the old photograph, and, curiously enough, while Marcia thinks it's comic, Joan, her nine-year-old daughter, agrees with her grandmother in thinking it very lovely. And so, in its quaintness and stiffness and bravery, it is.

While wine-colored silk wouldn't have done for a church wedding, it was quite all right at home; and Hannah Winter's had been a home wedding (the Winters lived in one of the old three-story red-bricks that may still be seen, in crumbling desuetude, over on Rush Street), so that wine-colored silk for a twenty-year-old bride was quite in the mode.

It is misleading, perhaps, to go on calling her Hannah Winter, for she married Hermie Slocum and became, according to law, Mrs. Hermie Slocum, but remained, somehow, Hannah Winter in spite of law and clergy, though with no such intent on her part. She had never even heard of Lucy Stone. It wasn't merely that her Chicago girlhood friends still spoke of her as Hannah Winter. Hannah Winter suited her—belonged to her and was characteristic. Mrs. Hermie Slocum sort of melted and ran down off her. Hermie was the sort of man who, christened Herman, is called Hermie. That all those who had known her before her marriage still spoke of her as Hannah Winter forty years later was merely another triumph of the strong over the weak.

At twenty Hannah Winter had been a rather sallow, lively, fun-loving girl, not pretty, but animated; and forceful, even then. The Winters were middle-class, respected, moderately well-to-do Chicago citizens—or had been moderately well-to-do before the fire of '71. Horace Winter had been caught in the financial funk that followed this disaster and the Rush Street household, almost ten years later, was rather put to it to supply the wine-colored silk and the supplementary gowns, linens, and bedding. In those days you married at twenty if a decent chance to marry at twenty presented itself. And Hermie Slocum seemed a decent chance, undoubtedly. A middle-class, respected, moderately well-to-do person himself, Hermie, with ten thousand dollars saved at thirty-five and just about to invest it in business in the thriving city of Indianapolis. A solid young man, Horace Winter said. Not much given to talk. That indicated depth and thinking. Thrifty and farsighted, as witness the good ten thousand in cash. Kind. Old enough, with his additional fifteen years, to balance the lively Hannah, who was considered rather flighty and too prone to find fun in things that others considered serious. A good thing she never quite lost that fault. Hannah resolutely and dutifully put out of her head (or nearly) all vagrant thoughts of Clint Darrow with the crisp black hair and the surprising blue eyes thereto, and the hat worn rakishly a little on one side, and the slender cane and the pointed shoes. A whippersnapper, according to Horace Winter. Not a solid businessman like Hermie Slocum. Hannah did not look upon herself as a human sacrifice. She was genuinely fond of Hermie. She was fond of her father, too, the rather harassed and henpecked Horace Winter; and of her mother, the voluble and quick-tongued and generous Bertha Winter, who was so often to be seen going down the street, shawl and bonnet strings flying, when she should have been at home minding her household. Much of the minding had fallen to Hannah.

And so they were married, and went to the thriving city of Indianapolis to live, and Hannah Winter was so busy with her new household goods, and the linens, and the wine-colored silk and its less magnificent satellites, that it was almost a fortnight before she realized fully that this solid young man, Hermie Slocum, was not only solid, but immovable; not merely thrifty, but stingy; not alone taciturn, but quite conversationless. His silences had not proceeded from the unplumbed depths of his knowledge. He merely had nothing to say. She learned, too, that the ten thousand dollars, soon dispelled, had been made for him by an energetic and shrewd business partner with whom he had quarreled and from whom he had separated a few months before.

There never was another lump sum of ten thousand of Hermie Slocum's earning.

Well. Forty years ago, having made the worst of it you made the best of it. No going home to Mother. The word "incompatibility" had not come into widespread use. Incompatibility was a thing to hide, not to flaunt. The years that followed were dramatic or commonplace, depending on one's sense of values. Certainly those years were like the married years of many another young woman of that unplastic day. Hannah Winter had her job cut out for her and she finished it well, and alone. No reproaches. Little complaint. Criticism she made in plenty, being the daughter of a voluble mother; and she never gave up hope of stiffening the spine of the invertebrate Hermie.

The ten thousand went in driblets. There never was anything dashing or romantic about Hermie Slocum's failures. The household never felt actual want, not anything so picturesque as poverty. Hannah saw to that.

You should have read her letters back home to Chicago—to her mother and father back home on Rush Street, in Chicago; and to her girlhood friends, Sarah Clapp, Vinie Harden, and Julia Pierce. They were letters that, for stiff-lipped pride and brazen boasting, were of a piece with those written by Sentimental Tommy's mother when things were going worst. "My wine-colored silk is almost worn out," she wrote. "I'm thinking of making it over into a tea gown with one of those new cream pongee panels down the front. Hermie says he's tired of seeing me in it, evenings. He wants me to get a blue, but I tell him I'm too black for blue. Aren't men stupid about clothes! Though I pretend to Hermie that I think his taste is excellent, even when he brings me home one of those expensive beaded mantles I detest."

Bald, bare-faced, brave lying.

The two children arrived with mathematical promptness—first Horace, named after his grandfather Winter, of course; then Martha, named after no one in particular, but so called because Hermie Slocum insisted, stubbornly, that Martha was a good name for a girl. Martha herself fixed all that by the simple process of signing herself Marcia in her twelfth year and forever after. Marcia was a throwback to her grandmother Winter—quick-tongued, restless, volatile. The boy was an admirable mixture of the best qualities of his father and mother; slow-going, like Hermie Slocum, but arriving surely at his goal like his mother. With something of her driving force mixed with anything his father had of gentleness. A fine boy, and uninteresting. It was Hannah Winter's boast that Horace never caused her a moment's sorrow or uneasiness in all his life; and so Marcia, the troublous, was naturally her pride and idol.

As Hermie's business slid gently downhill Hannah tried with all her strength to stop it. She had a shrewd latent business sense and this she vainly tried to instill into her husband. The children, stirring in their sleep in the bedroom adjoining that of their parents, would realize, vaguely, that she was urging him to try something to which he was opposed. They would grunt and whimper a little, and perhaps remonstrate sleepily at being thus disturbed, and then drop off to sleep again to the sound of her desperate murmurs. For she was desperate. She was resolved not to go to her people for help. And it seemed inevitable if Hermie did not heed her. She saw that he was unsuited for business of the mercantile sort; urged him to take up the selling of insurance, just then getting such a strong and wide hold on the country.

In the end he did take it up, and would have made a failure of that, too, had it not been for Hannah. It was Hannah who made friends for him, sought out prospective clients for him, led social conversation into business channels whenever chance presented itself. She had the boy and girl to think of and plan for. When Hermie objected to this or that luxury for them as being stuff and nonsense, Hannah would say, not without a touch of bitterness, "I want them to have every advantage I can give them. I want them to have all the advantages I never had when I was young."

"They'll never thank you for it."

"I don't want them to."

They had been married seventeen years when Hermie Slocum, fifty-two, died of pneumonia following a heavy cold. The thirty-seven-year-old widow was horrified (but not much surprised) to find that the insurance solicitor had allowed two of his own policies to lapse. The company was kind, but businesslike. The insurance amounted, in all, to about nine thousand dollars. Trust Hermie never quite to equal that ten again.

They offered her the agency left vacant by her husband, after her first two intelligent talks with them.

"No," she said, "not here. I'm going back to Chicago to sell insurance. Everybody knows me there. My father was an old settler in Chicago. There'll be my friends, and their husbands, and their sons. Besides, the children will have advantages there. I'm going back to Chicago."

She went. Horace and Bertha Winter had died five years before, within less than a year of each other. The old Rush Street house had been sold. The neighborhood was falling into decay. The widow and her two children took a little flat on the South Side. Widowed, one might with equanimity admit stress of circumstance. It was only when one had a husband that it was disgraceful to show him to the world as a bad provider.

"I suppose we lived too well," Hannah said when her old friends expressed concern at her plight. "Hermie was too generous. But I don't mind working. It keeps me young."

And so, truly, it did. She sold not only insurance, but coal, a thing which rather shocked her South Side friends. She took orders for tons of this and tons of that, making a neat commission thereby. She had a desk in the office of a big insurance company on Dearborn, near Monroe, and there you saw her every morning at ten in her neat sailor hat and her neat tailored suit. Four hours of work lay behind that ten-o'clock appearance. The children were off to school a little after eight. But there was the ordering to do; cleaning, sewing; preserving, mending. A woman came in for a few hours every day, but there was no room for a resident helper. At night there were a hundred tasks. She helped the boy and girl with their home lessons, as well, being naturally quick at mathematics. The boy, Horace, had early expressed the wish to be an engineer and Hannah contemplated sending him to the University of Wisconsin because she had heard that there the engineering courses were particularly fine. Not only that, she actually sent him.

Marcia showed no special talent. She was quick, clever, pretty, and usually more deeply engaged in some schoolgirl love affair than Hannah Winter approved. She would be an early bride, one could see that. No career for Marcia, though she sketched rather well, sewed cleverly, played the piano a little, sang just a bit, could trim a hat or turn a dress, danced the steps of the day. She could even cook a commendable dinner. Hannah saw to that. She saw to it, as well, that the boy and the girl went to the theater occasionally; heard a concert at rare intervals. There was little money for luxuries. Sometimes Marcia said, thoughtlessly, "Mother, why do you wear those stiff plain things all the time?"

Hannah, who had her own notion of humor, would reply, "The better to clothe you, my dear."

Her girlhood friends she saw seldom. Two of them had married. One was a spinster of forty. They had all moved to the South Side during the period of popularity briefly enjoyed by that section in the late nineties. Hannah had no time for their afternoon affairs. At night she was too tired or too busy for outside diversions. When they met her they said, "Hannah Winter, you don't grow a day older. How do you do it!"

"Hard work."

"A person never sees you. Why don't you take an afternoon off sometime? Or come in some evening? Henry was saying only yesterday that he enjoyed his talk with you so much, and that you were smarter than any man insurance agent. He said you sold him I don't know how many thousand dollars' worth before he knew it. Now I suppose I'll have to go without a new fur coat this winter."

Hannah smiled agreeably. "Well, Julia, it's better for you to do without a new fur coat this winter than for me to do without any."

The Clint Darrow of her girlhood dreams, grown rather paunchy and mottled now, and with his curling black hair but a sparse grizzled fringe, had belied Horace Winter's contemptuous opinion. He was a moneyed man now, with an extravagant wife but no children. Hannah underwrote him for a handsome sum, received his heavy compliments with a deft detachment, heard his complaints about his extravagant wife with a sympathetic expression but no comment—and that night spent the ten minutes before she dropped off to sleep in pondering the impenetrable mysteries of the institution called marriage. She had married the solid Hermie, and he had turned out to be quicksand. She had not married the whippersnapper Clint, and now he was one of the rich city's rich men. Had she married him against her parents' wishes would Clint Darrow now be complaining of her extravagance, perhaps, to some woman he had known in his youth? She laughed a little, to herself, there in the dark.

"What in the world are you giggling about, Mother?" called Marcia, who slept in the bedroom near by. Hannah occupied the davenport couch in the sitting room. There had been some argument about that. But Hannah had said she preferred it; and the boy and girl finally ceased to object. Horace in the back bedroom, Marcia in the front bedroom, Hannah in the sitting room. She made many mistakes like that. So, then, "What in the world are you giggling about, Mother?"

"Only a game," answered Hannah, "that some people were playing to-day."

"A new game?"

"Oh, my, no!" said Hannah, and laughed again. "It's old as the world."

Hannah was forty-seven when Marcia married. Marcia married well. Not brilliantly, of course, but well. Edward was with the firm of Gaige & Hoe, Importers. He had stock in the company and an excellent salary, with prospects. With Horace away at the engineering school Hannah's achievement of Marcia's trousseau was an almost superhuman feat. But it was a trousseau complete. As they selected the monogrammed linens, the hand-made lingerie, the satin-covered down quilts, the smart frocks, Hannah thought, quite without bitterness, of the wine-colored silk. Marcia was married in white. She was blond, with a fine fair skin, in her father's likeness, and she made a picture-book bride. She and Ed took a nice little six-room apartment on Hyde Park Boulevard, near the park and the lake. There was some talk of Hannah's coming to live with them, but she soon put that right.

"No," she had said, at once. "None of that. No flat was ever built that was big enough for two families."

"But you're not a family, Mother. You're us."

Hannah, though, was wiser than that.

She went up to Madison for Horace's commencement. He was very proud of his youthful-looking, well-dressed, intelligent mother. He introduced her, with pride, to the fellows. But there was more than pride in his tone when he brought up Louise. Hannah knew then, at once. Horace had said that he would start to pay back his mother for his university training with the money earned from his very first job. But now he and Hannah had a talk. Hannah hid her own pangs—quite natural pangs of jealousy and something very like resentment.

"There aren't many Louises," said Hannah. "And waiting doesn't do, somehow. You're an early marrier, Horace. The steady, dependable kind. I'd be a pretty poor sort of mother, wouldn't I, if——" etc.

Horace's first job took him out to South America. He was jubilant, excited, remorseful, eager, downcast, all at once. He and Louise were married a month before the time set for leaving and she went with him. It was a job for the young and hardy and adventurous. On the day he left, Hannah felt, for the first time in her life, bereaved, widowed, cheated.

There followed, then, ten years of hard work and rigid economy. She lived in good boardinghouses, and hated them. She hated them so much that, toward the end, she failed even to find amusement in the inevitable wall pictures of plump, partially draped ladies lounging on couches and

being tickled in their sleep by overfed cupids in midair. She saved and
scrimped with an eye to the time when she would no longer work. She
made some shrewd and well-advised investments. At the end of these ten
years she found herself possessed of a considerable sum whose investment
brought her a sufficient income, with careful management.

Life had tricked Hannah Winter, but it had not beaten her. And there,
commonplace or dramatic, depending on one's viewpoint, you have the first
sixty years of Hannah Winter's existence.

This is the curious thing about them. Though heavy, these years had
flown. The working, the planning, the hoping, had sped them by, somehow.
True, things that never used to tire her tired her now, and she acknowledged
it. She was older, of course. But she never thought of herself as old. Perhaps she did not allow herself to think thus. She had married, brought
children into the world, made their future sure, or as sure as is humanly
possible. And yet she never said, "My work is done. My life is over." About
the future she was still as eager as a girl. She was a grandmother. Marcia
and Ed had two children, Joan, nine, and Peter, seven (strong simple
names were the mode just then).

Perhaps you know that hotel on the lake front built during the World's
Fair days? A roomy, rambling, smoke-blackened, comfortable old structure,
ringed with verandas, its shabby façade shabbier by contrast with the beds
of tulips or geraniums or canna that jewel its lawn. There Hannah Winter
went to live. It was within five minutes' walk of Marcia's apartment.
Rather expensive, but as homelike as a hotel could be, and housing many
old-time Chicago friends.

She had one room, rather small, with a bit of the lake to be seen from
one window. The grim, old-fashioned hotel furniture she lightened and
supplemented with some of her own things. There was a day bed—a narrow and spindling affair for a woman of her height and comfortable plumpness. In the daytime this couch was decked out with taffeta pillows in rose
and blue, with silk fruit and flowers on them, and gold braid. There were
two silk-shaded lamps, a shelf of books, the photographs of the children in
flat silver frames, a leather writing set on the desk, curtains of pale-tan
English casement cloth at the windows. A cheerful enough little room.

There were many elderly widows like herself living in the hotel on
slender but sufficient incomes. They were well-dressed women in suits
and Field's special walking oxfords and small smart hats. They did a
little cooking in their rooms—not much, they hastened to tell you. Their
breakfasts only—a cup of coffee and a roll or a slice of toast, done on a little
electric grill, the coffee above, the toast below. The hotel dining room was
almost free of women in the morning. There were only the men, intent on

their papers and their eggs and the 8:40 I.C. train. It was like a men's club, except, perhaps, for an occasional businesswoman successful enough or indolent enough to do away with the cooking of the surreptitious matutinal egg in her own room. Sometimes, if they were to lunch at home, they carried in a bit of cold ham or cheese, rolls, butter, or small dry groceries concealed in muffs or handbags. They even had diminutive iceboxes in closets. The hotel, perforce, shut its eyes to this sort of thing. It was a harmless kind of cheating. Their good dinners they ate in the hotel dining room when not invited to dine with married sons or daughters or friends.

At ten or eleven in the morning you saw them issue forth, or you saw "little" manicurists going in. One spoke of these as "little" not because of their size, which was normal, but in definition of their prices. There were "little" dressmakers as well, and "little" tailors. In special session they confided to one another the names or addresses of any of these who happened to be especially deft, or cheap, or modish.

"I've found a little tailor over on Fifty-fifth. I don't want you to tell anyone else about him. He's wonderful. He's making me a suit that looks exactly like the model Hexter's got this year and guess what he's charging!" The guess was, of course, always a triumph for the discoverer of the little tailor.

The great lake dimpled or roared not twenty feet away. The park offered shade and quiet. The broad veranda invited one with its ample armchairs. You would have thought that peace and comfort had come at last to this shrewd, knowledgeable, hard-worked woman at sixty. She was handsomer than she had been at twenty or thirty. The white powdering her black hair softened her face, lightened her sallow skin, gave a finer luster to her dark eyes. She used a good powder and had an occasional facial massage. Her figure, though full, was erect, firm, neat.

Yet now, if ever in her life, Hannah Winter was a slave.

Every morning at eight o'clock Marcia telephoned her mother. The conversation would start with a formula.

"Hello—Mamma? How are you?"

"Fine."

"Sleep all right?"

"Oh, yes. I never sleep all night through any more."

"Oh, you probably just think you don't. Are you doing anything special this morning?"

"Well, I—— Why?"

"Nothing. I just wondered if you'd mind taking Joan to the dentist's. Her brace came off again this morning at breakfast. I don't see how I can take her because Elsie's giving that luncheon at one, you know, and the

man's coming about upholstering that big chair at ten. I'd call up and try
to get out of the luncheon, but I've promised, and there's bridge afterward
and it's too late now for Elsie to get a fourth. Besides, I did that to her
once before and she was furious. Of course, if you can't—— But I thought
if you haven't anything to do, really, why——"

Through Hannah Winter's mind would flash the events of the day as
she had planned it. She had meant to go downtown shopping that morning. Nothing special. Some business at the bank. Mandel's had advertised
a sale of prints. She hated prints with their ugly sprawling patterns.
A nice, elderly sort of material. Marcia was always urging her to get one.
Hannah knew she never would. She liked the shops in their spring vivid-
ness. She had a shrewd eye for a bargain. A bite of lunch somewhere; then
she had planned to drop in at that lecture at the Woman's Club. It was
by the man who wrote *Your Town*. He was said to be very lively and
insulting. She would be home by five, running in to see the children for a
minute before going to her hotel to rest before dinner.

A selfish day, perhaps. But forty years of unselfish ones had paid for it.
Well. Shopping with nine-year-old Joan was out of the question. So, too,
was the lecture. After the dentist had mended the brace Joan would have
to be brought home for her lunch. Peter would be there, too. It was Easter-
vacation time. Hannah probably would lunch with them, in Marcia's absence, nagging them a little about their spinach and chop and applesauce.
She hated to see the two children at table alone, though Marcia said that
was nonsense.

Hannah and Marcia differed about a lot of things. Hannah had fallen
into the bad habit of saying, "When you were children I didn't——"

"Yes, but things are different now, please remember, Mother. I want my
children to have all the advantages I can give them. I want them to have
all the advantages I never had."

If Ed was present at such times he would look up from his paper to say,
"The kids'll never thank you for it, Marsh."

"I don't want them to."

There was something strangely familiar about the whole thing as it
sounded in Hannah's ears.

The matter of the brace, alone. There was a tiny gap between Joan's
two front teeth and, strangely enough, between Peter's as well. It seemed
to Hannah that every well-to-do child in Hyde Park had developed this
gap between the two incisors and that all the soft pink child mouths in the
district parted to display a hideous and disfiguring arrangement of complicated wire and metal. The process of bringing these teeth together was
a long and costly one, totaling between six hundred and two thousand

dollars, depending on the reluctance with which the parted teeth met, and the financial standing of the teeth's progenitors. Peter's dental process was not to begin for another year. Eight was considered the age. It seemed to be as common as vaccination.

From Hannah: "I don't know what's the matter with children's teeth nowadays. My children's teeth never had to have all this contraption on them. You got your teeth and that was the end of it."

"Perhaps if they'd paid proper attention to them," Marcia would reply, "there wouldn't be so many people going about with disfigured jaws now."

Then there were the dancing lessons. Joan went twice a week, Peter once. Joan danced very well the highly technical steps of the sophisticated dances taught her at the Krisiloff School. Her sturdy little legs were trained at the practice bar. Her baby arms curved obediently above her head or in fixed relation to the curve of her body in the dance. She understood and carried into effect the French technical terms. It was called gymnastic and interpretive dancing. There was about it none of the spontaneity with which a child unconsciously endows impromptu dance steps. But it was graceful and lovely. Hannah thought Joan a second Pavlova, took vast delight in watching her. Taking Joan and Peter to these dancing classes was one of the duties that often devolved upon her. In the children's early years Marcia had attended a child-study class twice a week and Hannah had more or less minded the two in their mother's absence. The incongruity of this had never struck her. Or if it had, she had never mentioned it to Marcia. There were a good many things she never mentioned to Marcia. Marcia was undoubtedly a conscientious mother, thinking of her children, planning for her children, hourly: their food, their clothes, their training, their manners, their education. Asparagus; steak; French; health shoes; fingernails; dancing; teeth; hair; curtseys.

"Train all the independence out of 'em," Hannah said sometimes, grimly. Not to Marcia, though. She said it sometimes to her friends Julia Pierce or Sarah Clapp, or even to Vinie Harding, the spinster of sixty, for all three, including the spinster Vinie, who was a great-aunt, seemed to be living much the same life that had fallen to Hannah Winter's lot.

Hyde Park was full of pretty, well-dressed, energetic young mothers who were leaning hard upon the Hannah Winters of their own families. You saw any number of gray-haired, modishly gowned grandmothers trundling gocarts; walking slowly with a moist baby fist in their gentle clasp; seated on park benches before which blue rompers dug in the sand or gravel or tumbled on the grass. The pretty young mothers seemed very busy, too, in another direction. They attended classes, played bridge, marketed, shopped, managed their households. Some of them had gone in for careers.

None of them seemed conscious of the frequency with which they said, "Mother, will you take the children from two to five this afternoon?" Or, if they were conscious of it, they regarded it as a natural and normal request. What are grandmothers for?

Hannah Winter loved the feel of the small velvet hands in her own palm. The clear blue white of their eyes, the softness of their hair, the very feel of their firm, strong, bare legs gave her an actual pang of joy. But a half-hour—an hour—with them, and she grew restless, irritable. She didn't try to define this feeling.

"You say you love the children. And yet when I ask you to be with them for half a day——"

"I do love them. But they make me nervous."

"I don't see how they can make you nervous if you really care about them."

Joan was Hannah's favorite; resembled her. The boy, Peter, was blond, like his mother. In Joan was repeated the grandmother's sallow skin, dark eyes, vivacity, force. The two, so far apart in years, were united by a strong bond of sympathy and alikeness. When they were together on some errand or excursion they had a fine time. If it didn't last too long.

Sometimes the young married women would complain to each other about their mothers. "I don't ask her often, goodness knows. But I think she might offer to take the children one or two afternoons during their vacation, anyway. She hasn't a thing to do. Not a thing."

Among themselves the grandmothers did not say so much. They had gone to a sterner school. But it had come to this: Hannah was afraid to plan her day. So often had she found herself called upon to forego an afternoon at bridge, a morning's shopping, an hour's mending, even, or reading.

She often had dinner at Marcia's, but not as often as she was asked. More and more she longed for and appreciated the orderly quiet and solitude of her own little room. She never analyzed this, nor did Marcia or Ed. It was a craving for relaxation on the part of body and nerves strained throughout almost half a century of intensive living.

Ed and Marcia were always doing charming things for her; Marcia had made the cushions and the silk lamp shades for her room. Marcia was always bringing her jellies or a quarter of a freshly baked cake done in black Lutie's best style. Ed and Marcia insisted periodically on her going with them to the theater or downtown for dinner or to one of the gardens where there was music and dancing and dining. This was known as "taking Mother out." Hannah Winter didn't enjoy these affairs as much, perhaps, as she should have. She much preferred a mild spree with one of her own cronies. Ed was very careful of her at street crossings and going down steps, and joggled her elbow a good deal. This irked her, though she tried not to show it. She preferred a matinee or a good picture or a concert with Sarah, or Vinie, or Julia. They could giggle, and nudge and comment like girls together, and did. Indeed, they were girls in all but outward semblance. Among one another they recognized this. Their sense of enjoyment was undulled. They liked a double chocolate ice-cream soda as well as ever; a new gown, an interesting book. As for people! Why, at sixty the world walked before them, these elderly women, its mind unclothed, all-revealing. This was painful, sometimes, but interesting always. It was one of the penalties—and one of the rewards—of living.

After some such excursion Hannah couldn't very well refuse to take the children to see a picture on a Sunday afternoon when Ed and Marcia were spending the half day at the country club. Marcia was very strict about the children and the films.

And so sixty swung around. At sixty, Hannah Winter had a suitor. Inwardly she resented him. At sixty, Clint Darrow, a widower now and reverent in speech of the departed one whose extravagances he had deplored, came to live at the hotel in three-room grandeur, overlooking the lake. A ruddy, corpulent, paunchy little man, and rakish withal. The hotel widows made much of him. Hannah, holding herself aloof, was often surprised to find her girlhood flame hovering near now, speaking of loneliness, of trips abroad, of a string of pearls unused. There was something virgin about the way Hannah received these advances. Marriage was so far from her thoughts; this kindly, plump little man so entirely outside her plans. He told her his troubles, which should have warned her. She gave him some shrewd advice, which encouraged him. He rather fancied himself as a Lothario. He was secretly distressed about his rotund waistline and, theoretically, never ate a bite of lunch. "I never touch a morsel from breakfast until dinnertime." Still you might see him any day at noon at the Congress, or at the Athletic Club, or at one of the restaurants known for its savory food, busy with one of the richer luncheon dishes and two cups of thick, creamy coffee.

Though the entire hotel was watching her, Hannah was actually unconscious of Clint Darrow's attentions, or their markedness, until her son-in-law, Ed, teased her about him one day. "Some gal!" said Ed, and roared with laughter. She resented this indignantly; felt that they regarded her as senile. She looked upon Clint Darrow as a fat old thing, if she looked at him at all; but rather pathetic, too. Hence her kindliness toward him. Now she avoided him. Thus goaded, he actually proposed marriage and repeated the items of the European trip, the pearls, and the unused house on

Woodlawn Avenue. Hannah, feeling suddenly faint and white, refused him awkwardly. She was almost indignant. She did not speak of it, but the hotel, somehow, knew. Hyde Park knew. The thing leaked out.

"But why?" said Marcia, smiling—giggling, almost. "Why? I think it would have been wonderful for you, Mother!"

Hannah suddenly felt that she need not degrade herself to explain why —she who had once triumphed over her own ordeal of marriage.

Marcia herself was planning a new career. The children were seven and nine—very nearly eight and ten. Marcia said she wanted a chance at self-expression. She announced a course in landscape gardening—"landscape architecture" was the new term.

"Chicago's full of people who are moving to the suburbs and buying big places out north. They don't know a thing about gardens. They don't know a shrub from a tree when they see it. It's a new field for women and I'm dying to try it. That youngest Fraser girl makes heaps, and I never thought much of her intelligence. Of course, after I finish and am ready to take commissions, I'll have to be content with small jobs, at first. But later I may get a chance at grounds around public libraries and hospitals and railway stations. And if I can get one really big job at one of those new-rich North Shore places I'll be made."

The course required two years and was rather expensive. But Marcia said it would pay in the end. Besides, now that the war had knocked Ed's business into a cocked hat for the next five years or more, the extra money would come in very handy for the children and herself and the household.

Hannah thought the whole plan nonsense. "I can't see that you're pinched, exactly. You may have to think a minute before you buy fresh strawberries for a meringue in February. But you do buy them." She was remembering her own lean days, when February strawberries would have been as unattainable as though she had dwelt on a desert island.

On the day of the mirror accident in Peacock Alley, Hannah was meeting Marcia downtown for the purpose of helping her select spring outfits for the children. Later, Marcia explained, there would be no time. Her class met every morning except Saturday. Hannah tried to deny the little pang of terror at the prospect of new responsibility that this latest move of Marcia's seemed about to thrust upon her. Marcia wasn't covering her own job, she told herself. Why take another! She had given up an afternoon with Sarah because of this need of Marcia's today. Marcia depended upon her mother's shopping judgment more than she admitted. Thinking thus, and conscious of her tardiness (she had napped for ten minutes after lunch), Hannah Winter had met, face to face, with a crash, this strange, strained, rather haggard elderly woman in the mirror.

It was, then, ten minutes later than 2:07 when she finally came up to Marcia waiting, lips compressed, at the Michigan Avenue entrance, as planned.

"I bumped into that mirror——"

"Oh, Mom! I'm sorry. Are you hurt? How in the world? . . . Such a morning . . . wash day . . . children their lunch . . . marketing . . . wallpaper . . . Fifty-third Street . . . two o'clock . . ."

Suddenly, "Yes, I know," said Hannah Winter, tartly. "I had to do all those things and more, forty years ago."

Marcia had a list. "Let's see . . . Those smocked dresses for Joan would probably be all picked over by this time. . . . Lightweight underwear for Peter . . . Joan's cape . . ."

Hannah Winter felt herself suddenly remote from all this; done with it; finished years and years ago. What had she to do with smocked dresses, children's underwear, capes? But she went in and out of the shops, up and down the aisles, automatically gave expert opinion. By five it was over. Hannah felt tired, depressed. She was to have dinner at Marcia's tonight. She longed, now, for her own room. Wished she might go to it and stay there, quietly.

"Marcia, I don't think I'll come to dinner tonight. I'm so tired. I think I'll just go home——"

"But I got the broilers specially for you, and the sweet potatoes candied the way you like them, and a lemon cream pie."

When they reached home they found Joan, listless, on the steps. One of her sudden sore throats. Stomach, probably. A day in bed for her. By tomorrow she would be quite all right. Hannah Winter wondered why she did not feel more concern. Joan's throats had always thrown her into a greater panic than she had ever felt at her own children's illnesses. Today she felt apathetic, indifferent.

She helped tuck the rebellious Joan in bed. Joan was spluttering about some plan for tomorrow. And Marcia was saying, "But you can't go tomorrow, Joan. You know you can't, with that throat. Mother will have to stay home with you, too, and give up her plans to go to the country club with Daddy, and it's the last chance she'll have, too, for a long, long time. So you're not the only one to suffer." Hannah Winter said nothing.

They went in to dinner at six-thirty. It was a good dinner. Hannah Winter ate little, said little. Inside Hannah Winter a voice—a great, strong voice, shaking with its own earnestness and force—was shouting rebellion. And over and over it said, to the woman in the mirror at the north end of Peacock Alley: "Threescore—and ten to go." That's what it said—"and ten. And I haven't done a thing I've wanted to do. I'm afraid to do the things

I want to do. We all are, because of our sons and daughters. Ten years. I
don't want to spend those ten years taking care of my daughter's children.
I've taken care of my own. A good job, too. No one helped me. No one
helped me. Maybe I'm an unnatural grandmother, but I'm going to tell
Marcia the truth. Yes, I am. If she asks me to stay home with Joan and
Peter tomorrow, while she and Ed go off to the country club, I'm going to
say, 'No!' I'm going to say, 'Listen to me, Ed and Marcia. I don't intend to
spend the rest of my life toddling children to the park and playing second
assistant nursemaid. I'm too old—or too young. I've only got ten years to
go, according to the Bible, and I want to have my fun. I've sown. I want to
reap. My teeth are pretty good, and so is my stomach. They're better than
yours will be at my age, for all your smart new dentists. So are my heart
and my arteries and my liver and my nerves. Well. I don't want luxury.
What I want is leisure. I want to do the things I've wanted to do for forty
years, and couldn't. I want, if I feel like it, to start to learn French and
read Jane Austen and stay in bed till noon. I never could stay in bed till
noon, and I know I can't learn now, but I'm going to do it once, if it kills
me. I'm too old to bring up a second crop of children; I want to play. It's
terrible to realize that you don't learn how to live until you're ready to die;
and then it's too late. I know I sound like a selfish old woman, and I am,
and I don't care. I don't care. I want to be selfish. So will you, too, when
you're sixty, Martha Slocum. You think you're young. But all of a sudden
you'll be sixty, like me. All of a sudden you'll realize——' "

"Mother, you're not eating a thing," Ed's kindly voice.

Marcia, flushed of face, pushed her hair back from her forehead with
a frenzied gesture. "Eat! Who could eat with Joan making that insane
racket in there! Ed, will you tell her to stop! Can't you speak to her just
once! After all, she is your child, too, you know. . . . Peter, eat your lettuce
or you can't have any dessert."

How tired she looked, Hannah Winter thought. Little Martha. Two
babies, and she only a baby herself yesterday. How tired she looked.

"I wanna go!" wailed Joan, from her bedroom prison. "I wanna go tomorrow. You promised me. You said I could. I wanna *go!*"

"And I say you can't. Mother has to give up her holiday, too, because of
you. And yet you don't hear me——"

"*You!*" shouted the naughty Joan, great-granddaughter of her great-
grandmother, and granddaughter of her grandmamma. "*You* don't care.
Giving up's easy for you. You're an old lady."

And then Hannah Winter spoke up. "I'll stay with her tomorrow,
Marcia. You and Ed go and have a good time."

Classified

[1924]

The New York Working Girl, 1924 model. Curiously enough, she hasn't changed much in more than twenty years. She has even, for the moment at least, reverted to the identical style in hats and blouses. And her ultimate dream, born of the war years, is touchingly the same.

&§ TO SEE MISS BOBBY COMET EMERGE EACH WEEKDAY MORNING FROM that sunless black hole which was her bedroom was to behold each day a miracle performed. Compared with it, the trifling business of the butterfly and the chrysalis was humdrum. It seemed incredible that any human process could have produced from this dim cavern a creature so blond, so slim, so radiant, so perfumed. Yet eight-thirty each morning, six mornings in the week, saw the magic achievement. So palpably the work of overnight fairies, you were not surprised to learn that this elfin being regarded food with repugnance.

"I don't want any breakfast, Ma. I'm late as it is."

From Mrs. Henry Comet: "Now, you swallow a hot cup of coffee, late or no late. Come home at night and there's no living in the house with you, and no wonder. Not a thing on your stomach all day."

"Eat lunch, don't I?"

"Lunch! Ice-cream soda and a hunk of Danish pastry, if you call that lunch. Lookit how your skin looks! Old as I am, I wouldn't insult my insides by any such stuff, day in, day out——"

"Oh, all right, all right! Bring on your cup of coffee, then. I never heard that was so good for the complexion. . . . Ugh! Lookit that kid stuffing a soft-boiled egg into her. Makes me sick."

That kid (being Miss Jeannette Comet, aged nine, known in the Comet household as Din, a corruption springing from her own infantile inability to pronounce her given name) regarded her fastidious elder sister with wide eyes over the upturned rim of her milk cup. She put down the cup to retort with scorn as scathing as the decoration of her egg-and-milk-rimmed mouth would permit. "Is that so! Then don't look at me then, Miss Smarty."

To this, Miss Bobby Comet, sipping her coffee with wry face, paid only elegant indifference. The very crook of her little finger, aloof as she held her coffee cup, registered contempt. Elegant aloofness was the keynote of Miss Bobby Comet's manner. Yet, five minutes later, on her way to work, as she descended the outer steps of her home (a walk-up flat) in West Sixty-sixth Street, New York, you saw with certainty that, elegant and aloof as her manner might be, Miss Bobby Comet herself was only an imitation of the Real Thing. A flawless imitation, a perfect imitation—but an imitation.

How, seeing her, you knew this, it is difficult to say. If, by some feat of ocular gymnastics, regarding her with one eye, you could, at the same moment, have turned the other eye on any young lady of about Miss Bobby's age and manner emerging from her home in, say, East Sixty-sixth Street, New York, you might have been hard put to have discovered just wherein the difference lay. Understand that East Sixty-sixth Street is an address. West Sixty-sixth Street is merely a street. Between the two, east and west, lies only that narrow green oasis known as Central Park. It might as well be a continent. Yet West Sixty-sixth is never more than ten minutes late in adopting the style, dress, and manner of East Sixty-sixth.

So you saw Miss Bobby Comet on her way to work garbed as was the whole modish female world of the moment. Smart, slim *tailleur* (ready-made, hers); silk stockings so sheer as to seem no stockings at all; gay vivid scarf; brilliant blouse; tiny hat set well back from her face. A uniform. Every week she had her hair done by Emile. It cost her four dollars and a tip. She did not begrudge the money. Regularly she earned twenty-five dollars a week—sometimes thirty, frequently thirty-five, what with the system of commissions and prizes used by the manager of her office. Miss Comet was employed in the Classified Telephoned Want Ad department of a New York morning newspaper. She always spent the twenty-five or thirty or thirty-five down to the ultimate cent. Usually she was in debt for a fur coat, a crepe dress, a too-smart hat.

From her wage she contributed five dollars a week to the family budget; generally was late with it and always had to be asked for it. Sometimes—but rarely—she brought home a blouse, a pair of silk stockings, some bit of finery for her mother, or a toy for Din. These she would present carelessly, almost roughly. "Here, I'm sick of seeing you going around with those old socks of mine, full of runs." There was something shamefaced in her giving, as in their receiving. It was their fear of displaying fondness—emotion.

Forty-nine girls, besides Bobby Comet, were employed in the big bright want-ad room. And they, too, were imitations. Their presence, and hers, in a business office was one of the most absurd and paradoxical sights to be seen in a fantastic and ridiculous age. Their clothes, their faces, their voices, their bodies, their very postures were amusingly incongruous viewed in these surroundings made up of telephones, desks, pads, pencils, files, blackboards, racks.

Up one aisle and down the other the manager walked like an overseer eying his slaves. Yet there was nothing of serfdom in their manner or glances toward him. They were capable, independent, industrious. They knew their business. Now and then, in a dull moment, they tossed each other a word of conversation. It was always reminiscent of the night before, and bristling with the masculine pronoun, third person, singular. Their talk in the washroom at the noon hour would have made the occupants of a westbound Pullman smoker turn pale.

To present Miss Comet, sketchily, would be to present the other forty-nine, or nearly. She was twenty; not too pretty; wise, hard, knowledgeable, slim, cool, disdainful; a lovely painted mouth; eyes that stopped you dead at the entrance, though the sign on them read "Come In." Imitation pearls round her throat; a heavy scent of *Nuit Noire* at eight dollars the ounce; telephone receiver at ear, pencil in hand, pad on desk, lips close to mouthpiece.

The room buzzed and hummed and crackled with talk. The girls' voices were for the most part rackingly nasal. They articulated with such care as to render their syllables almost grotesque:

"Astorierr Thuh-rrrreee—uh-levun."

"Well, can you lemme talk to the owner of the gasoline station?"

"No, madam, I am not trying to tell you——"

"Thirty-fi' cents a line——"

"Well, I'm sawry you didn't get any satisfaction. Don't you want to——"

"If you have a vacancy again——"

". . . the largest circulation of any newspaper in New York——"

"I said Astorierr Thuh-rrrrreee-uh-levun!"

In the year and a half during which she had been employed in the Classified Want Ads, Bobby Comet had cultivated a soft, lilting, honeyed tone, yet businesslike withal. It was one of her most valuable trade assets. Prospects, hearing it, rarely slammed up the receiver in the middle of one of Bobby's sugared speeches. That voice, and a certain soft insistence, added up the extra ten a week in commissions and prizes for her. True, she uttered the same cockney New Yorkese to which the other girls gave speech. They all said verse for voice, and earl for oil, and berled for boiled; when they spoke of ersters they meant the succulent bivalve; and the winged creatures in the park trees were boids to them. It was a trick of speech characteristic of Bobby's class and type, born and reared in New York. If you had charged her with this linguistic peculiarity she would have uttered emphatic denial of its possession.

"My verse! What's the matter with it? I don't pronounce my woids different from any other goil. You got a noive!"

There was something likable about Bobby Comet's hardness. Perhaps it was the amiable frankness with which she confessed it. For the code of Bobby's life might be summed up in the six words with which she commented on her mother's existence, and condemned it. "They'll never get *me* that way." This, as she saw her mother at her duties about the five-room flat—daily duties in endless repetition; dishwashing, mopping, cooking, sewing. Tied to the house by a hundred dull tasks. To Bobby, her mother represented the thing which she was fighting—the fate to which she told herself (though not in just these words) she would never submit. Lower-middle-class drabness; childbearing, penny counting.

Not that Mrs. Henry Comet was a drudge. Not she! True, she was a morning slattern, careless as to hair and apron and shoes. But in the afternoon you were likely to see her blossom in Sixty-sixth Street, on her way to the el station and her shopping, in the gayer shades of crepe, and in a blithe hat and suede pumps and silk stockings (discarded as too faded by her daughter).

There was nothing pathetic about Mrs. Henry Comet, seen from the surface. A plump woman, fifty, and looking less than her age.

Between the two—mother and daughter—existed, unknown to either of them, a certain enmity. Neither would have recognized or acknowledged it. But to Bobby, this middle-aged unlovely woman represented the thing she must not become. And to the middle-aged unlovely woman, Bobby was the creature she would never again be. So when Bobby said, almost venomously, "Believe me, they'll never get *me* that way," there sprang up in Mrs. Comet a resentment mingled with a protective maternal fear for what was inevitably in store for this cool, remote, disdainful young thing with her slim ankles and her bobbed hair and her assurance and her cruelty and her soft red lips, like a puppy's.

"Yeh, I've heard that smart talk before. You'll wake up someday, young lady, and find you've gone and made a swell mess of it."

"Like hell I will," retorted Miss Bobby Comet. "I'm no sleepwalker."

There was another phrase of which Miss Bobby Comet was fond: "I can take care of myself." Simple enough sounding. To the uninitiated the words might even smack of a sturdy self-reliance. But beneath them was much that was sinister. "I can take care of myself." A murky saying, as the girl uttered it, and one that went fathoms deeper than its mere surface meaning would suggest.

To comprehend its full significance one should be allowed at least a glimpse of Miss Bobby Comet between the ages of eighteen months and eighteen years. For eighteen months she had been known as Barbara, a name she later regarded as lacking in chic, and for which she had substituted the briefer and more dashing nickname. When Bobby was Barbara, and eighteen months old, she had begun to take care of herself. At that time the Comets had lived on the fifth floor of a six-story walk-up in West Sixty-ninth Street. Their present abode in West Sixty-sixth was one of elegance and affluence compared to that.

The Sixty-ninth Street flat had been two blocks farther west, which put it definitely in an unsavory neighborhood swarming with dark-skinned men, slatternly women, bedraggled and unkempt children. Sidewalks and roadway crawled with these latter. There were two small Comet children older than the infant Barbara—Bess, aged four; Martin, three. Din had put in her tardy appearance almost ten years later. The dingy flat building cowered in the very shadow of the great menacing gas tower that reared its huge bulk at the foot of the sordid street so near the river.

Mrs. Comet had no time to take the infant out for an airing in the ramshackle old perambulator that had already done double duty. So Barbara, in her buggy, had been placed in front of the house at the foot of the short flight of dirty steps that led to the sidewalk. The boys of the district swarmed the street, playing baseball and handball in the middle of the road, roller skating, smoking, committing all manner of devilment. Baseballs and handballs whizzed around the infant's defenseless head. Her eyes grew quick and wary. She developed a genius for dodging an oncoming ball as a seasoned soldier senses the approach of a shell.

In this environment, too, she learned to talk surprisingly early. Before she was two she had a fluent if somewhat unintelligible vocabulary which, if anyone had been able to translate it, would have been found to be made up of odds and ends of gutter jargon, the language of baseball and the street, gossip between slatternly women in aprons and run-down slippers whose high heels proclaimed them declassed finery. At moments the small Barbara would sit up in her baby carriage with its soiled pillows and its grimy blanket and hurl invective at the street urchins in baby talk, her absurd rosebud of a mouth uttering obscenities in cheerful unconcern.

Such had been the early environment of Bobby Comet, and of Bess, her older sister now married, and of Mart, her brother. By the time of Din's belated arrival the Comets had moved by slow degrees from the West Side near the river to the West Side near the Park. The West Sixty-sixth Street flat in which they now lived represented a climax in decent comfort. That is, for Henry Comet and Mrs. Comet. Bobby designated it a dump. The rental paid was seventy dollars a month. Henry Comet, foreman in a hat-band factory, earned twenty-eight hundred a year. Mart, the son, who now at twenty-three earned more than his father at fifty-four, paid his weekly board and made no comment, being a silent and somewhat sinister young man who went his own mysterious way. Bess, now married and herself the mother of two, lived in Jersey. In Bobby's eyes, her married sister represented the very likeness of failure.

Bess had liked pretty clothes, had owned them before her marriage. Yet now she regarded Bobby's finery with a sort of wonder, as though she had forgotten that money could freely be spent for such things. Strangely enough, there was little of envy in her face and voice as Bobby flaunted before the older sister some wisp of chiffon or satin, a new hat, an absurd pair of slippers.

"My!" she would say, just a shade of wistfulness tinging her tone, "I'll bet that took a bite out of your pay, all right." Sometimes Bobby, in a burst of generosity, moved by she knew not what in the sight of this harried, disheveled woman who had been her pretty, careless sister of a few years ago, would thrust some piece of finery into her hand. "Here. Take this. It don't look very good on me, anyway. I liked it when I bought it, but—I don't know."

"Me? Where'd I wear it? Cooking?"

"Lookit her!" Miss Bobby Comet would say scornfully to her mother after one of Bess's rare and hurried visits to the parental flat. "Two squalling kids and another about due and not twenty-seven yet. And did you see that dress! I don't see how she can let herself go like that."

An expression saddened Mrs. Comet's plump face. "She did look pretty fierce, poor kid. She used to be so dressy, too, Bess did. Wasn't a girl in the block could touch her for style time we lived over in Sixty-ninth. I don't know—— I suppose——"

Bobby's mouth drew itself into a hard line. "No sense in letting herself go like that just because she's married. Fred earns good money. She looked like hell."

At which Mrs. Comet right-about-faced in quick defense of her first-born. "Is that so! Lookit the way she's bringing up those kids. Her money goes into good spinach and meat broth for them instead of everything on her back. You have a flat to take care of and two young ones and you'd soon see how much time you'd have for style."

"Me? Not a chance, lady. They'll never get *me* that way."

"Going to marry a millionaire, I suppose, soon's you get time."

"I might, at that."

"I heard they're tearing each other's coats off, trying to get beauties like you to take 'em."

"Yeh! Well, marriage isn't everything, you know."

A steely look narrowed Mrs. Comet's still fine eyes. "Looka here, young lady. Don't you go trying to pull any of that smart stuff or I'll have your father give you the whaling of your life, old as you are, and don't forget it. And Mart'll have something to say, too. I don't want no Tiernan talk around this flat, and just get that into your head, will you?—if there's any room in it for anything besides clothes and paint and powder and dates."

By Tiernan talk Mrs. Comet referred to the widow, Mrs. Tiernan, who lived in the flat next door. Her daughter came to see her briefly every month or two. A strangely luxurious figure she made as she flashed into this block of cheap flats, laundries, bootblack establishments, garages, riding stables, delicatessens, basement groceries. The girl came in a great, dark, silent motorcar which, with its chauffeur, she invariably left at the corner. She was swathed in rich dark mink. A tiny, beady-eyed dog poked its quivering nose just outside the furred curve of her elbow. Even Bobby could never hope successfully to imitate apparel such as this one wore.

"She sure married something elegant," Mrs. Tiernan would explain after these visits. "He's a big bug in Wall Street and makes money hand over fist and gives her anything she lays an eye on before she can as much as name it. Married grand, my Ellen—Eleanore."

To this statement Mrs. Comet did not even pay the doubtful compliment of contemptuous reply. She could even feel a little sorry for the widow Tiernan. "Married my foot," she remarked merely.

There was about the widow Tiernan's mouth a loose look which accounted largely, perhaps, for Ellen—Eleanore's befurred state. No such look marred the forthright features of Mrs. Henry Comet. Which was doubtless one reason why Bobby went minkless. Not that Miss Bobby Comet was a Puritan miss. She perhaps knew exactly what she meant when she said, "I can take care of myself." Certainly Mrs. Comet and Henry Comet knew little enough of the girl's life outside the five-room flat. For that matter, their son Mart's social life was pretty much a blank to them as well. There they were, the five of them, in a five-room flat. Parlor, front bedroom, back bedroom, dining room, kitchen. Mart slept on a bed couch in the parlor. Mr. and Mrs. Comet occupied the front bedroom. Bobby and Din shared the little dark bedroom with its single window that stared blindly out at the brick wall of an airless court.

It was incredible that a family living in such almost indecent proximity —dwelling in such physical intimacy—should still be able to lead lives so remote and detached from each other. Each had a separate and secret existence into which the others did not penetrate. Even Din, the elfin late-born, had hers. Din was a quiet almost wistful child given to startlingly frank statements. She could play by herself for hours, pale, self-contained, a trifle malicious. Sometimes Bobby thought she hated her. Sometimes she had for her a feeling of protective tenderness that surprised her.

Take Mart. In some way, at manual-training school and at nightwork in a technical school, Mart had picked up a knowledge of the electrician's craft. A few years at a decent technical college might have made him a trained and competent electrical engineer. But the Comets had had neither the money nor the imagination for that. The boy was skilled, uncommunicative, somewhat sinister, very male. His social life he lived quite outside the family circle. Between him and Bobby there existed a sort of fond feud.

They addressed each other mainly in terms of contumely.

"What you made up to represent?" would be his comment, perhaps, on Bobby's toilette for the evening.

Any display of emotion he considered effeminate. For that matter, there was little or no demonstration of affection in the Comet family. The children had never seen a fond look or gesture between the parents. Mrs. Comet now met with rebuff when she attempted to take the long-legged Din into her ams. A caress between Bobby and Mart was undreamed of. Yet for one another the two had a certain hard and astringent feeling of affection.

Mart ate at home, slept there, sometimes condescended to a game of ball after supper in the street before the house with certain hard, slim young men of the neighborhood, like himself dexterous, swift, silent. He never took Bobby out. It never occurred to either of them that he should. Mart had a quick catlike tread, a good deal like an Indian's. He was a marvelous dancer. His telephone communications were mysterious. His outgoing calls were not transacted on the home instrument. These he consummated for the most part at the corner cigar store at Sixty-sixth and Columbus. You saw him leaning indolently against the glass door of the booth, a cigarette waggling expertly in his lips.

But he had frequent incoming calls. Mrs. Comet was sometimes exasperated by the young ladies who called up, and sometimes sorry for them. "Is Mr. Comet in? I'd like to speak to him. . . . Oh, isn't he? Are you expecting him? . . . No. . . . No, I'll call again."

When they asked for Mr. Comet she knew well that these high, nasal voices were not craving the boon of conversation with the sparse, dry, caustic figure that was Comet *père*. They wanted Mart. Theirs was little enough satisfaction when they got him. Mart's telephonic conversation was as tight and terse as Mart himself. It seemed to consist almost entirely of brief negatives. One could just catch the plaintive interrogation of the female voice at the other end of the wire. Always the rising inflection. The pleading note. It was met by Mart's firm negation:

"No, I can't tonight. . . . No, I'm pretty busy this week. . . . No, you better not. . . . I'll give you a ring, maybe, later'n the week. . . . No, I tell you I ain't. . . . Well, I can't help that. . . . No, I might go outa town Sunday. . . . Huh? . . . No."

Sometimes there was wrung from Ma Comet, out of sheer sympathy for the unseen female pleaders, an objection in behalf of her sex.

"Mart Comet, I don't see how you can talk so stinkin' to those girls over the phone. I've a good notion to tell 'em next time they call you that they're fools to waste their time over a bum like you."

"Wisht you would."

"Time I was a girl, they didn't go chasing the fellas like that. Telephoning all the time, the silly things."

"Time you were a girl, you never heard of a telephone."

"Well, and if we had of, Mr. Smarty, we wouldn't of used it crying and slopping over no fella—least of all no fella like you."

Yet she admired this son of hers, and loved him, and was secretly gratified at his indifference to feminine wiles. She knew that he would marry someday suddenly and without preliminary announcement. She dreaded that day, yet longed for it; never spoke of it. Mart was never home in the evening. None of the family knew where he went.

Miss Bobby Comet, too, mysteriously disappeared almost every evening. She rarely was called for, though sometimes a yellow taxi waited, panting, for her in the street. Its occupant, having rung the bell marked Comet, did not come up. It was unbelievable that Mrs. Comet, lower-middle-class American mother, thus allowed her daughter nightly to fare forth. That she should do so was typical of her class.

Bobby, like Mart, ate and slept at home. But, unlike him, she sometimes stayed home evenings. On these evenings she was given to washing her hair, manicuring, doing odds and ends of sewing and refurbishing of finery, performing mysterious rites before the mirror. Often, as her older sister was dressing for the evening, Din would stand in the doorway or perch on the bed, watching her as she made up her face in the pattern of the day—cream, well rubbed in; powder; an expert application of rouge high up on the cheekbones and near the temples; then a dusting of powder again. A scarlet cupid's bow painted on her lips, deceiving no one, and not meant to. A black line marking the plucked eyebrows. Nail polish. A generous spray of perfume on hair and arms. A dab of it just behind the ears and just above the upper lip, for preparedness. Din's eyes were round and owlish in the little face that was losing its baby contours and emerging into adolescence. She was mathematically aware of every pair of silk stockings possessed by Bobby. Her information regarding Bobby's pink silk underwear, her bottles of perfume, toilet water, cold cream; her mysterious and somewhat grubby array of scissors, burnishers, and various red stuffs with which she was forever smearing lips, cheeks, and nails, was complete.

To Bobby's surprise and annoyance she had said gravely, one evening, after regarding in silence her elder sister in the complicated art of making up:

"When I grow up I'm not going to put stuff like that on my face all the time."

"Oh, aren't you, Miss Nosy! And why not?"

Din looked at her sister, straight. She shrugged her thin little shoulders with a startlingly grown-up air. "Oh, I won't. Not by the time I'm grown up. I'll be different from you."

Suddenly, then, Bobby Comet saw herself ten years hence, old, done for, out of it, the bloom gone. Din would be twenty, fresh, different. Different from her. Already she was learning different things at school, wearing clothes unlike those of Bobby's childhood.

Dressed, Bobby emerged with an unwonted dash of genuine scarlet flaming oddly beneath the artificial coloring on her cheeks. She addressed her mother seated in the parlor window overlooking the street.

"Pity a person can't even dress in this house without having that brat nosing around. Sitting right on top of you. No more privacy in this joint than in the street."

Mrs. Comet turned from the window to eye her irate and dressy daughter. "Are they wearing 'em as short as that again, for h'm sake! . . . And what's eating you now? What's she done? What you done, Din? Tell Mamma."

"Nothing," replied Din gravely. "I didn't do a single solitary thing."

"Tell Mamma! Tell Mamma!" mimicked Bobby in a cold fury. "She's the one that counts. It's always Din, Din! Look at the shoes you buy for her and what you used to buy for me when I was a kid. Anything was good enough for me. Now she's got to have the toes just so and the heels just right, and everything. She won't have corns like me when she's my age. Look at what she gets to eat, and what I got! She's got to have her chops and her spinach. And at school! French! And special this and special that, and all this new hygiene stuff. You learned on me and Bess, all right. We sure got the worst of it."

Mrs. Comet met this outburst mildly. "Done the best I could for you with what I had to do with. Your pa never was a big earner."

"Oh, I don't know." This from Henry Comet emerging from behind his evening paper. "I guess I've always provided as good as the next one. Good enough for me, anyway, if it isn't for your tony daughter."

"This dump!" In contempt, from Bobby, on the wing.

"If I could of had this, time I was married, I'd thought I was in paradise," began Mrs. Comet, in reminiscent mood. "Two rooms is what we had, over on Tenth Street, and had to go to the downstairs hall for every drop of water. And thought I was lucky to have that and maybe you will, too, someday if you're not——"

But Bobby Comet had flung out of the house.

Mrs. Comet returned to her window. Henry Comet went back to his paper. Din pursued some quiet game of her own. Sometimes you saw Henry Comet, silent, sparse, dried up, regarding this family of his over the top of his paper. And his eyes were the eyes of a stranger looking upon strangers. Henry Comet had come of a good old Vermont family of the codfish type. Perhaps he, too, had his secret thoughts as he squinted up through his cigar smoke. Sometimes Mr. and Mrs. Comet and Din went to the movies in the evening. Frequently Henry Comet went alone. He liked romantic pictures, with deeds of dash and daring in them.

Such was the Comet family life. Theirs was the spendthrift and almost luxurious existence of the American working class. Ready-made clothes, white shoes, Sunday papers, telephone, radio, pork roast, ice cream, the movies. A somewhat sordid household, certainly, but comfortable, too. Bookless, of course. Extravagant with its quarters, its half dollars, and its dollars.

If Miss Bobby Comet had been less imitative and less adaptable she might have been more content. But all about her, in a luxurious city, she saw luxury. Seeing it, she craved it. Craving it, she reached out for it and got, now and then, a handful. Being fundamentally a pretty decent girl, and further sustained by the fairly solid background of the Comet household, she worked hard, earned her money, spent it selfishly, took what was offered, and gave no thought for tomorrow.

For the most part, she went about with married men. She drove with them in taxis. You saw her and other girls of her type dining in famed restaurants and hotels along Broadway, Fifth Avenue, and the Forties. She dressed well and in excellent taste. She ate prettily and fastidiously. She had learned to eye the rose-shaded room with a look of indifference. She had caught the trick of ordering one dish, and that very special and expensive. She had learned to say, "Tell the waiter I want lemon, not vinegar." She was an excellent imitation.

Her escorts were, as a rule, dull and somewhat paunchy gentlemen grown weary in the pursuit of business. Her youth attracted them, and her commonplace prettiness, her flippant tongue, her audacity, her superciliousness. She possessed, too, a certain bubbling quality most refreshing to these doggishly inclined gallants approaching middle age and secretly weary of the connubial bathrobe and the humdrum of *geschäft*. Bobby

Comet took what these offered and gave little in return. She was alert, greedy, calculating, frank. There was nothing pathetic about Bobby's position with regard to these gentlemen. They were the victims. She the despoiler. If they protested, she left them. There were always others. When she had been younger—sixteen or seventeen—she had gone about with boys of her own class. She had frequented the public dance hall at the height of the craze, where she and her boy had performed with incredible expertness the intricate mechanical steps of the day, their bodies locked in a strangely sexless embrace. She almost never now went about with such as these.

During working hours she and the other girls discussed their social triumphs with a frankness and unconcern that would have appalled their victims of the preceding night.

"Any good?"

"Oh, yeh. Dinner at the Royale."

"Show?"

"Yeh, Music Box."

"Again!"

"My third time. But I've seen everything else. I didn't stick through the whole show, though. I told him I had to get home and grab my beauty sleep. Was he sore!"

But not so much of this as to interfere with the work of the day. Bobby rather enjoyed her work. It had in it the elements of change and of uncertainty. Unseen faces at the other end of the wire. Unknown voices. Rebuff or success—one never knew which might be encountered. Certain regulars came to know her over the telephone, and she them: boarding-house keepers, landladies of rooming houses. At home she would occasionally comment on them, caustically.

"The same rooms that were warm and cosy last winter are cool and airy now it's July. I could die at 'em."

Bobby, expert in her calling, no longer took incoming unsolicited ads. It was her duty to search out possible advertisers, many of whom had placed their want ads in the classified columns of rival papers. Others had advertised unsuccessfully once or twice, perhaps, in the columns of her own sheet. These last she urged to insert their ad for a full week, at a decreased weekly rate.

Bobby was very good at this. Her voice was sympathetic, clear, firm. She had had two years of high school, and a business-school course. Her English, when she pleased, was grammatical enough, though at home she spoke the slovenly speech of the household. She rarely met with failure, hence her increased weekly wage. A seven-day ad meant a fat commission. A set of them meant a prize plus the commission. Bobby Comet used a form; a

code. Lips close to the telephone mouthpiece, she got her number; waited;
then:

"This is Miss Comet talking. . . . Miss Comet. . . . Yes. . . . I want to talk
to the proprietor of the garage, please. . . . No, I want to talk to him personally. . . . Tell him Miss Comet wants to talk with him." Another wait.
Always just a tinge of trepidation, which added zest to the game.

Then: "Is this the proprietor of the garage? I want to know if you have
succeeded in selling your garage. You advertised it for sale, didn't you? . . .
Have you sold it? . . . No, I don't want to buy it. I want to help you
sell it. . . ."

More talk. Arguments. A strong friendly note in the voice. Nothing offensive. Her voice encouraging, not too insistent, but firm. It was surprising
to see how often she won them over. But it was hard, too, and a good deal
of a strain, this throwing one's personality into the telephone and trying to
make it penetrate the other end of the wire.

Sometimes an irate housewife, called to the telephone and sensing a pos-
sible bridge invitation or a bit of gossip, slammed up the receiver on hearing
Bobby's dulcet statement or request. But Bobby was undismayed by this.
Failure today might mean success tomorrow.

"Mr. Meyer? This is Miss Comet. I see you haven't sold your cottage yet
at Jamaica. . . . No, I'm not bothering you—at least I hope I'm not. I'm
just interested in seeing you sell that little cottage. I want to help you.
Now, why don't you give us a chance? You won't regret it. . . ."

It was thus she met Jesse—or, rather, met him again. For, as it turned
out, he had been a fellow student of Mart's at the technical night school
and had even come to the house with Mart once, briefly. Bobby had been
seventeen then. She did not remember him. Disguised as a mere telephone
number, he had advertised a storage garage for sale, using the classified
columns of a rival morning paper. Immediately Bobby was hot on the trail
of the unknown. The usual formula: "This is Miss Comet talking, I want
to speak to the owner of the garage. . . . Miss Comet. . . ."

"This is the owner. Who'd you say? . . . Spell it."

Bobby spelled it, graciously.

"Comet? Say, I used to know a—— You got a brother Mart?"

"Why—yes."

"Don't you remember? . . . Well, what do you know about that! It's a
small world. . . . Yeh. . . . Well, that's funny." They laughed a little, grew
friendly at once. His was a clipped way of speaking, very engaging. No, he
hadn't got any satisfaction out of that ad in the other paper. No, he didn't
want to try her paper. No use throwing good money after bad. They'd
soaked him hard enough already. You see it was like this. He had bought

this garage, thinking they were going to make a boulevard of this roadway. Yeh, fella he'd bought it from said they were. Showed him the plans, and everything. And they were, too, only they changed their minds. Something about graft, or city hall, or something. Anyway, there he was, stuck with the garage, and maybe five years before they began work on the street. He wanted to get out of it and go back to his regular job, working for somebody else. Let the other fella do the worrying. He'd take less than he'd paid for it, just to get out of it. No, he didn't think he'd advertise.

That ended the conversation for the day. Next day Bobby called him up again. Well, no, he hadn't sold it. We-e-e-ll, yes, he might try it once. A week! Oh, no! Well, four days then. Say, it's that voice of yours, I guess. It's the voice with the smile that wins. Yeh. Say, what'd you say your first name was? Huh? Bobby! Say, that's a h—a funny name for a girl. Bobby said it was no funnier than his name for a man. Well, that's right, too. Guess they'd better swap names. How'd you like to try my name for a change? Jesse Lloyd Whiting. Guess his mother must have read it in a book or something. Call me Jesse. Just Jesse. Ha! That's a good one!

She sold his garage for him, wording the ad herself, craftily. It was he, then, who called her on the telephone. He thanked her. He was jubilant. His old job again. Little old pay envelope looked pretty good to him. . . . Tonight? No, she had an engagement. Tomorrow night? Sawry.

A moment's meaningful silence at his end of the wire. Then his speech more clipped than ever. All right, Miss Comet. Much obliged for your kindness. See you at church sometime (a phrase). My regards to old Mart.

He had hung up. Bobby remained staring thoughtfully into the telephone.

That night at the supper table, she spoke of him to Mart.

"Who? Whitey! Sure I remember him. He was a swell kid. Smart, too, only always getting it in the neck. Invented a kind of a tire lock and somebody swiped it away from him and he never got anything out of it. Say, I'd like to see him sometime. Tell him, will you?"

"How'll I tell him?" said Bobby, loftily.

Mart threw her a swift, hard glance. "Oh. Yeh. Well. Strictly a business acquaintance, huh? One of these mechanic persons, what? Deah, deah! Listen to me, wench. Whitey's got it so all over these fat cloak-and-suiters I see you running around with that you wouldn't know how to talk to him if you did have a chance, which I bet you never did have. And don't you forget it."

She called the garage next day. No, he wasn't there any more. This place has changed hands. She might try him at such and such a number. She tried him. No, he was out. Any message? No, she'd call again. Something about this sounded vaguely familiar to her. That was what the girls said who called Mart unsuccessfully.

Anyway, he'd probably telephone her in a day or so. They always did. She waited. He did not call her. Two days passed. Three. Four. A week. Suddenly in an idle moment one afternoon, she called him again. When she heard his oddly clipped speech at the other end of the wire her heart gave a queer little leap. She gave him Mart's message as an excuse. Then, this time, it was she who said, "Tonight?" That little second of silence from his end.

Sorry, but he was working tonight. The silence again, and, oddly, she felt her cheeks burning. Then he said, coolly and without urge, "How about tomorrow night?"

At eight o'clock next night he rang the bell marked Comet. He negotiated the three flights of stairs and the dim hallways, rang the doorbell, came in, and was introduced to the family. Bobby hadn't remembered him as being so good-looking. Well, he wasn't, exactly, but—I don't know. His eyes, wide apart. And young! Just a kid. Like Mart.

He was quiet and a little shy, and yet he was self-possessed. He made a little fuss over Mrs. Comet without seeming to. Mart had stayed home to meet him. Bobby thought the two of them would never finish their stupid reminiscing. Had he come to see her or Mart? She tapped a restless toe. She wished she had never started anything. He'd take her to a movie, she supposed, and maybe an ice-cream soda afterward, and think he had had a big night.

He stood up, looked at her inquiringly. "I've got a car downstairs, Miss— Bobby. That is, I suppose you could call it a car. It goes on four wheels without pushing. I kind of made it myself out of a couple of tin cans and a piece of wire and an old cigar box or something. It's got parts in it of every car from a Rolls Royce to a Ford. If you'd like to run up along the river somewhere and have a bite and maybe dance——?"

The evening was warm, velvety, starlit. The mongrel car wasn't so bad-looking, its bar sinister hidden under a smart coating of maroon paint. Bobby Comet felt suddenly young, exhilarated, and very, very pure. Occasionally, as they wound along the river, she sang a bit of a song of the hour. Once she was faulty for a bar or two, at the end of a chorus, and he corrected her, whistling it softly, clearly, and in perfect rhythm.

He did not talk much. He reminded her, somehow, of Mart; and she liked him for that, which should have warned her. But she knew nothing of the theories of the psychoanalysts. They danced, easily and wordlessly and tirelessly, in the outdoor dancing pavilion of a roadhouse. Bobby loved the feel of his hard, muscular, flat body. The tired businessmen were convex where Jesse was concave; and they were, furthermore, what Mr. Mantalini would have called demned moist and unpleasant. Bobby Comet sighed; but blissfully.

"Tired?" Jesse asked her.

"No."

His hard, lean arm pressed her close to him. But when she looked up at him his young face was set and stern. Between dances they ate. At the figures on the supper card she hesitated—she who always ordered with such insolent unconcern. He sensed this at once. He grinned engagingly.

" 'S all right. You don't need to be scared. I'm not broke. You take just what you'd order with your—regular friends."

Her regular friends. She looked at him through narrowed lids. "What do you know about my regular friends?"

He glanced at her clothes—her smart clothes that were almost just right. He looked down at his hands, which he never could quite free from the grime of his calling. She thought she knew what he was going to say, but he surprised her.

"I could tell by the way you danced."

"Danced!" She rather prided herself on her dancing.

"Yeh. Kind of cautious. As if you'd forgotten how to let go. Dancing with the fat old boys who're short on the breath."

A flame of scarlet scorched her cheeks that hadn't felt such warmth in years.

He did not kiss her on the way home. They talked but little. Yet she felt strangely soothed, rested, serene, and, somehow, light. His manipulation of the crazy little car was smooth, expert, flawless. He did not ask to see her again. She waited, looking up at him. She waited.

"Well, good night. See you at church," he said.

An icy clamp coiled itself around her heart and squeezed it dry. She hesitated. He said nothing.

"Call me up sometime."

"Sure," he replied, gravely and politely.

Almost in horror she heard herself saying, "This week."

And in equal horror, his answer: "No, I'm busy this week," Mart's answer.

She turned and went up the steps. He climbed nimbly into the ramshackle little car and was off.

Oh, well, she told herself at the end of the week, what was he, anyway, but a greasy mechanic. A kid. Yet when she came home at six—"Anybody phone me?"

"No."

Bobby Comet took to staying home evenings. When the phone rang she flew to it, beating the impish Din by a scant second. Her voice, as she answered it, was low, vibrant. "Hello! . . . Oh." You would not have believed that a voice could change so in a breath; become flat, lifeless, without timbre. "Hold the wire. I'll call him." Then to Mart, "One of your dames."

Once Mart said, "Seen Whiting since?"

Her heart gave a great leap. Her face was impassive.

"Who?"

"Whiting. Jesse Whiting."

"Oh—him. No. Forgot all about him."

Mart's cold young eyes narrowed shrewdly, speculatively, "Then you're the first girl ever has."

She fought the impulse to ask her question, and lost.

"Why? Is he such a heartbreaker?"

"Is he! Why, say! He taught me all I know," said Mart modestly. The obvious answer to that rose to her lips and was spoken by them, lifelessly. She took no pleasure in the retort.

She'd show him. If he ever did call up again she'd show him. Let him ask her to go out with him again and she'd show him.

A week—ten days—two weeks. Then, unexpectedly, when she had quite given him up, his oddly clipped speech at the other end of the wire. And then her own voice, with a deep note in it, saying, "Tonight? Why—yes— I'd love to."

"And," said Mrs. Henry Comet, two months later, "what's he earn?"

"Enough," Miss Bobby Comet answered.

"How much?" asked Mrs. Comet again, insistently.

Bobby's head came up defiantly. "Forty a week."

"My God!" said Mrs. Comet piously. "Where you going to live on that! And how?"

A look of triumph came into Bobby's face. "We were looking at places Sunday. There's two rooms at a Hundred and Eighty-sixth Street——"

"Oh, my gosh to goodness!" said Mrs. Comet. Then suddenly, "Why, that's grand, Bobby. It's kind of far away from us, and all. But it'll be grand, to start on." Suddenly the two women were closer than they ever had been. A something had sprung up between them, binding them together for the moment. Love and pity shone in Mrs. Henry Comet's face, transfiguring it.

"Sure," said Miss Bobby Comet, happily; and looked about the five-room flat in West Sixty-sixth Street. The dump. "Say, we couldn't expect to have a place like this. Not to start with."

Holiday

[1924]

*They amble up and down the Atlantic City boardwalk, little family groups
on a brief holiday, bored with one another, with the ocean, with the walk,
with the shopwindows full of blue embroidery and salt-water taffy and
white woolly rabbits. The complaint about this story has been that it is sort
of frustrating, it doesn't get anywhere and leaves a lot of loose ends. But
then, I've heard the same complaint about life.*

❧ IT HAD BEEN RAINING FOR THREE DAYS IN NEWARK, NEW JERSEY.
Newark is unlovely enough on a gay May morning. After three days of
March rain it is sodden beyond bearing. It was the rain as much as anything else that caused the Cowans to decide on an Atlantic City holiday.
That and Pa Cowan's bronchial cold and Evelyn's everlasting telephone
and Evelyn's children's noise and the general state of irritability and wasp-
ishness to which the whole family was reduced after three days of being
cooped up. Six—not counting the girl—in a seven-room flat began to cut
jagged edges in each other's nerves even if they were a devoted family.

And the Cowans were a devoted family. They spoke of it often. "We're
very devoted." They were always saying, "Let me do that," or "I'll go. You
sit still," and "Here's a nice juicy piece just looking at you. Don't you want
it?" Naturally they quarreled a good deal. Take, for example, Evelyn's telephoning. It was enough, Carrie said, to drive a stone image crazy. Still,
before taking Evelyn's telephoning, it might be well to take the family one
by one.

There was Pa Cowan, sixty-nine; Ma, sixty-five; Evelyn, the widowed
daughter, thirty-three; Evelyn's two children, Dorothy and Junior, aged
four and seven respectively; and Carrie Cowan, the unmarried daughter,
aged—Carrie, the unmarried daughter. Not that Carrie seemed to mourn
her maiden condition; nor was she reticent about her years. She was always the first to speak of these, and jokingly. She was quite comical about
her virgin state and said in a roomful of Evelyn's married friends, "If you're
going to talk like that I guess a young gal like me had better leave the
room."

Evelyn, after her husband's death, had come back home to live. It was
pretty hard, she told her old Newark friends, after you've lived in New
York for nine years, and had your own lovely things and everything to do

with. Of course, she never said this in the presence of the family except
sometimes when Carrie was there.

Carrie went about almost exclusively with married people. She made a
fourth at bridge or gin rummy. She filled a last-minute vacancy at dinner.
She bought and presented dozens of baby jackets, rattles, and teething
rings. She heard the intimate talk and the innuendo of the married women
in Evelyn's group. She cried gaily, "Not knocking anybody's husband, but
I wouldn't change places with any of you." But within her someone else
cried out, "Oh, God!"

You saw a woman in the late thirties with a rather swarthy skin like her
mother's—Evelyn was fair—and the figure of the unwed woman approaching middle age, rather flat as to bust and ample below the waist. She made
a trim appearance, though, and was able to say with her married women
friends: "I know I don't look it. Nobody thinks I weigh within fifteen
pounds of that. It's because I carry all my weight right here. No, it doesn't
show, thank goodness, but it's almost impossible to take it off."

It wasn't as if Carrie hadn't had her chance. There was a good deal of
mystery about it. When she was twenty-nine there had been a man, and an
engagement with everything announced, and Pa Cowan was going to take
him into his own business. Cotton goods. Then Pa Cowan had made some
investigations and the man was no longer seen, and Ma Cowan said that
Carrie had had a lucky escape. Strangely enough, it was hard to make Carrie see her luck. Red-eyed and blotchy from weeping, she had said over
and over, "I don't care. I don't care. I'd have married him anyway."

"Yes," Ma Cowan had retorted, "and been miserable the rest of your
life."

"I'm miserable anyway."

"Not half as miserable as you would have been if you'd married him."

"How do you know? Anyway, I'd have had——" She stopped there and
her face had twisted comically and tragically and her hands had reached
out into the empty air, clutching futilely after something that was slipping
out of her life forever.

Carrie worked in her father's office now four days a week. She was most
efficient. At dinnertime she talked a good deal about the things that had
happened in the cotton-goods business during the day.

"We sent out the city salesman with some swatches and about three
o'clock they telephoned and said, 'Look here, I thought you were going to
send your city salesman——'"

From Evelyn, "Junior, eat your carrots."

Ma Cowan: "I'd get a black faille crepe if I had any place to wear it."

"You go out as much as most women your age, Mother."

"Where do I go?"

Pa Cowan, spruce, a little tremulous, brownish splotches on the backs of his hands and at the temples: "Seems nobody stays where they belong any more. Run, run, that's all they do. The world's gone crazy. Florida and Bermuda and I don't know where. Sailing on the Atlantic worst month of the whole year, January."

Pa Cowan, in the cotton-goods business, wanted to go to Florida and Bermuda and he didn't know where. Oh, how he wanted to go sailing on the Atlantic in January! He said to himself, "Here I am sixty-nine, and nothing's ever happened to me." Pa Cowan had always meant to live the life of a Robert Stevenson hero, though he had never read R. L. S. But he had gone into the cotton-goods business at twenty-four and there he still was at sixty-nine. Another writer with whom he was unfamiliar was Mr. Thoreau, so he did not know that the line about most men living lives of quiet desperation was applicable to himself. He dreamed a good deal about ships and the sea; about forests and tigers and mountains and beautiful maidens, blond and slim.

Ma Cowan had always been dark and heavy. In the last ten years the silvering of her hair had relieved the sallowness of her face. She had carried her weight well, but it always had distressed her, too. That which in a girl of twenty-five had been unsightly and disproportionate was now in the woman of sixty-five merely ample, comfortable, and not unfitting. Yet Ma Cowan, all unsuspected—perhaps even by herself—still had visions of herself suddenly transformed into a slim wisp of gold and cream and roses; a lily maid; a wraith, all flame and chiffon. This while she knew that her waist even in a stylish stout had never measured less than forty.

The Cowans lived in Tichenor Street, which, to one knowing Newark, definitely placed them. Tichenor Street was old, respectable, middle-class Newark. But like many other old streets it was beginning to grow shabby and careless and down at heel. Its respectability was leaning almost imperceptibly toward that unfastidiousness which degenerates into sordidness. Just around the corner you already noted those grisly harbingers of approaching decay—undertakers' parlors, private hospitals, midwives' signs, delicatessens, cheap new flats.

Since her return to the parental roof Evelyn was always urging her family to leave Tichenor Street and take a stucco and tile house in the Forest Park section, or on Parker Street, or even out of Newark in one of the Oranges. With that brief taste of New York still sweet in her mouth that now was filled with ashes and wormwood, Evelyn was secretly and fiercely ambitious for social prestige. Pretty, slim, and not without charm, she thought of herself as presiding at small, intimate dinners, rose-shaded, delicate, reticent; of queening it at evening affairs, large yet exclusive, at which people did not begin to arrive until ten. She loathed Tichenor Street. She actually humbled herself in order to scrape acquaintance with people who might be of benefit to herself or to the children, Dorothy and Junior, fifteen years hence.

"We've always been a very devoted family," said the Cowans. "We live for each other. . . . I'll go. . . . Don't you bother. . . . Let me do that for you. . . . Can I help you? . . ."

Ma Cowan, Pa Cowan, Evelyn, Carrie—four strangers living together. All unsuspected:

"Come, Adventure," cried Pa Cowan, "before I die!"

"Come, Beauty," cried Ma Cowan, "before it is too late!"

"Come, Love!" cried Carrie. "I am starving for want of you."

"Come, Power!" cried Evelyn. "I have always dreamed of you."

On coming back to Newark, Evelyn had said: "Let me take some of the housekeeping worries off your hands, Mamma. I'll do the marketing and things. It's little enough for me to do, goodness knows, after all you and Pa have——" Red-rimmed eyes and a quick handkerchief.

But that hadn't lasted long. Evelyn thought it foolish to walk a block to save two cents on a head of lettuce. Ma Cowan thought it criminal not to. House-cleaning under Evelyn's regime was a fairly painless process, with a scrubwoman in to help and a man to do the lifting and climbing. Mrs. Cowan made of the house-cleaning period a St. Bartholomew's Day.

Even in the summer, the Cowans stayed pretty close to Tichenor Street. They said that Newark was a regular summer resort, it was so cool, and you could get out to the beaches in a jiffy any time you wanted to. Besides, years of thrift had made them cautious. But this Atlantic City jaunt of three days' duration had come about almost of itself. Rain, coughs, snuffles, nerves, the noise of children housed too long, Evelyn's everlasting telephoning.

In the last three days she had, it seemed to Ma Cowan and Carrie, said the same thing over and over a hundred times, seated at the little wobbly black imitation-oak telephone table and jotting down meaningless figures and curlicues on the pad of paper as she talked.

"Hello! . . . Yes. . . . Oh, hello, Daisy. Isn't that weird! I was just this minute thinking of you. . . . Oh, I'm fine, but the rest of the family's laid low. Colds. I'm keeping Junior home from school because he has a little—— (Dorothy, Mother can't hear a word when you pound on the floor like that. Stop it, dear.) . . . He has a little temperature and I thought I'd just . . . What? What did you say? I couldn't catch that last—— (Lover, take that out of Sister's mouth this minute! You'll kill her.) . . . Aren't they terrible! They're simply fiendish after being cooped up. . . . I wanted to get out to see the blouses that Bamberger's adver—— (Put that down! Put it down, Mother said! Put it . . .)" Crash! Wails. Tears.

Ma and Carrie had a conference in Ma Cowan's bedroom. "If I have to stand much more of this I'll be a raving, tearing maniac, that's all."

It was decided suddenly that Ma and Pa Cowan were to go away. Atlantic City. The ocean air would do them good. Out-of-doors all day. One of the girls would go with them. "Evelyn, you go." "No, you. It'll do you good." "You need it more than I." "No, I won't leave the children." "You're with them too much, that's the trouble." "The trouble with whom, please?" "Oh, nobody."

In the end Carrie went. The three took the eleven-o'clock morning train. It was called the Atlantic City Special. Suddenly the sun had come out warm and golden after the three dour days. On Evelyn's face, as she stood in the doorway of the Tichenor Street house, waving them good-by in the spring sunshine, there was a look of anticipation and of release. Carrie saw plans maturing secretly in Evelyn's eyes. Carrie thought:

"I'll bet she's going to give a party while we're gone. The girls in for luncheon—or maybe even a dinner with the husbands too, and that bachelor brother-in-law of Daisy's. And her own silver and china and linen unpacked for it."

They bumbled away in the yellow taxi toward the station and Atlantic City. Evelyn went into the house and shut the door and began to telephone. Junior and Dorothy were drawing with colored crayons. "My angels," said Evelyn. "Mother's angels. It's brightening up. You can both go out just as soon as it gets a little drier. Hello. . . . Daisy? . . . Listen. The family's gone to Atlantic City. . . ."

The Atlantic City Special was filled with holiday seekers. Plump ladies in black crepe, with sly diamond clips fastened on one shoulder to no purpose. Sleek gentlemen in spats and yellow gloves which they did not remove, and a great many early-afternoon editions of the New York papers. Pa had brought along the *Newark News*. Carrie wished he'd stop reading it, all spread out like that. The sleek gentlemen ordered sparkling water in green bottles from the buffet car because ordering charged water from the buffet car was the thing to do on the Atlantic City Special.

Pa Cowan, on a holiday, was no niggard. Seats in the parlor car. No stopping at one of the picayune ramshackle side-street hotels but at a great fantastic rococo pile on the boardwalk itself. The doorman and elevator attendants wore uniforms of French blue with scarlet lapels and pipings and facings and gold buttons and white gloves. Their splendor would have made a French general on dress parade appear somber. They rather overawed Mr. and Mrs. Cowan, but they stimulated Carrie. Their backs were so flat and their waists so tapering and their buttons and gold braid glittered so delightfully.

Two bedrooms, connecting, with a bath for each, and you could see the ocean from both of them. There was cretonne. There were dressing-table lamps with pert little silken shades and a queer ventilator over the door and electric push buttons labeled "Maid," "Waiter," "Valet." A little rush of exhilaration shook the three as they unpacked. The women called between rooms.

"I'm not going to take out anything except just what I need."

"Do you want to have lunch here or somewhere down the boardwalk?"

From Pa Cowan: "Well, I think you ought to stop fussing over those valises and get out. That's what we came for. I'll meet you downstairs right out in front there. And don't be all day."

Pa was quite masterful when he took his womenfolk on a holiday. A false courage buoyed him. He was conscious of a little feeling of lawlessness within himself, as were the two women. Ruled as they were by each other, bound by a thousand clutching fingers of family devotion, each longed to be free for a brief moment; to fare forth, to prance, to seek the unaccustomed and forbidden.

As they started down the boardwalk in the seaside sunshine of brilliant noonday, you saw a family of three: father, mother, daughter—middle-class, respectable, well to do.

"This is great!" said Pa Cowan. "This salt air. Makes you want to step out. Come on, you girls. Step out!" He himself stepped out with what he fancied to be a jaunty, athletic stride, his shoulders held stiffly back, his head up. You saw merely an old man, rather rheumy-eyed from the salt tang, jerking along with a stiff and springhalt motion that was at once comic and pathetic. Every now and then he said, "Ha!" and breathed deeply. "Ha!" He thumped his chest. "My cold's better already. I can feel it breaking up."

They walked. They rode in wheel chairs pushed by a chair slave bent double with the load of the three of them. The women stopped and twittered before windows spread with Madeira embroidery, with drawn-work handkerchiefs, with Japanese kimonos showing vivid flashes of tomato-red linings, with silk and crepe-de-Chine lingerie in pink and orchid and rose.

"There's a pretty one. Look, Carrie. . . . No, not that one. The third on this side, with the two-toned ribbon. That would look good on you."

"I'm too dark for orchid."

"I used to wear it when I was a girl your age. I remember I had a waist, time I was engaged, trimmed with this passementerie across here in a kind of a yoke—that was when they wore basques. . . ."

"Oh, come on! What do you girls want to stand looking at that stuff all day for? Good gosh, I got a notion to go on by myself if you don't stop gawping in front of every window you see."

It was queer how remote the ocean seemed. You hardly noticed it at all, lying out there so flat and blue gray. Perhaps it was because of the people passing, repassing, marching up and down, up and down, like dream figures up and down, or sitting fatly swathed in wheel chairs with grotesquely bent black gnomes toiling flat-footedly behind. Canes, postcards, balloons, salt-water taffy, nut fudge, souvenirs, get-your-picture-taken-in-two-minutes.

They had their late luncheon at one of the restaurants on the boardwalk. "Dinner at the hotel's all right," said Pa Cowan, "but no use throwing good money away for lunch. They charge you twice as much in a hotel dining room as they do here, and the food's no better, if as good, and no service at all unless you tip like a drunken sailor."

They walked back to their hotel. The old man abandoned his springy stride. He was frankly weary, as was his wife. The Madeira embroidery and the souvenirs and the kimonos and the new spring models were much less interesting when you passed them a second time. Mrs. Cowan and Carrie did not stop more than twice on the return walk.

"We'll take a chair this afternoon," said Ma Cowan. "I've done all the walking I want for one day."

"Call this a walk!" scoffed Pa Cowan. But his eyes looked fagged.

"I certainly do. And I'm going right up to the room and have a nap and so are you. It wouldn't hurt you to lie down either, Carrie."

Carrie shook her head. "I'm going to wrap up and sit out on the porch in the sun. Why don't you lie down in my room, and Pa in yours? You'll rest better."

They separated to meet again at half-past three. From half-past three until five up and down in a wheel chair, almost to the Inlet and back. Up and down, up and down swam the dream figures, marching, riding. Madeira embroidery, balloons, kimonos, postcards, salt-water taffy. And there beyond, the flat blue-gray expanse that was the ocean.

Pa Cowan remarked it. "I don't ever remember seeing the ocean as quiet as it is today. Look at that!" He waved a patronizing arm. "Flat as a millpond. You forget it's there, that's a fact."

They talked little. They had little to say to each other. They spoke disconnectedly, fragmentarily.

"This air certainly makes you sleepy. Funny, though. Laid down and never closed an eye."

"I see those plain tailored suits are coming back."

"That was Gloria Dalton we just passed! It was, too. I'd know her anywhere. She looks a lot older than she does on the screen, though."

"Getting pretty chilly now, towards evening. Let's have him turn around. I guess I'll get out and walk awhile."

"You've walked enough, Pa."

Carrie and her mother dressed for dinner, Mrs. Cowan in her faille crepe and Carrie in her black velvet. The dining room was etched with black velvets.

"Yours looks as good as anybody's," said Mrs. Cowan. "And it's last year's, too."

"A good black velvet's always good."

The orchestra lent an air of gaiety, but the diners were solemn and constrained. Americans taking their holiday heavily. Carrie cut loose a bit and ordered hors-d'œuvres of sea food; braised celery, shad roe, chocolate meringue. "Things I don't get at home." But Ma and Pa Cowan were cautious, as they had been at luncheon. They ordered accustomed dishes. The old man had scant chance to do otherwise under his wife's watchful eye. For nineteen years a chronic ailment had made sweets, starches, and red meats forbidden delights for him. Mrs. Cowan made quite a ritual of his white meat of chicken, his spinach, his stewed fruit and sawdustlike biscuits. Sometimes he rebelled, but the revolt always came to nothing.

"Now you know you can't touch that stuff," she would caution him. "It's poison for you."

"I just wanted to taste it."

"No. If you're hungry you'll——"

"I'm sick and tired of this stuff."

But she was firm, vigilant, inexorable. "You know who'll suffer for it. You're like a child."

Indeed he did resemble a naughty child as he sat at table, sulking, rebellious, greedy.

After dinner there was little to do except sit in the rococo lounge with the other black velvets and listen to the orchestra and comment and speculate on the others sitting so stiffly about on the massive and ridiculous couches.

"I'll bet she's never married to him."

"Look at that. Isn't that terrible! And I suppose she thinks she looks grand."

Pa Cowan shook himself impatiently. "What do you say we go to a movie? I noticed there's one just a few steps down. Can't sit here all evening and it's too early to go to bed."

They saw the picture. They often went to the pictures in Newark and were glib and expert in their criticism. The picture was taken from a classic with a medieval setting full of iron doors and turrets and winding stairways and spears and doublets and oak-beamed halls. It gave the star an opportunity to wear pearl-encrusted robes, and be rescued from the slimy monarch, and let down her golden hair, and ride on a milk-white palfrey, and sit on a chair with a Gothic back, all robed in cloth of gold and velvet and ermine, and change to the ragged, tattered georgette crepe of a beggar maid. The picture had cost two million dollars. The Cowans viewed it with coldly critical eyes. When they emerged into the lights of the boardwalk they said that it was a pretty fair picture.

The old man and old woman in their room and the middle-aged spinster in hers slept well after their half day in the salt air. But they awoke at their accustomed early hour and could not sleep again.

"You up, Carrie?"

"Yes."

"It's only seven-thirty."

The day stretched empty ahead of them. Walk. Wheel chair. Windows. Some desultory shopping. Madeira embroidery, postcards, salt-water taffy.

Mrs. Cowan stopped again before the window full of pink and rose and orchid crepe de Chine. "I think that orchid set is lovely. I wonder how much it is."

"What do you want to know for?"

"Oh, I'd just like to know. For fun. Wait a minute." She entered the shop—came out again uninformed. "The woman says it's to be auctioned off this afternoon with a lot of other sets, and table linen, and lace."

"Well, I don't see——" said Carrie vaguely. The truth is she was bored. So was Ma Cowan bored. So was Pa Cowan bored. Bored with Atlantic City, with the Madeira embroidery and postcards; with each other; with walking; with riding in wheel chairs; with the flat, blue-gray ocean and the seaside sunshine so hard and brilliant and false.

"Great stuff, this sea air," Pa Cowan still said from time to time, but his heart wasn't in it.

By noon they were snapping at each other irritably. Well, what do you want to do, then? Well, why didn't you say so in the first place? Lunch? Pa Cowan didn't think he'd eat any lunch. No, he felt all right. Felt fine. But he had had breakfast at nine instead of at his accustomed hour of seven-thirty. He had eaten two eggs. The man had brought him two. Simply wasn't hungry, that's all. No use stuffing yourself if you're not hungry.

"Do you want to sit with us while we eat? Ma and I'll have a sandwich and a cup of tea in one of these tearooms."

No, he didn't think so. Just sitting there at the table. There was an exhibit up the walk a ways that he wanted to take in. Showed how they made Happy Days cigarettes. Not a human hand touched 'em. Everything by machinery—rolling, packing, labeling, everything. He turned to go.

"We-e-ell," said Ma Cowan, reluctantly, doubtfully. "You sure you feel all right?"

"Never felt better in my life. See you at the room later." He was off briskly. There was a new lift to his shoulders, almost a spring in his step. His faded old eyes burned momentarily with the light of anticipated adventure. He actually did go to the white-painted building in which you saw all the processes in the mechanical birth of Happy Days cigarettes. He had said he was going and he went. But by one o'clock he had struck off down a side street away from the boardwalk and toward the business district of the city. He went at a brisk pace, his face almost grim with determination. The light of daring—of adventure—was now aflame in his eyes. "Got shut of those womenfolks," he said to himself with satisfaction. He stopped a passer-by to ask, "Can you tell me the name of a first-class restaurant or lunchroom in town?"

"I'm a stranger here myself," said the man.

Pa Cowan continued his walk, away from the ocean and toward the business section. He'd find something. He walked spryly. The streets were busy here. More like Newark. Streetcars and trucks and traffic policemen. On a window, in fat raised white lettering, he read, "Steaks, Chops, Oysters." In the window, nestling amongst the crisp greenery of lettuce frills, Pa Cowan saw the red and white of forbidden foods. He entered.

"Um—bring me a steak," he said to the waitress. "Cut thick." He indicating a surprising thickness with thumb and forefinger.

"That's what we call an extra steak," said the girl. "Cost you two-fifty."

"I didn't ask what it would cost," retorted Old Man Cowan testily. "An order of French-fried. Got some lima beans? All right. With butter. Cup of coffee. Afterwards you can bring me piece of that chocolate layer cake I saw in the case up in front. Uh, make it a pot of coffee, you'd better." He sat waiting for his meal, fumbling with napkin, with salt shaker, breaking up matches from the little white china holder. The hands with the brownish splotches on the backs shook a little.

The girl brought rolls and butter, filled his glass with water. "Some oysters while you're waiting? Steak'll take about fifteen minutes."

"No." There was a dash of unwonted pink in the lean old cheeks. He broke off a piece of roll, buttered it, pushed it away. He would not dull the keen edge of this adventure.

The girl came with his laden tray. She placed the steak before him. "Is that the way you like it? You didn't say, but I told chef medium. Is that all right?"

He prodded it with his knife. "That's fine. Fine!"

As he munched the forbidden food he resembled in a startling degree a naughty boy, his eyes darting here and there as though even in this remote corner he was not safe from Ma's watchful scrutiny. He devoured all the monstrous meal. He drank the hot, stimulating coffee with plenty of cream and sugar. He glanced carelessly at his check, left an almost ostentatious tip for the girl, stopped at the cashier's desk near the door, took a paper-sheathed toothpick from the glass holder. He felt rakish, free, expansive, wicked. The cashier was a cool and insolent blonde. The wave of her hair, the glitter of her nails, the carmine of her lips proclaimed her aloofness from such poor things as Pa Cowan. The size of his check as he paid it brought no flicker of interest into the disdainful face. And yet Pa Cowan, bursting with beef and buoyance, had the temerity to address this splendid one airily, thus:

"Well, m'girl, I guess that five-dollar bill will look pretty sick time you get through with it." He picked up his change. "Fine weather you're giving us visitors."

The girl disregarded him with a cold blue eye. Her look did not spell active dislike. It was too remote even for disfavor. Still, she was not a vindictive person; and weather conversation was, after all, one of the duties of an Atlantic City dweller. People—visitors—talked to you about the weather and you answered automatically. They expected it. She answered now.

"Yeh."

Pa Cowan emerged from the portals of sin, satisfied. He thought with some distaste of going back to his hotel. He had no intention of confessing. But he had Ma to face, and Ma had a curious trick of finding things out. Pa Cowan hated unpleasant family scenes. He hated to be caught in some petty crime by his wife. On such occasions she spoke of him to his daughters as "your father."

The room reached, Ma Cowan was not there. Neither, on further investigation, was Carrie in her room. Out on the sun porch, probably. He was drowsy in spite of the unaccustomed coffee. He settled himself for a nap. As he dozed off he had the queer idea that two hundred-pound weights of iron had settled themselves on his chest.

He had been right about Carrie. Supine in a steamer chair, swathed in a rug, Carrie lay in the watery spring sunshine on the hotel veranda, sheltered from the breeze. She was holding a book which she did not read, and she was thinking: I suppose this is doing me good, out in the fresh air all day like this. . . . Good—for what? Suppose it is! Then what? . . . I wish

. . . No wonder Evelyn's so nice to Daisy, with that brother-in-law. . . . Poor Ev. A pretty bum time she has anyway, lumped in there with us. . . . I'll be glad to get back tomorrow. . . . What's Ma doing, I wonder? Sleeping. . . . I'll be old, too, in a few years now, and I've never lived a minute."

She shut her eyes, but not in sleep.

Down in the baths on the second floor—separate departments for men and women—Ma Cowan, alarmingly red of face, was seated in a white-enameled electric bath cabinet, her head sticking out of the round hole in the top, for all the world like a guillotine victim on exhibition. The bath attendant, a plump, dark-haired, eyeglassed woman with a good-natured face and strong, spatulate fingers, was leaning sociably against the cabinet, watching its temperature indicator warily even while she appeared not to. She had seen these stout old women go off into a sudden faint when they weren't used to bath cabinets. Ma Cowan was confiding in her. Patients always confided in her. She could hear without listening, thinking the while of many other things. Ma Cowan talked on.

"And another thing I always wanted to do was take a bath like this and a massage. But you know how it is. You think you'll do a thing and then you never get around to it. I've always had a kind of full figure and if I could have done the way lots of other women do, take massage and baths regular——"

"Don't you think you'd better come out now?" said the woman. "You've been in fifteen minutes and over. Usually we don't——" She regarded Ma's plump purple face a little anxiously. "You feeling all right?"

"Grand. I love it. I can just feel myself getting thin. How much do people usually lose in a treatment like this?"

"Well," said the woman, "half a pound or so."

"Imagine! Half a pound, and no effort. Time I was married to Mr. Cowan I had quite a nice figure. Real trim. They wore those tight-fitting things then, and I could carry them off to perfection. Those days, hips were natural and not something to be ashamed of."

"Don't you think you'd better come out now?" She flicked off a knob that controlled one set of lights within the cabinet.

"I'll sit here just another minute with the heat off. It's funny how I came to take this bath. I saw the sign up in my bathroom advertising them. I was just going to take a nap. And I thought to myself, why couldn't I treat myself to something I'd always wanted to do? I guess what I had done before started it. Don't you get the funniest wild notions when you're on a holiday? I sneaked off from my daughter Carrie who's here with me, and I bought an orchid silk set—nightgown and panties and slip—that I'll never wear. An old woman like me. But I've always wanted one. When I was married they never heard of such a thing as crepe-de-Chine underwear. My land, no! Muslin with ruffles of embroidery, and high-necked, long-sleeved nightgowns. My married daughter Evelyn doesn't have any sleeves at all in hers. That is, she *was* married. She's a widow now. I don't know what I'll do with the set. Give it to her probably. Another thing I always wanted was a red silk dress. I think dark women in red always——"

"You'd better come out now," said the attendant, firmly. She wrapped Ma Cowan in a sheet and the treatment proceeded. Soaping, hosing, shower, massage. Ma Cowan bulked huge on the flat table. The treatment ended, she was weighed. Happiness radiated her. "I've lost half a pound!" and she stepped down from the scales, shaking the room as she did so. It was as though a mountain were to rejoice because a pebble had rolled down from its peak.

Up in her room she found Pa sound asleep and breathing stertorously. She lay down in Carrie's unoccupied room, feeling delightfully languid and drowsy. She thought of the orchid crepe-de-Chine set in the bottom of her suitcase.

Carrie, coming in at five, found them both still asleep. Ma had started up at her entrance, but Pa had actually to be shaken before he could be roused. Both of them, as the lights were turned on, looked queer. Ma's face was very red and she said she felt as though she had one of her headaches coming on. Pa's face was drawn and strangely yellow—golden almost, and with a greenish tinge.

"Don't you feel well?" the two women asked him.

"Sure. I feel all right. Why shouldn't I? Slept too long, I guess. Foolish. Come here to Atlantic City and spend a lot of money for rooms and all and then sleep your time away."

At dinner he looked queerer than ever. He ate nothing, though he ordered almost defiantly. For that matter Mrs. Cowan looked queer too, with her flushed face and her bloodshot eyes. "I'm just going to have a plate of soup," she said. "My head's beginning."

No one suggested going to see a picture tonight. They sat again in the lounge.

"I'd like to take a walk," said Carrie.

"You don't want to walk alone. And I've had all the walking I can stand. I'm going to bed early, with this head of mine."

"I'm going now," said Pa Cowan suddenly. He got up. "Man at the door says it's turned rough out. And a fog. Says there'll probably be a storm by tomorrow."

Mrs. Cowan sat a half-hour longer with her daughter. Then she succumbed. "I'm dead. I've got to go up. You don't want to sit here alone, do you, Carrie?"

"A little while. Until the music stops. I'll be up. I'll read in bed. I never get a chance to at home."

She sat there alone in a corner of the great couch. Little groups sat all about. Men and women talking, smoking, relaxed, companionable. Carrie sat alone, watching them with hot eyes. The orchestra was playing "So This Is Love." The musicians were not particularly gifted, but the violinist had the trick of making his instrument wail. When the piece was finished the room seemed suddenly peopled with ghosts. Carrie rose and went up to her room.

"Getting rough," said the splendid elevator attendant, looking like a Coldstream Guard.

Carrie went into her own room. She heard her mother moving about next door. She opened the connecting door and stood a moment in the doorway. As she did so her mother thrust something hastily out of sight, turned toward her, her face redder than ever.

"My land, you scared me to death! I didn't hear you come in." She was in robe and slippers. She nodded toward the bed. "He's sleeping again. He was asleep when I came in and here it's only ten o'clock." The old man was breathing heavily.

"Out-of-doors so much," said Carrie vaguely. "Good night." She shut the door. She undressed slowly, washed some silk stockings, creamed her nails and the little fine lines under her eyes. Once in bed, she picked up the book that had failed to hold her in the afternoon. She read a page or two with her eyes only.

Suddenly she found herself listening. She was conscious of listening to something like a slow and regular drumbeat. Beat—beat—beat—went something pulselike, insistent. The sea. The great gray-blue waste that had irritated her so by day lying there beyond the boardwalk, so flat and smooth, like a backdrop in a theater. It had made her restless and moody. And now suddenly it had wakened. Boom—boom—boom. A drum, calling her. She turned out her bed light and went to the window in her bare feet. She shaded her eyes with her cupped hands and looked out. Strange how much nearer it seemed from her high window than it had been when she was passing it by day and on a level with it. Now, a great black beast, it lay below her window, calling to her.

She went back to bed. Lay there, listening. She found herself timing this pulsing sound with the beat of her own heart. She shut her eyes, very wide awake. Boom. Boom. Boom. Surging that fused with her heart. Between beats she could hear the unlovely sounds—those chokings, splutterings, in-halations, exhausts, and whistles—which marked her father's tryst with the nocturnal fairy. She listened closer to catch the sound of her mother's qui-eter breathing—that indomitable woman, her mother.

She lay there a moment longer. Then she got up quietly and dressed without turning on the light. She put on her long cloth coat and her round felt hat. She was very cunning and deft about it, as though she were in the habit of stealing out at night—as though for days, for years, she had planned this slipping out at night—as perhaps she had. Fully dressed, she began to open her door slowly, slowly, timing each turn of the knob and widening of the crack with the beat—beat—beat of the drum. Softly, softly. Sometimes the beat of the drum and the terrific snore from the next room came at the same time. She made great headway when this happened. She was out! She was out in the red-carpeted corridor. She pressed the elevator button. When the door was flung open she was a little afraid to face the surprise of the blue and gold and scarlet Coldstream Guard. But he evi-dently found nothing unusual in the sight of this plain woman in her heavy dark coat and small close hat bound for a walk at eleven at night. His flat, tapering back unbent just a little.

"Out for a nightcap?" said this splendid creature.

"Nightcap?"

"Yeh. 'S what we call a late stroll on the walk to make you sleep."

"Oh, yes!" said Carrie gratefully. "Yes. I couldn't get to sleep."

" 'S the best time, now is, when the crowd is gone and you got the works to yourself."

The door was flung splendidly open. She was out. Pearly gray chiffon veiled the walk, the ocean, the lights, the great turreted hotels. Fog. And beyond it the beat of the drum. A gold and mauve aura hung about each street lamp. The walk was black and slippery with moisture.

She began to walk briskly away from the hotel. She breathed deeply, feeling suddenly free, exhilarated, happy, almost young. The Atlantic City of the daylight—the shops, the Madeira embroidery, the balloons, the post-cards, the salt-water taffy, the Japanese kimonos, the dream people swim-ming up and down, up and down—all had vanished. Now there were only the ocean and the fog. The drumbeat and the banner. She walked perhaps a mile, happily. She turned, came back. Her cheeks felt fresh and cool, as though color had been whipped into them. Her eyes felt bright. She swerved suddenly and went to the railing that separated walk from beach. She leaned on her folded arms, staring out into the blackness—beyond. Boom—boom—boom. Come—come—come. You—you—you.

"Cer'nly is some foggy night," said a voice beside her. A man's voice.

"God pity the lads at sea on a night like this, say I." He laughed a little uncertainly.

A tall man. Broad-shouldered. A rakish cap pulled down over his eyes. A great overcoat. The scarlet eye of a cigarette blinking down at her. Carrie laughed too, and was surprised to hear her own laugh. She looked up at him, again faced the ocean, waited. Well, this was what happened to you when you walked alone on the boardwalk in Atlantic City at midnight. And why not? She waited as an experienced woman would have waited. Something told her that this was the thing to do.

"Out alone, girlie?"

Girlie. "Yes, I came out for a little nightcap. A walk."

"Say, that's a good one. Nightcap. That's a new one." He laughed appreciatively. His shoulder in the great rough coat just touched her arm. She did not move away. "That's a great little idea, I'll say."

"Nobody else seems to have thought of it," said Carrie. "I walked almost a mile and hardly met a soul."

"Afraid of the fog, I guess. I like it. The foggier the better. Give me a foggy night and a strange road and my car to drive and I'm happy. Some hate it, but not me."

"Oh, I don't know about driving in the fog!" How easy it was, this conversation. His car. He probably didn't have one. Just talk.

"Like to try it?"

"Try it? How do you mean?"

"Take a little run tonight in the fog. I know a little place between here and Philly where we can get something——"

She felt a little breathless. She must have time.

"Are—are you from Philadelphia?"

"Among other places. Florida, Philadelphia, California, Europe. A few of the places I'm from. Where're you from, girlie?" He leaned closer. She did not move away.

Newark. She could not bring herself to say Newark. Not after Florida, California, Europe. "I'm from New York."

"Yeh? New York's all right if you like it." They were silent a moment. "Say, that hat certainly's got me stumped. How can I tell whether you're a blonde or a brunette with that hat down over your head like that?"

"Perhaps it's just as well," said Carrie, and laughed. "Which do you like?"

"Brunette," said the man.

Carrie pulled off her hat and laughed up at him, her head thrown back, her face sparkling. "I aim to please," she retorted. Suddenly, swiftly, the great rough coat sleeve was about her. The man leaned down, breathing queerly, almost sobbingly. He kissed her. A long kiss. And Carrie's mind, working clearly, said: "So this is it. Well, I don't even like it. It feels as if I had fallen face down into a plate of wet sausages."

She jerked herself free.

"You're not sore, are you, girlie?"

"No." She put on her hat.

"Come on, take a ride with me in the fog. A nightcap." He laughed.

"Where's your car?"

"In the garage. It'll only take a minute. If you'll wait for me at the foot of this street——"

"I don't believe you've got a car."

"Don't believe! Why, say, come along with me to the garage, then. What do you think I drove to Atlantic City in? What do you think I'm going to Florida in next Tuesday, huh?"

"I'll come to the garage with you."

She was not at all clear in her mind as to her future course of action. Not that it mattered. Too careful all her life, that was the trouble with her. You had to meet things halfway.

The garage was a great cavern in which rubber-booted giants armed with hose and sponge were slaves to steeds of steel and enamel. She waited, a little fearfully, in the doorway. The man seemed taller, more masterful than ever now. He strode over to a huge and powerful car whose hooded engine loomed enormous under the garage lights.

"Taking the bus out," she heard him say to one of the men. "How's she fixed for gas?" And then something about valves. The garage attendant lifted the hood. Together the two men peered in. She could not hear what the garageman was saying. The noise of the hose, suddenly turned on a car, drowned his utterance. What he said was: "You taking out that dame? Say, your boss finds out you been joy riding again in the car I bet he fires you. He was shooting off this morning only about where had the gas went to that was put in yesterday."

"Shut up!" said the other, and climbed into the driver's seat as the mechanic clamped the hood.

As she saw this, terror possessed Carrie; and with terror, reason returned to her. The car began to throb gently. Without a last backward glance Carrie turned, fled, flew up the short street to the boardwalk.

"Well," said the elevator man—oh, the dear, accustomed elevator man in his friendly, homely blue and gold and scarlet! "You must of had quite a walk at that."

"Yes. Quite a walk." She could even smile.

She unlocked her door gently, gently, timing the sounds again with the beats of the faraway drum. She opened her door. Her room was flooded with light, so, too, was the room seen just beyond. Her mother, in robe and nightgown, was standing in the middle of the room. She was looking very wild and old and vast. A strange man, cool and competent and eyeglassed, stood at the bedside.

"Your father! He's been terribly sick. I thought he was dying. I don't know what—I had my headache and woke up all of a sudden and heard him breathing funny——" She stopped, regarded Carrie piercingly. "Where've you been, Carrie Cowan, I'd like to know? This time of night! And your father almost dying!"

Carrie took off her hat. Little drops of moisture, born of the fog, beaded her hair, her lashes. Her cheeks were pink. "I couldn't sleep. I took a walk. I——" Terror shook her. She went to the bed. An old, old man looked up at her with eyes that had known recent and terrible anguish. "Pa! Pa, you all right now?" She felt a sudden rush of tenderness toward him, so yellow and frail and suffering. The old man nodded; even attempted a grimacing smile.

"I'm fine. Never felt better in my life. Must have et something didn't agree with me, that's all."

"It's those two eggs," said Ma Cowan, "for breakfast." He looked at her gratefully.

The strange man at the bedside finished writing on a little pad. "I'll just leave this to be filled on my way down and the bellboy will bring it up. He'll be all right now. Won't you, sir? That's right. Only don't do that again, young man." He smiled with professional cheerfulness at the drawn old face on the pillow.

"Can we go home tomorrow?" inquired Ma Cowan, fearfully. "Will he be able?"

"I think so. I think so. I'll look in at about ten tomorrow morning."

He was gone. The old woman came to the bedside, put one plump hand on the lean shoulder under the bedclothes. "You scared my headache away," she said. She turned suddenly to where Carrie stood, drooping. "Crazy thing for you to do. Run out at this hour the night. What possessed you to do a thing like that?"

Carrie touched the crown of her hat with her forefinger. The hat was damp. She looked at it dully. "Oh, I don't know. You think of foolish things on a holiday that you wouldn't do at home. You get a kind of crazy feeling."

The old man stirred in the bed. The old woman put a hand to her head absently, as though the headache had not after all quite vanished.

By three next day they were back in Tichenor Street, Newark, these holiday seekers. Evelyn welcomed them. The children, Dorothy and Junior, fell upon their balloons and postcards and salt-water taffy with shouts and boundings. Evelyn, called to the telephone ten minutes after their return, could hardly hear for the noise.

"Hello! . . . Oh, it's you, Daisy. . . . Yes, it was nice. I'm glad you enjoyed it. . . . Uh, not now. Not now. . . . Yes, they're just back. . . . They say they had a fine time. (Junior, you oughtn't to eat that taffy with your brace. You'll break it as sure as anything.) . . . Oh, well, I suppose, they didn't do anything they couldn't do at home, but it's the—— (Sister, you mustn't sit on Lover's balloon. No. No! No, I say!) . . . She's sitting on Junior's balloon and I just know . . . I was saying it's the change that does you good. I don't care about Atlantic myself. Just the ocean and taffy and postcards and those hotels and Madeira embroi—— (There! I knew it! Don't cry now. It won't do you any good to cry now. Mother warned you.)"

Our Very Best People
[1924]

Here is an example of book-length material wasted in a short story. The story of the Tune twins could have been a novel of Western American railroad aristocracy. By this is not meant merely one of those galloping chronicles which might roughly be outlined as From Section Hand to Railroad President. Certainly there is a great and lusty and even important novel in the story of the people who built America's railroads. And when I say built, I mean with pick and shovel—foreman's shanty and brakeman's lantern, Harvey girl and switchman. You find these and their descendants now listed as First Families in the society columns of Kansas City, Omaha, Lincoln, Denver, San Francisco. Full of vitality and color and toughness and evil and romance it could be, that story.

⊰§ IF RUTGER G. TUNE HAD WAITED TWO WEEKS LONGER TO DIE HE would have had to do a lot of explaining. And he always had hated explanations. They bored him. He died as he had lived, soldier of fortune that he was, with his spats on. Not only that, they were fawn spats, setting off a gray morning suit further enhanced by a flower in the buttonhole. There were few other—if any—fawn spats, gray morning suits, or beflowered buttonholes in Kansas City, Missouri, twenty years ago.

A plump, high-colored, well-dressed, middle-aged man, he had just passed debonairly through the gates of the Kansas City Union Station on his way to take the eastbound train, a deferential dusky porter ahead of him, when suddenly he crumpled, sank, and became a mere heap of haberdashery on the station platform. Confusion, crowds, telegrams. And the Tune twins, already motherless, were summoned home from Vassar to find themselves pretty much in the position of the Two Orphans of drama fame, so far as finances and future were concerned.

One week after the funeral: "But what did he *do* with it?" demanded Hilda Tune, the beauty. Her tone was perhaps excusably querulous considering that she and her sister Hannah now found themselves possessed of exactly nine hundred and twenty dollars each, the lawyers having just finished explaining.

"He didn't have it," replied Hannah, the plain twin, composedly.

"Didn't have it! What nonsense, Hannah! What did we live on all these years! Our education and clothes, and this huge house, and Father's wine and food and horses and . . ." Her voice trailed off. Then again, in help-less wrath, "What did we *live* on?"

"Bunco," said Hannah.

Even then, stricken though she was, Hilda had the good taste to be of-fended. "I wish you wouldn't use words like that, Hannah. And I do wish you wouldn't be any more vulgar than you can help."

Hannah was good-humored enough about it, as always. "I'm not being a bit more vulgar than I can help. Besides, it's in the dictionary. Let's not quarrel now, Hilda. I simply meant that I don't think Father had much money, really, in the last few years. I think he must have been worrying for quite a while about how he was going to explain things. He'd have had to explain in another week or two. And he knew it couldn't be done."

"But Mother left heaps. And there was all that stock in the packing company."

"Yes, but Father squandered heaps. The stock must have gone years ago."

"But it was ours! Lots of it was ours! Yours and mine."

Hannah smiled grimly. "You must have understood something of what Mr. Patterson and that other lawyer meant when they said that Father had been unwise in his handling of the money. He gambled, among other things. So the money went, and the stocks went, and this house is mort-gaged right up to the shingles. Father died owing practically everybody in Kansas City from the First National Bank to the boy who delivers the eve-ning paper. We haven't any real right to this precious nine hundred and twenty dollars they've bestowed on us. . . . Well, if we've learned anything practical at school, Hilda, my gal, now's a grand chance to prove it."

An Eastern finishing school, followed by Vassar, had rarely turned out a more unfinished product than Hannah Tune, who was, she would explain to you, the elder of the Tune twins. Hannah resembled her simple, straightforward, plain-featured mother, who had been the Kansas City heiress of the stockyards stock. Hilda was undeniably her father's daughter —authentic offspring of Rutger G. Tune, of the Massachusetts Tunes who were born to be ancestors as some people are born singers, writers, drunk-ards. A true Tune, posing for a casual snapshot, always emerged looking like a portrait by Sir Joshua Reynolds.

Rutger G. Tune, having bestowed upon the plain Kansas City heiress his name, the charm of his occasional company, and the twin daughters, had considered his obligations ended and had set about enjoying what there was to enjoy in this Midwestern town to which he had come. Kansas City, though it sniggered at his lemon-colored spider phaeton with its two smart trotters, and a flunky seated up behind, really felt a thrill of pride in the picture it all made as Tune in his cream covert coat, perched high on the fawn-cushioned box, his whip held at an angle of ninety, his hat just a little on one side, clipped briskly down Gilham Boulevard and whirled into the Paseo at an hour when the rest of Kansas City's adult male population was turning nickels into mickles as fast as it could. He practically represented the city's male leisure class.

From his lofty vantage he would greet the townspeople with that specious air of democracy peculiar to the born snob. "H'are you, Lindsey! . . . 'Morning, Mrs. Horner!" his fine color high, his full lips smiling.

"Get on to the hat!" giggled Kansas City, nudging its neighbor. "He's fixed up like one of those dining-room pictures—*you* know. English prints, they call 'em." Nevertheless, the town felt a vicarious thrill when a Tune horse won an Eastern race. The racing sheet would read, "Twin Girls. Rutger G. Tune, Owner." His favorite racing horse, bought at about the time of their birth, had been named in compliment to Hilda and Hannah.

It had been part of his snobbishness that he had sent the girls in their very early teens to Eastern schools. Also, when the Tunes traveled it was always in the East, or in Europe. They knew practically nothing of the vast country that stretched thousands of miles west of Missouri to the Pacific. Mrs. Tune had loved her Middle West; had refused to live in the East, though her husband had urged it throughout her lifetime; and she had, during that lifetime and even after, made it financially difficult for her handsome husband to remain long away from the city whence her income had its source. The twins had once been taken to see the Colorado Rockies briefly and somewhat remotely, at Colorado Springs. Western railroad society was largely represented at the Antlers Hotel. Rutger G. Tune had not liked it. "A lot of brakemen," he had said, "who have worked their way up through promotions to superintendencies; and their wives who have been waitresses, probably, in the Harvey station eating houses."

Mrs. Tune, though plain, had been a woman of spirit. She had spoken up at this. "My father used to say that those Western railroad brakemen and Harvey lunchroom waitresses were the future aristocracy of the West. Fine stock, he used to say, for foundation material. 'Pick out,' he said, 'the wife of almost any well-dressed, intelligent ranch owner, Santa Fe railroad official, mining or oil man living within one thousand miles of the Mojave Desert, and ask her if she was born in the West. She'll answer, "Oh, no. I'm from Iowa" (or maybe Wisconsin, or Michigan, or Kansas, or even Ohio). "I used to be a Harvey girl." ' Pa always said they were a fine lot, those Harvey waitresses. Smart, independent. Had come West because they wanted to see the country, probably, and were tired of some kind of tyranny in the East. Pioneer stuff, Pa said. I used to like to hear him when he said that New England had its Lowells and Cabots and Lodges, and the South its Van Revels and Colonel Carters and its F.F.V.'s, but that out in Arizona and Texas and Colorado and New Mexico it was the children of the ranchers and railroad men and the ex-Harvey girls who would form the future backbone of——"

"Well," interrupted Rutger G. Tune, his mustache coming up under his nose. "I prefer my hired girls in the kitchen, not the parlor."

The Harvey system, with its chain of lunchrooms and dining rooms stretching across a continent, from Chicago through the very desert itself and beyond, to California, was the boast of any true Westerner. Mrs. Tune's pride in it was incomprehensible to her Eastern-born husband. "Beastly idea, anyway," he said, "having to get off a train for your meals, like that. And those cow towns!"

"We like it," said Mrs. Tune, spiritedly.

"We?"

"We Westerners. And I noticed that you liked the quail pretty well that they served you at the station of that cow town called Newton. You'd have paid ten dollars a portion for it in New York—and then it wouldn't have been fresh."

Still, they did not travel West again. But she loved it to the day she died.

At school the twins, Hilda and Hannah, had been known respectively as Tune and Cartoon. For nature, in her most prankish mood, having fashioned these two in like mold, yet had so slightly, so deftly, so fiendishly overemphasized in Hannah what was perfection in Hilda that perfection became grotesquerie—or almost that. It was only when they were together that the difference was strongly marked. People—strangers—seeing the two for the first time had a way of turning from the flawless purity of Hilda's contour to the exaggerated line that was Hannah's, and then blinking a little as though to rid themselves of an absurd optical illusion. It was as though Nature, having wrought this perfect thing, had said, pettishly, "What! You expect me to achieve this miracle a second time! No! Here, I'll make a rough copy of it. But a masterpiece is a masterpiece. One doesn't repeat."

Hence Tune and Cartoon. Whereas Hilda's nose was the most exquisite example of that ordinarily vulgar feature, straight, fine-pored, delicately fluted at the nostrils, Hannah's, being the minutest fraction of an inch longer, was just too long; and the fluting, being a trifle wider, gave her countenance that rather combative look so trying to the beholder. Whereas Hilda's cheekbones were just high enough to give her face its delicately heart-shaped outline and her eyes that shadowed look of fatigue which men find so fascinating, Hannah's cheekbones were broader, flatter, so that she had a somewhat Slavic cast. Still, if it had not been for Hilda's flawless beauty always there to mock her, Hannah might have been considered an average-looking girl, which she really was: healthy, high-spirited, wholesome. For that matter, there were those who might have thought Hilda's lips a shade too thin, just as others thought Hannah's mouth too large. That generous mouth of Hannah Tune's was the index of her character. It explained why she could be honestly proud and pleased when people exclaimed about her sister's loveliness. It made it possible for Hannah to say, as she watched the exquisite Hilda march across the greensward at the head of the historic Daisy Chain (the very day of the tragic telegram), that if the college had instituted a Poison-Ivy Chain she, Hannah, would have been a prominent entrant.

People who knew them well were aware that the difference between the twins was more than a surface one. It went deep, deep into their characters. It cropped out in all sorts of ways. You saw it in the accumulated dust of days in the seemingly dainty Hilda's hairbrush; in the condition of her bureau drawers; in the frequency with which she forgot to pay back money she had borrowed from Hannah; in her unfailing emphasis on the Tune side of her ancestry, ignoring quite the distaff or Packing-House side; her refusal to mingle with any but those whom she considered the most desirable type of girl at college. Her tone, in speaking of the undesirables, was startlingly like that of Rutger G. Tune when he had discussed the brakemen and Harvey waitresses years before. Hannah's familiar at college, on the other hand, had been a girl from Galena, Illinois, who had won a scholarship and was working her way through. Hannah's old red sweater and her careless tam were likely to give you no hint of the fastidious freshness of the garments worn beneath—the beribboned corset cover, the white embroidery petticoats, the lace-trimmed umbrella drawers of the period. Finally, this difference in face and character, less pronounced when they were children, became daily more noticeable as they grew older.

It had been June when Rutger G. Tune caused the little flurry in the Union Station and the great upheaval in the lives of his motherless twin daughters. In July the twins were to leave the big Tune house perched high on the hill that commanded such a sweeping and unobstructed Missouri view of nothing in particular.

"Father had it built up here," Hannah observed, a little grimly, perhaps, but without bitterness, "not because anything could be seen here from the top of the hill, but because everybody could see the house from the bottom of it. That's what our life has been, really, in the last ten years. A magnificent view of nothing at all."

The two had soberly been discussing that baffling problem known as

Ways and Means. Of Ways they had few. Of Means they had practically nothing.

"There's only one thing to do, of course," Hilda said; "that is, to get away from here. And there's only one place to go, and that's East. Our friends there know Father's dead, but they don't know how completely smashed we are. I shan't tell them until I have to. We both have enough invitations to last through the summer, if we manage properly. The Allisters' at Bar Harbor in July, and Isabel Kane's the first two weeks in August in the Adirondacks, and we might even manage Newport if we went about it properly and used a little——"

"And then what?" interrupted Hannah, bluntly.

"I don't know. But, at any rate, we'd have made a move in the right direction. Our friends in the East are numbered among the very best people. Those are the contacts we'll have to keep up."

"On nine hundred and twenty dollars per lifetime?"

"Yes. Why not! Until something turns up. And it will, with those people back of us. There's something picturesque about being twins. It's considered chic. And orphan twins, too."

"And penniless orphan twins makes it perfect, I suppose."

"All right, then. Suppose you suggest something better."

Hannah, for the moment, looked as nearly helpless as Hannah could, being handicapped by her height, her serenity of brow, and her aura of superb health. "I honestly haven't anything better to suggest, Hilda. I only know I can't go East with you and live on our very best people and be a chic twin."

"What are you going to do, then? What are you going to do? Stay here in Kansas City? Patronized by these people! What'll you live on? Really, Hannah, sometimes I think you're utterly——"

"I could teach school."

"Teach school?" Hilda echoed weakly. "You mean a girls' school somewhere in the East? But what? Your French isn't very good, and you know your English is—well, it's pure Kansas City. Your music is just passable. You hate history."

"Oh, I mean a school here somewhere in Kansas, maybe. A country school. It doesn't pay much, but it's a living, for the present at least. Besides, I like the West. You know that. I always have. A country school—and a horse to ride, maybe, Saturdays and Sundays. I'd like it."

"Hannah Tune, you must be crazy! A country school! A horse on Saturday!"

"And Sunday," put in Hannah, a trifle maliciously—for Hannah. Suddenly she became tremendously serious. "Look here, Hilda Tune. There's no use pretending we're not in a mess. We are. But we always have been. We simply didn't know it, that's all. But Father knew it, and shut his eyes to it, and pretended that something would turn up. Well, it didn't. Mercifully, he died before he had to do any explaining. Now, I'm not going on where he left off. I'm sick of pretending. I'm the plain Tune twin, with nine hundred and twenty dollars between me and whatever happens to you when your money's all gone. It's no use my trying to play the beautiful adventuress. I'm not equipped for it in face or temperament. It's July, and pretty late, but I'm going to try to get a school job by September, somewhere."

A sort of glaze crept over Hilda's beautiful face, hardening it. "All right, then. Be a schoolma'am. But don't expect me to stay here with you. Sometimes, Hannah, I think there isn't a drop of Tune blood in you."

Hannah seemed to consider this a compliment. "I know it. After all these years of pruning and snipping, here I am, just bristling all over with Kansas. I guess there's no help for it."

Hilda, looking lovely and fragile in black, went to the Allisters' at Bar Harbor. Hannah had not yet secured a school, but there were rumors of one to be had in Eldorado, Kansas. "Oh, my goodness!" Hilda had said, when she heard of it. At the last minute Hannah had stuffed five hundred of her own nine hundred and twenty into Hilda's bag. "I won't need it," she said, above Hilda's faint protests. "I'll be earning money soon. And you'll want it pretty badly if you're going to make any kind of showing in the among-those-present column in the Newport society news. Linsey-woolsey, whatever that is, will be all I'll need in Eldorado."

By the first of August Hannah was told the Eldorado school was hers. She wrote Hilda the news, jubilantly. Hilda was in the Adirondacks, according to schedule. Hannah got ready her linsey-woolseys, including the old red sweater of college skating days. In the middle of August Hannah was notified that Eldorado's last year's teacher was returning after all; and that here was one month's salary, and that it was hoped Miss Tune had been put to no inconvenience.

Miss Tune was not only inconvenienced but indignant, and a little frightened. Her first impulse was to telegraph Hilda; so she didn't. The Tune twins had been brought up on telegrams. Rutger G. Tune had hated letter writing. At this critical moment a telegram from Hilda (her father's daughter) said that she had a chance to go abroad in October with Mrs. Courtney Paige, as a sort of pet pampered companion. And what did Hannah think about it? Hannah, feeling suddenly alone in the world, and terribly twinless, answered: "It sounds heavenly. You must go." Then she began to read the want-ad columns of the *Kansas City Star*.

M-m-m-m-m-m—clerks wanted. Experienced. . . . Binders wanted. What was a binder? Hannah wondered. And what did they bind? . . . Ladies to solicit orders for marvelous new patent contrivance warranted to revolutionize housework. On commission only. . . . Waitresses wanted—oh, my goodness! what was there for her to do! Wait a minute! . . . waitresses wanted for Harvey hotel dining rooms and lunchrooms in Colorado, New Mexico, Arizona, and California. Apply Employment Department, Union Station, Room 15.

Something came creeping back into Hannah's consciousness like the fragments of a song once heard and long forgotten: ". . . fine stock . . . pioneer stuff . . . Harvey waitresses . . . future aristocracy . . ."

Hannah had been a very little girl when her mother, with that look of high pride and honest indignation, had delivered herself of that speech. But it came back to her now, as did the sneer on her father's face. Colorado—New Mexico—Arizona—California! Hannah took a long breath, exhaled it, and applied to the Employment Department, Union Station, Room 15.

She had a sick feeling at the pit of her stomach, and her knees seemed strangely fluid; but on the wall of the little waiting room there was a picture of the Grand Cañon, and a map whose black lines went bounding across mountains and deserts and plains and mesas in a way to take your breath away. Hannah regarded these, and they gave her courage and even a feeling of exaltation which always came to her, strangely enough, when she caught a remote hint of that which lay Pacificward from Missouri. A little soaring sensation. A feeling of freedom. If she had had wings she would have flapped them now.

There were five other girls in the anteroom. One of them had a foreign look—Polish or Bohemian, Hannah thought. Two, evidently friends, had entered together, exhaling a stench of perfume. Hannah thought they didn't look exactly pioneer material or future aristocrats. A fourth was a pale, quiet girl who appeared listless and limp. "She's going out for her health," Hannah decided. "Arizona, probably, if they'll take her." The fifth girl resembled Hannah's Vassar chum from Galena, Illinois. Hannah found herself smiling at this girl, companionably. The girl smiled back at her. Encouraged thus, Hannah moved to a chair next to her. "Are you—have you ever—are you going out West as a Harvey girl?"

"Yes—to stay this time, I hope."

"Oh, you've been before?"

"Two years ago. But only for the summer. I'm a schoolteacher. I took a Harvey job two summers ago because I thought it would be fun, kind of; and a cheap way to see something of the West. I'm from Albia, Iowa. You ought to have heard my folks when I said I was going as a waitress."

"And now you're going to stay?"

"Long as I want to, anyway. I'm lucky. They're sending me to the Cañon." Then, as Hannah looked blank—"Oh, I guess you don't know about the different stations. You see, all the girls are crazy to go to the hotels at the Grand Cañon, or Albuquerque, or big places like that. We call them heaven. Now, Needles, California, and Rincon, New Mexico, are purgatory. We say that's where bad Harvey girls go for punishment. Needles is two hundred miles from the Mojave Desert, in a sort of pocket. And hot! Phew! When it's a hundred and twenty-five there they think it's getting on toward summer."

Hannah looked a little worried. "Do you think a new girl——"

The other shook her head emphatically. "Some. But not you." Her glance encompassed Hannah's face, her clothes, her manner. "Gracious, no! You look like a Cañon girl, or Albuquerque, except that perhaps you'll lose out because you're too pretty."

Hannah stared, smiled. "Me!"

"You know, don't you, that Harvey's never hire girls that are awfully pretty. They found they couldn't keep them out West. They just melted away into marriage with some rancher or railroad man or mining——"

"Then it's true!"

But the other girl misunderstood. "Oh, my yes. They like to hire them neat, plain, and sensible. They're very strict, you know. You've got to behave just so during hours—and after hours, for that matter. In before twelve——" She broke off suddenly as the door to the inner office opened. She was next in the list of waiting applicants. "See you later. Wish you luck!"—over her shoulder.

Hannah never saw her again. Two days later Hannah Tune, daughter of the late Rutger G. Tune of the Massachusetts Tunes, to whom the Signers of the Declaration of Independence were mere upstarts, was on her way to San Querto, New Mexico, with a Harvey Santa Fe railroad pass in her handbag. She was enjoying herself immensely, though the ride was hot, dusty, and seemingly endless. Every now and then she went into the washroom and scraped prairie dust off her clothes and face and railroad cinders out of her hair. Then she washed for the sake of the relief the cool wet towel gave against her hot cheeks, and went back to her seat to resume her staring out of the window. Prairie, plain, corn, corn, corn, corn—hundreds of miles of it, an unmarine ocean, billowing away and away to the horizon. And, like the ocean, it makes the beholder content or restless. Hannah felt soothed, relaxed, satisfied.

With her Santa Fe pass was an identification card entitling her to meals free of charge at all stops where meals were regularly scheduled. At these

stations along the way passengers were notified that they would have half
an hour for lunch. They swarmed out of the coaches like ants from a disturbed anthill. The sound of a deep-throated brass gong greeted them as
they flocked toward the dining rooms and lunchrooms. Hannah soon discovered that she preferred the rush and scramble of the lunchroom to the
more dignified and orderly ceremony of the dining room. Her first meal in
the dining room at Hutchinson, Kansas, had been of immense interest to
her, flavored with almost hysterical amusement. She had never imagined
anything like it. A hundred or even two hundred passengers were fed
there in half an hour. The meal marched as inevitably, as irresistibly, as
death itself. Each table seated eight. The first course lay smoking before
you seated yourself. With that scant half-hour snapping at their heels the
passengers settled grimly, determinedly, to this business of consuming their
dollar's worth. It was a huge meal, hot, savory, appetizing. But the dining
hundreds made a ghastly ceremony of it. Not a murmur of conversation;
eyes on their plates. They were devastating, thorough. No sounds but the
clink of cutlery against china, the low voices of the white starched waitresses murmuring a chant of "Teacoffemilk? Teacoffeemilk? Teacoffeemilk?" Controlling, soothing this strange company, as unconvivial as the
elfin bowlers in Rip Van Winkle's mountain retreat, walked the Harvey
hotel manager, bland, watchful, weaving in and out among the tables,
hands behind his back. And as he walked he intoned: "Pas-sen-gers on
Number Nine have thirty minutes for dinner. Take—your—time!" Fifteen
minutes later, again as before: "Pas-sen-gers on Number Nine still have
fifteen minutes for dinner. Take—your—time!" Gobble, gobble. Clink,
clink. Gulp, gulp. Munch, munch. Soup, meat, vegetables, salad, olives,
iced tea, dessert. "Pas-sen-gers on Number Nine still have five minutes——"
They swept out like a horde of locusts, leaving a ravaged dining room.

No, Hannah decided, the dining room was not for her. She would eat
in the lunchroom, where ham and eggs, ordered one minute, appeared miraculously before you the next; where hovered the scent of coffee; where
blood-red half-moons of watermelon glowed at you from behind glass;
where you sat perched on a revolving stool before a white slab of counter,
with tiny cream pitchers and little butter chips and glasses of ice water
spinning and sliding all about you. Hannah became less and less a Tune;
more and more the daughter of her plain, democratic, high-spirited mother.

This trip had all the flavor of a stolen holiday, for the truth of it is that
at the last moment she had not had the courage to tell her plans to Hilda.
She lacked the courage to write to Hilda there in the Adirondacks at the
Kanes' elaborately rustic lodge, "I am going West to be a Harvey hired
girl." Instead, she had given Hilda to understand that her mission at San

Querto was to teach school. She dilated on it, in her guilt, and made it sound quite picturesque and charming. Much nicer, she said, than the Eldorado school, about which she had decided adversely.

Hannah had been in San Querto almost ten days before her twin's reply reached her. "I suppose," wrote Hilda, among other things, "you'll be the pretty Western schoolteacher of the movies, rescued from Indians by a rancher in chaps and frijoles, or whatever it is they wear, and marry him, and live happily ever after. Can you possibly spare me some money, Cartoon dear?"

Hannah, in her black uniform and white apron, read the letter as she stood behind the counter in a quiet hour at the San Querto station lunchroom. She had just emerged from the bewilderment, shock, and chaos of the past ten days. A certain accustomed serenity again sat on her brow. In those ten days she had learned much, suffered much, wept much, slept little. She had learned and suffered in the Harvey lunchroom; wept and lain awake in the little bare, clean, whitewashed bedroom on the top floor of the Santa Fe station, with the engines puffing, hissing, snorting, clanging in her racked head; grinding, it seemed, over her very knees. And yet, so miraculously do we adjust ourselves to environment (if we are Hannahs) that now the white-tiled lunchroom seemed a zestful, cheery place, and the little white-walled bedroom a snug refuge where she could be alone. The trains, after a fortnight, bothered her no more than does the chirping of birds the country dweller.

Now she read her letter in a quiet moment between trains, seated on a little stool behind the horseshoe of counter. It had just been handed her by the hotel manager. "Letter from home?" asked Louise, the red-haired girl.

"From my twin sister."

"Twins! Don't say! Do you look just alike?"

"Oh, no," Hannah said, rather absently, dipping into her letter again. "Not a bit. My sister's pretty."

Louise looked at her sharply as she sat there in her neat black and white, her hair done in the smooth simple fashion that the Harvey rules decreed, her throat rising so firm and white from the flat collar that finished the neckline of her blouse. "Well, you're no eyesore!" she exclaimed.

Hannah had smiled quietly. "You ought to see Hilda."

She sent Hilda two hundred dollars of the tiny sum that now remained of her original nine hundred and twenty.

By the end of the month Hannah had learned so much that it seemed to her as if, until now, she had merely been marking time. She had learned things pleasant and disagreeable; interesting and dull; exhilarating and depressing. She learned to call scheduled trains by their names, as if they were individuals—Number Nine—Number Thirteen—Number Five. Number Eight's due in from the West. There's Number Eleven from the East. She learned to remember six orders taken at one time in the rush of the crowd just off a waiting train. She learned to keep her head when under a fire of orders volleyed at her like hail.

"Ham 'n' eggs!"

"Apple pie! Glass milk!"

"Coffee!"

"Cheese on rye!"

"Liver 'n' onions!"

Short. Sharp. Relentless. Inescapable. Stinging.

She learned that San Querto itself, though an important Santa Fe railroad division point, was an ugly little Mexican town, squatting flat on the mesa, its new houses staring and unlovely, its Old Town, where the Mexicans lived, squalid and unpicturesque. Its roads were mud wallows; its main street was sordid; its Mexicans were lazy, dirty. Yet there was the Western mountain air, and there was the Western sky, and there, beyond the town, were the Spanish Peaks, those mysterious purple-black twin mountains rising abruptly, without warning, magically, from the flat mesa itself. They were, Hannah thought, like no other mountain peaks in the world. They thrilled her, bewitched her. When first they had loomed up before her as she gazed out of her train window she had given a little cry and had sat forward in her seat, staring. There stretched the sage-green mesa, for miles. Not a foothill. Not even a hillock. Then, suddenly, without preparation, rising out of this flat plateau and soaring straight up to snow, loomed the purple Spanish Peaks against the sunset sky. The tears had come to Hannah's eyes. She felt as if she had come home.

Now she had learned to look at them the first thing in the morning; to peer into the darkness in their direction the last thing at night. She learned to wash and iron her own shirtwaists. She learned to ride a Western horse on mountain roads. She learned to work "nights one week, days one week," without feeling sleepy during nightwork week. She learned that cowboys, though picturesque, do not change their shirts as often as they might. She learned those feats of legerdemain which all waitresses acquire through experience—a certain swing of the ketchup bottle, a juggling of hot coffee cups, a whisk of the towel.

And she learned to watch for the entrance of Dan Yard. Dan Yard was substitute brakeman on a branch-line freight train running into San Querto four nights a week. He had come off his train at 2 A.M. and had dropped into the lunchroom after washing up, as was the custom of brakemen, engineers, and conductors at the end of the run, for a cup of coffee and a sandwich or a couple of doughnuts. It was against rules for Harvey girls to carry on social conversation with lunch-counter patrons. No pretense of swishing imaginary crumbs off the slab while exchanging flirtatious pleasantries with the willing cowboys ranchmen or railroad men was allowed here. A greeting, yes. An amiable word or two. But that was all. Yet Hannah noticed a little intangible change come over the two girls on duty with her that night as Dan Yard swung open the screen door and, entering, threw one leg over a stool at the counter, pushed back his cap, and smiled. His smile was not the fictional smile of rare sweetness, lighting up his whole face. It was a schoolboy grin, engaging but tough.

"Any raspberries?" inquired Dan of the girl at whose station he was seated.

"Yes."

"Well, I don't want any."

"Thought you didn't." Having taken part in this brilliant dialogue which was evidently a formula, she set before him a cup of smoking coffee and his plate of doughnuts. Hannah, by now, was hardened to seeing monstrous quantities of food consumed at unseemly hours. Half hidden by the nickel coffee urn, she turned to look at him. He dumped three generous spoonfuls of sugar into his cup, emptied the contents of his cream pitcher, stirred the mixture, and took a great swallow of the scalding liquid. The size of that great gulp brought his head up and back so that he found himself staring at Hannah over the rim of his inverted cup. Hannah's gaze met his. Ting! went something like a bell inside her.

She saw a slim, hard, rather pugnacious-looking young Irishman of perhaps twenty-four or -five. Freckled. His eyes were wide apart, clear, singularly bright. She thought she had never seen anyone so wide awake at 2 A.M. He evidently had just washed with strong soap and slicked his hair after coming in off his run. His head was damp where the pocket comb had tidied it. Later Hannah learned that he was bowlegged and some three inches shorter than she. All their married life (for she married Dan Yard) she tried not to let him feel this difference in their height; did her hair flat and wore low-heeled shoes, for she loved him terribly and he was a sensitive and somewhat vain Irishman, as all good Irishmen are.

What Dan Yard saw of Hannah over the rim of his upturned coffee cup she never quite knew. He never seemed able to put it into coherent words. He would begin, when she asked him: "I said to myself, 'There she is!' like that. 'There's Mrs. Dan Yard.' I felt all the blood up in my head, fit to smother me."

"It was the hot coffee."

"It was hot love," said Dan, being the reverse of mincing.

He had finished his coffee that night, had reached for his glass of ice water, swallowed it in one long draught, sliding one piece of conveniently sized ice into his mouth along with the fluid, and had walked out, crunching the ice between his strong yellow teeth.

"Why!" said the girl who had waited on him. "Look! Dan Yard never touched his doughnuts at all."

For six weeks Hannah withstood him. In those six weeks she learned much about Dan Yard. He came from a family of railroad workers. When he talked of this it was as though he were descended from a long line of aristocrats. His father had been Engine Man John Yard, killed in the wreck at Algodones in 1899. His brother was an engineer on the Burlington. His uncle was an engineer on the Santa Fe. Another uncle was killed acting as yardmaster at La Junta. Two cousins were brakemen. Another a conductor. His family tree, and proud of it. He had almost gone through high school. Quit, his third year, because he had to go to work. By next January he would have his job as regular brakeman on the main line. Then they could be married.

"No!" said Hannah, trying to laugh. Terribly frightened, yet with a certain crazy feeling of warmth and happiness suffusing her whole being. Then "No," faintly, his eyes on hers and her own closing flutteringly as she felt his strong, hard, oil-grimed hand on her arm.

Hilda was in Europe. In January Hannah wrote her, fearfully yet boldly; and certainly baldly. "I am going to be married." They had been married some weeks before Hilda's reply reached them. "I hope he's one of those millionaire ranchers or oil kings that seem to grow exclusively out there in the West, where men are men, or whatever it is the poem says." The hot tears of resentment and indignation came to Hannah's eyes. She spent hard-earned dollars to cable her answer, unthriftily worded:

"He's a king, all right, but not the kind you mean. Dan's a brakeman on the Santa Fe railroad."

A cable from Hilda: "You must be insane cable if joke."

Hannah replied, tersely, "No joke."

Silence. Silence that lasted twenty years.

They went housekeeping in one of the ugly little San Querto houses and became part of the little bare railroad town where caste lines were drawn as definitely as in Mayfair. Brakemen's wives were beneath freight-train conductors' wives in the social scale. Stationmasters' wives patronized conductors' wives. The wife of a division superintendent queened it over the wives of both stationmasters and passenger-train conductors.

Hannah busied herself in the little house with its mission furniture and its Navajo rugs, but while Dan was gone she found time heavy on her hands, now that she had left the lunchroom. She decided to learn to be a telegrapher, learned with amazing speed, and was telegrapher at San Querto for two years, until her first child was born. They had two boys. Always there was with her that little fear ever present in the heart of the railroad worker's wife.

"Dan, I wish you'd stop railroading."

"Stop! What for?"

"I'm afraid you'll get k—hurt."

"Me! Naw! I won't get killed."

"They did."

"Not me."

The sound of the trains striding and elbowing their way in and out of this little railroad town, out to the prairies and mountains beyond, no longer disturbed her as mere noise. But she used to lie awake, always, on the nights when he was out on his run—wide awake, listening, until she heard the whistle of Number Seven. Dan's train. Dangerous work, braking. She knew that. They made him freight-train conductor one year later. Not so dangerous and better pay. A step up the ladder. By the time she had got accustomed to her duties as telegrapher in the little station at San Querto he was promoted to yardmaster at that point. Dangerous again. Sitting in the little bay window of the shabby red-brick station, her subconscious ear intent on the click of the keys, she would watch for him. It was his duty to shunt freight, direct the tangle of loaded and unloaded cars, see that they got in and out of the spiderweb of tracks, on their way East or West. When she saw the small wiry bowlegged figure crossing the tracks toward the station she would go to meet him, the old red sweater buttoned up tight about her full, firm figure. It seemed to her that all her married life she was watching for that little wiry bowlegged figure from some window or other, all the way from the dilapidated station at San Querto to the window of the great Spanish hacienda that they built in 1920, with its magnificent view of the Spanish Peaks. He never failed to appear just before fear had got its icy fingers on her heart. And she never let him know that she had been fearful.

The rise of Dan Yard is history in the annals of the Santa Fe road. They tell it as a sort of saga. Yet it all seemed natural enough in the actual happening. From brakeman to freight-train conductor; conductor to yardmaster; yardmaster to stationmaster at San Querto. Hannah with him all the time, toning down his roughness ("tuning him down," she called it); saying, quietly, "Now, Dan," when he became too coltish. He liked a pretty face and a trim figure, and she knew it, and kept her figure trim, for she knew that to hold an Irishman you must be vigilant and wary. He was the kind of husband who breaks out occasionally into playful tousling of hair and pinching of cheeks and bruising squeezes of shoulder. When he got too rough—"Now, Dan," with fine dignity and composure. He would subside. But she enjoyed it, nevertheless. Just enough Tune in her to keep him impressed. Plenty of her spirited mother to hold him.

At thirty he became an office man, clerk to the division superintendent at San Querto. At thirty-three he was Division Superintendent. Hannah, if she cared to, could now queen it over the conductors' wives. For the Division Superintendent has a private car, if you please. Not a very good private car, it is true. An old passenger coach, usually, carefully gutted out and made over, fitted with compartments and finished in the old red wood and gimcracky scroll work of a past era in railroad decoration. But a private car, nevertheless. They could use it to run to Omaha or to Kansas City, if they wanted to. Hannah Yard could take a carload of conductors' wives to the opera, if opera there happened to be within a distance of five hundred miles. But she never did.

From Division Superintendent he was promoted to District Superintendent. No trifling about it now. Dan Yard was an important man in the road. They say his wife had a lot to do with it. A smart woman, Mrs. Yard. And handsome isn't the name for it. They say she was the daughter of Rutger G. Tune. Don't you remember? Did you never hear of old Tune of Kansas City! Yeh. Used to be a big bug and a sport. Went through his wife's millions and died pretty shady. Well, nothing shady about this Mrs. Yard. And Dan! Say, he'll be General Manager yet. Watch him.

From District Superintendent to Assistant General Superintendent. Then, inevitably, General Superintendent. There is, after that, only one step; but it is a momentous step, a seven-league stride. It is the unrealized dream of every railroad official. It is not only the Chair at His Right Hand. It is the Right Hand. General Manager.

Dan Yard, at forty-six, was General Manager of the Santa Fe road. The Yards' private car now was a thing of rosewood and silken hangings and finest steel. They were Royalty. Yet, twenty years later, if you happened to be a guest in this private movable palace of theirs, and if, peering out of the window in the darkness you asked, "Where are we now, I wonder? What's this place we're coming to?" Hannah Yard could close her eyes and, listening intently a moment, say, "We're just coming into Trinidad. I can tell by the bump of the wheels over the rails. I was here when Dan laid out these yards."

During these twenty years she had thought of Hilda thousands of times, and sadly. She took *The New York Times* as soon as they could afford it, in the hope of seeing Hilda's name mentioned in the society columns, perhaps. She wrote her often. Her letters were unanswered. When she placed a return address on these letters they came back rubber-stamped, "Not at address given." Though Dan's position took him frequently to New York, Hannah rarely accompanied him. She dreaded it, somehow. Once she had tried to trace Hilda there, but had not succeeded. She thought of a detective agency, but shrank from the idea. After all, Hilda had not wanted her; Hilda had deserted her, ridiculed her just when she needed her love most. She seldom spoke to Dan of Hilda; as the years went on, Hilda's name was never mentioned. The two boys were at college—the elder at a school of engineering ("like his pa," laughed Dan Yard), the other at an agricultural school. He wanted to be a rancher, and raise stock and alfalfa and oranges and sugar beets and cantaloupes.

"All on one ranch!" laughed his mother. "That isn't a ranch. That's a paradise."

The Yard place, a great glowing creamy Spanish pile situated in the valley, but on a slight rise, and almost in the shadow of the purple and mysterious Spanish Peaks, was known throughout the West. You were likely to find as guests there anyone from the President of the United States to a flock of Harvey waitresses on a ten-day vacation. A Goya over the fireplace in the living room; a gorgeous old vestment of brocade and ancient velvet thrown over this screen bought in Granada. "Come on along to New York with me," said Dan Yard, in tousling mood. "Come on, old girl. Do you good. They sent me a catalogue of that Spanish stuff to be sold at Barrios'. There's one old tapestry velvet that sounds like the thing you want for that balcony railing, exactly. Come on. Let's take a look at it, anyway."

The General Manager's private car, summoned casually, like an automobile. Thousands of miles, over mountain passes, mesas, plains, prairies, cornfields, Omaha, Chicago, New York.

"I wired Barrios," said Dan at breakfast in New York, "and he just called up to say he was sending some stuff over here to the hotel. I thought, as long as your head didn't feel so good this morning——"

A wiry pugnacious bowlegged little Irishman, looking, in spite of graying hair and his carefully tailored suit and the dignity of his office, incredibly like the tough young brakeman of the San Querto lunchroom twenty years ago.

Like a cue in a play then, the telephone rang; Barrios' representative calling. And "Oh, dear!" said Hannah, glancing down at a foamy but informal negligee. "You talk to him for a minute, Dan. I'll do my hair and get into something. Don't let him sell you anything till I—— You remember that terrible table you——"

As she dressed hurriedly, she could hear him in the adjoining room.

"Well, say, that's pretty. . . . No, I don't like that one. . . . I don't know, I just don't like it. It doesn't look Spanish to me. My wife knows. She'll be in in a minute. She's . . . she may like it. . . . It don't look to me . . ."

A man's voice in low protest; then a woman's voice, high, hard, nervous, icy, "Not authentically Spanish! There are only two other pieces like it in the world. The other two were sold yesterday to a family representing our very best people. You will like it, I know, if you will just live with it awhile. . . ."

Hannah, at her dressing table, stood up, clutching her dressing gown to her breast. She whirled to face her husband, who had just come in. He was grinning. He dropped his voice to a rasping whisper. He even tiptoed in some absurd delusion of increased secrecy.

"Say, Hannah, there's three of 'em sent up with the stuff from Barrios'! A regular troupe. A kid to carry the bundles and a young Spanish feller, and he's got on a lavender shirt and perfume, so help me God. But listen. Don't get mad at me, Hannah, when you see her—the woman—say—she looks enough like you, in a kind of an awful way, to be a cartoon of you. By golly, she does! A lot older, but a kind of snaky dress, and too much red stuff on her mouth, and talks about our best people. . . ."

A sob of premonition shook Hannah Yard as she ran past her husband and into the next room to face the woman sent up from Barrios'.

Mother Knows Best

[1925]

That demon chaperone, the Stage Mother, is practically extinct. She reigned in the early 1900's and doubtless ruined the development of many a budding Bernhardt. Under the pretense of protecting her gifted off-spring's virtue and managing her business affairs, she usually succeeded in cramping her talents and twisting her love life. This particular story, though largely imaginary, was suggested by bits I'd been told of the early life of that gifted comedienne, Mabel Hite. I got into considerable trouble because another talented actress thought it was her story. It might have been that of many women whose fires had been dampened by the clammy hand of maternal solicitude.

⤳ THEY SAY THERE NEVER WAS SUCH A FUNERAL IN THE HISTORY OF New York's theatrical life. Though it was an eleven-o'clock service, the list of honorary pallbearers sounded like the cast of an all-star benefit. And not only that—they were present for duty. As for the flowers! A drop curtain of white orchids; a blanket of lilies of the valley; a pillow of creamy camellias; sheaves of roses; banks of violets. Why, the flowers alone, translated into money, would have supported the Actors' Home for years. Everything was on a similar scale. Satin where others have silk; silver where others have brass; twelve where ordinarily there are six. And her mother, Mrs. Quail ("Ma Quail"—and the term was not one of affection), swathed in expensive mourning which transformed her into a sable pillar of woe, through whose transparencies you somehow got the impression that she was automatically counting the house.

In the midst of it all lay Sally Quail, in white chiffon that was a replica of the full floating white chiffon dancing dress that she always wore at the close of her act. A consistent enough costume now. Sally was smiling a little; and all those telltale lines that she had fought during the past ten years—the tiny lines that, between thirty and forty, etch themselves about a woman's eyes and mouth and forehead—were wiped out magically, completely. What ten years of expert and indefatigable massage had never been able to do, the Mysterious Hand had accomplished in a single gesture. You almost expected her to say, in that thrillingly husky voice of hers, and with the girlish simper that she had adopted when she went on the professional stage at fourteen, and still had used—not so happily—at forty:

"I will now try to give you an imitation of Miss Sally Quail at twenty.

Miss . . . Sally . . . Quail . . . at twenty." And it had then turned out to be an uncanny piece of mimicry, embodying not only facial similarity, but something of the soul and spirit as well. Though in this particular imita‧ tion, according to the Scriptures, soul and spirit were supposed to have fled.

Crushed though she was by her sorrow, Ma Quail it had been who had seen to it that this, her talented daughter's last public appearance, should be in every detail as flawless as all her public appearances had been. A born impresario, Ma Quail. During the three days preceding the funeral she had insisted that they come to her for sanction in every arrangement, from motorcars to minister. And she supervised the seating arrangements like a producer on a first night.

"Sally'd have wanted me to," she explained. "She always said, 'Mother knows best.' "

Of course a lot of people know that Sally Quail's real name was Louisa Schlagel. Not that it matters. Even a name like that couldn't have stopped her climb toward fame.

The Schlagels, mother and daughter, had come from Neenah, Wisconsin, propelled rapidly by Mrs. Schlagel. Between Neenah, Wisconsin, and Chicago, Illinois, they had become Mrs. Quail and Sally Quail, respectively. Mrs. Schlagel had read Hall Caine's *The Christian*. Both book and play of that name were enormously in vogue at the time. She had thought the heroine's name a romantic and lovely-sounding thing and had appropriated its cadences for use in her daughter's stage career. "Glory Quayle . . . Flory Quayle . . . Sally . . . Sally Quayle . . . Sally Quail. . . . That's it! Sally Quail. That's short and easy to remember. And you don't run into anybody else with a name like that."

There's no doubt that if it hadn't been for this tireless general and terrible tyrant, her mother, Sally Quail would have remained Louisa Schlagel of Neenah, Wisconsin, to the end of her days. Though her natural gifts had evidenced themselves even in her very early childhood, it had been her mother—that driving and relentless force—who had lifted her to fame and fortune. That force of Ma Quail's in terms of power units—amperes, kilowatts, pounds—would have been sufficient to light a town, run a factory, move an engine. The girl had had plenty of spirit too, at first. But it had been as nothing compared to the woman's iron quality. If ever a girl owed everything to her mother, that girl was Sally Quail. She said so, frequently. So did Ma Quail.

Sally was forty when she died after an illness of but a few days. You were a little startled to learn this. Somehow, you had never thought of her as a mature woman, perhaps because she had never married, perhaps because of her mother's unceasing chaperonage. All her life she was duennaed like a Spanish infanta. Through her mother's tireless efforts Sally Quail had had everything in the world—except two things.

In announcing her death the newspaper headlines called her Our Sally. The news was cabled all over the world, and was certainly as important in London and Paris as in New York and Chicago and San Francisco. Hers had been international fame. Hundreds of thousands of people were conscious of a little pang born of shock and regret when they said, over the morning paper at breakfast:

"I see where Sally Quail's dead. Gosh, that's too bad! She was just a kid. First time I saw her was in—let's see—no, she couldn't have been so young, at that. Must have been around forty. But an artist, all right. They say she got five thousand a week every time she stepped into vaudeville. . . . Say, look here, this coffee's stone-cold again. Why is it you can't get a hot cup of coffee in this house!"

When Ma Quail was Mrs. Schlagel she had been the wife of Henry Schlagel, than whom there was nothing in Neenah less important. He was a small druggist of the kind who doesn't install a soda fountain in his drugstore. Even Mrs. Schlagel couldn't make a success of her husband, Henry, though she had early turned the full battery of her forces upon him; had tried to bully, bribe, cajole, threaten, nag, scold, and weep him into it. She was a fiercely ambitious woman, but there was no molding Henry. He was fluid, spineless. When you tried to shape him, he ran through your fingers. Henry came of better stock than she. Mrs. Schlagel had sprung from a rather common lot living the other side of the tracks. Her marriage with the meek and dusty little apothecary had been, technically, something of a social triumph for the girl. Her father had been a day laborer, her mother a slattern. The girl, lively, high-spirited, good-looking in a bold, dark sort of way, decided to lift herself out of this and did it in ten visits to the fusty little drugstore on fictitious errands. The little pharmacist, mixing drugs and grinding powders between mortar and pestle, knew nothing of the mysteries of human chemistry. His marriage was as much a surprise to him as it was to the rest of the town.

The girl Louisa was born fully six years after their marriage. By the time she was six years old the mothers of the neighborhood knew just where to find their offspring any summer evening after supper. They were certain to be gathered under the corner arc light with the June bugs blundering and bumping blindly all about and crackling under foot, while Louisa Schlagel recited "Little Orphant Annie" and sang "Jolly Old St. Nicholas" (with gestures) and gave imitations of the crowd's respective papas and mammas with uncanny fidelity. Stern parental voices, summoning children to bed, died away unheard on the summer air. Or, if heard:

"Willie! Clara! Come on now!"

No answer.

"Will Meyers, don't you let me call you again!"

"Well, Pete's sake, wait a minute, can't you! She's in the middle of it."

Sometimes an irate parent would come marching down to the corner, bent on violence, only to be held in thrall.

It was absurd, because she was a plain child, thin, big-eyed, sallow. By the time she was twelve she was speaking pieces at the Elks' Club Ladies' Evening and singing and giving imitations at church sociables and K.P. suppers. The little druggist objected to this, prompted by something fine and reticent within him. But his wife was tasting the first fruits of triumph. She had someone to manage, someone to control, someone on whom to turn the currents of her enormous directing energy. By the time Louisa was thirteen her mother was demanding five dollars a performance for her services, and getting it, which was in its way as much of a triumph in that day and place as was the five-thousand-a-week contract which she consummated in later years. At thirteen the girl was a long-legged, gangling creature, all eyes and arms and elbows and (luckily) soft brown curls. She had no singing voice, really, but the vocal organ possessed a certain husky tonal quality that had in it something of power, something of tragedy, much of flexibility. And when she smiled there was something most engaging about her. A frank, boyish sort of grin that took you into her confidence, that said, "Aren't we having a grand time!"

It is difficult to say how her mother recognized the gold mine in her. She induced the manager of the little local vaudeville theater to let Louisa go on one Monday night in an act made up of two songs and three imitations and one dance that was pretty terrible. It was before the day of the ubiquitous motion picture. The Bijou presented vaudeville of the Comic Tramp and the Family Four variety. Sandwiched in between these there appeared this tall, gawky girl with terrifically long legs and a queer husky voice and large soft brown eyes staring out from a too-thin face. The traveling men in the audience, hardened by the cruelties of Amateur Nights in vaudeville, began to laugh. But the girl finished her opening song and went into her imitations. She imitated Mansfield, Mabel Hite, and Rose Coghlan, all of whom her mother had taken her to see at the Appleton, Wisconsin, Opera House just twenty-five minutes distant by interurban streetcar. The one-night stand was flourishing then, and the stars of the theater were not so lofty that they would refuse to twinkle west of Chicago. Well, even the traveling men saw that here was a weird and unusual gift. Something in the sight of this awkward, white-faced child transforming herself miraculously before their eyes into the tragic mask of the buxom Coghlan or the impish grotesqueries of the clownish Hite or the impressive person of Mansfield moved the beholder to a sort of tearful laughter. Still, it cannot truthfully be said that there was anything spectacular about this, her first appearance on a professional stage. The opinion was that, while the kid was clever, she ought to be home in bed.

That trial served to crystallize into determination the half-formed plan in Mrs. Schlagel's mind. She took the child to Chicago, lied about her age, haunted such booking offices as that city afforded, hounded the vaudeville managers, fought the Gerry society, got a hearing, wrote her husband that she was not coming back, and the career of Sally Quail started.

To the day she died there always was something virginal and untouched-looking about Sally Quail. It was part of her charm. At twenty she looked seventeen. At twenty-nine she looked twenty. At thirty she looked twenty-five. At thirty-five she looked thirty—under that new amber lighting. And then, at thirty-nine, suddenly, she looked thirty-nine. Though she was massaged and manicured and brushed and creamed and exercised and packed in cotton wool she took on, in some mysterious way, the appearance of the woman of whom we say that she is well preserved.

For twenty-five years—from fifteen to forty—nothing could prevent Sally's progress, for the way was cleared for her by her mother. That remarkable woman pushed on as relentlessly, as irresistibly, as a glacier, sweeping before her every obstruction that stood in her path. Here was this girl who could sing a little, though she had no voice; dance a little, though she had too-long legs; act a little, though her dramatic gift was slight; mimic marvelously. No one ever made more out of little than did Ma Quail. She fought for contracts. She fought for plays. She fought for a better spot always in vaudeville, and even from the first Sally never closed the show. It was years before Sally became a real headliner in vaudeville, with the star's dressing room and her name in electric lights over the entrance. But her mother surrounded her with all the care, the glamour, the ceremony of stardom. She was tireless, indomitable, inescapable. Press agents featured Sally just to escape her mother. Office boys wilted at her approach. Managers and producers received her with a kind of grim and bitter admiration, recognizing this iron woman as one against whom their weapons were powerless.

"Now, look here, Mrs. Quail," they would say, in desperation, "you don't expect me to go to work and star a girl that hasn't got the stuff for it." Then, in anticipation of what was coming, from the look in Ma Quail's face, "Now, wait a minute! Wait a min-ute! I don't say she won't after a while. Give her time. She's only a kid. Wait till she has a little experience.

She'll grow. Prob'ly be a great artist someday. She's a great little kid, that kid of yours. Only——"

Though it was, perhaps, old Kiper himself speaking, here he floundered, hesitated, stopped. Ma Quail's steely glance ran him through. "Only what?"

A heartening champ at his unlighted cigar. "Well—uh—how old is Sally now? Between us, you know. I mean—how old is the kid?"

"Nineteen."

"Hm. Twenty-one, huh. Ever been in love?"

Ma Quail bridled. "Sally has always had a great deal of attention, and the boys all——"

"Ye-e-e-s, I know. I know. Has she ever been in love?"

Mrs. Quail pursed up her lips, bridled, tossed her head. "Sally is as unspoiled as a child, and as pure as one, too. She's never even been kissed. She——"

Ben Kiper brought one fat fist down on the mahogany of his office desk. "Yeh, and why! No fellah's going to kiss a girl when her mother's holding her hand. Now wait a minute. Don't get huffy. I'm telling you something for your own good, and nobody knows better than Ben Kiper that when he does that he loses a friend every time. But I'm going to tell you, just the same. You've been a wonderful mother to that kid, but if you're smart you'll let her alone now. Let her paddle her own canoe a little. Give her a chance. What if she does run on the rocks a little, and bump her nose, and stub her toe——" He was getting mixed in his metaphor, but his sincerity was undeniable.

"You're crazy," said Ma Quail. "Sally can't get along without me. She's said so a million times, and it's true. She can't get dressed without me, or make up. She can't go on unless I'm standing in the first entrance. She'd be lost without me."

"Yeh. Well." He made a little gesture of finality, of defeat. "All right, Ma. You win. Only, when she leaves you, don't come around and say I didn't warn you."

Ma Quail stood up, her diamond eardrops flashing with the vigor of her movements. She had started to buy diamonds in Sally's second year of stage success. At first they were rather smoky little diamonds of the kind that cluster around a turquoise for support. But as the years went on you could mark the degree of Sally's progress by the increasing whiteness, brilliance, and size of Ma Quail's gems. She bought them, she said, as an investment. At this moment they were only fair in size, refractive power, and color. But they took on life from the very energy of their wearer.

"And let me tell you this, Mr. Kiper. When the day comes that you offer my Sally twenty-five hundred a week, and she'll turn it down——"

"You'll turn it down, you mean," interrupted Kiper.

"All right. *I'll* turn it down. But just remember the time when you refused to star her for five hundred a week. You can tell the story on yourself if you want to. You're probably just fool enough."

Which is no way for a stage mamma to talk to a powerful and notoriously kindhearted old theatrical manager. But as it turned out, he was wrong and she was right, in the matter of predictions.

Ben Kiper, seeing that he had hit home, decided he might as well let Ma Quail have both barrels and make an enemy for life. He was interested in Sally's career and fond of the girl. And he was a wise old gargoyle.

Ma Quail was fastening her furs, an angry eye on the door. Kiper fixed upon her a look at once patriarchal and satyric—in itself no mean histrionic feat.

"Now, listen, Ma. You know's well as I do that no girl can make a hit in musical comedy unless she's got sex appeal. And how's anybody going to find out whether Sally's got it or not until you cut loose those apron strings you've got her all tied up with? My God—a stage nun! That's what she is. Let her fall in love and break her heart, and pick up the pieces, and marry, and have a terrible time, maybe; and fight, and make up, and get——"

Ma Quail was at the door. She looked every inch the stage mother. Suddenly her face was darkly stamped and twisted with jealousy and fear. "Sally doesn't want to marry. Sally doesn't want to marry. She's told me so."

"Yeh?" The old eyes, with the oyster pouches beneath, narrowed as they regarded her. Freud and fixations were not cant words at that time; and certainly old Ben Kiper foresaw nothing of the latter-day psychology. But he knew many of the tortuous paths that twist the human mind; and here he recognized something familiar and ugly. "Yeh? Who put that funny idea in her head? Give her a chance, why don't you?"

"If my Sally ever marries it'll be a prince."

"Prince! Hell! Not if she picks him," yelled old Kiper, just before she slammed the door behind her.

You would have thought that blunt talk like this might have opened her eyes, but such scenes only served to increase Ma Quail's watchfulness, her devotion, her tireless planning.

Sometimes headliners (female) used to resent the pomp and ceremony with which Ma Quail surrounded this young person who was only filling third spot on the vaudeville bill. A change of costume in the wings. A velvet curtain hung there for protection. A square of white sheeting on the floor before the emergency dressing tables so that the hem of her gown should not be sullied; a wicker clothesbasket, chastely covered with snowy

white, holding her quick change—gown, slippers, make-up. A special pan
of special resin in which to rub the soles of her satin slippers before she
went into her dance.

"Listen! who's headliner on this bill—me or Quail?" they would demand
of the house manager.

Mother and daughter went to the theater together. Ma Quail stood in
the wings throughout the time that Sally was on stage; dressed her; undressed her; made her up; criticized her; took her home. Put her to bed.
She brought her her breakfast in the morning. They ate their early dinner
together; their bite of late supper. Sally was an amiable and generous girl,
and devoted to her mother. But there were times when she was unaccountably irritable, restless, impatient. Ma Quail put this down to temperament and was rather pleased than otherwise.

Sally's big chance in musical comedy (*Miss Me* ran two solid years in
New York) did not come until she was twenty-four. Before she was starred
in that success she had won solid recognition in vaudeville, and in musical-
comedy roles that were not stellar. And always, just ahead of her, her
mother, inserting a wedge here, getting a toe in there, widening the opening that led to stardom.

It was when Sally was playing the old Olympic Theater in Chicago that
Ma Quail fell ill and was forced to take to her bed. It was influenza, of
which there was a particularly violent epidemic at the time. It was elegantly termed *la grippe;* or, as Mrs. Quail explained, "a touch of the *la
grippe.*" She literally had never been ill and thought that by treating this
illness with contempt she could vanquish it. For one afternoon and one
evening performance she stuck it out, appearing sunken-eyed and putty-
faced at the theater, there to stand alternately shivering and burning in
the wings until finally they forced her to go back to her hotel (they were
stopping at the old Sherman House) and to bed, where she just escaped
pneumonia. They got a nurse, though Ma Quail fought this.

Sick as she was, and even a bit delirious the first twenty-four hours, she
still ruled Sally from her bed. Sally was playing down on the bill, which
meant a good spot toward the end of the program in the second half. Ma
Quail fumed until Sally was off to the theater; tossed and turned and muttered during her absence; began to listen for her return a full hour before
the girl could possibly have finished the act. She thrashed about on her
pillows, sat up, threatened to get out of bed, quarreled chronically with
her long-suffering nurse, was as impatient and difficult as a sick man.

"Now she's putting on her make-up. She never gets it on right unless
I'm there. Chunks her grease paint. . . . Now she's dressing. There was a
hook that was working a little loose on her white. It may be off by now, for

all I know. I should have caught it when I noticed it, but I thought I'd do it next . . . Now it's almost time to go on. That Nixon is just ahead of her. I told them not to run those two acts next to each other. Not that that cheap hoofer's act is anything like my Sally's. But she ought to follow a sketch. If I was up I'd make them shift the bill. . . . Now she's on. . . ." She would hum a little tune, her eyes bright and heavy with fever, a dull glow in her sallow cheeks, her hair twisted into a careless knot on top of her aching head. . . . "That's right. That's right. Go on. . . . Now she's off. There's her bow music. She's taking her curtains. One . . . two . . . three . . . four—she could have had another if they'd taken the curtain up again. . . . She'll be home now in half an hour . . . twenty minutes . . . fifteen . . . ten. . . . What time is it, Miss Burke?"

The long-suffering Miss Burke would tell her the truth, having tried a professionally soothing lie on her first day with Ma Quail and having been caught in it, with effects not calculated to allay fever in a case of *la grippe*.

"Now, Mrs. Quail, you mustn't get yourself all worked up this way. Just see if you can't drop off a minute before Miss Sally gets back. She'll be here before you know it, and then won't you be surprised!"

"Talk like a fool," retorted Ma Quail. "What's keeping her, I wonder."

On the first day of her mother's illness Sally tore off her clothes, only half removed her make-up, flew back to the hotel, sat by her mother's bedside against the nurse's warnings and the halfhearted protests of her mother. The second matinee she returned to the hotel directly after her performance, but her haste was, perhaps a shade less feverish than it had been the night before. On the third night, after she had finished dressing, she came out to the first entrance and stood there to watch Nixon doing his act. Nixon was the hoofer of whom her mother had spoken with contempt. His act preceded hers. Ma Quail never permitted Sally to stand in the entrance, watching the other acts. "Keeping tabs," it was called; or catching the act; and Sally loved to do it, particularly when the act was a dancing act. She loved dancing, especially clog and soft shoe. At both of these Nixon seemed to be expert. Curiously enough, she found three pairs of eyes squinting through the tiny gap in the old red plush curtain that hung before the first entrance. High praise, certainly, for Nixon. Three—and now, with Sally, four—fellow actors on the bill keeping tabs on his act meant that Nixon's act was worth watching.

"New stuff?" whispered Sally to the nearest ear.

"Every time he goes on. Wait a minute. There now. Get that one. He didn't pull that one this afternoon. He makes every other hoofer I ever saw look like they was nailed to the floor."

Sally, standing in the entrance, applied a fascinated eye to an inch of slit in the curtain. Involuntarily the muscles in her long nimble legs ached to do these incredibly difficult feats that seemed so simple to the uninitiate. Nixon did a black-face single. His act was that of a dancing monologist, so that Ma Quail was justified in thinking that he should not have preceded Sally. His monologue was dullish stuff; his dancing nothing short of marvelous. His was perfect muscle control, exact rhythm sense, and an assumption of indolent ease in motion that carried with it a touch of humor. Sally had been on dozens of bills with him, knew him as a shy and quiet young man who called her Miss Sally and crushed himself up against the wall to let her pass—a decent young man, descended from a long line of hoofers, a personable enough young man with a lithe waist, a quick smile, white teeth, and a Midwestern accent. Born, he said, in Kansas City, but the world was his address. His costume—to which his black face lent the last touch of the ridiculous—was an exaggeration of the then fashionable male mode: peg-top trousers, wide silk lapels, saw-edged sailor, pointed shoes. In contrast with this grotesquerie he seemed, offstage, all the more shy and, somehow, engaging and boyish.

As he bounded off now, went on again for his bows, off, and turned toward the passage that led to his dressing room, Sally, ready to go on, forgot her own invariable nervousness in her interest at what she had just seen and envied.

"Where did you get that one?" She tried to do it. They were playing her cue music. It was time for her to go on.

"No," grinned Nixon, very earnest and polite behind the black smear that was his make-up. "Go on. You take 'em. I'll show you."

He was waiting for her when she came off—a thing that had never happened to her before. Trust Ma Quail for that.

"But I don't want to steal your stuff," Sally protested.

"Say, I'd be proud to have you even look at it, let alone want to catch it. Leave me show you how it goes."

"Mother's sick."

"Yeh. I heard. Say, that's too bad. How is she?"

"She's better, only she gets nervous if I don't come straight back to the room soon's I'm dressed. But maybe—just five minutes——"

They observed the proprieties by leaving her dressing-room door wide open. "Now look. . . . Naw! . . . Naw! . . . Look! One and two and three and slide and turn and one and two and three and slide and turn and . . . looka what I do with my knee there. . . . See? Naw! . . . Stiff. . . . That's it! You'll get it. Only you got to practice. I bet I was three months at it, mornings, before I put it in."

You got a mental picture of him, in dancing trunks, in his grubby hotel bedroom, solemnly and earnestly mastering the intricacies of this new step, his stage a carpet that had been worn gray and threadbare by many dancing, mirthless feet.

Sally meant to tell her mother the cause of her delay. She didn't dream of not telling her. After all, she had picked up a new dance step. But when she reached her mother's room she found there a woman in such a state of hysteria, brought on by anxiety and general devilment, that she heard herself, to her own horror, making up some tale about having had her spot changed—moved down on the bill—a change for the better. She felt stricken at what she had done. Then she realized that she would have to do it again tomorrow—and next day—and the next and the next. And suddenly a vista—not a wide one, but still a vista—opened out before her mind's eye. An hour to herself every day. Every day—an hour—to herself. She did not say this even to herself. She did not even think she thought it. Something seemed to say it for her. She did not even think of a way to explain her explanation, should her mother recover before the end of the week. But she wouldn't be able, surely, to come to the theater before the end of this week's bill. Sally hoped she would, of course—but she wouldn't.

Sally came out of the stage entrance after her afternoon performance that next day and stood a moment on the top step, blinking almost dazedly at the dim, slimy, dour Chicago alley. It looked strangely bright to her, that alley; a sort of golden light suffused it. An hour. She had an hour. As she stood there, blinking a little, she was like a prisoner who, released after long years of servitude, stands huddled at the prison gates, fighting the impulse to creep back into the cold embrace of the gray walls that have so long sheltered him. So Sally thought: Well, I guess I'll go right home.

But she didn't. Instead she began to stroll in a desultory manner down Clark Street, looking in the windows. She was conscious of a sensation of exhilaration, of buoyancy. That sordid thoroughfare, Clark Street, took on a fascination, a sparkle, a brilliance. Sally saw in the window of a candy store a great square pan of freshly dipped dark-brown chocolate creams. She went in and bought a little paper sackful. Her mother rarely allowed her to eat sweets. They were bad for her complexion. Sally now strolled on down the street, consuming her plump chocolates by a process as unladylike as it was difficult. You bit off the top of the cone-shaped sweet, or, if you preferred, you bit a small opening at the side, taking care not to make this too large, and including in this bite as little as possible of the creamy fondant beneath. This accomplished, the trick was to lick at the soft white filling with a little scooping flick of the tongue, much in the manner of a cat consuming a saucer of cream. Little by little, thus, the fondant melts on the tongue, disappears, leaving a hollow shell of chocolate, an empty cocoon.

So Sally Quail, in her new freedom, strolled exulting down Clark Street, staring into the windows, stopping before some of them, her little pointed red tongue working busily away at the sweet held in her fingers, her face beatifically blank as the sugary stuff trickled down her grateful throat. There was even a little unsuspected dab of chocolate on one cheek, near her mouth. It gave her a most juvenile and engaging look.

She was thus engaged when Nixon approached her, breathing a trifle rapidly, as though he had been running. She showed, queerly enough, no surprise at seeing him. He fell into step beside her.

"I didn't see you go out. I was getting dressed. You must've jumped into your clothes."

"Blm," said Sally, companionably, her mouth full of fondant; and held the sack out to him, hospitably. He took one, ate it, took another, ate that, suddenly noticed her method, which she was pursuing calmly and without affectation.

"Say, that's a great system you got, Miss Sally. How'd you like to have one six feet high, and lick your way right through it!"

Sally laughed heartily at this, and so did he, though it wasn't very bright. And so, still giggling, they reached the Sherman House. And a little stricken look of contrition came into Sally's face. He said, "Well, so long. See you tonight. Uh—say, there's a little spot of chocolate on your cheek."

"Where?" And rubbed the wrong place.

"Right—there." He whipped out a handkerchief, put it back hastily, took out another, neatly folded, and held it up, hesitating. "If you don't mind——"

She didn't mind. He rubbed it off, gently. There was something intimate, something protective, about the act.

"See you tonight, Miss Sally."

"See you tonight."

On the way up she gave the remaining chocolates to the elevator boy. And then the usual questions, the usual answers. How many curtains? How much applause? How was the house? Was the headliner still high-hatting her?

The evening show.

Nixon wanted to introduce a song into his act. No, he couldn't sing, he told her. Not what you'd call sing. But you know. One of those coon songs. Kind of fresh up the act. He asked her advice about it. He hung on her answer. Her decision. Sally Quail, for whom everything was decided. Sally Quail, who never was allowed to do anything for anyone. Everything done for her. No one allowed her to do for them. Not her capable martinet mother, surely. It was sweet to have someone dependent on you for a decision; someone who thought your advice valuable—not valuable only, but invaluable.

They watched each other's act, matinee and evening. She was there just the moment before he went on—that moment when the vaudeville actor "sets himself" for his entrance. She had seen them do all sorts of things for luck to last them through the concentrated fifteen minutes of an act. She had seen them cross themselves. She had seen them rub a tiny talisman. She had seen them mutter a prayer. Nixon, sprung from a long line of acrobats, blackface minstrels, hoofers, always went through a little series of meaningless motions before the final second that marked his entrance music. There was a little preliminary cough, a shuffle, a backward glance over his shoulder at nothing, a straightening of the absurd hat, tie, coat, a jerk at the coat lapel, a hunch of the shoulders, a setting of his features—all affording relief for strained nerves. Click! He was on, walking with that little exaggeration of the Negro shuffle, his arms hanging limp and loose and long, his eyes rolling tragically. He had rehearsed his new song and now he tried it out at the close of his act. It was one of those new songs and was called "I Guess I'll Have to Telegraph My Baby." It was the type of plaintive comic song that preceded the jazz blues of today. He had, really, no more singing voice than Sally. But he had a plaintive tonal quality and a melodious resonance that caught and held you. He got two extra curtains on it, thus cutting in on Sally's act time. She did not resent this, though when he came off he apologized with something resembling tears in his eyes.

"Why, say, I didn't go for to crab your act, Miss Sally. Why, say, I wouldn't have done that for the world. Why, say——" He was incoherent, agonized.

Sally, set to go on, looked up at him. No girl of experience would have shown unconsciously the look that Sally turned upon him. Certainly her mother had never seen that look in her eyes. Her face was sparkling, animated, glowing. Dimples flashed where dimples had not been. In that look you saw pride in the achievement of someone else—someone for whom she cared. She even said it.

"Don't be silly! I'm proud of you. Glad you stopped the show." And went on.

If Ma Quail had been there it would have taken the house manager, the stagehands, firemen, ushers, and doorman to hold her.

Ma Quail, in her hotel bedroom, had impatiently endured five days away from the theater, five days without seeing her Sally go on, five days of domination by a nurse. The nurse left, always, at eight. This evening, as

Ma Quail lay there, fuming, she was racked by a feeling of unrest, of danger to Sally. She had had that feeling before, and nothing had come of it. The feeling grew, took complete possession of her. Sally was in the theater. Sally was dressing; Sally would soon be going on. She could endure it no longer. Trembling and dizzy with the peculiar weakness that even a brief siege of this particular illness leaves, she dressed shakily, catching at chairs and tables for support. She was driven the short distance to the Olympic. Sick and shivering as she was, she actually seemed to take on a new strength and vigor as she passed the stage doorkeeper. She sniffed the theater smell sensitively, gratefully. For years it had been incense in her nostrils. Sally would be almost ready to go on, now that her act had been shifted to a spot down on the bill. She actually resented this advantage having come to Sally without her having fought for it. Up the winding iron stairway; down the narrow dim hall; a smile of anticipation on her face. She turned the knob of Sally's dressing-room door; she opened the door softly, softly, so as to surprise her Sally.

Sally Quail, with her head thrown back, was looking into the eyes of Jimmy Nixon, of the Dancing Nixons. Nixon's arms were close about her. Sally's eyes were half closed. Her chin was lifted with shy upward eagerness. Her mouth was tremulous and ripe and flexible—the lips of a woman who knows that she is about to be kissed. It was a kiss she never received.

"I love you, Sally," said Nixon.

And "Oh, I love you, too," said Sally Quail. Her voice was a breath, a whisper.

There was something terrible, something indecent about Ma Quail's ruthless tearing apart of these two young things. She did it so horribly, so brutally. Her jewel was being stolen. The flower that she had tended and nurtured was being plucked by clumsy alien hands. Ugly words bubbled to her lips and broke there.

"Get out of here!" She slammed the door, advanced menacingly. She actually seemed about to strike him. "Get out of here, you—you cheap hoofer, you! Get out or I'll have you thrown out!" She turned to the girl. "You fool! You damned little fool!"

Nixon unclasped the girl, but he still held her hand in his. As always, under emotion, he spoke the slow and drawling tongue of the born Kansan.

"You can't talk thataway to us, ma'am."

Sally said nothing. Her face was white and drawn and old. The sight of it whipped Ma Quail into fresh fury.

"Can't!" she spat out in a whisper that had all the vehemence of a scream. "I'll 'can't' you! Get out of here, you bum, you! I'll have you thrown out of the circuit. I'll fix it so you'll never show in any decent house again. I'll"—unconsciously she used a term she had heard somewhere in cheap melodrama—"I'll break you!"

He grinned at that. He took a step toward her, drawing the frightened girl with him. "Come on, Sally," he said quietly. "Come on away out of here."

"I'm afraid," whispered Sally. "I'm afraid. Where?"

"You know," he said. "What we were talking about. Nixon and Quail."

But at that, of course, Ma Quail fainted for the first time in her life. And when she had been revived she insisted that she was dying, and Nixon had been sent out of the room, and they took off her corset and rubbed her hands and gave her whisky, and she rolled her eyes, and groaned, and made Sally promise over and over that she would never see Nixon again. It was her dying wish. She was dying. Sally had killed her. And of course Sally promised, racked by self-reproach. And that was the end of that— and, everyone will admit, a good thing for Sally.

Ma Quail prevailed on the management to retain Sally's act for another week, which broke up contact with Nixon in the next week's bill, scheduled for Milwaukee.

Sally probably forgot all about it in later years. Curiously enough, she never would talk about it, even to her mother. And though the prince her mother was expecting never came, practically everything else in life did. Fame and fortune, and popularity, and friendship. A house in London, a house in New York, an apartment in Paris. Private trains. Maids. Secretaries. Perhaps no other woman of the theater ever made (honestly) such fantastic sums as Sally Quail earned yearly for twenty years. Under her indomitable mother's shrewd management she became polished, finished, exquisite in her art, though she managed somehow, miraculously, to retain something of her girlishness and simplicity and lovableness to the end. Still, sometimes, if you glimpsed the two driving on Fifth Avenue or in the Bois, you wondered about Sally. You saw them driving in one of those long foreign cars that are almost all engine. One of those cars that proclaim the fact that its owner has at least two others. It had a hood over the back, but no hood in the front, so that the chauffeur and a good half of the delicate upholstery were unprotected. It was a proud and insolent car that said, "I am a bibelot. I am a luxury. I am practically no good at all except when the sun is shining—but not shining too hotly. When it is fair, but not too cool. I am only to be used at special times by special people. I am the specialest kind of car for people who don't have to care a damn. I am money. Look about you. You won't see many like me."

Sally looked none too glowingly happy in the hooded depths of this gorgeous vehicle, a luxurious fur rug tucked about her gifted knees, a toy dog sticking his tongue out at passers-by in lesser cars.

Sally Quail's tragic and untimely death broke her mother completely—or almost completely. Small wonder. Still, she derived a crumb of comfort from the touching and heartbreaking last moment that preceded Sally's going. In the midst of the fever that consumed her she had what seemed to be a lucid last moment just before the end. Ma Quail told of it, often and often, over and over, to sympathetic friends.

For at the end, as she lay there, looking, in her terrible illness, much more than her forty years, suddenly her face had assumed the strangest look—the look of a girl of twenty. There was about it a delicacy, a glow. She sat up in bed as though she were strong and well again. All the little lines in her face were wiped out queerly, completely, as though by a magic hand. She lifted her chin a little with a shy, upward eagerness and her fever-dried lips took on the tremulousness and the flexibility of the lips of a woman who knows that she is about to be kissed. Her arms were outstretched, her eyes fixed on something that she found wonderful and beautiful.

"Sally!" Ma Quail had screamed. "Sally! What is it! Oh, my God! Look at me. It's Mother! Mother loves you!"

And "Oh, I love you, too!" said Sally Quail to someone unseen. Her voice was a breath, a whisper.

Every Other Thursday

[1926]

There came to me the not-very-brilliant idea that it might be amusing to do a series of stories depicting one day in the lives of people usually considered undramatic, commonplace, and even sordid. One of these was the taxi driver in "Hey! Taxi!" Another the garage mechanic in "The Afternoon of a Faun." Another, called "Fräulein," the one-day story of a nursemaid. This last does not appear in this collection because it seemed to have some of the characteristics of this particular story, which is the social life of a Finnish maid-of-all-work in New York. It was written because I heard a woman say, "I asked her to change her day off from Thursday to Wednesday. Just that once. She wouldn't do it. The selfish lump! What could she do on Thursday that she couldn't do just as well on Wednesday? Nothing!"

❧ FROM THE MOMENT SHE THRUST A SWIFT AND PRACTICED ARM FROM beneath the bedclothes to choke the seven-o'clock alarm, Helmi was suffused with the thought that it was Thursday. Not merely Thursday, but *Thursday*. Not only that: it was Every Other Thursday. And Every Other Thursday was Helmi's day out.

She lay there, snug, under the welter of gray blankets, savoring the delicious thought. Her mind leaped at one bound over the dull hours that intervened between 7 A.M. and 2 P.M. From two on and on the day lay before her, sparkling, golden, new-minted, to spend as she liked. She had it planned, down to the ultimate second.

A pioneer April fly buzzed drowsily at her tightly closed bedroom window. Here in America people slept with their windows wide open, but Helmi knew better than that. The night air is poisonous, as anyone can tell you. Helmi never opened her windows until the really hot June nights set in—sometimes not even then. Habit is strong; and there had been no steam heat in the Finland farmhouse of her girlhood, and Finnish nights are cold.

Next Sunday was Easter. At Eastertime, one year ago, she had had no new hat, no new dress, no new coat, no new slippers like the rest of New York. Last Easter she had been thankful just to be here. Lonely and homesick, but thankful. This Easter would be different. This very afternoon would find her on One Hundred and Twenty-fifth Street, East, which is New York's uptown Finland. There she would buy a blue dress and a

285

bright-blue silk hat such as Lempi Parta had worn at the Finnish Progressive Society hall last week; and pale-tan silk stockings, and slippers with bows.

For more than a year a great slice of her wages had gone to pay back her brother, Abel Seppala, and her brother's wife, Anni, for the money they had sent her to buy her passage over—her two passages over. Those terrible two passages, the first unsuccessful, so that she had seen New York's skyline approach and recede; the second dramatically successful. She could laugh now when she thought of that successful second landing. They had fooled them, all right, that time. It had cost one hundred and twenty-five dollars the first time, and one hundred and fifty to bribe the steamship steward the second time. Helmi had been almost a year and a half paying back that money to Abel and Anni.

This afternoon she would go to Anni's in Brooklyn, as usual. But not to stay. From there she would take the subway quickly to One Hundred and Twenty-fifth Street. She had so many things to do. So many lovely things. She ought to start before two, or how could she do all these things that must be done? That must be done today because it would be two weeks before Every Other Thursday came again. Perhaps she would get off at half-past one, or even one, if the work was finished. . . .

The sound of water rushing into the tub in the bathroom off Their Bedroom. Mr. Mawson! He had to have his breakfast at twenty minutes to eight, sharp. It was quarter-past seven! Helmi leaped out of bed, flung off her sturdy cotton nightgown, dived into the knitted union suit, the faded stockings with a run down the seam of one—discarded of Miss Zhoolie—the old sateen petticoat, the blue gingham work dress. Into the stuffy little bathroom off her bedroom. A dab at her face, a splash with her hands, a hasty running of the broken comb through her bobbed pale-yellow hair (that bob had been the first step in her Americanization). Helmi always combed her hair after she was fully dressed. It was interesting to hear Mrs. James G. Mawson on that subject, among others.

Out to the kitchen. Bang! The coffeepot. Rattle! The spoon. Slam! The icebox door. Clash! The silver. Clatter! The china. Whiff-woof! The swinging door. Three breakfasts to get at three different times, and the front room to be tidied in between.

Mr. Mawson had his breakfast in the dining room at twenty minutes to eight. James G. Mawson (the Mawson Optical Company) was a silent, grayish, neat man, behind glasses with special lenses. His breakfast never varied. Half a grapefruit or a glass of orange juice. Two four-minute eggs. Two pieces of whole-wheat bread, toasted. A cup of coffee. Two lumps of sugar. Plenty of cream. Out of the house at five minutes to eight.

In March he had essayed to diet. Mrs. Mawson had said he was getting paunchy, and decreed but one piece of toast, thinly buttered; black coffee with no sugar; one egg. For two mornings he had obediently sipped his coffee, though with a wry face, and had left half of it, a sable pool of bitterness, in his cup. Mrs. Mawson never breakfasted with him. The third morning he broke an oblong of sugar in half and slipped the piece into his coffee. The fourth he just tinged the blackness with one small splash of cream. The fifth Helmi brought him two pieces of toast. He ate them both. The sixth she prepared two eggs as usual, placed the sugar and cream at his hand, and left the room.

These men in America! These husbands! Poor, spineless things, treated like little boys by their wives and daughters. In Finland it was different. The women were independent, yes, like the men. But the men were not bossed by the women. These two women, they ran him. Do this, do that, go here, go there, I want thus, I want so. He hardly ever rebelled. Sometimes, but not often. Usually he just looked at them in silence, and a little line would come into his forehead. Between Helmi, the Finnish maidservant, and Mr. James G. Mawson of the Mawson Optical Company, there existed an unspoken and unsuspected sympathy and understanding. Helmi spoke rarely. She was an almost inspired cook.

Miss Zhoolie always dashed into the dining room just before nine, in a rush, and gulped her orange juice standing, in hat and coat. Mrs. Mawson's voice would be heard from her bedroom. "Zhoolie, you eat something hot before you go out."

"I can't. I've got a nine o'clock. I'm late now."

"I don't care how late you are. . . . Then get up ten minutes earlier. . . . Then don't stay out until one. . . . If it's only a cup of hot coffee. . . ." But Miss Zhoolie had gone to her class at Barnard.

The Mawsons lived in Eighty-sixth Street, West. Those lessons to which Miss Zhoolie dashed each weekday morning were in One Hundred and Sixteenth Street, Helmi knew. Evidently, in this country it made no difference if you reached these classes on time or not.

Mrs. Mawson's tray you brought to her bed every morning at nine, after the others had gone. It was quite a hearty breakfast, considering that Mrs. Mawson Wasn't Strong. She could not rise for breakfast because this brought on one of her headaches. She always spoke of these afflictions in the possessive. One of my headaches. It was as though she cherished them.

It was not hard, once you had got the hang of it. A year ago she could never have done it, but Helmi learned quickly. She had had to work much harder than this on the farm in Finland; had worked in the fields, not only from dawn to dark but far into the bright Northern summer nights. Still, this was hard in a different way. Here they were always changing things, doing things differently after you had learned to do them in one way. In Finland the work had been set, inevitable. Now the cabbages, now the rye, now the potatoes, now the corn, now the oats. The horses the cows the sheep the pigs. But here you never knew. With Mr. Mawson you knew. But not with Her. And not with Miss Zhoolie. Often, after they had told her to do a thing one way and she had learned it that way, they changed their minds and told her to do it another. But Helmi went ahead and did it in the original way, disregarding them. Mrs. Mawson said she didn't understand her.

"I must say I don't understand that girl. Really she's a closed book to me. You can't be friendly with her. She just looks at you. Her face is like a joss-house idol. I honestly think she could come in and find us all murdered and weltering in our blood and she wouldn't turn a hair—especially if it happened to be her Thursday."

The conversation was between Mrs. Mawson and her nineteen-year-old daughter, Zhoolie. Zhoolie had been christened Julia, after the departed distaff grandmamma. This, in her fourteenth year, she had Frenchified to Julie, which she insisted on pronouncing as though it were spelled with a *Zh* and a double *o*. It must even be stated that she frequently even signed herself thus, especially in the tenderer branches of her Barnard educational career.

James G. Mawson spoke up unexpectedly, as he sometimes did when they thought he had not been listening.

"Mighty good girl just the same," he said. "Knows her business and minds it."

"Helmi's a teep," said Zhoolie.

"A what?" inquired James G. Mawson, over the top of his newspaper.

"A teep."

"Spell it."

"T-y-p-e, teep. That's French."

"Well, you," retorted Mr. Mawson, "make me seek. S-i-c-k, seek. That's English."

Sometimes Zhoolie was driven to referring to Helmi as that Hunky. This usually when Helmi had succeeded in making an important (to Zhoolie) telephone message more than usually unsolvable. Her thick tongue and unaccustomed ear made a sorry business of these communications. "W'at? . . . Yeh, iss. . . . Who? . . . Yeh. . . . She ain't here. . . . Wait, I write. . . ."

Mrs. Mawson on her return home, or Zhoolie, would find a scrawl to the effect that someone named U-J-B-D-M had telephoned, and had asked her to call up as soon as she got in. Helmi's own telephone communications were as mysterious as they were private, being carried on in a guttural flood of Finnish, to Mrs. Mawson's bafflement. She always had a helpless feeling that she was being talked about.

Helmi would never make a modish-looking maid. Hers was a trim enough figure, in a broad-hipped ample-bosomed wide-shouldered peasant sort of way. But you always felt that her neat afternoon uniform of black and white confined her against her will, and that someday she would rend these garments from her in a furious burst of Nordic freedom. This irked Mrs. Mawson and Zhoolie.

"Still, if you have only one maid, what can you do? Of course"—hastily —"the Woman comes in to clean one day a week, and the Washwoman. But Zhoolie has so many friends. Half the time Helmi isn't presentable when people come to the door. And her room!" Mrs. Mawson would then gather the subject into a neat bundle and tie it with the sinister generality that they were all alike.

Helmi's bedroom undeniably was not the most exquisitely kept of bowers. Perhaps, after daily scouring, dusting, mopping, and wiping the rest of the Mawson apartment, there was a certain wholesome and nicely balanced defiance shown in the slightly musty disorder of her own private chamber. After all, your chef develops a personal indifference toward food; and walking is no treat for a mail carrier.

Mrs. Mawson had a way of investigating this room on Helmi's Thursday out. This she excused on the ground of housewifeliness. The room was always the same. On the lower shelf of her table reposed last summer's white shoes. There they had been throughout the winter. On her dresser a little mound of spilled talcum, a torn hair net; photographs of bridal couples in cataleptic attitudes, and family groups as stiff as woodcuts; a Sunday rotogravure picture of a motion-picture actress and an actor. Stuck to the sides of the dresser mirror were colored picture postcards that caused both Mrs. Mawson and Zhoolie some merriment. These were, they thought, pictures such as a six-year-old child would cherish. Done in crude greens and reds and pinks, they depicted an old man, white-bearded, got up like a Santa Claus in a pine forest; a white-robed princess-looking female floating on a wave, with stars and sunbursts shooting all about her; a brown-bearded man hammering at a forge like the Village Blacksmith. At the top of these pictures was printed the word *Kalevala*. Underneath, in finer print, unpronounceable words like Wainamoinen and Ilmatar and Joukahaimen.

"Some Finn fairy tale, don't you think?" Zhoolie said. "Poor thing. I'd like to take her up to school for a mental test. Outside her cooking and housework I'll bet she'd turn in an I.Q. of a child of eight."

Certainly Mrs. Mawson and Zhoolie never knew that the *Kalevala* is the national epic of Finland—the *Paradise Lost,* the Shakespeare of that Northern country; and that its rhythms, well known to Helmi and studied by her in her girlhood at the excellent Finnish country school, had been borrowed and stolen and copied by many a versifier included in Zhoolie's English course at Barnard. Zhoolie would have been startled if she could have translated the cadences of the thumbed and greasy volume that lay on the table shelf beside Helmi's last-summer shoes.

> On his back he bound his quiver,
> And his new bow on his shoulder,
> In his hands his pole grasped firmly,
> On the left shoe glided forward,
> And pushed onward with the right one,
> And he spoke the words which follow . . .

"My goodness, why doesn't she open her windows! And look at her lovely bedspread that I took such—why do they always sit on the edge of the bed and never on a chair! And just see this bathroom. I am simply going to tell her that she must bathe oftener than—— Oh, they're all alike!"

Always capable and energetic in a slapdash, lunging kind of way, Helmi, on this particular Thursday in April, was a tornado. There loomed ahead of her the regular Thursday routine which, on Every Other Thursday, was a rite. The kitchen linoleum must be made spotless. There was some American superstition about the sink faucets being left shining on Thursdays out. On the other hand, it was understood that lunch—if any—was to be most sketchy on Every Other Thursday; that Mrs. Mawson would go out for this meal, if possible. Zhoolie never lunched at home on weekdays. Helmi was free to go when her work was finished.

These things had come to be taken for granted, tacitly. There was little conversation between mistress and maid. Helmi practiced the verbal economy of her race. She spoke rarely, and then in monosyllables: "Yeh, iss. . . . I bake a cake wiss nuts. . . . What you want for eat? . . ." The iceman, the butcher boy, the grocer, the janitor, the service-elevator boy, in person or at the telephone, got short shrift from Helmi in any case. On Thursdays she was curt to the point of insult. Strangely enough—or perhaps not so strangely—this indifference to their advances gave Helmi a certain desirability in their eyes. When occasion presented itself they attempted to woo her in the patois of their kind.

"Say, you're a sketch. You hate the men, don't you? I bet the guy gets you'll have a right to wear a umpire's mask, all right. Listen, baby, don't you never go nowheres? How about a movie? Don't you dance or nothing?"

Did she dance? Did she dance! For what else did she live! To what other purpose was Every Other Thursday planned! Ask the girls and boys at the Finnish Progressive Society hall in One Hundred and Twenty-sixth Street. Especially (alas!) the girls, the girls who swarmed there on a Thursday night with their half dollar clutched tight in their big, capable palms. You went to those dances alone. If you were popular you danced with the boys. Otherwise you danced with the girls. By half-past eight the big dance hall on the top floor was comfortably filled. By half-past nine it was crowded. By half-past ten it was packed. The heavy-handed band boomed and pounded out the fox trot, the waltz, the German polka. Did she dance? Did she dance! These American boys were fools.

This Thursday night she would dance in her new blue dress to be purchased on One Hundred and Twenty-fifth Street. In her new silk stockings and her new kid slippers. And then perhaps Vaino Djerf would dance with her. Helmi danced very well indeed. She knew that. She had been the best dancer in her district in the old country. She had noted how Vaino watched her as she danced at the hall on Thursday nights.

But her clothes! It was not for such as Vaino to dance with her. Vaino, of all the Finnish chauffeurs, drove the finest car. It was big like a railway locomotive. It had great lamps like barrels, and glittering with silver. Often you saw this gorgeous vehicle outside Progressive Hall, where Vaino took his pleasures—had his Finnish steam bath, played pool, danced, boxed in the gymnasium. But when Helmi had her new clothes it would be different. He would dance with her then. She would talk to him (not much—but just enough to let him know that her people in Finland were not common farmers; that she had read the *Kalevala*; had gone to school; could figure; was a superb cook; owed nothing more on her passage money and could save from now on).

There! Mr. Mawson had almost finished his breakfast. Miss Zhoolie's orange juice on ice. A good half-hour in which to start the cleaning. She attacked the living room with fury. Ash trays. Papers. Plump the cushions. The carpet sweeper. Dust.

Usually she accomplished all this almost noiselessly. It was understood that Mrs. Mawson must not be disturbed. But this morning she need not be so careful, for Miss Zhoolie's voice, energetic in argument, and Mrs. Mawson's plaintive tones could be heard in unaccustomed early-morning dialogue. Zhoolie was in her mother's room, and dressing frenziedly as she talked.

"Well, you can *ask* her. . . . Well, Pete's sake, we do enough for her. . . . But I didn't know until last night. Jane asked me if I'd have them tonight instead of Saturday because they're going to Atlantic City on Friday, all of a sudden. And she's been so wonderful to me, and you know what it means on account of Len. Let her go out tomorrow instead of today. My gosh! It isn't as if she really *did* anything! Goes and squats at her sister's or whatever it is, in Brooklyn, and drinks coffee. . . ."

"Sh-sh-sh-sh!" Then Mrs. Mawson's voice, dulcet, plaintive. "Helmi! Helmi, will you come here just a minute?"

Helmi pretended not to hear; made a great to-do with her carpet sweeper. Wasn't it Every Other Thursday? Did not every minute count? Zhoolie opened her mother's bedroom door, poked her head out, called sharply, but with the edge of the sharpness illy concealed in a false sheath of velvet.

"Helmi, Mother wants to speak to you just a minute, please."

Helmi leaned the handle of the carpet sweeper against the table and came. Mrs. Mawson was in bed. She looked very plain and showed her age. Helmi, nineteen, wondered how it must feel to be as old as that; felt a stir of sympathy. In spite of the long period of passage-money payment, she had monthly sent money to her mother in Finland. It was well for Mrs. Mawson's peace of mind and pride that she could not read Helmi's thoughts behind that flat Finnish face. Miss Zhoolie stood in the background. She was fastening her blouse with absent-minded expertness. Little vibratory electric sparks of suspense seemed to dart out from her to Helmi.

Mrs. Mawson cleared her throat ever so slightly, pursed her mouth into the semblance of a placating smile.

"Helmi, Miss Zhoolie just learned last night that the guests she was expecting for dinner on Saturday night—three, you know—Mr. Mawson and I were going out—that makes four, with Miss Zhoolie——"

"Oh, Mother, do come to the point."

"Miss Zhoolie wants to know—they can't possibly come on Saturday—they're leaving town unexpectedly on Friday"—a sound from Zhoolie—"wants to know if you can't stay in today so that they can come to dinner tonight—she's to let them know this morning—and take Friday out instead. Will you do that?"

"No," said Helmi.

The monosyllable was so flat, so final, so direct that it had the effect of stunning her hearers slightly; they appeared not quite to understand. Mrs. Mawson actually repeated, painstakingly, as though Helmi had not grasped her meaning: "You could have tomorrow, Friday, instead of today. You probably have no plans. And it looks a little like rain anyway today, don't you think?"

"No," said Helmi.

"You mean no, you won't? Or——" Then, at the look on Zhoolie's face: "I'll tell you what, Helmi! You could take this Sunday instead. Easter Sunday. It isn't your Sunday, but you could have it——"

"No," said Helmi.

Zhoolie remained in the background no longer. She stamped her foot. Color suffused her pretty face.

"Well, I think you're a mean thing, Helmi! What have you got to do but go and sit at your sister's——"

"Zhoolie!"

"It's true. She hasn't."

Mrs. Mawson fixed her smile again, but not very successfully. It was really only pasted on, and crooked at that. "To tell you the truth, Helmi, one of the young men coming is someone Miss Zhoolie is very—she likes especially, do you see? And that's why she wanted them particularly to-night. This young man——"

This young man. Helmi turned and looked at Zhoolie in her soft girlish beige jersey frock, and her silk stockings, and her smart slippers. Her young man! Well, let her get him, then. Helmi had the getting of a young man to see to. So they stood staring at each other, these two girls: Helmi nineteen, immovable, inscrutable, implacable; Zhoolie nineteen, lovely, tearful, spoiled, furious. Helmi's thoughts, translated, would have read: "Get your young man, if you want him. I have seen your young men, and a poor lot they are, too. I would not exchange my Vaino for a half dozen of them." Zhoolie's flashing eyes and trembling lips meant: "Great clumsy Hunky! To think that you can actually spoil my day for me— maybe my life! Oh, damn! Oh, damn you!"

Aloud she said again, "But, Helmi, it isn't as if you really had anything special to do. What do you do on Thursday out that you couldn't do on Friday!"

What did she do on her Thursday out that she couldn't do on Friday! Within herself Helmi smiled and hugged her golden day to her. The Finnish girls uptown. Lempi Parta. Blue dress. The Finnish steam bath. Swim. Supper. The play at Finnish Hall. The dance. What did she do on Thursday that she couldn't do on Friday! She looked at Zhoolie, unmoved. She looked at Mrs. Mawson, her mistress. Looked at her stubbornly.

"No," said Helmi. Turned, and went back to her work in the living room; went back with redoubled and more furious energy to make up for precious time lost.

"I don't care!" cried Zhoolie, like a child. "She's a nasty, mean thing. What does she do! Nothing! Not a thing. She hasn't the intelligence to plan a holiday. She hasn't a thing to do."

Up the hall came Mr. James G. Mawson on his way to the Mawson
Optical Company downtown. He glanced in at the bedroom door. "What's
the row?" he asked. "What's the row?"

"Oh, nothing," said Mrs. Mawson wearily. "I can feel one of my headaches coming on."

Zhoolie turned a tearstained face to her father. "I want Helmi to take
tomorrow out instead of today, and she won't."

"Don't blame her," said James G. Mawson, maddeningly.

"Oh, you're always like that, Father! Abe Lincoln stuff. It's one of your
poses. What difference does it make what day she takes out, anyway!"

"Not any difference to you, Julia; might make a lot of difference to her.
. . . Well . . ." The front door slammed behind him.

"I've heard people say 'cold as a fish,'" observed Mrs. Mawson. "'Cold
as a Finn,' I'd say."

Helmi consumed little enough food as a rule, aside from copious and
unlimited cups of coffee and hunks of rye bread. Mrs. Mawson bought rye
bread studded with caraway, just for Helmi. In citing Helmi's virtues,
Mrs. Mawson was wont to include this. "She really doesn't eat a thing, I'll
say that for her. I don't know what she lives on. Eating and bathing seem
to be two habits that have never got much of a hold on Helmi."

Today Helmi ate even less than usual. She swept through the house like
a Juggernaut—living room, bedrooms, dining room, kitchen. By noon she
had done the work of three women; had done all the work there was to be
done. A cup of coffee taken standing at the kitchen table. By twelve-thirty
the smell of burning hair pervaded the Mawson flat. Mrs. Mawson had not
yet gone out. She sniffed the air with an expression of extreme distaste.
She walked down the hall to the kitchen. Helmi, fully dressed in her street
clothes except for her coat and hat, was heating her curling iron at the
gas stove.

"Not finished with your work already, are you, Helmi?"

"Yeh."

"Everything?"

"Sure."

"The icebox?"

"Thursday iss no icebox. Saturday iss icebox."

"Oh—well . . ." Mrs. Mawson drifted vaguely away. Helmi made the
final trip with her curling iron from the gas stove to her bedroom mirror.

It was not yet one o'clock as she sat stolidly in a subway train marked
Brooklyn. Seeing her, you would have known her for a foreign-born servant girl on her Thursday out. High, flat planes of cheekbones; low, full
breasts; broad shoulders; pale-blue eyes; frizzed bobbed hair; a pretty good

cloth coat; silk stockings; a velvet hat. Certainly you would never have guessed that golden hours filled with high adventure lay ahead of this lumpy creature; and that an exciting and dramatic year lay behind her.

Helmi Seppala was being slowly digested in the maw of New York. Her passage money had been sent her by her brother, Abel Seppala. She had sailed from Åbo. New York reached, she had been turned back at Ellis Island. Her country's quota was already filled. The thing had been overwhelming. Months passed. Again Abel sent money, against the protests of his wife, Anni. This time Helmi bribed the steward on the ship, and sailed as one of the stewardesses. One hundred and fifty dollars that had cost. How sick she had been! She was racked now at the thought of it. The boat reached New York. Unforeseen red tape bound Helmi to the ship. The stewardesses were not allowed to land. Frantic, she managed to get word to Abel.

The boat remained five days in New York. On the day it was due to return to Finland, Abel and Anni came on board, ostensibly to bid farewell to a Finnish friend who was going to his home country. Concealed, they carried on board with them American-made clothes—a dress, a coat, shoes, a hat, powder, rouge, eyeglasses. These had been smuggled to Helmi. Feverishly she had shed her uniform, had put on the American clothes, the rouge, the powder, the eyeglasses. When the call had come for visitors to go ashore, Helmi, with Abel and Anni, had passed down the gangplank under the very eyes of the chief steward himself—to the dock, to the street, into the amazing spring sunshine of a New York May morning. Spurned as an alien by her stepmotherland, she had disguised herself as a native daughter and achieved a home that way.

At once she had gone to work. At once she had gone to school. Anni had not been very cordial to this sister of her husband. But she had grudgingly helped the girl, nevertheless. She had got her a "place." The wage was small, for Helmi knew no English and was ignorant of American ways, of New York household usages. But from the first, part of that infinitesimal wage went to pay back the passage money loaned her by Abel and Anni. And from the first she had gone to night school, three nights a week. Three nights a week, from eight until ten, after her dinner dishes were washed, she attended the night-school class, sitting hunched over a scarred school desk used by fourth-grade children in the daytime. It was a class in English for both sexes.

Most of the women were servant girls like herself—Swedish, Finnish, Czech, Latvian, Polish, Hungarian. She had the look of the old country. A big-boned girl, with broad shoulders and great capable hands. She had worn her hair pulled away from her forehead and temples, held with side combs, and wound at the back in a bun of neat, slippery braids. In her ears she wore little gold hoops. Her hair was straw-colored, with no glint of gold in it; her eyes were blue, but not a deep blue. She was not pretty, but there had been about her a certain freshness of coloring and expression. Her hair clung in little damp tendrils at the back of her neck. There was great breadth between her cheekbones, her shoulders, her hipbones. Her legs were sturdy, slim, and quick. She listened earnestly. They read out of a child's reader. The lesson was, perhaps, a nature study.

"What is a frog, Miss Seppala?"

Miss Seppala would look startled, terrified, and uncomprehending, all at once.

Again, articulating painfully with tongue, teeth, palate: "What—is—a—frog, Miss Seppala?"

Much gabbling and hissing from those all about her. Suddenly a great light envelops Miss Seppala. She bounces up.

"A frock iss animal wiss legs iss jumping all the time and iss green." Triumph!

The lesson went on to say, "Dragonflies are called darning needles." Miss Speiser, the good-natured, spectacled teacher, spoke Upper West Side New York English. "Aw dawhning needles hawmful?" she inquired. The result was that Helmi's English accent turned out to be a mixture of early Finnish and late Bronx most mystifying to the hearer. Still it had served.

And now, a year later, her hair was bobbed, and her clothes were American, and she said, "I'll tell the vorld," and got twenty dollars each week at the Mawsons'. She had paid back her passage money down to the last cent, so now Anni, in one of her tempers, could never again call her a dirty Lapp —that insult of insults to the Finn or Swede. She had learned with amazing swiftness to prepare American dishes, being a naturally gifted cook. She knew how to serve from the left, to keep the water glasses filled, not to remove the service plates until the dinner plates were at hand, to keep thumb marks off glass salad dishes, to mix a pretty good Martini cocktail. She was, in short, an excellent middle-class American servant—spunky, independent, capable, unfriendly.

It was a long trip from West Eighty-sixth Street to Finntown, in Brooklyn, where Abel and Anni lived. Helmi begrudged the time this afternoon, but she went out of a sense of duty and custom and a certain tribal loyalty. Anni's house was a neat two-story brick, new, in West Forty-fourth Street, Brooklyn. The neighborhood was almost solidly Finnish. The houses were well kept, prosperous-looking, owned by Finn carpenters, mechanics, skilled workmen, whose wage was twelve, fourteen, sixteen dollars a day.

One of Anni's boys, Otto, aged four, was playing outside in the bit of yard. He eyed his aunt coolly, accepted a small sack of hard candies that she presented to him, followed her into the house, which she entered at the rear.

Anni was busy at her housework. Anni was always busy at her housework. Anni was twenty-seven and looked thirty-five. Between the two women no love was lost, but today their manner toward each other was indefinably changed. Helmi was no longer the debtor. Helmi was an independent and free woman, earning her twenty a week. Anni was a married woman bound, tied, and harried by a hundred household tasks and trials. The two talked in their native tongue.

"Well, how goes it?"

"Always the same. You are lucky. You have your day off, you can run out and have a good time."

"She wanted me to stay home today and go tomorrow instead. I soon showed her and that daughter of hers."

They went into that in detail. Their pale-blue eyes were triumphant.

"You are early today. Did you eat?"

"No. Coffee only."

"I'll fix you some *kaalikääreitä* left over from the children's lunch."

Helmi cast a glance of suspicion at her suddenly suave sister-in-law, but she pulled a chair up to the kitchen table and ate the savory stuffed cabbage with a good appetite. She had had no Finnish food for almost two weeks. It was good.

Well, she must be going. Going? Already? Where was she running? Helmi supped up the last of the gravy on her plate and rose. Oh, she had much to do! "Well, now you are so independent I suppose you will spend all your money." "Yes, and suppose I do? What then?" "Nothing, only Abel is so close with his money. I wish I had a dollar or two of my own to spend. I need so many things." Helmi gave her three dollars, grudgingly. She would do this again and again during the year. She was wild to be gone. She went into the bedroom to look at the baby; powdered her nose; drank a final and hasty cup of coffee, and was off. Anni watched her go, her eyes hard.

A long, long ride this time back to New York. Grand Central. Change. The East Side subway. She was spewed up with the crowd at One Hundred and Twenty-fifth Street; plunged vigorously into its colorful, cheerful hurly-burly. A hundred noises attracted her. A hundred sights lured her. But she knew what she wanted to do. She made straight for the shop where Lempi Parta had bought her dress. Bulging glittering plate-glass windows brilliant with blues and pinks and reds and gold.

Helmi entered. The place was full of girls like herself, with bobbed hair and flat faces and broad shoulders and pale-blue eyes. Upper East Side Finland was buying its Easter finery. A woman came forward—an enormous woman with an incredible bust and a measureless waist and bead trimming and carrot-colored hair. And what can I do for you, Miss? Helmi made known her wants. The woman emitted a vocal sound: a squawk.

"Miss S.! Oh, Miss S.! Step this way. . . . The young lady here wants you should show her something in a blue crepe."

You did not pay for it all at once, of course. You paid in part, and they took your name and address and the name of the people you worked for. (Helmi used to be most demanding about the accent over the *a*'s in Seppala, but she was no longer.) But they obligingly let you take the whole ravishing outfit: blue dress; blue coat lined with sand crepe and trimmed with embroidery; blue silk hat; silk stockings, very sheer; high-heeled slippers. She hung the boxes and bundles about herself, somehow, joyously. Miss S. was most gracious.

Into the five-and-ten-cent store. A mass of people surged up and down the aisles. They buffeted and banged Helmi's boxes, but she clung to them rigidly. A handkerchief, edged with blue lace. A small flask of perfume. A pocket comb that cunningly folded up on itself. An exhausting business, this shopping. More tiring than a day's housework. She stopped at an unspeakable counter and ordered and devoured a sandwich of wieners with mustard (10¢) and a glass of root beer (5¢). Thus refreshed, she fought her way out to the street.

It was midafternoon. She walked placidly up One Hundred and Twenty-fifth Street, enjoying the sights and sounds. Her strong arms made nothing of their burden. Music blared forth from the open door of a radio shop. She stopped to listen, entranced. Her feet could scarcely resist the rhythm. She wandered on, crossed the street. "Heh! Watch it!" yelled a tough taxi driver, just skimming her toes. He grinned back at her. She glared after him, gained the curb. A slim, slick, dark young fellow leaning limply against the corner cigar-store window spoke to her, his cigarette waggling between his lips.

"Watch your step, Swensky."

"Shod op!" retorted Helmi, haughtily.

An open-faced orange-drink bar offered peppermint taffy in ten-cent sacks. Helmi bought a sack and popped one of the sticky confections between her strong yellow teeth. A fake auction, conducted by a swarthy and Oriental-looking auctioneer, held her briefly. He was auctioning a leprous and swollen Chinese vase. A dollar! A dollar! Who offers a dollar? All right. Who says fifty cents! Twenty-five! Step inside. Come inside, lady, won't you? Don't stand like that in the door. She knew better than that; was on her way. Yet the vase would have looked lovely in a parlor. Still, she had no parlor.

Her pale eyes grew dreamy. She walked more quickly now. When she approached the Finnish Progressive Society building in One Hundred and Twenty-sixth Street there was the usual line of surprisingly important-looking cars parked outside. The portion of New York's Finnish chauffeurdom which had Thursday afternoon to itself was inside playing pool, eating in the building's restaurant, or boxing or wrestling in the big gymnasium. The most magnificent car of them all was not there. Helmi knew it would not be. Vaino was free on Thursday nights at ten. Her boxes and bundles in hand, Helmi passed swiftly through the little groups that stood about in the hallway. A flood of Finnish rose to her ears, engulfed her. She drew a long breath. Through the open doorway of the restaurant at the rear. The tables were half filled. Girls eating together. Men, with their hats on, eating together. She ordered a cup of coffee and a plate of Finnish bread—hardtack—*näkki leipä*—with its delicious pungent caraway. This she ate and drank quickly with a relish. The real joy of the day lay still ahead of her.

Into the hallway again and down a short flight of steps to the basement. Through the poolroom, murky with smoke, every table surrounded by pliant, plastic figures intent on the game. The men paid no attention to her, nor she to them. Through the door at the far end of the room. A little office. Down a flight of steps. The steam bath, beloved of every Finn.

All her life Helmi had had her steam bath not only weekly, but often two or three times a week. On the farm in Finland the bathhouse had been built before the farmhouse itself. You used the bathhouse not only for purposes of cleanliness, but for healing: in illness, when depressed. The Finnish women, in the first throes of childbirth, repaired to the soothing, steam-laden atmosphere of the bathhouse. The sick were carried there. In its shelves and on its platforms you lay dreamily for hours, your skin shining and slippery with water. The steam bath was not only an ablution; it was a ceremony, a rite.

On Tuesdays and Thursdays the Finnish Society's steam baths were used only by women. The bath woman, huge, blond, genial, met her, took her fifty cents, gave her a locker. Helmi opened her precious boxes and hung her finery away, carefully, lovingly. The room was full of naked girls. They were as lacking in self-consciousness as so many babies. They crowded round her—her friend Lempi Parta, and, too, Hilja Karbin, Saara Johnson, Matti Eskolin, Aili Juhola.

"Oh, Helmi! How beautiful! How much did you pay! The boys will dance with you tonight, all right!" they cried in Finnish.

She disrobed swiftly, and stood a moment in the moist warmth of that outer room. Her body was strong and astonishingly graceful, now rid of its cheap and bungling clothes. Her waist tapered slim and flexible below the breadth of the shoulders. She walked well. Now she went into the steam room. The hot breath of the place met her. She lifted her face to it, enchanted. She loved it. The air was thick, heavy with steam from the hot water that dropped endlessly down on to the hot steam pipes below, sending up a misty cloud. From out of this veil a half-dozen indolent heads were lifted from bunks that lined the walls. On each bunk lay an undraped figure.

Helmi sat a moment on the edge of a bunk. "Hello. Hello, Elli! How goes it, Mari? Oo, this is good!"

She reclined upon the bunk, gratefully, yieldingly. Every nerve, every fiber, every muscle of her being relaxed in the moist heat. This stolid Finn servant girl became a graceful plastic figure in repose, a living Greek statue. The mist enveloped her. Her eyes closed. So she lay for fifteen minutes, twenty, a half-hour. Out, then, with Lempi and a half-dozen others, into the cold green waters of the big pool, stopping first for a moment under a shower in the room adjoining the steam bath.

One after another they stood at the pool's edge, graceful, fearless, unaffected. This bath, to them, was a sacred institution. It was an important and necessary part of their lives. They dropped then, swiftly, beautifully, flashingly, into the pool's green depths. They swam like mermaids. They had learned to swim in the icy waters of the Finland lakes. Their voices were high and clear and eager, like the voices of children at play. They were relaxed, gay, happy, "Oo, look! Look at me!" they called to each other in Finnish. "Can you do this?"

Back, dripping, into the steam room again. Another half-hour. The shower again. The pool again. Helmi gave herself over to the luxury of a massage at the expert hands of the masseuse. The strong electric human fingers kneaded her flesh, spanked her smartly, anointed her with oils. She felt blissful, alive, newborn. The Mawson kitchen did not exist. Zhoolie Mawson was a bad dream. Mrs. Mawson did not matter—never had mattered. Vaino. Vaino only.

She was so long in donning the beautiful new blue finery that Lempi and the rest became impatient. But at last it was finished. She surveyed herself radiantly. The flat Finnish face glowed back at her from the mirror. Helmi could never be pretty. But she approached it as nearly now as she ever would.

She would not curl her hair now. That she would do after she had had her supper. She was ravenously hungry.

They would not eat at the building restaurant. They were tired of it. They would go to Mokki's, on Madison, just off One Hundred and Twenty-fifth. A real Finnish meal. Here they sat at a table for four and talked and laughed in subdued tones, as does your proper Finnish girl. And they ate! Mrs. Mawson would have opened her eyes. They ate first *marja soppa,* which is an incredible soup of cranberries and cornstarch and sugar. They had *mämmi* and cream. They had salt herrings with potatoes. They had *riisi puuro,* which is, after all, little more than rice pudding, but flavored in the Finnish manner. They drank great scalding cups of coffee. It was superb to see them eat.

It was nearly eight. Helmi must still curl her hair, carefully. This you did in the women's room at the Finnish Society's building. She scanned the line of motors at the curb for the great car—no, it was not there. That was as it should be. The hair-curling business took a half-hour. The room was full of girls changing their shoes; changing their stockings; changing their dresses; combing their hair, curling it; washing.

Helmi and Lempi were going to the play that was to be given in the theater two flights up. Another fifty cents. Helmi did not begrudge it. She loved to dance, but she would wait. She would be fresh for ten o'clock. At ten, though the play would not be finished, she would leave for the dance upstairs. She shut her ears determinedly to the music that could faintly be heard when the door opened to admit late-comers. The play was presented by members of the Finnish Society's theatrical group, made up of girls like Helmi and boys like Vaino. Helmi watched it absorbedly. It was, the program told you in Finnish, *The Second Mrs. Tanqueray.* Helmi and Lempi found it fascinating and true and convincing.

Ten o'clock. They vanished. They deserted Thalia for Terpsichore. They spent another ten minutes before the dressing-room mirrors. The dance hall was crowded. Rows of young men, stolid of face, slim, appraising, stood near the door and grouped at the end of the room, partnerless, watching the dancers. Straight as a shot Helmi's eyes found him. How beautiful he was in his blue suit and his shiny tan shoes! His hair shone like his shoes. His cold blue eyes met hers. Her expression did not change. His expression did not change. Yet she knew he had marked her blue dress, and her sheer silk stockings, and her new, shining slippers.

Wordlessly she and Lempi began to dance together. Lempi took the man's part. She was very strong and expert. She whirled Helmi around and around in the waltz so that her blue skirt billowed out, and one saw her straight, sturdy, slim legs to the knees. Her skirt swished against the line of stolid-faced boys as she whirled past; swished against Vaino's dear blue-serge legs. She did not look at him, yet she saw his every feature. He did not look at her. He saw the dress, the stockings, the slippers, the knees. True Finns.

The waltz was over. Soberly and decorously Helmi and Lempi sought chairs against the wall. They conversed in low tones. Helmi did not look at him. Five minutes. The band struck up again. The polka. He stood there a moment. All about were stolid young men advancing stolidly in search of their equally stolid partners. Helmi's heart sank. She looked away. He came toward her. She looked away. He stood before her. He looked at her. She rose. Wordlessly they danced. One, two, three, and a one, two, three, and turn, and turn, and turn, and turn. She danced very well. His expression did not change. Her expression did not change. She was perfectly, blissfully happy.

At twelve it was over. At twelve-fifteen she had deposited her boxes and bundles—the everyday clothes of Cinderella—in the back of the huge, proud car that had an engine like a locomotive. She was seated in the great proud car beside Vaino. She was driven home. She was properly kissed. She would see him Thursday. Not Thursday, but *Thursday*. He understood. Every Other Thursday.

The day was over. She let herself into the Mawson apartment, almost (but not quite) noiselessly. Mrs. Mawson, sharp-eared, heard her. Zhoolie, herself just returned and not so unhappy as she had been sixteen hours earlier, but still resentful, heard her. Helmi entered her own untidy little room, quickly shut the window which Mrs. Mawson had opened, took off the blue dress, kicked off the bright new slippers, peeled the silk stockings (a hole in each toe), flung her underwear to the winds, dived into the coarse cotton nightgown, and tumbled into her lumpy bed with a weary, satisfied, rapturous grunt.

Zhoolie, in her green enamel bed, thought bitterly: Stupid lump! Went and sat at her sister's or whatever it is, all day, swigging coffee. It isn't as if she had had anything to do, really. She didn't do a thing. Not a thing! And I've given her I don't know how many pairs of my old silk stockings.

Mrs. Mawson, in her walnut bed, thought: They're all alike.

Mr. James G. Mawson slept.

Blue Blood

[1927]

The Chicago of 1913–1924 was a lusty, eager city; a noisy, hearty, distinctive metropolis. From Halsted Street to the Lake Shore, from Evanston to the South Chicago steel mills, it was exuberant, rich, crammed with life. One cannot say this of it today. An isolationist and reactionary press, dirty politics, and racketeer rule have left their ugly mark on the great city situated so magnificently along the inland sea, Lake Michigan.

"Blue Blood" is the story of one small section of Chicago—the Stockyards aristocracy. It is the Yards, but not that part of the Yards which lives in Lake Forest or along the Lake Shore Drive and endows symphony orchestras. No; it lives on Emerald Avenue and knows a hog before it sees it on a blue plate. It was pleasant to learn that this story is used in the University of Chicago sociological courses.

&ᔕ DENNY REGAN WAS (AND IS) A HOG DRIVER AND AN ARISTOCRAT. IN order authentically to prove the cerulean hue of the fluid that flows in Denny's veins you will have to know something of Emerald Avenue, where he lives. But Emerald Avenue is only a street in the district called Canaryville. Canaryville is but a small part of Chicago's West Side. And Chicago's West Side is, after all, merely one huge arm of the sprawling, many-limbed giant, Chicago.

It would, perhaps, be simplest to tie the whole subject into one neat knot by saying that Denny, Emerald Avenue, Canaryville, West Side, and Chicago are dominated and permeated by that vast Augean acreage known as the Yards. The Yards is Chicago's fond abbreviation for the Union Stockyards.

Three generations of Regans—Old Dennis, who was Denny's grandfather, sixty-eight; Tim Regan, his father, forty-nine; and now Denny himself, twenty—spent their working hours in the Yards. All day long they worked in that Aesopian city, and at night they dwelt and slept within one block of it. Emerald Avenue is just east of Halsted Street. Halsted Street faces the Yards. Tim, the father, and Denny, the son, born and bred within shadow of the Yards, had olfactory nerves as insensitive to its peculiar malodors as were their auricular nerves to the din of the city. Certainly Old Dennis, with half a century of Yards work resting lightly on his fine shoulders, would have denied that any odor existed. In three generations of

Regans the Yards had risen from a bad-smelling joke to the dignity of an institution.

Old Dennis remembered well when the Yards had been outside the city limits, a reedy swamp wherein the croaking of bullfrogs mingled with the grunting of swine. Old Dennis's son, Tim, and Tim's son, Denny, had gone into the Yards as inevitably as a scion of the British nobility follows the law of primogeniture. As Old Dennis and Tim had started as hog drivers, so young Denny now followed that odoriferous calling as the first step in the course of porcine knowledge necessary to a true descendant of the house of Regan.

There is no attempting to describe this abattoir of the world. The Yards are—the Yards. But one might essay to convey an idea of Denny, and Canaryville and Emerald Avenue.

Canaryville is bounded on the north by Thirty-ninth Street, on the south by Fifty-fifth; on the east by Stewart Avenue, and on the west by Halsted Street. No one seems to know why it is so called. The origin of the district's name is lost in the city's fogs. Old Dennis claimed that in past days the prairies thereabouts were full of wild canaries—an explanation which sounds idyllic but improbable. But the origin of Emerald Avenue's nomenclature was simple enough: on this side of the Regans dwelt the Gallaghers, and on that side the Rourkes.

Emerald Avenue itself resembles a small-town street more than one to be found in the center of a gigantic commercial city. On either side of it two-story frame cottages are set in little green yards. Hedges of four-o'clocks wink their eyes at passers-by. There actually are catalpa trees amidst the grass plots, and, forming a pleasant vista, you see an occasional ancient willow swooping and dipping down the distance like a colossal old lady in hoops. Lace curtains in the front windows defy the hot black breath of Chicago's West Side. All about the street, like scavenger crows, hover grim factories, smoke-blackened chimneys, tumble-down tenements, waiting to pounce upon its comfortable plumpness. Here and there vacant lots, weed-infested, are grisly ghosts of past prairie days. Sometimes a neighborhood relic unconsciously traces the history of a bygone period. A dilapidated red barn just around the corner with rusty Fords and battered trucks spilling into the street bears under its sagging cornice the sign: "Sale Today. 50 mares and horses."

Doc McDermott's old place, as anyone in the district could tell you.

In the midst of this—cool, fresh, almost prim—lies Emerald Avenue, a little oasis. Most of its houses are cottages, but an occasional edifice rises almost to the dignity of a mansion, and then you know that here has been the dwelling of one of the early packing-house princes, content in past days to live near the Yards, but now kinging it over lawns and links and gardens in one of the city's North Shore suburbs.

The street is as Irish as its name. Emerald Avenue dwellers look down with pride on those swart workers who live in the district to the west, known as Back of the Yards. These are largely Poles, Lithuanians, Slovaks, and a few Bohemians. But a stanch handful of Irish of the old guard are still to be found Back of the Yards and these are as hoity-toity as the Emerald Avenue Irish themselves, owning their homes these many years past and refusing to be ousted by the dark-skinned newcomers contemptuously designated as Hunkies.

It was here, Back of the Yards, that Miss Norah McGowan lived, the lady oftenest seen with Denny Regan at the Saturday-night dances at Fairyland. A quiet, serious-eyed young woman, Miss McGowan, with a Yards lineage as aristocratic as that of young Denny himself. She herself had a good job as stenographer in the Exchange Building at the Yards, not to mention a father, two brothers, three uncles, and numberless male cousins employed in Packingtown, which is the factory section of the Yards.

Miss Norah McGowan didn't in the least mind dancing with Denny. She loved it. He was a divine dancer. Why wouldn't he be! Irish, twenty, slim, and the son of Tim and Molly Regan. But—she didn't in the least mind dancing with Denny. For when you live Back of the Yards, and yourself are employed in the Yards, and have a father, two brothers, three uncles, and numberless male cousins in Packingtown, you are all unaware of that something which so forcibly smites the stranger in Chicago, as he nears Halsted Street (and the breeze from the west). Suddenly, almost inevitably, he will throw up his head, sniff rapidly twice, look startled, and say, with emphasis, "What's *that!*"

"What's what?" the native will retort, perhaps a shade defensively.

"*That!* Don't you smell it!"

"I don't smell anything . . . but maybe you mean . . . it might be you imagine it's the Yards."

"Imagine! Why, say——!"

"I don't smell a thing," the native Chicagoan will repeat. And then, paradoxically enough, "I like it."

The faint whiff is but a zephyr of Araby, all laden with the scent of myrrh and attar of roses compared to the thing that Denny Regan encountered each weekday morning as, booted and overalled, he flung open door after door of the heavy-laden freight train packed with great two-hundred-pound hogs that had been traveling by day and by night from the farms of Illinois, or Iowa, or faraway Nebraska. It was Denny's job, as hog driver, to usher these porcine guests out into the Bluebeard hospitality of the

Stockyards hogpens. Before and after this daily rite he changed his clothes. He often shampooed his hair. He liked to simmer in the steaming benignancy of the inadequate little tub in the Emerald Avenue cottage. But the Yards were part of him; the pores of his skin, the roots of his hair, the nails of his hands, were of the Yards. For that matter, Denny himself, having grown up in the midst of it, was unaware of the breath of the Yards; all oblivious to it, as were his grandfather, his father, his fresh-faced mother, Molly Regan—all the members of the Regan household except his sister, the elegant Ellen. And you should have seen her turn up her nose until that feature threatened to be marred by permanent wrinkles.

The elegant Ellen worked in one of the huge offices housed in the People's Gas Company Building on Michigan Avenue, downtown, and she was renegade to the Yards. She called herself Aileen, and brought home to Emerald Avenue stories of high life as lived at the office in the People's Gas Company Building. She tried, too, to bring that elegance into the Regan household, and looked with disdain on the stamped plush parlor set that was the pride of Molly Regan's life, and ridiculed the pieces of tortured china and glass with which Molly decorated the parlor table and shelf.

"What's the matter with 'm?" Molly Regan would demand.

"They're terrible."

"Oh, they are, are they! Well, go and get yourself married to one of the millionaires or whatever it is that clutters up your office that you're always talking about, and then you can furnish your house the way you like it. This is my house."

"I could furnish my own place now, thank you. I earn as much as Pa does, or nearly, for all he's been working in the Yards for God knows how long. I could live in my own flat like some of the girls do."

Molly Regan's good-humored red face took on the unaccustomed pallor of white-hot anger. "Try it, Ellen Regan. You let me hear again about living your own life in any flat, other girls or no other girls, and I'll snatch you bald-headed."

Molly Regan, born in Chicago, had little or no brogue. Sometimes a word slipped out, or a sentence peculiarly Irish in its construction or phraseology. But only Old Dennis, of the lot, spoke with the tongue of the North of Ireland. What a woman, Molly Regan! A hearty, slam-bang, broad-breasted, light-footed creature who had always made life interesting for the quiet, moody, brooding Irishman who was her husband. Perhaps Tim Regan had married a little beneath him, for Molly had been in service over on the South Side. But it had been a lucky stroke for him. A dramatic woman, Molly, with the gift of making the commonplace seem glamorous. There was always a good deal going on in Molly Regan's household. At the dinner table she could tell a sordid story of the neighborhood—and immediately the incident and the actors in it were colored with the aspect of romanticism. Molly was not an especially good cook or housekeeper, though when she put her mind to it she sometimes turned out an amazing mess of dumplings or a triumph of pastry.

It was incredible what she and Tim had done on his thirty-five a week. They owned the frame cottage on Emerald. Ellen and young Denny and the oldest girl, Kitty (now married), had had decent schooling; had been fed, clothed. There had been insurance, church tithes, doctor bills. True, the children had started to work at seventeen, or earlier. But there had been, before that, seventeen years of prodigious eating, shoe scuffings, garment rending. Yet here they all were. And here was the stamped plush parlor set. All this, on thirty-five a week, cannot be accomplished by good management alone. It takes high faith, humor, courage, health, and a belief in fairies.

There were ways. For example, Tim always brought home the meat from the market belonging to the packing plant in which he worked. Sometimes he followed his own fancy. Usually he asked Molly, "What'll it be?"

Frequently Molly said, "Whatever they've got strikes you tasty." But when she was planning next day's meal she became more explicit. Tim would bring home in a brown-paper packet certain cuts that the average housewife never heard of. The big, spicy-smelling butcher shop, with sawdust covering the floor, was just next to the cold room in whose terrible numbing atmosphere Tim worked. Here Tim Regan would buy, perhaps, the succulent tender tips, sometimes called pork tips, for sixteen cents a pound. These, if ever they found their way into the fashionable butcher shops over east, would have brought forty cents a pound as pork tenderloins. He sometimes fancied beef, and bought T-strips very cheap, well knowing that the crafty butcher outside the Yards would have sold the same as beef tenderloin. He brought home bacon nuggets, which are the square chunks cut off the very end of the choicest bacon because they spoil the symmetry of the aristocratic slab. For this he paid fifteen cents a pound instead of your forty-five. Molly Regan would cook it with greens or beans or cabbage. It was superb.

Of course Old Dennis, living with them these twelve years past, since his wife's death, and stepping proudly to his work at the Yards daily as he did, contributed to the household's upkeep. A singularly gentle old Irishman, tall, gaunt, silver-haired, with a face amazingly like that seen in pictures of the more abstemious old medieval monks who later achieved saintship. His blue eyes had a wistful, other-world look. His job was that of wielding the nine-pound chopper that cut through the ribs of two-hundred-and-twenty-pound hogs. It was a Herculean task.

"I'm as good as ever I was!" boasted Old Dennis. It wasn't true, but they didn't tell him so. Gradually, in the last few years, they busied him with other jobs about the plant. They kept him occupied, happy. Overseer, they said. Dennis, you'd better oversee this, oversee that. You're the expert. The nine-pound chopper had grown heavy for the old arms, after half a century of service. But when important visitors came through he was often called from this or that job over which he was puttering.

"Here's Dennis," they said. "Fifty years with the company. Show them how a real hog chopper does it, Dennis."

He would step to the platform, king on his throne once more. He stood there, poised for a moment, chopper in hand. At his feet, dressed and pink and glistening, the great hog carcasses slid past him on their way to your kitchen. As each came directly in front of him he lifted the chopper high. Down it came through the massive shoulder of a two-hundred-and-twenty pounder. It was miraculous that he could wield this instrument with such precision. Two ribs made the cut a New York shoulder. Three ribs made it an English shoulder. One and a half ribs made it a picnic shoulder. And when Old Dennis's eye, in that fraction of a second, measured one and a half, then one and a half it was.

"I'm as good as ever I was!" boasted Old Dennis.

But he often took two swings of the nine-pound chopper now, instead of one, to cleave his way through the huge shoulder. "Sure you're as good as you ever were, Dennis," they told him. "You're a wonder."

In his place now you saw a giant Negro, a magnificent ebony creature with great prehensile arms, and a round head, a flat stomach, flat hips, an amazing breadth between the shoulders. From chest to ankles he narrowed down like an inverted pyramid. He raised those arms that were like flexible bronze, and effortlessly, almost languidly, as you would cut through a pat of soft butter, they descended in a splendid arc. Chuck! said the nine-pound chopper. One beautiful, epic gesture. The severed meat moved on, one of an endless procession of hundreds, thousands, millions.

"Fifty years an' more I've done that," Dennis would say complacently. "It's no more than play to me. I've bigger things to see after."

Such, then, was the heritage of aristocracy into which Denny Regan now took his natural place.

His own job wasn't pretty. But then, even princes must learn. There is, as has been the plaint of princelings ever since the king business began, no royal road to learning.

Perhaps it should be told that young Dennis was beautiful—and he would have knocked you down if he had heard you apply the term to him. Denny was a complete throwback to his North of Ireland ancestors. He had their high checkbones, and a certain deceptive look of frailty. His eyes were deep-sunk and of a peculiar blue gray, and the whites were very clear, with just a tinge of blue in them, like a child's. He had a dead-white skin, black hair, and heavy black brows that almost met over the bridge of his nose. His lashes were too long, perhaps, shading his eyes so that they imparted to them a mysterious and dreamy look, most misleading and certainly unexpected in a hog driver, but fatal, nevertheless, to female beholders. He was not a merry young man, and rarely smiled.

From the nature of his work, Denny's hours at the Yards were hard and concentrated. His was an eight-hour shift, supposedly, but often his actual working day was much shorter than that. It all depended upon when the hog trains were due to arrive. Monday and Tuesday were always big days. Wednesday was busy, Thursday just so-so, Friday and Saturday almost negligible. Often it was necessary for him to be on the unloading platform at four in the morning, for weeks together. Sometimes a hog train came in shortly after midnight. You were notified. You had to be there, ready with your tall ash or hickory pole in your hand.

Denny had already been promoted. He was assistant marker. They'd make him marker soon. He didn't mind the work—rather liked it, in spite of the hours, the filth, the rough labor. In detail it can, perhaps, hardly bear description.

Molly Regan was used to a household whose male members went to work at an hour which more favored wives and mothers would have considered the middle of the night—as often it was. It was one of her boasts that none of her menfolks had ever had to go to work breakfastless. The delicious aroma of coffee and bacon might be sniffed in the Regan household at the most incredible hours of the night and morning. In the years of her marriage Molly Regan had got breakfast by kerosene lamplight, by gaslight, by electricity. You saw her moving swiftly, deftly, about her kitchen, a shapeless figure in her inadequate kimono; the glow of light, the cheerful splutter of bacon, the scent of coffee, and her own cheerful red countenance combining to make mock of the black night that pressed its sinister face against the windowpane.

"Late nothin'! And late or no late you'll not go out of this house without you've got something hot in your stomach. Sit down, now, and drink this coffee if it scalds you."

Denny was accustomed to the gray black of the early-morning streets. There were in that neighborhood at that hour many swift figures like his own passing down Halsted Street, disappearing through the old gray-stone gate. In the Yards, through the cattle and hogpens you heard the cry to the gate-key men sounding eerily through the blackness. "O-key-oh!" they sounded the call now almost a century old. "O-key-oh!" Often, early though it was, drovers, buyers, commission men were already astir. You heard the clatter of their horses' hoofs on the pavement as they wheeled toward the pens, and glimpsed them, romantic figures in this day and age, looking for all the world, with their sombreros and long whips, their spurs and boots, like characters in a Western movie.

Down the long lane between the cattle pens went Denny on his way to the unloading platforms. The locker-room shed, which served, too, as a sort of waiting room in rough weather, abutted on the high platform. Here Denny swiftly changed his clothes, taking from his locker the high thick boots, the grimed corduroy pants, the rough coat, the hickory wand. Sometimes he covered this garb with overalls, but not often. What was the use? Nothing could escape the grime, the odor, of the hog cars.

On sharp winter mornings a fire glowed orange and scarlet in the pot-bellied stove in the center of the rough room, and the drivers, as they waited for their laden train, talked or dozed on the wooden benches. They were, for the most part, lean young fellows like Denny, and largely Irish. Som mes you saw among them a grizzled veteran who, through inertia, or misc. ice, or lack of enterprise or fitness, had never risen above the job of hog driver. In mild weather they lounged about the platform or perched on the fence, staff in hand, keeping a sharp eye out for the first glimpse of the puffing black engine coming round the bend. At sight of it they swarmed the platform, took their places. As the train approached, stopped, they pushed open the sliding doors, set the runway, and out poured the flood of squealing, scrambling, slipping, grunting porkers. The noise was terrific. The stench was appalling. The filth oozed under your boots. You prodded with your long hickory stick. You cried, "Soo-ey! Soo-ey!" and stepped nimbly this way and that, and just escaped being knocked down by a great, ponderous, charging mass of hog flesh. You pulled and tugged ₹ : this or that unwieldy bulk refused to take the step from car to runway. "Soo-ey! S-s-s-seeee!" Toward the end you entered the car itself to hasten the laggards. If, in one far end, you saw a mound that lay still and stiff, ɔu ːnd one of the others took hold of it and dragged it out and dumped it ⹁ ʰe platform, where it lay stark and, somehow, dreadful, even in the mids ⁝ ʰat city of slaughter. For the Enemy had stolen up and met it halfw.. en as it came, all unknowing, to the fatal rendezvous.

Train after train. Car after car. Hundreds, thousands, hundreds of thousands of hogs. Food for a nation—for the world, indeed. The stench in his nostrils, the grime in his clothes, the pandemonium in his ears. "Heh!

So-o-o! Soo-ey!" called Denny Regan, working with stick and arms and feet. "Sooey! S-s-seeee!"

Often by noon his day's work was finished. A change of clothes again (this job of his called for as many changes as a matinee idol's). His time was his own until tomorrow morning. He could go home to Emerald Avenue, there to snatch an hour or two of sleep. The movies. A ball game. The pool shack. The street corner. He was owner of a hybrid car of obscure origin and temperamental moods. You saw many such standing outside the frame cottages on Emerald Avenue, or Union or Wallace near by. Denny's car, and these others, were likely to be embellished with large and flapping muslin posters tacked across the radiator or the gas tank.

"Re-elect Tim Fitzgerald County Commissioner," commanded these posters in large blue letters.

Oddly enough, though it might be noon and her lunch hour, Denny never once thought of meeting Norah McGowan in front of the Exchange Building where she worked, though this was a scant five minutes' walk from the unloading platforms. The boys and girls in the Yards did not consider the lunch hour a time for dalliance. Dates were for hours of relaxation and ease, after the workday was over. She would have been scandalized at the suggestion of their meeting for lunch. Denny liked to be with Norah. She soothed and exhilarated him at once. She was easy to be with. Perhaps he had not concretely thought of marriage with her. He had not thought of marriage with anyone. But the Regans married young and stayed married. There was Norah, of course. Perhaps that was the trouble. There was Norah, dependable, laughing, hearty. And there was hidden, deep, a strong vein of the romantic in this silent, handsome, brooding, moody hog driver.

Denny never was at a loss for something with which to fill his afternoon. Halsted Street saw to that. The many saloons that lined that thoroughfare. Other neighborhood hangouts. Pappy the Greek's. Genzer's Soft Drink Parlor. The Range Cigar Store and Pool Room. Jake's Candy Kitchen. And, of course, the clubrooms. Denny had never run with any of the two or three powerful and sinister gangs that infested the neighborhood. Political clubs, they were called. Usually they had rooms above some store on Halsted; and police protection. Denny knew them. Tactfully, warily, he steered clear.

Coming into the locker room one May morning, he noticed a new driver. They came and went. You paid little attention to them. This young fellow had a locker next to Denny's. He was, too, about his own age, and undoubtedly Irish, but of the other type; sandy-haired, freckled, stocky, blue-eyed. His shoulders were too broad for his height, giving him a rather simian look, particularly as his arms were long. Still, it was a frank, good-natured face. He had some trouble with his locker key. Denny showed him how it worked. He offered Denny a cigarette. This was not according to hog drivers' ethics. Still, Denny took one. The brand was the same as that which he himself was accustomed to smoke.

"New guy, ain't you?"

"Yeh."

His heavy boots, his corduroy pants, his woolen shirt were new. Denny eyed them.

"Worked in the Yards before?"

"No."

"You want to be careful. First thing you know you're liable to get a spot on them clothes."

"Yeh, I was worrying about that," said the new one. "Give me the address of your dry cleaner, will you?"

"Don't get fresh, guy," Denny warned him.

"Why, say, take a joke, can't you!" The boy's blue eyes bore a look of hurt surprise. And as he spoke he lifted gently out of his way one of the benches that was preventing his locker door from opening to its full width.

It was a bench with a solid wooden seat and back and heavy iron legs. On it, at the moment, were two extremely substantial gentlemen in the hog-driving profession. He had lifted the bench almost without bending, and much as you would move a book from that side of the table to this. Just a cord in his great short pillar of a neck swelled ever so slightly. "Excuse me," he said, addressing the two on the bench. "I gotta get into my locker."

"That's all right, fella," said one of the two on the bench, palpably impressed. "Leave us know before you get ready to move the shack though, will you?"

Down the track came the hog train. The drivers swarmed the platform. The new man followed, uncertainly. Denny eyed him with a new respect. "Stick with me," he said. "I'll show you."

The new man stuck, gratefully. By noon his boots were as unspeakable as Denny's.

He was a friendly cuss. And he always had a cigarette pack. He and Denny become rather friendly in that remote, unquestioning way men have. He was known as Red. Sometimes, when they had cleaned up, they crossed Halsted to the drugstore on the corner and, straddling the high stools at the drugstore soda fountain, had ten minutes' laconic talk as they ate. Gravely and thoughtfully they would order and consume one of the monstrous messes with which the American male often regales his leisure moments. Their broad shoulders drooped over a miniature mountain of vanilla ice cream with cascades of chocolate sauce, topped by a snowcap of marshmallow. The white-coated Greek behind the counter seemed to find nothing unusual in providing such sticky and unadult provender to two powerfully built males. Sometimes this artless fare was abetted by one of the surprising sandwiches which made up the fantastic menu printed and pasted up on the mirror. Veal, ham, spaghetti, salmon salad, cheese-and-slaw. Denny and Red talked tersely. It was a pleasant enough place, with almost the comfort and informality of a clubroom. Telephone booths, cigarettes, cigars, chewing gum, candy; a soothing scent of spicy drugs, perfumery, fruit.

Denny never dreamed of inviting Red to the house on Emerald. Sometimes, though infrequently, the two went off together in Denny's makeshift car. They knew very little about each other. Their talk was a thing made up almost entirely of monosyllabic words.

From Denny: "You going to stick with the Yards?"

"Sure. You?"

"Yeh. We all been. My old man and his old man and all. All our life."

"Me, too."

"Yeh! You ain't said before. Right in the Yards, or what?"

"Packingtown's where I head in. Where my old man is, and all."

Sometimes they talked of women.

"You running with anybody?"

"Yeh, I got a girl. She lives Back of the Yards. Works over in the Exchange Building. She's a good kid, at that."

"What's she like?"

"Well, I don't know. She's a good kid. Easygoing. . . . No, I don't mean what you mean. No, not her. Say, she reminds me of my old woman more than anything, at that. Jolly, and a kidder, and laughing, and don't get sore. Not that you can get fresh with her, see, because I tried it and you can't."

"Figuring to marry her?"

"No!" said Denny, hotly, and a little surprised at the vehemence of his own denial. "I ain't figuring to marry anybody."

Red spoke simply. At something in his voice Denny looked up, quickly, and saw the other's features twisted with pain. What Red said was, "My girl turned me down because of the Yards." His round pink face was a deeper pink, and his blue eyes were suddenly dark.

"How do you mean—the Yards?"

"Well, I'm working in the Yards, see, and I can't stay out late much, and like that, because getting up so early and all, a guy can't. But that isn't all.

The stuff gets into your skin or something, and it doesn't matter how much you change and bathe and m—uh—bathe. And when we're dancing she says it makes her sick, see. And she wants to know if I'm going to stick with the Yards, and how long this is going to go on, and all, and I tell her years, though maybe later on I won't have a job that smells so bad, and at that she says it's either her or the job."

"Ha!" jeered Denny, and spat. "The nerve of 'm! Say, I hope you told that dame where to get off at."

"Yeh," croaked Red, miserably. "Yeh, I told her."

"Didn't want you to work in the Yards, huh? Say, I figure when I get married my kid's going to work in the Yards like me and my old man and his old man, see? Only different, see?"

Red, forgetting his own troubles momentarily, seemed interested. "How's that? How do you mean, different?"

"Well, I quit school when I was seventeen. My old man, he quit when he was thirteen. And his old man—my grampa—he quit when he was ten or before, even. Well, *my* kid, he's going to have an education in him, and don't you forget it, and then he's going to start like me in the pig driving or like that, but when he finishes he ain't going to have no lousy little job like my old man or like Grampa after he's been working a hundred years or better in the Yards. Grampa, he thinks all the old birds that started Packingtown and made their piles there—Old Cassidy and Martin Madden and like that—are like the guys in the Bible. What they do is right, see, even when it's wrong. He's always saying how good they been to him, and how old Madden, once when he happens to be in the Yards and sees him, shakes his mitt, see, and calls him Dennis. You'd think he'd give him a million. My old man, he's different again. He's in more with labor, and like that. Always beefin'. At that, he's headed in right, only he don't know what it's about. Grampa tells him about this meeting up with Madden, and Pa says, 'Well and all, what of it!'

" 'What of it!' Grampa says. 'He shook my hand and called me Dennis, didn't he?'

"Pa laughs and says, 'You worked for him all your life. You give 'em everything you got in you, didn't you? Well!'

" 'They paid me for it, didn't they!' the old man says.

" 'Like hell they did!' says Pa. At that, he's right. Only he don't know, like I do, that we're what counts now. My kid, he goes into the Yards, see. But he knows where he's headin' in when he goes, like I do. Only better."

The elegant Ellen, hearing something of this new friend of her brother, was languidly curious, but contemptuous, too. Each member of the family was likely to encounter, in its workday, certain characters or co-workers that so impressed them as to bring them into the talk that went around at the family supper table. Red said this. I was talking to Red and he said that.

The elegant Ellen's saga was all about a certain young lady named Genevieve who graced the office in which Ellen was employed downtown. The name occurred again and again in the table talk. All the graces, all the amenities, all the elegancies, were embodied in this young lady who, by now, had become a myth (and a jest) in the Regan household. Ellen had once unfortunately explained that the owner of the name insisted on the French pronunciation. She illustrated.

"Jenny-veeyave!" Molly Regan had exclaimed. "Save us all, what a name!"

"It's French," Ellen went on. "Her father was French."

"What's this Jenny-veeyave's last name?" Molly inquired.

"Duppy." Then, hurriedly, as a shout went up, "But that's only because of the way it's pronounced in America. Du Puis, that's what it used to be. Du Puis."

Denny Regan choked vulgarly over his hot coffee.

"Listen, did you ever tell her about your swell brother, Dennay?"

"She knows about you, all right," was Ellen's rather surprising reply to this.

"What do you mean, knows about me?"

"That Saturday you met me downtown when we went to buy the radio and you were waiting outside. She saw you. She said she thought you were a handsome guy and she'd like to know you."

Denny Regan, though he affected to be taken very ill on hearing this statement, was as palpably pleased as any male under like blandishments.

"Why'n't you bring your friend here sometime for Sunday dinner, or after work to supper?" inquired the hospitable Molly. "If she lives alone, like you say, with another girl, I bet she don't get any too much to eat."

"Here!" exclaimed the elegant Ellen, with a glance around.

"Leave me know when you do," said the gallant Denny, "and I'll be out."

But he was not out. When the exquisite Genevieve Duppy appeared, Denny was in. Not only in, but, having been warned of her coming, was bathed, shaved, lightly powdered, heavily sartorial, silent, magnetic, and less like a hog driver and more like Brian Boru than any youth named Denny Regan has a right to be.

Having, ever since adolescence, been relentlessly pursued by all manner of young ladies drawn by his good looks, his indifference, his silence, or all three, Denny's defenses were all planned for a mode of attack quite different from that now employed by Miss Duppy.

Miss Duppy was dainty. Miss Duppy was cool. She was good. She was elegant beyond words. She was frail, blond, lymphatic. You, having swept your plate clean, saw with dismay that her fork was mincing fastidiously about among the less gross tidbits that made up her own portion. She leaned toward you a good deal, rarely smiled and almost never when you expected her to; was altogether a thoroughly selfish and charming little defective. All the boys in Ellen's office were in love with her.

She succeeded in making Molly Regan feel a little sorry for her, which, with her equipment, was the most effective thing she could have done. She patronized Ellen. She was more silent than Denny so that, as he took her home (in the hybrid car), he found himself growing loquacious. Her diction and vocabulary were much less elegant and varied than her manner and Gallic background would have led you to expect.

"Can you imagine! . . . I'll say you're wonderful! . . . You slay me! . . . Honest! . . ."—all uttered in a small pale voice that made the memory of Miss Norah McGowan's hearty utterances seem Amazonian in comparison.

Did she like to dance? Yeh. Would she go sometime? Maybe. Next Saturday night? Uh, let's see, what's tonight? Call me up.

There began a series of tortures for Denny Regan. This office Borgia delighted in making her victims writhe. Her tricks were cheap, and Denny was deceived by them. She broke engagements, pretended offense when none had been offered, was deliberately provocative, and took refuge in false dignity. She made nothing of Denny's none-too-imposing weekly wage at the Yards. Through it all she disparaged the Yards, said the thought of it made her sick, and was none too delicate in stressing this fact as she danced with the miserable Denny.

Sometimes he encountered the forthright Miss Norah McGowan. "What's the matter, Denny? You sore at me?"

"No."

"I haven't seen you lately."

"I been busy."

As if she didn't know. Miss McGowan's hearty laugh had grown hollow; had ceased.

Denny stood outside the People's Gas Company Building on Michigan, waiting for Miss Duppy, on Saturday afternoon. He looked, somehow, different from the other boys stationed there at the curb on similar intent. The big office buildings along the avenue held many Genevieves. Denny's difference lay, perhaps, in the breadth of shoulder, the clearness of skin, the limpidness of eye, the co-ordination of muscle. Those others were, for the most part, office workers, male counterparts of Genevieve herself. Hog driving is an unromantic but healthful business, and keeps one out in the open air. Perhaps it was this quality—this difference—which after all had attracted the anemic Genevieve to him in the first place, and which attracted her with increasing strength, so that she now had some difficulty in pursuing her customary tactics by which she was to remain free and solvent while the victim was bound and broken. She found increasing fault with him. He was contrite. She made unreasonable demands. He was abject. She objected to his manners, clothes, conversation, friends, home, fingernails. He considered changing them all. He was in love.

She made a mistake. It was one night when he was having Sunday supper in the murky little kitchenette flat which was the home of Miss Duppy and two of her co-workers. The co-workers were out seeking social diversion. She gave him tea and a pallid and abominable dish known as Waldorf salad, a sickly concoction made up of diced apples and nuts and mayonnaise, and rightly despised of all virile males. Denny, bred to the vigorous stews and roasts and greens of Molly Regan's Emerald Avenue ménage, was dutifully consuming this unvital mess and finding it sawdust but ambrosia. The scene was domestic, intimate. Denny looked masterful. Perhaps this natural little parasite sensed in him potential success; saw in him something of the substantial future which was inevitably to be the lot of this serious, quiet, secretly romantic but clearheaded young Irishman.

She made a mistake.

She had dilated upon the aristocracy of her ancestry, the Gallic strain in her blood, the exquisiteness of her lineage. Her folks, she said, lived in a little town in Wisconsin. Her mother was dead, her father had remarried, her stepmother did not understand her. Common, that's what she was. She did not understand Genevieve's love for things that were fine and beautiful.

"And," said Miss Duppy, concluding the tale of her own elegance, "why don't you get a decent job somewheres downtown?"

"What?" said Denny, not as one who has not heard, but as one would ask who has failed to understand.

"Why don't you get a job downtown, like the other fellows I know? You could. If I'm going to keep on going with you I can't have the girls all laughing at me because you're a hog driver. It's terrible. It makes me sick." She shuddered. "The Stockyards. Killing and everything."

"Makes you sick, does it?" inquired Denny, with a quietness that she mistook for meekness.

"Oh, yes!" replied Miss Genevieve Duppy, and shuddered again and made a little face.

"Do you mean if I keep on a hog driver and in the Yards you'll quit going with me?"

"Well, yes, of course." Miss Duppy had hardly hoped her victory would be so immediate, so complete.

Denny crushed his cigarette into the midst of the Waldorf salad remaining on his plate, and rose. "Good night," he said.

Miss Duppy stood up, too, quickly. "What do you mean, good night!"

Denny's voice was not lifted above his usual conversational tone. If anything it took on a lower pitch with the passion of his outrage. "Listen, Frenchy. You ain't the only one has got blue blood in their veins, and don't you forget it. Me, I'm the son of a son of a hog driver. My grandfather remembers when they used to dump cattle and hogs on the sand hills outside the city limits and sell 'em for so much a head. That's how far back he goes. My uncle, John Daley, is the champion beef dresser of the world, see. Not of the Yards. The world! Twenty minutes from opening to dropping the hide. We been in the Yards since there was any. My grandfather and my father and me and my kid. You talk about your folks, will you! I guess when it comes to blue blood, we're there!"

"What do you mean, your kid?" asked Miss Genevieve Duppy, a little breathless.

"Why—I don't know," replied Denny, foolishly; and thought suddenly of Norah McGowan, who so strangely reminded him of his mother. Suddenly he strode out of the house, down the stairs, into the street. Miss Duppy's laugh, finely dramatic as it was, failed to reach his ears.

There were two people he wanted to see. Miss Norah McGowan. And Red. Red, whose girl had turned him down because he worked in the Yards and was redolent of the Yards. Hurt, angry, indignant, disillusioned. He'd go over to Norah's. But she was sore, and no wonder. He'd call up Red first, here in the corner cigar store. Red. Red what? He didn't even know Red's last name.

Norah? Norah was in. Not only was Norah to be found at home in the McGowan house Back of the Yards, but her mother was home, and her father, one of her two brothers, two of her three uncles, at least five of the cousins, and countless offspring of all these. There was about that family gathering something impressive, hearty, smacking of royalty, so sufficient were they unto themselves, so clannish, so established, so sure.

Denny they greeted as one of them; prince of another such line. Not a word of reproach from Norah. Not a glance of offense from Ma McGowan. Blue Blood. How's your ma? How's all the folks? Norah came forward. Her manner was hearty, but perhaps there was just a shade of reserve beneath. Her cheeks were pink, but it was the pink of sudden flush, and not her accustomed ruddy coloring.

"Hello, Norah."

"Hello yourself, Denny."

"Thought you might like to take in a movie or something."

She hesitated just the fraction of a second. "Kind of—late, isn't it?"

His voice dropped an octave, and vibrated. "Aw, Norah, it ain't late."

"I'll get my hat."

Denny, waiting, chatted laconically and easily with the clan. Their interests his, their viewpoint his, their life his. He and Norah stepped out of the warm, odorous, teeming little room into the warm, odorous, teeming city night.

"The old boneyard's certainly hitting it up tonight," said Denny.

Norah lifted her head and sniffed a little, but whether the sniff was one of pride or investigation it was difficult to know. "I don't smell anything," she said, a shade stiffly. And at that Denny Regan linked his arm through hers and brought hers sharply against his hard young ribs.

"Me neither," he said.

It was not until next day at noon, over one of the sticky mixtures at the drugstore soda fountain, that Denny had a chance to confide his story to Red. Red was all understanding, all attention. Didn't he know! Hadn't he suffered!

"And say," Denny concluded, "after I bawled her out, like that, telling her how I was a son of a gun myself when it come to family, see, why all of a sudden I wanted to get hold of you, see, and spill how I got the same deal from a dame that you'd got. Well, you could of knocked me for a goal when right in the telephone booth I remembered I didn't even know your last name and we been working together months, driving and all. Can you match that for brains! Say, what is your name anyway, Red? First and last."

"Madden," said Red, "Martin Madden."

"Yeh!" jeered Denny. "Mar——" A terrible thought struck him. He put down his spoon so that it clattered on the marble counter. He looked at Red and saw that gentleman's intensely rising color more than justify his nickname. "Say, listen. You ain't the son of the old—why, say——"

"Yeh," said Red. "Learning the business from the ground up, like you. What's the matter with that?"

"Jeez!" said Denny Regan.

Hey! Taxi!
[1928]

He hasn't changed much in almost twenty years—that charioteer to whom you entrust your life on the streets of New York. His likeness (unrecognizable in store clothes) looks down upon you from the smudged photograph required by the local constabulary. Loquacious, philosophical, sentimental, wise, tough, he is, perhaps, the real New Yorker.

☙ NERVOUS OLD LADIES FROM DUBUQUE, PEERING FEARFULLY AT THE placard confronting them as they rode in Ernie's taxi, waxed more timorous still as they read it. It conveyed a grisly warning. Attached thereto was a full-face photograph of Ernie. Upon viewing this, their appraising glance invariably leaped, startled, to where Ernie himself loomed before them in the driver's seat on the other side of the glass partition. Immediately there swept over them an impulse to act upon the printed instructions.

POLICE DEPARTMENT
CITY OF NEW YORK
ERNEST STEWIG

This is a photograph of the authorized driver. If another person is driving this cab notify a policeman.

Staring limpidly back at one from the official photograph was a sleek, personable, and bland young man. This Ernest Stewig who basked in police approval was modishly attired in a starched white collar, store clothes, and a not-too-rakish fedora. Trust me, he said.

From a survey of this alleged likeness the baffled eye swung, fascinated, to the corporeal and workaday Ernie seated just ahead, so clearly outlined against the intervening glass.

A pair of pugnacious red ears outstanding beneath a checked gray and black cap well pulled down over the head; a soft blue shirt, somewhat faded; or, in winter, a maroon sweater above whose roll rose a powerful and seemingly immovable neck. Somewhere between the defiant ears and the monolithic neck you sensed a jaw to which a photograph could have done justice only in profile. You further felt that situate between the cap's visor and the jaw was a pair of eyes before which the seraphic gaze of the

pictured Ernie would have quailed. The head never moved, never turned
to right or left; yet its vision seemed to encompass everything. It was like a
lighthouse tower, regnant, impregnable, raking the maelstrom below with
a coldly luminous scrutiny.

About the whole figure there was something pantherlike—a quietly
alert, formidable, and almost sinister quality—to convey which was in itself
no mean achievement for a young man slouched at the wheel of a palpably
repainted New York taxicab.

Stewig. Stewig! The name, too, held a degree of puzzlement. The passenger's brain, rejecting the eye's message, sent back a query: Stewig?
Isn't there a consonant missing?

Just here the n.o.l. from Dubuque had been known to tap on the glass
with an apprehensive but determined forefinger.

"Young man! Young man! Is this your taxicab you're driving?"

"What's that?"

"I said, are you driving this taxi?"

"Well, who'd you think was driving it, lady?"

"I mean are you the same young man as in the picture here?"

Then Ernie, to the horror of his fare, might thrust his head in at the
half-open window, unmindful of the traffic that swirled and eddied all
about him.

"Me? No. I'm a couple of other guys," he might say, and smile.

In spite of sweater, cap, jaw, ears, and general bearing, when Ernie
smiled you recognized in him the engaging and highly sartorial Ernest
Stewig photographically approved by the local constabulary. Apologetic
and reassured, the passenger would relax against the worn leather cushion.

About Ernie there was much that neither police nor passenger knew.
About police and passenger there was little that Ernie did not know. And
New York was the palm of his hand. Not only was Ernie the authorized
driver of this car; he was its owner. He had bought it secondhand for four
hundred dollars. Its four cylinders made rhythmic music in his ears. He
fed it oil, gas, and water as a mother feeds her babe. He was a member in
good standing of the United Taxi Men's Association. He belonged to
Mickey Dolan's Democratic Club for reasons more politic than political.

In his left coat pocket he carried the gray-bound booklet which was his
hack driver's license—a tiny telltale pamphlet of perhaps a dozen pages. At
the top of each left-hand page was printed the word VIOLATION. At the top
of each right-hand page was the word DISPOSITION. If, during the year,
Ernie had been up for speeding, for parking where he shouldn't, for wearing his hackman's badge on his left lapel instead of his right, for any one
of those myriad petty misdemeanors which swarm like insects above a

hackman's head, that small crime now would appear inevitably on the left-hand page, as would his punishment therefor on the right-hand.

Here it was, November. The pages of Ernie's little gray book were virgin.

It must not be assumed that this was entirely due to the high moral plane on which Ernie and his four-cylinder, secondhand cab (repainted) moved. He was careful, wise, crafty, and almost diabolically gifted at the wheel. When you rode with Ernie you got there—two new gray hairs, perhaps, and the eye pupils slightly dilated—but you got there. His was a gorgeous and uncanny sense of timing. You turned the green-light corner just one second before the sanguine glare of the stop light got you. Men passengers of his own age, thirtyish, seemed to recognize a certain quality in his manipulation of the wheel. They said, "What outfit were you with?"

There were many like him penduluming up and down the narrow tongue of land between the Hudson and the East River. He was of his day: hard, tough, disillusioned, vital, and engaging. He and his kind had a pitying contempt for those grizzled, red-faced old fellows whose hands at the wheel were not those of the mechanic, quick, deft, flexible, but those of the horseman, bred to the reins instead of the steering gear. These drove cautiously, their high-colored faces set in anxiety, their arms stiffly held. Theirs were rattling old cars for which they had no affection and some distrust. They sat in the driver's seat as though an invisible rug were tucked about their inflexible knees. In their eyes was an expectant look—imploring, almost—as though they hoped the greasy engine would turn somehow, magically, into a quadruped. Past these, Ernie's car flashed derisively.

Up and down, up and down the little island he raced. New York swore at him, growled at him, confided in him, overtipped him, undertipped him, borrowed money from him, cheated him, rewarded him, bribed him, invited him to crime. His knowledge of New York was fearful. He forever was talking of leaving it. He complained of the dullness of business, of the dullness of life. He never talked to you unless you first talked to him, after which you had some difficulty in shutting him up. He had a sweet, true, slightly nasal tenor which he sometimes obligingly loaned to college boys with an urge to harmonize while on a New York week end. His vocabulary in daily use consisted of perhaps not more than two hundred words. He was married. He was fond of his wife, Josie. His ambition, confided under the slightest encouragement, was to open a little country hotel somewhere up the river, with a quiet but brisk bar and liquor business on the side. To this end he worked fifteen hours a day; toward it he and Josie saved his money. It was to be their idyl.

"Yeh, hackin', there's nothing in it. Too many cabs, see? And overhead!

Sweet jeez, lookit. Insurance thirty bucks a month and you got to pay it. If you ain't got your sticker every month—yeh, that's it, that blue paper on the windshield, see?—you're drove off the street by the cops and you get a ticket. Sure. You gotta insure. Garage, twenty-five. Paint your car once a year anyway is fifty. Oil and gas, two-fifty a day. Five tires a year and a good shoe sets you back plenty. That says nothing about parts and repairs. Where are you, with anyway fifteen hunnerd a year and nearer two grand? No, I only got just this one hack. No, I wouldn't want no jockey. I drive it alone. They don't play square with you, see? It ain't worth the worry of an extra bus. Yeh, I see aplenty and hear aplenty. Keep your eyes and ears open in the hackin' game, and your mouth shut, and you won't never get into a jam is the way I figger."

Strange fragments of talk floated out to Ernie as he sat so stolidly there at the wheel, looking straight ahead:

"Don't! There! I've lost an earring."

". . . five dollars a quart . . ."

". . . sick and tired of your damn nagging . . ."

". . . You do trust me, don't you, babe?"

Up and down, up and down, putting a feverish city to bed. Like a racked and restless patient who tosses and turns and moans and whimpers, the town made all sorts of notional demands before finally it composed its hot limbs to fitful sleep.

Light! cried the patient. Light!

All right, said Ernie. And made for Broadway at Times Square.

I want a drink! I want a drink!

Sure, said Ernie. And stopped at a basement door with a little slit in it and an eye on the other side of the slit.

I want something to eat!

Right, said Ernie. And drove to a place whose doors never close and whose windows are plethoric with roast turkeys, jumbo olives, cheeses, and sugared hams.

It's hot! It's hot! I want to cool off before I go to sleep!

Ernie trundled his patient through the dim aisles of Central Park and up past the midnight velvet of Riverside Drive.

One thing more. Under his seat, just behind his heels and covered by the innocent roll of his raincoat, Ernie carried a venomous fourteen-inch section of cold, black, solid iron pipe. Its thickness was such that the hand could grasp it comfortably and quickly. A jack handle, it was called affectionately.

Though he affected to be bored by his trade he deceived no one by his complaints; not even himself. Its infinite variety held him; its chanciness;

the unlimited possibilities of his day's vagaries. Josie felt this. Josie said,
"You'll be hackin' when you're sixty and so stiff-knuckled your fingers
can't wrap around the wheel."

"Sixty, I'll be pushing you in a wheel chair if you don't take off some
that suet."

They loved each other.

Saturday. Any day in Ernie's life as a hackman might bring forth almost
anything, and frequently did. But Saturday was sure to. Saturday, in winter, was a long hard day and night, yet Ernie always awoke to it much as a
schoolboy contemplates his Saturday, bright and new-minted. It held all
sorts of delightful possibilities.

Saturday, in late November. Having got in at 4 A.M., he awoke at noon,
refreshed.

Josie had been up since eight. She did not keep hackman's hours. Josie's
was a rather lonely life. She complained sometimes, but not often; just
enough to keep Ernie interested and a little anxious. A plump, neat woman
with slim, quick ankles; deep-bosomed; a careful water wave; an excellent
natural cook; she dressed well and quietly, eschewing beige with a wisdom
that few plump women have. Ernie took pride in seeing her smartly turned
out on their rare holidays together. A lonely and perforce an idle wife, she
frequented the movies both afternoon and evening, finding in their shadowy love-making and lavishness a vicarious thrill and some solace during
Ernie's absence.

His breakfast was always the same. Fruit, toast, coffee—the light breakfast of a man who has had his morning appetite ruined by a late lunch
bolted before going to bed. Josie had eaten four hours earlier. She lunched
companionably with him as he breakfasted. It was, usually, their only meal
together. As she prepared it, moving deftly about the little kitchen in her
print dress and wave pins, Ernie went up on the roof, as was his wont, to
survey the world and to fool for five minutes with Big Bum, the family
police dog, named after Ernie's pet aversion, the night traffic cop at the
corner of Forty-fifth and Broadway. He it was who made life hard for
hackmen between the hours of nine-thirty and eleven, when they were
jockeying for the theater break.

The Stewigs' flat was one of the many brownstone walk-ups in West
Sixty-fifth Street, a sordid and reasonably respectable row of five-story ugli-
ness whose roofs bristled with a sapling forest of radio aerials. A little rick-
ety flight of stairs and a tiny tar-papered shed led to an exhilarating and
unexpected view of sky and other low-lying roofs, a glimpse of the pocket-
edition Statue of Liberty on top of the Liberty Storage Warehouse, and

even a bit of the Hudson if you leaned over the parapet and screwed your neck around.

Ernie liked it up there. It gave him a large sense of freedom, of dominance. He and Big Bum tussled and bounded and rolled about a bit within the narrow confines of their roof world. They surveyed the Western Hemisphere. Big Bum slavered and pawed and bowed and scraped his paws and wagged his tail and shimmied his flanks and went through all the flattering and sycophantic attitudes of the adoring canine who craves male company, being surfeited with female.

"Ernie!" a voice came up the airshaft. "Coffee's getting cold!"

Big Bum threw his whole heart into his effort to hold his master on the roof. He bared his fangs, growled, set his forefeet menacingly. Ernie slapped him on the rump, tousled his muzzle, tickled his stomach with a fond toe.

"Come on, Bum."

"Aw, no!" said Bum, with his eyes. "Let's not pay any attention to her. Couple of men like us."

"Ernie! Don't beef to me if your toast is leather."

"Come on, Bum." Down they went to domesticity.

"What time'll you be home, do you think?"

"How should I know?"

"You couldn't stop by for dinner, could you, late? Nice little steak for you, maybe, or a pork tenderloin and lemon pie?"

"On a Saturday? You're cuckoo!"

"Well, I just thought."

"Yeh! Don't go bragging."

They had discussed a child in rare conjugal moments. "Wait," Ernie had said, "till we got the place up the river with a back yard for the kid like I had time I was little and lived in Jersey, and he can fool with Bum and like that. Here, where'd he be but out on the street being run over?"

"Yes," said Josie, not too delicately. "Let's wait till I'm fifty."

She bade him good-by now, somewhat listlessly. "Well, anyway, you're not working tomorrow, are you, Ernie? Sunday?"

"No. Give the other guy a chance tomorrow. We'll go somewheres."

They did not kiss one another good-by. After seven years of marriage they would have considered such daytime demonstration queer, not to say offensive.

One o'clock. Over to the garage on Sixty-ninth for the hack. Gas, oil, and water. These services he himself performed, one of the few taxi men to whom the engine of a car was not as mysterious and unexplored as the heavenly constellations. It was a saying among hackmen that most of them did not know what to do when the engine was boiling over. Ernie's car had been cleaned during the morning. Still, he now extracted from beneath the seat cushion a flannel rag with which he briskly rubbed such metal parts as were, in his opinion, not sufficiently resplendent.

He had fitted the car with certain devices of his own of which he was extremely proud. Attached to the dashboard, at the right, was a little metal clip which held his pencil. Just below the meter box hung a change slot such as streetcar conductors wear. It held dimes, quarters, and nickels and saved Ernie much grubbing about in coat pockets while passengers waited, grumbling.

Out through the broad, open door of the garage and into the lemon-yellow sunshine of a sharp November Saturday. A vague nostalgia possessed him momentarily. Perhaps they were burning leaves on some cross street that still boasted an anemic tree or two. Saturday afternoons in Jersey—Jeez, it's a great day for football, he thought, idly, and swung into Sixty-eighth Street toward the Park.

Two elderly, gray-haired women twittered wrenlike at the curb in front of a mountainous apartment house near Central Park West. They looked this way and that. At sight of Ernie's cab they fluttered their wings. He swooped down on them. They retreated timidly, then gave him the address and were swallowed in the maw of his taxi.

Two o'clock. Ernie's Saturday had begun.

The number they had given was on Lexington Avenue in the Fifties. It turned out to be a small motion-picture theater.

"This where you meant, lady?"

They fumbled with the door. Ernie reached in, opened it. They stepped out, stiffly. The fare was fifty-five cents. One wren handed him a minutely folded green bill. He tapped the change slot three times and gave her two dimes and a quarter. The wren put the three coins into a small black purse. From the same purse she extracted a five-cent piece and offered it to him. He regarded it impersonally, took it.

A little superstitious shiver shook him. A swell start for a Saturday, all right. What those two old birds want to come 'way over here to a bum movie for, anyway! Curious, he glanced at the picture title. *Souls for Sale.* That didn't sound so hot. Oh, well, you couldn't never tell what people done things for. He tucked the folded bill into his upper left coat pocket. He always did that with his first fare, for luck.

Off down the street. Might pick up a matinee fare one the hotels on Madison. He came down to Forty-seventh, jockeyed along the Ritz. Little groups of two and three stood on the steps and came languidly down to the sidewalk at the Madison Avenue entrance. Orchids, fur, sheer silk stock-

ings; British topcoats, yellow sticks: au 'voir, darling . . . awfly nice. . . .
The doorman hailed him.

Two of the orchids skipped into his car. They waved good-by to a coat.
Whyn't the big stiff come along with'm, pay their fare and maybe a decent
tip instead of the dime these kind of mice give a guy?

"Listen, driver, can't you go faster?"

"Doing the best I can. You can't go through the lights."

Turn around the middle of the street front of the theater if the cop
wasn't looking. Yeh, he wasn't. "Forty-five cents."

"I've got it, dear. Please let me. Don't fuss. We're so late."

Oh, my Gawd!

The winning orchid handed him a dollar. He flipped a nickel and two
quarters into his palm, turned to look hard. "That's all right," said the
orchid. They skipped into the theater. Well, that was more like it. Cute
couple kids, at that.

He headed down Eighth Avenue toward the loft district in the Thirties
between Eighth and Fifth. The fur and cloak-and-suit manufacturers were
rushed with late Saturday orders to be delivered, to be shipped. Little dark
men ran up and down with swatches, with bundles, with packages of fur
and cloth and felt. Take me down to Tenth and Fifth. Take me up to
Thirty-second and Third. I want to go to Eighty-eight University Place.

It was tough driving through the packed, greasy streets. You couldn't
make time, but they were generous with their tips. Ernie preferred to stay
all afternoon in and out of the cloak-and-suit district. Being too far downtown, he headed uptown again toward the Thirties. In Thirteenth Street,
going west, vacant, he had a call from a gimlet-eyed young man at the curb
in front of an old brick building. The young man leaned very close to
Ernie. He made no move to enter the taxi. He glanced quickly up and
down the street. He said to Ernie, quietly:

"Take a sack of potatoes?"

"Sure," said Ernie. "Where to?"

"Broadway and Nine'y-foist."

"Sure," said Ernie.

The gimlet-eyed young man nodded ever so slightly toward an unseen
figure behind him. There emerged quickly from the doorway a short, mild-
looking blond man. He carried a suitcase and a brown-paper corded bundle. His strong short arms were tense-muscled under the weight of them.
It was as though they held stone. He deposited these gently in the bottom
of the cab. Glup-glup, came a soft gurgle. The younger man vanished as
the little fellow climbed ponderously into the taxi. He reappeared carrying
still another brown bundle. He sagged under it.

"Fi' bucks for you," he said to Ernie. "Take Ninth Avenue."

"Sure," said Ernie.

The young man closed the taxi door and disappeared into the brick building. Ernie and the mild blond fellow and the suitcase and the two stout, brown-paper parcels sped up Ninth Avenue, keeping always on the far side of an occasional traffic cop and observing all road rules meticulously.

The uptown Broadway address reached, the man paid him his fare and the five dollars. Ernie sat stolidly in his seat while the little man wrestled with suitcase and bundles. Not him! They wouldn't catch Ernie carrying the stuff with his own hands. As the bundles touched the curb he stepped on the gas and was off, quickly. He headed down Broadway again.

A plump, agitated little woman in an expensive-looking black fur coat hailed him at Eighty-fifth. "Take me to Eight-fifty-five West End. And I'm late for a bridge game."

"That's terrible," said Ernie, grimly. She did not hear him. She perched on the edge of the seat, her stout silken legs crossed at the ankles, both feet beating a nervous tattoo.

Ernie whirled west on Eighty-fifth, then north up West End. The dressy woman climbed laboriously out. She handed Ernie his exact fare and scurried into the marble-and-plush foyer of Number Eight-fifty-five.

"And I hope you lose your shirt," Ernie remarked feelingly.

He took out the five-dollar bill that the man had given him for carrying the sack of potatoes, smoothed it, and placed it in his billfold. Then he remembered the bill in his upper left coat pocket—his first fare given him by the fluttery old ladies bent on seeing *Souls for Sale*. He fished down with two fingers, extracted the bill, smoothed it, and said piously, "For the jeez!"

It was a ten-dollar bill. His mind jolted back. He pieced the events of the past two hours into neat little blocks. Hm. Gosh! Fifteen bones clean, he could call it a day and knock off and go home and have dinner with Jo. There was no possibility of returning the ten-dollar bill to its owner, even if he had thought remotely of so doing—which he emphatically had not.

The blue-and-gold doorman, guardian of Number Eight-fifty-five, now approached Ernie. "What you sticking around here blocking up this entrance?"

Ernie looked up absently. He tucked his bills tidily into the folder, rammed the folder into his hip pocket. "Do you want me to move on?" he inquired humbly.

"You heard me." But the doorman was suspicious of such meekness.

Ernie shifted to first. He eyed the doorman tenderly. "And just when I was beginning to love you," he crooned.

Four-fifteen. He bumbled slowly around the corner on Eighty-sixth and across to Columbus. Might go home, at that. No, Jo wouldn't be there, anyway. A white-tiled coffeeshop. A great wire basket of golden-brown doughnuts in the window, flaky-looking and flecked with powdered sugar. Pretty cold by now. Ernie stamped his feet. Guess he'd go in; have a cup of hot coffee and a couple sinkers.

There were other hackmen in the steaming little shop with its fragrance of coffee and its smell of sizzling fat. They did not speak to Ernie, nor he to them. The beverage was hot and stimulating. He ate three crullers. Feeling warm and gay, he climbed into the driver's seat again. He'd stick around a couple hours more. Then he'd go home and give the other guy a chance.

Down to Columbus Circle, across Fifty-ninth, down Seventh, across Fifty-seventh to Madison. Down Madison slowly. Not a call. Nearly five o'clock.

A girl gave him a call. Tall, slim, pale. Not New York. She had been standing at the curb. Ernie had seen her let vacant cabs go by. As she gave him the number she smiled a little. She looked him in the eye. Her accent was not New Yorkese. She got in. The number she had given turned out to be an office building near Fortieth.

"Wait here," she said and smiled again and looked into Ernie's eyes.

"Long?"

"No, just a minute. Please."

It didn't look so good. Still, he'd wait a couple minutes, anyway. Wonder was there another exit to this building.

She came out almost immediately. "The office was closed," she explained.

Ernie nodded. "Yeh, five o'clock, and Saturday afternoon. Close one o'clock."

She got into the taxi, gave another number. Ernie recognized it as that of still another office building. That, too, probably would be closed, he told her. He turned his head a little to look at her through the window.

She smiled and put her head on one side.

"I want to try, anyway." Then, as Ernie turned to face forward again, his hand on the gear shift, "Could I trouble you for a match?"

Hm. Thought so. When they asked you for a match, anything might happen. He gave her a light. She took it, lingeringly, and kept the matches. You want me to take you to that number, girlie? Yes. She did not resent the girlie. He took her to the number. Wait, please. In a minute she was back. Her voice was plaintive, her brow puckered.

"Seems like everybody's away," she said. She got in. "I love riding in taxis. I'm crazy about it." Her *I* was *Ah*. Her *ou* was double *o*, or nearly.

"You from out of town?"

"I'm from Birmingham. I'm all alone in town. I guess you better take me to my hotel. The Magnolia Hotel, West Twenty-ninth."

He started for it, waiting for the next move from his fare. She pushed down the little seat that folded up, one of a neat pair, against the front of the taxi. She changed over to it and opened the sliding window, leaning out a little.

"My train doesn't go till ten o'clock tonight, and I haven't a thing to do till then."

"That's too bad," said Ernie.

"If I keep my room after six they charge for it. It's almost half-past five now. And my train doesn't go till ten and I haven't a thing to do."

"Yeh?"

"If I got my suitcase and checked out, would you be back down here at six?" They had reached the hotel entrance.

"Sure," said Ernie. She stepped out, her slim ankles teetering in high heels. She turned to go.

"Ninety cents, girlie," said Ernie. She gave him a dollar. Her hand touched his.

"Six o'clock," she repeated. "Right here."

"Sure," said Ernie.

He drove briskly over to the manufacturing section again. They were great taxi riders, those little paunchy men, and a fare there around six o'clock meant a good call up to the Bronx, or over to Brooklyn. The manufacturers worked late now in the height of the season. Six o'clock and often seven. On the way he got a call to Twelfth Street, came back to the Thirties, and there picked up a Bronx call just as he had hoped. This was his lucky day, all right. Breaking good. Wonder was that Birmingham baby standing on the curb, waiting.

He drove briskly and expertly in and out of the welter of traffic. His fare wanted some newspapers, and Ernie obligingly stopped at a newsstand and got them for him—*Sun, Journal, Telegram.* The man read them under the dim light inside the cab, smoking fat black cigars the while. The rich scent of them floated out to Ernie even through the tightly closed windows. A long cold ride, but Ernie didn't mind. He deposited his fare in front of a gaudy new apartment house far uptown.

"Cold night, my boy," said the man.

"I'll say!" A fifty-cent tip. The fare had left the newspapers in the taxi. Ernie selected the *Journal.* He drove to a near-by lunchroom whose sign said Jack's Coffee Pot. Another cup of coffee and a ham-on-rye. He read his paper and studied its pictures, believing little of what he read. Sometimes, though rarely, he discussed notorious tabloid topics with a fellow worker, or with a talkative fare, or a lunchroom attendant. His tone was one of sly but judicious wisdom. In a murder trial he was not deceived by the antics of principals, witnesses, lawyers, or judges. "Yeh, well, that baby better watch herself, because she can't get away with that with no jury. Blonde or no blonde, I bet she fries."

Seven-thirty. Guessed he'd start downtown and get around the Eighties by eight o'clock, pick up a nice theater fare. Wonder if that Birmingham baby was waiting yet. No. Too late. Looked as mild as skim-milk, too. Never can tell, and that's a fact. He'd have to tell Jo about that one. Uh— no, guess he wouldn't, at that. Mightn't believe him. Women.

Central Park West. He turned in at Sixty-seventh, picked up a theater fare for Forty-fifth Street. Hoped that big bum on the corner Forty-fifth would leave him turn right, off Broadway. From Fifty-first to Forty-fifth his progress became a crawl, and the crawl became a series of dead stops punctuated by feeble and abortive attempts to move. The streets were packed solid. The sidewalks were a moving mass. Thousands of motors, tens of thousands of lights, hundreds of thousands of people.

Ernie sat unruffled, serene, watchful at his wheel. He rarely lost his temper, never became nervous, almost never cursed. It was too wearing. Hacking was no job for a nervous man. It was eight-thirty when he deposited his fare in front of the theater. Sometimes, on a good night, you could cover two theater calls. But this was not one of those nights. He went west to Ninth Avenue on his way to dinner uptown. Ninth would be fairly clear going. But at Forty-seventh and Ninth he reluctantly picked up a call headed for a nine-o'clock picture show. Oh, well, all right.

By nine he was again on his way uptown. He liked to eat dinner at Charley's place, the Amsterdam Lunch, on Amsterdam near Seventy-seventh. He could have stopped very well for a late dinner at home. But you never could tell. Besides, Jo getting a hot meal at nine—for what! The truth was that his palate had become accustomed to the tang of the pungent stews, the sharp sauces, and the hearty roughage of the lunchroom and the sandwich wagons. When possible he liked to drive uptown to Charley's, out of the welter of traffic, where he could eat in nine-o'clock peace.

Charley was noted for his Blue Plate, 65¢. He gave you stew or roast and always two fresh vegetables. Spinach and asparagus; corn and string beans. His peas were fresh. No canned stuff at Charley's. His potatoes were light and floury. Josie was an excellent cook. Yet, on the rare occasions when he ate at home, he consumed the meal listlessly, though dutifully. She went to endless trouble. She prepared delicate pastry dishes decorated with snarls of meringue or whipped cream. She cut potatoes into

tortured shapes. She beat up sauces, stuffed fowl. Yet Ernie perversely preferred Smitty McGlaughlin's lunch wagon at Seventh and Perry.

Charley's long, narrow slit of a shop was well filled. There were only
two empty stools along the glass-topped counter. Ernie had parked his car,
one of a line of ten taxis, outside the Amsterdam Lunch.

"What's good eating tonight, Charley?" Ernie swung a leg over the stool
at the counter.

Charley wore an artless toupee, a clean white apron, a serious look.
"Baked breast of lamb with peas and cauliflower and potatoes."

Ernie ordered it, and it was good. Rich brown gravy, and plenty of it.
But even if, in Charley's momentary absence, you had made your own
choice, you would not have gone wrong. Boiled ham knuckle, baked beans,
Ger. fr., 50¢. Broiled lamb chops, sliced tomatoes, Fr. fr., 55¢. As you ate
your Blue Plate there smirked up at you, through the transparent glass
shelf below, sly dishes of apple pie, custards, puddings, cakes. Here you
heard some of the gossip of the trade—tales of small adventure told in the
patois of New York.

"I'm going east on Thirty-eighth, see, and the big harp standing there
sees me, starts bawling me out, see? 'What the hell,' I says, 'what's eating
into you?' Well, he comes up slow, see, stops traffic and walks over to me
slow, looking at me, the big mick! 'Want a ticket, do you?' he says. 'Looking for it, are you?' he says. 'Asking for it? Well, take that,' he says, 'and
like it.' Can you match that, the big . . ." There followed a stream of effortless obscenity almost beautiful in its quivering fluidity.

Usually, though, the teller emerged triumphant from these verbal or
fistic encounters. "They give me a number up in Harlem. You ought to
seen the pans on them. Scared you. When we get there it's in front of a
light. So one of them pokes their head out of the window and says it ain't
the place. It's in the next block, halfway. Well, then I know I'm right. I
reach for the old jack handle under the seat and I climb down and open
the door. 'Oh, yes it is,' I says. 'This is the right place, all right, and you're
getting out.' At that the one guy starts to run. But the other swings back so
I clip him one in the jaw. I bet he ain't come to yet—lookit the skin of my
knuckles. . . ."

His fellow diners listened skeptically and said he was an artist, thus con-
veying that he was a romancer of high imagination but low credibility.
"Come on!" they said. "I heard you was hackin' at Mott Street Ferry all
evening."

Ernie paid for his meal, took a toothpick, and was on his way downtown for the theater break. Might as well make a day of it. Get a good rest
tomorrow. It was a grim business, this getting in line for the eleven-o'clock

show crowd. The cops wouldn't let you stand, they wouldn't let you move. You circled round and round and round, east on Thirty-eighth, back to Broadway, chased off Broadway by the cops, east again, back up Broadway, over to Eighth. "Come on! Come on! Come *on!*" bawled the cop, when you tried to get into Forty-fourth. "Come on! Come *on! Come on!*" chasing you up to Forty-sixth, on Eighth.

Ernie picked up a call in Forty-fourth. They wanted to go downtown to one of those Greenwich Village dumps. Pretty good call. Uptown again, and down again. He stopped at Smitty's and had a hamburger sandwich and a cup of coffee. Cold night, all right. How's hackin'? Good!

One o'clock. Might as well go over to the Sucker Clubs around the West Fifties. Saturday night you could pick up a 33⅓. One of the boys had cleaned up a hundred dollars one night last week. You picked up a call that wanted to go to a night club, a club where there was enough to drink. You took him in, if he looked all right to you, and you handed him over to the proprietor and you parked your hack outside and you came in, comfortably, and waited—you waited with one eye on him and the other on the cash register. And no matter what he spent, you got your 33⅓ per cent. One, two, three hundred.

Ernie cruised about a bit, but with no luck. Half-past one. Guessed he'd call it a day and go home to old Jo and the hay. Early, though, for a Saturday night. Pretty fair day.

He cruised across Fifty-first Street, slowly, looking carefully up at the grim old shuttered houses, so quiet, so quiet. A door opened. A bar of yellow light made a gash in the blackness. Ernie drew up at the curb. A man appeared at the top of the stairs. He was supporting a limp bundle that resembled another man. The bundle had legs that twisted like a scarecrow's.

"Hello, Al," said Ernie.

"Hey," called the man, softly, "give me a hand, will you?" •

Ernie ran up the stairs, took the scarecrow under the left arm as the man had it under the right arm. The bundle said, with dignity, "Cut the rough stuff, will you, you big ape!"

Ernie, surprised, looked inquiringly at Al. "His head is all right," Al explained. "He ain't got no legs, that's all."

Together they deposited the bundle in Ernie's hack. Ernie looked at the face. It was scarred again and again. There were scars all over it. Old scars. It was Benny Opfer.

"There!" said Al, affably, arranging the legs and stepping back to survey his handiwork. "Now, then. The address . . ."

"I'll give my own address," interrupted Mr. Opfer, with great distinctness, "you great big so-and-so."

Al withdrew. The yellow gash of light showed again briefly; vanished. The house was dark, quiet.

Benny Opfer gave his address. It was in Brooklyn.

"Oh, say," protested Ernie, with excusable reluctance, "I can't take no call to Brooklyn this time of night."

"Do you know who I am?" Ernie was no weakling; but that voice was a chill and horrid thing, coming even as it did from the limp and helpless body.

"Yeh, but listen, Mr. Opfer——"

"Brooklyn." He leaned forward ever so little by an almost superhuman effort of will. "I'm a rich man. When I was fourteen I was earning a hundred dollars a week."

"That right!" responded Ernie wretchedly.

"Do you know how?"

"Can't say I do."

"Gunning," said Mr. Benny Opfer modestly. And sank back.

They went to Brooklyn.

Arrived at the far Brooklyn destination, "I ain't got any money," announced Mr. Benny Opfer with engaging candor, as Ernie lifted him out.

"Aw, say, listen," objected Ernie plaintively. He hoisted Mr. Benny Opfer up the steps and supported him as he fitted the key.

"Get you some," Opfer promised him. "She's always got fi' dollars stuck away someplace. You wait."

"I'll wait inside," Ernie declared stoutly.

Ernie stood outside in the cold November morning. He looked up at a lighted upper window of the Brooklyn house. Sounds floated down, high shrill sounds. He waited. He mounted the steps again and rang the bell, three long hard rings. He came down to the street again and looked up at the window. 'Way over to Brooklyn, and then gypped out of his fare! He rang the bell again and again.

The window sash was lifted. A woman's head appeared silhouetted against the light behind it. "Here!" she called softly. Something dropped at Ernie's feet. It was the exact fare. Benny Opfer, limp as to legs, had been levelheaded enough when it came to reading the meter.

Half-past three.

Ernie was on his way home, coming up Third Avenue at a brisk clip. A man and a girl hailed him. The girl was pretty and crying. The man gave an address that was Riverside at One Hundred and Eighteenth Street. The streets were quiet now. Quiet. Sometimes New York was like that for one hour, between three-thirty and four-thirty. The front window was open an inch or two.

"You don't need him," said the man. "He's all washed up. You stick to me and everything'll be all right. He never was on the level with you, anyway."

"I'm crazy for him," whimpered the girl.

"You'll be crazy about me in a week. I'm telling you."

An early morning el train roared down her reply.

Cold. Getting colder all the time. Sitting here since one o'clock today. Today! Yesterday. Ernie sank his neck into his sweater and settled down for the grind up to One Hundred and Eighteenth. Last fare he'd take, not if it was the governor of New York State, he wouldn't.

The man and the girl got out. The girl's head drooped on the man's shoulder. The man paid Ernie. She wouldn't sit so pretty with that bimbo if the size of his tip was any sign and, if it wasn't, what was?

No more hackin' this night. He turned swiftly into Broadway.

Tired. Dead-tired. Kind of dreamy, too. This hackin'. Enough to make you sick to your stomach. Taking everybody home and putting them to bed. Just a goddam wet nurse, that's what. One Hundred and Fifteenth. Tenth. His eye caught a little line of ice that formed a trail down the middle of Broadway. The milk wagons that came down from the station at One Hundred and Twenty-fifth Street. The melting ice inside these trickled through the pipe to the pavement, making a thin line of ice in the cold November morning. One Hundredth. Ninety-fifth.

Half-past four.

The sound of a tremendous explosion. The crash of broken glass. Ernie, relaxed at the wheel, stiffened into wakeful attention. It was still dark. He drove swiftly down to Ninetieth Street. The remains of a white-painted milk wagon lay scattered near the curb. Broken glass was everywhere. A horse lay tangled in the reins. The sound of groans, low and unceasing, came from within the shattered wagon. Fifty feet away was a powerful car standing upright and trim on the sidewalk.

Ernie drew up, got out. All about, in the towering apartment houses lining the street, windows were flung open. Heads stuck out. Police whistles sounded. No policeman appeared. Ernie went over to the cart; peered in. A man lay there, covered with milk and blood and glass. Chunks of glass stuck in his cheeks, in his legs. They were embedded in his arms. He was bleeding terribly and groaning faintly as he bled. More faintly. Men appeared—funny fat men and lean men in pajamas with overcoats thrown on.

"Here, give me a hand with this guy," commanded Ernie. "He's bleeding to death."

No one came forward. Blood. They did not want to touch it. Ernie looked up and around. He saw a figure emerge from the queerly parked automobile and walk away, weaving crazily.

"Hey, get that bird," cried Ernie, "before he gets away. He's the one hit the wagon. Must of been going eighty miles an hour, the way this outfit looks."

A slim, pale young fellow, fully dressed, detached himself from the crowd that had now gathered—still no police—walked quickly across the street—seemed almost to flow across it, like a lean cat. He came up behind the man who had emerged from the reckless automobile. Swiftly he reached into his back hip pocket, took from it a blackjack, raised his arm lightly, brought it down on the man's head. The man crumpled slowly to the pavement. The pale young fellow vanished.

The groans within the shattered wagon were much fainter. "Give me a hand here," commanded Ernie again. "One you guys. What's eating you! Scared you'll get your hands dirty! Must of all been in the war, you guys."

Someone helped him bundle the ludicrous yet terrible figure into the taxi. Ernie knew the nearest hospital, not five minutes away. He drove there, carefully yet swiftly. The groans had ceased. Men in white uniforms received the ghastly burden.

Ernie looked ruefully at the inside of his hack. Pools of red lay on the floor, on the cushions; ran, a viscid stream, down the steps.

At the garage, "I won't clean no car like that," declared the washer.

"All right, sweetness, all right," snarled Ernie. "I'll clean it tomorrow myself."

The washer peered in, his eyes wide. "Jeez, where'd you bury him!" he said.

Josie was asleep, but she awoke at his entrance, as she almost always did. "How'd you make out, Ernie?"

"Pretty good," replied Ernie, yawning. "Made a lot of jack."

"You rest till late," Josie murmured drowsily. "Then in the afternoon we'll maybe go to a movie or somewhere. There's *Ride 'Em, Cowboy* at the Rivoli."

"The West," said Ernie, dreamily, as he took off his socks. "That's the place where I'd like to go. 'Ride 'em, cowboy!' That's the life. Nothing ever happens in this town."

The Light Touch

[1931]

This story was, I blush to confess, originally entitled "No Foolin'," and under that stomach-turning title it first appeared. It is a story of the period following the first World War when the Depression was spoken of as though it were some actual living monster. The youth of the United States had reached a degree of cynicism which should have been treated like a fit of the sulks. They spoke of themselves as the Lost Generation, but they were perhaps not so much lost as hiding behind their fears and disillusionment. They were so different from the adult, admirable, and knowledgeable young men and women of this troubled day as to make them now seem creatures from another planet.

❧ AS LONG AS THEY WERE GOING TO BE STUCK RIGHT THERE IN KARLS-bad, Mrs. Weeks said, for twenty-one whole days, they might as well buy Alice's trousseau linens. The windows of the linen shops on the Alte Wiese held her fascinated, writhing as they were with monograms, vine patterns, wreaths, curlicues, and hemstitching. There came a greedy glitter into Mrs. Weeks's eye, and her heart leaped in her housewifely breast. Dr. Goldschlagel had ruled that Father must stay for the full cure period of three weeks, with baths, waters, diet, packs, massage—everything.

"That gives us plenty of time to select. And even with the duty it'll come to much less than if we bought it at home. Such linen! And those monograms! They're like pictures."

Even a stranger might have remarked Alice's failure to meet this enthusiasm. George W. Weeks said, "A person would think this was your trousseau, Hattie, instead of Alice's."

So now you saw them marching up and down the Alte Wiese, in and out of the linen shops, a little procession. Mrs. Weeks led, American-woman fashion, plump, vigorous; Alice followed, cool, lovely, indifferent; George W. Weeks brought up the rear—gentle, shrewd, thinking his own thoughts. His face and his hair were the color of his good gray suit. When Mrs. Weeks noted that, it was as though a fiendish hand wrenched at her vitals.

The neat glistening stacks piled up, higher and higher: tablecloths doilies napkins; sheets pillow slips towels. Alice's monogram would afford a superb opportunity for the embroiderers' flourishes. A. W. T. Alice Weeks Tuckerman.

"This diamond-shaped monogram with the vine pattern wreathed around it is the prettiest, don't you think, Alice? Or maybe the shield pattern is richer."

"Whatever you say, Mother."

"*I* say! Who's marrying Phil Tuckerman—you or me?"

"Mom, darling, you know I never was the girl to throw open a linen closet and gloat. I can't get emotional about tablecloths and sheets, I don't care how lumpy they are with initials."

"Well, girls are certainly funny nowadays." Mrs. Weeks would turn again to the white drifts piled high on the counter. "I think the twelve-inch napkins are plenty big enough for luncheon size, and then the great big ones for dinner. Jane's best ones are as big as luncheon cloths, nearly. Aren't they?"

Alice had drifted toward the doorway where her father stood gazing out into the colorful panorama of the winding street. She linked her arm through his. Mrs. Weeks's tone flashed a warning edge of impatience.

"What? What did you say, Mother?"

Mrs. Weeks now turned her full attention upon her spoiled daughter. "Alice Corbin Weeks!" (Mrs. Weeks had been a Corbin.) "Now, you listen to me. If you are going to cut up any of your monkeyshines, you tell me right here and now. If you think your father can spend hundreds and hundreds and hundreds of dollars on linens, all monogrammed and everything, and then at the last minute have you change your mind again——"

"Oh, Mother! Really!"

But into Mrs. Weeks's memory had flashed the vision of her daughter's face as, two weeks ago, at the pier in New York, she had said farewell to the stricken and clinging Phil Tuckerman. Something then had warned Mamma Weeks that no damsel, parting thus from her betrothed for two months, should present even to a watching world so unanguished an exterior.

She came over to the two in the doorway. Her voice vibrated with emotion. "Tons of tablecloths and sheets and everything, all ordered embroidered in A. W. T. You're not a child. Changing your mind all the time. My land, you're twenty-three!"

George W. Weeks's interest in the matter of linens and monograms was less than negligible. American husband and father, he was required to be concerned in such matters only at the checkbook stage. Papa Weeks was something of a darling. There were strata in his make-up that Mrs. Weeks had never penetrated; of which she was, indeed, completely unaware.

His gray face now crinkled in a little secret smile.

" 'Put it down a we,' Hattie. 'Put it down a we.' "

But Hattie Weeks did not care for Dickens, and had never heard of

Tony Weller. "I don't know what you're talking about, George. Some of your nonsense." Yet, curiously enough, her next utterance unconsciously carried out her husband's cryptic suggestion.

"Do you know what? I've a good notion to have all the monogramming done in your initials. Some people do. Brides, in the old days, with hope chests. Just A.C.W. I swear, if I had to go back to New York with all this linen and then have somebody pick the *T* out of everything, it would just about kill me."

Alice now drew herself up to her full height—five feet one and a half. "Please, Mother. You make me feel so cheap." She turned to the bewildered Austrian saleswoman. "A. W. T."

The woman bowed a little, and smiled a little, and nodded her head a good deal. These Americans! she thought. *Gott im Himmel!*

Certainly there was some excuse for Mrs. Weeks's perturbation. Though things had never before actually reached the embroidered-monogram stage, Alice Weeks had, since her eighteenth birthday, been engaged to a procession of Phil Tuckermans. She was now twenty-three. Twenty-five, a warning milestone, was clearly to be seen up the road.

Her girl friends, back home in New York, had married, for good or for evil, and were even beginning to be bored with the novelty of their own apartments furnished with wedding gifts after the style of their day. It was the year 1912, and their bridal nooks were modish with mahogany or oak library tables, overstuffed chairs, sectional bookcases, Tiffany-glass lamps. Alice's two brothers, George Junior and Hobart, had married, and their Jane and Lillian had already presented them, respectively, with a daughter and a son.

Alice, the family agreed, was fickle and frivolous and spoiled. These accusations Alice vainly denied. She sensed, though she did not know clearly, that in her seeming capriciousness lay a genuine constancy. She became engaged to marry; she broke the engagement.

She could not clearly explain, even to herself, that each time she thought, in her willingness, in her eagerness to find love, that this was it— this was the perfect thing. Each time she had found that what she, in her rashness, had thought to be real was only a substitute; and she had refused to accept second-best. The family joked about it. "You ought to issue rain checks, Allie."

Only her father had not ridiculed her. "It's all right, Allie. You be as sure as you can. Of course you can't be sure. But you've got to think you are, anyway."

He spoiled her. Everybody spoiled her. Her father treated her as though she were a little girl, her brothers as though she were a rather annoying princess, according to the habit of American fathers and brothers. It was not her fault, certainly, that she had a heart-shaped face, eyes like animated pansies, and golden curls such as you saw on the magazine covers. In view of all this, the beholder naturally overlooked her square jaw and the firmness of her lips.

Then, too, her lack of height gave her an enormous advantage over the tall and broad-shouldered American male. Almost always she was obliged to look up at the person with whom she was speaking. This lent her a misleadingly melting look, and she thus was frequently surprised and even enraged to find herself suddenly swept into the great arms of a six-foot acquaintance to whom she was merely being politely attentive.

Thus equipped (or handicapped), she had gone her imperious way. Phil Tuckerman, a baffled fiancé, had rebelled in vain at her announced intention to spend two months in Europe with her parents. "But I do, Phil, really I do. I've told you over and over. And it's only for two months. I've never been to Europe, and goodness knows if I'll ever get another chance, and I've always been dying to go, and as long as there's that wonderful Dr. Goldschlagel, or whatever it is, in Karlsbad, and everyone tells Dad the cure there is absolutely what he needs, and after that we're going to Vienna and to Budapest and to Paris. Paris! Why——"

"Just the same," muttered Phil Tuckerman darkly, "just the same, if you really . . ."

Mrs. Weeks thought so, too, in private conversation with her husband. "Just the same," as though continuing a chant, "just the same, when I was engaged to you, if anyone had tried to make me go away for two months before we were married they'd have had to drag me by main force."

"Girls are different now. Alice is different."

"Girls aren't. Alice is."

So they were in Europe together, the three of them, and George Weeks was saying amiably, "Well, now, what do you girls want to do, huh? Whatever you say."

They always knew, and told him. It scarcely ever was what he wanted to do. He never thought of rebelling.

Karlsbad seemed to turn the trick. "But you won't feel the real benefit until next winter," Goldschlagel had said. "This cure is really a Christmas present." They thought that was a very original way of putting it until they discovered that all the Karlsbad doctors said the same thing to discharged cure patients.

When they reached Paris the two women shopped relentlessly, for Father Weeks had business of his own. George Weeks, in New York, had to do with stocks and bonds, and his European trip was not wholly in pursuit of health and pleasure. "Now I've got to see these fellows at the bank. You girls run along and enjoy yourselves."

Sometimes at dinner with his wife and daughter he let fall upon their inattentive ears some fragmentary account of his day's doings. "Dusty old-fashioned holes they've got for business. But smart! We think we're smart, in New York. Say, we're babies." He was thinking aloud, really. The women were not interested.

At his next words, however, they gave him their attention. "You girls meet me for lunch tomorrow, will you? I've invited Delage, of the Crédit International, and Tellier, his assistant. You see, they're kind of the French connection of our New York office. Like to show them a little attention."

George Weeks was not a New Yorker, born and bred. He had come East from the Middle West. His would always be the homely vernacular of his native region.

Alice Weeks said, "My French is terrible, and I don't think the Frenchmen are a bit good-looking."

"They speak English better than you do, young lady. And you're not expected to marry them. They're married, for all I know, so you can concentrate on your lunch and think about Phil, but be polite, will you, because this is kind of business."

Delage, chief of the investment department of the Crédit International, did turn out to be married; the rather snuffy type of prewar Paris professional or businessman, with a long parchment face, striped trousers, black coat, badly fitting collar. But Paul Tellier was different. Paul Tellier was so different that he took Alice Weeks's whole life as you take a piece of shapeless cloth, and fashioned it into the pattern he thought best for her.

He not only had been married, he was a widower, childless, and almost ten years older than Alice. He was tall, thin, incredibly graceful in speech and movements. His eyes, dark brown and velvety, would have been too soft and fine had they not possessed the saving and hardening alloy of intelligence.

He was nearly bald. This, in some curious way, only added to his attractiveness. He looked, Alice thought, like a young diplomat. She had never seen a diplomat, old or young. He spoke English perfectly, but with a little accent that made his most commonplace remark sound altogether enchanting.

She had extended her hand for the firm clasp with which one greeted new acquaintances back home. He brought it to his lips and lightly kissed it. He looked down at her. Alice Weeks, in the past five years, had been kissed on the lips, the eyelids, the back of the neck, the throat, the shoulder. No one had ever kissed her hand in that impersonal, magnificent, and altogether satisfactory way.

It made her feel more powerful, more helpless, more feminine than she had ever felt before. Phil Tuckerman's kisses faded into the limbo of such unadult delights as ice-cream cones, matinees, country-club dances, and orchids. Her protracted adolescence fell from her like an ill-fitting garment, and she stepped forth in that instant a woman.

They decided to get married. This was irregular and unusual, for Paul Tellier came of upper-middle-class French people. These, unlike the lower class or the nobility, both of which frequently lapse, almost invariably marry of their own. They were deeply in love. Seeing this, George and Hattie Weeks were alarmed, then really frightened.

"But you can't marry a Frenchman and live in France. Frenchmen are different. They're not like American husbands. You're engaged to Phil. Are you going on like this all your life?"

"No. No. No."

"You'll march yourself on that boat, young lady. It's the same thing all over again. You'll forget him before we're out of Plymouth Harbor." So they sailed according to schedule.

But when Mrs. Weeks saw her daughter's face as she parted from Paul at sailing she remembered how Alice had looked on leaving Phil Tuckerman in New York two months before. She knew, then, and resigned herself to the inevitable. This was the face of a woman terribly and passionately in love.

"I guess this is the real thing this time," George W. Weeks said. "Kind of tough on Phil, but anyway, Hattie, your *T* is safe on all those sheets and stuff."

Paul came to New York in September. They were married. Back they went to France. The girls all agreed that Paul was distinguished-looking, but not at all the type they had expected Alice to marry.

Alice had five thousand a year from her doting father. Paul's salary at the bank was almost four thousand a year, and another thousand or so inherited from his parents and his late wife. They could live in Paris comfortably, even luxuriously, on these combined sums.

They took an apartment in Passy with big, high-ceilinged rooms and handsome chandeliers, parquetry floors, and no hot water from July until September.

Their child was born a year later. They named him after his American grandfather, spelling it "Georges," in the French fashion. This, to his American relatives, by a process of family joking, and to avoid confusion, became "Gorgeous," and as Gorgeous they always spoke of him.

The Tellier apartment was furnished with care and taste. Paul had some excellent things of his own; Alice's wedding gifts had been liberally sprinkled with family checks. The pieces they bought were very French in the old manner, calculated to last a lifetime, and beyond. The apartment in Passy, and its furnishings, remained the same throughout the nineteen years of the Telliers' married life.

"*Planter le chou,*" Paul said. "To plant the cabbage," literally, but really an expression of the aim of every middle-class Frenchman. To put aside enough for a permanent house and a piece of ground in the country, there to live in serenity in one's later years.

When Mr. and Mrs. Weeks came again to France for a first look at their new grandchild, they gazed with amazement upon their erstwhile spoiled darling. France, the most material, the most thrifty, the most cynical nation in the world, had absorbed her and made her its own.

"Well, Paul, you certainly have made a woman of our little girl," Mrs. Weeks said sentimentally.

"Are not all little girls potential women?" Paul replied, rather pleased with his neatness.

Paul Tellier was head of his household. Alice Tellier had soon learned that the French husband is always head of his household and that the Frenchwoman rules by indirection. The result, she discovered, was much the same as that achieved at home by the more ruthless and less femininely diplomatic American woman.

At home, in New York, her father had been only the nominal head of the household; Mrs. Weeks always had ruled with a heavy hand. In her brothers' households George Junior and Hobart lived in a sort of pleasant subjection to their Jane and Lillian. These American wives decided where to go for the summer holidays; which people to invite for dinner; the schools to which their children were sent; the furnishings of the house; their husbands' very ties, shirts, pajamas, and even suit patterns.

All these things Paul Tellier decided, but Alice influenced that decision by suggestion. This, too, she had early learned. Paul engaged the servants, chose the furniture, selected a tutor for Georges, said the pictures were to be hung there and there, approved Alice's clothes, supervised the food and its cost. Yet behind all these decisions was Alice, who, perhaps through love, had learned tact and adaptability.

"It's such a lovely tapestry, Paul. Where do you think it should be hung? I suppose you'll decide on a place not too near the big picture there, and yet where it will get the proper light so as to bring out the colors."

"We shall hang the tapestry just there."

"Are you sure?"

"It is the one proper place for it."

It was hung. They surveyed it. "Oh, Paul, how right you are! It's perfect there. You always know."

It had been hung exactly where she had wanted it hung.

Their friends were French. Some of these things she had learned from them, for she was young and quick and intelligent and in love. It seemed that all Frenchwomen did as she did, and so they were a great power in the land. Every Frenchman was a Louis, and beside each was a Maintenon, guiding, suggesting, ever so delicately and persistently.

This diplomat, this stateman, this financier, this artist, all gently and with exquisite tact advised and swayed and influenced by the hard, unsentimental, straight-thinking brain of a Frenchwoman. So the Frenchmen kept their manhood and their self-esteem and the Frenchwomen kept their powerful feminine wiles and each was busy and content.

Sometimes, with a kind of unbelief, Alice recalled her young married friends back home, and her brothers and sisters-in-law.

"Bart, get four seats for a show tomorrow night. Bob and Helen are coming to dinner. Their bridge is impossible and I won't just sit and talk."

"That's a terrible tie. You do have the rottenest taste. You look as if you were going to a Polish wedding."

"I'm going to have the couch recovered in green. I called up the upholsterer today. It'll be one-seventy-five."

"Next spring I'm going to have our room done in peach."

"I'm going to apply at Lawrenceville for Peter."

"She's awful. If you want to talk business with him then ask him to lunch or out to the club or something. I won't have her here."

"Let's go to California for a month. Stell says it's lovely in the summer. I'm sick of Massachusetts."

In those first two years of her married life, from 1912 to 1914, Alice Weeks grew to be more French than the French. From the first, Paul had spoken her name in the French fashion, the second syllable stressed, the *i* given the long *e* sound. She had become Alice Tellier, through and through.

After Paul had come home from the bank that July day, white-faced, and had taken off his business suit, which he was not again to put on for four nightmare years, there came many frantic cabled messages from Mother and Father Weeks in New York.

"Come home. Come home immediately."

"I am home," she had cabled, in reply.

The French soldiers, unprepared, in ridiculous bright-red pants and bright-blue coats went scurrying in taxicabs to meet the gray-green horde just outside the gates of their beloved Paris. And thereafter, for four years, Alice Tellier lived in an exciting kind of hell. If she had failed to become completely adult in the past two years, certainly these next four accomplished it. Sometimes, as she walked up the Champs Élysées toward home in the late afternoon, with the Arc de Triomphe etched in grandeur against the sunset sky, she thought of America, of New York, dimly, fondly, as one remembers a childhood game, a schoolday sweetheart.

One slight arm wound, a brief period in hospital, Paul was back in it again. A second wound, almost at the close of the war, in the leg this time, a long business; not crippled, but he would limp a little for life. He came home.

Delage, his chief in the investment department at the bank, had not been so lucky. The striped trousers and the black coat and the frumpy collar had been laid aside forever. Paul stepped into his place as chief. He had seven thousand a year, now, as salary. A man of forty-odd, resembling in his dress and manner the American businessman of his own age and class.

They had changed much, in many outward aspects, the French. The comic-cartoon Parisian, with the black spade beard, the baggy trousers, the dramatic shoulders, the gesticulating hands, seemed, somehow, to have vanished in the trenches, never to reappear. Except for that tiny blood-red spot of ribbon in his buttonhole, Paul might have been any American businessman.

"Planter le chou."

So they bought a house near Mantes, in Normandy, about seventy miles from Paris. They went there in the summer. The flat in Passy remained unchanged. There was a cook, Marcelle, and her husband, Léon, houseman-chauffeur, for the Telliers had a small car of their own now. Little Georges had a tutor at home. When he was eight he would go off to the École des Roches, forty miles from Paris.

Georges learned to ride, and to fence, and to play tennis, and to speak German and English as well as his native tongue. They had a tennis court at the place in Normandy. Léon tended the small grounds and the really fine rose garden.

"We'll raise our own vegetables," Alice had said at first, making one of her few mistakes.

"Oh, no," Paul had answered. People in their class did not raise vegetables. It simply was not done. The very rich, with large estates, grew their own vegetables, and the peasant class, but not the middle class. It would have been beneath Léon's dignity to attend to vegetables. Roses were all right. He could care for a rose garden with propriety. Unwritten French rules.

It was in 1921, when Georges was eight, that Alice Tellier went home for her first visit since her marriage. Her father, she thought, looked ill and old. Things bewildered her, shocked her. There was about everything a vast and careless lavishness.

To her eye, accustomed to the postwar frugalities of Europe, the splendor all about her was Roman, was barbaric. The very streets seemed to be flowing with food; fruit stands were bursting with richness; every stenographer wore a fur coat and silk stockings glisteningly new; fat, glittering motorcars choked the streets; twenty-five a seat for the Follies; a dress seen in a window on Madison Avenue and bought as casually as though it were a handkerchief.

At home, in Paris, Alice had a new evening dress every year, a new dinner frock, a street costume, all well made. Throughout the winter she saw her friends, and they her, again and again in the same costume.

She spoke of these things to her father, feeling a little frightened and breathless. "Everybody's got too much of everything. Or perhaps it's just that I'm not used——"

He had smiled grimly. "Going to be an awful yelp when the piper comes around."

All the changes, too, bewildered her. Things had changed kaleidoscopically. All her friends had moved again. Everything, everyone, had moved. All the furnishings of the apartments of her sisters-in-law and her parents and all her friends had been whisked away—had vanished—and things of a completely different sort had taken their place. Buildings had changed, whole streets, districts, even.

"Oh, now, Alice. This is a young, vigorous country. We're a vital people. We don't sit in one place all our lives. Don't be so snooty and superior and old-world."

"I'm not. I didn't mean to be. I'm just not—— Doesn't it make you tired to get used to new things like that, all the time? Adjusting yourself constantly. Like a fresh shock every little while."

"Oh, say, listen!"

"I just mean it's so comfortable to have things where you expect them to be."

The visit wasn't much of a success. Everyone spoiled Gorgeous. He seemed very quiet and a little pale and even puny compared with the amazing precociousness of his young cousins; their physical development, their boundless vitality. There were Bill, young Bart, Ernie, and Sally (quaint names had come in for girls). Besides, he was, they thought privately, too pretty for a boy, having inherited Alice's curls and small-boned frame.

Little Gorgeous and his Grandpa Weeks became great friends. Curiously enough, they did not talk very much when together. "Gorgeous is such a quiet child, Allie," the family said. "Is he always quiet like that?"

"He isn't especially quiet. French children are different. They're different from American children."

"French! Oh, yes, I suppose he—— Seems funny, for a minute, your saying French children."

"Anyway," Hattie Weeks said, as bustling as ever, "I don't think a good tonic would do that child a mite of harm. I'd take him to Walsh and see what he says. Anemic, I'll bet."

"Leave the boy alone," George W. Weeks said, in his mild voice. "He's all right. He's different. He's not a rampager, like the others."

He looked down at the boy. Gorgeous looked up at him. At that instant there was, between the sick old man and the young child, a striking resemblance; a fleeting thing, more of the spirit than of the body.

"He looks like you, Father," Alice said suddenly.

"Fiddlesticks! He's the image of you," snapped Hattie Weeks.

George Weeks put a slow hand, with its skin so dry and splotched with brown spots, on the golden head of the eight-year-old boy. "No. It's just that we think alike about things, I guess." A strange statement.

She went back home to France with relief, with joy. The dear familiar figure, with its little limp, there on the pier at Le Havre. The flat at Passy, unchanged. The house at Mantes, unchanged. Marcelle, Léon, the same.

Five years went by, eight, nine. Always short, she had grown a little plumper. She must be careful. Marcelle cooked too well. Still, none of this starving such as her sisters-in-law in America practiced. She was so French by now that the tourists who thronged the Paris streets in the late spring and early summer, before the family went to Normandy to stay until autumn, seemed to her eyes almost as strange and alien as to the native Parisian; their dress, their walk, their voices, their gestures.

"Well, look, you and Gert go do your shopping and I'm beating it back to the hotel. . . . What'll I get for Aunt Gussie? I got to bring her something. . . . Someplace where I could get a real good cup of coffee . . . Lookit that cop. Say, the guy corner Forty-second and Fifth could eat that frog for a gumdrop."

The Telliers had survived the war. France had survived the war. The decade marched to its end. Paul Tellier the same—suave, charming, assured; older certainly. In another ten years, perhaps, there would be enough, and he would step down to make way for a younger man. Alice, still pretty, still youthful-looking, though the forties were upon her; the long-lasting youthfulness of the small woman blessed with good eyes and skin and hair.

The two lived the quiet, serene, well-ordered life of their class. But underneath there was a difference. Perhaps that difference lay in the boy, Georges. He had been brought up as millions of French boys before him had been brought up. But there was about him something not easily explained.

He was almost eighteen. There was about all the French boys of his generation that same inexplicable difference. It was as though, in the period between 1914 and 1924, a whole generation had been skipped, and these boys were decades ahead of their time.

Georges was still too beautiful. His hair was too soft and curling, his skin too fine, his hands and feet were too delicate. It was a fragility he had inherited from his mother. Strangers were misled by it. The lad was normal, male, intelligent, aware. He was more than this. About him, and the other boys from eighteen to twenty-five, there was an uncanny composure. The prewar frenzy had preceded them; the postwar bewilderment had found them too young. But they had felt the shock and the after-effects of both these periods, and now you saw them looking about, cool, wise, seeing.

Theirs was a curious adult hardness. They were like metal that has been through a furnace and has come out resilient, but harder, more powerful than when it went in. It was uncanny to see them as they surveyed a writhing and tortured world. Adages by which their fathers had lived were rendered ridiculous. "As solid as the Bank of England." "I could no more do that than fly." "As good as wheat."

Meaningless phrases now.

You've made a fine mess of it, they seemed to say to their elders. You and your sayings. Don't think we don't know.

It was as though civilization itself were in the balance, and upon them depended the outcome. They played games, they flirted, they sulked, laughed, loved, as generations before them had done. But the look of awareness was in their eyes. The young of France, the young of Germany, the young of England, world-conscious for the first time in the history of the world.

The market in America, that had been performing breath-taking stunts high in the sky, now collapsed in a nose dive. Mrs. George W. Weeks took the tumble very badly indeed. All of America took it very badly indeed. For a moment it stared, open-mouthed, dumb, eyes popping. Then it began to scream and scramble.

Mrs. Weeks screamed and scrambled. Elevator boys and policemen, millionaires, actresses, stenographers, grocery boys, doctors, policemen, lawyers,

Negro porters, shoe clerks, businessmen screamed and scrambled. Their money. Their money was gone. Where? Someone must have it. There was a mythical monster named They; and They had it.

Mrs. Weeks wrote frantic letters, which had been preceded by still more frantic cables.

Your father's income is hardly a third of what it was. Goodness knows what will become of us all. I'll probably never be able to come to Europe again, so if you want to see your father and mother you'll have to come here, that's all. . . . The money your father slaved for all his life just blown away. . . . Your father is a very sick man. . . .

The Telliers, in France, felt it, too. Calmly they arranged themselves. The house at Mantes was their own now, paid for. Georges was to enter the Polytechnique. He would be an engineer. Nothing must interfere with that. They would let nothing interfere.

Still, even the French cannot fight fate. Paul Tellier, on business connected with the bond department of his bank, booked passage on the big ten-passenger plane to Berlin. Three hours later, broken and charred, so that twisted metal and twisted human flesh were alike unrecognizable, the plane lay a blot in the middle of a neat German field planted thriftily with spring vegetables. Wild little figures, their arms waving, sprang out of what had seemed to be deserted countryside and ran toward the blazing pyre, and then stood helpless, shielding their faces.

Alice Tellier's eldest brother came over from New York. He attended to things. He was very kind. "Now look here, Allie. No use you and Gorgeous living here in Paris any more. Thing to do is to settle up everything here and come on back home. We're all broke, but we can be broke together. You and Gorgeous can take an apartment with Mother and Dad. Gorgeous can go to Boston Tech or Cornell or Harvard."

"I want to stay here. Georges wouldn't be happy . . . The house—Paul wouldn't have wanted us to . . ."

"Now, listen. Your home's America. Gorgeous has had about enough of France, anyway, I'd say. Do him good to mix with the kids at home. Bring him back to the good old U. S. A., where he'll get around with two-fisted guys with hair on their chests."

"I want to stay here. We want to stay here."

"On what? You could just scrape Gorgeous through his engineering, and that's about all. The house at Mantes is clear, all right. But there's precious little besides. You can't sit out there, alone."

She made a last desperate stand. "I don't want to be a burden. The depression over there. Mother's letters are always—and the girls', too. Lillian and Jane always write—and the racketeers and the drinking, and the noise and the——"

"Well, I certainly am ashamed of you, Alice Weeks. Your own country. The finest country that God ever . . ."

She and Georges sailed in June for America. The flat in Passy was dismantled and left forever. She had kept the house at Mantes. "Until the autumn," she said. "Until I know. How do I know?" Her pretty face was white and stricken.

Léon and Marcelle went out to the house at Mantes, as usual, and Léon began placidly to attend the roses, and Marcelle to buy and conserve fruits and berries as they came along—enormous strawberries the size of plums, and enormous raspberries the size of strawberries, and enormous currants the size of raspberries.

Unexpectedly enough, Gorgeous was eager to go, thrilled at the prospect. He had been in Germany; he had been in England. He knew German boys, and English. "I want to see what they're doing. Everything's upside down there. It will be fun to see what they are doing about it. It will be important. I want to know what Bill thinks, and Bart and Ernie."

They took small cabins on an obscure deck of an unimportant boat, but it was a French boat, and Paul Tellier had been a man of standing in his quiet way. They were given every courtesy, every attention.

Georges was enormously interested, more excited than she had ever seen him. He talked with everyone. He walked the deck with Americans and with the French and talked and asked innumerable questions. Alice knew a growing terror of America, of her mother, of her brothers, of their wives, Lil and Jane, and of their two-fisted sons with hair on their chests.

The Paris winter had been the usual Paris winter, intensified. Cold, with a penetrating cold from which there was no escape; gray, heavy, damp. The sky, for weeks at a time, was like a dirty canopy of wet gray cotton. The trip across the ocean was a succession of just such gray wet days.

Then, suddenly, on the morning of their arrival, they awoke at Quarantine to brilliant June sunshine. Scarlet-funneled ships on a blue bay lay bathed in golden sunshine. The air was clear, was brilliant. And suddenly Alice Tellier felt light, happy, almost gay for the first time in many weeks. They came majestically up the river. She felt American and a little hysterical as she stood at the rail with Gorgeous.

"Look! Oh, look at that one. That must be the Empire State. Look, Georges! Everything looks sort of pink. Rose color. It's beautiful. I didn't realize. It's been ten years."

The boy stood looking. It was curious, the look on his face. He had looked like that when they had put him, a small boy, on a horse for his first riding lesson. Frightened; determined not to show it.

At the tip end of the pier was an enormous bouquet that resolved itself into faces and hats and gay-colored frocks and waving handkerchiefs. Lil, Jane, Bart, Hattie.

"*Dar*-ling! How *won*-derful you look! You look simply *mar*-velous. *Gorgeous*, *how* you've grown! Isn't he *hand*-some! Look, he's blushing. The boys couldn't come down. Big, lazy things. They won't get up during vacation. Well, darling, how *are* you? You look *stun*-ning in black. Doesn't she, Mother? Bart, tend to the trunks. Bart, you know that man who's one of the inspectors or something. Get him to hustle Allie's things through. Now, go *on*!"

They were all so kind, so solicitous, so genuinely eager to make her comfortable. They all had dinner with Mother and Father—the whole family. It was lovely, but a little overpowering, too, after the journey, the rush, the excitement.

The boys, Bill and young Bart and Ernie, were stupendous enough to be an event in themselves, not to speak of the rest of the family. They looked amazingly alike; or perhaps this was due to their height, their breadth, their astounding color and vitality. Two-fisted guys, with hair on their chests. Compared with them Gorgeous seemed colorless, almost insignificant.

"H'are you, Gorgeous?" they said. Took his hand in their enormous grasp.

George W. Weeks was a shrunken old man. Alice was wrung with anguish as she looked at him. "Well, Dad, here's your wayward dotter back."

The depression. The talk at dinner was of the depression. They joked about it a good deal. Gorgeous began to ask questions. Alice almost wished he wouldn't. He was so eager, and the boys—Bill and young Bart and Ernie—seemed so offhand and big and careless.

"Say, what you birds in Europe lack is the light touch. Everything's on the toboggan. What the hell!"

It was the same when they had dinner at Lil's, next night, and at Jane's, the night following.

"Is this true? Is that true? What is being done about this and that?" Georges would say. He was terribly in earnest, and a little cuckoo, they thought.

"Call up Hoover," they would say, to his mystification.

He was tiresome with his questions, with his theories. He would hold forth. Young Bart would say, "No kiddin'." It was an expression uttered with the falling inflection, and contained no hint of interest. Rather, it expressed a bored sophistication.

Certainly Georges's phrases were not new; all Europe had mouthed them until they were frayed and shabby. But there were no others. The boy was terribly in earnest and deeply interested in what he saw, and they wished to Gawd he'd shut up.

"Vitality of America all that is left . . . eyes of Europe . . . end of Western civilization unless . . . crime . . . Prohibition . . . Communism . . . world credit . . . only the young can help . . ."

"No foolin'," said Bill, yawning.

"Get a soapbox," said young Bart.

"Yeah!" said Ernie.

Alice and Georges had dinner at Jane's, at Lil's. They had again moved into new apartments, both. In the first ten days since coming to New York, Alice could not recall having seen them in the same dress twice. They talked a great deal about the depression. This Depression, they said, as though it were an individual they hated.

Their furnishings were new. The details bewildered Alice. The hall closets and clothes closets were painted in brilliant colors, and hung with satins or chintzes. The shelves were edged with frills or pleatings. They looked like the tiny boudoirs of midget harlots.

"This one is done in Chinese," Lil would say, quite seriously, and open a closet door to reveal a riot of lacquer red and orange and green, with Bart's somber, masculine garments, or big Ernie's, hanging incongruously in its midst.

The bathrooms. Alice Tellier had forgotten about the lavish luxury of American bathrooms. Rose bathrooms, jade-green bathrooms, delft-blue bathrooms, modernistic bathrooms. On the side of the wall in each was a roll of paper, and that, too, was rose or blue or jade green to match the tilings, the rugs, the shower curtains.

Gorgeous had burst into shouts of laughter at sight of this. His Gallic sense of humor had been tickled. Jane and Lil were a little offended at his lack of delicacy.

"Haven't had anything new in ages," they said. "This Depression. I wanted to have the apartment done over in modernistic, but I suppose I'll have to wait to see how Things turn out."

Bill and Bart and Ernie all advised Gorgeous to go to Harvard. "Harvard's got the team this year," they said.

Gorgeous had seen that they scarcely glanced first at a newspaper's front page, with its stories of a world trembling on the brink of dissolution. England. Russia. Germany. India. Italy. Japan. China. Turmoil. Chaos.

Straightway they turned to the sports sheet.

"Schultzy got a homer, a double, and two singles off Weblin in the first."

"Yeah, but the Giants got it cinched with McGork."

"Who says so?"

"I say so."

"No kiddin'."

At the end of two weeks Alice said, "Oh, Georges, you can't judge people. You're too young and too ignorant of the ways of the country." They were speaking French, as they always did when alone together.

"Yeah?" said Georges, not without malice.

"This is a new world—not old and tired, like France. They're like children. Like beautiful, charming children."

"That isn't it at all," said the strange boy, Georges. "They talk and act like children, but I have been listening and they are bitter and disillusioned and they don't care any more, and that is why I think it is no use here. They are soft, from these last fifteen years. The first blow has felled them."

"Oh, Georges, you're really behaving like a terrible little prig. You go around looking so superior. Your father used to look that way, sometimes, after he had had a conference with an American business client. It always annoyed me, I don't know why, much as I loved France."

The boy was bewildered. He took to going about alone. He made amazing discoveries. He talked to his grandfather about what he had observed, for George W. Weeks alone of all the family seemed to find these items remarkable, or even interesting. The boy was very excited. He walked up and down the room as he talked. The old man sat in the wheel chair to which he was now bound.

"It's all very gay," the boy finished up, breathlessly, "and terribly exciting, you know, and you have to run like everything. But I'm so confused. No one ever does or says anything that I'm expecting them to do or say. Why is that?"

"Young folks, you mean? Or everybody?"

"Everybody. Everybody except you."

The old man, with his fingers clasped, chased his two thumbs one round the other, round and round. "That word they are all so slick with—psychology. Well, tell you, Gorgeous, it's a funny psychology—that of this country of ours. Of mine. We're still simpering and giggling, with a finger in our mouth, and saying, 'Oh, we're such a young, young country.' Reminds me of a skittish old maid. We used to be a young and wild and headstrong country. But that's past now, or should be. That was finished fifty years ago. I kind of wish America would be its age."

Georges went to his mother.

"I have talked to Grandfather," the boy said.

"Yes," Alice said absently. "That's nice. You are sweet to Grandpa, dear. The boys never seem to talk to him, really. Sitting there, all day."

The boys always came in, big, glowing, rather overpowering. "Hello, Gramp! H'are you? Hello, George W. Weeks, old socks! How's the boy?" Very hearty. They never really talked with him.

"I have talked to Grandfather," Georges Tellier said again, slowly. Something in his tone made her look at him, then, attentively. And in that instant his voice sounded so like that of Paul Tellier, his whole aspect was so terribly that of his dead father, so little did he resemble his mother, whose very form and features he had, that Alice Tellier knew a moment of actual terror.

"Hear me." He spoke rapidly, in French. "We are leaving America. We will sail for home next Tuesday, on the *Paris*."

"We can't."

"We will."

She felt helpless. She was shocked into helplessness. But glad, too. Glad. "Georges! Do you mean it?"

"No foolin'," said Gorgeous grimly.

They Brought Their Women

[1932]

On my way to Mexico by train some years ago, I was reading a book by Ernest Gruening. It was on the subject of the early settling of America by the pioneers. In it was a paragraph about the exalted position held by women in this country. Women in the early days were scarce and rare, hence they became something precious. When the American settler went pioneering, his womenfolk came along. "The North American settlers brought their women," wrote Mr. Gruening.

This gave me an idea for the story of a modern hag-ridden husband journeying, perhaps, to a dazzling and romantic country such as Mexico. Into the mouth of this nagging wife I put certain speeches definitely uncomplimentary to Mexico itself, but these were strictly in character and certainly no reflection of my own opinion of that country. Unfortunately, the Mexican government misunderstood. After the short story appeared I was stunned to read in a New York newspaper that I was forever barred from Mexico.

I hope they have by now relented.

◆§ MURIEL IS A NAME YOU CANNOT TRIFLE WITH. SHE HERSELF WAS like that. Even her husband called her Muriel. It was queer about her. Her skin was so fair, her eyes were so blue, her hair held such glints, that unobservant strangers, dazzled by all that pink and white and gold, failed to notice her jawline and the set of her thin red lips. They soon learned.

All the other youngish married women of her crowd were known by nicknames, or by cozy abbreviations—Bunny, Bee, Lil, Peg. Jeff Boyd's wife, Claire, actually was known to everyone as Hank Boyd, so that her own lovely name was almost forgotten. When first she had come, a bride, to Chicago's far South Side, Jeff had declaimed, "It's just a rag, a bone, and a hank of hair—a poor thing, but mine own." Hence Hank.

Then, as now, after nine years of marriage and two children, she was a skinny little thing: enormous brown eyes in a sallow, pointed face; white teeth in a rare grin; a straight bob; a beret hung precariously over one ear; her fists jammed into the shapeless pockets of a leather jacket against the stiff Lake Michigan winds. She was Hank Boyd to the whole crowd of steel-mill aristocracy living in the Chicago suburb that was a magic circle of green just within sight of the searing glare of the steel-mill chimneys—those stark chimneys bristling high above the slag-tortured Illinois prairie.

Muriel never called her Hank. She addressed her as Mrs. Boyd; or—somehow, it sounded even more formal—occasionally Claire. But Hank never called Muriel anything but Mrs. Starrett. "It—it's the long *u*," she said once, in unconvincing explanation. "Funniest thing. I can't pronounce it. I've struggled with it since childhood. I think I must have been marked, prenatally. I was sixteen before I could say funeral."

"Rilly!" said Muriel Starrett.

The two women, so nearly of an age, yet so unlike, probably never would have exchanged ten words had it not been for the friendship existing between their husbands. And that was strange, for the two men were as unlike as their wives. They had been classmates—Leonard Starrett, the son of a South Chicago steel millionaire; Jeff Boyd, a pseudo-Socialist, working his way through the engineering course with the help of a scholarship.

Jeff was not one of your gloomy, portentous haranguers. Gay, redheaded, loud-voiced, free, he was possessed of a genius for friendship. He talked too much, he made execrable puns, he ramped and roared; and was fundamentally as sound as Marx himself, and ten times as charming.

The first thing that welded the friendship between the two men was an accidental look at a portfolio of drawings Jeff had idly come across while waiting in Starrett's room at college. Leonard Starrett, entering hurriedly, late and apologetic, had found a red-faced and vociferous Boyd charging about the room, the drawings spread on every table, chair, cushion, and shelf.

"Listen. Whose are these?"

"They're mine."

"No, no, fathead! I mean, who did them! Who drew 'em!"

"I did."

"The hell you did!"

"Why not?"

"Say! Gosh!" He was so moved that Starrett was a little embarrassed.

They were drawings, in charcoal and in pencil, of steel-mill workers and their girls and their wives and their smoke-blackened dwellings. Hunkies. Bohemians, Poles, Hungarians, Czechs, Lithuanians, Negroes. There were men, stripped to the thighs, feeding the furnaces. You could see the muscles, like coiled pythons, writhing under the skin; smell the sweat; feel the strain of the eye sockets.

There were puddlers and rollers, in their shoddy store clothes and their silk shirts, their yellow snub-nosed shoes and round haircuts, the Saturday-night cigar between their teeth, standing on the street corner watching the high-heeled girls switch by. The watchers' Slavic eyes were narrower still, their lips more sensually curled. Their shoulders threatened the seams of their ridiculous clothing. There were big-hipped women in shanty doorways, a child at the breast. Through the open door a glimpse of a man sprawled asleep on a cot, in his mill clothes, his mouth open, his limbs distorted in dreadful repose.

"Holy gosh!" said Jeff Boyd again, inadequately.

Leonard Starrett explained, politely. "That one I call *The Boarder.* Couple of rooms, family of seven, then they take in a boarder or two. Half of them work on the night shift and sleep in the beds during the day; the other half work the day shift and they use the beds at night. Neat little arrangement, what?"

"Say, listen, Len. Len, listen——"

"I call this one *The Open Hearth*, which isn't very bright of me because that's what it is. The big furnace where the stuff flows out white-hot. It's called the open hearth. One splash and you're burned through to the bone. It's exactly like a Doré picture of hell. I love the name of it. So cozy and homelike."

"You mean to tell me you been doing those things and never said a—— Why, say, Starrett, you've got to exhibit these, see! Exhibition of original drawings by Leonard Starrett. Boy, won't Prexy sit up!"

"Don't be dumb. I can't do that."

"Why can't you?"

"Can't."

"Now, listen. I don't know what I like, but I know about drawing. And you know's well as I do that these things are so good they're god-awful, so don't simper. Why, they're—they'll bust something wide open. You wait."

"I'm not simpering." He was gathering up the drawings and stacking them neatly into the portfolio. "My old man would have a stroke."

"Let him." Suddenly Jeff Boyd's high-colored, boyish face grew thoughtful and almost stern. "What're you doing here, engineering and chemistry and slop, when you can draw like that, my God!"

"Oh, these are just—amuse myself."

"Amuse, hell! This is important stuff and you know it. What's the idea —Papa'll have a stroke!"

Leonard Starrett hesitated a moment. Confidences came hard to him who had known a misunderstood childhood. He even looked a little sheepish.

"Uh—well, my father's a great guy but he's one of those from-the-ground-up boys. That's the way he began, and so that's the way he wanted me to start. Summers, since I was sixteen, I used to have one month in Europe and two months in the mills. Can you beat it! That's how I began

to draw. When the time came for me to start here in the scientific end I
got kind of desperate and blabbed I wanted to go abroad and study.

"I showed him and my mother some sketches—these, and some others.
What a row! White hair in sorrow to the grave, and all that stuff. So I
agreed to come here for four years, anyway, and learn to be a good little
steel official. Mother took me aside and explained that if these things
ever came to light they'd let Dad down the toboggan. I guess they might,
at that. He got in early, of course, and made his pile, but he isn't one of
the big shots."

Jeff Boyd lowered his head pugnaciously. "I'll tell you what. When you
get through here, if your father's got enough soaked away to live on—
which you damn well know he will have—and you don't go on drawing
and refuse to go into the mills if they won't let you exhibit, I'll never speak
to you again, so help me, for a white-livered, sniveling this-and-that."

But Leonard Starrett did not exhibit, and Jeff broke his oath, though the
portfolio of drawings lay dusty and neglected through the months, through
the years. For along came the war, and then along came Muriel, and then
along came Junior. The big steel mills became monster mills, breathing fire
and sulphur and gas over the sand dunes, over the prairie, over the lake,
so that steel might be made wherewith Len and Jeff might kill the Germans and the Germans might kill Len and Jeff.

But the two came back, miraculously, whole; Leonard to his father's steel
mills and to Muriel—Muriel so strong, so enveloping, so misleadingly pink
and white and gold, so terrible in her possessive love. And Jeff took a job
there in the South Chicago mills, for there was the postwar disillusionment, and there was Hank. And Leonard Starrett went back and forth between the roar of the steel-mill offices and the quiet of his big house facing
the lake. And the boy must have this and the boy must have that and the
Whatnots are coming for dinner and bridge and Oh, darling, what a lovely
bracelet, you shouldn't have done it.

Jeff Boyd was known as a brilliant engineer, but too quick on the trig-
ger, and what's this about his palling around with the Bohunks? He sounds
like a Red, or something. His name came up occasionally and uneasily at
board meetings.

"There's nothing red about Jeff except his hair," Leonard Starrett would
say, smiling. "You pay him less than men who are worth half as much to
us as he is. He doesn't ask for a raise. The Youngstown people would grab
him at double the salary if he'd go."

Muriel protested, too, the sharp edge of her dislike sheathed in the velvet of loving pretense.

"Darling, I don't know what you see in that Boyd."

"That's all right, Muriel. You needn't."

"But it is important, in a way, dear, because it's kind of embarrassing for me. If you're a friend of his, and ask him here, I have to invite his wife."

"Have to invite her! Why, everybody's crazy about her. She's a wonderful girl. Jeff says she——" He broke off. "And she runs that house with one maid, sees to the kids, and keeps her job at the Welfare Station three full days a week."

"I always say, welfare begins at home. I don't think those Boyd children look any too well cared for, if you ask me."

"They're not Little Lord Fauntleroys, if that's what you mean." His tone was tinged with bitterness.

"Fauntleroy! You don't think I've made a Fauntleroy of Junior, do you?"

"You'll pin a lace collar and curls on him yet."

"You're not very kind, dear. But that's because you're not well. Goodness knows I'm not the sort of wife to come between her husband and his friends. But it does seem queer for you, whose father was one of the founders of the mills—they say the Boyds often have the Hunkies in, evenings, not for welfare work, but as friends, as social equals. They had four of the mill Negroes in to sing last week. Imagine!"

"Yeah, that's terrible. We met Robeson at Alice Longworth's in Washington last year."

"Oh, well, look at her father!"

"Yes. Low character he was."

"Darling, you hurt me very much when you talk like that, so bitterly. If you were really well you wouldn't do it. You couldn't."

It was a queer thing about Leonard's health. Muriel explained that he wasn't really ill. He was delicate. Not strong. The least thing upset him. That was why she never left him. When he traveled, she traveled with him. I've left Junior many a time when it almost broke my heart. But a wife's place is with her husband. Leonard comes first.

Jeff and Hank Boyd sometimes talked of it. "He was strong as an ox at college. Crew man, and out of training could drink beer like a Munich Vereiner."

"It's her," said Hank, earnest and ungrammatical. "She wants him to be sick so that she can have him all to herself."

"That," he agreed thoughtfully, "and not doing what he wants. He has hated the mills for—oh, almost twenty years, I suppose. I told you about the way he can draw—or could. Well, you take twenty years of frustration, and believe me you've got enough poison in you to put you in a wheel chair."

"Can't we do something about her?"

"They hang you for murder in Illinois."

When the plan for the Mexican business trip first came up Muriel fought it like a tigress.

"Mexico! You simply can't go. I won't hear of it. Let them send somebody else. Why do you have to go?"

"Because we need what they've got, and because I think I can get it, and because we can't afford to overlook any bets these days and because the steel business, along with a lot of others, is, if I may coin a phrase, Mrs. Starrett, shot to hell-and-gone."

"That Boyd. Why are we taking that Boyd?"

He ignored the plural pronoun. "I'm taking Jeff because he speaks Spanish and because he knows more about manganese than any white man in North America and because he's a swell person to travel with."

"He won't be with us all the time, will he?"

"Now listen, Muriel. This is a trip you can't possibly take with me."

"But I'm going."

"It's impossible. You don't know Mexico. The altitude's seventy-five hundred feet. It's in the tropics. The air's cool and the sun knocks you flat. They say the food is terrible, you can't drink the water, the country's full of typhoid and malaria and dysentery." He was improvising and rather overdoing it.

When she set her jaw like that he knew it was no use. "I can stand it better than you can. I'm stronger. I come of pioneer stock. If my great-grandmother could cross the country from New England to Illinois in a covered wagon, with Indians and drought and all sorts of hardship, and if her great-grandmother could come over the ocean from England . . ."

He had heard all this many times. So had everyone else. Muriel was very proud of her ancestry. Her family had been "old North Side." Her marriage to Leonard Starrett, which had brought her, perforce, to dwell on the despised South Side, amounted in itself to a pioneer pilgrimage. Muriel, fortunately, was all ignorant of the fact that, among the more ribald of the younger mill office set, she was known as The Covered Wagon.

Her overweening pride of ancestry had once caused even Hank Boyd to show a rare claw. It was at a dinner at the Starretts' and Muriel had been more queenly than usual. In evening clothes Muriel looked her best and Hank her worst. Hank was the cardigan type. Muriel was all creamy shoulders and snowy bosom and dimpled back and copper-gold wave and exquisite scent and lace over flesh-colored satin. Hank, in careless and unbecoming black, looked as if she had slipped the dress over her shoulders, run a comb through her hair, and called it a costume. Which she had.

Muriel's blue eyes were fixed on Hank. There were eight at dinner—

four North Siders of cerulean corpuscles; the Boyds; Muriel and Leonard. "You can't know what it means to one like myself, whose ancestors—well, I'm afraid that sounds like boasting—but I mean, when I read of all these dreadful, new, vulgar people crowding in, getting their names on committees, trying to push the fine old families out of their rightful place!"

"Oh, but I do know," said Hank warmly. Her voice was clear and light. "At least, I can imagine how my ancestors must have felt."

"Your an——"

"Yes indeedy. There they were, down at the dock, to welcome the *May-flower* girlies when they stepped off the boat onto Plymouth Rock."

Muriel allowed herself a cool smile as her contribution to the shout that went up. Then, slowly, that smile stiffened into something resembling a grimace of horror, as the possible import of Hank's words was realized. She stared, frozen, at the smiling, impish face, the eyes so deeply brown as to seem black, the straight black hair, that dusky tint of the bosom above the crepe of her gown.

"You don't—mean you've got Indian blood!"

"Only about one eighth, I'm afraid. My great-great-grandpappy, they tell me, was old Mud-in-Your-Eye, or approximately that."

It got round. Perhaps Starrett himself told it, or the jovial Jeff. For days it enlivened South Side bridge tables, dinner tables, golf games, office meetings. "And then she kind of stiffened and said, 'You don't mean you've got Indian blood!'"

Hank was a little ashamed of herself—but not much.

Leonard Starrett quietly went ahead with his preparations for the Mexican trip. So, less quietly, did Muriel. He might have uttered, simply, the truth. I don't want you. I want to be alone. Remember the man in *The Moon and Sixpence*. He did say something like this, finally, when it was too late.

"The firm won't pay your expenses, Muriel. This isn't a pleasure jaunt."

"Then I'll pay my own—if you won't pay them."

"How do I know how long I'll have to be down there! It may be a week, it may be a month. How about Junior? Planning to take him along, too, I suppose."

"Mother'll move right in for as long as we need her."

"Remember the last time, when we came home from Europe? She'd darned near ruined him. Now listen, Muriel. I want to make this trip alone. I've taken a drawing room for Jeff and me from here to St. Louis, and from St. Louis on the Sunshine straight through to Mexico City. Please understand that interior Mexico is no tourist country, no matter what the ads say."

"I know more about it than you do," Muriel retorted. "I've been reading Gruening and Stuart Chase and Beals and all of them. I wouldn't let you go down there alone for a million dollars, with your indigestion and your colds and your——"

"Stop making an invalid of me, will you!" he shouted.

"There! You're a bundle of nerves."

"Oh——"

"What kind of clothes, I wonder. They say it's cold, evenings, and in the shade. Knitted things, I imagine, for daytime."

Defeat.

Hank Boyd, when she heard of it, flushed in deep rage—the slow, rare flush of the dark-skinned woman. "It's a rotten, filthy shame, that's what it is."

"Oh, I won't let her bother me much."

"I wasn't thinking so much of you—you'll have an interesting time, no matter what. But poor Len."

"I wish you were going along, Hank."

"No, you don't, dolling. Thanks just the same. Though I've wanted all my life to see Mexico. Maybe, someday. Maybe it isn't as dazzling as they say it is. But, Jeff, manganese or no manganese, find out all you can about the Indians; you know—if they're really as superb as I think they are, after the dirty deal Cortés gave them. Take a good look at the Riveras in Mexico City—and the ones at Cuernavaca, too. Find out if they pronounce Popocatepetl the way we were taught in school. Betcha dollar they don't. If you bring me home a serape, I'll make you wear it to the office. Those things look terrible outside their native background. If there are any bandits or shooting, you run. I don't want no dead hero for a husband. I would relish one of those lumpy old gold Aztec necklaces, though I understand you have to tunnel a pyramid to get one. Don't touch water, except bottled. . . ."

Hank and some of their friends came down to the train to bid Jeff goodby. Two men and a girl. They were very cheerful. Muriel watched them from her drawing-room window as, at the last moment, they shouted to Jeff on the car platform.

"Good-by, dolling!" Hank called, above the noise of departure. "Remember, drink three Bacardis for me the minute you strike Mexican soil."

"Don't do anything I wouldn't do!" From one of the men. Then they all roared, as at something exquisitely witty. Then the four of them, arm in arm, began to execute a little tap dance there on the station platform, chanting meanwhile a doggerel which—Jeff explained, later—Hank had made up at the farewell cocktail party.

Tap-tap-tappity-tap.

> *If you would live a life of ease,*
> *Go hunt the wary manganese,*
> *The manganese so shy and yet so docile.*
> *The manganese it aims to please,*
> *The thing to do is just to seize*
> *Upon it, be it fowl or fish or fossil.*
> *The manganese . . .*

The train moved; the quartet began to recede from view. Muriel and Len, at their window, caught just a glimpse of Hank's face, the smile wiped from it. One of the men tucked his hand under Hank's arm. They turned to go. The train sped through Chicago's hideous outskirts.

"Well," said Muriel, taking off her topcoat. "She didn't seem to be very brokenhearted."

Jeff appeared in the drawing-room doorway. He had a lower in the same car. His face was wreathed in smiles.

"What a gal!" he said. "What a kid!"

"I was just saying to Leonard, you two don't seem to be much cut up at parting." Her voice was playful; her eyes were cold.

"The smile that hides a br-r-reaking heart." He glanced at his wrist watch. "Well, I'm going in and feed the featyures before the stampede begins. You people coming in, or is it too early for you?"

"We had an early dinner before we left at six," Leonard said.

Muriel took off her hat, began to open a suitcase, rang the bell for the porter. She was the kind of woman who starts housekeeping instantly she sets foot on a train. "I don't eat any more meals on a diner than I can possibly help. Miserable, indigestible stuff."

Jeff laughed good-naturedly. "Ever since I could afford it I've liked to eat on a train. You'd think I'd be cured of it by now. I guess it comes of having watched the trains go by, when I was a kid on the farm in Ohio, with all the grand people eating at tables with flowers and lamps. I thought it must be heaven to be able to do that. I always order things you only get on trains. You know—dining-car stuff. Individual chicken pie and planked shad and those figs with cream that come in a bottle, and deep-dish blueberry tart and pork chops with candied yams. It's never as good as it sounds, but I just won't learn."

Leonard laughed. "That's the way to travel."

"Doesn't it make you sick?" Muriel asked primly.

"Sick as a dawg. That's part of traveling. You can be careful at home." He was off down the car aisle, humming.

"Where's that porter!" Muriel demanded. "If a drawing room can't get service I'd like to know what can."

By the time Jeff returned from the diner she evidently had got the porter, for the drawing room was swathed in sheets like a mortuary chamber. Shrouded coats, like angry ghosts, leaped out at you from hooks. Books were neatly stacked, bottles stood on shelves, an apple sat primly on a plate, flanked by a knife; an open suitcase over which Muriel was busy revealed almost geometric contents.

Jeff stood surveying this domestic scene. "Len, didn't you break the news to Muriel?"

She turned from her housewifely tasks. "News? What!"

Jeff grinned. "We get off this train, you know, Muriel, at St. Louis, and take another whole entirely different train for Mexico City."

"This is nothing," Len replied for her, rather wearily. "Muriel puts up sash curtains and a rubber plant when she's in a telephone booth."

Muriel bridled. "I can't help it. I'm a home woman. And I'm not ashamed of it."

"You'd have a fit at the way Hank and I travel. But boy! Do we see things!"

Muriel sniffed. "We'll see you in the morning, Jeff."

"Say, what do you mean—morning! It's only eight-thirty. Come on back in the buffet car, Len. I met a fellow in the diner name of Shields. Lives in Mexico City. Knows the whole works. He says Mateos is square enough, but the Monterey outfit is crooked as a dog's hind leg. He's with the Universal people at San Luis Potosí. Quite a guy! He wants to meet you. Good idea, too, I think. Come on back."

"Now, Leonard, dear, you're going to do nothing of the kind. Sitting there smoking and drinking till all hours. You need a good night's sleep after the week you've had. You look perfectly haggard."

During the days and nights of steady travel that followed the change of trains at St. Louis, Jeff Boyd was up and down the length of the train and in and out of it at every stop of more than thirty seconds. He talked to passengers, conductor, waiters, porters, brakemen, and loungers at railway stations. He spoke Spanish, English, and bad German, as occasion demanded.

Muriel read and sewed. The scene in the Starrett drawing room was very domestic. Muriel kept the shades down about halfway, and a sheet across the windows because of the Texas glare and dust. She read books on Mexico. The very first day out of St. Louis, she had looked up from her book with a little exclamation. Then, leaning toward Len, she had pointed a triumphant finger at a paragraph.

"Listen to this, Leonard! Listen to what Gruening says." She began to read aloud.

" 'The diversity between the two cultures south and north of the Rio Grande is sharply discernible in the respective status of their women. The North American settlers brought their women. The squaw man was outcast. The exalted position of woman in the American ideology dates from the pioneer days of companionate hardship and effort. . . . The Aztec female, on the other hand, played the part of handmaiden to the warrior male.' "

She looked up, beaming. "There!"

Len looked about him, one eyebrow cocked a little, as when he was amused. "A drawing room on a limited train may be your idea of companionate hardship and effort——"

He went back to his book. It was not a book on Mexico, but a slim little volume given him by Hank as a parting gift. Muriel had picked it up and looked at it. *Walden,* by David Henry Thoreau.

"Well, what in the world did she give you that for!"

He had wondered, too, at her choice of the plain chronicle of the man who had lived alone, in rigorous simplicity, at Walden Pond. He had opened the book, idly. He read a few pages. On page five he came to a line. Something shot straight to his heart, so that he jumped a little, as though he had been hit. Then he knew.

The mass of men lead lives of quiet desperation.

"You seem to be enjoying that book Mrs. Boyd gave you."

"Yes."

Every two or three hours Jeff charged in, bursting with facts valuable or fascinating or both. "That fat fellow with the fancy vest and one arm used to be the richest man in Mexico. They got him in the Revolution and did they take him for a ride! Burned down his hacienda, destroyed the crops, chopped up a couple of daughters, shot his right arm off. . . . Next time the conductor goes by get a load of him. He's Mex, named Cordoba, wears a wing collar and a plaid tie with an opal in it as big as your eye, and a gold cable watch chain from here to here, with a sixteen-peso gold piece size of a dinner plate as a charm. . . . Say, Muriel, if you'll take down that Turkish-harem drape at the window and look at what's going by, you'll learn more about Mexico than from any book on Mexico—*How to Tell the Flora from the Fauna.*"

At San Antonio they had had an hour and a half. The train drew in at eight. It would not leave until half-past nine.

"Come on, folks. Let's shake a leg. Get some of the train stiffness out of our bones. We can walk up into town, take a look around, and beat it back in plenty of time."

"Walk! At night! Through this district!"

Then it began in maddening futility: "But what do you want to ride for, Muriel, when we've been riding for days? . . ." "Well, you two go and I'll just wait here. . . ." "No, I wouldn't do that. . . ." "But I don't mind being here all alone at the station, really. I can just sit in the train. . . ." "A walk will do you good. . . ." "Jeff, you walk, and Muriel and I will take a taxi. . . ." "Good God, you can't see anything in a taxi. Besides, the idea is the walk. . . ." "What is there to see? . . ." "Well, good gosh, let's not stand here arguing, or none of us will be able to go. . . ." "Leonard, this porter says it's a good mile and a half to the main street. . . ." "Well, what if it is? . . ." "Now listen, fifteen minutes wasted . . ."

After the train passed the border at Laredo and they were in Mexico, Leonard put down his book to stare out of the window, denuded now of Muriel's protecting sheet. She continued to read, placidly, while all the stark, cruel beauty of Mexico went by. The mesa; a cluster of adobe walls and huts, half-naked children, dogs, chickens, mules; cactus as high as a man's head marching like an army of meager Indians across the desert; dusky women in pink petticoats and dark *rebozos*; swarthy men in dirty white pajamas, their unwashed, powerful toes thrust into rope sandals; enormous straw sombreros, brilliant serapes flung across shoulders; white fences; crumbling Spanish churches, pale pink and white and misty gray—and always, against the sky, purple at dusk, rose at sunrise, the Sierras.

"God, it's beautiful! I didn't know Mexico was so beautiful."

"Look at them!" Jeff explained. "Look, Len. Those are the peons Rivera's been painting. Some magnificent, what! Makes you realize how darn good he is, doesn't it?"

Leonard Starrett said nothing.

"My, they're dirty!" Muriel exclaimed.

"That woman with the child slung in the *rebozo* and the jar balanced on her shoulder."

The hotel to which they went in Mexico City had been recommended because it was said to be clean and to have artesian-well water. These turned out to be its only virtues. In all other respects it was like one of those fourth-rate little Paris hotels on the Left Bank in which the chambermaids run up and down the corridors on their heels, doors and windows slam, voices bellow or screech across the echoing court, and the mysterious custom of hurling what seem to be stove lids occurs every morning at five.

They could eat nothing there, though Muriel took her morning coffee and orange juice in her room. Len and Jeff breakfasted at Sanborn's, in the

Avenida Madero. After three days of visiting other recommended restaurants, Muriel insisted on Sanborn's three times a day. In its American-Spanish patio hung with red velvet and bird cages she found, in all Mexico, the cleanliness, the familiar American language, and the creamed chicken, buttered beets, and apple pie to which she was accustomed.

"But this isn't Mexico," Len objected. "Might as well be eating at Childs. The other restaurants are full of people who seem healthy."

"'When you're in Rome——'" quoted Jeff.

Muriel was adamant. "At least you're not getting malaria and typhoid. Those other places are impossible."

Jeff said she had pleasantly condensed two hackneyed sayings into the single "When you are in Rome, do as the Romans do, and die."

Jeff bounded off alone. He tried them all—native restaurants, open-front cafés, cantinas and *pulquerías*—while Len accompanied Muriel drearily to Sanborn's. Jeff took a good deal of bicarb, but he ate all the fearful native dishes, the frijoles, the enchiladas, the tortillas. "Hot dog! They burn the vitals to a cinder. Len, you got to taste *mole de guajolote*. Turkey cooked in twenty spices, any one of them guaranteed to eat a hole through asbestos." He even drank pulque. He insisted that they go with him for cocktails to a place he had discovered called Mac's Bar. He was enthusiastic about it. "Mac's an Irishman. He's lived in Mexico for forty years, without leaving it. He speaks of the United States as 'the old country.' Wait till you taste his Mac Special."

It turned out to be a dingy little vestibule of a place. Muriel said she certainly didn't think much of it. Jeff seemed a little chagrined and even bewildered. "I don't know. I guess I was wrong. I thought it was swell before. It doesn't seem like much. I guess it was just——"

They found time during that first week, occupied though the two men were with their business, to make a short trip or two. They lunched well in the sun-drenched patio of the inn at San Angel, once a monastery. They drifted down the Xochimilco canals and came home with armloads of violets and roses. They whirled down the dusty roads across the plains to the pyramids at San Juan Teotihuacán.

Leonard Starrett, long silent as he looked out at the Mexican countryside unfolding before their eyes, said slowly, "It's more mysterious than Egypt."

"Egypt's finished and done. This thing's just begun. You can feel the Indians boiling and seething underneath. Someday—bingo!"

Muriel looked about mildly. She was very careful to protect her fair skin from the straight rays of the Mexican sun. "Mysterious! Why, I was just thinking it looked a lot like the places outside of Los Angeles."

Muriel had a tiny camera, not more than four inches square. With it she took pictures of pyramids, mountains, rivers, cathedrals, and plazas. She had difficulty in pronouncing the Mexican names.

"Just call everything Ixcaxco," Jeff cheerfully advised her, "and let it go at that."

After a week Leonard came to her in some distress. "We're not getting anywhere. At least, we've just made a start. They don't do business here the way we do at home. They talk for hours. They only work about four hours a day. Jeff and I will have to be here a month, at least—maybe longer. I'd like to put you on the boat at Vera Cruz. They say it's a beautiful five-day trip. You'll land in New York, take the Century home, and we'll all be happier."

"I'm sorry my being here has made you and your friend unhappy."

"Oh, Muriel, for God's sake!"

"Please don't think I'm enjoying it. But I know what my duty is. And if you have to be here a month, I'm going to look for an apartment."

"No!"

But for the next three days Jeff, stricken with dysentery, was wan and limp. That decided it. Muriel, with the aid of an agent, found an apartment in a good new building just off the magnificent Paseo de la Reforma. It was the apartment of some Americans named Sykes. They were returning to the United States for three months. Sykes was a mining expert. Mrs. Sykes showed Muriel all over the place. Very nicely furnished, and in good taste. A grand piano. There were even some good American antiques. A mahogany four-poster, a drop-leaf table, a fine old couch.

"These have been in the family for generations," Mrs. Sykes explained. "I'm very much attached to them. That's why I've never rented this apartment before, to strangers."

"I understand," Muriel said, with some hauteur. "I am a member and, in fact, an officer of the Pioneer Daughters of Illinois."

"Oh, well, then," Mrs. Sykes said, reassured. She looked happily, pridefully, about her at her dear belongings. "You'd never know you were in Mexico, would you!"

Muriel repeated this to Leonard and to Jeff as she, in turn, showed them the apartment. "You'd never know you were in Mexico."

"You certainly wouldn't," they both said; and roared with laughter.

"What's so funny about that?"

Mrs. Sykes had left her servants with Muriel. "They're very good," she had assured her. "As good as you can get—in Mexico. Jovita—the bigger one—she's rather handsome, don't you think?—is the cook. She's a—uh—I mean to say, she's a very good cook. She's used to having her own way. I wouldn't interfere with her if I were you." Then, as Muriel's eyebrows went up, "I mean, unless you're used to Indian ways—yes, she's Indian, and very proud of her ancestry—you might not understand. She does all the marketing."

"I always prefer to do my own marketing. It's the only way to get the freshest, the best. In Chicago——"

"But this isn't Chicago. Mexico is different. They wouldn't understand. Another thing. You'll find she sometimes has one or two of her children here for a day or so. They're very quiet. She has four."

"Oh, she's married!"

"No."

"Oh, I understood you to say four——"

"Jovita has four children, of four different fathers. She has never married. She does not believe in marriage. She is the finest cook in Mexico City. She used to pose for artists. She is highly respected. I wouldn't part with her for the world. I'd rather not let the apartment, really, if you——"

Muriel related this to Len and Jeff, expecting from them masculine indignation. They seemed impressed, but not in the way she had expected. At their first dinner in the new apartment—Jeff dined with them—she saw the two men regarding Jovita, who assisted Lola in serving. The Indian girl, Jovita, bore herself magnificently. Her eyes were large and black; her skin was a rich copper; her bosom was deep; her shoulders were superb; her hair was straight, black, abundant.

"I really don't feel quite comfortable about Jovita," Muriel confided to the men, as they sat sipping their very good coffee, after dinner. "Having her here in the house, I mean."

"Well, I shouldn't think you would," Jeff agreed, with a great laugh. Muriel said, afterward, that she never realized how vulgar Jeff was, until the last two weeks. You really have to travel with people to know them.

Besides Jovita and Lola, there was the Indian boy, Jesús. Muriel had objected to the name, but Mrs. Sykes had assured her that it was very common in Mexico among the Indians, and that he would be terribly offended if called by another name. The three servants were capable, quiet, and rather consistently dishonest about small things, according to American standards.

"Custom of the country," said Len. "Don't fuss about it. You're not going to live here. Take it as it comes."

"Jeff is always talking about how magnificent the Indians are, and how the race has survived in spite of everything, and how they'll rule someday. A lot he knows about it. If he can tell his precious Hank about her cousins the Indians I guess I can tell her a few things, myself."

Muriel was horrified to learn that Jovita usually slept on the floor of her little bedroom, rolled in her blanket, instead of on the very decent little cot bed provided for her. The boy, Jesús, had conceived an enormous and instant liking for Leonard. They discovered that he was in the habit of sleeping outside their bedroom door, like a faithful dog.

"I'd like to send them packing," said Muriel, again and again. "The whole dreadful kit of them. Oh, how wonderful it will be to get back to my own lovely clean house, and to Junior, and to Katy and Ellen, and a good thick steak and sweet butter and fresh cream and waffles and a big devil's-food cake with fudge icing."

They had asked Jeff to share the apartment with them, but he had declined, a little embarrassment in his high-colored, boyish face.

"It's mighty nice of you to want me. But I think I'll just stay on at the hotel. I kind of like to bum around the restaurants and cafés and streets. I like to see the way the people live, and talk to them. But if you'll ask me to dinner once in a while I'll certainly appreciate it."

Muriel, with her fine, fair skin, her coils of copper-gold hair, her plump, firm figure, attracted attention when she went out alone. She was accustomed, at home, to walking. All her Chicago friends walked for the good of their figures. She found that almost always now she was followed home by some amorous Mexican.

Her admirer always used the same tactics. He would pass and repass her. He would double on his tracks. He would appear at unexpected and impossible corners. She would think she had evaded him. She would jump hurriedly into one of the crazy little Ford taxis marked Libre. But when she reached her own flat there he would be, miraculously, lounging against the building, in his bright-blue suit, his feet, in their American tan shoes, negligently crossed, a cigarette between his slim brown fingers.

She complained to Leonard and Jeff about this. "Horrid creatures!"

"Hank would get a kick out of that," Jeff grinned.

"I suppose she would."

"They don't mean anything," Leonard assured her. "It's the Latin way of showing admiration."

"They frighten me, the nasty leering things."

"Try taking Jovita along as bodyguard."

"Oh, well, if that's all you care. I don't understand you lately, Leonard."

"It's the altitude," fliply.

The servants made her nervous. They were in and out of the room without a sound. She would look up from a letter she was writing to find Jovita standing there, silent, waiting.

"Goodness, how you startled me. What is it?"

Jovita spoke very little English, understood a little, thanks to the Sykeses. Jeff came to dinner two or three times a week. He and Jovita would speak together in Spanish. Suddenly Jovita's dusky, impassive face would grow vivid with a flashing smile.

Muriel didn't like it. "What are they talking about?" she demanded of Leonard.

"He's going down to Milpa Alta on business Thursday. She heard us talking and caught the name. She's telling him it's her native village, where two of her children are. She says it's very beautiful, and that there is a festival down there next week—an important festival when everyone dresses up and there are fireworks and dances and big doings. Let's all go."

"Don't be foolish, Leonard. Those festivals are childish and stupid; the sun blazes down; you can't eat the filthy food, nor drink the water. You know it as well as I do. It's a mercy Jeff has been able to take the necessary business trips into the other districts. I'm glad, now, that you brought him along. I'd never have let you take them. Never. You would have, though, if I hadn't been here. You're like a child. Really, sometimes I think you need as much looking after as Junior."

"Yes," Len said thoughtfully. "I would have taken all those trips into the country, by motor and by mule, with the hot sun beating down by day and the cold coming on at night; sleeping, perhaps, on straw mats on the floor of some pueblo hut—if it hadn't been for you."

"Well, then! And the way Jeff looked last time. Remember? Though you can't tell me that was only the hardship of the trip."

Jeff was off to Milpa Alta. If this trip proved successful they could leave at the end of the week; the last, then, of their six weeks' stay. Jeff would be gone four days.

Next morning Jovita was not there. She simply was not there. No word, no explanation. Lola and Jesús shook their heads, spread their palms in innocent denial.

"I'll tell you what I think," said Muriel, with the abrupt coarseness of the good woman. "She's gone down there to be with Jeff, that's what I think."

"I hope so," said Leonard.

"What do you mean, Leonard Starrett!"

"I was just thinking."

"Thinking what?"

"I was just thinking how pleasant it would be to live for a year or two with Jovita in an old pink house, with a garden, in Cuernavaca, and paint pictures of the Indians, and of Jovita and her children, and sit in the sun, and in the evening look at Popocatepetl and the Sleeping Woman against the sky."

"Leonard Starrett, have you gone crazy!"

"A little," said Leonard, "a little. But not enough."

Glamour
[1932]

Another one-day story. Knowing something about the life of a successful actress during the ordeal of rehearsals I fancied the title would carry a fine ironic flavor. That was before the word "glamour" had become thumb-marked and shabby. Katharine Cornell, Helen Hayes, and Lynn Fontanne, among others, thought they detected bits and pieces of themselves in the story. And how right they were.

Still, this description of a nerve-shattering day in the life of a star will not serve to discourage or deter an aspiring young actress. And it may soften the flinty heart of some first-nighter.

Of course, nothing much happens, really, in this tale. Just detail piled on detail, like the torte—thin layer on layer—that one used to get at Sacher's in Vienna.

&⸎ OF ALL WORDS IN THE ENGLISH (OR ANY OTHER) LANGUAGE, LINDA Fayne most hated the word "glamorous." Yet invariably the newspapers coupled her name with this shopworn adjective. That glamorous actress, Linda Fayne, they said. Photographs in the magazines showed her glamorous apartment—triplex, with balcony overhanging the East River—and Miss Fayne herself seated therein, attired in glamorous velvet. At her feet was a dog so overbred that all its points seemed out of drawing; lining her walls were books richly dark and oily of binding, picked out with gold tooling that gleamed like the dentistry in a Negro's mouth.

She was, perhaps, the only actress in America for whom a line nightly waited outside the stage door after her performance, just as people used to do in the simple and sentimental nineties, long before her day. All this may have been due, partly at least, to the fact that Miss Fayne, unlike her contemporaries, never dined in popular restaurants, and hated shopping on Fifth, Madison, or any other avenue.

When her Public wanted to see her it had to pay admission or stand out in the cold. It knew her, therefore, through her stage characters, through the newspapers and her publicity department. It was not aware that she liked to dress in old sweaters, easy shoes, and battered berets; that she worked like a truck horse and practically never had time to sit in that book-lined room overlooking the river, except when she was having photographs done for publicity for her next production.

Sometimes, haggard and spent after a three-matinee week following the merry Yuletide, she would say, as she sipped her midnight cocoa or hot milk, her lean and weary body wrapped in an old flannel dressing gown, "Glamorous, eh!" But she was not bitter about it.

For the past three weeks she had been playing the usual six nights a week and two matinees in *Parrakeet*, which was closing, while rehearsing daily in *Cadogan Square*, due to open in Cleveland the following Wednesday. This pleasing state of affairs was enhanced by four hours' sleep a night and an obsession that she would never be able to play the part.

Linda Fayne lay now asleep, alone, in her bed. It was seven o'clock. The unlovely light of a New York January morning spread its clay-colored pallor over her face. The farther window was open on the river, the curtain not quite drawn. A gray day, and the river flowing sluggishly by was gray, too, and icily thick.

One of the sleeper's long arms was flung outside the coverlet, and the hand was clenched, instead of normally relaxed in sleep. A strange hand to be attached to the lovely body of the glamorous Linda Fayne. Yet not so strange, perhaps; for it was the nervous, lean, big-knuckled hand of the intelligent and masterful woman.

Like most very successful actresses, Miss Fayne was not beautiful. That is, she possessed few of the attributes which the adolescent taste of America usually demands of its beauties. She had a broad free brow, eyes set well apart and slightly protuberant, high cheekbones, and a wide scarlet mouth like a venomous flower. The effect of all this was arresting—even startling. So her great following, baffled by this mask which gave the effect of beauty without actually being beautiful, fell back on the trite word "glamorous" and clung to it.

Linda awoke now, not drowsily, deliciously, as one who has been deep sunk in refreshing slumber, but suddenly, with a look very like terror on her face, as though she had yielded unwillingly to sleep and resented the hours spent in its embrace. The instant she awoke her hand reached quickly under her pillow and brought forth a scuffed and dogeared booklet, crudely bound in heavy yellow paper and fastened with clips. Typed on the cover were the words CADOGAN SQUARE.

It contained the seventy-three typewritten sheets of her enormous and overpowering part in the new play now in rehearsal, her own speeches typed in black, her cues typed in red. Any actor will tell you that if you place the script of your new part under your pillow at night, the good fairies will help fix it in your memory while you sleep; and that lines conned late at night will stay with you when you awake next morning.

In the gray light of the early January morning she peered at the typewritten pages. She began to mouth words in an undertone. She passed one tense flat palm over her forehead and hair as she crouched over the book, while with the other hand she covered the black-typed lines of her speeches, leaving exposed only the red-inked lines of her cues; and so on, down the page, and over to the next page, absorbed, shadowy in the half-light.

Her cues she mumbled in an undertone, her own speeches she uttered more clearly, but she rocked her body to and fro in the effort of bringing the words forth from her memory, and the whole effect was strangely that of a woman in the agonies of parturition.

> *. . . Then I'd be better off!*
> No, stay here, I can't see him. I don't feel up to it. I can't.
> *. . . told me yesterday . . .*
> I know. I know. But I really don't feel that I can see him now.
> *. . . showed him into the library, Miss.*
> But I—I'd much rather not see him.
> *. . . romantic-looking and quite the dandy.*
> Is—is my hair tidy!

She got gingerly out of bed now, shivering a little, closed the window, tied the cord of her pajama trousers a little tighter, and began her morning exercises. Usually she stopped these horrors altogether during rehearsal weeks, but yesterday she had noticed the suspicion of a roll about the waist-line.

She marched across the room with a shattering form of locomotion a good deal like the goose step, except that her knees, right, left, right, left, were brought sharply up to her chin as she marched. The typewritten booklet was propped against her pillow, open, and each time, as she passed it, she peered at it and mumbled as she peered and marched as she mumbled.

> *. . . at last! At last!*
> I—I've had to put off the pleasure of seeing you much longer than I wished.
> *. . . looked down on me often before.*
> No, really!
> *. . . top of the wardrobe, and . . .*

An outsider, chancing upon her thus physically and orally engaged, would have put her down at once as a lunatic. Yet these were stern antics, and the seemingly disjointed sentences were wise, orderly, and meaningful.

The dachshund, Blitzen, roused from his pillow, shook his comic length, and lurched toward her to join in the game. "Go 'way, Blitz! Lie down.

Geh weg! Was machts du!" He stood regarding her with the worried look of his breed.

She thought, fleetingly, of a cold shower, decided against it, and popped back into bed. There, for another fifteen minutes, she mumbled and rocked. Quarter of eight. Ruthlessly she pressed the button that would summon Miss Grassie. Miss Grassie, young, tweed, terribly executive, Bryn Mawr, her secretary, would appear in ten minutes, ready to cue her until, exhausted, she rang for breakfast. Chester wouldn't be awake until ten, at the earliest. No four-hour sleep for him.

Wrapping her warm robe about her, she was out of bed again and padding softly up the stairway to the top floor and into a many-windowed room which, incredibly enough, had the effect of being filled with sunshine on this spectral morning. This was, perhaps, due to the fact that the walls and curtains were a warm yellow, as was the hair of the young person seated in a low chair and inexpertly ramming spoonfuls of cereal into her mouth.

"My darling!" exclaimed Miss Fayne, and swooped upon the yellow head. "Mother's precious!" Then, to a stern female domestically engaged at the tiny wardrobe door: "Good morning, Nana."

" 'Ning, madam," replied the stern female, with a look which said, "What right have you to come in disturbing our feeding time at this hour of the day?" Mother's precious, likewise, showed an absence of enthusiasm about this early-morning visit. She peered around the maternal arms to· squeal at Blitzen standing bowlegged and friendly and haggard in the doorway. She then made a whirring and puffing sound with her lips, causing a spray of cereal to descend upon her gifted parent.

"Ellen Fayne *Davis!*" chided Nana, pretending to be shocked, but really quite pleased.

Linda Fayne wiped her face with her sleeve and kissed Ellen's cheek just as a laden spoon was halfway to her lips, whereupon Ellen lurched, dropped her spoon, and began to howl.

"Here, darling. Mother'll feed you."

"If you please, madam, we don't feed her. It's bad for her now that we're training her to feed herself."

"But, Nana, look, it's so hard for her. Here's a bit on her ear. She hardly knows where her mouth is."

"Plenty old enough, madam. My last fed herself at twenty months, the MacArthur baby."

"I'm sick of your old MacArthur baby," said Miss Fayne, in a pet. "Nana, she'll need the heavy white leggings and the fur-lined coat. The wind from the river is like a wet blanket."

"I had intended to, madam."

"Mother's precious. Mother's darling. . . . Bring her into my room before you take her to the park."

"Oh. I thought you'd be busy with Miss Grassie, half-past nine, with rehearsal at eleven and all."

"I will. I am. What of it? Bring her in. Whose child is she, anyway—yours or mine!"

Nana's eyebrows, Nana's whole aspect said, "Mine, all mine."

Linda Fayne sped back to her bedroom, followed by the careening Blitzen. And there sat Miss Grassie, cap-a-pie, calm, cool, ready for the typed sheets that Linda had carried with her to the nursery. She pulled the window curtains wide, she drew a chair to the bedside. Miss Fayne sat back amongst her pillows.

"Top of page ten," said Miss Fayne.

" '. . . you promise me that?' " began Miss Grassie promptly.

" 'I promise.' "

" 'Very well . . . Shall I go now?' "

" 'Please.' "

" '. . . done to deserve it.' "

"Oh—uh—wait a minute, don't tell me, Grassie—uh—'I had'—oh, yes—uh—'Oh, I had forgotten! You've just come from the palace. I have never seen the Queen. What is she like?' "

At quarter of nine two breakfast trays appeared in a little procession made up of Walker, the houseman, with the light tray, and Millie, the housemaid, with the heavy one, and Blitzen bringing up the rear. Walker in a white coat, Millie in blue linen.

"Mawnin', Miss Linda!" Ebony above the white and the blue, smiling, friendly.

"Dinner at six-thirty sharp, Walker, on a tray up here."

"Anything specially tasty, Miss Linda?"

"No; I——"

"It's going to be a fierce day for you," said Miss Grassie. "Mutton barley broth, very hot, Walker. Lamb chops, creamed celery, chopped fresh pineapple. That's nourishing, but light."

Miss Grassie threw her the next cue, and began to eat the breakfast placed before her on a little table. Miss Fayne caught the cue, fumblingly.

"Oh, God, Grassie, what's the use! I'll never get it. Here it is Friday, we open Wednesday; I don't even know my lines. What'll I do? It's the part. I haven't got it. It eludes me. It——"

"Drink your coffee."

"All right. But go on, go on!"

They went on indefatigably. Miss Fayne ate her breakfast: orange juice, coffee, a flat dry biscuit libelously attributed to the Swedes and resembling in appearance and taste a confection of baked ashes.

Miss Grassie ate her breakfast: grapefruit, little golden pancakes, hot and hot-buttered; country sausages, toast, coffee. Walker came to collect the trays.

"Mr. Davis awake, Walker?"

"Oh, no, ma'am!" said Walker, as though shocked by the question. He handed Miss Fayne a sheaf of letters. Miss Fayne cast a lackluster eye upon them, saw a particularly lurid one marked air mail, special delivery, urgent, postmarked Cincinnati.

"Did you forget to mail that check to my cousin, Grassie?"

"Yesterday morning, air mail. It'll be there by now." Miss Fayne tossed the bundle of letters in her direction.

"You'll have to start to dress in ten minutes. Fitting at ten, and it will take nearly an hour."

"All right, all right. Go on."

Miss Grassie went on:

"'. . . *married lady for almost a week . . .*'"

Twenty minutes to ten. Miss Fayne threw aside the bedclothes, snatched a pair of stockings from a drawer, drew them swiftly up her slim legs. Her head was cocked toward Miss Grassie, her eyes strained and fixed with the intensity of her effort of memorizing. Brown kid pumps, step-in, slim wool dress.

My dear, my dear, you think I don't understand! Oh, but I do! And I feel for you and pity you with all my heart! I can do nothing to help you. I daren't even advise you. But never lose hope—never lose——

A quick, martial step up the hall, into the room. Her mother, Mrs. Fayne, handsome, dressed in smart dark street clothes, bristling.

"Oh, Mother, I didn't know you were—I didn't hear you come in."

"I came just a minute ago. I went straight up to the nursery. She's already taken her out. I should think when I come in at this hour of the morning I could see my own grandchild."

"But, Mother, you know Ellen's always out by nine-thirty."

"What for, I'd like to know! What good will it do her, a bitter, damp, miserable day like this?"

"But she can't be out yet. I told Nana to bring her in to me before she took her out."

"I wouldn't have that woman in my house!"

"She's a wonderful nurse, and she loves Ellen. She knows what's best for her. Ellen's used to being out in the cold."

"Look at you! You're shivering, indoors."

"That's because I'm so terribly nervous."

"Get out and get a little exercise, instead of staying in bed half the morning."

"Exercise! Good God, Mother, I'm on my feet from ten in the morning until two the next morning! Ex-er——"

A rather heavy man of forty or thereabouts appeared in dressing gown and slippers, a piece of toast in one hand. Handsome eyes, no chin to speak of, a good figure that was losing ground.

"Hello, darling," said Linda Fayne, pulling her hat down over one eye. "Grassie, where's that brown bag? I had it last night. Oh, I know, I left it downstairs on the table in the——"

"What a stinkin' day," said Chester Davis, strolling to the window and looking down upon the river flowing lumpishly by under a gray sky. In passing he had nodded to his mother-in-law, and the two had exchanged looks of richest dislike.

"Everybody living the life of Riley in this establishment," Mrs. Fayne remarked with a false breeziness. "You certainly keep funny hours for a Wall Street man, Chester."

"Wall Street, my pretty, is just a lot of brick-and-stone mausoleums these days. I might as well go and sit in Trinity churchyard."

"Mr. Fayne was out of the house at seven this morning."

"I'll bet he was!" said her son-in-law, very distinctly.

Linda Fayne snatched the paper-bound booklet from Grassie. She thrust an arm into the sleeve of a rather shabby broadtail coat.

"Linda, I want to have a little talk with you about your father," commanded Mrs. Fayne. She always spoke of her husband as "your father" when talking to Linda, as though disclaiming responsibility for that erratic gentleman.

"Not now, Mother. Not now."

"When, then?"

"I don't know. Next week. No. After we get back from the road. After we've opened."

"Everyone's more important than your own mother and father."

Walker appeared. "Connelly phoned they's something the matter with the car, Miss Fayne; says he'll be another hour, anyway, fixing it; says——"

"Get me a taxi. Is he on the wire? Tell him the theater at three-thirty; tell him it's got to be fixed by then." She was halfway down the stairs. "Home for dinner, Chester?"

"No!"

"Home at six-thirty?"

"Nope. Playing squash at the club."

Jolts, bumps, skids, traffic jams on the way to the dressmaker's, but she paid little heed except, now and then, for a frantic glance at her watch and another at the maelstrom surging about her cab. Her eyes were on the worn and tattered pages of the booklet in her hand; her lips moved.

Here she was. Ten past ten. Ten minutes late. Connelly could have made it on time. He had secret ways of worming in and out of traffic.

There were three dresses to be fitted, voluminous petticoats, slippers, hats. *Cadogan Square* was a costume play, the period the middle of the nineteenth century. They were ready for her in the big, mirrored fitting room. They understood. Madame Renée, head of the workroom, a stout, red-cheeked Arlésienne, sound, hard, astringent as the wine of her own native province; Mrs. Carewe, head of the French room, who wore a hat all day long, and smoked cigarettes at the end of a long holder, and said, "That red is wonderful on you. I knew it would be. Now don't fuss. Everything will be there for the dress rehearsal on Sunday. Have we ever fallen down? Well, then!" And on her knees on the floor, little plump Tasie, the fitter, a craftsman to whom the figure standing before her was only a structure of velvet and silk and lace and flesh and bone to be made into a perfect whole by the magic of her pins and needle and scissors.

"That is well," said Madame Renée, from time to time; or, "No, no, no! *Le mouvement.* Leave it. You must not break the line!" Like a top sergeant.

Miss Fayne looked up from the pages in her hand. She had been standing almost an hour. "I think it could be an inch longer. It ought to dip the floor all around. It'll be filthy in ten minutes, but it ought to, just the same."

"That's right," said Mrs. Carewe. "And the sleeves tighter at the elbow, but wide at the wrist."

The three women moved around her, around and around.

Suddenly, "Quick!" said Linda. "It's almost eleven. Take it off." She never was late for rehearsal. She was horrified at stars who kept their company waiting. She dashed out, leaving behind her a whirlwind of French adjectives, velvet skirts and muslin petticoats and plumes. No one recognized Linda Fayne, a slim girl in a rather ratty fur coat and a hat jammed down over her hair.

She reached the theater, miraculously, on time; not her own theater, where she was playing at night, but another, untenanted, and available for rehearsals during these past three weeks. She was, in fact, early, for the director, Mr. Ibsen (no relation), had not yet come in. Nesbitt was there, her leading man, that intelligent and responsible young Englishman brought over for the part. There he stood, in a corner, and his head was bent, and in his hand, too, was that familiar dogeared book of typed paper, and his lips moved, silently. Dear Nesbitt, with his solemn spectacles on his fair young face, and his pleasant English voice, and his beautiful English trousers, and his feeling for the theater, and his great good taste in it.

"Good morning. Good morning. Good morning." And then straight over to him. After her performance the night before they had come back to her apartment to go over the third act together from midnight until two, and had parted inarticulate with weariness. Yet here he was fresh, rosy, tubbed-looking. They began where they had left off, without a preliminary word.

"I think I know how we can get around that scene. Let's just try it now, for sight lines, while we're waiting. It came to me after you left last night. Here." They moved to the center of the stage. "Where I say—uh—what's that? Oh, yeah—I say, 'You don't know what he says. You don't know how frightening he can be.' Well, I can turn away from you there, like this. And if you'll sway forward—you won't need to take a step that would break the scene—just sway out and sort of toward me as I lean away, and they'll be able to see you beautifully. Let's try it."

They tried it, solemnly. She turned away, he swayed forward, she put out her right hand, palm out, in a gesture that cut an imaginary line from the lower right stage box to the spot on which they stood. "There! That does it!"

"Splendid!" said young Nesbitt. "I say, Miss Fayne, you're amazing!"

Ibsen came in, brisk, nervous, irritating. He clapped his hands together sharply. "Now, then. Second act. Mr. Logan! Please!" Just as if they had not all been waiting for him.

Miss Fayne and the three other women of the company thereupon quickly tied about their waists flounced skirts of very mussed muslin and crinoline. Part of Linda Fayne's exquisite technique was her insistence on a geometrical study of position. As the play required voluminous crinoline skirts, rehearsals must be conducted with makeshifts of the same, so that positions, distance, sight lines, attitudes standing and sitting might be gauged. The women now moved about, serious, intent on their parts, serenely oblivious of the grotesquerie of flounced crinoline below the stern severity of their modish little modern felt hats.

An hour of this, broken by stark tragedy in the person of Simon Ludwig, the scenic artist, who entered, followed by three men carrying panels of the first-act set. These turned out to be a blue green which would prove poisonous as a background for Miss Fayne's first-act costume, a purplish red, hand-embroidered, and three weeks in the making.

"But, Mr. Ibsen, it's impossible. You must see that. You see it, don't you, Simon? It would make me look as if I had jaundice."

"But it's the color of the sample we submitted, Miss Fayne, weeks ago, and you approved, and so did Mr. Ibsen and Mr. Wolfe."

"Where's Mr. Wolfe?" demanded Linda Fayne. Oscar Wolfe was the producer.

Mr. Wolfe. Mr. Wolfe. Mr. Wolfe was in his office in Forty-fifth Street, talking long distance to Cleveland.

Miss Fayne became dreadfully calm. "It's foolish to waste toll rates on long distance to Cleveland, because we're not going to open there Wednesday, anyway. We can't."

"Oh, now, Miss Fayne, it'll all be ironed out by the time——"

"When? How? Look at that green! You simply haven't seen my red, or don't remember it. Miss Grassie! Send over, will you, and get a sample of the red to show Mr.——"

"I've seen it. I've seen it. Listen, Miss Fayne. At the very worst you can wear it on the road and order a new one in another color for the New York opening."

Simon Ludwig, looking suicidal, said he might tone down the green, making it more of a yellow green, but then he certainly couldn't have it ready for the dress rehearsal on Sunday.

The stage doorman. "Say, Miss Fayne, there's a girl here says she's got color samples of red. She says for shoes."

"Tell her never mind. I'm not going to wear the dress, anyway. . . . Hey, Dolan, wait a minute. I'll just look at them, anyway. Tell her to come here. The shoes might as well be right, even for the road."

Jimmy New, the publicity man, who had been lying in wait to snatch her at the first pause in rehearsal.

"Hello, Miss Fayne! Gee, you're looking wonderful this morning. The harder you slave the better you——"

"All right, Jimmy. Let's have it."

"Well, we got to have some new pictures."

"You've got thousands. Millions!"

"Yes, but we want new ones for this play. This is different. I'm getting out an advance story for Cleveland."

"Oh, Cleveland." With the falling inflection.

"And there's a man here from the *Times* wants to make a head-and-shoulders sketch while you're rehearsing. Just a head-and-sh——"

Ibsen's sharp spat of the hands, like a pistol shot for those overstrained nerves. "First act! First act! Everybody! Please!"

The red samples thrust into the errand girl's hand. "This one. Tell Mrs.

Carewe this one, please. Thank you. . . . All right, Jimmy. Photographs. I
don't know when I can. . . . I've a permanent at three-thirty for the new
hairdress. He's got to do it. You know. Curls. It'll take almost three hours.
Tomorrow. Tomorrow, before rehearsal. No, I've a fitting again at ten.
How about tomor—no, tomorrow's matinee. Noon, tomorrow. I won't need
any lunch. Head? Oh, the head. Why don't we wait until I get the new
hair-do, and then have the *Times* artist do the—— All right, Mr. Ibsen.
Sorry."

Another hour of rehearsal. Almost one-thirty. "Only half an hour for
lunch, please, ladies and gentlemen. We must get on, and Miss Fayne
won't be able to rehearse tomorrow afternoon, matinee day. Everybody
back here at two, please." Hober, the stage manager. He caught Miss
Fayne on her way out. She and Nesbitt were in the habit of lunching together at the Narragansett Quick Lunch just next door, which was not so
grand and not so crowded as Childs, across the way. There, during the half-
hour, they could talk over a scene; decide whether today's treatment of it
was, after all, an improvement over yesterday's.

"Miss Fayne, that young fella's here."

"What young——"

"The new boy for the bit in the third act. I think he'll do, but you'd
better see him. I'll rehearse him, if he's right."

She turned to Nesbitt. "You go on. I'll be there in a minute. Order me
a pot of tea—black—and a chicken sandwich, all white. Irma'll understand."

It required five tactful minutes to bring about a state of coherence in the
new boy for the bit in the third act, and another five minutes to decide that
he would do, with Hober's grinding private coaching. That left a scant
twenty minutes for lunch.

Beside the plate of each was the battered booklet, open at Act Two.
Irma brought the pot of tea, black. Irma set before her the chicken sandwich, all white. Irma knew that she was serving, daily, at the Narragansett
Quick Lunch, the glamorous Linda Fayne, but Irma was too much a
woman of the world to take advantage of that fact. Irma, with her yellow
wave that seemed cut out of wood, and her disillusioned eyes, and her
slim, quick legs. The lights of Broadway were her sun, the Bronx express
her chariot. Wise, tolerant, friendly, hard, and urban. To her Linda Fayne
was a hard-working actress in a bum hat, and looked like she needed a rest,
if you ask me. "There's your hot water with it."

"You think of everything, Irma."

"I guess I got a right to know by now." Often Irma's speech was unintelligible to the ear unaccustomed to New Yorkese.

Linda and Nesbitt ate and drank. "How's your little boy?"

"Oh, he's right as rain now. Just a cold. Change in climate, I suppose."

"Did Mrs. Nesbitt find an apartment?"

"Not yet. They do seem fearfully expensive, don't they? We can't manage hotels, you see, with the boy. Not that they're cheap. But furnished flats—really, it's ghastly."

"I'll tell Grassie. With Grassie on the job you'll get something in no time."

"I say, that's kind of you, Miss Fayne."

"Oh no," vaguely. She was thinking of something else, palpably. "It didn't go a bit better this morning, that scene. And I'll tell you why. It isn't written, that's why."

"It does need rewriting. Won't he do it—Korber?"

"He says it isn't a lack in the writing, it's in the interpretation. Then I ask him what it means and he can't tell me, and then he goes away and sulks and doesn't come to rehearsal, because he can't fix it."

"Perhaps he'll be round this afternoon."

"It's no use. We'll have to try it out on the road, and show him it's wrong, and that they won't take it. Then he'll have to do something about it." Two minutes to two. She paid for her lunch; he paid for his. "I'll tell you what I think. I think he's got away from the mood and tempo of his play, in that scene, for the sake of a bright line. It's a good line, and I'll get a laugh on it, but it's out of key. There you are, imploring me to marry you. Would I be likely to wisecrack at a time like that? It isn't in character. She'd say something like . . ."

The musty dimness of the theater enveloped them. Wolfe was there, round, gentle, charming, shrewd. "Oh, Oscar. Where've you been hiding?"

"Me! Hiding!"

"It's no use saying we'll open in Cleveland on Wednesday. The set's wrong, I'm ragged in the part, it needs rewriting; we're trying out a new boy for the first time this afternoon in the part of Charles; my clothes aren't right; I'm rotten in it, anyway."

"All right, Linda. All right. Then we don't open in Cleveland on Wednesday. The thing is, you should be happy. You've got the part of your life here. Last year, you remember, you did nineteen thousand your Cleveland week. You'll do even better this trip. It doesn't matter. We can stay out another week. Cleveland is crazy about you, but you're the one——"

"We'll see. Maybe, by Sunday, it won't seem so hopeless."

Hober at her elbow. "Miss Fayne, the man's here with the couch. He said you wanted to see it today against the green of the set, so that if it wasn't right you'd have time to change."

"Oh, I'm on in a minute. Where is he? . . . Doesn't that seem awfully yellow to you? The sample looked more gold, didn't it? Gold? Of course if Ludwig tones the set into a more yellowish green—otherwise this would be awful. Still, maybe under the other lights . . . That's my cue. . . . 'No! No, Wilson, don't touch me!' "

Three-thirty. The hairdresser. I can't help it. I must go. It's my permanent for the hair-do. Mr. Nesbitt, will you come round after the play tonight? We can get in an hour or so, at my house. Do you mind? That's sweet of you. It's got to come right. Maybe that scene on the couch . . .

"Miss Fayne, will you try this book?" Otto, the property man.

"Book?"

"It's your book in the first act. The real one. I think it's the right weight you wanted it. You better sit down and hold it; see if it feels good."

She sat down. She held it. She leaned back indolently and weighed the book in her hand, and by some miracle it was right, and she beamed on Otto and he took the book and went off, full of other momentous affairs.

Connelly was there with the newly repaired car. He was all for elaborating on the story of his struggles with it. "That's fine, Connelly. You're sure it's going to be all right now? After Tuesday I shan't mind, but just now! . . . Frederic, the hairdresser, on Fifty-seventh Street."

Frederic was waiting with his comb, his scissors, his bowl, his bottles, his bend from the waist, his elbows in air, and his little finger of each hand elegantly crooked.

"I must—I mean, I simply must—be home by six-thirty, Frederic. Now, then, the part. She wears crinoline. It is about 1840, in England. She is not beautiful, but interesting and fragile. Curls, but not a young girl's curls, you understand. A woman."

"Ah! I know. George Eliot!" said the surprising Frederic. "The mind, yet a woman. The story of the play? Just in rough, you understand. It is better that I know, for the artistic result."

She told him. It sounded, she thought, in a panic, rather silly. Silly, too, to be sitting here with her hair being clamped into shining metal tubes, trapped for a period of three hours, and all for a play that might never see a performance.

"Oh, but amazing!" exclaimed Frederic. She had forgotten about him. "You will be ravishing in this play. You will see. Here your hair must be cut more thin on the sides, so. Then here flat, and here more full. You will be like a cameo, exquisite."

"Really, Frederic? Do you really think so?" She felt better. She wondered how she could sit there until after six. Just sit there. But Grassie had promised to come and cue her for these hours of enforced idleness. Where was she?

"Hello!" Grassie's reassuring voice, Grassie's intelligent, cheerful face in the glaring white light of the little booth. "Good God," said Miss Grassie, "if your dear public could see you now!"

"Here." Linda thrust the part at her.

Miss Grassie sat down, pushed her hat on the back of her head. "Last?"

"Yes."

"'... room in the carpetbag....'"

"Oh, say, I think Jimmy's cuckoo. When I told him you were trapped here for three hours he was all for sending that *Herald Trib* girl over for a special story she wanted to run the Sunday before we open here. And you looking like Medusa."

Panic. "But she isn't...!"

"No. He doesn't even know the name of the hairdresser. Besides, I explained to him why I thought he'd gone balmy. So don't worry. Uh...

"'... room in the carpetbag.'"

"'Never mind.'"

"'... forgotten nothing else.'"

"'And if we have, it won't matter much.'"

Five o'clock. Six o'clock. A row of stiff, little, dark, cylindrical curls bobbing like corks about her neck. "But soft, soft!" pleaded Frederic.

"No, I can't. Not till Sunday. I've got tonight's performance to play, and two tomorrow, with my hair absolutely modern. Heaven knows how I'll do it."

The gray morning had kept its promise of a rainy night. The apartment on the river was warm, bright, inviting. New York, Linda thought aloud, was full of lucky women who would put on velvet house gowns to dine cozily at home at seven-thirty, at their leisure.

"Nonsense!" said Grassie briskly. "All tearing into evening clothes to gobble their dinner to get down to the theater to see you at eight-thirty."

"You're a duck," said Miss Fayne.

Ellen had one degree of temperature. It was nothing, madam, Nana said. "But don't you think you'd better call Becker?" "Certainly not, madam." "Well, if she isn't perfectly all right by morning." "She will be." "I'll look in when I get home tonight." "We'll be sound asleep."

She took off her clothes and got into bed with a little grunt of weariness and relief. Six-forty. She had one whole delicious hour before she need start for the theater. Snug, warm, comfortable. This morning seemed far away. Years away. She must relax. Here eyes turned toward her bedside table, where her part lay, open at Act Two, Scene One, as she had placed it when she came in. Her hand reached for it.

Walker entered with her tray. She surveyed it listlessly. A bunch of violets on the tray—thrilling, as violets are in January. Chester? No. A card scrawled in the great dashing hand that tried to hide a timid, defeated soul. Papa. Henry Fayne. "For my Favorite Actress, from An Admirer." The tears, hot and stinging, came to her eyes. She neglected him. Everyone neglected him. He was that kind of person. He was worth a thousand like her mother, that devil-woman.

"Soup's right hot, Miss Lindy. Don't burn your tongue so you can't say your piece tonight."

The hot, thick mutton broth, soothing, revivifying. The lamb chop, creamed celery, chopped fresh pineapple, a little cup of black coffee. She ate it all, gratefully. That was better. There now. A half-hour, almost, in which to rest completely. Try to sleep. That would be wonderful.

No, I can't sleep. It's no use. Turn out the light. There. Relax. Don't think of your lines. Think of being a lake. I'm a lake . . . fluid . . . a lake. . . . Open my hands; they're tight. There. . . . My shoulder is tight. Relax. . . . There, I'm relaxed. But my mind is tight. I can't make my mind loose. . . .

"Seven-forty-five, Miss Lindy."

On her way to the theater she leaned back in a corner of the car and thought, suddenly, of tonight's performance. It was the first time she had given it a thought during the entire day. It was important. Every performance was important. She was too tired to do it. All that dressing and undressing and going on and being glamorous. If only she didn't have to talk to people. If only they would keep those people away from her. The doorman. She'd have to say good evening to the doorman. Her maid. That was silly. You're just nervous about the play.

"Evening, John."

"Get in quick, Miss Fayne. They's two girls from New Rochelle high school been waiting since seven o'clock. I told 'em you always come in the front way round so they won't be back here for a while."

"Miss Holstrom here?"

"Waitin'."

Miss Holstrom, the Swedish masseuse, the calm, impassive woman with the magic hands. As soon as Linda Fayne was out of her street clothes and wrapped in a dressing gown, the electric hands were performing the miracle that would bring the blood away from her head, take the pains of neuritis out of her shoulder. Just ten minutes. Better? Oh, much better, thank you, Holstrom. I couldn't go on without you. Miss Holstrom put on her shabby cloth coat and her mashed hat and vanished with her little bag, like a benevolent fairy.

Cora, her maid, answering a knock at her dressing-room door. "Box office wants to know if they can use your seats tonight, Miss Fayne, if you're not using them for anybody."

"Yes. . . . No! No! Tell him no. I forgot. I promised them to Frederic, the hairdresser. I thought closing tomorrow night we wouldn't——"

Three notes demanding autographs—one from the New Rochelle high-school girls. Suddenly, "Cora, I don't know what's the matter with me. I can't remember my lines. My lines for tonight."

"Why, Miss Fayne, you've played it for ten months and over. You're just nervous, that's all. Now you just relax. I'll open the door; listen for your cue. You just relax. . . . There's your cue, Miss Fayne."

A box of flowers. Dutch-pink roses. She loathed Dutch-pink roses. A card which read, "Happy memories from Pittsburgh. See you after the show. How about some supper?"

Oh, my God, who were they? Vaguely she remembered that she might have met them, somehow, somewhere, while trying out this play, a year ago, in the West. . . . There they were, after the last curtain. . . . Tell them—in a minute. Yes. Come in. How do you do! Yes, indeed I do.

Two shirt fronts, two silk hats. One red velvet evening coat, one brocade. Charming. Lovely. Wonderful. Charming. Charming. Oh, I couldn't possibly. I have to work. Mr. Nesbitt. No, not my husband. The leading man in the new play.

They were gone. Get me out of my face. Get me out of my dress. Tell Mr. Nesbitt in just a minute.

She and the young Englishman driving home through the dark cold streets to the river. In the library sounds of voices, laughter. Chester must have brought his friends home with him. She'd have to go in and speak to them.

"Only a second. Do you mind? I'm terribly sorry. We won't even sit down. I'll explain."

In the drawing-room doorway. "Hello! Hello! Come on in, Linda."

"Mr. Nesbitt. Mr. Nesbitt's over here from London to play the lead in *Cadogan*. Have you got everything? Walker will bring you sandwiches in a minute. No, we can't. Really. We've got to rehearse."

Eyebrows lifted. Eyes sliding round.

Up to the little sitting room on the second floor.

"I want to dash up to the nursery just a minute. Ellen had a little cold. No, nothing. You know how they run a temperature the minute they . . ."

Silence, darkness, peace in the room on the top floor. A passing river boat tooted hoarsely in the fog. She tiptoed in, peered at the cocoon in the little bed, felt the cheek, the forehead in the dark. Warm, but not hot. Unnecessarily, she tucked a cover. She tiptoed out, satisfied.

Nesbitt, pacing the sitting room, had an idea. "D'you know, Miss Fayne, I think this couch is a much better shape for our second act than the one they showed us today. Look. Where I lean toward you and run my arm along the back, I think it's just right because it gives the effect, you see, of my virtually having my arm about you without really quite daring to. That other couch has a higher back and the effect is awkward, don't you think?"

They tried it. Solemnly they went through the love scene—pleading, refusal, passion, capitulation, embrace.

"It *is* better!" agreed Linda. "I'll tell you what. I'll simply have this couch sent down to the theater tomorrow, and we'll throw the other one out. This scene's got to be right."

This settled, they ate scrambled eggs and hot cocoa, and Nesbitt mixed himself a highball. One o'clock. Two o'clock. Chester's friends departed, and Chester came upstairs and leaned in the doorway and said, "God's sake, Lin, you look like your own grandmother. You two better call it a day. What have you done to your hair? Those corkscrews! Well, unless the new play is *Uncle Tom's Cabin* and you're playing Topsy, I don't think much of that coiffure, if you ask me!"

"Is it really two o'clock? Connelly'll drive you home, Mr. Nesbitt. He's waiting."

After all, it was a favor to her, this rehearsing late at night when she was playing. It was only decent to see that he got home comfortably. She had felt nervous, though, about Connelly, up so late. Still, she herself had been hard at work since seven, and he hadn't. Oh, well. He'd probably be surly tomorrow.

Chester had gone off to his room. "Chester! Chet, did you turn off the lights downstairs?" No answer. She leaned over the railing, looked down. They were burning. Had Millie remembered to take Blitzen out? She went swiftly downstairs, turned out the lights. The library, the drawing room, were a welter of glasses, cigarette stubs, crushed cushions. Well, she simply couldn't cope with that, at this hour.

Upstairs in her own room. A hot bath. That would help her relax. Hot, and lots of pine bath salts. There. Oh, my heavens, I wonder if Grassie remembered to send a telegram to Cissie Reynolds for her opening tonight. Did I tell her?

I'm frightened. I'm frightened. It isn't the play. The play's good enough, except for that one scene Korber's such a mule about. It's me. I'll never do it. Open Wednesday! They're crazy. I won't. I can't. . . . Out of the bath. Her dressing gown. Into Chester's room.

"Chester! Chester!"

"What? What's matter?"

"Darling, I'm so scared."

"Scared of what?"

"You know. Scared. I can't do it."

She was shivering. Her teeth chattered. He drew her down to him. He tucked a corner of the comforter about her shoulder. He was half asleep, and a little tight, and the whisky and cigarettes of the evening party were heavy about him, but he knew the right words to say.

"You're crazy. You'll be swell. Say, you'll knock 'em cold. You always have. You always will."

"Oh, Chet, do you think so?"

"Do I—— Listen, if you were ever dead sure of yourself in a new part I'd know you were through. You're always like this. Don't you know that? Look at you before you opened in *Parrakeet!*"

"Was I nervous?"

"Jittering! And look what you've done in it! Nobody can touch you. You're the works, I tell you."

"Maybe it's just because I'm tired. Will you come to the dress rehearsal Sunday night?"

"Sure. Sure." He drew a long breath. It was as though sleep could no longer be fought off. He succumbed to it like a child—like Ellen. He was a child.

But he was right. Of course. She would be able to conquer the part, once this week was over. This week, and the next.

She was back in her own bed. Three o'clock. She must get some sleep. She'd be awake at seven, she knew. Rehearsal at ten tomorrow because of the matinee at two-thirty. Rehearsal, matinee, night performance—the last. There'd be flowers, and people and—she must relax. Quiet, now. Open the window. She had forgotten. The river flowed below, mysterious, black.

She crept, shivering, between the sheets and felt with her feet for the hot-water bag. A boat whistled, and she liked the sound. It was accustomed and real and friendly. Somebody else was awake. She reached for the paper-bound typewritten sheets, and tucked them under her pillow, and made a wish, and brushed the little stiff curls of the new hair-do away from her cheek. And slept.

Keep It Holy

[1933]

It is a trite truth that the stranger can be lonesomer in New York than in the desert. Linny's Sunday is that of thousands of girls who, on a bright spring morning, issue forth from their rooming houses and one-room flats and third-rate hotels. This little ghost may pass you in the park next week.

SUNDAYS WERE THE WORST. THERE WERE THE EVENINGS DURING the week, of course, but they weren't so terrible. An evening comes to an end. By the time she had eaten her dinner and read the tabloid and perhaps gone to a movie it was ten or after. There were always Things To Do, evenings; stockings to mend, gloves to wash, a dress to press, a letter to write, hair to shampoo, nails to manicure. Then, too, you were tired and sleepy after stitching hats all day, and trying them on customers' heads, and rushing them through for delivery. But Sunday! Sundays stretched endless hours ahead. You got nowhere. They were like a bad dream in which you walked and walked and made no progress.

This was her third Sunday in New York. You couldn't count that first Sunday because she had gone back home to Hartford for that. Well, she knew better now. She closed her eyes as though to shut out the memory of that first Sunday when she had gone back home to Hartford to see the folks.

As she lay in bed now, on Sunday morning at ten o'clock of a brilliant February New York day, she said to herself as she often had said in the past four weeks, Linny Mashek, you're a lucky girl to be in New York and have a good job and do what you want to. Having told herself this, firmly, she stared hard at a modernistic pattern sketched brightly on the ceiling by the bold spring sunshine and began to cry. So then she sat up in bed, looking very plain indeed, and remarked, aloud, "You need a good cup of hot coffee, that's what you need."

Luck had played a small part in the drama that had landed her in New York. She knew nothing of that. She knew nothing of the letter which had lifted her out of Hartford, Connecticut, and deposited her in Miss Kitchell's millinery shop on upper Madison Avenue, and in this rooming-house bedroom (five dollars a week and no cooking allowed, but everyone knew that didn't mean coffee).

DEAR KITCH,

Well, I'm married to a Hunky up here in the sticks believe it or not.
He owns a nice house and a Buick here in Hartford and a tobacco farm
about ten miles out with an old farmhouse on it like you see pictures in
the magazines I'm going to fix it up quaint later. Maybe I was a fool but
I don't think so. I was good and tired of working and anyway things the
way they are a person is lucky to have a home and I'm no spring chicken
any more. When I came up here to take charge of this hick millinery
department last fall I never dreamed I'd end up living here. He's Polish
extraction and real good-looking his wife was a Swede died a year ago.
He has got two sons married to Polack wives live near by but I can settle
their hash all right. I put on my little black Lanvin copy and talk New
York and they run like I had hoofs and horns. But look there is a girl too
a dead loss lives at home unmarried and probably always will be. And
that is where you come in Kitch. Her name is Linny—Linny Mashek. I
I am Mrs. Mashek now can you beat it. I asked her what do you mean
Linny and she said that was short for Linne or even Linnaeus he was a
Swede botanist discovered something about flowers and her Swede
mother was crazy about flowers always raising them in the yard and
named her after him is that goofy or isn't it I ask you. Well anyway
Kitch here is my proposition. Now listen Kitch. This Linny is an A 1
milliner. I know because she worked under me here and has got natural
style and knack and an eye for line. They laid her off here with others
because business is terrible the factories all shut down and the boobs not
buying hats and I guess they will go back to shawls if this keeps on. She
lays around the house all day and I am going crazy. She worshiped her
Swede ma. She is twenty-three looks more though she is little. The way
I met her pa was she asked me to come to the house for supper on Sunday night they had schnapps and beer and goose and fixings you'd be
surprised the way these Hunkies live. Well, this Linny is as smart a
milliner as I ever worked with I'm telling you straight. A girl with her
eye for line and copying would stand you forty a week in New York
even in these times. She can copy anything and original too I don't know
where she gets it. She can do them on the head, too. She'll work for
twenty a week. I will send you three weeks wages that is sixty dollars
and you will have an A 1 worker in the busy spring season won't cost
you a red cent for three weeks. After that if you want to keep her it's
your own lookout but if I once get her out of the house, she stays out.
I don't mean I am a mean stepmother or anything but the way she
mopes around the house and looks at me drives me crazy. Do this little
thing for me will you Kitch you won't lose by it. She isn't a bad little
thing quiet and homely but not a bad egg. I have done many a favor for
you in the past and you know it. Me and my old man will probably be

driving down to New York in March in the Buick when the weather gets milder and I'll be seeing you. Now do this will you Kitch for old times sakes.

> Your old pal Tessie.
> MRS. GUS MASHEK
> (Couldn't you die)!

Miss Kitchell, Millinery, Hats Made on the Head, sold guaranteed copies of French models at five to seven dollars. Miss Kitchell had unvenerable white hair, a basalt eye, and a black-clad figure which was the battleground on which Miss Kitchell's strong will waged perpetual war against the flesh. Miss Kitchell's voice, firm yet furry, was lifted hour upon hour in phrases that had become a chant through repetition.

This just came in. . . . You can't tell a thing in the hand. . . . I love it on you. . . . More over the eye. . . . It's a little Suzanne Talbot. . . . It's a little Rose Descat. . . . It's a little Yvonne. . . . This just came in. . . . I love it on you. . . . More over the eye. . . . You can't tell a thing in . . .

In the littered workroom behind the showroom, Linny Mashek stitched and folded and steamed and pressed and cut. It's promised for tonight, it's promised for tonight, it's promised for tonight.

At the close of the first bewildering week Miss Kitchell, glancing sharply and not unkindly at the girl's white face and twitching hands, had said, "Well, thank God even Saturdays come to an end. Listen, Mashek. If I was you I'd catch myself a good rest in bed all tomorrow morning and then go out and see New York. You got some friends here?"

"No," said Linny. "No."

"Well, you'll soon make friends. Anyway, there's lots to interest a young girl in New York. There's the Metropolitan Museum and the Natural History Museum and the Aquarium and the Bronx Zoo. A person," concluded Miss Kitchell, "can live here in New York all their life and not see the half of it."

"I think," said Linny, "I'll go up home to Connecticut this Sunday, see the folks, and come back on the late train Sunday night."

"Don't do that!"

Linny was a little startled at the vehemence of Miss Kitchell's tone. "Why not?"

"It's foolish. What do you want to go and spend your money like that for? Why'n't you stay here in New York and see the sights?"

"I will, next week. I guess I'm kind of lonely for—for—not lonely exactly, but I just thought I'd run up home and see the folks. I wrote a letter Thursday and told them I was coming, just for Sunday. Anyway, I want to bring back a couple of things. Little things I didn't bring when I first came, like a picture of my—of my folks, and some things like that."

Miss Kitchell shrugged her shoulders in a gesture of resignation.

"You tell your—you tell Mrs. Mashek I said you'd be better off staying here, having a good time seeing the sights."

"I'll tell her," said Linny, mystified but polite. "She'll be glad to hear from you."

"Oh, my God!" exclaimed Miss Kitchell.

Well, Linny knew better now. She had come home to a closed house at Hartford. Everything closed tight. Doors locked, windows locked, shades pulled down. She rang, knocked, pounded. The cellar door locked, the garage door locked, even the back pantry window that had never had a lock before. They had gone to the farm, most likely, for the day. They had never got her letter and they had gone out to the farm for Sunday.

At the rear of the house, in a last foray before going to her brother's, her eye was caught by the stunted old apple tree whose bare limbs just reached the roof of the back porch. She smiled then, a wide grin of delight. A childhood spent with two older brothers had taught her a trick to foil locked doors and downstairs windows. She took off her good Sunday coat and her smart new hat and placed them on the back porch steps, with her gloves and bag neatly on top. With a swift glance around she tucked her skirt about her belt and was up the tree, onto the flat roof of the porch like a cat, and through the second-story window. It was fun. She would tell the boys about it, later. The back hall was dark. She dusted off her hands, pulled down her skirt, opened the hall door, and came face to face with her stepmother.

They stared at each other. Their opening words sounded like the dialogue in a bad translation of a Chekhov play.

"My! A new dress!"

"It was locked. You locked it!"

"Your pa's at the farm."

Well, she knew better now.

On the second Saturday, at closing, "Miss Kitchell, what do you think is the most interesting thing to see in the Metropolitan Museum, to start with?"

"Well, I've never really been. I meant to go a million times. But Sundays I'm so dead I'm glad to be off my feet, let alone tramping around looking at pictures and like that. Weekdays I'd look swell, wouldn't I, running to museums with a living to make!"

That first New York Sunday she had awakened to rain. The rain had turned to a soggy snow. The combination had formed a slush that made galoshes a necessity. Still, she had started out with an almost gay feeling of adventure. Anything might happen. The movies had taught her that Romance, in the person of lithe young men with cleft chins and quizzical eyebrows, roamed the parks, the streets of New York. Later in the day she decided that Romance was blighted by galoshes and an umbrella. Certainly the start had not been propitious. She was not certain about the location of the Metropolitan Museum. Fifth Avenue in the Eighties somewhere. Coming from her rooming house she stood a moment at the corner of Lexington and Eighty-sixth. Fifth Avenue was over there—uh—no, over —let me see. A man with his coat collar turned up and a cigarette dangling limply from a corner of his lips was standing slouched in the doorway of the cigar store. Not a young man; shabby, with pimples. A man.

"I beg your pardon——" That was the way you approached strangers in Hartford. "I beg your pardon, but could you tell me—is that the way to the Metropolitan Museum?"

"The what?"

"The Metropolitan Museum on Fifth Avenue."

"Not today, sister," the man said.

She walked away, her chin up. He could have given her a civil answer to a civil question. Making fun of her like that. It didn't even make sense. Not today. Through there was the park. She could see the bare branches of the trees. That was Fifth Avenue. It must be right there, somewhere, the Metropolitan Museum.

She was wearing a brown coat with a good fox-fur collar, and a nice little hat she had made herself; and excellent gloves and stockings, and neat pumps beneath the galoshes. Everything she had on was good and modish, in the manner of the American working girl. She had added a tiny veil, for coquettishness, but it was not right. Her sharp nose poked it out, and a black dot in the wrong place gave one eye a drooping look. She was short and very slight, but her smallness had not the appealing and miniature quality that endears babies and kittens, and that arouses the protective instinct. It was, rather, a meagerness, as though nature had skimped.

Up the broad steps of the vast edifice. Check your umbrella here. The great marble halls of the Metropolitan were swarming with people, for the day was cold and wet and gray.

She stood alone in the center of the huge entrance hall. She looked up at the stairway ahead. She glanced to the right, to the left. Things Egyptian leered at her. Undraped Greeks in athletic poses stared at her with sightless marble eyes. Mythological monsters yawned in her face.

Everyone seemed to be there in couples, in families, or in hordes. Italian

families of five or six children, all strangely of a size, regarded the statuary
with the accustomed gaze of people to whom Michelangelo's *David* is a
thing you see always in the piazza on market days. They dragged themselves over miles of floor, past endless walls glowing with the blues and
crimsons of holy groups and the mild moonfaces of Neapolitan madonnas.
The boys were in full regalia of American kiddie clothes. Their swimming
Italian eyes looked out from beneath hatbands on which were printed in
gold letters u.s.s. MINNEWASKA. The husband, in his Sunday blacks,
seemed to shrink and fade into the background. The woman always held
a lunging lump of a child in her arms. With staring eyes and pendulous
cheeks, he hung perilously over her shoulder to peer into glass cases containing aristocratic Tang figures with disdainful, evasive faces.

I bet she isn't any older than I am, Linny thought. And look at her.
All those kids, and no more shape than our cow back home. I wouldn't
change places with her. . . . And then: I bet she don't know what lonesome
is, all those kids squawking.

The place was remote, in spite of the swarms, and overpowering. It's
real interesting, though, she reminded herself. In one of the picture gal-
leries she stopped before an Inness—a valley bathed in golden light. It
made her think of Connecticut, in the autumn, back in the hills. It made
her happy to look at it, but it was a sad happiness. Since last week—since
last Sunday—she had had a curiously heavy feeling—a feeling of uncertainty. She had experienced, crudely and ruthlessly, the sensation of not
being wanted. It had shaken the very core of her self-confidence. She did
not know this. She only felt it in some obscure and painful way.

Sargent's portrait of Mme X, a figure of great elegance in her black
velvet with its tiny waist and swelling hips and bosom. Her cold, passionate
profile was turned away from the girl staring up at her. Snooty old thing,
Linny thought. Chase's devilish portrait of Whistler she passed with a
blank gaze. Rembrandt's *Old Lady Cutting Her Nails*. Degas' ballet girls
with their muscular legs and distorted feet. Well, what did people want
to go and paint things like that for!

People whispered. They tiptoed and whispered. Linny found herself
tiptoeing, too. She went up to a guard (elderly) and whispered, "It says
the American Wing."

"Second corridor straight ahead turn to your left turn to your right turn
to your left turn to——"

"Thank you so much," said Linny. "I'm ever so much obliged." Miraculously she found it, but it seemed to her to be poor stuff. They had as good
as that in the farm attic back home, stuck away in dusty corners. Stuff that

had been there years, long before Pa had bought the old place. And old tables, scarred and hacked like the chopping block in Vogelsang's butcher shop in Hartford. A placard said 1650–1675.

Cool court ladies done in ivory miniatures framed in jewels and resting on velvet. Do Not Lean on the Glass. Twelfth-Century Armor. Brocades. Mummies.

"Oh, fine!" said Linny, next day, in answer to Miss Kitchell's question. "There's so much to see you can't see it all in one day."

"It's a wonderful city, New York is. People who live here don't half appreciate it."

The pimply man on the cigar-store corner was sometimes lounging there, evenings, when she came home from the movies or from work. She passed the corner on her way to her room in Eighty-sixth. "Hello, sister!" She turned her head away, disdainfully, like that picture of the woman in the black velvet at the Metropolitan. The old fool, as if anybody would want to speak to him.

It was funny, though. A week would go by and she would have spoken to no one except Miss Kitchell and women and women. Never a man. You couldn't count Florida Cream, the colored errand boy who swept out and delivered the hats and brought materials up from the wholesale district. He slapped about in a torn red sweater and shapeless cap and fringed pants. But he must have a large social life of his own, after hours. There had been, one night, some confusion about the promised delivery of a hat, with hysterics on the part of the customer. Linny had been summoned from her rooming house and Florida Cream from Harlem. He had appeared in such a blaze of pinch-waist French-blue topcoat and fawn-topped shoes and yellow stick and pearl-gray fedora as to leave her gasping.

She remembered a Hartford girl she knew who had gone to New York to work in a beauty parlor. That was over a year ago. Emma Hovak. On her rare visits back to Hartford, Emma had been all fur-trimmed coat, glinting hair, troughlike wave, and scarlet nails. Linny searched her memory for the name of the beauty parlor. She called Emma Hovak.

"Hel-lo!" said Emma, summoned to the telephone. The expectant note in her voice amounted almost to a trill. Linny had not given her name.

"This is Linny."

"Who?"

"Linny Mashek."

"I guess you got the wrong party."

"No. Linny Mashek, from Hartford. Linny Mashek."

"Oh. Oh, hello." It was another word altogether, that hello. A silence. "You down for the day?"

"I'm living here in New York. I'm working here."

"Yeah?"

"I thought—what're you doing—I mean I thought we could fix up a date for next Sunday, maybe——"

"Listen, Linny, I'm all dated up for Sunday. This Sunday and the Sunday after and—I'll give you a ring, see. Listen, I got a client, see, I'm giving her a henna, she'll have a fit; we're not supposed to answer the telephone when we're doing a henna. Listen, I'll give you a ring real soon——"

She had not even asked where Linny worked or lived.

That third Sunday had been one of those piercingly brilliant New York days, blue and gold and sharp. She had slept late, and then, awakened by the sunshine, she had prepared her own good breakfast—the coffee she loved, and coffee cake and a surreptitious egg, and a slice of ham bought at the delicatessen the night before. Sustained and almost happy, for the coffee had been strong and the day was bright and she was twenty-three, she strolled across Central Park toward the Natural History Museum. Florida Cream had told her something of the wonders it contained.

"Animals," he had said, his eyes rolling, "called denasserusses, bigger than any elephants you ever see, used to roam the earth, one lick of their tail would knock down a tree; and Indians, stuffed, and tigers and meterites fell down from the sky as big as this here room. Boy! I sure hate get hit by one them!"

Groups of girls and groups of boys and Sunday fathers with their offspring, pompous and a little bored. And couples and couples and couples. The couples had cameras. The girl was forever taking a snapshot of the boy or the boy of the girl, accompanied by giggling, pouting, and general coquetting on the part of the girl and embarrassed comedy from the boy.

"Aw, Merton, stand still and straighten your hat, woncha! Lookit how you look, your face."

"Well, can I help it if you don't like my face! It's the only face I got." Salvos of laughter rewarded this bit of repartee. There were young men, alone, on park benches in the cold sunshine, but there was nothing relaxed and indolent about their lolling. They had the look of this year's young men to whom park benches were no luxury. Linny glanced at them, shyly. Their gaze was blank; or it slid past her, unheld.

There was a pleasant informality about the crowds that swarmed the Natural History Museum. They had nothing of the stiffness and rather puzzled awe of last week's Metropolitan Museum hordes, made self-conscious by supercilious Gainsboroughs and nude Greeks. Small boys raced the aisles, pointing pop-eyed at monsters and snakes and tepees. Still smaller boys said, "Lift me up, Pa!"

"It's only a canoe, a Indian canoe, says seagoing war canoe of the—uh—Haida Indians live on the coast of Alaska——"

"I wanna see in! I wanna see in! Lift me up!"

Linny liked the giant trees; the California sequoias, enormous blocks of wood grown for centuries, for a thousand years, as large in circumference as a room. "Lookit! Ut's a tree!" The small boys pointed, scuttled on.

Middle-aged couples stood together before glass-enclosed exhibits, their faces upturned in the pure expression of learning. For the moment they had the eager receptive look of children. They stood, boy and girl fashion, the man's arm loosely about the woman's broad waist. His hand rested on her hip; thick, spatulate fingers with work-stained nails, rather touching in their Sunday idleness. He read aloud from the placard, being the learned of the two. "The Struggle for Existence. Every living thing, plant or animal, is engaged in an unconscious struggle for existence with other living things. In order to live, the meadow mouse must be able to escape its enemies such as the cat, the skunk, weasel, hawk, owl, and snake. It is the survival of the fittest——"

The two stood gazing with new respect and understanding at the family of meadow mice in the glass case. Meadow mice themselves, that waist and that broad hand, struggling for existence against the skunk, the weasel, the hawk, the snake.

Two nuns in their anachronistic garb bent their wimpled heads over a chaste display of waxen blossoms under glass; Color Inheritance in the Flower of the Four-O'clock, Red and White. Above the delicate petals of the four-o'clocks was a small portrait of a man in priest's garb, a cross upon his breast. Gregor Johann Mendel, discoverer of the Mendelian law of heredity.

"Cute," said the younger of the two black-shrouded figures, with a last glance at the four-o'clocks. They turned toward the case showing the evolution of the polliwog.

Glyptodonts, mammoths, dinosaurs. Tyrannosaurus Rex. The largest flesh-eater of all times. The Alaskan moose. Peninsular giant bear. Florida panther. The American bison. The tsine or banteng. Sumatran rhinoceros. Forest, river, and ocean life. Linny found herself sidling into groups, in order to hear them speak. Once a couple glanced at her over their shoulders and moved on, pointedly annoyed. She felt her face get hot.

"You getting acquainted with New York?" Miss Kitchell asked, on Monday.

"Oh, yes."

"It don't take long. First thing you know you'll be a real New Yorker. I ought to get out more, Sundays. I'm so dead I do my sight-seeing in bed, with the papers. Time I get myself pulled together it's six and some of the crowd begins coming in."

Now, on this fourth Sunday, as she lay in bed staring at the pattern of sunshine on the wall, these things went through her head, not in orderly fashion, but disconnectedly, in pictures and flashes. Her father now fifty-three, a zestful fellow with a stocky, muscular body and a dark, ruddy skin and iron gray in his hair. He was better-looking now than when he had married the Swedish girl who had worked with him on the farm a quarter of a century ago. His new wife's face. Linny did not even call her "stepmother" in her mind. The shop. Miss Kitchell. Hartford Sunday. Portrait of Mme X. Not today, sister. It's a little Suzanne Talbot. Lift me up, Pa. The American Wing, 1650. I'm dated up this Sunday and next Sunday; I'll give you a ring sometime, see. Then some of the crowd begins coming in. . . .

It was then that she had begun to cry, her face screwing up absurdly. It was after that that she had said, aloud, to herself, "You need a good cup of hot coffee, that's what you need."

She rather enjoyed these Sunday breakfasts, after the weekly morning scramble and gulp. She had two meals only on Sunday—her leisurely coffee and bakery coffee cake and her egg when it was nearly noon; her dinner at the Werner cafeteria at six. She drank a great deal of coffee, a habit inherited, perhaps, from her Swedish mother. There always had been a pot of the strong brew simmering on the stove back home.

This five-dollar room was not sordid or uncomfortable. It was small and not very bright. Most of the furniture had some minor disability—a chair rung missing, a knob broken, a caster off, a mirror crazed. But the landlady had learned about cretonne, and the one window caught briefly the late-morning sun.

Peering out, after breakfast, Linny was aware of something odd in the air, something different. She felt it when she stuck her head out of the window, but it did not penetrate her room or the dank subway.

The mazes of the Sunday subway bewildered her. There were no guards in sight. The whole thing seemed to function without human aid. Trains rushed into stations, unguided. Doors opened and shut mysteriously. People were spewed forth, others flowed in, the train fled into the black cavern. There was no one of whom to ask a question. New York assumed that, having come, you knew your way about. If not, you could damn well find it. Linny plucked up courage to ask direction of middle-aged family men with wives. There were young men, too, in gray fedoras and belted overcoats and gay mufflers, but Linny was too shy to approach these. After the rush of boarding the train, the passengers, seated or standing, fell into a kind of catalepsy, staring glassy-eyed before them or up at the advertising placards overhead. They did not speak. Couples sat sedately, their eyes sliding round. There was color and life, though, in the smart Negro girls, resplendent in fine red or green cloth coats with big fur collars framing the flashing vivacity of their faces. Their chocolate cheeks were delicately rouged, enhancing the liquid brightness of their eyes. Occasionally, when a door rolled open, there tumbled in a laughing, jostling group of boys and girls. They carried the inevitable camera. They never could find seats all together. They called across to one another and made personal jokes, shoving, nudging, giggling. Linny sat regarding these with an expression which she intended as a blending of hauteur with contemptuous amusement. She envied them.

Once out of the subway at the end of the line, walking through Battery Park on her way to the Aquarium, Linny knew, suddenly, the name of the thing that had vaguely troubled her when she had stuck her head out of the bedroom window to sniff the air.

It was spring.

There in Battery Park, for the first time since coming to New York, she had a feeling of freedom, of exhilaration, and of peace. All that blue sky, all that tossing bay, all those clouds, white and puffy, the scarlet funnels of the ships; that vast bank of towering buildings left behind, like a prison wall from which you have escaped.

Peanuts! Popcorn! Crackerjack! Chocolate bars! Pretzels! Everyone seemed to be eating something. Jaws worked rhythmically. Gum. Apples. Bananas. Linny bought a bag of peanuts and entered the close-smelling circular hall of the Aquarium. At once she was caught up in the fascination of the unknown and unusual and fantastic. She followed the crowd, munching her peanuts, staring, held. With the rest she pressed against the rail above the circular pool. It held cormorants. They stepped about, stiff-kneed, mincing. Linny was puzzled by their resemblance to someone she knew. One cormorant in particular—the biggest one. Its craw hung down like a double chin. It stuck out in front and it stuck out behind. It looked about with a cold and bawdy eye. It bridled and leered and minced, elegantly. It had a way of ducking the head and drawing in the chin, with horrible coquetry. Its unvenerable white head was close-clipped and neat.

"Miss Kitchell, of course!" said Linny, aloud. She blushed with embarrassment then, but the Sunday crowd did not heed her.

As Linny became accustomed to the dim green light of the room she saw that it was infested with bleary bums asleep on benches tucked around the supporting pillars—scabrous gentlemen with a peculiar bluish cast to the skin and loose, open mouths. Defeat had stamped her iron heel on their faces, distorting their features into strange lumps and depressions. All about them, in pale, sparkling tanks of water, glass-enclosed, flashed brilliant living things—orange and scarlet and jade and lavender things. They were like no fish she had ever seen. Rather, they seemed orchids endowed with the power of locomotion. In another tank a vast fleshy thing waggled majestically up to the very confines of the glass wall and stared superciliously at the gaping crowd outside like a fat dowager gazing with lackluster fishy eye through the plate-glass window of her limousine.

On one of the little circular seats a blond boy lay asleep. His clothes proclaimed him a sailor from one of the battleships anchored up the Hudson. A sailor on a busman's holiday, visiting the Battery and the Aquarium. As he lounged there, relaxed in slumber, his huge hands were open and defenseless. His head had fallen on his breast. His shock of yellow hair was like a pompon. He was, perhaps, twenty. Childlike and helpless there in sleep. Linny Mashek, looking at him, suddenly longed to sit beside him and very gently place her body so that the yellow pompon should be pillowed on her breast. The impulse was so strong as to frighten her. Abruptly she turned away, pushed through the crowd massed in front of the tank containing the sea horses—miniature monsters, and unbelievable, like something out of *Alice in Wonderland*. Just ahead of her stood a boy and a girl. Under the guise of gallant attention the boy touched the girl whenever possible. He helped make way for her through the crowd toward the tank, protected her from the crowd, again made way out of it, and always his hands touched her—her shoulder, her arm, her waist, her hip—mutely wooing her. The girl wasn't pretty. She wore eyeglasses. Linny hated her. She walked behind the two, toward the doorway. In a niche in the wall near the main exit was a white marble bust of a woman. Beneath it was a tablet, engraved:

JENNY LIND

Presented by the New York Zoological Society in Commemoration of the First Appearance in America of the Swedish Nightingale at Castle Garden.

Linny knew about Jenny Lind. She had heard about her from her mother.

The boy with the insistent fingers and the eyeglassed girl stood a moment gazing up at the bust and the placard.

"Who's she?" said the boy.

"You're asking me!" retorted the young lady, with fine irony. "It says

Swedish nightingale, I guess she got her dates mixed. She ought to be up in the birdhouse at Bronx Park."

The young man went into a flattering paroxysm of mirth. "No kidding!" he said. "You're a sketch!"

I could have told him, Linny thought, hotly. I could have told him all about Jenny Lind, the way my mother told me. But then the young man would never have laughed and squeezed her arm and said she was a sketch.

When she emerged, blinking, into the midafternoon February sunshine, the Battery Park photographer was taking a picture. Ranged before him in a wooden pose stood the young man and the girl with the eyeglasses. They were smiling self-consciously. The photographer ducked beneath his little black cloth, he emerged with a worried look. His business instinct battled with his artist soul. The artist won.

"Lady," he demanded, mournfully, "you keeping your glasses on?"

"Sure," replied the young lady, blithely.

"Sure she's keeping them on," the young man shouted, belligerently. "Go on duck into your tent and snap it up."

The young lady smiled her reward upon her love-blinded knight: "Hold still now!"

Linny turned away in an absurd fury.

"Boat for the Statue of Liberty just leaving, thirty-five-cent round trip! Just leaving! Statue of Liberty! Takes forty-five minutes round trip, lady. Just leaving."

The boat's cabin was hot. In every corner was a couple, low-voiced, intent. The boat's cabin seemed to be all corners, all snugly occupied and each corner protected by a shimmering haze of amorous mystery.

Linny went outside, banging the door behind her, and stood, bracing herself, on the forward deck. The air was biting. The top-heavy island receded. The wind whipped her cheeks. The tears sprang to her eyes. She denied them to herself. It was the cold. This was fine. This was what she liked. That was the Swede in her, like her mother and her mother's folks, she thought.

But when they reached the little island that held the Statue of Liberty, and the crowd swarmed up the gangplank and hurried toward the statue's base, she decided, suddenly, not to wait for the next boat, not to climb the statue's many stairs, not to see the View. She wanted to go back, unreasonably, at once, with this boat which even now was being filled with the new crowd returning from its inspection of the statue.

Two lantern-jawed military police, deceptively impressive in their olive-drab uniforms, stood guard on either side of the gangplank. From the

corrugated metal shed on shore came the sound of a radio, whiling away
the Sunday hours of the military police off duty. "Wha-wha-wha-wha,"
whined a crooner.

Linny turned, blindly, and stumbled down the gangplank to the boat.
The S.S. *Hook Mountain* cast off.

"Take her away!" yelled the military police. Linny shrank. It was like a
personal insult.

Battery Park reached, it was half-past five. The Aquarium was closed.
The crowds had thinned. The air was sharp. By the time she got uptown
to Werner's cafeteria it would be six. The day was nearly over.

Werner's cafeteria, uptown on Lexington, showed a half block of cheerful plate-glass window. Those who sat within had no dietary secrets from
the world.

Linny almost always ate her dinner at Werner's cafeteria. It was cheap,
bright, good, clean. You got your tray, you selected your food, you served
yourself. A long counter stretched the length of the farthest room. On it
was ranged a bewildering variety of food. To choose amongst it was to
illustrate the impressive power of decision in the human mind. Enormous
roasts of beef and pork and lamb; pans of fish; mounds of vegetables, green,
white, gold; bowls of salad; quarter sections of fruit tarts, mosaics of plum
and apple and apricot; acres of coffee cake. The catch in it was that, the
decision once made, the soup was found to taste strangely like the roast,
and the roast like the vegetables, and the vegetables like nothing at all.
Still, it was almost hot, and nourishing. The place was crowded, as always.
Linny was forced to choose a table at which sat a man, eating. He kept his
hat on. He ate, keeping his eyes on his food. He did not even glance up at
Linny when she sat down. He was a middle-aged man. Pieces of food kept
clinging to his pale-tan mustache. Linny kept her eyes cast down, too.

A movie. I'm sick of movies, she said to herself. Good and sick and tired
of movies. Always the same thing. All that necking. And the couples
around holding hands, too, and carrying on. It was always too hot in the
movies. She might go over to the room, first and change her shoes, and
rest a minute before going to the movie. Her feet were tired, walking
around all day in new Sunday pumps.

She had finished her dinner. Strawberry tart—fresh strawberries, too,
in February! It had looked delectable beyond words and had tasted like
raw cucumbers.

She had selected her food in silence, pointing. She had eaten in silence.
She was out again in the February dusk. Suddenly, without warning, panic
clutched her. You could live in New York, and go around all day, and have
nothing happen. Not one thing. All day long she had talked to no one.

From the moment of her awakening this morning until now, standing on the street corner in the early spring dusk, she had talked to no human being. Not one. She was a ghost, unreal, immaterial, drifting like fog through an indifferent city, mingling with the throng, but no part of it. She was nothing. She was nobody.

Chatter, chatter; talk, talk; laugh, laugh. Heh, buddy, where you going, what do you want to do now, let's hop a bus, meet my friend Mr. Sweeney. All about her people talked to people, walked arm in arm.

She began to run. Her face was distorted. Her head was down. She bumped into someone. It brought her to her senses. She slowed her pace to a walk, straightened her hat, her smart little spring hat that she had made herself. I guess I'm tired, standing around all day. I'll go to the room, lay down on the bed a minute, rest myself. But at the thought of the room —the dark, quiet little grave of a room—her footsteps lagged. Lagged. Eighty-fifth street. Eighty-sixth and Lexington.

"Hello, sister!" It was the pimply, oldish man slouching there, as usual, against the pillar of the cigar store on the corner, a limp cigarette in his mouth. "Hello, sister!"

"Hello yourself!" croaked Linny, to her own monstrous surprise. Her lips were stiff with distaste.

Blue Glasses

[1936]

Autograph hounds in bobby sox who envy the slim, fur-swathed goddesses who occasionally bejewel the streets and theaters and restaurants of New York know little or nothing of the working day of these spangle-eyed damsels. Motion-picture publicity departments prefer that we of the humdrum world dream on, all ignorant of the weary haggard woman who drags herself from her bed at five in the morning to begin her grinding Hollywood chore and who returns gratefully to her pillow at nine at night. Still, perhaps her life has its less heart-rending side.

❧ CERTAINLY SHE SHOULD HAVE BEEN USED TO LUXURY BY NOW. TEN months of it, and they say it takes only ten days. She should have got the feel of success, too. But at fifty-nine, body and mind had taken on a rigidity that fitted awkwardly into the curves of a new environment.

Try as she might, she could not get over the feeling that her coach would turn into a pumpkin any minute. Her comfortable house perched on the hills above Coldwater Canyon, her two cars, her swimming pool, her dear two Scotties (which comically resembled her), her good California food with all those buttery green vegetables, that nice little pint of iced champagne with her dinner in bed at the end of a twelve-hour day at the studio—all these might vanish as they had come, overnight, and Minna Dixon (late of Hainey & Dixon) might find herself back in any one of the hundreds of fly-by-night rooming-house bedrooms that had been her only home for over forty years.

When she had a bad dream it was always of this, or of the smoke-blackened wooden shack in the mill section outside of Pittsburgh where she had spent her childhood, with her last conscious moment at night and her first waking moment in the early morning filled with the complaints of her mother's nagging voice as she berated her dour husband. Frequently these tirades had mounted to actual combat in which the curses of the man, the screeching of the woman, the cries of the huddled, frightened children mingled in dreadful cacophony. A hand on her shrinking shoulder, shaking her, her arm up to shield her head from a blow—and she would awaken to find Colly's firm, gentle hand on her shoulder, and Colly's black face, concerned and reassuring, bent over her in solicitude.

"Five-thirty, Miss Minna. Here's your hot-water lemon juice. You must been having a bad dream, fighting them bedclothes like they was wild tigers coming at you."

Haggard, wild-eyed, she stared up at the smiling Negress; she gazed bewildered at the big comfortable room; she saw the blank gray wall of fog that was California's early morning. The relief was almost too intense. She would sink back on her pillows, safe, safe. It was real. The great soft bed, the smooth sheets, the satin puff, warm yet light, all were real. "God's sakes, go 'way, Colly; let me sleep."

"Five-thirty and after. You got jest half-hour git yourself down to that lot and you know it. Want I should pull them bedcovers offen you!"

"Call up the studio, tell'm I'm sick."

But she didn't mean it. Half-past five of a January morning or no, she didn't mean it. And Colly knew she didn't mean it. Half-past-five rising in the morning was only another Hollywood indication of your success, paradoxical though it might seem. After her many years of midday rising with the rest of the vaudeville and theatrical world, it had been difficult for Minna Dixon to comprehend this. At some very formal low-cut Hollywood dinner to which she was bidden because of her spectacular success she would embarrass the pompous producers, the first-string directors, the current glamour girls and idol boys who formed the impressive company.

Minna alone talked frankly of her shabby past. The tall gods in tails and the slim beauties in tulles looked down their classic noses in self-conscious disapproval. Any one of them could have matched her story. But the vulgar and robust day was a thing of the past in pictures. Hollywood had gone in for elegance, French lessons, ranch life, and only eight of us for dinner.

Her friendly glance, her warm Midwestern voice, encompassed them. "This sure is a goofy town. When I was a kid back in Youngstown, Ohio, and Pittsburgh, getting up half-past five meant you were a failure. Half-past five my old man was starting out on the mill day shift. Us kids would hear Ma nagging at him and slamming the dishes around and packing his lunch pail, yelling how she wished she was dead before she married a Hunky like him.

" 'Course he wasn't a Hunky. Pa was decent-enough Scotch, and I suppose if he'd of soaked away his first dime the way Carnegie did, why, I'd be living on Fifth Avenue. Wait a minute! I could anyway, couldn't I? Now, I mean.

"Well, anyway, Ma she'd been a girl come to town with a tent show and he married her to make an honest woman of her—the poor ignorant fella— and she never forgave him, I guess. Her being sore at him all the time, I guess that's how it got into my head that getting up to work before daylight was proof your name was mud. At that, I bet Hollywood is the only town in the whole world where if you have to get up at five every morning to go to work, and hit the hay at nine every night to get your sleep, why, it means you're a hell of a success."

Milt Marks, head of the studio publicity department, had wanted to do a piece about her entitled:

$$\text{\$UCCE\$\$ AT \$IXTY}$$
$$\text{THE OLD LADY SHOWS HER}$$
$$\text{METAL}$$

"No you don't!" Minna had said when she heard of it. "Listen, young fella. I'm fifty-nine. I don't like it, but I'm fifty-nine. And if you don't know the difference—to a woman—between fifty-nine and sixty, why, you better read a book or meet some girls."

She was right. There was nothing of the old lady about Minna Dixon. A hearty, zestful woman, plump but not fat. In youth, her face had been a handicap in her career and in her love life. She looked like a nice horse with tragic eyes. It was the face of a woman who would always be surprised at the ruthlessness of life and the faithlessness of men. But to a world of movie fans the long muzzle, the wide upper lip, the arching neck, the cavernous nostrils spelled pure comedy.

The fine eyes, with their brooding sadness, only served to heighten their appreciation of the comic mask. Since her very first appearance in pictures (a mere trial bit ten months ago) any audience could be counted on to burst into a roar of laughter the moment her face was flashed upon the screen.

As she rose from her bed in the dim light of this January morning she looked every second of her age. She had had barely five hours' sleep. They were doing retakes on this last picture. They had worked until nearly midnight last night; they probably would work until midnight tonight so that tomorrow the two stars, Minna Dixon and Dinah Crewe, could leave for a ten-day vacation before starting their next picture.

She was numb with weariness; her legs felt wooden, yet the knee joints pained like a toothache. These last months had accustomed her to a fixed period of sleep while working. Up at five-thirty, yes; but in bed at seven, one of Colly's hot, savory dinners on a tray, Swedish Hulda's electric fingers massaging her weary body; asleep by nine.

Oh, well, she thought now, as she dashed cold water on her swollen eyelids, into that plane tomorrow. Planing to New York, they called it in Hollywood, as you would say, carelessly, motoring to Santa Barbara. Can you beat it, she said to herself as she pulled a soft woolly white sweater over her head, me, Minnie Dixon, in a plane to New York? Personal appearances and interviews and a suite at a smart hotel and first nights and flowers and ermines. Dixon, old girl, it just ain't true. Any minute now you'll wake up back in that rooming house over on West Forty-fifth near the river—the one where you couldn't tell the rats from the horses, only the one was inside the house and the other outside.

She shivered a little, what with the memory of past days and consciousness of the present one—a foggy winter California morning. Her eyes were mere slits, her cheeks still creased from the pillow; her hair was combed carelessly back and away from her face in straight and stringy strands.

She knew it didn't matter. By half-past six she would be in the hands of the make-up man at the studio dressing room. Her face would be done, her hair redipped, curled, waved, dressed. Her underclothes, her shoes, her gowns, her hats, would be placed on her in exact duplication of their line and position the day before. Photographs, exact measurements, guided them.

A lick and a promise was what her mother would have called her morning method of dressing. Tweeds, sweater, brimmed sport hat, fur sport coat of nutria. Cold, driving down the canyon this time of day. The young things wore slacks to work—some of them not so darned young, either, she reflected. Minna said she guessed she was more the old-fashioned feminine kind, especially in the beam. Better leave the pants to the girls who needed the publicity.

She did not glance at herself in the many-mirrored room. Bad to get scared on an empty stomach, she told herself grimly. At that, I don't look much worse mornings than some of those kids driving down to work. Their public could see those baby lambs at 6 A.M., driving in from Santa Monica and Bel Air and Laurel Canyon and everywheres, with their golden curls all stringy and their eyes gummed shut and their noses red, I bet they'd be back home in Ashtabula with their dear ones in no time.

As she started down the stairs, the grateful scent of bacon and eggs was wafted up to her. Colly had made good her threat, as always. Breakfast on the table and there it stayed, hot or cold. It was the only way to cure her of tardiness. She hated cold eggs and lukewarm coffee. The hall clock grudgingly gave her four minutes for breakfast and nine minutes to drive down the canyon to the studio. Have to step on it.

A pile of last night's mail on the hall table. She did not stop. Secretary to take care of that. Past the open doorway of the big library and the drawing room beyond. She scarcely ever had time to set foot in them, much less relax in the depths of one of the great soft chairs or couches.

With the proceeds of her third picture she had bought the house out-right from a fallen star. "But take out that white bedroom and that white sitting room," she had said to the decorator. "They put me in mind of Kindlund's Undertaking Parlors back home. I want the place to be hand-some but comfortable, so every time you spill a cocktail you don't feel like you'd desecrated an altar."

She went on through the dining room, past the swinging doors into the butler's pantry and the kitchen. No one about at this hour but herself and Colly. It was so every working morning. If she was up at five-thirty, Colly was up at five. Her secretary slept, the houseman slept, the waitress slept, such waifs and derelicts as she always had as house guests slept. But Colly evidently had learned the secret of life and health without sleep. A hand-some black woman with immense vitality and the cooking gift; a mixture of Negro, Indian, and white blood. Her mother had solved the problem of nomenclature by simple process of calling this child Colorado, after that state in which she was born; Colly for short.

She was not deceived by the glittering ones of Hollywood, but surveyed their antics with a keen and merciless eye. An encyclopedia of moviedom, Colly knew the dates, duration, and intensity of every stellar love affair; scandal came to her by some grapevine route. She was something of a witch and was said to be able to predict with astronomical exactness the rise or fall of a star in the film constellation.

She had presided over a hundred palatial plaster households and had seen their owners crumble with the shoddy walls. Colly never worked for failures; was unsentimental, capable, and rumored to be writing her mem-oirs, which rumor caused considerable malaise in certain quarters; preferred solid, middle-aged mistresses to the flighty type of young-girl star.

"Don't know or care what they put in their stomachs so long's it keeps 'em thin. Lettuce leaf and orange juice, rye cracker and raw pineapple. I won't run no kitchen thataway. Time I stand an hour stirring a hollandaise smooth I want it et. And look the way they dress theirself! Slop around all day and night in pants and sweatshirts like hitchhikers."

On working days (which had been every day for the past ten months) Minna Dixon had her hasty breakfast at the kitchen table. A cup of coffee, a bite of toast, an egg, or a strip of bacon, eaten with utter disregard for digestion.

"Look, Colly, tell Miss Sanford to wire the hotel see if my trunks came. They ought to be there by now. Wouldn't it be awful if I got in by plane and no trunks? . . . Ouch! this coffee's hot! . . . Don't count on dinner; we'll probably be working till midnight. . . . What'll I look like taking that plane at nine tomorrow morning? . . . How about coming down to the dressing room, cooking me a little something hot at six; that commissary stuff makes me sick when I'm nervous and tired like this. . . . Oh, Colly, I wish you were going along to New York."

"You don't want no colored maid in and out, with them reporters interviewing you in New York, Miss Minna. No class. New York office'll fix you up with one those kind of mean, middle-age French ones in black can flat herself against the wall like a cat. Better git going now. 'Less I hear different I'll be down at six, but something light on account you don't want no upset stomach with that plane."

Eddie was there in the drive with the little car throbbing, his impassive mechanic's face opening the merest slit to return her greeting.

"I'm late."

"Yeah."

"Can you make it?"

"Foggy."

She turned up her coat collar. They shot out into the road, were off down the canyon. The gray fog that rolled in from the Pacific made a sea of the valley below. Beverly Hills had vanished; Los Angeles was a Pompeii buried under layers of gray. The palm trees were like horrible giant cormorants with their heads hidden in their bedraggled feathers.

Minna's eyes were puffy and red. They smarted under the sharp wet breeze. Cars flashed past her, whirred behind her. Like comic caricatures of their screen likenesses you saw them in their speeding motorcars emerging from the mists, the fog beading their eyelashes. The glamour boys and girls on their way to work at six in the morning; the villains and comics; the million-dollar babies; the English importations; the hoofers; sopranos from the Met, with mouths and noses swathed against the damp chill, wondering if it was worth even all that money.

From Laurel Canyon and Coldwater, from Santa Monica and Bel Air and Beverly Hills and Hollywood and Culver, in station wagons and sport cars; themselves hunched at the wheel in camel's-hair coats and mufflers, or solemnly under glass with chauffeurs in too-correct uniform. Every morning, every morning, in every kind of weather. Minna thought she knew every inch of the road from the house on the hilltop to the studio gates. Yet it still seemed unreal, after three months in the house, after three months of spectacular success.

After all, only ten months of Hollywood altogether.

That first tiny bit in *Visitors Ashore*. They had almost cut it out, had decided not to, and magically it had been the hit of the picture. A character part in *Over the Fence Is Out*.

They had rushed her into stardom after that, but bad as the picture was, she had got notices as good as even Crewe's in *You As in Yuma*. They had worked her like a truck horse, but she hadn't minded.

Pretty tired, though, she reflected, after this one. Maybe these ten days in New York wouldn't turn out to be such a hot idea, at that.

But the studio had wanted it, and Leider said her public expected it of her. New York. New York as she had never known it. Fifth Avenue instead of Eighth; Fifty-seventh Street instead of Fourteenth. It just couldn't be. It wasn't true.

Down Coldwater Canyon in the mist, past the firehouse, past the ivy wall (she liked that unexpected ivy, planted by someone with a nostalgia for the hardy, crisp North in a land of the lotus); past the Swiss chalet where the woman had killed herself with a chloroform-soaked cloth while her phonograph played on, record after record, for an hour in the room that was suddenly empty, though she still lay there.

There was Will Rogers' house that he'd never lived in, really, and now would never need to; and now you were on Sunset Boulevard and done with the Canyon drive. Over to Santa Monica Boulevard, turn right past the Hillcrest Golf Club. A shabby little yellow station wagon edged past them, scuttled ahead. A brown, bare hand flashed out in the briefest of passing salutes.

Dinah Crewe driving herself down to work.

"I'm taking the nine-o'clock plane for New York tomorrow, Eddie."

"That right?"

"Have you ever been East?" she asked.

"I was born East."

"Is that so! Where?"

"Kansas City."

The columns of the studio entrance loomed up ahead of them in the fog. The cynical face of Burke, the gateman, ex-detective and strong-arm, nodding his unsmiling greeting as they drove in. Harder for a stranger to pass Burke at the studio gates than for a tourist to pass a royal guard at Buckingham.

Minna leaned out, like a child. "I'm planing East tomorrow, Mr. Burke. You won't see me for another two weeks. New York."

The gimlet eye gave forth no fire. She slipped a bill into his hand. He did not look at it. "'Anks. New York, huh? Well, I've seen 'em go and I've seen 'em come back." Sinisterly he spat into the grit of the concrete.

Two hours of it, then. Two hours of that long and tedious daily process. Hair, nails, hands, face, clothes. Then on the set. Hours of retakes and waits, retakes and waits.

The waits were the worst. Ordinarily, a star would be expected to go back to her dressing room between waits. But in today's concentrated program the waits were too uncertain in length. They might be five minutes; they might be an hour. Besides, it was a lonesome business, going back to sit in your dressing room in stately solitude, with only your maid for company.

At first Minna had been dazzled by this luxurious apartment which they called a dressing room. It occupied a whole first-floor corner of the whitewashed building in this town of whitewashed buildings known as the studio. A reception hall in which Miss Sanford, the secretary, usually sat; living room, dining room, bedroom, dressing room, bathroom, kitchenette; flowers, books, sunshine, couches, pillows, mirrors.

"Dressing room!" Minna had said to Leider on that day when he had inducted her into stardom. He himself had escorted her to her new quarters on the lot; had shown her about with a flourish of the arms, like a magician waving an unseen wand. "My God, Mr. Leider, you ought to seen the ratholes I called dressing rooms when I was playing vaudeville. Half the size of that kitchenette there, no more window than the grave, and smelled like a zoo. Four to a dressing room if we was lucky."

Leider had raised a protesting palm and V-shaped eyebrows. "We will forget such topics like these, Miss Dixon. Such topics like these are things of the past."

She shook her head. "You can't take off your past, Mr. Leider, like you'd peel off a union suit."

The novelty of the dressing room had soon palled. She was a sociable woman, Minna; she liked people; she craved the warmth of human contact. She talked to everyone: cameramen, script girls, stand-ins, grips, gaffers, property men, carpenters, electricians, Alonzo the cop. She talked to the other actors in the picture, too, but they usually were off in a corner with a script and you could hear them mumbling a line over and over, like children trying to memorize an errand on the way to the grocery store. Eggs bread vanilla mustard; eggs bread vanilla mustard.

Dinah Crewe was the hardest of all to talk to. It wasn't that she was snooty, Minna told herself. It was just that she didn't seem to be there, kind of. Always reading a book or listening to one of the technicians, or studying something about lighting as if she were a cameraman instead of the most popular star in pictures. She came to work looking like a hired man going to the barn to milk—pants, sweater, wool shirt. Not the dressy kind of mannish stuff that those imported stars wore, but shabby duds that looked as if she'd borrowed them from her kid brother. Bet she had, at that.

Crewe was polite when you spoke to her. She would look up from her book or whatever she was so busy with, and she would answer you nicely enough. It wasn't that. Why, noontime she was as likely as not to eat in the big commissary with the electricians and cameramen, perched on a stool at the counter with a glass of milk in front of her.

Today, Minna Dixon found the waiting intolerable. Maybe I'm nervous about that plane trip, she thought. And that crowd in New York waiting for me. No, that'll be fun; that'll be swell; you're shot with luck, you old fool.

Crewe's maid had just handed her her powder puff, her make-up box; she was freshening herself for the next retake. Her book—a great fat volume—lay face down on the chair beside her. Minna strolled over to her, elaborately careless.

"I hear you're fl—uh—planing to New York tomorrow, too."

"I always fly." That clear young voice, that strong young voice. She stared with distaste into the hand mirror at the little flock of freckles across her nose.

"This'll be my first time."

"Really? What fun for you! Next year I'll have my own plane and a pilot's license. Then I won't have to wait for these poky old things."

"That'll be nice," Minna said feebly.

Crewe put down her mirror; her hand went toward the book. It was always, Minna had noticed, a fat book with big black letters on the cover that said *Napoleon* or *Biology* or *Psychology* or *Decline* of something. Another minute and Minna knew she would flash that little, friendly, fleeting smile and plunge again into the book.

"What you reading?"

"It's a book on perennials. Gardening."

"For land sakes! You like gardens?"

"Oh, yes. I have a darling garden in Connecticut."

"Connecticut. Yeah. That's the way, where you have to coax 'em. I always thought if I could have a garden, why, I'd be in heaven. A geranium in a tin can was a garden to me, those days. But I don't know; my garden here, it don't seem like flowers, somehow. No smell to them, and kind of fall to pieces like ashes, overnight. Same with trees. Acacia and pepper and palm and eucalyptus, but I'd swap 'em all for one good elm."

The girl nodded in agreement. "I know. I can't wait. It's been such a hard winter back East, they say the privet and box and ivy have suffered terribly. I can't wait till I get out to my farm in Connecticut to see if I've lost much."

Minna stared. "You mean when you get back to New York you're going to spend your vacation on a farm in Connecticut!"

"Well—perhaps not the whole time."

"I should hope not—young thing like you. I guess the crowds and the shops and the shows and all will look pretty good to you. Night clubs and dances."

"I never go near them. I hate crowds."

"Crowds is only people. You go round wearing those blue glasses all the time, hiding. You can't see the people's faces."

"I don't want to see their faces—the horrors!"

"Oh, now, look here, Miss Crewe. You get a kick out of being a big picture star, like the rest of us."

"I like playing in pictures, if that's what you mean."

"Pictures, yes, but I mean having 'em crazy about you."

"If you mean fan mail and the crowds gaping at you and the autograph fiends and the whole filthy bunk of publicity, I hate it."

Minna sat down, sociably. Here was the sort of conversation she liked. She smoothed the skirt of her dress with the ample gesture of one who is settled. "I guess you never knew what it was to be poor. And ugly. And nobody liking you. I'm so glad to have them even know me that I'll autograph anything from a tablecloth to a gas bill if they shove it at me. I love to have them like me."

The girl stared at this middle-aged woman with the look of an adult regarding a child. "You don't really think they care anything about you and me, do you?"

"Why, sure they do."

"And I know they don't. You wait. You'll see. We're just symbols to them—love or success or beauty or money or clothes or whatever it is they want. The things they used to believe in have—I don't know—something's happened to them. So they've set us up in their place, for a little while, each of us. It's a pretty thin time we've come to when millions of people have to idolize pieces of asbestos paper like us."

Abruptly the girl opened the volume on her knee.

"You been reading too many books, Miss Crewe. You've gone and read yourself right out of the real world, that's what."

"That isn't the world. When I'm making a picture, that's that. I give it everything I've got; I work as hard as I can. My own personal private life, that's my world. That's what I want. I want to be left alone. I've got my farm in Connecticut and my little house in New York, on the river. When I'm through in pictures, there they'll be. Why don't they let us live our own lives!"

The director, the cameramen, the electricians were coming out of their huddle. They would be ready for Dixon's scene in a minute. She stood up, beckoned her maid, who hastened to her with make-up box and mirror. She talked hurriedly as she peered at her own reflection.

"I don't want any personal life. Any woman wants to put her whole soul into a garden, or ordering two pounds of top round and be sure and throw in a piece of suet, is welcome to it. I had it, married to Ted Hainey. I had it even playing four a day on the small time. Nobody knew I was alive, or cared. If I hadn't showed up on the bill they'd have shoved in a trained seal or a Japanese acrobat and nobody'd have known the diff. No, sir! When I get to New York I want to do and see every single thing there is. Milt Marks says it'll be wonderful."

The look on Dinah Crewe's face then was one of purest pity. "Do you mean The Works? D'you mean you're letting them give you The Works!"

But Minna Dixon must go on the set. She turned away. "Quiet, please! Quiet, please!" from the assistant director. Minna was on. Through the brief scene she tried not to think of their conversation. Yet bits of things she wished she had said kept running through her head. Private life, huh? When I was first married to Hainey, and there I would be with the little hot dinner I'd about broke a leg to go out and buy and cook over the hot plate, and then him telephoning he couldn't make it, he had to see a fella owed him some money, and all the time I knew he was phoning from the N.V.A., shooting pool and drinking beer with the boys. I'll have to tell Crewe about that. Wonder what did she mean by The Works.

But the next scene was Dinah Crewe's. And then the girl seemed to vanish between scenes. She had a trick of vanishing, Minna had noticed. Next morning, for example. You wouldn't think that any human being could vanish in a transcontinental plane, but Dinah Crewe seemed never to be in sight. She had arrived five seconds before they took off. Minna Dixon meant to speak to her, but it wasn't until the plane was actually taxiing down the New York airport that she realized she hadn't seen her at all.

But then, the whole trip had been something of a blur to Minna. At first she had been scared. No one else seemed scared. Then she had been sick. No one else was sick. Albuquerque. Scared. Sick. Dallas. Kansas City. St. Louis. At each stop the newspaper reporters and the cameramen descended on her, a flock of them.

As the plane alighted, the little black figures came hopping and clustering about it, like crows about an eagle. And when Minna descended, a little dazed, a little sick, trying to look like an important and successful motion-picture star and realizing that she felt and looked like a wretched and travel-worn hag, they swarmed on her.

"Look this way, Miss Dixon! Hi, Miss Dixon, turn your head this way, willya? Give us a smile, Miss Dixon. Now, hold it!" She held it. She felt yellow green; her hat was askew; the cold wind whipped her skirts; her nose was red; the cameras clicked. "Hi, where's Crewe?" they demanded. "Where's Dinah Crewe?"

Crewe had vanished. How she did it was a mystery. She wasn't in the plane; she wasn't in the lunchroom at any port. "Do you know where Miss Crewe is, Miss Dixon? She's on this plane, isn't she?"

"She got on, anyway, at Los Angeles." Minna Dixon was a little fed up with the question. With the other questions too, for that matter. How do you like pictures? What's your new salary contract? Is it true they're giving you six thousand a week whether you work or not? Are you going to marry again? How much did that mink coat cost?

As they came nearer and nearer to the Eastern seaboard she noticed that the newspapermen and women became younger, harder, more pressing, less eager, tougher to answer. Is it true you left Ted Hainey and he starved to death? Are you a permanent fifty-nine? Where's Crewe? Where's Crewe? Have you seen Dinah Crewe?

New York was the worst. New York at five in the morning. Minna Dixon felt a thousand, and crippled. There they were, swarming on the plane at the airport. Their faces were haggard and unsmiling, their coat collars turned up; their hands were lean, gloveless, the first two fingers golden brown to the second knuckle.

"Hello, boys!" said Minna Dixon. "You're not going to take my picture now, are you? I look a sight. Have a heart! No woman is young enough to have her picture taken at five A.——"

They did not return her smile. Their faces were grim. There even seemed to her to be a touch of distaste in those stern young countenances. "Look, Crewe flew with you, didn't she?"

"Well, she got on at Los Angeles."

"Yeah, I told you," one of them said to the rest.

"All right, then, where the hell is she? She didn't parachute down, did she!"

A belated member of their company came up to the little group. A cigarette waggled between his lips as he talked. "She took a private plane from Pittsburgh. Just got a phone from Kearney."

"The little so-and-so."

They melted away. There was a little halfhearted clicking of cameras. Then the cameramen, too, vanished into the Jersey mist.

The bright luxury of the hotel suite. Brocade and crystal, rich strong coffee, pink roses in tall vases, a little heap of telegrams on the table, the roar of Park Avenue traffic outside. In the five-o'clock murk of the airport, Minna had firmly decided that, once in her hotel apartment, she would go to bed and sleep until noon at least. Strangely enough, she wasn't sleepy now. She wasn't even weary. She felt buoyant, gay. The early-morning sky was a brilliant blue, the fantastic buildings a dazzling white in contrast.

She decided to have a bath and then breakfast—not just coffee, but breakfast. Little hot rolls, and curls of butter; bacon; maybe an omelet; strawberry jam. Then she'd dress and go out and shop and look in the windows. To look in the windows on Madison and Fifth and know that she could buy the fabulous objects with which they were decked—that alone would be worth the trip to New York.

Her immersion in the tub was, apparently, the signal for the telephone. It rang with a New York shrillness and vitality, peal on peal on peal. Dripping and inadequately wrapped, "Who?" she said. "My what!"

"Your secretary and your maid are here. Do you want them to come up?"

The hall door left open a crack, a scurry back into her tub. Five minutes. A discreet cough from the sitting room, then an even more discreet knock at the bathroom door.

"Your breakfast is here, madame." That must be the French maid Colly had predicted. Wish it was Colly, Minna thought, all comfortable and knowing everything about everybody, the way she always does.

Telephones. Doorbells. The clink of china and silver. Voices. Scurryings. Telephone bells. Telephone bells. In dressing gown and slippers Minna Dixon entered her hotel sitting room to a scene which was a publicity man's dream. Flowers in boxes and vases and bowls. The mean, middle-aged French one in black who could flat herself against the wall like a cat was there, exactly as specified. And there was a neat secretary in knitted jersey. And there were two boys with very young faces and old eyes. These leaped at her, shook her hands, grinned, said it was wonderful to see her, said she was wonderful, said everything was wonderful, got out notebooks, and began to read off an astounding program.

"Now, just a minute," interrupted Minna Dixon. "If it isn't asking too much—who are you?"

The slightly older one now seemed covered with boyish confusion, and turned on all his charm, which was considerable. "Oh, Miss Dixon. How awful! We feel we know you so well through your wonderful—— I guess we took for granted you knew we were the New York office publicity—— Look, this is Ott Spring, my assistant; that's Miss Schwerin, your secretary while you're here, I hope she'll be—I'm sure she—— That's the maid—uh—Louise—and I'm Dicky Kane. I guess you've—— Well, it doesn't m——"

"All right, Dicky, all right. I just thought I'd ask. Does anybody want

breakfast? Well, then, **Louise**, you go in and open those trunks, will you?
Here's the keys. Miss Sch—uh—Schwerin, is it?—thanks—Schwerin, will
you take a look at those telegrams and flower cards and mail and so on——"

"Oh, that's all right," Dicky Kane interrupted. "That's stuff we arranged,
Ott and I. Look, I believe I will have a cup of coffee, at that. Up at the crack
of dawn. Thanks. Three lumps. How about you, Ott?" Ott thought not.

Minna Dixon took another bite of buttered roll, but thoughtfully. "Arranged?" She looked around the flower-laden room; she saw Miss Schwerin
ripping her orderly way through telegrams, letters, cards. "Is that what
Dinah Crewe meant when she s——"

Ott, the silent, spoke at last. "That one! Look. Wouldn't even see **me**.
Wouldn't come to the telephone. Wouldn't——"

"Shut up, Ott," said Dicky Kane. "Ott isn't quite bright, Miss Dixon.
Crewe pretends to hate publicity. She'll suffer for it. You can't treat 'em
that way. They'll turn on her. The public won't stand for it."

"Merely the biggest draw in pictures, that's all Crewe is." Things went
more smoothly, perhaps, when Ott did not speak.

"Look, Ott, go away, will you? There's enough stuff waiting for you at
the office, without your making a nuisance of yourself here. Go on, beat it."

"Nuts to you. I sold a piece to a magazine. Who wants to be a slick press
agent? Goo'by, Miss Dixon. I'll call for you at seven-fifteen sharp tomorrow night." Was gone.

"Call for me?" She turned a bewildered face toward the urbane Dicky
Kane. "Look here, what are you two kids up to, anyway? What kind of
monkeyshines are you pulling up here? Who do you think——"

He flipped the pages of a small notebook. "Oh, that's all right, Miss
Dixon. He's taking you on tomorrow night—dinner and show and supper
or night club if you want it. I take you tonight, see? Now, then, any special shows you want to see? Of course I've already arranged for the important openings, and so on. How about furs?"

"Furs?" echoed Minna. She noticed that Miss Schwerin, too, had taken
out a little notebook.

"Yeah, for evening. Noticed you've got a mink for daytime. Anything
for evenings? Ermine, white-fox cape, chinchilla wrap, silver fox, sables?"

"Ten months in pictures and only four or five in the money. Where do
you think I——"

Miss Schwerin here began to read from her notebook, even before the
nod of assent from Dicky Kane. "Slott says he'll send an ermine swagger.
Barré Frères, a sable coat, but says we'll have to pay half the insurance for
each night used. Littendorf, a white-fox, full-length tiered cape. That's the
one, I'd say. More showy. I wouldn't bother with chinchilla. It's old-

fashioned, and anyway always looks like old sweetbreads, my idea of it."

"How about it, Miss Dixon? What do you say to the ermine for tonight, and the sable for tomorrow night, and then the white-fox full-length for the big Gordon opening on Saturday night?"

"I never wore borrowed clothes in my life. If I couldn't have a thing I went without."

"Oh, but this is different. Isn't that so, Miss Schwerin?" Miss Schwerin said it certainly was. "Your public expects you to look like a million dollars, and these fur people are happy to have you appear in their garments. Now, then. The newspapers showed up, didn't they, all along the route? The reporters and cameramen and so on? I wired them."

"Yes," Minna said. Somehow, it wasn't the same. She had staggered out of the plane and had talked to them and posed for those pictures because she had thought they wanted her to; because she was important, because the world wanted to see her and hear about her. "Listen, Mr.—uh—listen, I think if you folks'll excuse me I'm going to take a walk and kind of look around. I haven't seen New York since——"

"Oh, you can't do that! Here's the schedule. You check with me, Miss Schwerin, see if it's O.K. Bunch of afternoon-paper people coming in for a feature interview at eleven. That gives you an hour or more to get yourself dolled up. The first-string motion-picture daily-paper editors are asked for lunch right here. Ten of 'em. The bunch that's coming in for tea and cocktails isn't so important. The magazine crowd tomorrow lunch.

"Fashion sittings—hats, shoes, dresses, gloves, jewelry—that'll have to wait over until day after tomorrow, I guess. Check that, Miss Schwerin. We thought we'd go out for the older-woman kind of thing—not try to be young—the best-dressed woman among the—uh—more mature movie stars, see? The fashion magazines will tell you what to wear. They'll have the stuff. All you'll have to do is put it on and pose.

"Now. The fan-magazine editors end of the week, I guess, unless they get sore at having to wait. They'll want—you know—are you ever going to marry again? Does a career and success make up for a life alone? Better let me write you the stuff for that, and you learn it. Let's see, now. Where were—oh, yes—we've got three radio outlets. You'll have an interview with Sadie Norris on her hour, and guest star with Buddy Powell on his. They want you in a sketch with Georgie Hawkes and Lee Devine, but we're holding out for three thousand——

"May throw a big cocktail party, but those things aren't so hot any more, and besides, they don't get a chance for the personal stuff with you. . . . Steer off that stuff about your personal life. . . . And of course I'll be taking you to the shows one night and Ott the next all the time you're here, unless there's somebody you'd . . . and you wouldn't want to be seen with just anybody because naturally your public . . ."

The Works.

Minna asserted herself finally, but not with her usual vigor. She felt bewildered, beset. "What's the use of seeing all these people unless they want to see me?"

"Huh? Oh. Uh—they do! Sure they do! They're crazy about you, Miss Dixon. Say, you're the big new sensation in pictures. You wait. The papers'll look like a Dixon special edition tonight."

"But I thought I'd like to go around alone a little—the place—the rooming house where I used to live over on Ninth Avenue."

He rose to go. His thoughts seemed already to be on something more remote and rare than the plans for this flustered, middle-aged woman. Something in Miss Schwerin's rigid attitude—an emanation of disapproval that was like a spoken warning—brought the words to him after they had ceased to sound. "What? No. No, don't do that. That's no good any more. Rags to riches. They don't like it. Well, Miss Schwerin here and Louise'll take care of you. The boys will be here at eleven. I'll be back."

The boys did not come together. Their interview hours had been arranged, one at a time—staggered, they called it. The boys turned out to be not at all the gay and roistering blades of the press as shown in stage and fiction. Quiet, they were, and almost sinister. Their eyes swept her, swept the apartment and all its contents, with the cold raking thoroughness of a searchlight. The men were boys in wool mufflers and careless clothes; and with Eastern-college accents. The girls were young and sharp and pretty, but not like the California girls. There was an edge to them.

Minna wanted to talk about her work, about her house, about California. "Well, it's wonderful. People who say California isn't wonderful have got me to fight. I've got a swimming pool—course I'm no bathing beauty, but just the same—tennis court—roses—my new picture——"

But they brushed this aside. "Are you going to get married again? How much did that dress cost? Is it true you go around with a twenty-year-old movie actor named Pedro Sandro?"

The good-humored, comic face had the hurt look of a child who has been struck by a hand she had trusted. An uncertain smile that was little more than a grimace seemed pasted precariously on the wide mouth.

Still, it was wonderful—at first—to walk along the city's streets. The blue of the January sky was so different from the blue of California. The shops were richer in spoils than those of any other city in the world. The finest pelts, the rarest jewels, the most lustrous fabrics were piled in unbelievable profusion in this, the greatest of bazaars.

In Beverly Hills one never saw a soul on the streets, but here everyone walked briskly, head up. The women were smart with a sort of uniform richness: mink coats or broadtail with enormous silver-fox scarfs; exquisite shoes; handmade hats, so unlike the sloppy informality of Hollywood's streets, with the women's curly heads burnished but unbrushed; hatless, rouged, in cotton print pajamas.

As Minna walked up Fifth Avenue or Madison there accompanied her a little murmur of recognition. She loved it. They made no effort to drop their voices. "Look! That's Minna Dixon . . . Minna Dixon . . . Dixon . . ."

Minna smiled on them in a friendly way. Curiously, they did not return the smile. They stopped or turned to look after this woman whom they had recognized, and it was as if they were weighing her, estimating her. Their faces were as expressionless and staring as the faces of fish in a bowl: goggle-eyed, open-mouthed.

Following the publication of the newspaper interviews and special articles, they were gathered outside the hotel when she emerged, and at theater openings they massed themselves at the curb. They were, for the most part, young boys and girls. This made her happy, in the beginning. They set upon her with their books, with their scraps of paper, with their pens and pencils.

But it came to the friendly, flattered woman that there was about them a very expert and businesslike quality. They thrust their pens and pencils at her with a hard ruthlessness. It was almost impersonal, though they touched her, talked to her.

"Here," they commanded. "Sign here. Do this one." They almost guided her hand; their eyes were hard and keen; it was as if they were collecting her autograph as one would add stock to a business.

When she stepped out of the motorcar in front of the theater, with the voluble Dicky or the less suave Ott Spring as escort, they would press about her.

"Hello, kids!" Minna would say heartily, liking it. Still, she wished they wouldn't push and shove quite so roughly. "Hello! Wait a minute, dearie. Ouch!" Two of them had trod on her feet. She wrote her name for all of them on anything they thrust at her. Hundreds of them.

Their gaze was coldly devouring. The emotionally starved, middle-aged woman read into it the warmth and friendly affection she craved.

"Ain't it wonderful!" she said to Ott or Dicky, barging breathless through the crowd. "Hi, look out, sonny! You're tearing the coat off me."

"Yeah," the saturnine Mr. Spring would say, or the too-sprightly Kane. "Yeah, it's wonderful, all right."

Minna Dixon would adjust her wrap, set herself for her entrance down the aisle to those two good first-night seats in Row C. A grand feeling to know that millions of people love you.

She did not confess to herself that the New York visit of triumph had lacked something. Yet on the last night of this ten-day holiday she was conscious of a feeling of relief that it was nearly over. A strangely haggard and dull-eyed Dixon she was, emerging from the Booth Theater, where the first night of *Avalanche* had just been launched. She thought, as she wrapped the borrowed ermines about her, Well, Dixon old girl, back to the mines. That house up there on the hill, and Colly, and even the palm trees will look pretty good, after this. I don't know. Maybe I expected too much.

Dicky Kane was thinking his own thoughts. A tough ten days, lugging the old girl around. But not much worse than the young ones, at that. She got a kick out of it, anyway. Bet she still believed in Santa Claus.

There they were, out on the sidewalk, the autograph hounds, jostling the outcoming theater crowds, pushing, shoving; scavengers of fame. The first of them elbowed his way toward her. Minna adjusted her little smile, a tarnished copy of the bright thing it had been a fortnight ago. But even as she graciously took the grimy pad and pencil from the boy's hand, another hand grasped his arm; a raucous voice, shrill with excitement of the chase, screamed in his ear, heedless of the fact that she, too, heard.

"Crewe's next door at the Plymouth! Scud seen her!"

"Ya, she never goes to openings."

"It ain't a opening. That's why she's there. He seen her comin' out. C'mon, you nut. Whaddyha want wit' 'at old bag! You can get her autograph any time. She's all washed up, anyway."

Trees Die at the Top

[1937]

Madam was in bed. Evidently she had been there ever since this luxury train started its northbound journey from Florida. I got aboard at South Carolina; New York was our destination. She and her husband and assorted children were occupying what amounted to quite a spacious New York apartment in one of the cars. I had a cocktail with them in their drawing room before dinner, surrounded by such luxury of silken sheets, books, trays, pillows, flowers as to give the impression that this Pullman car was her permanent home.

This doubtless gave impetus to the working plan for this long short story. For years, gazing out of the car window on trains between New York and California or Chicago and Denver, I had been fascinated by what I saw—magnificence and squalor; beauty and hideous sordidness; mountains and plains and prairies. Behind this interest was a feeling of concern about the fantastic luxury in which a large part of the United States seemed to be cushioned at the time.

The wagon train of 1849 and the streamliner of 1939 began their parallel journey in my mind—one day, one month; two days, two months; three days, three months. Perhaps, one day soon, we of the three-day supertrain will seem like hardy pioneers to the passenger winging his way from New York to San Francisco in an hour or two.

~§ THERE WAS NO DOUBT ABOUT IT THIS TIME. OLD JARED CONTENT WAS dying. High time, too. He had been almost a century at it. All that vitality, all those millions, could not save him now. He had clung to both long after he had any real use for either, the family thought (privately). The San Francisco newspapers had had his obituary filed away in their morgues for half a century and more. The men who had written it and rewritten it were themselves dead and gone while old Jared lived triumphantly on, grown to fabulous age and rugged grandeur, like one of California's native sequoia trees.

Like all good San Franciscans, he had only contempt for that part of California which lay south of his beloved city. For years, relatives and friends and physicians had tried to coax him out of the fogs and cold of Russian Hill to the sun-drenched groves of the lower country. He had resisted them with all the strength of his formidable will. The heady air of San Francisco, its scud and winds and hard, rare sun were elixir to him. It was, he said, the most civilized city in the United States, and San Franciscans themselves were a race of gods who had vanquished the elements; conquered the desert, harnessed the ocean, wrung gold from the mountains, and built their own Olympus on the seven hills.

"Look at 'em!" he had been known to shout, brandishing his arms in the midst of Post Street traffic, to the bewilderment of the throngs of passersby. "Where else do you find men like that! And women like goddesses! Walk like race horses, and cheeks like cream and roses. . . . Don't talk to me about Los Angeles. They're all pulp and thick yellow skin down there, like their damned sour oranges."

When that first blow struck him at ninety-five, depriving him of speech and of locomotion, they had carried him, helpless, to the south. There, by a miracle of sheer will, he had partially regained his powers. They said it was the sun and the solitude (both of which he always had hated). He knew it was his iron determination not to die out of sight of his own golden hills and the Golden Gate spread before his vast bedroom window. Like a figure out of the New Testament he took up his bed and walked. Safely back in his beloved San Francisco, clearheaded and undeceived, he made ready for the second blow which he well knew might be the last. He thought about the family, not sentimentally, but with the same grim detachment with which he surveyed his own approaching end.

They had not come to him. On one pretext or another they had stayed away from what they must have thought to be his deathbed. Eager for him to die and get it over with, like those scavenger birds that hover at a distance, wings spread, waiting for the final tremor to cease before they swoop on their prey. Fooled 'em, he thought; but not triumphantly. He had been generous enough with the Content millions, but he had had, too, an old-fashioned notion that these offspring of pioneer people should make their own way, partially at least. Well, they had. But his own holdings had pyramided there in the West: mines, banks, real estate. Mansions had gone up where shanties had stood; skyscrapers had mushroomed on the mansion sites. Old Jared had been canny and courageous. To trace the source of those attributes you would have needed to do no more than to glance at the faded tintypes of his father, Jared Content, and his mother, Tamsen. Hadn't he, a lad of seven, made with them the incredibly courageous journey overland inch by inch in '49?

There were strangely few branches of this dying giant tree. Through almost a century he had seen them wither and fall, and now he, the topmost branch, gnarled and sapless, was about to crash. There was left his widowed daughter, nearing seventy, herself more helpless than he, living in Santa Barbara, renegade San Franciscan that she was. There were two grandsons only; five great-grandchildren. The East had claimed them— Chicago and New York. One by one, the family had deserted him, so that he was like a lone eagle now in his eyrie on the hill overlooking the bay. Yet their very being had come out of San Francisco. Old Jared had never ceased to be bewildered at their leaving it.

Let them come back to it now, he thought. Let them see what lay between the Atlantic and the Pacific. He had seen it at seven, every step of it, every inch of it; not only that, he had walked a good bit of it on his own sturdy little legs. After almost a century of living, that journey remained his clearest memory. His actual will had been made long ago, an amazingly brief and simple document for the disposal of riches so vast. This he would not alter.

"But let them come and get it," he said, "the whole kit and boodle of 'em. Grandchildren and great-grandchildren. Have that a provision of the will. I'll make them see this country, by God, if I have to die to do it."

His speech, once so vigorous, was strangely thick and painful now, but his meaning was as plain as his words were homely and American. So the lawyers wrote it down and he signed it with his own great fist, once so powerful, now grown so reluctant. Let them come back to pay final homage, not to him, but to a continent which they took for granted and to a city which they had flouted.

Two weeks later the second blow struck, paralyzing him almost completely, so that he lay like a lightning-struck old sequoia. Still miraculously alive, the muted face wore a look not of defeat but of triumph.

FIRST NIGHT

Mrs. Jay Content said she wouldn't fly. Not with the children. Furious at the summons, she put it plainly. Frances Content was not a word mincer at any time. "I don't care whose grandfather, or how nearly dead, and how many millions depend on it—though heaven knows we need them. I won't fly across the continent with the children."

They had just opened the house in Lake Geneva for the summer. Luckily, late in the day though it was, they were able because of Jay's influence to get what even Frances Content considered proper accommodations on the San Francisco Streamliner out of Chicago for that night at six-fifteen. Frances Content prided herself on not being a nagging wife, but she allowed herself a decent meed of protest in the few frenzied hours preceding their departure for the West. She unburdened herself as she and Jay and

Turkey, the children's nurse, and Katharine, her maid, plunged into the grim business of packing. Jay was studying neckties, surveying each one with passionate intensity before stowing it reverently in the case.

"I think his mind is gone. I don't want to hurt your feelings, Jay, but really! Dragging little children across a continent for a dying old man's whim. You'd think, wouldn't you, that in a hundred years of living he'd have learned something about life?"

"Not quite a hundred."

"Ninety-five, then. What's the difference! And just to hear his will read while he's alive! I never heard of such a thing. It makes me all creepy. . . . Two thousand miles in this heat. I know they're air-conditioned, but just the same . . . Miss Turck, did they absolutely promise to have the twelve quarts of Grade A certified milk down at the train? I can't have the children drinking that wretched train stuff. . . . We'll reach San Francisco half dead ourselves, and he'll probably meet us hale and hearty. He'll live to be one hundred and fifty. . . . Jay, for heaven's sake, don't take that red necktie, you know you can't wear red at a f—— Miss Turck, pack their light sweaters right on top where you can get at them first thing. . . . Yes, it's blazing here, but the train's air-cooled and you can get pneumonia and Tam had a little sniffle yesterday. . . . If that child's going to develop hay fever . . . Look, Jay, I think it would be a good idea to have Griswold stop in at Tebbett's and pick up some of that wonderful smoked salmon and smoked sturgeon and we could give it to the chief steward to put on ice. Train food is so horrible."

"I like it," said Jay Content. "Planked whitefish and chicken potpie and raisin muffins." He stowed a bottle of rye and a bottle of Scotch in the capacious maw of his pigskin bag. "Stuff you never get at home."

"You wouldn't touch it at home. . . . Katharine, I'll take my Persian-lamb sport coat; it's freezing in San Francisco after five. . . . The minute the children and everything are settled on the train I'm going to bed and not get up for twenty-four hours."

"Only takes thirty-six to get there."

"Thirty-six! And I hate the very smell of a train. Honestly, Jay, if we hadn't been so broke these last few years, and all those millions of his, and the children's future to think of, I'd just refuse to go at all!"

Jay was big, sandy-haired, ruddy, and as much the American husband as this black-haired, gray-eyed Frances was the managing and arrogant American wife. But Jay Content was no worm, and he had his quiet humor.

"That's my brave little pioneer woman," he said, and snapped his bag shut.

"Oh, pioneers!" As Frances said it, it sounded like an epithet.

They made quite an imposing procession this steaming July evening as they crossed the Chicago Northwestern station platform to their train. Of course, Griswold, the chauffeur, wasn't going along, nor Miss Kennedy, Jay's secretary, but they were there in their last-minute official capacity, and working at it. Turck, with little Tam (Tamsen, after her great-great-grandmother) and Jerry (Jared IV, but too confusing); Katharine, the maid; Mr. and Mrs. Content; and a squad of porters carrying such a variety and profusion of bags, boxes, bundles, tins, cases, and toys as to give the parade the look of a safari on the march.

Miss Turck, Tam, and Jerry had the drawing room. Jay Content's compartment adjoined it. Mrs. Content's was just next to that. Thus protected, she would not hear the children's early-morning clamor. When the doors were open right through, the three little rooms gave the effect of quite a spacious apartment on wheels. Katharine had a lower in the next car. They pulled out at six-fifteen in such a welter of Chicago July heat as to make the train's cooled interior a haven.

Within half an hour they had practically set up housekeeping. Frances Content was a wonderful manager. Everything shipshape. She and Miss Turck and Katharine made short work of it. The children's hats, coats, the garments they would need next day, the sleeping garments for tonight, all were hung in the little clothes cupboard so cleverly set into the room. Mrs. Content's clothes were similarly bestowed. The Persian-lamb coat, being bulky, was hung behind the door in the room proper, all swathed in a clean sheet provided by the porter. As the great metal train took curves at high speed the sheeted thing swooped out like a wraith to snatch her. There were the necessary jars and bottles that Mrs. Content needed. Katharine placed these on the glass shelves in the medicine cabinet sunk in the wall. Katharine did a hundred things, but then Mrs. Content was terribly busy, too. She glanced in at her husband, to see how he was getting on with his unpacking. "Need any help, dear? I'm up to my ears just now, but later Katharine could——"

But he was deep in the Chicago *Evening News*. "My stuff's all out. Everything I need."

"The children are going to have their supper. They're late."

"I'll be in to see them before they go to bed."

"Turkey's taking them into the diner because he's making up their room. I wish you'd go in and see to them. I'm too exhausted to cope. It always helps to—uh—see the chief steward, and we've got that stuff to put on ice. Tam's never been in a diner before; she may bully Turck into giving her ice cream or something instead of egg and applesauce."

"Bully Turck! Nobody could." But he went. Early though it was, the dining car was crowded. Mr. Wiener, the chief steward, was making a great to-do about pulling out chairs and thrusting menus under people's noses, while the colored waiters, dexterous, flexible, tray-laden, swam in and out of the aisle with the agility of porpoises.

Turck, with Tam beside her and Jerry seated opposite, had a fourth at their table in the person of a large blond lady in pink. The children were starry-eyed and flushed with excitement. Tam, the seeker after truth, was pointing with a relentless finger and saying with terrible distinctness, "Why is that lady sitting at our table?"

"Sh-sh-sh, Tam. Eat your egg."

"But why is she! I don't like her. Make her go away."

Jay to the rescue. He stood beside the table. "How are you doing, Miss Turck? Children all right?" He turned to the pink blonde; he smiled his winning smile. "I hope they're not annoying you."

She looked up at him. Widower? The white mask of fury was miraculously transformed into dimpled tenderness. "I just love kiddies."

"That's fine. Their mother is tired, so I came in to see how they were getting along."

"Pahdon me, suh, pahdon me, suh." He was obstructing a waiter, fearfully laden.

The mask of hate, stiffened by disillusion, again slipped down over the blonde. "Pity she couldn't spare the time to teach her kids manners, if their nurse can't."

"Look, waiter, see that they get everything they want. Let me speak to the chief steward."

"Chief's busy, suh. You kin'ly step outta the aisle?" A dollar bill thrust into his mauve palm. "Yessah, Cap'n. Ah get'm for you. Just step up the end of the car. Yes*suh!* Mistah Wienah!"

"Are you on to the end of the run?" Jay was taking no chances with Mr. Wiener.

"Yes, sir." Mr. Wiener was distrait, what with his duties and his sense of importance. "All the way to 'Frisco."

Ten dollars for Mr. Wiener. "Look, we're in the drawing room and compartments B and C in Car 69. The porter's got some stuff to put on ice. All right?"

"Certainly, certainly. Anything. Now, would you like your dinner here, or served in your drawing room? Would you like to order now?"

"I'll eat here, later. Mrs. Content will probably come in with me when she's rested. Seven-thirty, say."

"Fine. Fine. What's the name? I didn't catch——"

"Content. Jared Content. Chicago."

"Ho! Well! Say! Content! I should think everybody . . . I'll save a nice table for you and the madam, seven-thirty. Now then, could I make a couple little suggestions, Mr. Content? We get to Omaha about two in the morning. And there we take on for our special passengers some of the grandest little beef tenderloins you ever sunk a tooth in. Special Omaha prize beef. Sweet," Mr. Wiener assured him earnestly, "as sugar. We serve 'em for breakfast, just to special people, you understand, on hot toast. No bigger than this. Two bites a piece, about four pieces a portion. The tastiest little breakfast dish you ever ate. Melt in the mouth."

Jay Content swallowed. "That sounds great. Not for Mrs. Content, though. She eats very lightly in the morning."

"Now, at Cheyenne we take on fresh-caught mountain trout hustled down specially for us, caught that morning; we serve 'em for lunch, just about two three dozen altogether; they eat like butter, sauté meunière, lemon parsley, and lyonnaise potatoes. The madam won't say no to those."

A lot you know about what the madam will say no to, Jay thought. He waved to Miss Turck and to Tam, who had a spoon in her mouth, very far down. Arrived at the vestibule of his Car 69 (it was named Winnemucca, he noticed, with some distaste), he stopped and drew a deep breath and lighted a cigarette. The vestibule was fantastically hot in contrast to the cars through which he had passed. It was like the withering breath that came from the open hearth of the Gary steel mills in which so much of his money lay sunk these last seven years. He was enough of a sensualist to welcome the outdoor heat of the vestibule so that he might the more relish the cool of the car. He leaned there, swaying easily with the motion, watching the Illinois prairie landscape flashing by in a torrid July haze. The Old Boy's money must have shrunk with everybody else's. The damned income tax and probably a lot of bad paper. Inheritance tax would take a fierce bite out of it, too. Must be a little cuckoo. Frances probably right. Making them come and watch him die, like royalty. If you failed to show up, you were out of the will, eh? Bet you could break a will like that on the grounds of mental incompetence. Magnificent old devil, at that. Across the continent in a covered wagon when he was no more than Jerry's age. Guts, that crowd. Suppose he and Frances and Jerry and Tam . . . Heat, dust, desert. Oxen. Mountains. He looked out at the shimmering farmlands, exhaled, dropped his cigarette, and carefully stepped on it. As he entered 69 the cool air was as refreshing as water to one thirsty.

Frances was standing before the mirror in his compartment, creaming her face. She looked as lovely as a Benda mask with all that smear of white,

and her dark smooth hair and deep-set gray eyes. The porter, aided by
Katharine, was making up her room for the night, though outside was
brilliant summer daylight.

"What in the world, Jay! I thought you were never coming back. Are
they all right?"

"Sure. They're seeing life. Good for 'em. The chief steward said he'd
have a table for us. Oh, damn, I forgot to tell him to send me a bottle of
water. Heh, porter! Bottle of water. How about a little drinkie, Mrs. C.,
before dinner?"

"I wouldn't go in to dinner tonight," said Mrs. C., patting cream, "if I
were starving to death. I may get up for dinner tomorrow night, if I feel
rested. I'm having my dinner in bed."

"Oh. Well." He was disappointed. He hated eating alone. "How about
ordering, then? I'll tell them. What do you want?"

"I'll have a tiny highball with you before you go in. Just cold chicken—
white meat—and chicory salad. Tell them oil, lemon, ice, and a bowl.
Katharine will mix it; their dressing is always foul. I might have some
cream cheese and a jar of Bar-le-Duc, with salt wafers. Katharine will heat
me some milk at ten."

Katharine now knocked discreetly at the open door. "It's all made up,
madam." Frances, still patting, passed into her own room. Scotch or rye,
said Jay, in the doorway. Her room was indeed made up. The drab Pullman bed had become a couch of luxury. Her own pale-peach crepe-de-
Chine sheets scenting the air delicately with heliotrope; a nest of peach
pillows, hemstitched; her own satin-edged, summer-weight blanket neatly
sheathed in a silk slip; her plainest little tailored bed jacket laid out.

The children were coming along the corridor. Tam was squealing, Jerry
was roaring, Miss Turck was saying "Children, children" in her clipped
Canadian accents. "Oh, dear, they're on the rampage. I knew it." Frances
tied tighter the cord of her robe and prepared to do battle in the drawing
room. She passed through Jay's room into theirs. Jay was mixing the high-
balls and whistling softly between his teeth.

"Let Turkey wrestle with them."

The unwonted excitement, the unusual hours, had got them completely
out of hand. They bounced on the beds, they splashed water, pressed push
buttons, turned on the electric fan, yelled. Tam suddenly remembered a
dreadful dismembered doll which she always took to bed with her, and
whose mangled remains had been forgotten in the rush of packing. She
now set up a keening that could be heard in the next car. Turck gathered
her up.

"Just let me cope, Mrs. Content. I'll quiet them. Not so many people is better. . . . Sh-sh. . . . Look, she's asleep." Tam had indeed gone off in the middle of a sob. "Jerry, you haven't brushed your teeth. See, you're to sleep up there, and a little fence thing to keep from falling out. . . . No, it isn't a baby crib. Nothing of the kind. Only big boys can sleep way up there." A tower of strength, Miss Turck; fortyish, neat blue-gray uniform, sensible flat oxfords with rubber heels, broad, flat fingernails with little white flecks in them; a bosom, flat, too, and composed of some wooden material like a Japanese pillow, unyielding; fine on formulae; Jerry and Tam were exactly the proper weight for their years.

"Oh-o-o-o-o!" breathed Mrs. Content, closing the drawing-room door behind her, thus shutting it off from Jay's room. "No," as he offered her a frosty glass, "not here. I'm going to get into bed first. Bring it to me, dear. I'm exhausted. Simply sunk."

"How about a bite of that smoked salmon with your highball? I'll tell the steward. It'll give you an appetite for your chicken, later."

He saw her settled among her pillows with her book and a bottle of fresh-smelling toilet water and a mild highball. The little room, cool, perfumed, had actually taken on an air of elegance.

"Well, Fran, I think I'll go in and have my dinner." He glanced about the compartment. "Got everything you want?" The American husband, hugging his chains. "The waiter will be along with your tray any minute now. I've got the chief steward all buttered up."

By the time he had finished dinner it was nearly nine, but the Western sky was still aglow. Luckily he had met two men he knew. The three had dined together and had sat smoking and talking for an hour after that in the club car. The radio was on and they heard the late evening news from Chicago and New York. There was among the passengers a table or two of bridge. Others were deep in books or magazines. Jay Content was pleasantly tired, but not sleepy. The thought of his own bedroom did not appeal to him; stuffy; and besides, no place to sit, and Frances probably asleep. He'd turn in at eleven and read for an hour or so. It was agreeable talking about business, Roosevelt, Europe, recovery, taxes, politics, golf. At eleven they broke up. Well, mighty nice running into you like this. . . . See you tomorrow. . . . Might have a little bridge. . . . How long you going to be in 'Frisco, Jay? . . . Well, hard to say. Not long. My grandfather's very sick, dying, in fact. . . . Well, say, I'm sorry to hear that. Lives out there, does he? . . . Oh, yes, he's an old settler. Crossed the country with his parents in a covered wagon when he was a kid. They were Forty-niners, you know, my great-grandparents. . . . Is that right! Well, great stock, that bunch. Yessir, it took guts. . . . Well, see you tomorrow."

The door between his room and hers was open; her lights were on. "Jay!

Jay, we've had the most awful time with Jerry. I was going to send for you, and then I hated—— He won't go to sleep, he's keeping Tam awake, Turck can't do a thing with him, it's overexcitement, he keeps hanging his head over the edge of the berth, if the train lurches he'll dash out his brains——"

The drawing room was a shambles. Even Miss Turck had a wild look. The boy's eyes were at once brilliant and heavy, his black hair stood on end, his legs were in the air, and he was enjoying the novelty of paddling his bare feet against the car ceiling from the vantage point of the upper berth. He was balancing on his head to do so.

Jay Content gathered the boy up, blanket and all. "Come on, son. We menfolks will go off by ourselves a little while, shall we?"

"Jay, what——" she called from her room as he entered his.

He closed the drawing-room door behind him, leaving Turck and Tam in peace. "Go to sleep, France. Never mind, we're all right. I'll attend to this. You go to sleep." He shut the door between his room and hers, laid the boy on the bed, and covered him. He took off his suit coat, got into his dressing gown, and lay down beside him, cozily. "Let's talk. What'll we talk about, son?"

"Indians."

"Indians!"

"That lady at supper, the one at our table, said everything around here used to be Indians, they were all the way to California, they used to sneak up at night and cut the tops of people's heads off with the hair on and wear it, and they shot arrows with poison on the end and you died."

"She did, eh? Well, a lot of the Indians were pretty decent, considering what the white people did to them. Your great-grandfather that we're going to San Francisco to see was just about your age when he went from Illinois to California. His father and mother took him and his little sister. His father's name was Jared Content, like yours, and his mother's name was Tamsen, like Tam's. We keep on naming people Jared and Tamsen in our family. That was almost a hundred years ago, before there was a railroad or anything. Come to think of it, they made almost the same trip that you and Mother and Tam and I are making now, only they didn't have soft beds to sleep in, and waiters and cooks and electric lights and hot water. It took them three months."

"Will it take us three months?"

"No, son. We'll be there day after tomorrow. They traveled all the way, over prairie and desert and mountains, in a prairie schooner."

"What's a prairie schooner? You're fooling. I know a schooner's a boat; you can't go over mountains in a boat."

"This wasn't a boat; it was a big wagon. They called it a prairie schooner because the top of the wagon was canvas and it made a kind of round tent. . . ."

FIRST MONTH

The top of the wagon was canvas and made a kind of round tent. There were scores of them drawn up here at Independence, Missouri. They billowed white against the prairie horizon like waves of the ocean. Not that she had ever seen an ocean. Here they were, bound for the Pacific, but she didn't want to see it. The little creek that ran through the farm back home in Illinois was ocean enough for Tamsen Content. Jared had told her that Independence, Missouri, was the real start of the trip to California. She knew now what he had meant. All these wagons drawn up, ready for the start in the morning, their white canvas tops like a fleet of schooners. Of course, that was why they called them prairie schooners, she said to herself, rather foolishly. When the morning had come she sat tight-lipped and staring hard to keep from crying. Jared picked up the reins and the ox goad, shouted to the oxen; they gathered themselves together, their great flanks moved, their muscles rippled beneath the brown hide. Jared's mare was tied and following behind. And the wagon with the supplies was behind theirs. Jacob, the hired man, and Lavina, the hired girl, had charge of that. They had married, conveniently, before starting. Jarry was back there with them. She could hear him whooping and shouting to the oxen. The milch cow, faithful Velvet, was tied behind their wagon—Velvet because of her eyes and because of the richness of her creamy milk. There was a third supply wagon, but the Contents had only a half interest in that. They shared it with their erstwhile neighbors back in Illinois, now their traveling companions to California, the Haskins, Ambrose and Sarah.

Little Tam lay asleep in her arms, up there on the wagon seat, perched so high. "You can't hold her like that all the way to California," Jared said. "From May to August. She's a big girl. Three years and past."

"I know. But she didn't get her sleep out, up before daybreak for this early start. Look, the sun's just coming up now. It's going to be fair. That's a good sign, isn't it, Jared?"

"That left hind wheel's squeaking again, before we're rightly started. And I paid that wheelwright two bits at Independence, like a fool."

She looked down at the child's face, rosy in the folds of her shawl, the sunrise flushing it pinker. "It was all a pother, back there. Nobody closed an eye last night, I'll be bound. We're well away from it, only——"

She left the sentence unfinished. For a moment her mind held the pic-

ture of last night's vigil. May in Missouri, the night was sharp but not too
cold. They had slept in the wagons, of course; Jared and Tamsen in the
big wagon, with Jarry and Tam. Jacob and Lavina in the other. Tamsen
never lay down in the wagon that she did not think of her four-post bed
with the calico valance and the candlewick spread she herself had made.
It was all there in the second wagon, with the other household goods, tied
and wrapped. How luxurious it seemed! When would she sleep in it again?
The stars had been brilliant last night. Millions of them, big and blue
white like the diamond she had seen in the brooch worn by Mrs. Squire
Reade, back home. Back home. The safe little farm back there in Illinois.
But Jared had the roving spirit; his people had come to Illinois from Connecticut, and before that to Connecticut from England. Besides, the Illinois winters had not agreed with him. He coughed, and his cheeks had
hollow places in them so that his long Anglo-Saxon head looked longer. He
had heard the stories of this California of gold and sunshine. People were
flocking there from all over Illinois and Missouri and even back East. Jared
did not talk much. But once his mind was made up it was no use. She had
learned that.

Last night had been torture. No matter how far they had come before,
Independence, Missouri, was the starting place, the jumping-off place.
Once well out of it, there was no turning back. The camp was in a jitter
of nerves and anticipation. It seemed no one slept. From sunset to dawn
there were sounds. Lanterns flashing. The stamp of hoofs—oxen, mules,
horses. The long bray of a mule, a horse's whinny. A shout of laughter.
Someone singing. Drunk, probably.

> *When you start for San Francisco*
> *They treat you like a dog,*
> *The victuals you're compelled to eat*
> *Ain't fit to feed a hog.*

The slap-slap of cards. A whimper of fear from the recesses of some dark
wagon. An old man with his family around a late campfire, his bearded,
patriarchal face, his hollow voice uplifted in supplication: Whither shall I
go from thy spirit? Whither shall I flee from thy presence? If I ascend up
into heaven, thou art there. If I make my bed in hell, behold, thou art
there. If I take the wings of the morning, even there thy hand shall lead
me. . . . Whee-yip! Ee-yow! Roisterers; or cow hands, maybe. The night
had seemed endless, but the dawn had come too soon.

"Only what?" Jared said, to her unfinished sentence. She came out of
her thoughts with a start. Stared. "Only what?" he insisted, rather testily,
for him.

"Nothing, really. I was just thinking—I mean—once you're well away from Independence, Missouri, why, there's no turning back, ever."

"I should think not! Every stick and stone and dollar we possess is right here in these wagons. Turn back, indeed!"

How many times, in the months that followed, she thought of that first morning out of Independence. They were a small wagon train, as California-bound parties counted in that day. Twenty-five wagons. The Contents owned two of these and half of another. Their world was contained therein. Her most precious belongings: her sheet-iron stove, her feather beds and pillows, her pots and kettles, her precious willow-pattern dishes, her four-poster bed, her cherished walnut table (that made awkward luggage indeed), her dresses and the children's in trunks; her little box of water colors and her brushes, for she loved to sketch; she had even brought books, this Tamsen Content, who had been briefly the pretty schoolmistress of the district school before she had married Jared. As for Jared, his luggage was sterner stuff: an anvil and bellows, crowbar, auger, ax, chisel, harness, kegs. Jacob, the hired man, had brought his accordion. Then there were, of course, hundreds of pounds of flour, besides ham, bacon, sugar, coffee, tea, cream of tartar, soda, salt, dried fruit, beans, rice, pilot bread, pepper, ginger, tartaric acid. They well knew what to take along. Jared wasn't long-headed for nothing. So they traveled that first month—farmers, lawyers, merchants, preachers, laborers. As Tamsen, last night, had fitfully dreamed of the Illinois farm, so they had dreamed of their Vermont hills, their Kentucky fields, the lakes of Maine, the Massachusetts woodlands, the Indiana prairies. Gold! Adventure! Twenty-two hundred miles lay before them.

At the conclave held by every member of the wagon train on the second day out they had offered Jared Content the captaincy, but he had refused. "An older, wiser head for captain," he had said. "Let me be lieutenant, like. Besides I'm subject to little spells of feeling poorly, and might fail you in a pinch. I thank you for the honor, folks. If I could make a suggestion I'd say Ambrose Haskins for captain; he is a neighbor of mine back in Illinois—was, I should say—and can turn his hand to anything, with a wise head to guide it, and us."

Ambrose, elected, had risen and had spoken briefly, grimly. "Folks, neighbors, fellow travelers, we've got twenty-two hundred miles to go to Hangtown, Californy. Between here and there we got a sight of high mountains, broad desert, great rivers, and hostile Indians. But it ain't those that'll give us most grief. You can figger it out for yourself. May, June, July, part of August; about one hundred twenty days. How much a day, every cussed day, rain or shine, hail, cholera, breakdowns, floods, dust storms, washouts, lost critters? . . . That's right, folks. Above eighteen miles

a day. Eighteen miles a day, no matter what, or you get stuck in the autumn snows on the High Sierras and eat each other like the Donner party
done, in '46."

A scream from one of the women. The rest, white-faced, turned to look
at her in disapproving silence.

Still, that first month wasn't so bad, Tamsen thought, as June came on
them. May in Missouri, in Kansas, in Nebraska; winding their slow, dog-
ged way across the prairies and the plains. She was surprised to find that
the prairies had knolls and even hills. She always had thought they were
flat like the farmland back home. Why, they had talked of the California
Trail as though it were a plainly marked wagon road. But on the high
plateaus there was never a wagon track at all; the wind covered with dust
and sand every boot or wheel track an hour after it was made. The wind!
Tamsen looked ruefully at her face and neck and arms and hands and hair.
The sun and the wind and the dust had wrought their will on them. A
farm woman, inured to manual labor, used to battling with the elements,
eight years a wife, she still had kept her pretty ways; she prided herself on
her clear creamy skin, her slender hands, shapely in spite of the drudgery.
But this was different. There was no fighting this.

They crossed the Kansas River, the widest stream they would encounter
in the whole twenty-two hundred miles. "But not the trickiest," old Uncle
Bob McGlashan said. "Wait till you git to the Platte. Three feet deep,
mebbe, but a current kin sweep ye, oxen and all, to the bottom of a mud
trap, and gone. She flows bottom side up, old Platte does."

You got used to it. You learned a kind of Oriental patience. Tamsen recalled with amusement how irked they had been at having to wait their
turn seven hours in order to ferry across the Kaw. Heat and dust. Men and
women, horses, mules, oxen, tortured by enormous, venomous flies. That
had been the first week in May. It seemed nothing now. Past graves,
marked with an elk horn, for wood was too precious to be used thus. Bones
of animals whitening on the plains. Broken-down outfits bogged near the
Big Blue, trapped in the rich wet spring soil of eastern Kansas.

By the end of May certain things stood out stark and clear, good and
bad. They kept track of the days, she and Jared. One month had gone. The
children were well, though thinnish. Velvet's milk was not what it had
been. Jared was well—that is, you might say, well enough. He'd always had
those hollows in the cheeks. Not dark like that, though, Tamsen thought,
as if dirty fingers had smeared beneath the cheekbones.

The evening of May 31 they took stock of the month past as they sat
around the campfire after supper. Bacon, beans, bread. Abiah Pinney, who
knew the route having once before gone beyond the Sweetwater, said they

soon would have fresh meat in plenty—or should. Antelope and buffalo meat. Buffalo hump, Abiah vowed, was the sweetest eating meat there was. Tamsen thought it sounded fairly sickening. She envisioned a plump frying chicken with hot biscuits and cream gravy for Jared and the children—such food as they had not known since they left the farm. She must not think of such things; it was greedy. Besides, hadn't Lavina baked an apple pie tonight as a special treat, to celebrate the first month passed? Dried fruit, of course, but delicious, with a little of Velvet's scant cream poured over each portion.

At home on the farm she had prided herself on having kept things "nice" in the household. A checked tablecloth even at breakfast instead of the oilcloth of the average farm kitchen; napkins to match; the butter kept firm and sweet in the cold spring water; red geraniums in the kitchen window. Now their table was the ground, their tablecloth a piece of rubber which was used as a cloak when it rained. Dishes of tin, spoons of iron. At first it had been like a picnic, but the novelty had long worn off. Even the children felt the discomfort of sitting cross-legged on the ground three times a day, and they refused to eat the coarse stuff called mountain bread, which was simply flour and water mixed and fried in grease. She tried not to think of the angel cake for which she had been famous in the countryside. The whites of a dozen new-laid eggs went into it. It was sweet and light and melted like snow on the tongue.

"End of the first week in June," Abiah Pinney was saying, "with any luck, that is, we ought to be in Fort Laramie, Wyoming."

Wyoming! thought Tamsen. What a wild-sounding place! She, Tamsen Hoyt Content, with Jared and Jarry and little Tam—what were they doing, headed for a place called Wyoming? Around the next campfire they were singing in chorus, pleasant to hear, though some of the songs were too rough for her taste.

> *Hangtown gals are plump and rosy,*
> *Hair in ringlets mighty cozy;*
> *Painted cheeks and gassy bonnets,*
> *Touch them and they'll sting like ho'nets.*

She liked better such songs as "Auld Lang Syne" and "Bonnie Charlie" and "I Remember, I Remember." Or "Oh! Susanna" with its heartening chorus:

> *Oh! Susanna, oh, don't you cry for me,*
> *I've come from Alabama, wid my banjo on my knee.*

"Last week in June," Abiah went on, "we should by rights reach the South Pass, summit of the Rockies and the Continental Divide."

"The Rocky Mountains!" Lavina exclaimed, rather incredulously, as though she had not expected this. Lavina had only such book learning as Tamsen, her mistress, had been able to give her at odd moments when the farmhouse work was done.

"Certainly, girl, certainly. Did you expect to git to Californy without noticing the Rocky Mountains!" Abiah said humorously.

"South Pass they'll need their songs," Ambrose Haskins predicted grimly. He nodded toward the singing campfire group. "That is, if they can spare the breath to sing 'em."

Tam and Jarry were supposed to be sound asleep in the wagon. The singing must have wakened them. Tamsen saw their tousled heads poking out of the canvas flap. "Tam! Jared Content! Get back to bed this minute!" They grinned impishly in the firelight and did not budge. They were getting out of hand with this rough life, living like gypsies. Tomorrow she'd start lessons, though it wasn't easy now that she was doing part of the driving each day when Jared began to look too queer and drawn. It wasn't driving. You walked along by the side of the oxen in the blazing sun and the wind. Sometimes you could rest a brief while up in the wagon seat. But they were stupid creatures, the oxen, and had to be guided and prodded. The mule-drawn wagons seemed to get on faster. She wished Jared hadn't been so set on oxen.

"Time will come," Jared was saying gravely, "when they'll have a railway all the way from New York State to Californy. I predict it, and soon."

"Yah!" hooted Jacob, the hired man, who had grown very free. "And git mule teams to haul the enjines over the mountains!"

Lavina tittered at her husband's wit.

But Uncle Bob McGlashan nodded his grizzly head sagely, in agreement with Jared. "There are wonders to come never dreamt of on land or sea. I say with Jared here the day will come they'll make the trip by railway in three weeks."

Tamsen looked about her proudly. "Jared's right, likely. Jared's always right. But they'll never see what we've seen, this trip. Not rushing along like that, they won't."

Sarah Haskins looked up from her knitting. "I was thinking today, the sights we've seen this past month, and the strange things have happened. Things I'll never forget, not if I live to be a hundred. The man who cut his horses free midstream in the current to save them, and he on the back of one of them, and let his wife and children in the wagon bed float downstream to their death if it hadn't been for Abiah and Uncle Bob catching hold of it at the narrow bend in the stream. Never will I forget the poor wife's face, and the screams of the little ones."

"Dirtier skunk never drew breath," agreed Uncle Bob. "I pity the outfit he's traveling with. Our boys were for stringing him up from a wagon tongue if Ambrose here hadn't stopped 'em. I reckon he figgered wives come cheap but horses is worth their weight in gold in Californy."

Lavina snuggled closer to her Jacob. "I keep thinking, nights, of those first Indians we saw when we was along the Little Blue. Pawnees, wasn't they, Jacob? How they rode along on their ponies, looking neither to right or left, over two hundred of them; it froze me to the bone. Nobody can't make me believe they are friendly. Red devils!"

"That child," Tamsen said, almost in a whisper, "that had splintered his leg and they'd never set it and it began to gangrene and how they tried finally to cut it off and he——" She shuddered and buried her face in her hands.

They all chimed in, then. . . . The man who'd traveled seven hundred miles and turned back because his mother-in-law made him: she said she'd made a living before she ever heard of Californy. . . . The man who drank too much cold water at Alcove Spring, poor feller, to die of that. . . . The coffin they made for that Mormon widow's man, out of pieces of their own precious wagon beds. . . . The groves of wild plum trees on the Little Blue, where they had camped amidst loveliness, and the terrible downpour at dawn, so that they found themselves camped in a lake at daybreak. And the call of a humorous camp sentry at the waking hour: "Five o'clock and all is wet!"

"Well," said Tamsen, "it's bedtime. Coming, Jared?"

Sarah Haskins neatly rolled her knitting. "I never thought to see the day —night, rather—when I could lay my bones down on a wagon-bed mattress week on week and sleep sound. It just shows."

"Doesn't it!" Tamsen agreed brightly. She put her hand on Jared's shoulder; he slipped his arm around her.

"No fair for married couples spoonin'," yelled Uncle Bob McGlashan.

FIRST DAY

It seemed to Jay Content that for hours he had been feverishly aware of the children's early-morning clamor and Turck's unavailing efforts to quiet them. "But he never sleeps this late, Turkey. He gets up and goes to the office. I want to see him shaving."

"He isn't going to the office. He's on a train. Now hush, Jerry, do. It was you kept him and all of us awake till midnight, and after. It was well past that when we brought you back to your own bed, like a great baby."

"Don't call me a baby. I'll tell my father."

"Do."

Tam's voice. "I want to see Mummy."

"Mummy's sleeping."

"I want a cooky. I'm hungry."

"Likely story, this time of morning, a cooky. Besides, you had your breakfast only an hour ago."

Haggard, groaning, Jay looked at his watch. Half-past nine! Well, I must have had some sleep, after all. That damned racket at Omaha, just as I was dropping off. Omaha. Oma—those little steaks. Don't feel quite up to steaks, after telling bedtime stories until all hours. Still, maybe a shower and shave—— No, I guess I'll have the train barber give me a shave after breakfast. Ten o'clock before I get in to breakfast as it is.

He listened at her door, opened it cautiously, and peered in. The room was dim, silent. He sneaked down the corridor; he had a refreshing shower, hot and cold. When he returned, the children fell on him, but he silenced them with promises and threats.

"No, you can't come in to breakfast with me. I want you to stay in your room, with the door shut, so that you won't wake Mother. If you are good and quiet I'll have lunch with you, we'll all eat together in the dining car. Oh, God, I won't be able to eat mountain trout at twelve-thirty when I'm having breakfast steaks at ten-thirty—— Well, anyway, I'll sit with you."

"May we have ice cream for lunch?"

"Yes." Rashly. Miss Turck cast him a reproachful look.

"A certain young person has a tiny little c-o-l-d."

"Pooh, I know what that spells," Jerry announced. "It spells cold. Tam's got a cold, she prolly can't have any ice cream."

Tam opened her mouth to scream; Turck said, "Yes you can, too, lovely, but come here and let Turkey put drops up your nose."

"I won't."

"Why don't you take them back to the lounge car and let them listen to the radio, Miss Turck? Lots of magazines with pictures, too."

Miss Turck's features took on a British glaze before his very eyes. "Please, Mr. Content. Tam mustn't have a change of room temperature—it's bad enough in here, this cold-air system. Besides, they've their own books and toys—dozens of them."

But the damage had been done. "We want to go to the lounge car. Daddy said we could. I want to listen to the radio. You're not the boss of us. Daddy said we could. He said it himself."

Jay Content fled to the dining car and the undesired and promised bits
of tenderloin steak that would melt in the mouth.

It was, somehow, eleven before he had dealt with the beef and Mr.
Wiener and the strange morning paper which, like all train newspapers
picked up en route, seemed to have column after column of nothing in it.
When he returned to his compartment it was made up and tidied for the
day. The children's room looked like a State Street toy shop at Christmas.
Mechanical sets, dolls, books, games. Tam, somewhat smeared, was busy
with paper, a brush, and water colors in a precarious state.

"She's making a lovely water-color painting for her mummy when she
wakes up, aren't you, ducky?" Turck said, and rescued the red just in time.

"Let her say it herself," Jay found himself snapping at her, to his own
surprise.

"She's only three, after all," Miss Turck said, defending her darling as
though he had accused her of crime.

"If she's old enough to use water colors on a train she's old enough to say
so for herself." What was he talking about, he thought. Those steaks must
have disagreed with him. Too heavy and rich for breakfast. Miaowing at
Turkey like an old she-cat.

He heard Katharine's voice in compartment C. Then Frances was awake.
He knocked; he opened the door between his room and hers. "Hello!
How'd you sleep?"

"Sleep! Look, darling, don't come in, this place is a shambles, three people in here would call for a traffic cop. How are the children? Tell Turck
to come here a minute. I didn't close an eye all night. Not an eye. I look
like Dracula."

"How about breakfast?"

"Katharine rang. I'm just having orange juice and black coffee."

"Well, I guess I'll go to the barbershop and get a shave. If you think
you look like Dracula you ought to see me as Tarzan."

When he returned Frances was sitting up in bed among her rosy pillows, looking fresh and cool and young. She had on a bed jacket with a
pattern of tiny sprigged flowers, quaint and fetching. The little room had a
refreshing woodsy smell, Frances' kiss was delicately scented, her dark hair
was fragrant and soft and neat, her gray eyes were clear; her little stack of
books on the shelf above her head, her needlework bag at her feet, her
smart traveling clock on the window sill, her robe folded at the foot of the
bed, she was jotting things down in a small blue leather notebook. Frances
always made orderly little notes in bed, night and morning, under a list
entitled "Things to Do." Cryptic notes: "tel upholst. extra man try Winky.
send blue cleanr. Tam drops. brdg lamp."

"Had breakfast?"

"The orange juice was warm and the coffee cold. Wouldn't you think, on a train that's supposed to be good—— And last night they stopped somewhere for hours and hours and people outside yelled to each other, all named Bill. No wonder it takes thirty-six hours."

"Well, they have to do something about ice and food and fuel, you know, like any household."

"What in the world were you talking to Jerry about last night! You rumbled on and on; that's no way to quiet a child. What were you saying?"

"Oh, I was telling him the yarn about the way Grandfather and his folks made the trip in '49. I told him it was almost exactly the same route we're taking on this train. He was interested."

She glanced idly out at the Western landscape. "Was it? Where are we? Look, darling, Tam drew me a picture in water colors, isn't it touching! It seems it is supposed to be a house."

"How about getting up for lunch? Come on, be a sport. Fresh trout."

"I simply couldn't. Do be sweet about it, Jay. I'll get up for dinner tonight, I promise."

He went into the dining car with the children and Turck at twelve-thirty, but he did not eat. He watched them and approved as they ate their vegetables. Ice cream, yes, but you've got to drink your milk. Their special certified milk was brought them, each bottle dated like vintage wine. Replete, they were brought into their mother's room before their nap. Frances was stitching on her tapestry, an ambitious work intended for a chair covering, on which she had been sewing, like a medieval princess, for a year or more. The wools were green and gold and deep red and cathedral blue, a delicious melange of color. Tam loved to play with them, though it was forbidden.

Tam, the precocious, regarded her recumbent parent with the merciless, steady stare of the very young. She and Jerry knew about breakfast-in-bed-for-Mother. But this was afternoon; and on a train.

"Why are you in bed, Mummy?"

"Because Mother's tired, sweetie."

"Why?"

"She had to work so hard to get everything ready for all of us on this trip."

"Why?"

"So that you and Jerry and Daddy would be comfortable."

"Why?"

Frances discarded the sweetly maternal tone and all her child-psychology training. She sat bolt upright. Her voice rang above the roar of the train.

"Turkey! Miss Turck! Come and get Tam. She's driving me crazy. Anyway, it's time for their nap."

"I'm too big for naps," Jerry announced. "I'm never going to nap again, 'specially on a train."

Turck came in, crisp and capable, and Turck thought not. "No nap? And you've been up half the night and keeping everybody else awake. You'll pop right off. Come along." Turkey's large-knuckled hand closed over Tam's soft pink fingers like a cactus pad on a rose.

"Anyway, I'm sick of this old train," Jerry shouted.

"Hush. Come along, there's a good boy, and I've a treat for you."

"What? What kind of a treat? I don't believe it."

"Your father says we come to a place called Ogden-utah, at half-past four; it's quite a large city, I believe; we stay ten minutes; you may walk out on the platform, you and Tam, if you're both good and take your naps; and we'll buy picture postcards. So, now!"

"Oh, pooh, old picture postcards!" Tam, slave and adorer of her brother, found this an arresting phrase and now echoed it as best she could as the two were gently hustled off. It came out "pitty potard" or some such matter, but the boredom in her tone was a triumph of slavish imitation.

Frances' needle plunged in and out of the tapestry stretched tightly over the frame. It made a popping sound.

Jay stuck his head in at the door. "I'm going to have lunch with some fellows I met. One of them is that young Murchison who's with the Flint people. I've been trying to get at him for a couple of years. It's a break, meeting him like this on the train. Look, Fran, do something for me, will you?"

"Within reason. But no bringing him in for a chat and a drink. I'm no Du Barry."

"His wife's on the train, and their little girl. She isn't well—Mrs. Murchison, I mean—and she has to spend the winter in Tucson. He says it's bronchial, but sounds like lungs to me. They've got a section three cars back. Murchison hasn't any money—the Flint people don't pay him enough —and he's worth twice his salary to me if I can persuade him to—— Look, go back and talk to her, will you? She's spending a week in San Francisco with him before she goes to Tucson. We'll ask them to have dinner with us there, but I'd like to get going with him right now. Will you do that, honey?"

But over honey's face there slipped the icy mask of negation. He knew it well. "Darling, dinner in San Francisco, yes—if you think that business dinners and deathbeds go well together. But please don't ask me to be the hostess and the little woman today."

"I just thought if you were getting up, why——"

"But I'm not. And Tam's got a cold already. I won't have her playing with strange train children."

"All right. Forget I ever brought it up. Aren't you going to have some lunch?"

"Later perhaps. I'm not hungry now. Run along, dear." She smiled tolerantly. "Tell the porter to send Katharine to me." She ceased her stitching and lay back a moment, her eyes shut. There was a discreet knock at the door. Katharine, in neat black, came to her bedside. "Katharine, see if there's a manicure on this train. There must be. My nails are frightful. I didn't have time, rushing off this way. I think she'd better do it—rather than you, I mean—because she's probably used to the train lurching, and all. Tell her I'll want her at about half-past two. And get out my own polish. Their stuff is awful. At three order me a grilled sardine sandwich on whole-wheat toast and half a grapefruit. And tell them for heaven's sake the sandwich hot and the grapefruit cold."

Katharine closed the door softly behind her. They were slowing down a little as they approached a town. Frances glanced out to view the burning Western landscape. A Chamber of Commerce sign said WELCOME TO GREEN RIVER WYOMING. A little station came into sight, with men standing on the platform, gaping at the train. Frances pulled down her window shade. She lay back in her little nest of cool pink crepe and closed her eyes. Welcome to Green River, Wyoming. She shuddered. People actually lived here. The train came to the briefest stop. In another moment they were moving. Again the luxury train cleft the continent.

SECOND MONTH

Jared had traded some of his oxen for mules—his beautiful, costly oxen for these vulgar little beasts. But at Fort Laramie they had told him that he'd never make the mountain passes without mules. Oxen were all right for the plains, they said, but mules for the mountains. Besides, not so much feed and water. These Midwestern farmers had no knowledge of mountain and desert. They knew about crops, about the four seasons, woods, water, weather, animals of their own section of the vast continent. But Western trail signs, canyons, deserts, arroyos; Indians, buffalo; blazing hot days followed by freezing nights; these things were new, bewildering. They had no knowledge to cope with these.

It was queer how you took for granted—and even found commonplace, finally—things which you had never expected to see or experience. That first vast herd of buffalo. Abiah Pinney, with his superior knowledge of the plains, had been the first to spy them. Riding his mare, Nancy, ahead of the wagon train, as he often did, he had suddenly wheeled and ridden back at high speed, one arm with its pointing finger waving frantically toward a black spot on the horizon. The black spot moved, grew larger, came nearer.

"Buff'lo!" he yelled. "They must be millions of them coming up from the river. Turn your teams around so you're headin' with the herd, and hold on to your critters, and keep your young'uns in the wagons." On they swept, thundering nearer and nearer, a river, a sea of buffalo. You heard the rifles crack in every direction; some of the men were shooting from their horses, others from the wagons in which they sat. The herds swept on and on, running between the wagons like flowing water. The mules danced and snorted.

"Buffalo meat for supper and till kingdom come, looks like," Jared said.

That night Tamsen looked up from her plate of broiled buffalo hump. The air of distaste with which she had at first regarded it had vanished. "Why, it's good! It's delicious!" Abiah Pinney, his mouth full, munched and nodded with an air of I-told-you-so.

Jared and Tamsen agreed that everything seemed suddenly to change after they had left Fort Laramie. You felt it once you had left the adobe walls of the Fort, situated there near the Oglala and Brûlé divisions of the Sioux nation and not far from the tribes of the Cheyenne and Arapaho. The sky seemed vaster as the horizon broadened. The men of the party looked to their axes, their shovels and crowbars. Serious, even grave, they said it was heavy going from now on, with the mountains just ahead of them. The trail became rougher; there were steep hills for the first time— so steep that the women and children got out and slid down as best they could, holding on here and there to a rock or a bit of brush to check their slipping feet. By now Tamsen and Jared and even Jarry and little Tam often walked to save their bones the hideous jolting of the wagon over the ruts. They had learned to sway with the motion of the schooner, but sometimes when she lay down to rest at night it seemed to Tamsen that every bone in her body was broken. She and Jared drove turn and turn about now. Jared would walk or ride his mare or even lie resting in the back of the wagon. Tamsen pretended not to think it strange that Jared should be lying down in the daytime.

They began to pass queer objects by the trailside. Bleaching bones they were used to; camp refuse, carcasses of dead animals, even an occasional broken wagon-wheel rim. But now, suddenly, as the way became rougher, steeper, deeper in dust, they came upon articles once thought invaluable, now abandoned. Large blacksmiths' anvils, plows, grindstones, harness, cooking stoves; even clothing and bacon and beans, thrown out by wagon trains that had gone before.

Jared stared at these, then turned to look down at Tamsen seated there beside him. "Overloaded." Something in his tone made her stare at him, but he was looking straight ahead now, his young face set and stern. "So are we. Ambrose and Pinney both said we most of us are. Overloaded. Iron stuff. Crockery. That big walnut bedstead."

"No!" cried Tamsen. "I won't let you. I'll get out and carry it myself. No, not my four-poster that I've thought about a thousand times! Jared Content, it's for our new house in California! What does he know! What does that Ambrose Haskins know, more than we do! Let Sarah throw away her——"

"She's agoing to," Jared interrupted quietly. "So're you, Tamsen. There's no way out, if we want to reach Californy before snowfall."

But before the end of June she could look back at this and wonder that she had ever considered it important, or even worth a second thought. By the end of June, Velvet, alkalied, had gone dry and there was no milk for Tam. "She'll get on without milk," Jared assured her, making light of it. "She's a great big girl now. She can eat and drink as the rest of us eat and drink."

It's for you I want milk, Tamsen thought. Milk and eggs and greens. You need them more than Tam does. But she gave no utterance to her anguished thoughts.

They were encamped for the night by the Green River, so pleasant and cool. For days they had looked forward to the Green River as travelers in the desert long for the oasis. In their fevered imagination it had become a mirage, green against the horizon, always just beyond their reach. Yet here they were at the Green River. They had reached it at five in the afternoon at the end of a fifteen-mile drive ankle-deep in dust, and against a wind that had whipped the dust in their faces until they looked as if they wore masks of gray clay. Tamsen had made Jared tie a handkerchief across his mouth and nose because the fine dust made him cough so. Wonderful Green River! The hundreds who had gone before them had devoured all the grass along its banks, but the water itself was there, cool, refreshing, truly green as it ran its emerald course to California.

Tonight it would be cold. Last night there had been half an inch of ice on the water buckets. Now the Wyoming sunset suddenly became night. Tamsen, clearing the tin dishes and basins and iron spoons from their supper table, looked over her shoulder for the children playing by the campfire. Jarry, with little Abner Haskins, was deep in some boys' game. "Jarry, where's Tam? Go get her. It's bedtime."

The small Jared, busy with his own devices, did not look up. "She's here." But she wasn't. Tamsen looked into the group at the next campfire, at the next; she stood up as though jerked by a cord; she stared this way and that into the dusk. "Tam! Tam!"

"Round by the wagons, likely," Jared said. He walked swiftly over and peered into them; called. Quickly, then, he went from group to group. "Tam here with you folks? My little girl here? Tam?" Like a crazed thing, Tamsen began to run from spot to spot, her hands open and reaching ahead of her. "Tam! Tam!" in a voice that was high and cracked like a crone's.

They all recalled the story of the child who suddenly was missing in the McAlastair wagon train, California bound. It was as well known as the story of the Donner party. Three, the child had been, like Tam. They remembered now how that other party had called, searched; how the men had mounted and ridden in all directions; how the whole wagon train had waited a day—two days—three—four—and then had had to move on, sternly, or perish all. The mother, with another small child and a third on the way, had sat stony-faced on the wagon seat, searching the terrible horizon with dry, staring eyes as the wagon rolled on toward California.

They were all on their feet now, running this way and that. Leather creaked as the men saddled their weary horses. It was the child, Jarry, who found her curled up asleep under a pile of buffalo robes that Eli Wheeler had left out to dry on the bank of a little knoll a hundred feet from camp.

As she held the sleepy, bewildered child in her arms Tamsen began to cry hysterically. Her usually serene face worked with her agony and relief. She gripped her husband's arm with frantic fingers. "I want to go home! Let's go back, Jared. Let's go back home!"

He tried to calm her with soothing words, his arm about her and the child. But Abiah Pinney, the practical, brought her to her senses.

"You can't go back, ma'am. Why, you're in Wyoming. You're facing towards home this minute—your future home. And that's Californy."

Jacob Cobbins, the hired hand, grinned with relief and laid his great sunburned paw on the shoulder of little Jarry, the hero of the moment. "Betcher life! Ain't nobody going to turn back now, is there, Jarry! Californy or bust! Like the feller says, there's gold in them there hills."

SECOND NIGHT

Jay discovered he'd have to have his suit pressed. The porter said the valet was piled up with work and wouldn't be able to press it for a couple of hours, anyway. "God, what kind of a train is this!" Jay shouted. Everything had gone wrong. It had been discovered that Tam's sniffle was worse and she had a little temperature. The New York market reports had come in over the radio late that afternoon. Jay and his two business friends had listened with narrowed eyes and lips pursed over cigars. It had been most depressing. He had come back to Frances for comfort at six and found her still not up.

"For God's sake, France, you're not going to be carried off this train on a stretcher tomorrow morning, are you! What's the matter with you, anyway? Turned into an invalid or something?"

"Nothing's the matter with me, thank you. But there will be if you don't take that filthy thing out of this room. What's that you're smoking?"

Jay removed it from his mouth and looked at it as though seeing it for the first time. He looked at its lighted end, with the fine collar of thick gray ash. Then he put it back in his mouth, rolling it a little with his tongue and lips as he spoke.

"This, dear lady, is what's known as a cigar. Product of Cuba. Made of the tobacco plant, first brought to England, they say, by Sir Walter Ral——"

"Well, it's a nasty, stinking thing; you never smoke cigars. I suppose it's those big-business boys have made you go so male and Western all of a sudden." She began to sprinkle the woodsy toilet water all about the little room. "After all, I'm resting so as to have the strength to go through this wretched week we're facing. I should think you'd be delighted to have me take it this way. Perhaps you'd rather have me running up and down this miserable train, swapping cooking recipes with your Mrs. Murchison while she breathes germs all over me."

He strode into his own room and slammed the door. Jerry was sitting there curled up by the window, reading in the fading light. "Hello, son, what's the matter with your own room?"

"Tam's got a worse cold, I'm not allowed near her, Turkey says maybe I'd better even sleep here with you tonight. It's—uh—very con-ta-jus, colds are."

Jay threw his cigar into the cuspidor. He didn't like them, really. Jerry was deep in his book. Jay sat staring out of the window. What was the matter with everything? Fran was pretty and smart. Two swell kids. Not always enough money, but that was going to be all right now. Yet something was wrong. They all took everything for granted. He, too. Too easy, or something. Soft. He ought to be happy as hell, and he wasn't.

Jerry closed his book. The eerie whistle of the train came back to them as they hurtled across the continent. "This is a poky old train. I'd rather go in an airplane."

Jay Content was still staring out of the car window. Desert, sagebrush, mountains, the blue-gray dome of a pitiless sky. Something clicked in his memory, and he saw a little wagon train plodding against the far horizon. The white-topped wagons, gray now with dust, the slow, wearied pace of oxen and mules, the dwindling string of horses, the lean dogs, the under-fed men and women and children, the wooden wheels grinding the sand and sinking into it, the animals' flanks dark with sweat.

"Look, Dad, tell me a story about how Great-grandfather Jared Content when he was a little boy no older than me had to drive a whole lot of oxen and mules. Gee! I'd like to do that, cracking the ol' whip. Whoa, there! Giddap! You won't even let me drive the pony cart alone. Go on, tell me about it. It isn't true though, is it? You just make it up."

"Of course, it's true. Don't be silly. It's history. American history. No use starting a story now, though, because the train stenographer's coming in any minute. He's due now to take a lot of letters and telegrams. By the time I've finished dictating to him it'll be your suppertime, son."

"Can't you do your letters and things afterwards?"

"No. They'll have to be ready to send by air mail when we stop at Reno tonight."

"Can I see it? Reno?"

"You'll be tight asleep. One o'clock in the morning. Besides, we only stop a few minutes. Everybody'll be asleep. There's nothing to see."

The boy wriggled impatiently. "Everybody's always busy. Just till he comes—the man who is going to fix your letters—won't you tell about it? You know—about the wagons and the Indians and the oxen, the way your father told it to you when you were a little boy, and his father told it to him."

"Well—but he'll be here any minute and I'll have to stop in the middle, and then it will be your suppertime. Let's see—uh—well, your Great-great-grandmother Tamsen Content, she was quite a girl. Once when they were near a place called Soda Springs—that's not far from where we are this minute on the train—an old one-eyed, mean-looking cuss of an Indian, with two or three other Indians behind him, bounced out of the brush when the party was camped. Most of the men were off looking for game and getting water and so on. There were only a couple of teamsters left. The Indians began to pillage the wagons——"

"What's pillage?"

"Steal. They began to steal things, and the teamsters were scared out of their wits and didn't even try to fight, but Tamsen Content was in the back of her wagon and she just leaned over and went after their hands with a hatchet. They began to howl, and then the teamsters pulled themselves together and got their guns and began to shoot——"

The door buzzer sounded. "Good evening, Mr. Content. Stenographer."

THIRD MONTH

Desert, sagebrush, mountains, the great blue-gray dome of a pitiless sky. That May day seemed so long ago, so terribly long ago, when Ambrose Haskins, newly elected captain of the wagon train, had said grimly, ". . . high mountains, broad desert, great rivers, and hostile Indians. It ain't those that'll give us most grief. . . . Eighteen miles a day, rain or shine, eighteen miles a day, no matter what."

Tamsen was up in the wagon seat most of the day, now. She looked ahead toward California, but her eyes no longer really saw the train of wagons, their canvas tops bleached dead white with the sun like the drying bones along the trail; the slow-pacing oxen, the dwindling string of horses, the great wheels grinding the sand and sinking into it, the animals' flanks dark with sweat.

"You all right, Jared?" she would call over her shoulder.

"I'm fine. I'm getting up in a minute now," Jared's queer thin voice from the wagon bed. Little Jarry sat beside her on the wagon seat now, and often he actually drove, though there was little enough to driving really, with these weary animals plodding ahead through the sand. "Whoa!" shouted little Jarry, enjoying it enormously. "Whoa! Gee! Haw!" Little Tam sat up there, too, or with Jacob and Lavina in the second wagon. Tam's hair was bleached almost white from the sun and wind; she was tall and thin. Too thin. All except Lavina. Lavina had grown plump, and she was ill, mornings. The wives nodded their heads and told her to eat bits of dry pilot bread to stop the morning sickness. Everyone else was thin and irritable and oversilent. There was a sort of poisonous unseen thing running through the whole wagon train. Frayed nerves, blistered feet, sunburned eyes, lips swollen and blotched with the dust as though they had tasted poison ivy; filthy, alkaline water, no proper food for the animals. These and a thousand other things combined to lower the morale of the party. The Valley of the Humboldt, it was called, this long, brutal, killing stretch. The final, heartbreaking pull before you reached California. The Valley of the Shadow, Tamsen thought, bitterly, listening to Jared's breathing, seeing how the ribs of the oxen and mules stuck out almost comically under the dust-covered hides.

How old she felt! She was fifty years older than she had been that May morning when they had pulled out of Independence, Missouri. Her fine walnut bed was gone, her precious walnut table, her iron stove—all left to rot by the roadside. Velvet was gone, killed one night by the thieving Indians. They had let her out to graze on a bit of rare green growing in the midst of an alkali stream, and an Indian arrow had got her.

Well, she had learned a lot of queer things. How smart Jared had been— was, she said, quickly, fear clutching her. Was? *Is.* That cream of tartar made this horrible alkali water drinkable. He had known that. That vinegar and tartaric acid had kept them from having the scurvy. Mule steaks were not so bad. And if you were out of salt and pepper, a little gunpowder made them palatable. Jacob's accordion! In her rage and grief she had said, "Make him throw that away if I have to throw away my bed and my table and stove and iron pots and dishes and everything I love."

"We need that accordion," Jared had said. "A wagon train can do well without a bedstead and a table and even an iron stove. But the music of an accordion, evenings, can make you feel you can push on next day."

Jared knew everything. Little Jarry was like him. Smart and quiet and longheaded. Oh, God, let us get to where there's milk and eggs. Let him not die, dear God. Just milk and eggs and my good cooking and he'll be all right, and the children, too.

Dust. Sun. Jolting, racking, over the mountain roads. Eighteen miles a day, rain or shine, or you land in the snow in the High Sierras——

They should tell people how awful it was, before they ever got started. But they didn't come back to tell. They either stayed or they fell by the way. She had seen them. Crazy men and women trudging back by foot, or trying to, and dying by the way. Animals crazed with heat and drought, or dropping suddenly in their tracks without warning. She had seen them, often, in the past month, going along slowly, patiently, in this desert, and then, as if shot, they would fall and die instantly. As you passed them on the trail the desert sand in the dead animals' eyes gave them an unearthly glitter.

What had she not seen! Soda springs; ice ponds in July; skulking Indians with poison-tipped arrows; books thrown away with other litter by the side of the trail; dust that made it impossible to see the wagon ten feet ahead of you; oxen dying in heaps; men dying of cholera; children being born on the trail; a wedding in an oxcart.

In desperation she resolved to go to Ambrose Haskins, leader and captain of the wagon train.

"Mr. Haskins—it's about Jared. He isn't sick—not really, I mean. Only tired. If we could only stop for one whole day, and rest. It's the going on day after day, all these weeks and months without stopping. It's wearing him out. It's killing——"

"We're all of us worn out, Mrs. Content, and that's a fact. But Jared's going to pull through fine with the rest of us. Less than a month more of it, and you'll be wearing gold nuggets for a necklace."

"I want no necklace." She felt hysteria coming into her voice and was powerless to check it. "He'll die, I tell you! He'll die if he doesn't get a little rest. That terrible jolting in the wagon, or else the sun beating down on his head, walking; and the dust and alkali. It would be like heaven not to feel your bones being racked. Oh, Mr. Haskins, please, for God's sake, let him rest a day. When we make camp today or maybe tomorrow, if it's a spot where there's some water and maybe even a tree, let's stay there a day. Just a day, quiet. Please, Ambrose. Just a day, for Jared."

His voice, his face, were compassionate but stern. "We can't, ma'am. You well know why." He pointed across the burning desert toward the direction of the mountains, the last barrier between them and their goal. "There's the mountains ahead of us. We've got to get over them before snowfall or we'll perish, all of us. Dust or storm, sickness or death, we must go on, eighteen miles a day. One day lost may mean a day too late. A blizzard in the mountains, and we're done for. Remember Hagar in the wilderness, ma'am. Remember Sarah, mother of nations. So will you be, mother of a nation. Strength for two, Mrs. Content, that's what you'll have to have. And let's hear no more about stopping."

She went back to the wagon. As she climbed up over the wheel she heard someone in the next cart singing a bitter parody of her favorite song:

> *Oh! Susanna,*
> *Go to hell for all of me;*
> *We're all of us the livin' dead*
> *Bound for Californ-i-ee.*

"You all right, Jared?"

"I'm fine. I'm getting up now. I was just thinking, Tamsen. Those of us that get to Californy and settle there, we'll be fit to face anything after this. We'll be the iron it takes to dig gold. We'll be a race of giants in Californy."

"Yes, Jared."

ARRIVAL

It had been a ghastly scramble to be up and dressed by the time they were due in San Francisco. Seven-fifty-two in the morning.

"If they dawdle around at Omaha and Reno and heaven knows where—

as they did—why don't they dawdle a little longer!" Frances Content suggested. "Then we might get in at a fairly decent hour; nine o'clock, at least. I'll have to have a cup of coffee. Katharine, ring and tell him a cup of coffee, here. I'll die if I don't have it right away."

"They'll have breakfast waiting as soon as we get to the house," Jay called from his room.

"I know. But if I don't have coffee as soon as I'm up I get one of my headaches. You know that."

"Do I know it! Listen, tell him coffee for two, will you? I feel rotten. Maybe a cup of coffee will buck me up. I'll bet I didn't sleep two hours."

"Funny they didn't answer your last telegram."

"Maybe nothing to say. The wire at Reno said he was holding his own—whatever that means—and conscious. No change, I guess."

Frances passed through his room to the children's. She looked very smart and fresh in a dark print and a tiny turban. "Don't put their coats on yet, Miss Turck. It'll be hours. Well, half an hour, at least. . . . No, Tam, no faces, darling. You're not sick any more. Turkey took your temperature and you haven't a speck. . . . Did they drink all their milk? They can have a good breakfast at Grandpa's. Much better than this stale train food—I hope. I had a lamb chop last night that was simply rubber. And asparagus the size of my little finger. Heaven knows I eat little enough on a train, but I do want that little decently—— Jerry, what *are* you doing, shouting so? You'll be worn out before we get there."

"He's driving oxen, he says; he's been at it ever since he got up. I couldn't get him dressed, he wriggled so," Turkey explained, good-humoredly enough.

Jerry's face grew red. "I'm not. Ol' fool! And you didn't. I dress myself. I aren't a baby, like Tam."

"Jared Content, don't you let me hear you talk——"

Jay stuck his head in at the door. "Coffee, France. Better swallow it. We'll be there in less than fifteen minutes."

He was feeling better this morning. Must have been a touch of indigestion made him feel so low yesterday. Too much food without exercise, and those cigars. Frances, too, was her gay, vital self, bright-eyed, capable, chic.

"I've had a lovely rest. Did you see the mountains early? Divine! Jay, sometime if we're—when we have—well, with the money—you know—anyway, let's go to one of those Western mountain snow resorts for the skiing, shall we? It would be fun."

"Winter, you mean?"

"Yes, way up high, where the snow's very deep and the sun hot. Mimi Bayliss went last winter. She said she never saw such luxury. Imagine!

Even Mimi! Something-or-other Lodge, it's called. Sun traps, and priceless skiing and skating and such food! The mountains in winter! Exciting!"

Jay's brother, Jacob Content, was there to meet them as they stepped off the train. Frances took one look at him and whispered a quick aside to Jay. "He's trying to look mournful, but he's really pleased about something. Grandpa Content is dead—that's it. I feel it."

He and Frances had never got on. Jacob Content did not look a Content. He favored the other side of the family: the Cobbinses, offspring of Jacob Cobbins and Lavina, the hired man and servant girl of the old Forty-niner days, among the first of that wagon train to strike it rich in California. It was their daughter that Jared Content had married in 1862. He's common-looking, Frances thought now, as he came toward them, and slick. Jacob Content and his wife and children lived in New York. Frances resented that, too, with a fierce, Chicago resentment.

"Hello, Jay," he now said somberly. "How are you, Frances? Hello, kiddies."

"It's nice of you to meet us," Frances said quickly. "How is he?"

Jacob wore the unctuous look of one who bears tidings. "I've got sad news for you. He—went—at six this morning. Adele and I were with him at the end. And the children—in the next room of course—the children."

"I'm sorry," Jay said.

Frances echoed it, hollowly. "Sorry." Then her resentment of him flared into anger. "We got here as soon as we could. We took the very first train."

Jacob Content flicked an eye at the great transcontinental monster that had hurled them across thousands of miles. "We flew."

The little procession moved toward the waiting car. Jay Content looked a trifle dashed. "But we came." As though continuing an unspoken train of thought.

Frances was not one to beat about the bush, especially with so thick-skinned an antagonist as her brother-in-law. "The telegram said that we were to come, all of us, and that it was imperative. And we came. So they can't say—uh——"

"Oh, you're all right," Jacob assured her jocularly. "You finished at the post, and you qualify."

"Oh, say, look here!" Jay's tone was protesting.

"But now the wretched, boring trip was for nothing," Frances concluded. "That is, in a way. We thought he wanted to see us all and that he'd probably live for weeks and weeks. The way he did the last time."

Jacob Content had a San Francisco morning paper in his hand. He unfolded it now. There was a three-column photograph of old Jared Content, a magnificent towering figure, rugged, keen-eyed, looking out at them with the quizzical gaze of the undeceived. But it was not to the picture that Jacob Content pointed. He indicated the headline:

CENTENARIAN '49ER
LEAVES FIFTY MILLION

Jacob Content almost smiled before he remembered he mustn't. "Oh, I wouldn't say the trip was exactly for nothing, Frances. There's gold in them thar hills."

ARRIVAL

That first glimpse of the Promised Land had come on August 15. Somehow, they could not realize it. The weeks, the months, had been too long. Through those last days the journey had had a dreamlike quality of unreality. The weary, jaded wagon train had ascended painfully through forests of evergreen timber, up and up on the last stretch of the fantastic climb until they reached timber line. The trees were only stunted, twisted things. The snow was old and as hard as ice. They were more than nine thousand feet above sea level. The thin air seemed to agree miraculously with Jared. Sallow and peaked though he was, there came a freshness into his face and movements, a sparkle into his eyes.

"But he won't be fit to do anything when we get there," Tamsen had confided to Sarah Haskins. Her tone was not one of complaint. She spoke as though facing a fact squarely. "He couldn't dig and shovel, the way they'll have to in the gold fields. Gold fields. It's funny. I don't care a thing about whether there's gold or not. Just Jared, to be well again, and the children happy."

Sarah Haskins was quick to reassure her. "He'll pick up in no time now. They say the sun and the air are like wine and a tonic."

"He can hardly turn his pillow. Well, I can work. I can cook and wash and sew. Surely they'll need work like that to be done in Hangtown. Jared said he heard they were planning to change the name to Placerville. I wish they would, time we get there. It's so much nicer-sounding."

North, south, east, and west lay the golden plains seen from the heights, threaded by a line of blue. Ambrose Haskins pointed with one dust-grimed finger. "That line there, it's the coast range of mountains near the Pacific. In between is the valley of the Sacramento and the Joaquin rivers. And that there beyond is the west slope of the Sierra Nevadas." The pointing hand came up above his head then in a fist of triumph. "Yessir, we've made it, by God!"

"By God," echoed Tamsen quietly.

Now they began the steep descent. Some of them rushed down the precipitous slopes. You found their wagons in a heap at the bottom, the precious belongings which they had carried over two thousand miles now strewn like debris in the dust. The thin, clear air was deceptive. The diggings looked so near, though they still were days away. It was three days later that Tamsen, dragging a painful way through the dust and sun, suddenly raised her drooping head, as though listening. She was seated perched high on the driver's seat, early, early in the morning. Through the jangle of the trace chains, the grunts of the mules, the clop of the oxen's hoofs, the grind of wagon wheels on dust, the shouts of the drivers, she heard a lovely sound and then another. Her face grew radiant, was transfigured as though celestial music filled the air.

Across the plains on the morning breeze was borne the sound of a cowbell. And then a cock crowed.

Nobody's in Town

[1937]

Altitude does strange things to low-blood-pressure people. Nine thousand feet up in the Colorado Rockies makes me feel much as the average person does who has had two dry Martinis. In that exhilarated mood and accelerated tempo I write a story such as "Nobody's in Town" or "The Afternoon of a Faun." Somewhat lightheaded, I find that the story is written easily and almost gaily by one to whom the process of writing ordinarily is a dour and painful ordeal. My high-altitude stories are likely to have a fey quality.

One steaming midsummer New York morning I read a snobbish line in the society gossip column of the Herald Tribune. "New York is deserted," it said. "Nobody's in town."

I looked all about me. Nobody, I thought, except seven million people. Nobody except all the people who make New York habitable. So I leaped from Central Park to Washington Market, here, there, and everywhere in New York; gathered together typewriter, paper, luggage, and went up nine thousand feet to set down what I had seen and felt.

ONLY LAST WEEK IT HAD BEEN COOL—COLD, REALLY. YESTERDAY HAD been merely warmish. But this! This was it. Mrs. Alan Career, waking at eight, knew at once. Her nostrils, bred to New York City's effluvia, sensed hot rubber, melting tar, sunburned gasoline and oil; poisonous gases, blazing heat on brick and stone and steel; murk shot through with smoky sun. Born in the Sixties (streets, not years), she knew that summer had come to New York.

They had predicted a cold summer. A lot they knew about it, the idiots. Just because May had been bearable, and the first two weeks in June. She had stripped the apartment down to the airy essentials. She had replenished the broken set of tall frosty glasses meant for iced tea and mint juleps and Tom Collinses. And she went about saying, as she had said every June for the past five years, "I simply adore New York in the summer. It's so restful. The roof restaurants and the air-cooled movies and Long Island week ends; and first thing you know it's September and everyone's coming back half dead and their skin looking like potato chips."

"Really!" her women friends said. "I must try it sometime. We're sailing Wednesday. Bark wants to motor through France and Italy; and then we'll have two weeks in Salzburg for the Festival."

Every time she left the apartment there were piles of luggage downstairs in the foyer or at the curb—smart beige bags with brilliant red and green and yellow sashes painted about their middles, and little, luxurious dressing cases softly jacketed in buff. Tags and labels read: *Queen Mary, Île de France, Rex.*

Always noisy, there now was a rush in the streets, a louder buzz in the air, stronger vibrations underground. A roaring of airplanes overhead. The engines of vast ships turned, and their rudders churned the bay. The hum of a million motorcars filled the countryside. Automobiles darted and swept up the lanes of New England or nosed toward Colorado and California and Canada. At Pennsylvania and Grand Central stations the crowds milled like stampeding cattle.

Day by day, bit by bit, as the blasting heat continued unabated, New York cast off her French corsets, sent her furs to cold storage, took off her hat, rolled her stockings. Ungirdled, in bare legs and sandals, she let the hot, odorous breezes from the Hudson and the East River blow through her hair. The great, proud apartment buildings fell into their long summer sleep. One by one they pulled down the shades and awnings that were the eyelids over their hard, bright window eyes and allowed themselves to be draped in their summer shrouds of slip covers. Their guardians relaxed. The doorman unfastened the two top buttons of his taupe-and-blue summer uniform. Superintendents, usually so dapper and double-breasted, could be detected lurking in shirt sleeves and no collar in the shadows of foyer pillars. The big old brownstone houses and the newer Georgian pink bricks and the vast white marble palaces on Fifth Avenue and Park and the East Sixties and Seventies were boarded up tight, with only little crescent moons showing in doors and windows like slits of eyes squinting suspiciously down upon the rare passer-by.

One by one, furtively, almost fearfully, the Little People now crept out of their tenements, their walk-ups, their fire-escape flats, and claimed the New York which was rightly theirs. Gratefully they poured into the parks and squares whose grass they watered, whose gravel they raked, whose shrubs and trees they planted, whose walks they swept. They wandered free in the proud streets whose homes they lighted, whose food they supplied and delivered. You saw them sprawled on the courageous grass, timidly displaying their clean, worn undergarments to an understanding world. Their tired, unlovely feet were bared to the sun and wind. Their gray-white skin knew the ardor of the elements. Gangs of kids in ragged knickers and limp shirts and nothing beneath these yelped along the avenues; urchins in bathing trunks followed in the blessed wake of the sprinkling cart. They poured out to the streets, the fire escapes, the parks, the el trains, the subways, the beaches, benches, squares, curbs, roofs, doorsteps—the six and a half millions of people left in deserted New York.

And now, for the first time, you saw the contours of the city, no longer winter-choked. Its bone structure was there; its ribs and muscles stood out. It was like an overfat person from whom the excess weight had been peeled, pound by pound, so that now at last the actual body may be seen in its real outline, stripped and lean.

That second week in July the Alan Careers had it out at the breakfast table. Usually Patty Career had her breakfast in bed, but she said it was too horribly hot to have it there—to have it anywhere. She sipped her iced orange juice and glanced at her *Herald Tribune*. He sipped his iced orange juice and read the *Times* front-page headlines and glanced at the market, saving his more intensive perusal for the subway.

It was eight-thirty in the morning, it was hot, it was hell, it was unbearable. Patty Career burst out with it, though she had meant to wait until evening. Hysteria, probably, induced by heat and sleeplessness; and intensified by certain Talks with her mother.

She set her glass down now with a queer little clatter and pushed aside her plate of thin toast so that it executed quite a nice little spin. "Look, Alan, I can't stand this any longer. Honestly I can't. I can't face another summer in New York."

He looked at her over his paper. Then he put it aside altogether. She went on with a rush now. It had been pent up for weeks.

"Everybody's gone this year. Everybody! During the Depression it was—— We all—— I didn't mind so much—practically all our friends in the same fix. But now it's different. The Depression seems to be over for everyone but us. It isn't fair. It isn't fair to me or to Susan."

Susan had been born very mathematically, so that she now was four. Her appearance had coincided with the vogue for quaint, old-fashioned names bestowed by rather hard-bitten modern parents. All Susan's little friends were named Susan, Ann, Jane, Mary, Kate, Prue, Betsy.

Alan Career's mouth was etched with lines that one would expect to see on the face of an embattled man of fifty rather than on one of thirty-three. The past ten years had done some very odd artwork on the faces of Alan Career's generation. "Two more years," he now said, as though he had said it to himself many times, "and I'll be out of the woods."

"Who knows what'll happen in two more years! I'll be dead, for one thing, and Susan, too, probably, in this poisonous heat and gas."

"Oh, now, listen, Patty. It isn't as bad as that. I can manage a couple of weeks somewhere up in the mountains, or Maine. There are little cabins. This heat won't last."

"Oh, Alan, for heaven's sake! Little cabins! Tourist camps, I suppose."

Now it was he who pushed back his plate with unnecessary force. "We could afford something better if we didn't live beyond our means. If we didn't live in this damned, silly, expensive apartment, we might clear out for a couple of months in the summer. But you can't live anywhere but the East Sixties or Seventies. Why! It's the ugliest stone pile in the world. A million people like you trying to edge into it because it's fashionable. Fashionable! It's a ghetto of the rich and people like us who are pretending to be rich. We're a couple of young people trying to get along. Hell! Why don't we live like it! We pay thirty-two hundred a year for this stinking little third-floor back apartment, and that's why we can't have a house in the country or a trip to wherever it is you want to go. Why! What for!"

She now spoke in very controlled tones, using her broadest New York accent with a tinge of London. Alan Career hailed originally from Chillicothe, Ohio. "I always have lived in this section of New York. One naturally is accustomed to having a decent place in which to receive one's friends."

"If they're friends they'll come if you're living up in Fordham. As for most of the gang that comes here to eat our dinners and guzzle my whisky all winter so that we can go there and eat their dinners—it's a merry-go-round—it's silly—it's idiotic!"

"Will you please not shout so that Dahlia and Miss Mapes will think we're quarreling."

"We are."

"Perhaps you are. I'm not. I'm simply trying to talk to you like an intelligent adult. For one thing, living here is good for your business. And Susan's future depends on her making the right social contacts——"

"Susan!" he now yelled. "My God, the kid's four years old! The right social contacts for an infant just out of diapers."

"Isn't it just about time that you lost your Ohio viewpoint, Alan? When I was four my mother——"

"A lot of good it did her. What did it get you? You had dancing school and Miss-Gipp's-on-the-Hudson and all the Right People and Southampton and your picture in the rotogravures, and when you grew up you married a hick from Ohio who can't even afford to take two months off in the summer. Maybe if you hadn't made the right social contacts you'd have married a millionaire or the King."

"He doesn't care for women under forty," Patty reminded him icily.

"You knew I had a few thousand dollars and a job with a future and not another damned thing. Why did you marry me? I didn't try to put anything over on you or your family."

"I married you because I was crazy about you."

"Well, I'm just what I was then: a boy from the Middle West trying to make good in the Big Town."

"No, you're not. That's the trouble with you Midwestern men. You all have adolescent Abraham Lincoln complexes and go around with your mental socks rolled down, and black string ties and square-toed Congress boots inside you."

He turned back his coat to show her the label stitched on the lining. It was dated. "Nineteen thirty-two. But Betzel made it and it cost me one hundred and thirty-five bucks."

"I know, I know. But dated clothes aren't so amusing any more. The time is past when it was considered chic to be poor and stay home and get your evening clothes at Macy's. But everything's going to be brocade and fur and lumps of gold next winter. You can't get a box at the opera for love or money."

"Thank God."

"Here. Look at this." She picked up her *Herald Tribune* and pointed with one forefinger tipped by its cool, coral nail to a line at the head of that paper's society gossip column.

"The summer exodus is complete," it read. "New York is deserted. Nobody's in town."

"That's pretty silly. There are millions of people in New York all summer."

"Don't quibble, Alan. There's nobody that counts. Nobody important."

He pushed back his chair, stood up. "Well, what'll we do about it, Patty? I'm not holding out on you. I'll do anything I can. I wish to God I could——"

She brought it out, then, with a little rush.

"Mother has offered to take Susan and me to Europe for the rest of the summer. And even Miss Mapes, if she'll take a cut in wages. A lot of Mother's stocks and things have come back. She got some reservations through Bill Snowden's pull—— Of course I told her if you absolutely—but I was sure you'd—— The *Champlain* sails Thursday—I think it's just wonderful of her, but if you——"

"Yeh, wonderful." Dully. Then, as though the words had just penetrated his consciousness, "Thursday! You mean this Thursday! That's day after tomorrow!"

"Well, I sort of—after Mother asked me I sort of—not packed, but went over things."

"I see."

So then, quite amazingly, it was tomorrow and immediately it was

Thursday and in a moment Patty and Susan became two little specks among hundreds of other specks that were growing smaller and smaller as the distance between the French Line dock and the *Champlain*'s deck rail widened. He felt very odd and alone, standing there among the perspiring, close-packed crowd massed at the pier end, waving and shouting futile last-minute messages. He turned and made his way through the throng. They looked a good deal like the people who had sailed, he thought. . . . Nobody that counts. Nobody important.

The ship had timed its sailing with the tide. As Alan Career looked at his watch he saw that the afternoon was gone. It was hardly worth while going back to the office, except for the afternoon mail, and Miss Voss could take care of that, unless it was something colossal. Fine chance of that in the middle of July, end of the week, end of the day. Good old Voss. Nobody important, eh? Well, she was pretty damned important, with a memory that never slipped up and a head for figures like an Einstein.

Her brisk, unlovely, reassuring voice on the telephone. "No, there isn't a thing, Mr. Career. The Street's as dead as Trinity churchyard and the thermometer outside your window says ninety-nine. . . . I can take care of the mail, what there is. . . . Kunz's is the only one that needs your signature, and I can forge that. . . . Newbold phoned and I told them fifty or no dice, like you said. . . . I made an appointment with Mr. De Palma for ten Tuesday because he's taking the plane, is that O.K.? . . . Did the folks get away all right? I sent the fruit and all, and wired the purser. I hope everything's the way you wanted it. . . . Shall I phone your house you're on the way up?"

Good old Voss. Important, vital old Voss, who lived in the Bronx and would die in the Bronx, and who was to him as his own right hand. Back, he thought, to an empty flat, an empty town, an empty life. . . . Everything next winter is going to be brocade and fur and lumps of gold. . . . Maybe Friday night he'd pack a bag and go out to the Beach Club if Jay or somebody would put him up. Noisy bunch, though, and a lot of drinking. . . . Bet the apartment is an oven this time of day. . . . Warm and cold shower and a cold drink. . . . Wonder what Dahlia's got for dinner. No lunch, in the rush to clear things at the office before taking the girls to the boat.

He had been wrong. The apartment, when he had let himself in, was almost cool in comparison with the torrid streets. The shades were down, the windows shut. Dahlia had straightened and picked up and tidied after the flurry of packing and departure. What dignity and poise and intelligence behind those broad black features. Her face had worked comically, tragically, when she had said good-by to Susan, her darling. When she had come to work for them, five years ago, at the beginning of their marriage,

Patty had said, amused, "Dahlia? Your mother was fond of flowers, I suppose. Is that how she happened to name you Dahlia?" "No, ma'am," Dahlia had said in her calm, rich voice. "It's out of the Bible, the one who was the wife of Samson."

Alan Career went into the bedroom and stripped. It was pleasant, walking around naked, no one in the house but Dahlia humming in the kitchen. The tiles of the bathroom floor were hot to his bare feet, and the perspiration was like a wet coat of oil all over his body. He'd have a lukewarm bath first and use some of Patty's scented bath salts like a big sissy and just lie in it, and then he'd have a shower, cool and cooler and cold, and he'd stand under it for hours until his veins ran ice water and to hell with the doctors who said it was bad for you. Clean clothes and then a highball—no, a gin fizz or a julep with a big spray of mint stuck in the side of the glass. Boy! He might have it right now and wait half an hour for his bath. He wrapped a bath towel about his middle and padded to the swinging door of the pantry.

"Heh, Dahlia! Got any mint?"

"Any what?"

"Mint. To put in a julep. I'm parched."

Her dusky face was almost beautiful in its regret, its suffering. "Oh, Mr. Ca-reer! I ain't got a sprig. Not a sprig. Tell you what. I'll just skip over to Lexington get you a bunch of mint."

"Oh, never mind. It's too hot. Don't you bother."

"I'm going. When a person got their face fixed for mint, they want mint."

"Well, if you—uh—— Look, Dahlia, what've you got for dinner? Hm?"

"What you want? What you got a hankering for?"

"Oh, it's late. It's probably too late to do anything about it now."

"Not onless you want roast beef or leg of lamb. Hot night like this, you don't. I can get it same time I'm getting the mint. Too late for what? What you want?"

"I know what I don't want. I don't want any of that damned cold jellied soup, nor yet I don't want cold salmon with green sauce. That's Patty's idea of a—uh—Mrs. Career probably planned——"

Dahlia knew the male free and untrammeled. She threw her dinner menu to the winds. "Ain't that the truth, Mr. Career! That ain't vittles, it's like swallowing a lump of cold mud, it's bad for your stomach, any weather. What you got your mind fixed on, makes your mouth all spitty when you think of it? Hm?"

His voice took on a dreamy note as he leaned there in the doorway, the towel clutched around him. "Dahlia, I want soft-shell crabs, little ones, a million of them; and sweet corn, yellow bantam, cut off the cob and mixed up with butter and little green peppers. And I want French-fried potatoes, and then I want an enormous bowl—not a sauce-dish, but a bowl—of big red raspberries, cold and sugared so the sugar is kind of crusty. That, madam, is what Ah craves. Do you think you could get it?"

"It's as good as got," said Dahlia. Then a look came into her face. "When you're all through dinner and it tasted good, is it all right if I go uptown tonight right early after dinner?"

"Why not?"

He slapped back to the bathroom. He turned the cold-water faucet all the way, and the hot-water faucet one third. He turned them again. Nothing happened. He stared like one struck by nameless horror. No water. No water! He turned on the taps over the wash bowl then. Nothing. Grabbing the towel again he rushed toward the kitchen, bawling, "Dahlia! Dahlia!" But he arrived there just in time to hear her friendly voice greeting the back-elevator man and then the slam of the heavy metal door as they began to descend. He bounded to the house telephone, which was at the side of the pantry door. "Look!" he shouted to the voice of the hall man who answered, "there's no water! What's the matter with this place on a day like—— Well, let me talk to the superintendent then. What's his name? The new man. Bauers. Let me talk to Bauers. . . . Hello? Is this the superintendent? You're the new man, aren't you? Well, what the hell kind of a note is this, anyway! No water, and a hundred in the shade!"

WATER

Brophy always said that many a millionaire would like to live where he spent the whole of his days, there in the stone house on a lake, with the breeze blowing through the park across the water, and always cool in summer and warm (or warm enough) in the winter. He called it his Town House. To the Board of Water Supply of the City of New York it was known as the South Gatehouse of the water-supply system; and familiarly as the Central Park Reservoir. And there daily from eight to four Dan Brophy reigned a king and had for thirty-five years. At home in the crowded little flat on West Sixty-fifth there was the Old Lady, who was ailing, and Ellen and her husband, and he always sore since he was out of a job and come to live with her folks; and their two little ones, and Katie who'd never married and religious-cracked and forever in a corner with her beads. A man couldn't find a spot to sit with his paper and his pipe that there wasn't a screeching and pother and the Old Lady sitting there in her wheel chair with a look that turned your heart over. But here—here in the

Park Gatehouse—all was peace and dignity and order, and he loved it.

And now it was gone. By four o'clock this afternoon his robes would drop from him, his scepter would be taken from his hand, and he would be only an old man of seventy, out of a job. Seventy you were through, and they took your job away from you. Well, the young folks had to have their chance.

It was thirty-five years ago that Dan Brophy had got his papers as stationary engineer and come to take charge of the big Central Park Reservoir. He knew it better, he loved it more than any other place on earth: the smooth fresh lake that was the reservoir water, the little stone house jutting into it. A little damp in the winter, perhaps, but you got used to it. He was supposed to come on at eight in the morning, but almost always he was there a little after seven, especially in the summertime. Dan Brophy was one of the hundreds who controlled the water fed to New York's millions. It gave him an enormous feeling of responsibility, power, importance.

And now young Noonan would take over tomorrow morning at eight. He was coming in this afternoon to get last-minute instructions from Dan Brophy. The night man came on at four. Noonan was to have been here by three. It was half-past, and after, and he wasn't here yet.

Dan Brophy didn't in the least look his seventy years. A slim, tight little Irishman with a fine long head. He would have denied its looking more English than Irish. He always had color in his face; thin cheeks with the red rather high on the cheekbones, and lined but not wrinkled. His eyes were an unexpected hazel and they made you think of the eyes of an Irish setter: fine, faithful, trusting eyes. Thick iron-gray hair and a trim little gray mustache like a smart colonel's. He looked sound and clean and fresh, and he was.

New York politics had come and gone over his head—dirty politics and criminal administrations; crooked men and honest men of various breeds and stocks had held the vast rich city in their hands for a few years, but Dan Brophy had quietly gone on attending to the water that must always be on tap.

During his daily hours of work he ruled alone. No one was allowed within the Gatehouse without his permission. There were folding iron gates, so that you could leave the big wooden doors open and still be locked securely within. Daily his program was the same. First thing, at eight, he descended to the operating chamber far underground down in the bowels of the earth, to try out the motor. For thirty-five years he had done this at eight and never missed a day. Down the narrow spiral steps, round and round, sixty-one steps down, sixty-one steps up, a dozen times a day for thirty-five years. No wonder he had kept a nice flat stomach and never got winded like the inspector when he came his rounds, though he was forty and slim.

The reservoir was fed by the sweet waters of the Catskills. Dan liked to say it. The sweet waters of the Catskills, drinkable, washable, mixable. No copper in it. He knew all the names of the vast main reservoirs and the rivers and dams that fed the water to New York's millions, and he loved to tell them off. The kids—Nelly's kids, his married daughter—and before that his own kids used to ask him to say them and Nelly had made a kind of song out of the names to sing them to sleep when they were babies. Good, hard-sounding Indian names, and Dutch, like music. He knew them all, without Nelly's song to guide.

> Schoharie and Catskill and Mohawk,
> Shandaken and Kaaterskill Creek,
> Esopus and Croton, Kensico, Ashokan,
> Hush now and the fairies will peek.

Byram, Jamaica, Richmond, Manhattan, and Queens. Bronx. Silver Lake. The words were honey on his tongue.

This morning he had gone about his work as usual. He had seen that everything was in apple-pie order. The little stone house was cool and shady, but when you stepped outside it was like putting your head into an oven. But he liked a taste of the sun now and then. It felt fine on his skin. Part of his job—assumed by himself—was to keep clipped and neat the little privet hedge that bordered the Gatehouse stone steps and coping. He liked clipping, snipping. Vaguely, something stirred in him. A throwback, probably, to peasant or gardener ancestors in Ireland or England. He always had been handy with tools; clipping a hedge or seeing that an engine ran sweet and smooth, it was all one.

Brophy glanced at his control board. First Avenue—Second—Third. Fifth. Tenth. All in order. Here, on his left, the East Bay, there the West Bay, tidy little oblongs of water there below the flooring, like indoor swimming pools. And outside, through the rear door, open now, the shining silver expanse of the lake itself, the July sun glaring down upon it and the lake giving back as good as it sent.

There were all sorts of interesting things in that lake. Most of the people walking round the two-mile reservoir circular path didn't notice. Only he and the Regulars. He knew them and they knew him. There was Bernie Baruch and Groucho Marx and Greta Garbo and Gilbert Miller and Katharine Cornell and George M. Cohan and many another as famous. They knew him, and sometimes they stopped a moment to chat. Hello, Dan! How are you, Brophy! He had seen some of them grow from youth to middle age. He never presumed on his knowledge of them. Hard-working people, like himself, serious about their jobs and walking to refresh the strength that was in them, and recharge their batteries. He had seen them walking around the reservoir in sun and in snow, happy and in trouble; a sparkle in their eye or a glance that never left the pathway.

In the big lake itself there were all manner of living things, but you didn't tell people about that because they wouldn't understand; they'd think they dirtied the water when really they kept it clean. There were turtles, for instance, and ducks and fish. Pike as big as your leg that had been there for years and years. And the pigeons and gulls that rode the water.

He had got into the way of talking aloud to himself. He stepped out now to the little balcony overhanging the lake, at the rear. Fifth Avenue to the east and Central Park West opposite—he had seen amazing things happen to those skylines. He had seen palaces go up and come down. There was Andy Carnegie's house at Fifth and Ninetieth still standing. Few enough of them left now. When he first came on gatekeeper, the whole of Fifth Avenue was nothing but fine, big houses—the Vanderbilts and Goulds and Astors. Gone now, and square stone apartment houses, twenty stories high, in their places.

He minded the day they had come to take down the little iron fence, dated 1858, that ran all the way around the reservoir stone coping. A nice neat little fence. Victorian, they called it, after the old girl herself, doubtless, though that was queer here in America. They had carted it away and put up an ugly wire fence in its place, eight feet high and hideous, to keep people from throwing themselves in the water, they said. A lot of good that had done. If a person wanted to kill himself bad enough he'd climb an eight-foot wire fence as soon as a three-foot iron one—and they had, too, as he knew they would.

That very first week he had come on the job, years and years ago, that young woman had jumped in the lake up there at the far end, near Ninety-sixth East. By the time they got to her with a boat and fished her out she was dead enough, poor girl. And that man who had run out on the ice itself that bitter winter when the lake had frozen over except for a little open water hole where the old fountain pipe ran. Crazy, he must have been. He remembered how the man had just shoved himself down into that hole in the ice. He couldn't get to him in time, though he had shouted as he ran. A job it had been, fishing him out that afternoon. Bitter work. What did they want to go and throw themselves in the pretty reservoir water for! Untidy and thoughtless. But then, you didn't think of such things when you were crazed with grief and that. When the boy Michael,

his only son, had died, and when the Old Lady had got the stroke, and
when Nell and Ed and the kids had come to the flat to live, why, then he
sometimes had thought that life wasn't much to go on with. But there
always was the quiet and peace and responsibility of the Gatehouse to hold
him up. . . .

He stopped thinking about that and went indoors. No good thinking of
things like that now. He knocked the ash out of his pipe, carefully, into the
big brass spittoon that Boyle had given him when that crazy Prohibition
had come in and closed his place over on Columbus and Sixty-fifth.

Quarter to four. He had done everything there was to do. For the last
time he had had his lunch in the little wooden enclosure that he liked to
call his office, there in one corner of the big stone-walled room. He always
brought his lunch with him, put up by Nell. (Not as good as the Old
Lady's had been, though Nell said her way was more nourishing and
healthy for him. Vitamins, God save us all!) He had brewed his cup of tea,
strong and black, the way he liked it, in spite of the heat outdoors. It put
new life into him. He had washed his dishes and made everything shipshape. He saw that all was in order—his report blanks, a pencil (he'd give
that pencil to Noonan as a present, just to show there were no hard
feelings).

He had polished the brass parts. He had rubbed the control board until
it glittered. Then down in the operating chamber for a last look. For the
first time the climb up the stairs seemed wearisome, endless. Fifty-eight,
fifty-nine, sixty—sixty-one.

What could be keeping Noonan? They were like that nowadays. No
sense of responsibility, not caring whether the job suffered or not. He had
the right to go at four if he wanted to, Noonan or no Noonan, but he
didn't want the night man to show him the ropes. The last of it, but his job
just the same, showing the new man around, explaining where this was
and that, what time the calls came in, how the report should be made out.
And to tell him never to leave the Gatehouse while on duty. Never. He
remembered the one time he had left the place. His rule was not to step
more than ten feet from the door to where the privet hedge grew, so that if
the phone rang he could hear it. That one time when the girl had been
thrown from her horse in the bridle path right there below the bridge facing the Gatehouse south door. He had run to pick her up as she lay there
in the road, cut and bleeding so that her golden hair was dark and sticky.
That minute the phone must have rung and kept on ringing, and he hadn't
heard it with all the hullabaloo and the girl lying there like death.

"Brophy! Where've you been?" The inspector's voice on the telephone,
hard as nails. "I've been ringing for ten minutes straight, and more. Don't

try to tell me you were down in the operating chamber." So then he had told him about the girl and how she looked like done for. The inspector had toned down a little then, but he'd barked just the same that the mounted police was there on the bridle path, it was his duty to attend to runaways and accidents on the beat.

"The cop wasn't there to see. I'm a man and a human being. Would I see a girl stretched there in the road, white as death and the blood streaming from her head, and not help! I'll give you my job now if that's what's expected of me!" Dan always had been proud of the way he spoke up to the inspector that day.

Five minutes to four. He looked out through the folding metal gate at the south door, facing the bridge and the bridle path. A cruel, blistering day. Mothers with their babies in gocarts with wobbly wheels. They spread their bits of blanket on the parched grass beneath the trees and lay there through the long drowsy afternoon and got the good of the park. They were the ones needed it, he reflected. The usual group of starched, white-clad nursemaids were seated on the stone coping near the building itself, in the scant shade. Talking to their park beaux, good-for-nothing bums most of them, meeting the nursegirls and coaxing small change out of them and pretending to be crazy about them, while the poor kids were left squalling or else running out into the bridle path, not being watched. He never had let Michael when he was alive, or Nelly and her kids, come and play in or around the Gatehouse. It wasn't business. If they came to the park they had to take what they could get of it like all the rest, and no favors, just because their pa and grampa was a Gatehouse tender. Engineer. Gatehouse Engineer.

Well! Two minutes to four. Four, you might say, and no Noonan. He turned back into the cool of the house. Guessed he'd call up the High-Pressure Station down on Oliver Street. Noonan had been oiler at the High-Pressure till he passed his stationary examination and got promoted to this. Oiler on one of the big engines. Great, shining, black-and-gold giants that reminded him for all the world of some people he had seen once in a circus—The Egyptian Queen's Eunuchs, they were called—he didn't know how that one word was pronounced, but great, black, oily giants they had been, too, with gold on their wrists and arms and around their middles. Slaves.

There was a breeze between the two open doors, north and south. He loved the north door best. That great circle of water, blazing and still this July afternoon. There were winter days the wind whipped it up and made waves you'd think it was the ocean. Other times, like today, it was like a sheet of hot glass. In the winter the ice went shush-clink, shush-clink, like music. Staring at it now he tried to decide when he liked it best. Well, sir, hard to say, and that's a fact. He stood. He glanced all around and up. Like a good-by. On the wall over the lake-side doorway there was a plaque, bronze, with a lot of names on it. One stood out: FAIRCHILD, CONTRACTOR. 1858. He had built the stone house that had been Dan Brophy's castle these thirty-five years. And thanks to you, Mr. Fairchild, sir.

"Hi, Pop!"

Dan whirled. Yes, there he was. Noonan. His big shoulders blocked the south doorway. He rattled the bars of the folding gate that was kept locked. He peered in facetiously, making a face like a prisoner behind bars, or an ape. Kids sometimes did that. It always made Dan mad.

"Oh, it's you, Noonan. I thought you wasn't coming, maybe you'd changed your mind about would you accept the job or not." There, he had said something he hadn't meant to. But Noonan wasn't put out.

"What's the hurry! I'll be cooped up here till I'm seventy, like you, and that's a good thirty-five years. Time enough to sit in this death house and get rheumatism, I'll say."

"I've got no rheumatism," Dan said. "I'm strong and hearty as ever I was."

"Sure, Grampa. You're a tough guy. How's for a scrap? Want to fight?" He doubled his fists and danced around Dan like a prize fighter.

"I bet I could give you a good scrap at that, for all you're so young and cocky."

"Save it for the girls, Pop. Look, where'll I put my things?" He had brought a little bundle.

Dan became official. "Here." He led the way to the little office enclosure. "I'm all ready to go. I want to show you the ropes first so you'll get the hang of the place. Maybe we'd better start down below in the operating chamber, that's the important place."

"Oh, take it easy. I'll find my way around." He looked all about the bare, cool, gray room and glanced at the lake through the open north door. "That's the puddle, huh? Well, I guess after the High-Pressure Station I can manage this one-horse machine."

Dan's face was set and stern. He went on, doggedly, "This here is the control board——"

"O.K., O.K., Pop. I catch on."

"Look here, you think you're smart, but this place is important. It isn't what you're used to, Greasy Pants, with nothing to do but oil a black engine every so often—a child could do it. Stationary engineers in the Waterworks, we're important men, and the running of the stations and resavoys and gates depends on us. It's us provides water for the kids to bathe, and for cooking and washing and drinking for millions and millions of folks in New York. Where'd they be without us! You got to think of that when you take on a job like this, young feller, me lad."

"Yeh, we're great little guys, all right. What's that? That shed thing in the corner?"

"That's my office—the office. You can make yourself a nice hot cup of tea in here, too, when the damp gets you, winters."

"Tea!" He roared with laughter.

Dan regarded him searchingly. "You're not a drinking man, I hope. Drink don't mix with this job, let me tell you."

"Oh, I take a drink now and then with the boys. But working, I have a bottle of milk with my lunch."

"You'll find tea keeps you warmer."

"I don't need nothing to keep me warm. I'm a hot baby just the way I stand." He slapped his chest a resounding blow.

Just so he had felt thirty-five years ago, Dan reflected. Not such a big fella maybe, but strong and tough.

This is the east bay, this here is the west bay.

Noonan listened as an adult listens to a child's prattle; he seemed to be enjoying some private joke. He grinned as he listened and nodded his head. It was well after four now, and Quirk, the night man, had come on. Dan introduced the two men, stiffly. He was going to do his duty to the end.

The telephone rang. There was something sharply insistent about its ring, as though the very tone of its bell divulged its emergency. Dan started toward it. Then he looked at Noonan, but Quirk answered it. His face then became an almost childlike study in surprise, unbelief, horror. He glanced at the control board. "Why, no, sir. They're all O.K. It must've been something else—— Is it—— You say it's on again now—— Well, nothing's happened here. . . . No, Brophy's off, you know, for good. . . . He's still here in the Gatehouse, but he's leaving. . . . Oh, no, he wouldn't do a thing like that. Not Dan. . . . Yessir, I'll call you back."

He leaped to the control board, examined it. All was in order.

"What's wrong?" Dan Brophy demanded, "What's that about me you said?"

"That was the Chief. Main office says they been swamped with calls the water in this section's been off for five good minutes."

Noonan began to laugh aloud now. Not so heartily, perhaps, as he had planned, but loudly enough, nevertheless, and the effect was aided by the way he slapped his own thighs. "The joke's on old Dan! I was just having a bit of fun when you turned your back and was explaining so solemn about this was the east and this was the west and this the north and that the south, why, I just snapped her off for a minute, for a joke, see?"

The two men stared at him. "I'll have you fired," said Quirk.

"Not me, buddy. I got my papers."

Silent, Dan walked with dignity to the office and gathered up his things: his little spirit lamp, his cup and saucer, his pencil (let him get his own pencil now, the ape), his old sweater that Annie had knitted for him years ago against the cold and damp, his rubbers for winter days down in the operating chamber.

He came out. His bundle under his arm, he shook hands in silence with Quirk. He turned and looked at Noonan and the effect was that of a tall man looking down at an insect, though Noonan towered inches above him.

"It's you," Dan said very low, for there were people outside the open south door, in the shade, "it's you and your kind they call the younger generation is ruining the world. Nothing is sacred to you—jobs nor duty nor responsibility nor nothing. Joke, is it! It's jokers like you scum will bring the country to ruin and the world to an end. Mark me!"

"Aw, it was just in fun, Pop! Can't you take a joke?"

Dan Brophy unlocked the folding iron gate and stepped out into the withering July sunshine. The reservoir path stretched ahead of him, a last long mile.

"You're to keep the hedge clipped," he called over his shoulder to Noonan grinning in the doorway.

"Sure thing, Pop. I'll bite it off every morning before breakfast."

LOVE IN HARLEM

Alan Career had eaten six of the hot, delicate little soft-shell crabs, their white meat melting on the tongue. He had eaten the buttery sweet corn and crisp stacks of French-fried potatoes and a vast bowl of red raspberries, iced and sugared. He had drunk his long, cold drink with the mint stuck in the side of the glass. He hoped he wouldn't have a stomach-ache. You couldn't, he argued to himself, when you had enjoyed a meal as he had that one. The digestive juices or something took care of that. Instead of iced coffee Dahlia brought him a small cup of black hot. He felt soothed, rested, incredibly refreshed, and not at all lonely.

When he had found that the water mysteriously was not running, and after his irate protest to Bauers, the new superintendent, he had thrown himself on the bed a moment to cool off and wait for the water. And he had slept briefly, in spite of the heat. He had wakened feeling curiously free and light and happy. He was a little ashamed of the feeling, with

Patty and Susan hardly more than an hour out at sea. But he enjoyed the soaring sensation, nevertheless. He had barely had time for his bath and a cigarette and a long cold drink before Dahlia had summoned him to dinner. And what a dinner!

So now he sat by the window with the electric fan going, feeling fine. He left the lamps unlighted. It was very early, and brilliant daylight. He heard Dahlia stirring about in the kitchen as though she were hurrying with the dishes. She wanted to get up to Harlem, that was it. Vaguely he wondered how she had the energy on a night like this. He thought idly of what he should do with his evening. It was nice to do nothing. Might go over to the newsreel, later. Air-conditioned. But those damned war pictures, or travel films. The canals of Holland. He might just stroll over to that cool place by the pond in the park at Seventy-second and sit there and breathe the fresh air. He heard Dahlia telephoning briefly, in a low voice with a certain timbre. Dahlia rarely telephoned. It was one of the things Patty liked about her.

Suddenly she appeared before him now, lounging there by the window, a transformed Dahlia. She was wearing a chocolate-brown and white print, very smart, and a large brown hat. She had rouged her cheeks and her lips just a little and her eyes looked large and lustrous. She wore neat, high-heeled pumps so that her badly articulated shanks seemed slim and almost shapely. Big-bosomed, trim, she looked handsome now.

"I just thought I'd let you know I'm going, Mr. Career."

"All right, Dahlia. That was a grand dinner you gave me."

"Well, those raspberries was awful high. Terrible. Seems they're scarce or something; it's the wet spring we had and then this heat all of a sudden, the man said. I had to go three places to get 'em, and high! Miz Career would be wild." She giggled a little, nervously.

"That's all right. They were worth it. . . . How did you eat your dinner and get dressed so fast?"

"I didn't eat. I'm eating uptown."

Uptown. It was a term she always applied to Harlem, that mysterious city within a city. "A beau, eh? Good girl, Dahlia. Just so you're back for my breakfast."

She laughed lightly, evasively.

He took out his billfold; he held out a five-dollar bill. "All that extra work packing for Mrs. Career and Susan and Miss Mapes, and that running around in the heat on Lexington and that good dinner——"

"Mrs. Career gave me a dollar." She hesitated.

He was furious. He took out another five, recklessly, and put it in her light palm with the other. Her eyes widened, "Oh, Mr. Ca-reeah!"

She was off. He heard the bump and slam of the service elevator. He reflected that they knew nothing about her, really. She had lived in their apartment, a daily and necessary part of their lives, and they knew nothing about her except that she was good and kind and honest and sympathetic; a gifted cook; and that she loved Susan. As if that weren't enough to know about anybody, he thought. When she came to them Patty had asked if she was married and she had said, no'm, she had been married, but not at present. Dahlia Thomas. Sometimes—rarely—she had telephone calls. They were brief, but her voice and manner changed. They took on another note, a fine informality. When she answered the telephone in a call from one of Patty's friends she was very correct.

"Mrs. Career's apartment. . . . Yes. . . . I'll see if she's in. . . . What's the name, please?" But in her own private talks, "Yeh? . . . Oh, hello, there! . . . Sure am! . . . Where was you last night?" A soft-throated giggle. She could speak correctly enough, but now she lapsed into an easy illiteracy as though dropping a stage role.

Five years in the house, he reflected, and they really knew nothing about her.

Dahlia got off the subway, came up the stairs at One Hundred and Thirty-fifth Street, and emerged into the full light of Harlem's Lenox Avenue. It was almost eight o'clock and she hurried, stepping along with a free stride in spite of her stilted heels. Lenox was not yet blooming for the night. Harlem's workday was a long one. Its neon lights were not yet turned on, its music had not yet started. They had just begun to stream home to Harlem—the truck drivers, the seamstresses, the part-time maids, the girls who slept "out," the lavatory attendants, the dock hands, the switchboard operators, the elevator boys. They poured out of the el trains and subways to savory suppers and dark, noisome rooms, to leisure and music and dancing and sleep. Housewives and returning workers scurried into the neighborhood pork and sausage and fish shops. From open windows, block on block, you smelled food in frying fat, you heard snatches of melody—a mouth harmonica, a banjo or guitar, a voice in song. Never unrhythmic, never unvital music.

Dahlia's quick, light step carried her past the dozens of beauty parlors that dotted the region and she wished she had time to have her hair done fresh and clean and chick. The beauty-parlor-window signs announced, "Croquignole Wave, 75¢."

She had telephoned him to put on the stove, in water, the chunk of fat pork that was in the icebox, but she couldn't be sure that he had done it. He had no head for things like that, and why should he? Maybe he hadn't even stayed home. You never knew whether he would stay or go. That was part of the thrill of it.

She came to the row of strangely blackened houses, once good middle-class brownstone fronts, on One Hundred and Thirty-seventh just off Lenox. Up the stairs, one flight, two, three, four, quickly, quickly. She could smell the pork bubbling. Cooking too fast. She'd fix all that. Wouldn't it be like him wanting pork and cabbage a night like this! As she put the key in the door she heard the sound of the piano, one phrase over and over again. Her heart beat fast.

There he was at the piano, sitting half turned away from it in the grotesque position he always assumed during the long hours when he sat there composing. His lean, flexible legs crossed at the knees and sort of twined around each other, yet his feet managing to reach the pedals; his long fingers seeming to flow over the keys like chocolate sauce on vanilla ice cream. He was in his sleeveless white undershirt and a pair of wrinkled, white linen pants. He glanced up as she came in, but his face remained immobile. Only his eyes changed a little, grew wider then half closed again as before. He went on playing, his head jerking in time to the music, one great flat foot in its sockless bedroom slipper beating out the rhythm with a gentle slap-slap. From the top of the smudged and scarred piano his clarinet grinned at him with all its teeth.

She had stopped at the grocer's and now she dumped her bundles on the kitchen table, crossed to him at the piano, bent over him. She kissed the back of his long, lean bare neck as a mother kisses a child. He went on playing. His face and head might have been used as a portrait of the tragedy of his race—the tortured eyes, the lines of dignity and submission, the pouting childlike mouth, the amazing flash of white teeth so unexpectedly brilliant, like a lightning flash in the somber cloud of his mask. She looked at him, he looked up at her from the piano stool, he nodded and smiled and went on with his music. She was quick, lively, capable; he was slow moving, slow talking, dreamy. You couldn't tell, half the time, whether he had heard what you said. He was thinking of something else. His music, usually. A tune running through his head. He had made up dozens of them. She never ceased to marvel at the wonder of it. "Listen at this," he said now, playing.

She listened, her head cocked carefully to one side. She knew little about music. She had only the unerring rhythm sense of her race.

"Listen at this," he said again, like a man in his sleep.

It was a complicated thing, yet slyly simple, too. "It's grand," Dahlia said. "It's just wonderful, Lacy. It's hot licks, that's what."

She always said that. He repeated, patiently, like a child who is tugging at his mother's skirts, wanting attention, "No, but listen at this, Dahlia."

"Um-hmm, Lacy." She went into the bedroom and peeled off her smart print dress and her pink slip and girdle and came back in her all-over work dress that buttoned right down the front, neat and fresh. There were only two rooms: the kitchen-sitting room where the piano and the stove mingled affably, and the dark, stifling bedroom with its double bed. She went to the stove now, lifted the cover off the pot, clapped it back on, and brought the kettle to the sink. There she poured off the salt water and covered the meat with fresh. She put it back on the stove and began to cut a head of cabbage into the simmering pot.

She was ten years older than he. Sometimes she was frightened by her own luck. It couldn't last. Here she was, thirty-six, and Lacy only twenty-six. She was only working out and he was Lacy Bigger playing piano and clarinet, both, in the Jungle Ballroom with Chick Trueblood's Famous Rhythm Orchestra. White and black swarmed up there every night, enchanted, held, hypnotized by the perfection of the swing music that issued from that group of music-bewitched Negroes. All over Harlem they knew and applauded Lacy when he played a clarinet or piano solo or when they announced one of his own original compositions. And he stayed with her. He let her pay for this flat, for the installments on the piano. Let her cook his dinners on her days off. Curiously enough, though he loved fine clothes he would not let her pay for those. On Sunday afternoon in the Lenox Avenue style parade or on St. Nicholas Avenue in the late autumn or the first spring days when the Harlem bucks were out in their new finery—French-blue topcoats, postillion style, pockets dashingly slashed, patent-leather shoes, pearl-gray fedoras, bright-yellow walking sticks, pink or blue shirts—Lacy appeared a somber figure, but never drab. In his dark brown or navy blue or black he had an effortless grace and even some distinction.

As Dahlia set the table for supper she chatted through the music. If he heard he gave no sign. "She left today. My, they looked swell! Susan was like a rose. Blue, one of her handmade French, and a coat and hat to match, though it was too hot for the coat, but you know how Miz Career is —Susan had to look traveling correct, like her ma. She gave me a dollar when she left and said take good care of him, as if I wouldn't anyway. And he up and gave me ten, I thought I'd bust, you could of knocked me down with a breath. It'll pay the piano installment and part of the rent money. I made him a mess of soft-shell crabs, he said it was the best dinner he ever eat. He's a sweet fella, that's what he is." She laughed fondly. Then, as an afterthought, "She don't rightly understand him."

"Listen at this, Dal," said Lacy patiently. He played the air again, just a few bars, listening intently as though to something far away and elusive. "Mm-hmm, Lacy. It's wonderful. It's the best yet." Just to be near him was enough, to know that he was here in the flat, playing, this wonder boy, Lacy Bigger. Lazy Beggar they called him at the Jungle, but she knew different. She knew he was working all the time in his mind. He never stopped working. Tunes ran through his head by day, by night.

"Hongry?"

"Hm?"

"I says, hongry?"

"Not much. Had me ham 'n' eggs for breakfast, big saucer huckleberries and cream, and some hot bread."

"My land, what time, Lacy! What time you have all that?"

"Usual time. 'Bout three."

"But when I phoned, asked you what you'd like for supper, you said fat meat and cabbage. If you ain't hongry."

He did not answer. She went on with her preparations for dinner. She seasoned the contents of the pot—a handful of fresh celery tops to give delicacy of flavor; pepper, a pinch of kitchen bouquet. The cabbage was simmering with the meat in a pool of golden fat. She went into the other room and stripped the tumbled bed, replacing the rumpled sheets with fresh ones, sheathed the pillows in neatly laundered cases. Over all she spread the rose taffeta cover that Mrs. Career had given her when she changed her bedroom color scheme. "In case you ever get married again," she had said laughingly. "Though heaven forbid."

Dahlia dusted the bedroom and wiped up the floor with a mop. Artlessly she shook the small matting rug out of the window and laid it again. Her face was wet with the heat and exertion. Now and then she peered into the bubbling kettle. Lacy continued to play. He would play one bar over and over a score of times, a hundred times, his eyes glazed. A cigarette dangled from his lips, cold. Sometimes he made little marks on a piece of paper propped up on the music rack.

"Wonder is it too hot for light biscuits. I'd have to use the oven, but they'd go good with the pork gravy. But maybe it's too hot with you at the piano, so near."

"Biscuits would go good," Lacy said almost a full minute later, as though the words had just penetrated his consciousness. "I ain't hot."

It was as though he had given her an accolade. Swiftly she got out the mixing bowl, spoon, flour, baking powder. She beat and stirred and rolled and cut. She had worked since six that morning, packing for Mrs. Career, cleaning the apartment after the travelers' departure, cooking Alan Career's dinner. Yet all her movements were brisk and sure and full of vitality. Now and then she glanced at him as a work-driven mother throws a reassuring glance at a child playing in the room. He went on with his repetitious strumming.

"Bring an evening paper with you?"

"Oh, Lacy, I forgot! I was in such a tear to get here I forgot."

He said nothing. He went on with his music. She slid the pan of biscuits into the oven, looked down at herself worriedly, brushed the flour off her skirt, then with a little shrug as though, after all, nothing mattered but Lacy, she opened the door and ran down the four flights of steps to the street, just as she was. In less than five minutes she was back, the illustrated tabloid in her hand. She held it out to him. With a flicker of his eyelids he indicated that she was to put it on the piano top.

They sat down to supper at quarter of ten. The room was stifling. She heaped his plate with cabbage and the slices of pork, ruddy and gold; with biscuits and cream gravy. She ate a little, but he, after a mouthful or two, ate nothing. He smoked cigarette after cigarette. They talked little. Her glance lingered anxiously on his face. She did not ask if the food suited him, if he was not hungry, or why he did not eat. She knew that, for the time, she did not exist for him, the food did not exist, that only music marched in his brain. The hot, heavy victuals lay on his plate, almost untouched.

She brought out the vast slice of chilled watermelon that she had carried with her when she first came in. He looked at it as a strange object. She had seen him distrait before, but never like this. Her patient, adoring eyes searched his face. His cheeks seemed hollower than when she came in, his eyes were dull and leaden, the cigarette dangled limp from a corner of his mouth. He sat, staring into space. Sometimes his head waggled jerkily in time to some ghostly, unheard tune.

Suddenly his face kindled. The transformation was frightening. His eyeballs seemed ready to start from their sockets, the muscles around his jaw worked, the veins stood out on his temples. He shoved his plate away so roughly that the gravy slopped on the clean cloth she had spread. He reached the piano in two strides of his long legs, his slippers slapping after him, he melted to the piano stool, he seemed to take the battered instrument into his long arms. He began to play now, not uncertainly, not querulously as he had before, but masterfully, triumphantly.

"Listen at this!" he shouted above the paean. "Listen at this!"

She sat there. Then she rose; she seemed pulled to her feet by the compelling rhythm. She stood a moment as if listening, then she began to dance alone, trucking at first, then her steps became more and more intricate, her movements took on a barbaric frenzy. Faster and faster he played.

Her body writhed and twisted and whirled to keep pace with it. "Listen at this!" he yelled. "Boy! Listen at this!" Exultation in his voice.

He stopped at last. She dropped, dripping and exhausted, into her chair. Now the sweat was dripping, too, from his hands and face that had been so clammy. He got up from the piano and went over to the sink and sluiced his head and arms and mopped them, grinning. He came over to her and kissed her, roughly, and ran his hands over her. He sat down at the table and began to eat, voraciously.

"Honey boy, don't eat that! It's all cold. Let me get you a plate of fresh from the stove."

"It's grand." His mouth was full and running over. He stabbed great forkfuls of the dripping pork and cabbage, wolfing them down. He sloshed halves of biscuit around in the gravy. "That's the tune I been rassling with since way back last spring and couldn't make it come right no way. Good hot July weather and it clears my head, makes me feel good. What'll I call it? 'Hot July.' How's that for name? 'Hot July.' You wait. You see. They'll be playing it dance music all next autumn and winter, every band in Harlem'll be playing it—— Harlem, hell! Every band in New York! Benny Goodman'll be playing it, and Duchin and all of 'em, and Whiteman. You wait. You see. Jeez, I feel like I'd come out of a fever. Leave me have a glass of beer, will you, honey?"

She hesitated, then fetched it and poured him a scant glass. "You know you never drink before you work, sugar. Eat slower. You'll make yourself sick, hot night like this."

"I ain't hot. I feel fine."

It was almost eleven. He got up, lighted a cigarette, took a long drag at it, then stretched his arms high above his head and kicked his legs out, first one and then the other, as though he were trying to get the stiffness out of them after a long sleep.

As she cleared the supper things, she heard him dressing in the bedroom. Presently he came out and began to pack his clarinet and his music. He had on his smart white coat and his black pants with the broad satin stripe up the side, and his patent-leather pumps and the romantic black cummerbund wound around his slim, flat waist. She came over and straightened his black tie, though it did not need straightening. He held out his hand and she put five dollars into it. She put up her face; he bent and kissed her.

"We got to rehearse. I want they should play this tonight. They got to get it right for tonight." He was talking, not to her but to himself. He lighted another cigarette and was out of the room; she heard his feet, incredibly swift and light on the stairs.

Neatly she put the remaining food into the refrigerator, she made the room tidy. She washed his socks and handkerchiefs and underwear and hung them to dry. In the bedroom she turned back the spread and lay down to rest briefly and she groaned with weariness as her body sank down in the breathless little room. She slept half an hour. Awake, she washed her body at the bowl and patted herself with pungent toilet water and powder and felt refreshed. By the time she had dressed again carefully and made up it was well after midnight.

She tucked a five-dollar bill—her second—into an old envelope, placed the envelope on the piano keys where his eye must fall on it first thing tomorrow, and closed down the piano lid. She looked all about her. The flat was neat and clean. She turned off the light, shut the door after herself, and locked it. The streets were brilliant and alive; the sidewalks were thronged as for a festival. Shuffling feet, music, gay, rich, caressing voices, girls in brilliant red and green and yellow and pink. Violent color, violent sound, carnival spirit. But she hurried along, no part of it, with her serious, gentle face and her quiet brown print.

At the Jungle Ballroom they knew her well; she went to her little corner table near the orchestra platform almost hidden by the artificial palms. She sat demurely at the table and ordered her small glass of light beer from Stompy Sam, the waiter.

There he was at the piano, her Lacy boy. His clarinet lay on top of it. The orchestra was playing "Swingin' Earth" and the floor was crowded with white people and black, men and women. The vast room was artificially cooled. The music stopped, there was perfunctory applause, the dancers drifted to their tables and booths. She leaned forward, Lacy swung round on the piano stool, his eyes sought her corner and his eyelids just flickered. That was all, but it was enough. She leaned back, satisfied.

That little Fredi Buzzell, the blue singer, slithered out from behind the palms to do her number. The roll of the drum. They threw the spot on her in the center of the bare floor in her tight white satin that was only a skirt and a shield over her breasts, a scarlet chiffon handkerchief dripping like blood from her hand. She sang and wriggled. Nothing extra and never was, Dahlia thought. Only her figgah, you had to hand it to her there. Dahlia looked down at herself and sighed a little.

Fredi Buzzell gave a last screech, a final wiggle, and a wave of the scarlet handkerchief and was gone to fair applause. Hundreds as good as Fredi in Harlem, and better, Dahlia knew. Sex appeal, probably, like that Josephine Baker, she couldn't sing or dance or anything, but they say dukes and lords go for her in Paris and Europe.

An interval, then Chick Trueblood, the orchestra leader, stood up and raised his right hand. There was a ruffle of the drums. Her eyes went to

Lacy seated there at the piano, his hands listless on his knees, his face dreamy, remote.

"La-dees an' gen-tel-men! This evenin' I have the honor to announce that Chick Trueblood's orchestra—yes'm, that's me, thank you—will now endeavor to present for the first time in this or any other country an original numbah by one of our own members of our own celebrated orchestra. The numbah, entitled 'Hot July,' is composed and arranged entirely and especially for this orchestra and played here and now for the first time by Mr. Lacy Bigger. . . . Stand up, Lacy, let the girls see you and let the folks all give you a great big hand. *Mistah Lacy Biggah!*"

Lacy looked around, still seated. Then, inch by inch, he uncoiled his long, lean body and stood a moment, drooping, his head averted from the perfunctory applause.

"You wait," Dahlia said aloud, fiercely, though no one heard her but Stompy Sam. "Just you wait!"

Lacy melted fluidly into his chair again. He struck the opening chord of "Hot July" and the orchestra swung into it with him. They were to play it all next winter, and the winter after that and after that, though they didn't know it then. It was to be incorporated into the music language of America; and orchestras in Cairo and Paris and Venice and Budapest and London were to play it, wherever people gathered to dance; and it was to be played at Carnegie Hall by the Symphony Orchestra, and the red plush boxes were to shout bravos at the lank, limp, black man who so lackadaisically came out to take his bow.

The floor had been crowded before; now it was a maelstrom. They were not merely dancing couples; they danced, seemingly, like a ballet, moved by one emotion, swayed by a common rhythm. It was like *Prince Igor,* like *Petrouchka,* like *Scheherazade,* in color, movement, frenzy, that crowd.

When it was finished they stood a split second. Then they began to stamp and shout and smack their hands together sharply. There was nothing forced about this. This was the real thing.

Dahlia was looking at him. Her eyes were enormous; they seemed to glow as though a lamp were lighted somewhere behind them. Her bosom rose and fell as though she had been running.

Suddenly, out of the mob, a little figure that had been dancing with the rest darted free and leaped to the orchestra platform. It was a white satin figure, slim and lithe, with a scarlet handkerchief streaming after it like a banner. Like a cat she gained the platform, screamed shrilly, sprang high, and hung herself about the standing Lacy's limp frame, her thin brown arms about his lean neck, her bare legs with the scarlet satin-shod feet locked about his legs. So she hung for a moment, a she-panther on its prey.

Dahlia Thomas stood up. The knuckles of her black hand gleamed white where she clutched the chair, her lips drew back from her teeth in a snarl, the room reeled and swayed before her eyes, she started forward.

But Lacy's strong, wiry hand reached up then and unclasped the brown arms from about his neck; gently, yet with power and firmness and a terrible deliberation, he turned the little figure over and slapped her soundly, just once, on her white satin bottom. Then, still gently, he tossed her onto the unused bass drum, where she landed with a conclusive boom. "Scat!" Lacy said lazily.

The crowd howled. Shaking, Dahlia sank back into her chair. Her eyes were on him. Unsmiling, he sleepily raised his palm to her—just a barely perceptible gesture—the opening of the palm, a little jerk at the top of it as the hand came up. That was all.

"Another beer, Miz' Thomas?" said Stompy Sam.

She shook her head. Blindly she paid for her beer. She felt she must choke with happiness if she did not get out. Out into the air she walked a few blocks, but then her feet began to hurt in the high heels. She had scarcely sat down these past twenty hours. She sank into the subway seat but she was not conscious of weariness. She was not conscious of anything. Happy. That was all. She let herself into the Career back entrance and flicked on the kitchen light. A saucer and a spoon in the sink. He had had a little snack. She washed the plate and spoon and put them in their place. She wound her alarm clock, yawning fearfully so that all her strong white teeth showed against the red mouth. Two o'clock, and after. She was beat, she told herself. Dead on her feet. She rolled into her narrow bed in the stifling back room with the hot-water pipes running through it and she slept, and as she slept there was a half smile on her gentle, good face.

DANCING IN THE PARK

It was surprisingly cool in the center of the park, there by the pond near Seventy-second Street. Alan Career sat on a bench looking over the water. It was actually cool enough for a pipe. It putt-putted peacefully as he sat there. The place was almost deserted. People didn't know about it much, hidden there in a sort of hollow among the trees. Some small boys were playing near the edge of the pool in the fading light. There was a splash, and another. Two of them had jumped in and were swimming in the shallow water while the others kept a sharp watch out for the cop. Bathing was forbidden in this pond. Boys sailed their toy boats in it, and grown men, too, frequently. Once or twice Alan Career had strolled over here on Sunday morning and he had seen men his own age, and older, absorbed in the

maneuvers of tiny ships they themselves had fashioned—exquisite miniatures of the yacht builders' craft. Carefully they placed their boats in the
pond, these nautical men who were moored to the land, and they fed their
starved urge for the sea and the salt breeze by bending all morning over
the stone parapet, watching the little land breeze fill the sails of their beloved boat, fancying themselves actually aboard a slim beauty like this,
with a line like a scimitar, and a hundred times its size.

He had never been here before at this time of day. Patty wasn't one to
come out to the park of an evening, like a servant girl.

The young ragamuffins were coming out now with hoarse, triumphant
shouts, having bested the law, and were dressing in the near-by bushes. It
was almost dark. A grateful freshness seemed to emanate from the trees,
the grass, the water.

I'm sitting here, he thought, like an old married man, the kind you used
to see in the funny papers before *The New Yorker* and *Esquire*. What was
that song? "My Wife's Gone to the Country, Hurray! Hurray!" I guess
they don't have jokes about summer widowers in *Esquire*. They've gone
out of fashion. Fashion. I'm fashionable. Hell, yes! Me and my wife, both.
Alan Career photographed at El Morocco with his lovely young wife, the
former Patty Mallett. . . .

Chillicothe, Ohio. Local boy makes good in New York. Good and lousy.
Had to have her mother take her to Europe, like a damned failure.

There came to his ears the sound of music. Some fools in the park with
a radio; or maybe just a radio taxi waiting for a fare along a Fifth Avenue
side street. No, it was a real band playing hard. Must be one of those band
concerts they had over near the Mall somewhere. But it didn't sound like
anything as conventional as a band concert. It had the insistent rhythm of
swing. He rose after a minute or two and strolled in the direction of the
music.

There was the bleat of the saxophone, the beat of the drum, the pipe of
the cornet, the blare of brass. Vaguely he remembered that there was some
sort of municipal park dance in the summer. Keep the kids off the streets,
or on 'em, he didn't know which. He was not prepared for what he now
saw as he turned off the walk, crossed the wide roadway, and came upon
the vast space in front of the bandstand.

Thousands of them. Thousands and thousands of boys and girls—eighteen, twenty, twenty-five—dancing on the cement in the open air. The arc
lights cast a golden glow upon them. As he came to the outer edge of the
watchers that encircled the dancing floor, the music stopped with a final
blare and the dancers swarmed off the floor. They brushed past him, they
jostled him, they made for the shadowy spaces that lay so invitingly beyond

the dance floor. Hatless, all of them. The boys were the kind he saw in shipping rooms, at minor desks, standing behind chain-store grocery counters, delivering packages, driving bundle vans—working for twenty or twenty-five dollars a week. They had on clean blue shirts, their hair was slicked back, they had a pleasant city sunburn. They wore suit coats. One or two even sported white coats smartly pinched in at the waist.

The girls were in summer prints and little wash frocks and organdies. Thin stuff, and transparent for the most part. They wore their hair as Patty wore hers, he noticed—simple and cut rather long so that it curled where the ends just touched their shoulders. Their hair looked as if it had just been washed. It sprang alive and shining. The style was flattering and made a frame for their faces so that they seemed very young and wide-eyed.

Almost immediately the band struck up. They played "Whoa Babe." A second before the floor had been a deserted gray expanse. That first alert couple darted across the immense space like a pair of swallows in flight. Then the thousands swarmed upon it. Not an inch was left bare. Alan Career found himself grinning as he knocked the ash out of his pipe and edged his way to the rim of the dance floor, the better to see this exhilarating sight.

They danced in the curious style of the day and age. They jerked and twirled in the intricate St. Vitus steps of the Howdy Hop. Then, quite simply, they withdrew a little, and, arms about each other's waists, they ambled lackadaisically for all the world like young calves in a meadow. Suddenly the youth would catch the girl to him and twirl her in a breathtaking spin that made the onlooker's head whirl. They then kicked up their legs, swooped, dipped, jounced, and glided. As Alan Career watched their childlike antics he felt suddenly old and out of it. They were so young, so lacking in self-consciousness. Any boy, he noticed, would approach the lady of his choice and say, "Would you like to dance?" Very self-possessed, like a Yale blood at a Christmas dance at Pierre's. Usually the girl would nod her head, wordlessly. They were off. He was surprised to see that the girls, for the most part, wore rather sturdy shoes with heavy soles and sensible heels. Coquettish footgear seemed to be the exception. The boys had their trousers well turned up at the cuff so that you saw their lively shanks as they capered. He thought that some of them must have danced together for months, so expert were they, so intuitive each with the other's signals. Miles of practice must have been covered to perfect this amazing routine. Some of their steps were as intricate and exquisitely planned as those of a pair of professional entertainers at the Rainbow Room or the Waldorf. Yet there were others who had met at that moment and never before. An introduction evidently was not necessary. The music was their chaperon. Then Alan Career saw that this was not quite true, for here and there on the dance floor and at the fringe of the crowd were stern-faced and somewhat weary-looking women in khaki skirts and blouses and little military-looking caps. They kept an alert eye on the dancers and when a couple showed signs of too much energy even for that lively gathering, or too much emotion for the park proprieties, they stepped quickly forward and tapped the offending pair on the shoulders.

Amused, he edged his way over to one of these rather formidable and martial figures.

"Uh—many dances like this?"

The observant eyes looked up at him and at what they saw, melted. "Every Tuesday and Thursday night. All over town."

"Great thing," he remarked, conversationally. "I wouldn't mind having a whirl myself." Then, aghast at the thought that she might consider this an invitation, "That is—uh—makes a fellow feel young again—you know."

But he need have had no fear. She had moved away, her basilisk eye sweeping the dance floor. He felt like a schoolboy who had talked out of turn to teacher. The music stopped again. Again they swarmed off the dance floor. They gathered into little groups, they stormed the ice-cream-cone wagon, they indulged in heavy-handed banter, they shoved; there was a good deal of horseplay, heavy coquetry; and girlless boys marching lock step through the crowd, followed by scuffling and unconvincing shrieks

"Stop it! Stop your shoving!"

"Look, Myrna's sore!" They pronounced it Moyna's so-ah.

"Whyn't you daincing?"

"I wouldn't daince with a stick like you, not if I was to staind here all night."

Or two boys huddled in dark conference. "I seen a couple of nice ones together, but you was hoofing with that rock you picked up."

"Well, she looked O.K. How would I know she was paralyzed from the hips down?"

The music struck up. That new song. They were rhyming ring time with swing time instead of springtime as they used to when he was a kid back in Chillicothe, Ohio. There was a kind of cult of this new-old jazz among the boys and girls Alan remembered having heard. They worshiped it, the old gods having been destroyed, and having nothing better upon which to lavish their bewildered, undirected young devotion. As they sped forth now at its summons they were magically transformed from the rather vulgar and commonplace giggling girls and oafish boys of a moment before into lovely pixies, fauns, and sprites, free, graceful, uninhibited, disporting themselves in this urban concrete grove.

Alan Career's feet were tapping in time with the infectious rhythm. Someone brushed softly but unmistakably against the sleeve of his tweed coat. He looked down. A girl's voice said, "Oh, pardon!" He thought, Well, my gosh, I'm being picked up in the park like a grocery boy. She was a funny-looking little thing, not pretty.

"Oh, hello!"

She looked a little disdainful. "Hello—if you want to start that way."

Well!

She nodded toward the madly whirling crowd on the dance floor. "Isn't this delicious!" in an affected little tone.

In the second glance, encompassed in a moment, he decided that, though the average boy in this mob would have passed her by in favor of one of the more obvious golden-haired sprites, she had a kind of charm. The word piquant came to his mind. She wore a gray dress that had a sort of ruching edging the square-cut neckline, rather low. Tight in the bodice, full in the skirt. Patty had one something like it. She had told him it was a dirndl, copied from the Austrian peasant girls' dresses. This particular little ersatz Austrian peasant had a wide red mouth, made wider and redder purposely, rather protuberant blue eyes, a nose that was too short. She was a good deal like a Pekingese. She looked up at him under her lashes as though she had been practicing looking up under her lashes. Not very good at it yet.

"My name's—uh—Alan. And you——? As they say in the novels."

"I'm Miss Lonely Heart like you read about in the papers."

This was going to be all right.

"Dance?"

She nodded. They danced. The floor was very unyielding and not smooth. It had been waxed with a soapy preparation. He knew now why the girls wore practical shoes and the boys turned up their trousers. She danced effortlessly and rhythmically. Her body was pliant and slim. She was little and light and it was pleasant. Patty was a tall girl, tennis and swimming, biggish bones, and a lot of expert dieting to keep the thirty-four, with her shoulders. Miss Lonely Heart did not talk as she danced. At first he led her in the conventional steps to which he was accustomed. But little by little, and almost without his noticing it, she was guiding him into the steps in use by those about them. They essayed some of the convolutions he had watched from the side lines. Not so bad. They whirled. Then, arms about each other's waists, they strolled. He felt young, foolish, irresponsible, and rather happy. He was sorry when the dance was finished. Hot, though.

"How about an ice-cream cone?"

She shuddered. Oh, no.

He was puzzled. He couldn't for the life of him make out whether she was a nice girl trying to be not too common, or a not-too-common girl trying to be refined. That was it. Refinement. Terrible word.

"What is a young and lovely and fashionable gal like you doing in New York on a night like this?" He was rather proud of that lead in. Slick.

"It's no hotter than Long Island or Connecticut."

(You don't say.) "Is that where you'd be if you weren't here?"

"Maybe. Where would you be?"

(No dice.) "I like it fine right where I am. I'd rather be here this minute than any place in the world." (Phew!)

She turned on him another of those under-eyelash looks. Where had he seen that kind of eyework before? The movies, that was it. Pictures.

The music again. "Dance?"

She pointed to his fawn flannel trousers, very smart. "You'd better turn those up. They'll be ruined." Nice little thing. Practical for a kid. He began to feel rather paternal about her and wished he wouldn't. He turned up his trouser cuffs, displaying an alarming pattern of fawn and gray and scarlet plaid English socks which Patty had given him for Christmas.

Out on the floor they skimmed again. He felt expert and confident now. "Hi, Hot Socks!" yelled a demon lad from the side lines. "Hot Socks!" his gang echoed with gusto. Alan didn't care at all. He kicked up his heels. They skimmed, dived, swooped, pranced, strolled, whirled. She was a feather in his arms; he swung her with one arm as he remembered having seen that Argentine fellow swing his partner at the Plaza Persian Room. Almost at once one of the khaki basilisks touched him on the shoulder. "Sorry. We don't permit that."

Oh, very well. We've got plenty of other elegant steps and try and stop us. He smiled down at her, she smiled up at him (eyelash business). He held her a little closer. Her face became serious, dreamy. They were all serious, he noticed. He had remarked that from the first. They were lively but unsmiling. They did not talk, they did not laugh. They were enjoying themselves, but it was a surface gaiety with an air of routine about it. From somewhere in the back of his head there popped a line from a play that he and Patty had seen. He hadn't liked the play much. Ibsen. *A Doll's House*. Thorvald, stricken at his wife's leaving, had cried to her, "But haven't you been happy?" And she had replied, sadly, "Not happy. Only merry."

That was what these youngsters were, dancing. Not happy. Only merry. Only merry. He must have said it aloud, unconsciously, for she looked up sharply. "What's that?"

Rather shamefacedly he explained, "I was just reminded of a line in a play. You young people today. Not happy—only merry."

Evidently she had never heard of it, wasn't interested, didn't understand. "I suppose you think you're a hundred."

"I'm thirty-four," he said gravely.

"I hate kids."

"You're a sweet thing."

They danced cheek to cheek. Her skin was fresh and smooth and resilient. If he had turned his head just half an inch he could have kissed her. He said so.

"Yes, and get put off the floor for good." Sharply.

"They can't see everything."

"Yes, they can—those old drizzle-pusses."

"When are you going to break down and tell me all about yourself?"

But she was evasive. There was something guarded, calculated about her. "You're not one of those girl reporters, are you? Sent out to get a feature story on New York in the summertime, and I'll read all my brilliant cracks in next Sunday's tabloid?"

"Don't you wisht you knew."

"Wish."

"Pardon?"

"Wish, not wisht. And don't say pardon all the time like that. Who do you think you're fooling! Stop pretending and be yourself. Your own little darling self. Come on, before I get rough. Where do you live and who are you?"

"You married?"

"Yep."

"All the nice ones are married."

She was cute but hardly original, he thought. "Now I've told you, you tell——"

The band struck up "Home, Sweet Home."

They danced wordlessly then, very close, and when the music ended he stood holding her in his arms for a moment because he wanted to, and she wanted him to, and all the others were doing the same, and the drizzle-pusses couldn't chase them off the floor now when they had to go, anyway.

The boys and girls were drifting off the floor and into the park shadows. There was a dreamlike quality about their going. Back to the stuffy flats, the nagging, harassed parents, the squalling brothers and sisters, the roar of the el trains outside their bedroom windows, the heat, tomorrow's job.

The cops, their smart coupés lined up at the roadside, were watching sharply. Outta the park, boys and girls. Kindly, but no nonsense about them. Outta the park and home with you.

"Well," said dirndl, "good night. It's been—I mean I've had a swell time."

"O.K., pleased to've metcha, hope we meet again sometime, sister. There. How's that? Now let's stop pretending. It's too hot. Where do you want to go for a drink?"

"A drink?"

"Yes. You know—wet libation in a glass, preferably alcoholic."

"Oh, I don't think I——" Looking up at him, very little and gray and gold and wide-eyed.

"Cut it, won't you! A joke's a joke. Do you want to go downtown? Or how about the Carlyle bar just over on Madison? Or Longchamps? It's air-cooled."

"Well," she agreed reluctantly. "Only for a minute, though. You wouldn't ply a girl with liquor, would you?"

He hustled her into a taxi at Fifth. "Vulgar little baggage, aren't you? Is that the right answer? Now you've given a very fine performance. Very. Stop it! . . . No, not you, driver. I was talking to—— Go to Longchamps, will you, Madison and Seventy-eighth."

She giggled. "Oh, sir!"

He shook her then, not seriously, but as one who is exasperated. She slapped him. He kissed her hard. She screamed. The taxi stopped before Longchamps' lime-and-raspberry-colored front.

"Well, that's over," Alan said. "Now we can be comfortable." And gave the driver a dollar on a twenty-five-cent ride for which the driver did not thank him, being a true New York taxi driver. For a moment he thought she actually was going to leave him. She started south on Madison, just a step, but he grasped her arm firmly and held her before him in the same compartment as they went through the revolving door.

"What will you drink? And wouldn't you like something to eat, after all that dancing?"

He didn't feel like eating; but a long cold drink! He was suddenly tired. Rye highball. Or a brandy and soda. No. Keep him awake.

"I'll have an Alexander cocktail."

He was aghast. "Oh, listen, you don't want that sickish sweet stuff this time of night."

"I do so!"

"All right." He was a little bored with it. "Only when you wake up with that oopsy feeling at three A.M., remember Papa warned you. Look, where do you live?"

"Over on Park—near Park, I mean."

"Make up your mind. Anyway, Park Avenue's a long street with lots of little streets cutting into it. I'll tell you what. I'll tell you all. I'm married. My wife's in Europe. I think you're sweet. I——"

"What's your job? I mean, where are you employed?"

"Ma'am, I ain't employed. I employ myself when I can get any business, which they say it's picking up and the Depression's over, but they'll have to show me. I'm a desk worker. How's that? I work over a desk, a handsome desk, I'll admit, with a view and a secretary and push buttons and telephones and an office boy. But a wage slave just the same. And now won't you be honest and cozy, and I wish to God you wouldn't crook your little finger like that when you drink. You're not fooling me, you know. Not any more."

"I don't know what you mean."

"All right, all right. You're a bitter-ender, I can see that."

She bridled. "I think it's about time you apologized for kissing me in the taxi like that, if you're a gentleman."

"I'm no gentleman, but how about that sock in the jaw you gave me? I suppose that's being a lady, eh?"

"Don't you talk——"

"Girl, you're as good as apologized to. One more drink and I'm down on my knees, though Grampa's knees feel a little wore down after all that cavorting. Now then. Where do *you* work? Junior League?"

She threw him a sharp glance. "What makes you think I work anywhere?"

"I'm going to kiss you again when I take you home."

"You ain't—— You're not going to take me home."

"You never were more mistaken in your life."

She was up, she was through the revolving door and down the street. His astounded gaze saw the elfin figure flash past the big plate-glass window, headed south. One shocked second and he, too, was on his feet, he was dashing after her. The headwaiter, suave but firm, blocked him at the door. "Pardon me, sir. You are forgetting your check."

Alan Career fished in his pockets, he opened his billfold, there was nothing smaller than a ten-dollar bill. You couldn't, after all. Habit was too strong. He clutched his change after what seemed like hours, and whirled through the revolving door so that it spun like an electric fan after him. The kid was crazy. Cute, but crazy. Out on the sidewalk he looked up the street as he ran. He could just discern her tiny figure tinier still in the Madison Avenue distance.

He had been a good runner in the Chillicothe high-school track meets and at Dartmouth. But as he ran, the caution of the past ten years of conventional New York training tugged at his coattails and told him he should not be doing this. The little dim gray figure darted round a corner and vanished. He made the corner in what would have been record-breaking time even in his Dartmouth days and it turned out to be his corner, his street. He could just see her. She was not running now. Poor little kid. Heh, wait a minute, Alan, my boy. You can't be seen chasing a girl down the street at one o'clock in the morning. The cops have a word for it. You'd look nice in nine-o'clock police court, up for molesting women on the street. Patty'd like that in the Paris *Herald*. He glanced over his shoulder to see if he was being watched, and when he faced forward again she had vanished completely. He stopped running then and was conscious that the sweat was streaming down his face; his whole body was wet. Dancing in the park was one thing; running hotfoot down these closed-in streets was another. He hoped that none of his elevator boys or the night doorman had been standing outside, seeing him chasing a girl up the street in the middle of the night, and Patty just sailed this afternoon.

But where had she gone? He turned into the foyer of his apartment house, in order not to pass it. He'd beetle up to the corner in a second to see if she was racing up Park Avenue. But he heard the voice of Bauers, the new superintendent, raised in an angry shout, and Bauers himself, in shirt sleeves, warm and wroth, was denouncing someone who had just vanished around the corner at the rear in the direction of service and the superintendent's basement apartment.

"A fine time for you to be coming home, young lady! Your ma's been half crazy. Said you was going out for a walk and it's after one. Where you been?"

A voice from the rear. "Oh, shut up, Pa. I been to the park."

"Park! I'll learn you to bum around the p——"

He saw Career. He coughed apologetically. "Excuse me, Mr. Career. My shirt sleeves and all. I was just worrying about my daughter, where she was. Of course it's hot down in the basement where we live, but young folks nowdays, honest to God, Mr. Career, I don't know what they're coming to."

"That's right," agreed Alan Career feebly. Bauers himself took him up in the elevator, still apologizing. Bauers said it was too hot to sleep and that's a fact. Career said, vaguely, was it, and Mr. Bauers decided privately that he had been drinking. You could smell it on his breath, and his face was like a beet.

He let himself into the apartment, he flicked on the light, he stood there swaying a little as if he were drunk, which he was not. The place was stifling. He felt as if he were choking. Ice water. That was it. He went to the kitchen. Dahlia's room off the kitchen was dark and her door open. The back hall door was not chained from the inside. She hadn't come in yet. He poured a glass of water from the iced bottle in the refrigerator, dumped ice into it, swallowed it thirstily and then another, though the chill burned his throat and made it ache. As he was closing the refrigerator door he saw a little saucedish of red raspberries looking rosily up at him, sugared and tempting. Holding out on him, was she? Thought he'd had the whole box for dinner. Saving this for his breakfast, probably. He got a spoon and ate the saucerful, leaving the icebox comfortably open until its warning burr protested against such treatment. He put the plate and spoon in the sink.

A cold bath before he turned in. Nope, couldn't stand it, too tired. He peeled his clothes, he lay a moment staring at the empty bed next his all primly dressed in its dotted-Swiss summer flounces. He turned out the light and rolled over.

The superintendent's daughter. If Patty ever knew she'd have a stroke. . . . Poor little kid.

FOOD

The Swiebacks had everything lovely. Or almost everything. Mrs. Swieback would have been—was, in fact—the first to tell you so.

"We got everything lovely. The apartment you couldn't ask for anything grander, we can see the park from our bathroom, around the corner it practically is from us. Either I or the girl takes little Manning every day he should play by the pond in the grass, it's perfect. My Mannie is a gorgeous husband and father, if I say so. I don't want to brag. Even I don't have to open my mouth to ask for something already I got it. I was born lucky, like Mannie says I am shot with luck, it's a slang expression. All my life I wanted to live on the East Side—I mean below Hundert and Tenth, naturally—and so I'm living, the hall downstairs, the foyer, it's like a palace, especially in the winter, with Turkish rugs and drapes and everything done in Italian, the furniture. I got tickets the fourth Monday regular as clockwork we go to the Guild opening, not the opening night it isn't of course, but for us subscribers it is like an opening till the tickets are for sale with outsiders like you. I got my mink, Manning goes like a little prince, everything at Best's. But what is the good—I got no husband. Well, I don't mean I ain't got my Mannie, God forbid. But on Saturday night only, like a fella, not a husband. It's the business. I ought to be ashamed to talk like that about a grand business brings us in such a wonderful living. Only it's like I am married and got no husband, God forbid. Mannie, he does all the buying fruit and vegetables for the whole three stores. It is some job. One o'clock in the middle of the night he is got to be up to go to Washington Market, it's downtown by the river. So daytime he sleeps, it's like you was married to a factory hand, or something. I shouldn't ought to say that, a king like my Mannie. Five, six o'clock in the morning he comes home, he has got to sleep again. Day in, day out, ony Saturday nights he can sleep like a person, account Sunday is closed the stores, naturally. Ony he can't sleep because he is by now so used to sleeping crazy like that he wakes up anyway the same as usual. Sunday mornings he just lays there like a mouse so he doesn't wake me, but I hear him anyway. Him and little Manning—he is got his own room, Manning—they can't wink a eyelash I don't hear it right away. I am like that. Day in, day out, so it goes like that. The worst is he don't hardly see little Manning, his own son, from one week's end to the other. He leaves, the boy is asleep, naturally. He comes home the boy is in bed. It's sh-sh-sh! you wake your papa, all the time. Manning might as well got no papa, God forbid, ony Sundays. Oh, well, I couldn't complain when I see what others got and how grand I got it, Mannie a wonderful provider and the sun rises and sets in me and Manning, and this gorgeous apartment on Lexington and a maid—the girl she can't cook anything extra, but that I don't mind, I like to cook, she is with little Manning wonderful, she is crazy about the child, you would think she is the mother, not me. Yes, we got everything lovely, if ony Mannie didn't have to get up such a hour, rain or shine, summer and winter. Every morning till five and six down there in that place, it's like crazy. A hour for a grand man like my Mannie he should be up!"

This July night Mannie Swieback had slept badly, for the day and the night had been insufferably hot. He had awakened at ten, at eleven, at twelve, he had lain there, tortured with heat and sleeplessness. And even when he slept, fitfully, he muttered in his sleep. Delphine Swieback (Della to her folks) listened and made out his mumblings to be about raspberries. My poor darling, always the business on his mind. Raspberries. Suddenly he shouted, "Raspberries!" in quite a loud voice so that he woke himself up and sat upright in his bed, sweating freely and staring wildly about in the midnight blackness.

"Sh-sh, Mannie, you wake the child!"

She got up and padded heavily into the adjoining room, but the round brown sausage that was Manning II (out of Emanuel) lay peacefully asleep in his bed, his breathing steady, his chest and belly barrel-like with good living from the Aye Wun Stores, Emanuel Swieback, Prop.

His wife and child came first, of course. But the business was part of him, part of them all, it was his first thought when he wakened, his last when he fell asleep. All through the day he was immersed in it, happy as a fish in water. Sometimes he wondered if the name—Aye Wun Stores—was quite the thing. It had been all right up in the Bronx, where he had started. But now with a store on Lexington near Seventy-first and another at Eighty-sixth and still another at Fifty-sixth and Third he had his doubts. Something like The De Luxe Markets would have been the thing. But that Sophy Lieber called her market by that name. The Widow Lieber, his ruthless enemy and competitor on Lexington. In gold letters on the Aye Wun plate-glass store windows you read, "Long Island And Westchester Deliveries Tuesday Thursday Saturday." He had even contemplated adding Newport to these gold letters, but he had decided against it, though reluctantly. These deliveries were mostly mythical, for his customers could avail themselves of local markets near their summer homes. But it was true that when they wanted something special, something rare, something precious in the food line, then the Aye Wun Stores, Emanuel Swieback, Prop., could supply it. Mannie made a specialty of fruits, vegetables, and poultry out of season. No dainty too exquisite, no source too remote, for his providing. The Widow Lieber had been quick to follow his lead in this, and the rivalry between them was of vendetta proportions. The neighborhood was what Mannie called classy. A customer caught with a rare dainty was often a customer gained for life. "If It's Edible The Aye Wun Has It" was the store motto. It was becoming difficult to get things out of season because now practically everything seemed to be in season all the year round. New York palates were overpampered.

"It used to be," Mannie complained, "you got watermelon in August and grapes in September and strawberries in June and spring chickens in the spring and turkeys at Thanksgiving and so on. But now! Turkeys you get in May, and strawberries in January, and peaches in March and all of them the year around. Folks is spoiled, thank God. Now it is so if you got something in season in season, you understand, why, it's considered out of season. A crazy world."

Now, at Mannie's nocturnal shouts Mrs. Swieback was disturbed but not too distressed. She knew it was business on his mind. And the heat. She came back to bed now. "You woke yourself up, Mannie, with your business worries. Isn't that a foolishness! What you want to worry? We got everything lovely. Leave be. Raspberries! Who cares raspberries!"

"I tell you what," he said to the plump, black-haired armful in the vaguely French bed beside his own, "I tell you what, it's too hot you and Mannie staying here in New York. You go up to the mountains anyway a month."

"And leave you here alone in the flat, with that girl's cooking, and if you should get sick! If it ain't too hot you should stand it, it ain't too hot for me. And Manning is brown and healthy like a Indian—knock on wood."

He rose now, for it was nearly one o'clock, and began to dress hurriedly like a soldier going into battle, with necessity for speed but reluctance to face the turmoil. "I'm going down early, I can't sleep anyway, the heat. And I want I should get the first chance at the raspberries."

"Raspberries, raspberries!" echoed Mrs. Swieback in sleepy irritation. "What is it with raspberries all the time! Never in all my life have I heard so much from raspberr——" But she was caught up in sleep like a living Rubens painting, all black hair and scarlet cheeks and white flesh on the tumbled sheets.

He rarely stopped even for a cup of coffee. He could get that later, in the market. He went to the garage around the corner and got the little battered car. He wouldn't dream of using the good car that he and Delphine had for evenings and occasional Sunday driving. They scarcely used it even then, for that matter. It was more symbol than a toy or a convenience. Mannie was dressed a trifle shabbily, too, for the night's fray. But though the suit was shabby, it was well made, and so was his shirt, but they were old and unfit for his wearing in any place other than Washington Market with its slippery streets, its piled-up produce, its rush and almost savage strife.

He was not a dashing driver; Mannie had no head for mechanics. He eased his pudgy figure behind the wheel now, then sat tense and watchful as he trundled down the streets. Over to Park, down to Fourteenth, across to Twelfth, past the docks of the steamship lines and the freight sheds. The waters of the North River were almost hidden by the great piers and warehouses; only now and then you had a glimpse of it, smooth and oily under the hot July night sky.

As always he had some difficulty in finding a parking place, though he left his car on the fringe of the Washington Market maelstrom. The Aye Wun trucks would pick up his purchased merchandise, both fruit and vegetables. But they were somewhere within the battle line itself by now. His notebook and order book in his pocket, a cigarette between his lips, he went forward into battle, a gargoyle little figure, shrewd, sentimental. The short, bandy legs bespoke an undernourished childhood down on New York's swarming East Side; the round belly and the plump cheeks testified to his marital content and his present affluent state. A bad foundation, a top-heavy upper part; but the sound heart and kidneys would see him through.

Half-past one. Washington Market was a brilliant bazaar—a mass of

color and sound and fury. Thousands of men labored here all night so that
New York's millions should be fed next day. From midnight until six in
the morning it was the most vital spot in all New York; it was more male
than Wall Street itself at midday. Every street—north and south, east and
west—in the Washington Market area was chock-a-block. A thousand vast
trucks loomed up like freight cars, their rubber-shod double wheels pro-
portioned like a juggernaut's. Drays, vans, carts, wagons, horses were
wedged like pieces in a jigsaw puzzle. Huge draft-horses, pudding-footed,
clopped the pavement in a day when a horse was thought to be an anach-
ronism. On the driver's seat of the great trucks backed up at the curb men
lay asleep in the midst of incredible turmoil as the load was being taken off.
They had driven these hundreds of tons a distance of fifty, a hundred, one
hundred and fifty miles that day; they would drive back tonight; tomorrow
they would repeat the trip with a fresh load. They must snatch repose
where they could. Food for millions, perishable, costly, it must be moved
before the sun was high. By seven the streets would be almost empty, by
noon as deserted as the catacombs. Hard, tough, concentrated work; shrewd,
competitive, realistic men.

Through this brilliant carnival of color and sound Mannie Swieback
made his way. It required lively stepping and expert dodging as the siren
of an ambulance occasionally testified. The pavement was slippery, the
sidewalk worse; the street crossings were blocked so that he was forced to
worm his way in and out of a tangle of vehicles. All about was the stamping of iron-shod hoofs on stone; the rattling of trace chains, the snort of
engines, the nerve-racking report of backfire, the rumble of heavy barrows,
the shouts and yells of men.

On the sidewalks outside the commission houses were piled boxes and
bales, crates, bags, baskets of fruits and vegetables. They were stacked
higher than a man's head, forming narrow, perilous aisles for pedestrians.
Down these aisles charged a constant stream of giant Negroes pushing
laden hand trucks. These they kept upright by some miracle of balancing
skill. The muscles stood out on their bare black arms and chests; their eyes
rolled and seemed to start from their sockets with the strain of the load.
"Watch it!" they yelled not a second too soon as a buyer or commission man
leaped nimbly to flatten himself against a bank of boxed lettuce or oranges
or apples.

Mannie was looking for his own trucks and drivers. They had an ap-
proximate stand, but one never knew from night to night what luck the
crowded street might bring. Force and ingenuity and ruthlessness decided
the location of your truck. As he squirmed and dodged to avoid this driver,
that hurtling box, Mannie kept a sharp and experienced eye on the night's

produce. This was the height of the summer season. Even August would
bring no greater variety of growing things. Melons from North Carolina.
Cherries from Oregon. Peaches from Colorado. Pears, apples, oranges,
strawberries. The currants were the size of cherries, the cherries as big
as plums. Peas and beans from Jersey. Eggplant from Virginia, iridescent
purple like an Oriental empress, too majestic to be mere food. Cauliflower
like a bride's bouquet. Carrots, onions, potatoes, lettuce, celery; leeks, corn,
spinach, asparagus, alligator pears. Tops of sample boxes were laid craftily
open so that the rosy cheeks and plump firm flesh caught the eye of the
passing buyer and tempted him, as slaves were displayed on the block in
the Far East. Vitamins for swarming New York in July; the lettuce in a
drugstore sandwich; the tomatoes in a noonday salad; the greens for soup;
the mint in Alan Career's julep, the peppers for his corn sauté. The raspberries——

No raspberries, dusty red and downy like the lips of a Spanish beauty.
Huckleberries, yes; blackberries, unseasonable strawberries. "What's the
matter no raspberries?" Mannie demanded of this commissioner and that.
The commission men in white aprons and straw hats stood outside their
doorways, plump and rosy as their own fruits. They smoked large cigars
nervously.

"Well, I tell you, Mannie, they ain't none. How about some nice blackberries, I got some extra select huckle——"

But he was off down the street, poking, smelling, pinching. Raspberries.
He had to have raspberries for the week-end trade. Raspberries to pour,
crushed, over their Sunday ice cream at dinner; or for the heaped-up bowl
at breakfast. His Park Avenue trade wanted raspberries because they were
scarce and expensive. Only yesterday that colored girl from the Careers',
she had come in, she is got to have raspberries. Peaches, currants, huckleberries, blackberries—no. The boss says raspberries he wants. And who has
got raspberries? Nobody on the whole street, nobody on the East Side,
only that Lieber, that black widow Lieber. She must, then, have got them
from Sam Klug, that cutthroat, a widower, he was always after Lieber,
that cow; everybody knew he wanted to marry her only for her good business.

Morosely he dug a plump finger into a watermelon's broad sides. "Heh,
watch it!" A hand truck overturned with a crash as the forewheel tipped
crazily, negotiating the high curb, and encountered a backing van.

Out of nowhere appeared Garbage Hannah with her string bag. She
was a nightly prowler. Her rheumy eye scanned the curbs and the sidewalks for stray greens and bits of fruit—a carrot loosened from the pile, an
orange half crushed under a horse's hoof, an apple that had rolled into the

gutter. Into the string bag they went. No one knew whether she ate this refuse or sold it. She roamed and searched, and cursed the truckmen when they hooted at her. Bet she's got a million dollars, the market was fond of saying. I bet when old Garbage Hannah dies they find about seventy bankbooks and her trunk choked with twenty-dollar bills. I bet she's stinkin' with dough. They always are.

As Mannie searched, he did not waste time. He bought, too, his transactions brief and his conversation terse; out came his notebook. The truck would pick up the stuff later. Here, there, everywhere he trotted, scenting a delicacy, ferreting out a rare lot of fruit or a consignment of vegetables made scarce by the withering heat.

He came to Sam Klug's place, its front piled high with every conceivable fruit, the lights beating down from the roof of the protecting shed. Sam himself, irate, in the doorway.

"Hi, get that truck outta there!" An empty truck was wedged just in front of the curb, locked there, seemingly, in a hopeless jam of cars and wagons and vans.

The driver surveyed the teeming street; he cast a look of scorn on Klug. "Yeh, where'll I put it!" he yelled. No one spoke, merely, in Washington Market; they yelled. It was part of the technique of the whole opera.

The answer to this was obvious. Mr. Klug was not one to deny himself a conversational opening such as this. He told him.

"A minute," interrupted Mannie. "That's my truck. What's the matter all of a sudden you're so high and mighty he's got to move——" Then he remembered his errand. Diplomacy, not rancor, must be the keynote. "Look, Sam, you got right he's blocking the street. I'll see he gets away from there. Only first let's do a little business, hm? You ain't too busy to sell something, maybe?" The crook. The murderer. Widows he's got to have, yet. A honest father of a family isn't good enough for a customer.

He bought this and that to cover his real purpose.

"Seen Sophy Lieber?" he inquired with crafty casualness. "I got a message for her."

"Not this evening I ain't. I'm expecting her any minute, though."

So. If there were raspberries hidden away for her by her suitor she had not yet secured them.

"Uh—how much for them strawberries? Watery."

"Ten to you."

"Keep 'em."

He closed his notebook, he made as though to leave. "Now I'll get that fella out of there for you—— Oh, by the way, I need a few raspberries. How's your raspberries?"

"No raspberries."

"I got to have a few raspberries just to dress the window, y'understand. I can't make a cent on 'em and I don't expect to. So come on. I'll pay for them."

"What do you mean—got to! It's been raining, all of a sudden it is hot enough to burn everything on the bushes—they ain't no raspberries. If they ain't raspberries, so people do without seeing them in the window of the Aye Wun Market."

"Yes, but that's just the trouble, Sam. People don't want to do without. They go till they get them somewhere and it's maybe a customer lost. I pay any price. You know me when I want something. I'm no piker. So come on now, Sam, hustle out that crate raspberries you're holding out on me. You can't fool Mannie Swieback."

"All right, I got a crate. Just one. But I already promised 'em."

"Who to?"

"What's the difference who to—they ain't for sale." Coyly. The rhinoceros.

"Look, Sam, I ask you as a favor. To you maybe it's nothing. To me, either I got the choicest things in and out of season in my market on the swell East Side, or I ain't."

"Well, then, you ain't."

Mannie now threw pretense to the winds. "Look. If Soph—if the Dee Looks don't want 'em, will you let me have 'em? That's fair enough, ain't it? If she—if they don't come for them by, say, four o'clock—it's after three now—will you sell 'em to me?"

"If the berries is still here at four you can have 'em."

"No, that ain't good enough. I says, if the Dee Looks hasn't picked them up by four will you save them for me, word of honor?"

Sam Klug now assumed an injured air and appealed to the sense of justice of an imaginary audience. "Listen to him! He don't trust a man I've been dealing with him for how many years! Did you ever——"

"You will or you won't. . . . Here—Mike!" He called to the boy on the truck backed against the curb. "If by four o'clock the Dee Looks, God forbid, ain't picked up a crate raspberries here with Sam Klug, you get 'em and hang on to 'em, you hear?"

"All right, all right," said Klug, still injured innocence. "But she—the Dee Looks wants them."

"He'll watch," Mannie threatened grimly. And was off.

He had bought prodigiously for the week-end trade, but now this single crate of berries loomed more important than all the rest. The artist in Mannie Swieback was aroused. Perfection or nothing. The most infuriating thought was that his rival was a woman—the one woman buyer in Washington Market. It was no place for a woman. Why didn't she let a manager or a man buyer come down here in this crazy market and do her buying? No, she had to come. She took a shameful advantage of her sex. Not that the Widow Lieber was lovely or alluring. She was a monster, swarthy, big-bosomed, broad-hipped, sharp-tongued. Her husband had died, leaving her with the business and two children. A formidable woman, ruthless as an Amazon, tireless, working all day, all night. The son was to go to college. The daughter was training to be a dancer. Talented, Sophy said. Unusual, her children. All right, if she wanted to work like a man, let her take a man's chances in the market.

He was hungry now, but he would not stop to eat. He passed the lunch-rooms that dotted the streets, their neon lights beckoning him, their smells enticing to a breakfastless man. A cup of coffee was what he craved, but he put the thought aside. Later. Inside the lunchrooms the truck drivers were fortifying themselves against the long drive home. They wolfed gargantuan breakfasts on this hot July morning; pigs' knuckles and sauerkraut, liver and bacon, ham and eggs, beef stew swimming in gravy, mops of bread; coffee and coffee rings. The scent of the coffee was too much for Mannie. He darted into the Ritz Lunch and swallowed a burning cup of heavily creamed coffee and a coffee ring. Immediately he felt livelier, more confident. He sallied forth again to the fray.

"Cigarscigaretteschewinggumcandy!" The battered visage of Cigarette Sarah with her basket appeared around a small mountain of crates. He bought a packet of cigarettes just for luck, told her to keep the change out of a quarter, and shuddered away from her witchlike grin. On the sidewalk in front of a closed warehouse door a group of colored boys were shooting craps with murmured adjurations and rolling eyes. Mannie paused a moment to look over a shoulder and the boy won. A good sign. "Stay here wid me, boss!" said the boy. But he hurried on. He peered into the open door of every commission house, he stared at every group on the sidewalk. He even told himself that he was being foolish—crazy with the heat, Mannie thought. But he went on.

There she was at last, a massive, unlovely mountain of flesh in her gingham dress tightly strained across her tumultuous bosom; wrinkled brown stockings, a battered straw hat, of no determinate age or sex. She was standing at the shelf desk in Louie Pinello's place, writing in her order book and stowing a memorandum away in the capacious pocket of her skirt. She did not bother with so feminine an adjunct as a handbag, this formidable female. Mannie entered breezily.

"Hiyah, Louie! Hi, Sophy! How's the little woman?"

She threw him a brief and malevolent look and went on copying. Chunk of suet, Mannie thought. A woman! "I ain't seen you lately, Mrs. Lieber. I thought maybe you wasn't coming down these days, such heat, a woman."

"Heat or no heat, a woman is got to live, the same as a man."

Mannie laughed at this and wagged his head in admiring agreement. "You got me there, Sophy. Well, how's about a cup of coffee with me? I was just going to have one."

"I got no time for coffee," the fair widow rasped sourly.

"O.K. No offense, my girl," benevolently. He now raised his voice well above the clamor of the streets, addressing Louie in a more masculine tone as it were. "How about blackberries, Louie?" Then, before Louie could answer, Mannie held up a plump palm and continued, "And when I say blackberries, Louie, I ask blackberries, so don't tell me you got red raspberries as big as tomatoes because I ain't in the market to buy poison raspberries, so don't think you can unload raspberries on Mannie Swieback."

Out of the tail of his eye he saw Sophy's busy pencil slow its caperings.

"Raspberries!" snorted Louie Pinello. "You know damn well I nor nobody else ain't got raspberries, and if they did——"

"You don't have to tell me. I know. If they did they'd have poison and not raspberries. I guess Louie Pinello is too smart a boy to get himself put in jail for a child poisoner like the fella in this morning's paper."

Sophy's pencil was still. Her back was toward him, but it was vibrant with attention.

Louie Pinello stared. "What do you mean—child poisoning?"

Mannie only laughed. "No, you don't know. Certainly not!"

Sophy Lieber now abandoned pretense. She turned slowly, ponderously, like a freighter changing its course. Her face was a mask of suspicion. Mannie, that superb actor, now appeared to abandon the subject. He cut through Louie Pinello's amazed protests. "These here huckleberries you got, Louie. My opinion, they ain't so hot, but——"

"What do you mean—poison?" Sophy demanded with elephantine directness.

"Huh?" said Mannie, absent-mindedly, as though deep in other thoughts. He nibbled a huckleberry between his strong yellow teeth.

"You heard me. What do you mean, poison in the morning papers, raspberries!"

"Don't you read the paper, Sophy? You got your mind always too much on money and business, you get into trouble yet, mark my words. You get a million dollars, what good does it do you if you are in jail and your children disgraced forever!"

She shouted now like any truck driver. "What are you talking, you big mouth! If you don't—— What are you talking, poison and jail!"

"Sh-sh! Sophy! What is with you? I was just saying, no offense. They're all poison. Maybe they hushed it up in the later editions. I get the early-morning paper, first thing when I drive down. They're all poison, it said. That's why you can't buy a crate raspberries—or a box, that matter—for love or money. Scairt to sell them, scairt to buy them. Naturally."

"It's a lie. Raspberries is scarce account the wet weather and now the heat."

"All right, Soph. It's all right by me. Only the paper says raspberry blight, it is very seldom it happens, the growers they used some kind of spray, it had poison in it, not only it kills the blight, it kills who eats the raspberries, even washed. So the food officers say it's forbidden raspberries, and they lay in the warehouses, rotting. Of course, a crate might not have the blight at all, then again it might be enough to kill a whole family. Family! Say! A neighborhood! Convulsions they get first, it's terrible. I don't take no chances. Believe me, huckleberries is good enough for Mannie Swieback's customers this week end." He turned. "Hi, Louie! Where's that loafer? I ain't got all night and day I should spend over a handful huckleberries."

Louie Pinello laughed scornfully. "I never heard such a lot of hooey in my life. You're nuts, Mannie."

Mannie surveyed him more in sorrow than in anger. "Am I a stool pigeon or something, Louie, you got to be afraid to talk in front of me? You ain't got any raspberries. I ain't got any raspberries. The Widow Lieber here ain't——" A sudden terrible suspicion then seemed to dart like an adder through his mind. "Sophy, my poor woman, you ain't stuck with a lot of poison raspberries, are you? Bought and paid for? Somebody didn't do that to a woman is trying to make a living for herself and her childr——"

"No!" snarled Sophy Lieber. "I am too smart for that. I am as smart as you are any day, Mr. Mannie Swieback. I knew all the time they was poison. Say, what do you think? I can't read!"

Mannie smiled affably at this and wagged his head again in silent admiration. He breathed a deep sigh. He looked about him with an air of finality. "Well, I guess I go home. I'm just about finished up for the day. . . . You look tired, Mrs. Lieber. It's terrible work for a woman, the market. I'm surprised you don't marry again—a fine woman like you. I hear there is plenty grand boys would be glad to marry you and run the business for you and be a father to your wonderful children. I hear that Sam Klug—there is a wonderful fella for you, I hear he is crazy about——"

"Klug!" roared the Widow Lieber, a tinge of purple enriching the already ruddy color in her cheeks. "That bum! That cutthroat! Him I don't go near, even to buy!"

She charged out of the shop. Mannie Swieback, humming a little tune, followed her leisurely to the doorway and stood idly a moment, watching the ponderous figure waddling up the street away from the direction of Sam Klug's commission house.

GARBAGE

He was being pursued by devils with English plaid socks over their hoofs. Beating cymbals to the tune of "Whoa Babe," they chased him through the park to Trinity churchyard, calling attention to the fact that he was stark-naked in the midst of Wall Street's noonday throng. The girl stenographers perched on the ancient gravestones, eating their lunches with elegantly crooked little fingers, jumped up at sight of him and joined in the chase, only suddenly it was he who was chasing them.

Alan Career awoke in a hot-and-cold sweat—hot because of the temperature of the sweltering July morning; cold because of terror. He found himself half out of bed, one foot on the floor, the other flexed for running as he used to gauge his stride when he was the crack man in the hurdles and the four-forty dash at the Interscholastic Field Meet in Chillicothe, Ohio.

He sat there on the edge of his bed, breathing fast, as though he actually had been running. His hand went to his forehead in fright and bewilderment and the palm came away wet. The bedroom was hot, bright, breathless. He looked at his watch. Seven o'clock. The clashing noise that, in his nightmare, had been devil's cymbals now resolved itself into an actual sound. It was a sound all too familiar to New York apartment dwellers. Fiends of another sort were at work in their gifted way. The garbage men were collecting the morning cans.

In a neighborhood such as the Careers' they always came around two hours later than this. A region inhabited by the wealthy and late-sleeping, the Department of Sanitation knew that the clatter of early garbage and ash cans would result in too many telephone calls from highly indignant voices threatening to report the outrage to their friend the Mayor and their friend the Chief of Police.

"Leave 'em lay," the order had gone forth from the new Department of Sanitation Head. It was the lesser neighborhoods, the more obscure streets, the walk-up apartments, that submitted to the six- and seven-o'clock clatter and bang.

But this, they must have figured, was summer, and the occupants of the proud piles were absent in some cool haven redolent of balsam and far removed from such urban vulgarities as ash and garbage cans. The shaded and shuttered windows on Fifth and Park and the stately side streets testified to the soundness of this reasoning. And now toss and catch, with a high percentage of misses, seemed to be going on below Alan Career's bedroom window, three stories up. (The higher, the dearer, in New York's rental arithmetic.)

As if this were not enough, one of the tossers or catchers was singing at the top of a not very true tenor voice the more difficult passages from Pagliaccio's lament.

Alan Career staggered to the window, unmindful of the fact that he had slept minus a pajama top. He stuck his head out into the glaring heat of the day. Five hours of sleep! Five hours after a day like yesterday.

"Heh, you! Yes, you! What the hell do you mean yapping and banging and waking people up in the middle of the night!"

There were three men on the wagon: one driving, two wrestling cans. It was one of those modern garbage trucks, smart, enameled, buff-colored, discreetly hooded, and as different from the old odorous one-horse affair as an airplane is unlike a prairie schooner. The song broke off abruptly. The three looked up at the tousled head and the bare brown torso protruding from the stately edifice of brick and stone. They fell into frozen attitudes of attention like privates when an officer catches them off guard. Indeed, they wore khaki-colored uniforms and their caps had a military aspect. One —the one who had been singing—had a jaunty sprig of mountain laurel stuck in his cap band. It was this one who said, "Sorry, mister." The face upturned to Alan Career's window was boyish, olive-skinned, and cameo-cut, with a profile designed for the movies. Career, wide awake now, suddenly wished he hadn't bawled out of the window at these men working.

The second man of the pair who had been hurling ash cans now grinned and pointed to the singer. "Tony's feeling good. He's going to be married tomorrow."

Alan Career thought that *Pagliacci* was not quite the medium through which to express a state of amorous joy. He felt a fresh pang of remorse. "Well, what do you know about that!" he said, inadequately.

The man at the wheel now entered the conversation, which was taking on the aspect of an urban version of a small-town, back-fence gossip interlude. "Yeh, and he's through tomorrow."

"Fired?" yelled Alan Career, shocked.

"Fired nothin'! Promoted. Assistant Foreman, that's what. Twenny-one hunderd a year. That's how he's getting married." There was vicarious pride in the voice of Tony's confrere.

Tony now took up the explanation. No one seemed to find anything odd in this casual morning scene. "We thought the building was empty, see. We figgered everybody was to the country, we'd make the rounds early and get off." As one man to another.

"Well, sure," Alan agreed, surveying the dead-eyed walls up and down the street. "I'm all alone on the island. Me and you and a few other million like us." Then a thought struck him. "You fellows come up and have a drink?"

"It ain't allowed. . . . It's against regulations."

A fresh thought now came to him; a better one. "Too early, anyway. Listen, wait a minute, will you? Don't go away. I got something for you, Tony. Wedding present."

The head was withdrawn. As he padded back to the little bar off the front hall he remembered how he used to deliver the morning papers back in Chillicothe. They came in on the early train from the city. Only the well to do took the out-of-town paper. He used to make the rounds on his bike, twisting the paper into a firm knob and hurling it at the front door with a vicious thud. I guess that'll wake you up, he had thought, though he hadn't known it.

Somewhere in the liquor cabinet there was a quart of champagne left over from their fifth-wedding-anniversary celebration. He couldn't remember how this strange phenomenon had come about. But as he rummaged and finally found it he was somewhat dashed to see that the quart was a magnum. Probably everybody had had enough, and a magnum, opened, would have been sheer waste. Patty had figured that one out. The closet contained little besides this: a bottle or two of half-emptied Scotch, some gin, some of that sweet red stuff that women put into cocktails. With a passing pang of regret he slapped barefooted back to the window and held up the bottle. "Minute!" he shouted. About the neck of the bottle he firmly knotted a corner of his bed sheet, making a cradle of it. He then knotted a second sheet to a corner of the first. Inspired by his own brilliance, his roving eye now hit upon the fourteen-foot telephone cord with which Patty liked to roam about the bedroom when conversing with friends on the wire; now telephoning from her bed, now from the dressing table, now from the chaise longue. With some difficulty he tied the cord, its mouth-piece dangling, to the sheet end and gently, cautiously, lowered his fragile glass burden foot by foot out of the window to the region of the sidewalk below. There it hung, a surprising object, within easy reach of Tony's nimble brown fingers.

Alan Career bawled a final message before he hauled up his ingenious rope. "It's for your wedding. Health to the bride and groom, see! Put it on ice. It's got to be cold. Ice!" He withdrew his head. Despairing of further sleep he turned on the cold-water bath tap.

Tony Marucci looked at the vast rounded sides of the big green bottle in his hands. He spelled out the word letter by letter. B-o-l-l-i-n-g-e-r. 1921. Champagne.

"It's wine," he announced to his curious mates. "Champagne wine. What do you figger he wanted to go to work and do that for?"

"Hangover."

"No, he talked all right, only nothing on."

"I bet it ain't any good."

"No, he was an all-right guy. He just felt like giving away, and he thought of this."

"Let's see. Whyn't you open it?"

"Nope. Health of the bride and groom, the guy says. And that's how it's going to be."

The equipage, garbage-laden, rolled ponderously down the street, Tony's sprig of mountain laurel, plucked from who knows what ash can, nodding gaily in the sun.

In the Department of Sanitation they called them G Men, facetiously. But the G Men were proud of their occupation. A good city job, and no limit, practically, to your chances of promotion. Hadn't Ben Gourley himself, now Head of the Sanitation Department of the City of New York, started collecting garbage back in the days when there was one man to a wagon, and that wagon a crude two-wheeled lumbering affair drawn by one decrepit nag? At department banquets and picnics Ben liked to reminisce about those days when he was driver, collector, and dumper, working from six in the morning until six or even eight at night, and all for fourteen dollars a week, and glad to get it. The hundreds of hard-muscled G Men listened respectfully. You said it, they thought. They knew that after three years as collector you were in line for Assistant Foreman at $2100 a year if your record was tops. After that, with the breaks, you could be Foreman at $2385. Listen. You could be Superintendent at $3085. You could be Head—— But Tony Marucci's brain always reeled at that. Not Iolanda's, though. Iolanda would be Mrs. Tony Marucci tomorrow, and her brain never reeled.

It had been Iolanda's unswerving determination and boundless ambition that had prodded Tony into his assistant foremanship. They had been "going together" since she was seventeen. She was twenty now, and Tony had been no languid suitor. But Iolanda was as unsentimental as any daughter of the new Italy, though she never had seen her parents' native land.

"I'm not going to marry any guy can't give me a nice place to live and nice things. You'll be slinging garbage cans all your life if you don't figure ahead and get things started right now. I'm not going to look like Ma when I'm her age—old as a squaw and never has any fun. You get yourself a job as foreman and then we'll get married, and not before. Lots of girls would marry you right now. Well, let 'em. It ain't that I'm not crazy about you. But young people today can't be like that. Look at Pa, working for the WPA. Look at Angelica, married four years and she hasn't had a new dress since, and babies all over the dump. Well, I know I sound hardboiled, but when she married Marino she married a sap. And now look. Not me. So get busy. Three years you'll be twenty-five—and Assistant Foreman."

Tony the romantic got busy. His record was flawless, he had used every ounce of influence in his precinct, he had pitched his ball team to victory, he had sung in the glee club, he was the garbage and ash man par excellence. But sometimes, during those three years, he had wished that Iolanda had had not quite so much character.

With his last load he trundled with the truck and crew into the new garbage incinerator on the far West Side near the water front. The vast building was as bright and clean and airy as a watch factory. True, there was about it a certain acrid odor that might elevate a more sensitive and unaccustomed nose. Tony and the boys did not even notice it. They dumped the load into the receiving pit, an immense cavern that ran the length of the block-long building on the ground floor. Tony had carefully removed his great green bottle from the driver's cab up in front. Now, while the truck was being emptied, and before the truck and crew made their way uptown to report for final roll call, he went rather shyly about making his farewells. Assistant Foreman after tonight. Well, so long, Mike! Hi, Gus! Just thought I'd say good-by. He raised a palm in farewell to the furnace tenders raking the final fires of the day in the six great flaming pits. The traveling cranes overhead jerked open the yawning buckets whose jaws scooped up mouthful after mouthful of the tonnage below, dropped the stuff into the bins, the bins opened and released the mass into the furnace pits. Tony even went up the stairs that led to the bin floor. The men up there whose job it was to prod the laden bins as they emptied into the furnaces below were chained by the belt to posts. There was a job for you! The chains kept them from losing their balance and slipping over the bin edge should their poles catch and jerk them. A dumb bunch, Tony thought, for they often unbuckled their chains on the sly, though it was forbidden by the rules. Then sometimes they mysteriously disappeared and there was only a belt buckle or some such telltale bit of metal in the furnace siftings next day to tell the tragic, sordid tale.

"So long, boys!"

"Big boss now, eh, Tony?" But their tone was not grudging.

Hugging his bottle wrapped now in a piece of coarse brown paper, he reported at the uptown station for line-up and roll call. His last roll call as collector.

There they stood in khaki pants and brown shirts, the one hundred and fifty men of the district. The names, as they fell from the lips of the inspector, made a picture of America. The men stood straight and fit, at attention.

Polacheck? Here! Monahan? Here! Cohn? Here! Scott — Podzulski — Tonetti — Dietenhofer — Brennan — Wells — Tregouboff — Popoudopoulos? Here! here! here!

Tony made a rush for the shower and washroom. Iolanda was expecting him at five. Usually he stopped at the Elite Diner across the street for a sandwich and a cup of coffee, but not today. When he emerged an almost incredible metamorphosis had taken place. Here was a modish young blood in gray trousers, blue shirt, trim tie, perforated buckskin shoes. He had not stopped to shave. The blue-black stubble only served to enhance his Latin look of romance and virility. It was a stubborn beard and a tender skin. He'd shave twice over tomorrow morning before the wedding.

He found an extremely busy and somewhat waspish Iolanda in the crowded walk-up flat which was her home. The shop people from whom she was renting the white satin wedding dress and the voluminous cloud of trailing white net veil had said they couldn't send the outfit until midnight because it was being used for a six-o'clock wedding this evening.

"Tell them to keep it," Tony advised her lightheartedly. "Let's get married just like we are, in regular clothes."

Iolanda withered him with a look. "Yeh, that would be dandy, that would be a swell wedding to wait three years for." Iolanda was having six bridesmaids in pink and her married sister, Angelica, only slightly pregnant, as matron of honor. Her father, not being irked by his WPA duties on Saturday, would give the bride away. Iolanda's head presented a strange aspect, like that of a Medusa of the machine age. It was tiered in wooden waves and all about her ears and neck hung little metal rolls that held her hair in a viselike grip. She was wearing a shapeless overall apron and a pair of run-down shoes, palpably the dregs of her wardrobe, for her clothes already hung in the closet of their own little flat in which they would sleep as bride and bridegroom tomorrow night.

Now Iolanda's distracted gaze fell upon the bulging package under Tony's arm. "What's that you got?"

Tony grinned. "Champagne for the wedding."

"What do you mean—champagne for the wedding?"

He unwrapped the bottle. He held it up so that the label on its bulging sides was plain for her to read. A look of horror came into her face. "Tony Marucci, you ain't gone and blown good money on stuff like that! You take that right——"

At the concentrated fury in her tone he hastily presented the truth.

"Fella give it to me. Guy was cuckoo or something, handed it to me out a window tied to a sheet."

"I don't believe it. Champagne! It costs money. Look, come on in here." She pushed him toward the front room and shut the door so that they were momentarily alone, with only the Family in crude crayon staring down at them from gold frames on the wall. "Now come on, Tony. Where'd you get it?"

Simply, he told her. She believed him. The story was too absurd to make up. Iolanda now examined the bottle with a calculating eye.

"And he says," Tony concluded triumphantly, "it was to drink the health of the bride and groom and to put it on ice. We'll be drinking champagne at our own wedding, Landa, like real Park Avenue millionaires."

Iolanda was still examining the oversized bottle, turning it over and over in her capable hands. That practical look which Tony knew so well was in her pretty face, making it look sharp and somehow, older.

"We will not. How'd we look, drinking champagne, there isn't near enough with fifty people eating, and the rest drinking the red wine Pa made."

"Let's drink it now," Tony suggested. "Let's put it on ice and drink it tonight, you and me. I never tasted champagne. That's what we'll do. Or look, we'll take it home with us tomorrow night."

"No. Listen. Is this good champagne? Because if it is it's worth real money. I heard where a bottle of champagne if it's good costs as much as five dollars and this is bigger than any bottle of wine I ever saw. It's double, and more. We'll sell it and get the money for it."

Inured though he was to the practical side of his young bride's nature, Tony recoiled at this. "You're crazy. Sell it! To who? Anyway, the guy says health to the bride and groom and put it on——"

"Who cares what he said? He must have been crazy, anyway. A bottle like that can bring ten dollars. Maybe fifteen. That's half a month's rent, and more. You go on right over to Crespi's place and ask him will be buy it off you."

"I will not. Fifteen dollars. Who ever heard of a bottle of wine bringing fifteen dollars? The heat's got you."

She was tired, she was cross, she was worried, she was a little scared, she was hot, and her nerves were on edge. She blazed out at him now, a virago. "Tony Marucci, you march out of here and down to Crespi's or someplace with that bottle and sell it or I'll call the whole wedding off. I've saved and got me nice things and my own money for sheets and curtains that I worked three years for at Blum's. I ain't going to guzzle down no fifteen dollars in champagne when Pa's made red wine that's good enough for anybody. I mean it. I'm through." She was working at the dim little diamond chip ring on her engagement finger.

For three years he had been a browbeaten and faithful lover. Habit was strong; and this, he sensed, was a nerve-torn and desperate woman. If he could have looked into her subconscious mind he would have beheld a poisonous jumble made up of tardy wedding dress, three years' uncomfortable continence, a flat crowded with a voluble Latin family, a job made up of long days in Blum's bargain basement.

She thrust the bottle into his arms. He hated it now. He would have liked to smash it on the pavement. He would have liked to smash it over the head of that nut that had let it down out of the window. Sullen, morose, he walked miserably down the street toward Crespi's. Masculine wisdom told him that if this bottle really was worth what his shrewd fiancée said it was then Crespi would have no use for it. Crespi's neighborhood had no call for double bottles of champagne. Tony saw himself trudging shamefacedly from liquor store to liquor store, probably farther and farther removed from his own squalid neighborhood, trying to dispose of this burden of riches like a thief with a too-rare jewel.

He stood outside Crespi's liquor store, wavering as though he had drunk the contents of the bottle in his arms. He went in. In a neighborhood largely talented enough in the making of its own wine Crespi's was a thinnish stock, and unimpressive. Rafe Crespi emerged from the murk of the back room which probably explained the existence of his shop. He eyed the great green bottle which Tony now unwrapped for his inspection. He looked at its label. His glance traveled up to Tony's flushed face.

"So what?"

"How much'll you give me for it?"

"I ain't got no call for stuff like that around here." He stared at Tony now, suspiciously. "Is that the real stuff?"

"Well, sure. What do you think!"

"I ain't buying no Bollinger '21 champagne. You must work in a night club or something, with a bottle like that to hock. Bottle like that is worth twenty-five bucks in a night-club joint. What do you think I am? A fence!"

He walked deliberately back to the curtained rear room.

Ordinarily Tony would have hit him or any man who talked to him like that. But his anger now was transferred to the absent Iolanda. She had got him into this. But twenty-five dollars for a bottle of wine! Jeez!

He wrapped it in its paper. He hated it. He wanted to drop it on the sidewalk. He passed the diner run by George the Greek, and the tantalizing smell of frying hamburgers was wafted out to his grateful nostrils. He had missed that five-o'clock coffee and sandwich and now he was suddenly ravenous. He slid onto a stool in front of the shiny white slab and placed the bottle awkwardly at his elbow, where it loomed gigantic among the pygmy salts and peppers and ketchups. Things were sizzling on the flat black surface of the stove behind the counter. George the Greek greeted him, his hamburger turner in his hand. "Hi, Tony! How's the boy!" His eye fell on the vast green bottle whose paper wrapping had slipped, revealing its majestic bulging sides. "What you got there! Mineral water?"

"It's champagne. Bottle of champagne," Tony said wretchedly. "Give me a couple hamburgers, German-fried, cup of coffee."

"Yeh, champagne!" jeered George the Greek. The men eating at the counter now looked up, eying the bottle, their mouths full.

"All right," Tony said hotly. "If it ain't champagne, what is it then?" And tore away the brown paper. Bottle, label stood revealed to the full moist eye of George the Greek. George had been a bus boy at Reisenweber's over twenty years ago when bottles like this had actually circulated. He read the label with its name and date. His mouth dropped open. He stared at Tony.

"What's matter, you been robbing the Ritz or something!"

"Is it any good?" Tony asked miserably.

"Ha! Is Bollinger good! Look, twenny-five dollars they used to get for a bottle like that at Reisenweber's, it wasn't no fifteen year old, neither. What you doing with it?"

"Nothing."

"Saving it for the wedding, eh, Tony? Some swell wedding, champagne."

"No."

George the Greek was now frankly curious. He slapped an order of ham and eggs on a plate, he cut a wedge of peach pie, slid them along the counter to their various destinations, and returned, fascinated, to this reminder of former glories. "Well, what you going to do? Huh? Wash the hair in it?"

"If it was cold," Tony said loftily, "I'd drink it. It's got to be cold, on ice."

"Sure thing. I know. Look, I'll put it on ice for you. Half an hour it's cold as hell."

"I'd look good sitting here half an hour."

"Go on next door, get a shave. You look like a crook or something, them whiskers. Go on. I'll serve your hamburgers to somebody else and make you fresh. Be a sport. Where'd you get it, anyway?"

"Fella give it to me, wedding present. My girl, she don't—uh—she don't like champagne." A sudden thought struck him. He'd get rid of it. He waved an arm to include the counter company. "Look, everybody'll have a drink. Stick it on ice good, George. I'll be right back."

A shave. Hot and cold towel, though the weather was smothering. He'd have another tomorrow. You only got married once. Looked like once would be enough, he reflected grimly. He tipped the barber a quarter in a gesture of defiance toward Iolanda, and felt strangely better for it.

Back at George the Greek's he found that though some of his fellow diners had eaten and gone there were others who had learned of the mysterious bottle. George was twirling it in an ice-filled mop bucket which served as cooler.

"That's-a boy! Now you look swell, like you ought to be drinking champagne. Same order?"

"Do hamburgers go good with champagne?"

"Sure. Anything goes good with champagne." George gave the bottle a final twirl in the crushed ice, but there was a little worried frown between his eyes. "Ain't no glasses, you have to drink it out of tumblers, it don't taste so good. It ought to have fine glasses like this." His hands described in the air fragile-stemmed glasses, bubble-bowled.

He poured a tumblerful and it brimmed over, the foam forming a pool on the counter. He dropped a small piece of ice into the glass as a precaution. "Set 'em up!" commanded Tony. "Have one yourself."

"Not for me," three or four said. Three others only drank with him and George.

Tony tossed down the tumblerful as though it were beer and he thirsty. The others followed suit, all except George the Greek. He sipped his. A look of having been cheated now came over the faces of the drinkers. "Thanks, buddy, but if that's champagne I'll take beer for mine, or a slug of whisky. It tastes like ginger pop."

"It sure does," Tony agreed, bewildered. He began to eat his hamburger and German-fried, a disillusioned man.

"That ain't the way," George the Greek protested. "You got to drink it slow, like this, a sip, and taste it. Ah!" He smacked his lips and put down his glass. Then he poured another bumper for Tony. "Try that. It's colder. And not so fast."

Tony drank the glass thoughtfully. Slowly a thousand years of wine-drinking ancestors who had grown the grapes on the sun-drenched slopes of Italian hills took possession of him. He looked up at George the Greek, dreamily. "Why, say, this stuff, it's got a wonderful taste. Like you said, you got to take it slow, and taste it going down. . . . Have another—and fill mine up. Hamburgers go good with this. Fry me another, will you, George. Onions."

"What'll your girl say, onions?"

Tony let a half glass of the golden, bubbling liquid slide down his throat. He drew in his breath. He drank the remaining half. George filled his glass from the great bottle, three quarters empty now. "She's got nothing to say," Tony announced. "Only what I tell her."

"That's the way. Treat 'em rough right from the start. They like it."

"Like it or lump it, it's all the same to me. . . . Have another glass, George—and give me one, if you don't mind." He was very polite. He felt fine. He hadn't felt so well in years. Strong, clearheaded, purposeful, carefree, light. It was wonderful. George the Greek was grinning. Tony looked at him scornfully. "Think I'm drunk, don't you? You're crazy. I was brought up on wine, see? My folks used to give me my glass of wine when I was a baby, right along with 'em. Used to it. Of course," he added as though to be strictly fair and aboveboard, "not like this. Not cha—champagne—Bolllll—not like this." He drank his sixth and final tumbler. The bottle was empty. His plate, too, was empty. He stood up, smiling, he fished in his pocket and produced a dollar bill. "Keep the change, George. You're a great guy, George."

He felt marvelous, and the amazing part of it was that he knew he felt marvelous. He felt that he could do anything. He was strong, powerful, potent, happy. He went straight to Iolanda's house, though he had no recollection of how he had got there. The store windows had skimmed by him obligingly, that was all. And there he was. Up the three flights of stairs in the same fluid way, very delightful.

"Well?" demanded Iolanda, seeing him without the big bottle. "Did he take it? How much?"

"Who?"

"Who! Crespi."

"Oh, him. No, he didn't want it. Said it was worth twen—twenny-fi' dollars."

"Well, where is it? What did you do with it?"

"Drank it."

Then, for the first time, she looked concentratedly at him. "You—you ain't—you didn't drink that—— Tony Marucci, you're drunk! You great big bum you, you dirty little rat, you went and drank that whole twenny-five-dollar bottle of champagne would have paid a whole——"

Still smiling, Tony walked over to her and slapped her smartly on the cheek, a light stinging blow. He saw her face staring at him as her own hand flew to her outraged cheek—her eyes, her mouth, round as the letter O.

"I'm doing what I please with what is mine, see, and that bottle was gave to me by a friend. Scratching around for money the night before you're getting married, like I was a beggar or something. I'll buy your sheets and curtains off you that you was yapping about. You can go back to work at Blum's. Me, I'm Tony Marucci, see, Assis'ant Foreman of the New York Depar'men' of San—uh—Santion, and I pull down twenny-one hunnerd a year. I'll prolly be head of the whole works someday. I'm going to be boss in this family, see. Get that in your head righ' now, or no wedding."

Iolanda's round eyes, Iolanda's round mouth, crinkled now into lines of anguish and woe. Iolanda, the termagant, melted before the ruthlessness of the dominating male, Tony Marucci. "Tony!" she cried, her arms thrown about his neck, her cheek on his, "Tony, I didn't mean it, say you didn't mean what you said, too. Tony, you love me, don't you, Tony? Say it!"

At breakfast Alan Career remembered that he hadn't told them to discontinue Patty's paper. There it lay beside his *Times*. "Dahlia, tell the boy to stop Mrs. Career's morning paper until she gets back." He paged it through, idly. There, on the society page, was a picture of Patty leaning ornamentally against the boat-deck rail. They must have snapped it—the newspapermen—while he was below, arranging for their dining-room and deck-chair reservations. Patty smiled out at him, young and chic and triumphant. Among those sailing on the *Champlain*: Mrs. Alan Career. Mrs. Rutger Oliphant with her prize-winning Bedlington Lambheart II. Rhinelander Coudert . . .

"Riffraff!" said Alan Career distinctly, as Dahlia put his buttered toast before him. Then, at her startled look, "No, not you, Dahlia. Uh, look, I think I'll go to the country over the week end. Get a swim and cool off. As Mrs. Career says, nobody's in town."

No Room at the Inn

[1939]

Here is pure plagiarism. My source is the Eternal Best Seller. I happened to read in The New York Times *the brief and poignant news paragraph quoted at the top of this story. The persecution, torture, and death of six million European Jews had actually brought little or no protest from a Christian world whose religion was based on the teachings of a Jew.*

I took the story and characters involved in the birth of the infant Jesus and modernized these to fit the German Nazi pattern. So Joe, Mary, Lisabeth, and Zach are rather well known to you—I hope. It is to be regretted that this story, written in 1939, is not what we call dated even today in 1946.

"NOBODY" IS BORN IN NO MAN'S LAND

Prague, Oct. 25 (U.P.)—A baby born in the no man's land south of Brno, where 200 Jewish refugees have been living in a ditch between Germany and Czechoslovakia for two weeks, was named Niemand (Nobody) today.

⮥ SHE HAD MADE EVERY STITCH HERSELF. LITERALLY, EVERY STITCH, and the sewing was so fairylike that the eye scarcely could see it. Everything was new, too. She had been almost unreasonable about that, considering Joe's meager and uncertain wage and the frightening time that had come upon the world. Cousin Elisabeth had offered to give her some of the clothing that her baby had outgrown, but Mary had refused, politely, to accept these.

"That is dear and good of you, 'Lisbeth," Mary had said. "I know it seems ungrateful, maybe, and even silly not to take them. It's hard to tell you how I feel. I want everything of his to be new. I want to make everything myself. Every little bit myself."

Cousin Elisabeth was more than twice as old as Mary. She understood everything. It was a great comfort to have Elisabeth so near, with her wisdom and her warm sympathy. "No, I don't think it's silly at all. I know just how you feel. I felt the same way when my John was coming." She laughed then, teasingly: "How does it happen you're so sure it's going to be a boy? You keep saying 'he' all the time."

Mary had gone calmly on with her sewing, one infinitesimal stitch after

515

the other, her face serene. "I know. I know." She glanced up at her older cousin, fondly. "I only hope he'll be half as smart and good as your little John."

Elisabeth's eyes went to the crib where the infant lay asleep. "Well, if I say so myself, John certainly is smart for his age. But then"—hastily, for fear that she should seem too proud—"but, then, Zach and I are both kind of middle-aged. And they say the first child of middle-aged parents is likely to be unusually smart."

The eighteen-year-old Mary beamed at this. "Joe's middle-aged!" she boasted happily. Then she blushed the deep, flaming crimson of youth and innocence; for Joe's astonishment at the first news of the child's coming had been as great as her own. It was like a miracle wrought by some outside force.

Cousin Elisabeth had really made the match between the young girl and the man well on in years. People had thought it strange; but this Mary, for all her youth, had a wisdom and sedateness beyond her years, and an unexpected humor, too, quiet and strangely dry, such as one usually finds associated with long observation and experience. Joe was husband, father, brother to the girl. It was wonderful. They were well mated. And now, when life in this strange world had become so frightening, so brutal, so terrible, it was more than ever wonderful to have his strength and goodness and judgment as a shield and staff. She knew of younger men, hotheaded, who had been taken away in the night and never again heard from. Joe went quietly about his business. But each morning as he left her he said, "Stay at home until I come back this evening. Or, if you must do your marketing, take Elisabeth with you. I'll stop by and tell her to call for you. Don't go into the streets alone."

"I'll be all right," she said. "Nobody would hurt me." For here pregnant women were given special attention. The government wanted children for future armies.

"Not our children," Joe said bitterly.

So they lived quietly, quietly they obeyed the laws; they went nowhere. Two lower-middle-class people. Dreadful, unspeakable things were happening; but such things did not happen to her and to her husband and to her unborn child. Everything would right itself. It must.

Her days were full. There were the two rooms to keep clean, the marketing, the cooking, the sewing. The marketing was a tiring task, for one had to run from shop to shop to get a bit of butter, an egg for Joe, a piece of meat however coarse and tough. Sometimes when she came back to the little flat in the narrow street and climbed the three flights of stairs, the beads of sweat stood on her lip and forehead and her breath came pain-

fully, for all her youth. Still, it was glorious to be able at night to show
Joe a pan of coffeecake or a meat ball, or even a pat of pretty good butter.
On Friday she always tried her hardest to get a fowl, however skinny, or
a bit of beef or lamb because Friday was the eve of the Sabbath. She rarely
could manage it; but that made all the sweeter her triumph when she did
come home, panting up the stairs, with her scrap of booty.

Mary kept her sewing in a wicker basket neatly covered over with a
clean white cloth. The little pile grew and grew. Joe did not know that
she had regularly gone without a midday meal in order to save even that
penny or two for the boy's furnishings. Sometimes Joe would take the
sewing from her busy hands and hold it up, an absurd fragment of cloth,
a miniature garment that looked the smaller in contrast with his great,
work-worn hand. He would laugh as he held it, dangling. It seemed so
improbable that anything alive and sentient should be small enough to
fit into this scrap of cloth. Then, in the midst of his laugh, he would grow
serious. He would stare at her and she at him and they would listen,
hushed, as for a dreaded and expected sound on the stairs.

Floors to scrub, pots and pans to scour, clothes to wash, food to cook,
garments to sew. It was her life, it was for Joe, it was enough and brim-
ming over. Hers was an enormous pride in keeping things in order, the
pride of possession inherited from peasant ancestors. Self-respect.

The men swarmed up the stairway so swiftly that Mary and Joe had
scarcely heard their heavy boots on the first landing before they were
kicking at the door and banging it with their fists. Joe sprang to his feet
and she stood up, one hand at her breast and in that hand a pink knitted
hood, no bigger than a fist, that she was knitting. Then they were in the
room; they filled the little clean room with their clamor and their oaths and
their great brown-clad bodies. They hardly looked at Joe and Mary, they
ransacked the cupboards, they pulled out the linen and the dishes, they
trampled these. One of the men snatched the pink cap from her hand and
held it up and then put it on his own big, round head, capering with a
finger in his mouth.

"Stop that!" said one in charge. "We've no time for such foolishness."
And snatched off the pink hood, and blew his nose into it, and threw
it in a corner.

In the cupboard they came upon the little cakes. She had saved drip-
pings, she had skimmed such bits of rare fat as came their way, she had
used these to fashion shortening for four little cakes, each with a dab of
dried plum on top. Joe had eaten two for his supper and there had been
two left for his breakfast. She had said she did not want any. Cakes made
her too fat. It was bad for the boy.

"Look!" yelled the man who had found these. "Cakes! These swine have cakes to eat, so many that they can leave them uneaten in the cakebox." He broke one between his fingers, sniffed it like a dog, then bolted it greedily.

"Enough of this!" yelled the man in authority. "Stop fooling and come on! You want to stay in this pigsty all night! There's a hundred more. Come on. Out!"

Then they saw Mary, big as she was, and they made a joke of this, and one of them poked her a little with his finger, and still Joe did nothing; he was like a man standing asleep with his eyes wide open. Then they shoved them both from the room. As they went, Mary made a gesture toward the basket in the corner—the basket that had been covered so neatly with the clean white cloth. Her hand was outstretched; her eyes were terrible. The little stitches so small that even she had scarcely been able to see them, once she had pricked them into the cloth.

The man who had stuffed the cakes into his mouth was now hurriedly wiping his soiled boots with a bit of soft white, kneeling by the overturned basket as he did so. He was very industrious and concentrated about it, as they were taught to be thorough about everything. His tongue was out a little way between his strong yellow teeth and he rubbed away industriously. Then, at an impatient oath from the leader, he threw the piece of cloth into a corner with the rest of the muddied, trampled garments and hurried after so that he was there to help load them into the truck with the others huddled close.

Out of the truck and on the train they bumped along for hours—or it may have been days. Mary had no sense of time. Joe pillowed her head on his breast and she even slept a little, like a drugged thing, her long lashes meeting the black smudges under her eyes. There was no proper space for them all; they huddled on the floor and in the passages. Soon the scene was one of indescribable filth. Children cried, sometimes women screamed hysterically, oftenest they sat, men and women, staring into space. The train puffed briskly along with the businesslike efficiency characteristic of the country.

It was interesting to see these decent middle-class people reduced to dreadful squalor, to a sordidness unthought of in their lives. From time to time the women tried to straighten their clothing, to wash their bodies, but the cup of water here and there was needed for refreshment. Amidst these stenches and sounds, amidst the horror and degradation, Joe and Mary sat, part of the scene, yet apart from it. She had wakened curiously refreshed. It was as though a dream she had dreamed again and again, only to awake in horror, had really come to pass, and so, seeing it come true, she was better able to bear it, knowing the worst of it. Awake, she now laid his head in its turn on her breast and through exhaustion he slept, his eyes closed flutteringly but his face and hands clenched even in sleep. Joe had aged before her eyes, overnight. A strong and robust man, of sturdy frame, he had withered; there were queer hollows in his temples and blue veins throbbed there in welts she had never before seen.

Big though she was with her burden, she tried to help women younger and older than she. She was, in fact, strangely full of strength and energy, as often is the case with pregnant women.

The train stopped, and they looked out, and there was nothing. It started again, and they came to the border of the next country. Men in uniform swarmed amongst them, stepping over them and even on them as if they were vermin. Then they talked together and alighted from the train, and the train backed until it came again to the open fields where there was nothing. Barren land, and no sign of habitation. It was nowhere. It was nothing. It was neither their country nor the adjoining country. It was no man's land.

They could not enter here, they could not turn back there. Out they went, shoved and pushed, between heaven and hell, into purgatory. Lost souls.

They stumbled out into the twilight. It was October, it was today. Nonsense, such things do not happen, this is a civilized world, they told themselves. Not like this, to wander until they dropped and died.

They walked forward together, the two hundred of them, dazedly but with absurd purposefulness, too, as if they were going somewhere. The children stumbled and cried and stumbled again. Shed, barn, shelter there was none. There was nothing.

And then that which Mary had expected began to take place. Her pains began, wave on wave. Her eyes grew enormous and her face grew very little and thin and old. Presently she could no longer walk with the rest. They came upon a little flock of sheep grazing in a spot left still green in the autumn, and near by were two shepherds and a tiny donkey hardly bigger than a dog.

Joe went to the shepherds, desperate. "My wife is ill. She is terribly ill. Let me take your donkey. There must be some place near by—an inn. Some place."

One of the shepherds, less oafish than the other, and older, said, "There's an inn, but they won't take her."

"Here," said Joe, and held out a few poor coins that had been in his pocket. "Let her ride just a little way."

The fellow took the coins. "All right. A little way. I'm going home. It's suppertime. She can ride a little way."

So they hoisted her to the donkey's back and she crouched there, but presently it was her time, and she slipped off and they helped her to the ditch by the side of the road.

She was a little silly by now, what with agony and horror. "Get all the nice clean things, Joe. The linen things, they're in the box in the cupboard. And call Elisabeth. Put the kettle on to boil. No, not my best nightgown, that comes later, when everything is over and I am tidy again. Men don't know."

Her earth rocked and roared and faces were blurred and distorted and she was rent and tortured and she heard someone making strange noises like an animal in pain, and then there came merciful blackness.

When she awoke there were women bending over her, and they had built a fire from bits of wood and dried grass, and in some miraculous way there was warm water and strips of cloth and she felt and then saw the child by her side in the ditch and he was swaddled in decent wrappings. She was beyond the effort of questioning, but at the look in her eyes the woman bending over her said, "It's a boy. A fine boy." And she held him up. He waved his tiny arms and his hair was bright in the reflection of the fire behind him. But they crowded too close around her, and Joseph waved them away with one arm and slipped his other under her head and she looked up at him and even managed to smile.

As the crowd parted there was the sound of an automobile that came to a grinding halt. They were officials, you could see that easily enough, with their uniforms and their boots and their proud way of walking.

"Hr-r-rmph!" they said. "Here, all of you. Now then, what's all this! We had a hell of a time finding you, we never would have got here if we hadn't seen the light in the sky from your fire. Now, then, answer to roll call; we've got the names of all of you, so speak up or you'll wish you had."

They called the roll of the two hundred and each answered, some timidly, some scornfully, some weeping, some cringing, some courageously.

"Mary!" they called. "Mary."

She opened her eyes. "Mary," she said, in little more than a whisper.

"That must be the one," they said amongst themselves, the three. "That's the one had the kid just born." They came forward then and saw the woman Mary and the newborn babe in the ditch. "Yep, that's it. Born in a ditch to one of these damned Jews."

"Well, let's put it on the roll call. Might as well get it in now, before it grows up and tries to sneak out. What d'you call it? Heh, Mary?" He prodded her a little, not too roughly, with the toe of his boot.

She opened her eyes again and smiled a little as she looked up at him and then at the boy in her arm. She smiled while her eyes were clouded with agony.

"Niemand," she whispered.

"What's that? Speak up! Can't hear you."

She concentrated all her energies, she formed her lips to make sound again, and licked them because they were quite dry, and said once more, "Niemand . . . Nobody."

One man wrote it down, but the first man stared as though he resented being joked with, a man of his position. But at the look in her eyes he decided that she had not been joking. He stared and stared at the boy, the firelight shining on his tiny face, making a sort of halo of his hair.

"Niemand, eh? That the best you can do for him! . . . Jesus! . . . Well, cheer up, he's a fine-looking boy. He might grow up to be quite a kid, at that."

You're Not the Type

[1940]

We were casting a play in 1940. It was one of those meager periods in the theater, when the Fabulous Invalid was temporarily in a wheel chair. Swarms of talented and untalented stage-struck boys and girls were trudging Broadway as they had for a century. But these were somehow different. There was about them something gallant vital and terribly serious. The play required a large cast and we interviewed scores of young actors and actresses. Off stage there was about them almost no pretense, affectation, meretriciousness. Flat-heeled, hatless, straightforward, wise, they were a new breed in the theater. Made of sterner stuff, through the times, than their predecessors, they were less glamorous it is true. They were admirable, they knew their job. But there's no denying that out of the lot there has arisen no great dimensional figure of the stage. Perhaps, after all, it is temperament and not intelligence that turns the magic key to the world of make-believe.

◆§ ALL HER LIFE—THAT IS, ALL HER PROFESSIONAL LIFE—VIVIAN LANDE had been cast in society plays. A consistent enough line of conduct. The Lande family was listed in that weirdly anachronistic volume, the New York *Social Register*. Naturally, Vivian's name had been hastily dropped into the oubliette of the outcast when she made her first professional appearance. That had been twenty-five years ago. Ironically enough, the Landes, still clinging to the run-down old mansion in East Seventy-fifth, had held their heads above the social waters these past few years in a strange and frightening world only by their connection with the more or less gifted Vivian.

Miss Lande's reputation as an actress had survived the period during which the Lande money had vanished down the big drain called Wall Street. From her professional niche (now none too secure), she surveyed with considerable hostility the antics of the daughters of New York's first and second families. These, mistaking exhibitionism for talent, went stumbling about the stage in the hope that a Hollywood scout out front, struck by their beauty and histrionic powers, would rush back to woo them with the dotted line.

"They don't want to act or learn to act," Vivian said contemptuously. "They just want to be called actresses. Noisy little brats with their unbrushed hair! They use the stage as a place in which to exhibit themselves until time for the night clubs to open. I wouldn't be surprised at any performance to see one of them waving from the stage in the middle of a scene and yelling yoo-hoo to a friend in the audience."

The Lande family worshiped this, their slightly tarnished golden calf. In the past quarter century the wealthy little clan, together with its fortunes, had dwindled in such nice proportion that they now balanced one with the other. There remained in the Seventy-fifth Street house only Benjamin Lande, head of the family and brother of Vivian; his daughter, Dinah; and his son, Hapgood (Happy to the family). Mrs. Lande, confronted with what she considered poverty, had elegantly chosen to pine and die rather than do without the services of a personal maid.

On Vivian's first nights you always saw the three of them, burnished and alight with pride and anxiety, seated in the third row center. Benjamin's face was rather wattled and wan above the expanse of fine white linen. Habitually, now, it wore a faint look of bewilderment, ghostly reminder of that October a decade ago when the bottom had dropped out of the twentieth-story offices of Lande, Hapgood, Watkins & Glenn, landing the firm in the basement. Dinah, her hand in her father's, was vivid in one of those $19.95 evening dresses that only the young size 12 can wear. In contrast, her brother Happy's face was gaunt and somewhat sullen. A man in years and stature, there yet was about him something vaguely incomplete, as though in early youth he had been halted in ambitions and ideals and hopes; and, bewildered, had not known how to go on. Paradoxically, his somber face wore a twisted half smile, as though he suspected that a joke was being played on him, yet hadn't the spirit to resent it.

"My sister, Vivian Lande."

"My aunt Vivian."

"Old Viv."

After the play they crowded eagerly back to the little dressing room that wasn't so feverish now as it once had been. It wasn't the star dressing room. It never had been. In the comparative quiet of Vivian's little nook you heard a bedlam of jovial sound from the more splendid quarters whose door was marked with the symbolic star. Down the corridor of twenty-five years Vivian Lande, removing her make-up, had heard these noises—the little friendly or false bleats of congratulations from across the hall, the extravagant adjectives, shabby now from too much use, the ecstatic shrieks of "Jane!" or "Ethel!" With the years the names had changed, that was all. "Talloo! . . . Lynn! . . . Kit! . . . Helen! Divine! Marvelous! Thrilled!"

Still, Vivian's friends rallied backstage, too, on these occasions. Rather surprisingly young men who kissed you on the cheek and used little waving gestures of admiration; women of her own age, looking very well in their good fur coats, though slightly green under the merciless dressing-room lights. These uttered rather two-way compliments. "You never were better, Vivian darling!" But the family was there, the Landes were there; you could always be sure of them, admiring, sustaining, but not too posses-sive. You were wonderful, Viv. You walked away with the play. You stole the show. You simply couldn't see her when you were on. You looked heavenly.

But never stardom. Yet she probably was the best-known and certainly the best-dressed second lead on Broadway. To the layman, the distinction may not be clear. To the professional, it represents the difference between queen and lady in waiting. Never once had the billing read:

VIVIAN LANDE

in

Lemon or Cream

It was always:

LEMON OR CREAM

with

Vivian Lande

A whole world of theatrical standing lies between the two prepositions.

Still, she had built up a solid following—if anything can be said to be solid in a medium so ephemeral as the theater. When the curtain rose on all that flowered chintz, the family portrait, the garden backdrop with the vivid green muslin hedge, the audience settled back and relaxed. They knew that sooner or later Vivian Lande would be expertly occupied with the silver sugar tongs. Her "Lemon or cream?" would be uttered with just the right degree of solicitude.

In fact, her roles came to be known as lemon-or-cream parts. The women in the audience waited for her entrance in that dressy suit trimmed with broad bands of expensive fur. They copied the sensational third-act dinner dress into which she must have been poured. They went home and tried to ape the style in which she did her hair, but by the time they had caught the trick Vivian was wearing a new coiffure.

It wasn't that she lacked a degree of talent. Hers was a genuine enough, though by no means a great, acting gift. But she lacked certain essential attributes of the first-rate actress. Vivian was not beautiful or homely or arresting—merely pretty. In her youth the dreadful adjective dainty had been applied to her. Nature had not bestowed on her the big, bold features so necessary to stage success: the wide mouth, the breadth of cheekbone, the eyes set well apart, the challenging line of nose and jaw. Until she was forty, her hair had been a true and shining gold. Even now, at forty-nine, her eyes were that deep, delphinium blue rarely seen except in English county girls and young A. & P. grocery clerks fresh from Ireland.

The men or women stars to whom she was subordinate usually had no single glowing facial attribute. Nature had wisely given them merely hair-color hair, eyes medium brown or blue, skin of no remarkable texture or brilliance. Equipped thus with a neutral background, these more fortunate ones could limn thereon such characters or colorings as their fancies or the part demanded.

Vivian was in demand, though. No doubt of that—at least, not until recently. She had those jaunty little fur jackets for spring, those lavish fur wraps for winter. Her own bright, luxurious little apartment in the East Sixties, with the wood-burning fireplace and the soft-spoken, light-colored maid and the pots of blooming jonquils and hyacinths and tulips in February. Managers instructed their secretaries: "Let me know the minute Miss Lande comes in. I'm expecting her at three."

At five minutes after three she would be ushered past whole rows of the unarrived who had been waiting patient hours in the outer office as is the brutal custom of the theater. Unconsciously she set herself as for a stage entrance as she hesitated a moment before the door marked Private. Then there were little glad cries of, "Bernie darling! How are you? How brown you are! Did you have a good crossing? I've read the play—it's divine, though my part is a weensy bit thin, don't you think?"

Bernie would say laconically, "Hello, Vivian, you're looking good. Sit down." They then would begin to haggle grimly about salary. For years it had been the best possible for her type of part. Three fat figures made it up, and it had even swelled to four on one or two occasions. Yet there was no denying that she had remained merely a sort of back wall against which the star, male or female, bounced all the effective dialogue. The autograph hounds rarely followed her in full bay as she emerged from the stage door. Usually she was permitted to pass by unscathed and privately chagrined, while the ravenous young faces waited for *him* or *her* to emerge.

Then the world began to take on a grim aspect indeed, and the smaller sphere of the theater did likewise. Vivian, between plays, did a bit part in a picture or two, but they seemed to lose interest after that. The whole structure of the theater began to wobble and crack. The Bernies of Broadway began to take the Super-Chief to Hollywood with greater and greater frequency, and then they began to take planes back to New York fewer and fewer times and for shorter periods. Looking very sunburned and babbling of golf, they spent forty-eight hours in their New York offices and, pressed for plans, spoke vaguely of next season if business picks up.

"It's the plays," Vivian stormed. "Who wants to spend time and money listening to plays about the Soil, or the Bronx or War or God! And who plays in them! Kids who couldn't have got jobs as ushers in my"—she had almost said day—"in my opinion."

It was early in this phase, before it really had taken on menacing proportions, that Dinah Lande had announced one day to her aunt, "I'm going to be an actress, Aunt Vivian."

"Are you, dear?" Vivian said with amused tolerance, as one who listens to the prattle of a charming infant. She took it merely as a compliment to herself; the flattery of would-be imitation. "Duse or Bernhardt?" She expected Dinah to say, "You."

Dinah said, "Neither. They're as dated as last year's hat. If they were to try to come back to the stage today nobody'd——"

"Oh, wouldn't they! A lot you know about it. They were magnificent! They were superb! They were divine!"

Dinah Lande twisted her hair (shoulder-length bob) into a little washer-woman knot and then let it untwist itself as though released by a spring, which was a way she had when intense.

"They chewed scenery. I heard a Bernhardt *Camille* record on the phonograph. It was terrible. She couldn't get a job in stock."

Vivian Lande now sat up in bed and stopped patting cold cream under her eyes. Dinah, in slacks, was perched in the bright bedroom window seat. It was two o'clock of a nonmatinee day and Vivian was having her breakfast in bed. All her young life Dinah had loved being at Vivian's apartment. Life there seemed so exciting, so enchantingly different from the prosaic stuffiness of the Lande house. At Vivian's, telegrams were always arriving; her friends seemed never to use the mails, they always telegraphed, even for the most trivial things. Masses of flowers; great white pasteboard boxes from whose tissue-paper cocoons there emerged dream dresses bearing the names of New York's most stonyhearted dressmakers.

The telephone rang and rang, though Vivian's was an unlisted number. "I'd love to, but I'm having supper with Lennie, he sails tomorrow. . . . We go into rehearsal on the eighth. . . . No, I never dine out on matinee days, but how about next Friday if you don't mind eating early? . . . A perfectly thrilling hat, yet it doesn't look important. I hate important hats. . . . We had just a cozy little bottle of champagne to celebrate, though the stuff simply poisons me. . . . If we close in July I'll hop the first boat for Europe. . . ."

This had been going on for years—until recently. Dinah loved to fetch and carry for Aunt Vivian; to touch the bottles and jars on her dressing table, so sweet-smelling and pink and exotic. Foam baths. Dollar soap. She never saw Vivian when she wasn't scented and curled and lovely in the chiffon and satin of nightgown and negligee or smart and slim in street clothes and furs. Perhaps Dinah never really saw this woman as she was today. She still regarded her with the dazzled eyes of the child of fifteen years ago. So, happily, she had thought of Aunt Vivian as a fabulous person who somehow happened to be her father's sister; and the apartment was to her a place of pure enchantment. Happily she carried trays, fetched books, arranged flowers, wrote notes, walked the dachshund, answered the telephone, "This is Miss Lande's secretary, I'll see if she's in," with a smothered giggle of delight.

Vivian accepted this worship as her due. She was an actress; she was entitled to special hours, special food, special attention, special consideration. There was about her nothing unkind or mean. She simply revolved around herself. She was generous when it cost her no sacrifice; fond but not affectionate: "You may have it, pet. It isn't becoming to me, anyway. I'll try to get you two seats if I think of it, but I've got so much on my mind."

And now, suddenly, the adoring slave had turned critic. Unreasonably enough, Vivian Lande sensed that a criticism of Duse and Bernhardt implied a criticism of herself. "Well, my gifted niece," she now said, with a little laugh that would have surprised her usual audience, "if you knew anything about the theater, except what you've seen on your side of the footlights, I might be more impressed with your contempt for the greatest actresses of our day."

Dinah looked out across the rooftops to where the park glinted emerald and sapphire in the autumn sun. Then she turned her face toward the woman in the bed; and it was no longer the face of a worshiping child. Suddenly, as she turned her eyes from park to pillow, she was nineteen, purposeful, adult.

"Not my day. If any student of acting today tried to pull those tremolo stops to get an effect, Schatzy would bawl the bejinks out of her."

"Schatzy?"

Dinah stood up and, with an unconscious gesture of preparedness for flight, reached for her somewhat shabby fur coat (a Vivian castoff). "Last week I enrolled with the Modern Stage School."

Vivian sank back among her pillows, a little angry flush showing beneath the film of cold cream. "Going to school to learn to be an actress! Ha!"

"Your precious Bernhardt did it. And if she found it tough going when she tried to make the Conservatoire, I just wish she could go up against

Schatzy at the Modern School. That vocal stuff wouldn't get her by. One girl tried it in the auditions, and Schatzy said, 'You've come to the wrong school, haven't you, young lady? They teach singing at Carnegie.'"

"They accepted you, of course. My niece. Though why you should want to be an actress—I should think one actress in the family would be enough. Of course it's flattering to me, darling—uh—you're a kind of grown-up niece for an actress to have——"

"I didn't do it to flatter anybody. I didn't do it for any reason except that I want to learn the technique of acting in order to be a really good actress. And—don't be cross, ducky—I didn't tell them you're my aunt. I wanted to get by on my own, see? If Bernhardt's life motto was '*Quand même,*' mine is, 'Don't do me no favors.' I registered under the name of Dina Ladd, and that's the name you're going to see in big lights someday, my fine-feathered friend. I hope you don't mind my wanting to be an actress, Viv darling. Good-by. I've got to run; I've got a class. I'll have to kiss just the tip of your nose—all that cold cream."

"Class! In those slacks! On the street!" Which wasn't what she meant.

"Coat covers most of it. We get pretty acrobatic. No pretties."

The front door slammed.

Vivian Lande lay very still—one might almost say rigid—except that the lace on her bosom rose and fell, rose and fell with her rapid breathing. Suddenly, with an almost violent gesture, she flung aside the covers and, barefooted, crossed to her dressing table. She did not sit down. Instead, she pushed aside the chair and, leaning on both hands, peered at her reflection in the mirror, close, close. With one hand she reached for the container of face tissues. She wiped the film of grease from her eyes and mouth and forehead, still staring. The little fine lines around the eyes, around the mouth; that queer little canal that had hollowed its way under her chin and down her throat.

"No!" shouted Vivian Lande to the staring woman, the frightened, staring woman. "No! No! No!"

"You call me, Miss Vivian?" said a soft voice from the doorway. Essie came briskly into the room, and immediately her eyes, her mouth, her hands registered shocked solicitude. "You running around in your bare feet catching your death!" She caught a glimpse of the stricken face. "What happen, Miss Vivian? You sick?"

"No, I'm not sick, don't be silly. . . . Essie, she says she's going to be an actress. Dinah." Resentment, jealousy, fear were in the voice, were stamped on her face.

With the magic intuition of a race born to suffering the brown girl understood. She laughed. It was a superb imitation of mirth. "Land, everybody says they going to be an actress. Look at me! I was going to be an actress; nothing would do, I was born to act. But I never did. That's how come I'm maid for Miss Vivian Lande, the famous Broadway star. It was the nearest to acting I could get. Same way with Miss Dinah. Next thing Mr. Benjamin, he say he's going to be a actor. That's because we wish we was you, see? Now, how'd you like I give you a tonic rub, make you smell like a garden and feel like one those drunk debs."

But before long there was no Essie. In her place was a slattern by the day who nipped Vivian's precious imported perfume and who seemed to have the same mysterious attraction for stockings and handkerchiefs that a magnet has for steel filings. There were no hyacinths and jonquils scenting the apartment out of season. There were no little new jaunty fur jackets. There were no society plays in which to say lemon-or-cream. There was, in Vivian Lande's opinion, no society, for that matter. She was bitter about it.

"The newspapers used to have snapshots of the homeless sitting on benches in Madison Square. Remember? Bleary-eyed. I suppose the papers stopped thinking that was picturesque when unemployment came in. Now they have the new homeless. Café society! They sit on benches, too. In night clubs. They're just as bleary as the old-time bums but not as interesting."

No society plays; no society playwrights. Vivian thought playwrights should look like Lonsdale and Clyde Fitch and Noel Coward. But these new boys—the strange lads who wrote about mill hands and the Bronx—were bewildering, incredible, outrageous, in Vivian's estimation. Hatless, sockless, bone-rimmed, often unshaven; their talk terse, their written dialogue sanguinary—their very presence in a producer's office seemed to her to constitute an affront to the theater.

And they didn't want Vivian Lande in their plays. Some of them had never heard of her. The type of play she always had graced they regarded as a joke; or as dim and unimportant history. "Oh, that. Yeh, I've heard of it. But I didn't see it. That was before my time; that was way back in 1929, wasn't it?"

Vivian couldn't be cast for a factory hand, a tenement dweller, a Comrade, a Dust Bowl victim. Nobody sent her playscripts now; producers did not instruct their secretaries to notify them of Miss Lande's arrival. Her talent was not pungent enough for character parts. She battled. She kept her figure through sheer heroism, for, paradoxically enough, these lean times made her plumper. Massage is costly and dieting even costlier, when the regimen is lamb chops, steak, pineapple, lobster, chicken. I'll have to watch myself, she thought. I mustn't look middle-aged. I mustn't act middle-aged. She had got into the habit of humming with the orchestra when they played Victor Herbert airs, and she knew all the words of "Absinthe Frappé" and the *Merry Widow* choruses.

She had no play that season; then there was nothing in the early spring and, with the approach of hot weather, not even a few weeks in summer stock. In the autumn she let her charming apartment, furnished, and spent four disastrous weeks on the road, touring with the second company of *Give Me a Ring*. They closed in Cincinnati Christmas week. Back in New York, she found herself jobless and homeless.

Benjamin Lande said, "Come on and live at the house with us, Viv. We're all busted together. There's plenty of room. You can have the whole third floor, and Dinah'll move upstairs, won't you, Di?"

"Pleasure," said Dinah a shade grimly. "And if I'm missing some morning you'll find me buried under the plaster that's fallen down on my bed during the night."

The Lande house reflected clearly and definitely the Lande family fortunes. Though they had not been rich as money was accounted in the Arabian Nights of New York's postwar period, they had been among the affluent in a city and day bursting with luxury. The house in Seventy-fifth was one of a block of fine substantial residences standing shoulder to shoulder in international amity—Georgian, French, Colonial, Tudor, Italian Renaissance. Richly curtained against the gaze of passers-by; polished brass, glistening doorstep, shining paint, speckless windows. But now, up and down the street, you saw discreet signs like fingers mutely pointing toward a strange new world: SALE OR RENT. *Inquire Picket & Reese*. One of these protruded from the Lande doorway in the vain hope of catching the eye of the roving new-rich.

The basement delivery-and-service entrance that had known the haughty tread of butlers and had seen processions of tenderloins, crowns of lamb, cases of good red Burgundy, long pasteboard boxes stamped with Fifth Avenue names, now wore a sign even more significant than the one above-stairs. It was a neat blue-and-white enamel sign: DR. HOPNER. WALK IN. The basement had been let as a physician's office. The kitchen had been moved upstairs.

It is the minutiae that achieve significance in a general cataclysm. Perhaps the item of the daily newspapers would serve as well as anything to illustrate the depths to which the Lande family economies had fallen. A newspaper it was that caused the first emotional upset between Vivian Lande and her erstwhile adoring niece, Dinah.

In the good old days of wanton waste there had been an imposing stack of newspapers delivered daily, morning and evening, to the house in

Seventy-fifth. Benjamin Lande had gulped at least two newspapers with his breakfast and had carried them down to Wall Street for further digestion. Martin, the chauffeur, waiting in the car at the curb, had his tabloid. In the servants' quarters there were the dailies stuffed with murders, recipes, advice to the lovelorn and love-nest bits. A French paper for Mad'moiselle, a Swedish one for the upstairs maid. Mrs. Lande had had her paper with her breakfast tray, in bed.

On Sundays the bulky printed sheets were stacked like cordwood in the hall, awaiting the family's awakening. The market; society; sports; the theater; scandal; crime; politics; shops; clothes. Each according to his or her interests. Altogether, if one added the whole thing up at the end of the year (which no one dreamed of doing), quite a nice little forest of trees must have perished to provide that five minutes of newspaper perusal, morning and evening, for the Lande family.

One newspaper was delivered now, and like the loaves and fishes it was multiplied magically and made to do for all. Benjamin Lande devoured the first-page headlines, said, "Good God, what next!" and took the market report downtown with him, having neatly dissected it from the whole. Happy took the sports page. Dinah's eye flew to the theatrical news. Benjamin Lande thriftily read his afternoon papers at the Bridge Club to which he had cannily taken a life membership in the old days.

Aunt Vivian's third-floor apartment in the Lande house had immediately taken on an atmosphere of careless richness and gaiety at variance with the decayed splendor of the rest of the house. Unable to let her own apartment again, she had brought with her such pieces as she wanted, and stored the rest. Her own bed, her own satin coverlet, her lacy pillows foaming over the chaise longue; chintz; silver or pickled-wood photograph frames out of which dramatic and rather improbable faces stared at you from behind an embroidery of scrawled inscriptions, couched in terms of extravagant endearment. *To darling Viv, ever devotedly, Bruce. To the most wonderful actress in the world, from her adoring Mimsie.* The dates were somewhere in the twenties, and the faces, though familiar, were more youthful than you had last remembered seeing them.

In all her professional life Vivian had never had her breakfast out of bed except for those few grisly weeks in Hollywood when she had been obliged to report, red-eyed and haggard, at the studio at what she considered the crack of dawn. The household staff, a broken reed now, consisted only of a general cook and housemaid, with a woman-by-the-day two days a week. Benjamin Lande, his face more drawn than usual, had said to his daughter, "Sorry, baby, but we'll have to choose between the second housemaid and the house. It's all I can do to scrape together the taxes. Nobody'll buy the damned white elephant, and nobody wants to rent it these days."

"Pooh!" said Dinah. "I'll make the beds. Besides, we're all gone all day, from breakfast to dinner. Second maid me eye!"

That first morning after she was settled in, Vivian rang the bell for breakfast. It was eleven o'clock. She waited, lying there, wondering if she ought to ring up that agent at eleven-thirty or wait for him to call her. He had said that he would telephone yesterday, but he hadn't. Her change of address and the new telephone number. That was it. She had given both to him, but some stupid secretary had probably forgotten and called the old apartment number. Better call him after breakfast.

She rang again for breakfast, holding a rather vicious thumb on the button. She got up, brushed her teeth, stared at herself in the mirror, shivered a little in the drafty old house, being accustomed to the hothouse temperature of a modern flat. She popped back into bed and drew the covers up to her chin. No answer. No scent of coffee pricking the nostrils deliciously. No sound except a kind of thump-thump from below. She rang a third time. Then, furious, she wrapped a quilted satin robe about her, slipped into mules, and clumped rather heavily down one flight of stairs, two.

"Dinah! Hello! Where's everybody?" She peered into the darkish dining room that had been the library in a previous existence. A vague mound on the floor in one corner now took on human semblance and revealed itself at the same time as the source of the thumpings. The woman-by-the-day was doing the dining-room floor.

Blue satin stared at calico and raveled sweater. "Why don't you answer the bell!"

"What bell? I ain't heard no bell."

"My bedroom bell. I rang for breakfast."

"Oh, that bell up there. It don't ring. They don't none of them ring up there, them upstairs bells."

"Tell what's-her-name—the cook—I want my breakfast. Coffee, melba toast; and I always have hot water and the juice of half a lemon first. Tell her to bring that up before the tray."

"She ain't here."

"Who ain—isn't?"

"Annie. She's went over to Third to do her marketing."

"This is fantastic. I never heard of such a—Dinah! Dinah!"

The bundle stood up, wiping her hands on herself. "She ain't here neither; she's to her school, mornings. Nobody ain't here, only me. I'll get you your coffee, or would you rather go down and fix it yourself the way you want it, mella, or what you called it."

Vivian stood a moment, a blue satin statue, frozen thus. "I'll do it. . . . Where's the morning paper?"

The bundle glanced down to where she had been kneeling. She stooped and picked up a few damp sheets, taking pains to shuffle and fold them into a semblance of neatness as she thrust them toward Vivian's shrinking hand. Vivian took them gingerly. The early risers had neatly disemboweled it of all the news sheets. Vivian's disdainful gaze was rewarded by the want ads, the shipping news, the real-estate transfers, and the obituaries. She flung it down in disgust, burst into tears that shocked even herself by their hysterical suddenness, and ran from the room, up the stairs, into the realms of her own ghostly luxuriousness.

There was quite a scene that evening. Dinah arranged things after that, privately. "Look, Annie darling, bring her her breakfast, won't you, like an angel? Please. She's used to it, and she's not well, and sort of sad and old— not really old, but not so young, I mean. And when I'm a great successful actress I won't forget it; I'll send you seats to all my first nights, and a diamond-studded cigarette case, and pork and cabbage that you love so, every day."

"Yeh, successful actress like her." Annie had her sardonic side.

"No." Dinah's young face was stern. "No, not like her."

For though she had had no encouragement at all, other than the rare and cryptic grunts that might have been approval or disapproval from the insatiable Schatzinow, head of the Modern Stage School; and though she was finishing her second and final year there with the knowledge that the theater appeared to be dying of malnutrition; and though the face that looked back at her from the mirror was far remote from the conventional pattern of beauty—in spite of all these, she knew. She knew she was good; she knew that her voice and her timing sense and her flexible body were natural stage equipment for which most beginners had to work years. Good face bones, too, and features bold enough to register across the footlights; a deep emotional feeling for the theater. She had few illusions about it and a firm belief in its importance, not only as a career and an art, but as an institution of civilized society.

When Dinah talked in these terms Aunt Vivian said, "You sound like the Madam Chairman of the Passaic Drama Study Luncheon Club."

Vivian Lande's tongue was tipped with acid these days. She seemed definitely to have made her choice between lemon and cream.

The household began almost imperceptibly to be regulated for Vivian's comfort. She slept in a little zone sacred to quiet. Sh! Aunt Vivian's sleeping. Do be quiet and stop slamming doors, Happy! Aunt Vivian's resting.

Happy Lande, moving about the house like a sardonic ghost, would raise a quizzical eyebrow. "The Bide-a-Wee Home for Broken-Down and Budding Actresses. Attendants will please leave their shoes outside and talk in whipers.... Resting!... Not on me, she ain't."

Benjamin Lande or Dinah would chide him. "Shame on you. You know she's having a tough break just now."

"Too bad, too bad. Nothing but fun and fuss and feathers for about fifty years, and now she's having a tough break. You won't think it unmanly, will you, if I break down and sob like a child?"

Vivian certainly did demand a good deal of attention. Dinah, before and after school hours, whirled like a top in order to make Aunt Vivian comfortable. Dinah, call up Lederer, will you, and ask him if he got that script of Behrman's new play? There must be something in it for me. Dinah, take my blue to the cleaner's and tell him I've simply got to have it back by Wednesday. It's the only decent rag I've got. Tell Annie, for God's sake, not to put butter on my toast; if I've told her once I've told her a million times. Drop by the Shubert box office, will you, and get those two matinee seats for me—they've promised me the house seats. Bring me a jar of Caress Cold Cream on your way home tonight; the drugstore at Seventy-sixth and Madison has it.

Slowly Dinah, the worshipful, the adoring, saw Aunt Vivian go to bits and pieces before her eyes. She never before had seen her when she wasn't made up. Now the woman forever resting in the somewhat tumbled bed seemed surprisingly haggard and ocherous. Later in the day she spent hours at her dressing table. In the evening she would emerge dressed for a party or for an important first night looking radiant, her skin unlined and softly blooming, her eyes lustrous. But after midnight the skillfully erected structure began to crumble. It was as though a bad fairy had waved a wand. A weary middle-aged woman stared out from behind the pink-and-white mask.

Vivian almost never asked Dinah to accompany her on these theater evenings or late supper parties. She gave her reason to the unreproachful Dinah, imparting at the same time some advice that she considered sage.

"Don't go around with women, evenings. It's bad publicity for an actress. It dates her and makes her seem unpopular and frumpy. Better stay home with a book and cold cream on your face than be seen at first nights with girl friends."

Vivian usually procured the theater tickets through the management or the star. Her escort was likely to be a very young man in faultless evening clothes minus small change for taxi fare.

Dinah Lande (Dina Ladd on the program) graduated from the Modern Stage School. Vivian, Benjamin Lande, and even the morose Happy attended the exercises at the Lyceum Theater. Dinah's face, high-cheekboned, arresting, seemed to stand out from the rest.

"Say, Viv," Benjamin whispered, nudging his sister, "is the kid kind of more attractive than the rest—stands out, I mean—or do I just think so because I'm her father?"

"She is." It was wrung from her.

How young she is, Aunt Vivian thought. How young they all look! Oh, God, how young they are!

So now there were two actresses in the house in Seventy-fifth, one with a slipping reputation, one with no reputation to lose. Every morning, like a stenographer or a clerk or a housemaid out of work, Dina Ladd went job hunting. Ignoring wars, rumors of war, civilization's threatened destruction, and all such minor matters, she turned straight to the newspaper's theatrical news, combing it for possible jobs. Berg's going to produce that Barry play. Sherwood's casting. Kaufman's writing a new one. Almost always she wrote these names and addresses in a notebook for the day's future reference. But once or twice, in her eagerness, she forgot and marked the column itself, tearing it out and tucking it into her purse.

"Where's the theatrical page? Somebody's torn out the theater news!" Vivian's outraged voice.

"Oh, darling, I'm so sorry. I forgot. Look, I'll run down to corner and get you another."

"Really! After all, Dinah, I happen to be the one who's the actress in this family, not you. I think perhaps you'd better get your first job before you put on this act as an actress."

Dinah, the young, the strong, the hopeful, took this in good part. "I can't just tramp onto a stage and begin to recite. They say, 'What have you played in?' and I say, 'Nothing.' And they say, 'Come back when you've had experience.' And I say, 'I can't have stage experience if you won't let me act.' And that's the way it goes, merry and carefree as a lark, all the livelong day."

Vivian, propped up among her pillows, would survey her young niece, armed for the fray. "Do you mean to say that you're going job hunting in those clothes!"

"Soitinly. Shoes, stockings, dress—I've even got a hat on! What's wrong with 'em?"

"You look as if you were dressed for a barn dance."

Dinah and all this new lot of young actors certainly were casual about clothes. They seemed dressed for the campus rather than Broadway. From office to office they tramped, they compared notes, they fought office boys and ice-locked secretaries and indifferent agents. Sometimes Dinah, goaded to fury, would try a thrust with that sharp tongue of hers, inherited doubt-less from her aunt. "Look," she might say to a manager who was ruder than usual, "you don't object to my wanting to act in your play, do you?"

"You're kind of sassy like your aunt, ain't you?"

"What aunt?"

"Your aunt's Vivian Lande, isn't she? What's she doing? I haven't seen her for years."

"She's—uh—she's resting just now."

"Uh-huh."

They lunched on milk and a sandwich at the Penn Drugstore; they sat around at a Ralph's; they were frank, matter-of-fact, terribly in earnest, debunked about everything but the theater.

If Dinah was shabby, Vivian was not. It was, of course, unthinkable for her to hunt openly for a job, even though jobless. But she contrived and schemed to lunch where managers were lunching; she said to the play-wrights encountered at cocktail parties or after-theater suppers, "Drop round and have a cocktail Friday at my house. I'm living in ye olde manse in Seventy-fifth, you know, to help out the fading family fortunes. But I'm going back to my own apartment in the spring. Friday?"

"Uh—Friday—Friday—there's something—— Oh, yes, I've promised to go up to Boston take a look at Oscar's show; the last act is sort of sick."

"Monday?"

"Guild meeting Monday at five. I'm one of the directors, God help me."

"I hope you're writing a part for me in your new play, dee-rie. You know —a Vivian Lande part, with lots of wonderful lines and good meaty situations."

His eye would begin to rove wildly about the room. "Well—ah—this is a kind of serious play, though it sounds silly of me to say so. There are only two women's parts: a young girl and a woman of about thirty, she——"

"But that's just my dish—thirty."

"Mmmm—no. You're not the type, Vivian. Sorry. There's Kay calling me. She wants to go, I guess. Excuse me. . . ."

Her furs were good, her clothes well cut, her hats—you can't do much about last season's hat, and the cheap ready-made ones looked tacky on her, she said. Even at the professional discount, the new hats cost twenty-five dollars each.

Sometimes when she came home at night there would be a great babble of talk and laughter from the big high-ceilinged drawing room. Dinah was having a party. The refreshments for those parties were likely to be rather sketchy—Scotch and beer and cheese with crackers—but the kids seemed to find nothing lacking. They talked in little rapt groups; they sat on the floor, heads close together, and there were bursts of laughter. They stood up and acted for dear life. Their talk was of the theater, the theater, the theater.

In the old days, when she was sixteen, seventeen, Dinah had said, "This is my aunt, Vivian Lande." Her friends would blush and stammer, impressed. They had seen her at matinees; this gracious, scented, other-world divinity actually was Dinah's aunt.

Now, when she strolled into the room to meet Dinah's funny little friends, a sort of pall seemed to fall upon the gathering. They all scrambled to their feet and said, "How do you do, Miss Lande?" very respectfully, but they seemed vague about her plays and one or two dreadful little upstarts hadn't even known who she was. Dinah had introduced one grubby-looking boy as a playwright—he had written one of those PWA things. This boy actually had called her Miss Ladd. Dan Korah, like something out of the Old Testament, that was his name.

Furious, she rather took it out on Dinah, later. "Why, if you think you want to be an actress, don't you try to make some contacts that will do you some good! You do go around with the queerest people. That dreadful little Bronx number you had here last night. Don't tell me that's a playwright. He looks as if he couldn't write his name."

"He can, though. There are public schools up in the Bronx, too, you'd be surprised. He can write his name, all right, and before long you'll see it up in lights or my name isn't Dina Ladd—or isn't it!"

She almost never became impatient with the embittered older woman. It was as though, young as she was, the girl sensed the tragedy of prestige and assurance lost. In the past months she had got into the habit of taking charge of Vivian's breakfast tray herself, carrying it up to her before going out on the hunt for a job. Annie had rebelled at the work and the stairs. Perhaps in the aging actress Dinah saw something of her own road ahead. But this she rejected in thought. I'll never be like that. That was the phony theater. They acted off as well as on. Maybe that's the way, though. Maybe I'm too everydayish to be an actress. No, that's a lie. I'm good. I'm good! If they'll only let me act just once so I can show them.

Then, by a miracle, she actually got a walk-on part and understudy in a bleak little folk play that lasted three weeks. She hadn't a chance in it, but the family went to the opening, Vivian very dressy entering with the two men and saying very gaily between the acts, "My little niece is in this, it's her first appearance, she's only a babe, stage-struck." But it was queer, sitting there in the audience, watching for Dinah's appearance, when for years it had been the other way around. It gave her a sinking in the pit of her stomach.

Dinah was in heaven for those three weeks; she was working, she was a member of Equity, she was an actress though she didn't utter a line and never had a chance to play as understudy. She came home rather late at night now, for there usually was a bite somewhere and a little talk after the performance. The first two weeks, though, she dragged herself awake for Vivian's breakfast tray. Then, on Tuesday of the third week of the play's run, Vivian awoke, rang (her bell had been mended), and there was no answer. She called. It was almost eleven. Annie was out marketing, no doubt. She'd rather not eat than get her own breakfast. There was something about facing a kitchen before you'd had your coffee—well, she couldn't, that was all there was to it.

"Dinah!" There was no answer. She wrapped her robe about her and made swift though somewhat heavy ascent to the floor above.

Dinah lay asleep in the shabby top-floor room with the peeling wallpaper and the crazily cracked plaster. Her head was half cradled in one upflung arm, her long lashes rested on her cheeks, and there were shadows where they rested. Fathoms deep in sleep, she looked young, old, spent, fresh, tragic, comic, ugly, lovely; disarmed by sleep, revealed by sleep, she looked —Vivian groped for the elusive resemblance—something she had once read —Maurice Baring's description of a great actress: "She had received from nature the gift of wearied and melancholy dignity." That was it. Dinah, lying there asleep, looked what she was—an actress.

Something inside Vivian Lande stirred for the first time, and turned over and came feebly to life. She leaned forward and, with an age-old gesture, folded a corner of the blanket over the bare arm on the pillow. Then she crept as softly as might be down the creaking stairs.

She went to the kitchen, heated a cup of coffee that had been fresh for Benjamin and Happy Lande at eight o'clock. She drank it standing. It was the first time she had entered the kitchen in the weeks of her residence in the house. She looked about her with considerable distaste. Annie was the type of houseworker whose breakfast dishes stand unwashed until lunchtime. Egg yolk, congealed; coffee dregs; bits of toast; orange skins. This was what Dinah wrestled with daily. Vivian's breakfast tray, brought up two flights of stairs by Dinah, had always been fresh, tempting. Poor kid, poor little kid.

She saw the tray standing, upended, in a corner of the pantry shelf. She'd bring up Dinah's breakfast for a change. The idea gave her a warm feeling; a little surge of well-being permeated her. She began to search for a fresh cup and saucer and plate; she would carry it up herself and surprise her.

As she pattered about the grubby kitchen in her mules and her quilted satin robe she thought a shade grimly, My God, middle age isn't making me mellow, is it!

The telephone rang. For Vivian and Dinah the telephone had become an instrument of hope and of torture. Their voices, when they answered its summons, were dramatic and vibrant and pitched for an entrance line.

Now Vivian dropped the bread knife and sprinted for the hall with the most amazing agility. She made it just before Dinah, in her nightgown, seemed to pour herself down the second flight of stairs. Dinah leaned over the stair rail now, hugging her thin shoulders in the drafty old hall. She whispered, making the facial contortions so maddening to the one who is engaged at the telephone. Is it for me? her lips and eyes said. Is it for me?

But Vivian Lande did not hear her, did not see her; her eyes were fixed on a vision of unseen bliss. "Yes, this is Miss Lande. . . . Oh, yes, Miss Rosen. . . . Oh, I'm wonderful, thank you. . . . Yes, I've missed you, too." Her mouth was wreathed in the set smile of social insincerity; she was being polite to the secretary and wishing she'd get down to business or drop dead or something. Now she listened breathlessly, the amenities finished. She spoke then, her voice velvet. "I think I can make it, Miss Rosen. Will you tell dear Mr. Outlander? I had another engagement but I'll rearrange it and come down. Of course it was naughty of him not to send me the script first. Oh, well—I'll run in. I think I can make it by twelve."

She hung up. For a fraction of a second she stared, starry-eyed, at Dinah. Then she gathered her robe about her and pounded up the stairs, trailing a comet of ecstatic words behind her. "It's Bernie. . . . Bernie's back from the Coast. . . . He's got a play he's crazy about. . . . He's going to do it right away. . . . The author wants me for the girl. . . ."

At the foot of the stairs where she stood looking after her sprightly aunt, Dinah repeated the words, and her voice sounded hollow and ghostly, like that of a person calling from the bottom of a well. "For the girl!"

Aunt Vivian's voice, lilting, trilled down to her. "Thank heaven it's cold enough for my short fur cape and fur hat. Oh, Dinah, I smell the coffee— I left it on the gas stove, it's boiling over, I was going to bring up your tray, wasn't that sweet of me, and when the phone rang I forgot——"

Stockings sheer. Girdle snug. No time for a bath, oh, the hell with a bath. Make-up careful, not too much eye shadow. Pull in your stomach. Throw up your head, your chin isn't—well, maybe it isn't as clear a line as it used to be, but it certainly doesn't sag. I must get a massage course next week and have one a day, with the Scotch hose afterward, to get really slimmed down.

As she peered into the mirror for a last searching look at the completed picture, Dinah stuck her head in at the door. She had a terry-cloth bathrobe over her shoulders; she was holding a half-empty coffee cup in her hand.

"You look lovely, Aunt Viv. Uh—are you sure you want to wear that fur jacket—I mean, it's stunning, but those bulky jackets are kind of thickening. Why don't you wear the suit with just your sable scarf knotted——"

"Please don't tell me how to dress for a manager's office."

"I didn't mean—— I just thought—— Did you say it was for the part of the girl, Aunt Viv?"

"Certainly the girl. Why not!" She turned to go. Something stricken in Dinah's face made her pause a moment. "Maybe there's something in it for you, pet. I'll speak to Bernie." She was off down the stairs.

The telephone rang. Let it ring. It couldn't taunt her now. She heard Dinah's high young voice answering it as she held up a finger for the taxi across the way. In the taxi she took out her compact and again surveyed the face whose every feature she had searched in her bedroom mirror only a moment ago. The girl. Certainly she could make up for it. A pinkish make-up, perhaps. But why not?

There at last was Bernie's dear familiar office, with the hopeful unknowns waiting in the outer room. Miss Rosen jumped up as she entered.

"Oh, Miss Lande, I'm so sorry, I——"

"That's quite all right, Miss Rosen. I don't really mind coming down, I had a luncheon engagement anyway." Vivian brushed her aside; she made straight for the door of the private office; she even tapped a little tattoo gaily before she opened it. "Hello, Bernie darling, how are you? How brown you are! Was it fun in Hollywood? You bad boy deserting us like that for months and months."

"Hello, Vivian, you're looking—uh—you're looking good." He shuffled the papers on his desk; he looked very strange. He coughed; he waved a hand toward a young man who had risen as Vivian entered. His back was toward the window; she had scarcely noticed him. He came forward now, and to her nearsighted eyes he seemed vaguely familiar. He, too, seemed embarrassed. A dreadful premonition seized Vivian.

"Aren't you the young man from the Br—the young man who is a friend of my niece, Dina Ladd?"

Bernie Outlander tried to wed the two with a gesture of introduction. "Vivian, meet Dan Korah; he's the author of this play. Dan, my boy, this is a great lady of the stage. I've known her work for—well, never mind—only Miss Rosen, here, she certainly mixed things up. You'll laugh when I tell you, Vivian."

"Will I?" Her tone made this promise seem improbable. This boy, this nobody, lounging at home in Bernie Outlander's office. He had no place in her world of the theater. She turned away from him; she confined her attention to her professional equal. Bernie Outlander. "Do you mean that the play Miss Rosen spoke about on the telephone was written by this young man?"

Miss Rosen, who had been hovering agitatedly in the vicinity of the door, now uttered a little squawk of dismay, and fled.

"Look at her!" shouted Bernie. "That old hen. Makes a monkey out of me and embarrasses that young fella there, a talented kid, and brings a great actress like you, Vivian, down here practically in the middle of the morning when you ought to be getting your beauty sleep——"

Vivian Lande opened her furs at the throat and drew herself up with a slow uncoiling rhythm like that of a cobra preparing to strike. When she spoke her voice had none of the lilting, dulcet tones of the actress bent on charming the producer. "What are you trying to tell me, Bernie Outlander? Because if it's what I think it is——"

"Now, Vivian—now, let me explain. Did I know you had a grown-up niece, a young girl like you, let alone she's on the stage? I've been away from Broadway a year—anyway, the name was the same, Lande. Now he says it isn't Lande; it's Ladd. I wouldn't have this happen for the world, my girl . . ."

His voice trailed off into nothingness as the door opened quietly; one could just glimpse Miss Rosen peering with beseeching eyes over the shoulder of the tall, slim and casually clothed figure of Dinah Lande. The girl had on a tweed skirt and a sweater under a gnawed-looking camel's-hair coat that Vivian recognized as belonging to her nephew Happy. No hat. No make-up. Her hair was electric with life, her face was luminous with emotion, her voice was vibrant with feeling, her body was flexible with unstudied gestures; she made Vivian Lande seem a museum piece.

"Oh, Aunt Viv, I'm so sorry! I ran out to catch you after I'd answered the phone, but you'd gone." She turned to the older man. "I'm Dina Ladd, Mr. Outlander." She looked toward the boy. "Hello, Dan." He moved near to her so that they stood together, the two young people, brave beginners in a world from whose grim realities the older two seemed to shrink in sallow dismay.

"See what I mean, Mr. Outlander?" said the boy. "She could walk on as she is, in the part. And wait till you hear her in the scene where she tells her mother what she—— Here, Dinah, read this, from here where she gives her mother the works—it's the big speech—— Wait, maybe you don't want to jump right into it—start back a little and sneak up on it." He glanced swiftly around the room with the eye of the instinctively stage-wise; he snatched another dogeared manuscript from Bernie's desk. "Look, Miss Lande, will you read the mother part so that Dinah can play against you? This mother's always been jealous of the girl, see, and she resents her; she's one of those old belles who won't give in." He thrust the typed page into her hands; his finger pointed to the first line of the chosen speech.

Vivian's eyes blazed at him; her lips drew back from her teeth. "Why, you little——" She felt herself choking.

"That's it, that's great! Go on!" said the boy.

She stared at Dinah, and Dinah's eyes, understanding, beseeching, looked back at her. Vivian Lande looked down at the page that blurred and swam and then cleared. "Why, you little——" read the first three words of the speech.

Bernie Outlander had not been a half century in the theater for nothing. His stubby hand patted her befurred shoulder; his kindly gargoyle face was full of wisdom. "Go on, Vivian, be a sport; help give the kid a chance, just read the mother part against the girl here, will you, Viv?"

"Why, yes," said Vivian Lande. "Yes, of course." Suddenly she stopped pretending. She stopped pretending to be younger than she was and more beautiful than she was, and as she stood there with the manuscript in her hand, she experienced a feeling of relief, of lightness and of freedom; and her voice, as she plunged into the first speech, took a note of human emotion and reality that never had sounded in her lemon-or-cream days.

" '. . . you don't know what it is to feel young inside and to look at yourself in the glass and see this raddled stranger looking back at you—— It's like the old woman in the Mother Goose rhyme; you say, "Can this be I!" ' "

Dinah's voice taking the next speech: " 'You've had your life. It isn't my fault if you haven't made the most of it. You can't have mine too.' "

It was good theater. Not only that, it was a superb first reading. On to the end of the scene.

"Hi!" exclaimed the boy as they finished. His tone was jubilant.

Bernie Outlander nodded sagely. "Yes, she's got something. A little amateurish maybe, still; but with the right direction she can make it."

Dan Korah waved this aside brusquely. "Oh, you mean Dinah. I knew she'd be all right. But Miss Lande here! For the mother part! She's perfect!"

"Me!" shouted Vivian Lande. "You mean me—in a mother part!"

Dinah came forward swiftly. "You were wonderful, Aunt Viv. And you helped me so. It's the star part, really, the mother."

Vivian reached for the chair beside her and sat down abruptly; her legs seemed suddenly to lack bone and muscle. "Well, I—— Perhaps it would be rather amusing to try it just for a change. I—I might make up for it—the mother part. If it's a terribly good part I might make up for it."

"Sure," said Bernie Outlander, his voice kindly, reassuring. "Sure, Vivian. You could make up for it."

Grandma Isn't Playing

[1942]

This is a story written to order. Only during World War I and World War II have I ever written according to plan or theme ordered or suggested by someone else. But throughout the 1941–1945 years, many professional writers in this country wrote to order—that is, wrote propaganda, requested or ordered by a governmental or military agency. The result often was not very good. A writer of integrity and genuine creative ability does not write well under outside compulsion. The urge must come from within. A number of such stories, written by me in the past four or five years, are not included in this volume simply because they definitely date and because they rather heavy-handedly drive home their intent. For example, a story called "Life Boat" was written at the request of the Maritime Commission. I wrote it with inward rebellion and it shows this emotion, though there is some good writing in it. In "Grandma Isn't Playing," one can detect, too, the somewhat heavy tool of propaganda. A necessary and an important wartime weapon, but often unwieldy in unaccustomed hands.

 SHE SHOULD, BY NOW, HAVE BEEN A WRINKLED CRONE WITH STRAGGling white hair and a dim eye. Certainly her mother in the Old Country had been that at forty. Yet here was Anna Krupek, a great-grandmother at sixty, with half a century of backbreaking work behind her, her lean hard body straight as a girl's, her abundant hair just streaked with iron gray, her zest for life undiminished. The brown eyes were bright and quizzical in the parchment face; the whole being denoted a core of soundness in a largely worm-eaten world. Not only did this vital sexagenarian enjoy living; she had the gift of communicating that enjoyment to others. When, with enormous gusto, she described a dish she had cooked, a movie she had seen, a flower that had bloomed in her garden, you vicariously tasted the flavor of the dish, you marked the picture for seeing, you smelled the garden blossom.

She never had been pretty, even as a girl in her Old World peasant finery, bright-hued and coquettish. But there was about her a sturdy independence, an unexpected sweetness such as you find in a hardy brown sprig of mignonette.

On first seeing Anna Krupek in her best black, you were plagued by her resemblance to someone you could not for the moment recall—someone as plain, sustaining, and unpretentious as a loaf of homemade bread. Then memory flashed back to those photographs of that iron woman Letizia Bonaparte, mother of the ill-starred Emperor—she who, alone of all that foolish family, had been undeceived and unimpressed by the glittering world around her.

It wasn't that Anna didn't show her years. She looked sixty—but a salty sixty, with heart and arteries valiantly pumping blood to the brain. Her speech still was flavored with the tang of her native tongue, though forty-four years had passed since she had crossed the ocean alone to marry Zyg Krupek and live with him in Bridgeport, Connecticut. This linguistic lack was only one of many traits in Anna which irked her daughter-in-law, Mae, and rather delighted her grandson, Mart, and her granddaughter, Gloria.

"Heh, Gram, that's double talk," Mart would say.

Anna's son, Steve, would rather mildly defend his mother from the waspish attacks of his wife, Mae. "Now, Mae, leave Ma alone. If you don't like the way she does things why'n't you do 'em yourself?"

For Anna Krupek lived in that household and the household lived on Anna, though none of them realized it, least of all she. It was Anna who kept the house spotless; it was Anna who cooked, washed, darned, mended. But then, she had been used to that all her life; she was a dynamo that functioned tirelessly, faithfully, with a minimum of noise and fuss, needing only a drop or two of the oil of human kindness to keep her going.

Mae, the refined, the elegant, perhaps pricked a little by her conscience, would say, perversely, "I wish I had your energy. You never sit still. It makes me tired just to watch you rushing around."

"Inside is only," Anna would say above the buzz of the vacuum or the whir of the mixer, for Mae's house was equipped with all the gadgets of the luxury-loving American home.

"'Inside is only.' Only what, for God's sake! Drives me crazy the way you never finish your sentences. Fifty years in this country and you'd think you landed yesterday. Inside is only what?"

Mildly Anna would elaborate. "Your legs and arms isn't tired, and back, like is good tired from work. Inside you only is tired because you ain't got like you want. You got a good husband, Steve, you got Mart and Glory, is swell kids, you got a nice house and everything fixed fine, only is like all the time fighting inside yourself you would like big and rich like in the movies. Is foolish."

"I don't know what you're talking about."

But she knew well enough. Mae Krupek definitely felt she had married beneath her when she, with generations of thin native blood in her veins, had condescended to Steve Krupek, son of that Bohunk Anna Krupek.

Steve had been all right, a nice boy, and earning pretty good money in the Bridgeport General Electric, but everybody knew his mother had supported herself and her children and educated them by doing scrubbing and washing for Bridgeport's comfortable households. Before her marriage to Steve twenty years ago, Mae had taken the secretarial course in a Bridgeport business school, but she never could learn to spell and her typed letters looked like sheet music. She never had kept a job more than a week or two. But she knew what was what; she never had worn white shoes to work; and now her nails were maroon, she pronounced "and" with two dots over the *a*, her picture even sometimes appeared in the club and society page of the *Bridgeport Post* when there were local drives or community doings or large municipal activities of an inclusive nature. Still, she wasn't a complete fool. Though she thought it would be wonderful to have the house to herself with her husband, Steve, and her son, Mart, and her daughter, Gloria, she knew, did Mae, that her mother-in-law was a pearl of great price when it came to cooking the family meals, doing the family dishes, scrubbing the family floors, all of which tasks are death on maroon nail polish.

But if the second generation, embodied in Anna Krupek's son and his wife, took her for granted or grudgingly accepted her, the third generation, surprisingly enough, seemed to meet her on common ground. Mae had managed to get herself and her husband on the membership roll of a second-rate country club. Mart and Gloria never went near it. Mae and Steve, in the century's twenties and thirties, had dutifully followed the pattern of hip flask and high speed and cheap verbal cynicism. Theirs had been a curious grocer's list vocabulary of rejection: "Nuts!" "Applesauce!" "Banana oil!" "Boloney!" To the ears of Mart and Gloria this would have sounded as dated and ineffectual as the "nit," "rubberneck," "skiddoo" of a still earlier day.

When Gloria Krupek had been born, almost eighteen years ago, the first thing that struck her family's eye was her resemblance to her Grandmother Krupek. It was fantastic—the little face with its wrinkles and its somewhat anxious look; thin, wiry, independent. The Connecticut neighbors said, "She's the spit of her grammaw, the way she looks at you. Look, she's trying to set up!"

They had named her Gloria (influence of the movies on Mae), and Anna Krupek had not interfered, though her nice sense of fitness told her that it somehow didn't sound well with Krupek. She thought that a plain name like Sophie or Mary or Anna would have been better. She did not know why.

Perhaps the day and age into which they were born had given young Mart and Gloria their curiously adult outlook, their healthy curiosity about the world. The years of the Depression had been followed by the war years. These two young things never had known a world other than that. Emotional, economic, and financial turmoil, all were accepted by them as the normal background to living. They had been catapulted into chaos and had adjusted themselves to it. Their parents, Mae and Steve, were like spoiled, foolish children to them. They were fond of them, tolerant of them, but not impressed. But the old woman of peasant stock—hardy, astringent, shrewd, debunked—this one they understood and respected. They knew the simple story of her early days—a trite enough story in American annals. They never thought of it, consciously, but they knew her for a courageous human being who had faced her fight with life, and fought it. She didn't bore them as she bored Mae and—sometimes—Steve. Mae and Steve were impatient and even contemptuous: "Oh, Ma, you're a pain in the neck! This isn't the Old Country."

The Old Country. Anna Krupek never thought of it now, except when she saw the familiar name in the newspapers. War-torn now, the peaceful village in which she had been born. Ravaged, blood-sodden, gruesome. Anna had been fourteen when Zyg Krupek sailed away to America. She would have married him before he left, but he had no money for her passage and her parents forbade his marrying her and leaving her, though he had promised to send the passage money as soon as he should begin to work in the rich New World overseas.

"Yes, a fine thing!" they scoffed. "Marry and off he goes and that's the last of him. And then you'll be here on our hands with a baby more likely than not, and who will marry you then!"

They had tried to make her marry Stas after Zyg had gone—Stas, who was an old man of thirty or more, with a fine farm of his own and cows and pigs and God knows what all besides, and a silk dress and gold earrings and a big gold brooch containing a lock of his first wife's hair—she who had died giving birth to her fifth. It was the old plot of a trite story, but it wasn't trite to Anna. She had held out against them in the face of a constant storm of threats and pleadings. For months she wept until her eyes were slits in her swollen face, but her tears were shed only in the privacy of her pillow and quietly, quietly, so that the other seven children should not hear. And then when she was sixteen and faced with spinsterhood in that little village from which the young strong men had fled to the golden shores of the New World—then Zyg's letter had come with the passage money. It was like a draught of new life to one dying. Pleadings and remonstrance meant nothing now. The child of sixteen packed her clothes and the linen she herself had woven and she embarked alone on the nightmarish journey.

Conn-ec-ti-cut. Bridgeport, Conn-ec-ti-cut. A place you couldn't say, even. She stepped off the gangplank in New York Harbor in her best dress, very full-skirted and tight-bodiced, with six good petticoats underneath and her bright shawl over her hair and the boots that came up to her shins. And there in the crowd stood a grand young man who looked like Zyg, but older, in a bright-blue suit and a fashionable hat with a brim and a white linen shirt and a blue satin necktie and yellow leather shoes and a gold ring on his finger. When he saw her he looked startled and then his face got red and then for one frightful moment she thought he was about to turn and run through the crowd, away from her. But then he laughed, and as she came toward him his face grew serious and then he took her in his arms and he was Zyg again, he was no longer the startled stranger in the splendid American clothes, he was Zyg again.

Sixteen to sixty. There was nothing startling or even fresh about the story. The Central European peasant girl had joined her sweetheart in America, had married him, had borne four children, all sons, and had settled in a community in which there were many from her own native land, so that she spoke with them, and her English remained bad. She had lived her lifetime, or most of it, an hour's train ride from the dazzling city of New York; she never had seen it, for you could not count that brief moment of her landing when she had been too blinded by love, happiness, bewilderment, weariness, and the effects of three weeks of seasickness in an unspeakable steerage to see or understand anything.

She had been widowed at twenty-six. Then life would have been a really grim business for anyone but a woman of Anna Krupek's iron determination. Strong, young, bred to physical labor, with centuries of toiling ancestors in her bones and blood and muscles, she had turned scrubwoman, washerwoman, cleaning woman, emergency cook for as many Bridgeport families as her day would allow. She had fed her four, she had clothed them, sent them to school; they had turned out well, not a black sheep among the lot of them. Sig, the first-born, had settled in the West and Tony had followed him and both had married. Anna had never seen their children, her grandchildren. She had thought to see them next year and next year and next, but she never had. Andy had a farm in Nebraska. None of these three of peasant farm stock had found the rocky soil of New England to their liking. Only Steve, of the four, had stayed in Bridgeport and had married there.

It was Mae who had stopped the scrubbing and the washing and the cooking and cleaning by the day.

"She's got to stop it, I tell you, Steve Krupek! It isn't fair to the children, having a washwoman for a grandmother. When Gloria grows up and marries——"

"Oh, now, listen! She's five years old!"

"What of it! She won't stay five forever. She'll be going to school and everything and the other girls won't have anything to do with her."

"Well, if they're stinkers like that I don't care if they don't."

"You don't know what you're talking about. I know, I tell you. And I just won't have people saying that my children's grandmother is a common washwoman!"

"Just take that back, will you!"

"All right then. Washwoman. An elegant washwoman."

"I can't support two households, not the way things are now."

"What about those brothers of yours?"

"They're having a tough time, crops and prices and weather and all. You only have to read the papers. Fifty dollars every three months for her would look big to them. Me too, for that matter."

So it was that Anna Krupek had come to live with her son Steve, and her daughter-in-law Mae, and her grandchildren Martin and Gloria, in the neat white house with the bright-blue shutters and the garage attached and the four trim tall cedars and the single red maple in the front yard. It was then situated on a new street in what had been a subdivision of the sprawling smoke-etched factory town; but the town had crept up on them. It still was a neat street of comfortable six- or seven-room houses with a garage for every house and a car for every garage. Lawn mowers whirred, radios whanged, vacuums buzzed, telephones rang, beef roast or chicken or loin of pork scented the Sunday noontime air.

Anna Krupek's group of Bridgeport households had been stricken at her abandoning them. "What'll we do without you, Anna! The washing! The cleaning! Your cakes! Who'll iron my net curtains?"

"You get somebody all right."

"Not like you, Anna."

"Maybe I come and help for fun sometime, I don't say nothing to my folks."

But she never did. Mae wouldn't have it. Besides, there was enough to keep Anna busy the whole day through in the house on Wilson Street. Hers was the little room off the kitchen in which Mae had fondly hoped to have a maid installed when Steve's income should soar to meet her ambitions. The maid never had materialized, but the room was a bright, neat little box, and after Anna's green thumb had worked its magic in the back yard, the hollyhocks and delphinium and dahlias looked in at her window.

Anna Krupek had made this adjustment as she had all her life sur-mounted adverse or unfamiliar circumstance. She missed her independ-ence, but she loved the proximity of her grandchildren. When, in the be-ginning, it had been explained to her that a grandmother who went out to clean by the day was not considered a social asset in Mae's set she had turned bewildered eyes on her son Steve.

"All my life I work." She looked down at her gnarled brown hands, veinous, big-knuckled. She looked at them as you would look at two faith-ful friends who have served you a lifetime. "I worked you and the boys should have everything nice, school and nice shoes and good to eat so you grow big, like your pa wanted." It was not said in reproach. It was a simple statement of fact uttered in bewilderment.

"I know, Ma. I know." Steve was shamefaced. "You been swell. It's only that Mae thinks—we think you've worked hard enough all your life and now you ought to take it easy."

"I got no money to take it easy." This, too, was not said in reproach. The truth only, spoken by a realist.

Then Mae took matters in hand. The children of the people you scrub and wash for . . . same school as Gloria and Martin . . . it isn't fair to them . . . won't want to play with a washwoman's grandchildren . . .

Anna turned and looked at her son, and his eyes dropped and a sick feeling gripped him at the pit of his stomach. A little silence beat in the room. Hammered. Pounded. Then Anna Krupek's hands that had been fists of defiance opened, palms up, on her knees in a gesture of acceptance.

"I don't want I should do anything would hurt Glory or Mart. I guess things is different. I been so used to work all the time, but maybe I like to play like a lady now."

"Sure, Ma. Sure!" Steve, hearty and jocular so that the hurt look might vanish from her eyes.

She had five dollars each month from one of the four sons, turn and turn about, and usually ten dollars from each of them at Christmastime. Her wants were few. Her neat starched gingham dresses in the house, her black for best, a bus into Bridgeport's Main Street for a little shopping and an occasional motion picture. Ten cents for an ice-cream cone for Glory; a quarter surreptitiously slipped to Mart for one of his mechanical con-traptions.

For a time, in her late forties and early fifties, she had felt very shaky and queer; there were times when she could scarcely get through a day's work. But that passed and then a new strength had seemed to flow back into her body; it was almost as if she were young again. There seemed little enough that she could do with this new energy. The housework had become routine, the rooms shone, the meals were hot and punctual, the flowers bloomed in the garden, she even planted some vegetables each year because she loved to tend them and to pluck the succulent leaves and roots and pods.

A shining car in the garage—two, in fact, if you counted the rackety, snorting vehicle that Mart had contrived out of such parts and pieces as he could collect from derelict and seemingly dead motors of ancient vintage. Overstuffed furniture in the living room. A radio that looked like a bookcase. Silk stockings so taken for granted that Gloria never had heard of anything else. Movies. They never walked. They jumped into the car to go down to the corner to get a loaf of bread, to buy a pack of cigarettes at the neighborhood drugstore.

Anna should have been content and happy, but she was uneasy. Here was more of luxury than she and her compatriots had ever dreamed of in the days of the Central European village, even when they had talked of the wonders of the golden New World. Something was missing, something was wrong. She began to be fussy, she was overneat, the two women bickered increasingly. But there was Mart and there was Gloria. Anna drank new life and new meaning in life from the wellspring of their youth and vitality.

Mart, from his fourteenth year, had lived a mysterious life of his own in a world made up of mechanical things that inhabited a corner of the cellar. He was nearly twenty now. Bolts, nuts, screws, rods, struts, engines, fuselages, jigs, tanks, wings, presses, drills, filled his life, made up his vocabulary. Food scarcely interested him except as fuel. He stoked absentmindedly and oftenest alone and at odd hours, his face turned away from his plate as he read the latest magazine on mechanics. His boyish incisive voice would be heard from the cellar depths.

"I can't come up now. I'm busy. Put it on a plate somewhere, will you, Gram?"

"Everything gets cold."

"Naw." When he emerged an hour later, grease-stained and sooty-faced, there was his food, neatly covered over and somehow miraculously hot and succulent, awaiting him.

"Is good?"

"Huh? Oh. Yeah. Swell." His eyes on the book, his mouth full, his legs wound round the chair rungs. But, finished, he would carry his plate to the kitchen sink and scrape it neatly and even make as though to wash it.

"Go away. I do that."

"I might as well learn kitchen police right now."

Suddenly he would grab her, he would twist his lean frame into the latest jitterbug contortions, he would whirl her yelping through space. He would set her down carefully, soberly, and disappear into the cellar workshop, where a single bulb lighted the metal-strewn bench.

Breathless, enchanted, she would screech down the cellar stairs, "Crazy fool! I tell your pa!"

"Madam, close that door. Visitors not allowed in private office of aviation experts."

Gloria, going on eighteen, was a modern streamlined version of her grandmother; the firm chin, the clear-eyed look, the mouth that curled up a little at the corners. Usually her dark hair hung softly to her shoulders, but sometimes, busy at some task, she slicked it away from her face and then the resemblance between the old and the young was startling. In shorts or slacks, uncorseted, bare-legged, sandaled, Gloria moved with the freedom of a winged thing.

"Skinny is all the go now," Anna Krupek would say, her fond eyes following the girl. "Your age I used to cry I was so thin. Zyg, your grampaw, he made fun; he said I was like a chicken, scrawny. It was then stylish to be fat. Now girls got legs like boys, thinner even, and on top too."

The two were like the upper and lower halves of a wholesome bread sandwich, and between them was Mae Krupek of the middle generation, a limp lettuce leaf spiked with factory mayonnaise, serving only to bind the two together.

There were plans of great elegance for Gloria. Mae wanted her to attend a private school after she had finished at the high school. "Well, I guess I could swing it," Steve said, "if she wants it. I didn't know there was a place in Bridgeport where——"

"Not Bridgeport," Mae interrupted, and trying to make it sound casual. "There's a lovely girls' school in Boston, near Harvard; that Denning girl went there; she married Christopher Houghton, Third; they live in New York."

"You're crazy," Steve said, but without heat, as one would state a fact.

"I knew you'd say that. What chance has she got in a town like this! We're nobody. Away at a good school they meet other girls, and they have brothers, and Gloria meets them and she's invited to their houses, week ends and everything."

"Yeah. Only maybe it would work in reverse, see. Gloria's got a brother too, you know. And maybe one these dames would meet him, low as we are, and she might fall for him, and then you'd have nothing but a daughter-in-law on your hands instead of What's-his-name Third."

But as it turned out they needn't have bothered. The neat white house on Wilson Street began to shake and tremble with the roar of traffic.

Trucks, cars, jeeps, busses packed with workingmen and—a little later—women, all headed for the airplane factory that was two miles distant. Until now it had been rather a modest plant, an experimental thing, really, reached by way of another street. Now it had doubled, trebled, quadrupled in size; its hum could be heard for miles; it was served not by hundreds but by thousands, and you could hardly tell which were men and which women, for they all wore pants and shirts and the girls had their heads bound in snoods or kerchiefs. "Like was in the Old Country, only not pants," Anna Krupek said interestedly. She followed the news avidly; she read of the country of her birth, of the horror that had befallen it; her kind eyes were stern. "We got to do something. Quick we got to do or is here in America like over in Old Country, people is killed, people is hungry, everything goes in pieces, houses, and towns and churches and schools. We got to do quick."

Young Mart did quick. He came in at suppertime one evening with a young fellow in uniform.

"Them wings is pretty," Anna Krupek said. "You get you a suit like that, Marty, and I make you embroidery wings on it the way this young man is got."

They had roared at that.

"Yup, I'm getting me a suit, Gram," Mart said. "And I hope I'll have the wings, too. Only they come already embroidered."

The young fellow with him was Lieutenant Gurk; the family gathered that he had been stationed in Texas, he was out at Mitchell Field on some special mission, he hoped to go overseas very soon. He was unloquacious, like Mart. He and Gloria seemed to know a number of people in common, which was strange.

"Gurk," said Mae, pronouncing the name with considerable distaste. "From Texas?"

"No, ma'am, I'm——"

"There were some Gurks—let me see—they had a garage and filling station—remember, Steve? We pass it near the bridge—Gurk's Garage. But of course you wouldn't be re——"

"Yes. That's me, Mike Gurk. That's my father's place."

Mae was furious. She spoke to Mart about it later, after the young man had gone. She addressed herself not only to Mart but to her husband and to Gloria and even Anna, as one who knows herself to be right and expects the support of the family against an erring member of the group.

"I'm upset enough about your being in it, and risking your life, and goodness knows aviation's the most dangerous—but at least there are wonderful boys in it of the best families, and why you have to pick one like that to bring home, a common mechanic out of a garage in greasy overalls!"

"Hi, you're getting mixed, Mom." His tone was light, but his face was scarlet.

"You could think of your sister once in a while. There are perfectly stunning aviators. This is a wonderful chance for Gloria—and you too, for that matter—to meet the most——"

But he left the room then, to Mae's chagrined bewilderment. Gloria was about to follow him. Then she began to laugh; she laughed as you would at a vexatious but dear child. "Look, cooky, this war wasn't arranged so that I could meet dazzling members of the Air Force, exactly."

"But it wouldn't hurt the war if you did! And I don't need you to tell me about the war, thank you. I'm doing my share."

Mae was serving on committees, she was busy at jobs that entailed calling people on the telephone or going to their houses. She seemed particularly occupied with the war work which necessitated canvassing the houses in the more impressive residence sections—Brooklawn, the more fashionable end of old South Park Avenue, and the tree-shaded, sizable houses on Toilsome Hill. She would return to her own home after one of these sorties, her mood gay or sullen depending on what she had seen or heard. She would glance with new eyes at the interior of the house on Wilson Street, and even at its outside aspect.

"Well, I wouldn't have believed it. With all their money, and the place looks like a junk shop. Not even good antiques." Or, with a baleful look around the living room, "These curtains are dated and stuffy. They don't use that heavy material any more. Chintz, or silk with net glass curtains, or that cream kind of linen stuff, or wool. That's what's smart now. Those old things are hideous!"

Steve's job with the G. E. was a war job now, automatically. He worked early, he worked late, he looked tired and older, but he had the air of one who knows that his work is good and useful. Gloria said she was going to be a Wave, she was going to join the WACs; she applied for Red Cross Motor Service, she worked as Nurse's Aide, she gave her fresh young blood to the blood bank; she collected this and that, she was on committees, she grew thinner, her eyes were bigger, but there was a sort of bloom about her, too. She said, "This is no damn good, this is silly, I'm not really doing anything, I wish I could be a ferry bomber pilot, I wish I could go overseas, I wish, I wish, I wish."

Anna Krupek was not one to avoid fundamental truths. "You wish, you wish—I know what you wish. You wish you got a husband and baby, that is what you wish."

A look of desperation leaped into Gloria's eyes. "They're all going away, the men. Pretty soon there won't be any to marry."

Anna Krupek, standing at the stove, stirring something in a pot like a benevolent witch, said comfortably over her shoulder, "They come back. You wait."

"I don't want to wait."

"Or you go where he is. Like me. I betcha I cried like anything, my folks was mad with me, but I went where Zyg was, across the ocean even I went."

"That was different. You were different."

"Nothing is different. On top only."

Mae confronted Gloria one day. "Who was that man in uniform I saw you with on Fairfield Avenue?"

Gloria flushed, but she was unable to resist paraphrasing the classic reply. "That wasn't no man in uniform, that was my beau."

"It looked like that Gurk."

"It was Lieutenant Gurk."

"How did you happen to run into him?"

"I didn't. I telephoned him."

"I thought he was at Mitchell Field, or Texas, or—didn't he say he was going overseas?"

"He's being sent to Seattle, Washington, first. And then probably Alaska —the Aleutians—up where——" She turned her face away.

"Gloria, I hope to goodness you haven't been seeing that—that—I hope you haven't been seeing him, even with Mart."

Gloria's voice had an even edge like cold steel. "You couldn't call it just seeing him, exactly. I've been chasing him. I've been breaking my legs running after him."

"You must be out of your mind!"

"You never said a truer word."

Mae started to make a thing of it, a family to-do, with tears, reproaches, and name-calling, but then Lieutenant Gurk vanished not only physically but in all his manifestations so far as Mae was concerned, because Mart went, too; he wasn't Mart any more, he was Martin Krupek of the American Air Forces. The psychopathic dreams of a mad paperhanger had reached across thousands of miles of ocean and land and had changed the carefree boy into a purposeful man.

Each member of the family took it in his or her own way. Mae moped and cried and put up photographs of him all over the house, including rather repulsive studies taken at the age of two months. Steve looked older and more careworn than ever, but there was nothing of age or care in his voice when he spoke of him. "My son, Martin. He's in the Air Force, you know. Aviation. Don't know yet whether he's going to be a pilot or a bombardier. Yep, aviation. That's the thing. God, if I was twenty years younger! But it's kids these days. Boys."

Gloria said little. She was working hard in a confused and scattered effort. She was gone from morning until night. She spent her free time writing letters, and all her small change on air-mail stamps.

Anna Krupek went about her business. She was quieter. She was alone in the house now for the greater part of the day. Mae did practically nothing in the way of household work. "My Red Cross," she said possessively as she whisked out of the house, usually taking the car for her exclusive use. "My Bundles Committee. My Drive Committee."

Then a queer thing happened. The neighbors noticed that the house seemed closed almost daily for hours during the middle of the day. Anna Krupek would board a bus after the others had breakfasted and gone. She would return in midafternoon or even later sometimes.

"Where were you, Ma? I tried to get the house on the phone and no answer."

"Maybe out in the yard or to the store."

The meals were prompt and good in spite of the rationing. When they complained about meat shortage she said, "We cook *haluski* in Old Country, not meat all the time like here. Morning it would be dark yet, the men would get up and go to the farm, it was miles away, not like here in America, farmers live on the farm like Sig and Tony and Andy got it good. We would get up too, pitch-black, and make the housework and cook *haluski*, it was like little noodles, only cut with a spoon in little pieces, not like noodles with a knife. And we would put in pot hot with hot stones and we take it out to the men, miles, and they would eat it for their breakfast and it was good."

"Sounds awful," Mae said.

"You yell about no coffee. Maybe once a week we had coffee, it was out of barley roasted in our oven, not real coffee like you got. It tasted fine I can tell you. We had only Sunday. Meat once a month, it taste like a piece of cake, so sweet."

"Well, thank God Mart's getting meat; steaks and things."

"Plenty of food," Steve said, crossly for him. "People bellyaching. Ought to be working. Planes, that's what we need. They could use twice the help they've got. Men and women."

"You betcha!" Anna Krupek said with enormous energy. Then again in what amounted almost to a shout, "You betcha!"

She jumped up from the table and brought in the meat. She had managed to get a ham, juicy and tender; she served with it a hot sauce blended of homemade grape jelly and prepared mustard; it was smooth and piquant on the tongue. It was like a Sunday dinner, or a holiday.

"Gosh, you certainly did yourself proud, Ma," Steve said. "I'll bet there's no other country in the world where a family can sit down to a meal like this, middle of the week. Is it somebody's birthday or something I've forgotten?"

"No," said Anna Krupek, and brought in a lemon chiffon pie.

There was nothing to warn them. When Mae Krupek came home next day at five her mother-in-law was not there. Gloria had just come in, the early spring day was unseasonably hot, there was no dinner in preparation, the kitchen was silent except for the taunting whir of the refrigerator.

"Well, really!" Mae snatched off her hat, ran a hand through her hair, and glared at the white enamel cabinets which gave her as good as she sent, glare for glare. "After five! Your father'll be home and no dinner. She's probably gone to a movie or something, or running around with those everlasting points. I'm dead. Simply dead."

Gloria, sprawled on the couch in the living room, jumped up and came into the kitchen. "Well, let's get things started. I hope nothing's happened to Gram."

"Never fear," Mae retorted.

"If it weren't for Gram you'd have to get dinner every day, and breakfast too, and everything."

"And how about yourself!"

"Oh, me too. Sure. I'd like to learn to cook."

"Why?" snapped Mae, whirling on her.

"Well, my goodness, why not?" Gloria said, reasonably enough. "Anyway, Gram's a kind of unpaid slavey around here."

"She gets her room and board and everything."

"So do you."

"You're crazy. I happen to be your father's wife."

"Gram's his mother."

The heat, the annoyance, and the prospect of wrestling with the contents of the refrigerator caused Mae's taut nerves to snap. "Oh, shut up!" she yelled, her refinement temporarily cast off like a too-tight garment. Steve Krupek, coming in at the moment, blinked mildly.

"What's the ruckus?"

"Nothing. Dinner'll be late. Your ma isn't home."

"O.K. Too hot to eat, anyway. Wonder where Ma is."

The three stood there in the clean, white kitchen with its gay, painted border and its polka-dotted, ruffled curtains and its geranium blooming in the window pot. Queer not to see the neat, deft figure performing expert magic with pots and pans and spoons.

Someone passed the kitchen window. Grandma Krupek always came in the back way. The kitchen door was locked. You heard her key click.

Grandma Krupek stood framed in the doorway with the new green of the backyard lawn behind her. Then she stepped into the kitchen.

They stared at her, the three of them. It is noteworthy that no one of them laughed. It was not only amazement that kept them from this; it was something in her face, a look of shyness, a look of courage, a look of resolve, a curious mixture of all three that blended to make an effect of nobility.

Then, "Well, my God!" said Mae Krupek, and dropped a pan in the sink with a clatter and spatter.

Anna Krupek was dressed in slacks and shirt, the one blue, the other gray, and her hair was bound in a colored kerchief. On her feet were neat, serviceable, flat-heeled shoes, in her hand was a lunch box such as workmen carry.

"Hello," said Grandma Krupek inadequately. She put down her lunch box, went to the sink, and retrieved the pan and its contents.

Between them Steve and Mae said all the things that people say in astonishment, disapproval, and minor panic: "What does this mean!" "Have you lost your mind!" "You can't do a thing like this!" "What will people say!" "We'll put a stop to it." "You're making a fool of yourself and all of us."

Only Gloria, between tears and laughter, kissed her grandmother and gave her a hearty smack behind and said, surveying the slim little figure in trousers and shirt, "Sexagenarian is right!"

Anna Krupek stood her ground. Quietly, stubbornly, over and over again she said, "I work in airplane factory. Is defense. Is fine. I like. I make plane for Mart. In a week only I learned so quick."

"You can't do that kind of work. You're too old. You'll be sick."

Anna's was a limited vocabulary, but she succeeded in making things reasonably plain.

"Say, in factory is a cinch. Easier as housework and cooking, you betcha." Then, fearful of having hurt them, "I cook again and make everything nice in the house after we fight the war, like always. But now I make airplane for Mart." She just glanced at Gloria. "For Mart and other boys."

Mae drew a long breath, as though she had come up after being under water. "We'll see about that. Steve, you've got to speak to them. You have her fired. I won't stand for it."

"My boss is Ben Chester. I don't get fired. Years and years I work for his ma, cleaning and washing. Ben, he is crazy for me. I don't get fired. No, sir!"

Mae's lips were compressed. She was too angry for tears. "The neighbors! And everybody laughing at us! At your age!"

Grandma Krupek wagged her head. "Oh, is plenty old ladies working in airplanes." She shot another lightning glance at Gloria. "Old ladies and kids too. Next to me is old lady she is getting new false teeth for hundred and fifty dollar! And her hair marcel each week. I save my money, maybe I travel."

"Travel!" echoed Mae, weakly.

But Gloria leaped the gap at last. "Could I get a job there, do you think? Could I do it?"

"Sure thing. Two, three weeks you could travel—oh—New York or—uh—Seattle—or——" with elaborate carelessness. "And back."

Mae turned to Steve. "Well, your mother won't stay here any longer, that's one sure thing. I won't have it."

"O.K.," said Anna Krupek, without rancor.

Steve spoke quietly. "You're staying here, Ma. This is your home."

Anna's face was placid but firm. "On day shift I am through I am home five o'clock. I help you, Mae. You ain't such a bad cook; you got to learn only. I was afraid in factory first, but I learn. Like when I cross the ocean alone to come to this country. I was afraid. But I learn."

She looked at her two hands as she had once before, almost as though they belonged to someone else. She looked at them and turned them as she looked, palms in and then palms out, curiously, as at some rare jewels whose every facet reflected a brilliant new light.

"What you think! I make airplane. I sit in chair, comfortable, I put a little piece in a little hole it should fit nice, and for this I am pay fifty dollar a week." She shook her head as though to rid it of a dream. "Zyg, he won't believe it."

The Barn Cuts Off the View

[1940]

Beneath the banter and persiflage of this story lurks that grim-visaged thing known as a Message. This may be so thoroughly concealed that the reader never can discover it. I shall, therefore, rather annoyingly point it out.

Before doing so, I should like to say that this story differs from any other in the collection. It follows the meeting and eventual mating of two young-ish people who are intellectual equals. They are worldly, urban, modern. Once again this is a short story which might have served as the outline for a novel of present-day New York life. Blix's San Francisco background is only hurriedly sketched in. Her mother, I should think, is a meal in herself. Blix's New York beginning and her rise in the fashion-magazine profession might well have been amusing. Myself, I'd have been interested to know something more of the somewhat ruthless Mark Speed. The story was written well before the United States entered World War II.

As for the hidden Message: in 1938 I built a house in Connecticut on a hilltop commanding a view of practically the Western Hemisphere. For years I had scoured the region in the hope of finding that dream dwelling already made. The process of construction has certain terrors for one who never before has built a house. Down little lanes I scurried, across roads, up hills, but invariably the house sat too near the road and the great red New England barn just across the road cut off the view. The New England farmer had wanted to keep a vigilant eye on his livestock. This, I concluded, might have been not only a practical but a mental character-istic of the region. Perhaps in many cases the reactionary barn is still cut-ting off the New England view.

⋘§ HER MOTHER HAD NAMED HER BLIX AFTER THE FRANK NORRIS NOVEL of that title. Later, Blix realized that a mother who names you for a hero-ine in a novel is a mother given to daydreaming rather than dishwashing. Certainly Mrs. Carewe, faced with impecunious widowhood, had success-fully daydreamed herself right out of bleak reality into cozy semi-invalid-ism. From the horizontal security of the sitting-room sofa she surveyed Blix's frantic lunges at the housework, preparatory to catching the early ferry which took her across the bay to her job as stenographer in San Francisco.

The folks in Sausalito and San Francisco understood about the name, naturally. But when she finally arrived in New York, it needed quite a lot of explaining. People would say, "Blix! That's a nickname, isn't it?" Or, "What's that short for? Beatrice?"

"No, that's my real name. Blix. It's after a girl in a book by a California writer, Frank Norris."

"Oh! Well, it's a cute name, but it doesn't sound like you. I mean, Lucy or Martha or something like that, more."

At this left-handed compliment Blix's eyes would take on a steely sort of look.

From the shabby Carewe cottage, perched on the Sausalito hill, the view was as fine as when Balboa first beheld the Pacific. Mrs. Carewe graciously divided her daydreams between this panorama and the latest novel from the lending library. At noon, perforce, she rose in Blix's absence and sustained herself with a rather astonishing list of indigestibles commonly supposed to be successfully combated only by pick-and-shovel men.

She had been one of those San Francisco beauties, all fresh coloring and glinting hair and springing stride. The goddess type.

As so often is the case, the daughter had inherited almost none of the mother's good points. Those she had inherited, nature prankishly had exaggerated. As assets, Blix had the poreless skin and the rose-and-cream coloring of women who live in damp, foggy climates like the British Isles and San Francisco; fine eyes; a low, warm speaking voice which frequently deceived people into thinking her a person of poise and calm. But her nose was too long and dominating, where her mother's had been modeled with fine arrogance; her mouth was too wide, where her mother's had been luscious; her bone structure was that of a big woman, not a goddess. Even at fifteen, her clothes had been on the severe side; she required size eighteen, which never is planned for the frivolous. Because of her very plainness, the girl Blix worshiped beauty. Curiously enough, she wasn't bitter; merely acid on occasion. With what may have been unconscious malice, the ex-beauty on the living-room couch tried to break down the girl's morale under the pretense of building it up.

"Blix darling, try not to walk so heavily. My head. You shake the house with every step. . . . I wouldn't wear that hat with your nose. The nose sticks out like a signpost below it. . . . Blix dear, try not to be so wholehearted when you smile. Sort of keep your lips more like this, so that your mouth doesn't spread all over your face. . . . Well, if I don't tell you these things, who will?"

"Nobody," Blix said with terrible distinctness.

Blix was twenty-one when her mother married an inhibited young man with middle-aged habits who had been boring Blix with his Sunday-afternoon attentions. Mrs. Carewe always coquetted with her daughter's infrequent beaux, throwing herself into Récamier poses and letting the light from the window fall on her hair and away from her face. Blix had been busy in the kitchen, preparing the Sunday-night supper. Entering the living room with that lightness of step which her mother had advised, she discovered the pair in the spring dusk looking like one of those close-ups in a sexy motion picture. The beau had deserted his chair for the edge of the couch and was doing a good deal of breathing.

"Camera!" said Blix gaily, having once gone to Hollywood on a two-day excursion.

Once safely landed in New York—if a boxlike bedroom and a precarious secretarial job can be said to constitute urban safety—Blix missed nothing about the old life except the bay view, the tonic fogs, and the *moules marinières*.

It happened that the autumn of her coming to New York was the year 1929. That she, a stranger, had actually got a job in that catastrophic period was perhaps due to her very naïveté. The newspapers were strange to her West Coast eyes; the tempo of the city was exhilarating but bewildering. If she did notice that an extraordinary number of gentlemen seemed to be jumping out of twenty-story office buildings she probably thought this was New York's way of remonstrating against life. In San Francisco, one had the cliffs, which was tidier.

She had gone about hunting a job exactly as though no panic were shaking the country's very gizzard. With her sensible nose, her matronly clothes, her quiet, reassuring voice, her intelligent eyes, she deceived Hedda Gale into choosing her from among fifty applicants for a secretarial job. Hedda Gale was the shrewd and forceful fashion editor on *Fig Leaf*. *Fig Leaf* is a woman's fashion-and-fiction magazine so expensive that the average female reads it only at the hairdresser's. Its style drawings are authentic and Parisian. Its photographed models invariably are gleaned from the reigning stage success or from decayed French, Russian, or English nobility. When you peruse its pages, it is difficult to tell where fashion ends and fiction begins.

At the end of five years, Blix, using the well-known bootstrap method, had lifted herself from the position of eighteen-dollar stenographer to that of assistant editor. By this time, Hedda Gale had discovered that the long nose meant executive power; that the voice was not only low but vibrant, and that the intelligent eyes saw clearly and wisely for everyone except their owner.

Once Hedda Gale said, "If you weren't so good I'd fire you."

"Why?"

"Because if I don't you'll probably have my job in another three or four years."

Blix considered this with her air of childlike candor. "I shouldn't think so. In the first place, the editor of a fashion-and-beauty magazine should be fashionable and beautiful. And second, I make a better lieutenant than captain. My mother booted most of the self-confidence out of me before I was ten."

She went to important openings, and even wrote occasional editorials, besides doing most of the palsie descriptions beneath the fashion photographs. There was a basic formula for these captions. Blix was required to freshen them. You never, for example, simply said, "This picture shows a white dress with a red jacket." You said:

Though it returns each year, spring is always news. So is white. They're wearing it already under scarlet coats in Paris. Derrière was inspired to name this model from the Russian campaign. It is called Blood on Snow. Palm Beach is mad about it.

Perhaps because her job required her to write about winter wools and furs when the sweat was trickling down her spine in August, and about chiffons and strapless sun suits in midwinter, Blix spent little time or thought on her own clothes. Then, too, it had early been impressed on her that clothes could do very little to disguise nature's handiwork. In the past three years, however, Hedda Gale's harping had begun to show an effect. "This year's clothes are heaven-sent for you, Blix. Long classic lines and broad shoulders. It's old-fashioned to be pretty. You've got distinction. Why don't you hold up your head and admit it?"

Blix lavished her feeling for beauty upon the inanimate things with which she had surrounded herself. From the little room at five a week Blix had, in ten years, lifted herself up into a charming three-room apartment with a wood-burning fireplace, pots of ivy on the mantel, nice bits picked up at auction, an elevator man who said who-shall-I-say-is-calling, and a maid by the day. She loved it. It was wonderful to come home at night to soft warmth, gleaming fire, good food. She dressed now with taste and intelligence and carried her big-boned frame with considerable distinction. She walked like a San Franciscan. Hill climbing does it. Then, too, she lately had learned to emphasize her bad points. Hedda Gale's handiwork showed there.

"Look. Your mouth is big. Make it bigger. You can't hide it, so brag about it. Your hair's unruly, so wear it slap-bang away from your face like a Ubangi. You've been trying for years to soften up your nose line with bangs. No good. Clean-cut is your best bet; and one good, big piece of jewelry that'll knock their eye out."

That winter a newspaper fashion column said, "Blix Carewe at the Gavotte in Ainsi's newest model called Wicked Widow, gray crepe with lavender gloves and flower hat."

Men. She didn't use much guile or sense about men. She had beaux, what with her fine eyes, her sympathetic voice, her nice wit. But infrequently that wit contained a barb so sharp that you didn't know you were hit until some minutes after the point had got under your skin. Those early years of hardship and her life with the frustrated, fading beauty had made her strong and self-reliant, qualities which do not, she found, endear you to the male. The truth was that she was stronger than most of the men she knew. They sensed this and unconsciously resented it. Then, too, many of them were not what you would call marrying men. She met them often in the course of her work. There was about them a certain softness—an elusive quality frequently found in men who work in the semicreative professions. They were glib, quick, slightly malicious, often witty; they liked to talk about themselves. They didn't live in hotels or with their immediate families, though unmarried. They had their own apartments in which they kept house with astonishing expertness. They even gave little dinners with all the right silver and spring flowers in the center and a new meat dish over which they were shrilly triumphant—sour-cream gravy and you brown the onions first.

They liked Blix. They took her out to dinner and the theater and told her their troubles at the office. She was sympathetic, understanding; she made them laugh, though they sometimes wished she wouldn't see the humorous side of everything. Most of her energy and emotion went into her work. This, as well as her tendency to be amusing about tragedy, was due to the fact that she was sad at heart, and even beginning to be a little frightened. She would stay overlate at the office, in spite of a dinner date. Then, in a panic, she would scurry home, stopping at the florist's on Lexington for a bunch of spring tulips in winter and a fan of glossy huckleberry branches for the bronze bowl on the foyer console. Then, instead of slapping a good thick antiwrinkle mask on her face and taking a leisurely hot bath full of sweet-smelling stuff and maybe having a guilty preliminary cocktail while dressing, with a quick, strong gargle to whisk away the breath, she fussed about the house. It was an unadult throwback to the days when, neglecting herself, she had had to fuss about her mother, fuss about the cottage, fuss about the meals after her day's work was done. But this she did not know. She would start a fire in the fireplace for coziness.

She would arrange the flowers in a clear crystal vase and the huckleberry in the hall, and stand back and view and rearrange. She would pull down the Venetian blinds and plump the pillows and tidy up the row of varied magazines on the living-room table. When the doorbell rang and the swain was admitted, Blix would emerge rather wild-eyed and haggard, with her hair not quite what she had meant it to be.

He practically never noticed the flowers, or the fire, or the magazines. He only sensed that the girl was flustered and fidgety, and he would begin to finger his tie and then he'd say, "Well, come on, Sugar, let's get the hell out of here. Do you want a real dinner and late for the show or a quick snack and supper afterward?"

It wasn't that she didn't know or want love. Her attitude toward it was motivated by the same feeling which caused her sometimes to buy a beautiful and quite unsuitable hat which she never wore. She would place it on the hat stick in the closet and look at it admiringly from time to time, as one gazes at a flower on its stalk without ever wanting to pluck it or wear it. Certain lovely things were not for her, but she could look at them and even touch them, sensuously. Continued, this was going to be bad for her nerves, she half suspected.

The men, after six months or a year or even two years of confidences and fun and banter and some desultory or episodic love-making, would vanish for a month or more, reappear with affectionate protestations, vanish for a still longer period, then turn up one day with, "Look, Blix, I want you to meet Nancy"—or Gay or Bee or Ernestine. And there, twinkling up at her, would be a little something with lashes and Dubonnet nails and a dimpled mouth and shrewd eyes, and they would say, both, that Blix must be the very first person to have dinner at the apartment as soon as they were settled. The dimpler would add, "Ben has talked so much about you I honestly was jealous." But the look accompanying these honeyed words said as plainly as though the words themselves had been spoken, "I see now I needn't have worried."

After the wedding—she always sent a nicer present than she really could afford—they did ask her to dinner. Dimples, at the telephone, said, "We're not asking anybody else. Just the three of us. We're being selfish because we want you all to ourselves. We'll have a good visit and really get acquainted."

Blix never had had the courage to say that the very idea bored her glassy-eyed. She came, cooed over the new furnishings, admired the bedroom of which Dimples seemed to make quite a point (or maybe it was her own warped imagination, Blix told herself, chidingly). These grisly evenings did not really poison her, however, for next day she would regale Hedda with the choicest bits. She wasn't bitter about it; she was just terribly factual and devastatingly right.

"She wore a negligee of the kind I haven't seen since *Lulu Belle*. The bedroom looked like a big pink bassinet and the living room's modern with plumbing pipes and lots of glass and beige. She spent most of the evening telling the story of the struggle Ben had had to get her away from another man who had threatened to kill her if she married anyone else. Ben believes it. Roast beef and drugstore ice cream. I went home and patted all my furniture. It was heavenly to stand there in the middle of my living room and be alone. Ben's thin, you know, or used to be, but he's acquired a funny little stomach from conjugal happiness or drugstore ice cream or lack of exercise or something. He looked like a lead pencil that has swallowed an olive."

Hedda Gale laughed, as Blix had meant she should. Then said the wise Hedda, who was not only as good as she was beautiful, but better, "There's more here than meets the eye. You're too vehement and explicit about all this, honey. You're not trying to justify yourself, are you?"

"What we used to call sour grapes back home in Sausalito? Before emotions were all explained in terms of psychiatry?"

"We-e-ell, if you weren't such a dear, and wonderful, I'd say it might be something like that."

"You're wrong. If ever I see a man I really want to marry I'll hit him over the head and drag him to my lair before he knows what struck him."

"No, you won't. You'll pile up obstacles against your emotional door."

"Oh, you make me tired since you've been going to that Austrian mumbo-jumbo man. I can manage my own life without a soul doctor, thank you."

"That's what you think," retorted Hedda, who had a pretty good husband and two nice children with braces on their front teeth.

So then suddenly Blix was thirty-one, a big-boned, rather distinguished-looking woman with a wistful quality at variance with her size, and a liking for the poems of Emily Dickinson. No use kidding myself, she told herself. I'm an old maid, no matter what they call it. And, she said, a woman who doesn't get the kind of husband she wants by the time she's thirty is a failure, no matter how successful.

The girls she knew or had known were thirtyish, too, and had married. They had quit their jobs or they had vanished for a surprisingly brief period, to emerge with figures only slightly less slim, an eye on their diet and stories of how the baby was the smartest or the biggest or the pink-and-whitest or the hairiest of any baby the hospital had produced in its

history. They then showed pictures as they sipped their luncheon cocktails.

Blix wasn't frightened. She was thoughtful. The new girls who had unimportant jobs in the office seemed incredibly young and pert and they
thought hats were as dated as red flannel underwear—in fact, they wore
red flannel underwear for skiing, but no hats. You had to be an acrobat,
Blix thought grimly, to adjust yourself to life, which now was conducted
like a two-way traffic street.

She took a good look around inside herself. At this rate, she thought,
what's the best that can happen? In another five years I probably will have
Hedda's job, though I don't really want it. I'll then be able to have a five-
room apartment instead of three, but I don't want that, either. Three dinner dresses instead of two. Buy a good picture for over the mantel. I don't
want that, either.

The next time Ben and Dimples asked her to dinner, "Just the three of
us, pot luck, and we'll have a cozy talk," Blix replied over the safe distance
of the telephone, cold:

"Three of us, me eye! I'm a gal that's got her own way to make. We
know everything we want to know about each other. You tell Ben to pull
up his socks," she continued with deliberate coarseness, "and get an extra
man for me if you want me to come to dinner. And none of those snuffy
old boys with livers. While I'm up I may as well tell you that I don't want
pot luck, either. I'm company and hard to get. Delicacies. Aspics. Soufflés.
Vintage wines. Birds. I know Ben's salary."

Dimples tittered nervously. "Blix, you're a sketch."

Blix said, "Tell Ben to come to the phone." She then repeated it for
Ben. As she talked she thought: This must have been rankling in me for
years.

When she had finished, Ben was silent for a moment with that silence
which, over the telephone, is deeper than the tomb. Then he said thoughtfully, "That's telling 'em. All right. Orders are orders. I'll try to get Mark
Speed. He doesn't go to dinners, but anyway I'll try. Do you know him?
. . . Uh, say, Blix, you sound different. What's come over you?"

"Light. A clear, white light."

Mark Speed, eh! Well, that was more like it. Mark Speed, the brilliant
bad boy of the Big Three magazines. There was the solid one published
for the Big Business Boys at a dollar a copy. It was called *Power*. There
was the newsy one for clubwomen and for men who say, "I don't get time
to read." Its name was *Now*. The third, for people who couldn't read at all,
evidently, was made up entirely of illustrations. It was called *See*. The

circulation of each was enormous, the advertising fabulous, the editorial staff so high-powered that they were said to give out sparks when touched by ordinary fingers. Mark Speed was associate editor; Blix knew about him: a terrific salary as magazine editors' salaries are reckoned; a reputation for ruthlessness, inventiveness, rudeness, brilliance, unconventionality.

She wore her new dinner dress which came up to her throat and down to the floor, giving a false effect of severe simplicity until you realized that it was designed to show up the wearer's figure like a Rubens nude. Long legs, flat hips, firm, proportionate waist, small round bosom, broad shoulders, she looked at once arresting and provocative, a protean feat more than which no woman can ask.

She planned to be late, which was naïve of her. Mark Speed was there. He was not wearing dinner clothes. They had all had a cocktail. Dimples looked baffled. Speed said, without waiting for an introduction, "An entrance, by God! I didn't know they made them any more. Very nice, too."

"All for you," said Blix in her lowest and quietest voice, but giving it all the vibrance she could manage without sounding tremolo.

Lamely, Ben stumbled along with the introduction. "Blix, this is Mark Speed. Miss Blix Carewe."

"I suppose if you'd been a boy she'd have named you McTeague, eh?"

"I didn't know anyone read him any more except us Californians."

"It's been years. Probably couldn't wade through him now. Must have another look some time. *The Pit*, maybe."

"My name book's kind of soppy now. I tried to get interested after a couple of—well—decades, if you must know. But kind of terrible."

"Say, what the hell are you two talking about!" yelled Ben. "I haven't made sense out of anything you've said since Blix came in."

Mark Speed explained graciously. "We're talking literachoor, you big baboon. You wouldn't know about Frank Norris."

The dinner was definitely fancy. Speed said, "I can't understand why women put snarls of whipped cream on top of otherwise decent food. It must date back to pioneer days when cream was scarce. Or maybe it's the bourgeois blight of the women's magazines."

Dimples looked as though she might cry. "It's my fault if you don't like it," Blix hastily confessed. "I demanded a company dinner."

"Shows what you know about men. Women's idea of company food is vile. Now, men——"

"Thick steaks, French-fried, large coffee, and any dessert that's chocolate," chanted Blix.

"Now men," Speed went on, relentlessly, "don't like a lot of things, including wisecracking women."

"I ordered you, too," Blix murmured. "Seems as though everything I do is a failure."

Dimples struck out desperately in the dark. "You two children stop. You know you're crazy about each other." Vaguely she sensed that some strange chemical was working in reverse between these two.

Ben laughed the hollow laugh of the uncomfortable host. "What's the matter with you folks?"

"Sex antagonism," Blix announced calmly.

Speed leaned forward, speaking very slowly and looking her straight in the eye. "Look, Blix, I'm not a marrying man. You may as well know it now and spare your ammunition."

Dimples gave a little scream which she tried to muffle with a giggle, deceiving no one. But then, no one knew she was present by now.

Blix leaned back in her chair, instinctively reversing her adversary's method. Her voice was gentle, almost caressing; her lids came down a little over her eyes as she returned his gaze. "I'm a marrying woman, Mr. Speed."

"Then why aren't you married—at your age?"

A little silence fell upon the table. Blix's hand reached toward him across the table with a little gesture of appeal, of reasonableness. "But I only met you tonight."

For the rest of the evening all was as merry as a funeral knell. Speed criticized the furniture as he had the food, brutally; but his heart wasn't in it. For Blix had fallen silent. "Why do people jam their flats with the kind of furniture they see in interior-decorating magazines? Some precious boy opens a shop in Fifty-seventh Street full of Victorian gyps he found in a junk store in Newark. Next thing you know there's a picture of it in *Home and Humbug,* and next thing after that it's right here."

The palpable unfairness of this even the distracted bride could refute. "Pardon me, Mr. Speed, but this room is done in modern."

Blix waited. If he says, "What makes you think so?" or something completely malicious and rotten like that, he's a really twisted fellow and I want no part of it. She waited.

"So it is. And mighty nice, too. . . . That reminds me. I brought you a thing." He disappeared into the entrance hall; he returned with a brown-paper parcel, which he ripped open. He then walked to the mantel and placed squarely in the center of it (first displacing a gimcrack) a superb and authentic head done by Mrovic. Immediately the fireplace, the wall, the whole room took on distinction and authority.

"It's darling!" cried Dimples. She didn't know what it was, but even she sensed that it was right and good.

"Say, Speed, that's darned nice of you. It just fits this room, doesn't it, Blix?" Blix said nothing. The thing was stunning—and valuable.

"It fits any room," Speed snarled. He looked at Blix. "You've played this quiet, mysterious stuff long enough. Speak, sibyl, if that's what you're waiting for. Give out."

"It's so glorious, Mr. Speed, that I forgive you everything."

"That's big of you. Ten years from now it'll be worth ten times what it is now."

"Is that why you bought it?"

"Sure. Isn't that all right? Ten years from now Ben may be out on his ear."

But by now she felt that she knew him. Knew him deeply. She looked at him quietly, with satisfaction. Carelessly assembled features, carelessly assembled dress, but both were fundamentally good and right, like the figure on the mantel. He looks a little like Lincoln, but his ears stick out, and not enough compassion. Maybe that will come later, when he loosens up. He's been hurt worse than I have, and he's even more scared. He fights, not because he's been hit, but because he's afraid he will be. She felt herself stirred as she sat there looking at him—stirred, too, by purely masculine outward things—his ankle in its neat black lisle sock, his big foot in the rather worn-looking black oxford into which he evidently never put shoe trees. When I'm his wife I'll put trees in his shoes every night. His hand, holding a cigarette, was relaxed yet vital. He'll always drop ashes on the carpet, she thought. I mustn't care. He's like a little boy who won't take your hand when he's crossing the street. This, Blix, my girl, is it. God help you!

"It's been awfully nice, Dimples, I've loved it. Ben, I've got to go—working gal, you know. Good night, Mr. Speed." She moved toward the hall.

"I'll take you home."

"Thanks. That's sweet of you."

"Don't thank men for common courtesies."

"I use the same etiquette toward men as toward women, when they're politely attentive. What do the women you know do? Roll their eyes and simper!"

She did not see him or hear from him again for two months. It was April when he telephoned her. She felt her heart turn over like a great lumpish thing that had been sleeping. Then it began to whirl so that she pressed her hand over it as though to quiet it. I didn't know people really did that, she thought.

"Look, I'm driving up to Connecticut Sunday, rain or shine. Want to go? We'll have a late lunch at a good place I know. I want to look at some houses."

"Oh, are you buying a house in Connecticut?"

"What's it to you!"

His car was good, though battered, like his suit and his hat. His driving was rather erratic. She had a little car of her own and she found herself stiffening when he missed fenders by fractions and ignored his side of the road and jammed on the brakes instead of calculating distances.

"Just stop being executive," he said. "And relax. This is Sunday. You're not nagging a lot of office girls."

"But I haven't said a syllable."

"Just the same, I could feel you draped over the steering wheel like a hoop skirt."

"Isn't it heavenly, the way we get each other's vibrations!"

It was cold in the Connecticut countryside, but the promise of spring was in the air. He seemed to know the region; he talked about it; his ancestors had been New Englanders who had abandoned the rocky fields for the grateful black loam of the Midwest. There was a house up here one of them had lived in; he had heard it was for sale; he began to describe it. She closed her eyes and sat quiet, quiet, while the sound of his voice flowed over her, laved her. His voice took on the rising inflection, he ceased to talk; she opened her eyes, she realized with a start that he had asked her a question.

"You haven't heard a damn word I've said. You weren't even listening."

"I was listening to your voice," she said. "I've been so hungry for the sound of it."

"Sensual little puss, aren't you?"

"Yes."

"It'll make a slave of you when you fall in love."

"I'll manage—when the time comes."

Because they were afraid of each other they advanced warily, retreated, crept forward again cautiously. She did not cross him, she was deliberately feminine, she talked little, she talked about him and about herself a little. She was attracted to this man against all reason; it was a thing about which she herself needed to make no decision; it was made for her by a force inside herself. She felt that she understood him; she wanted him to understand her.

"That's lovely," she would say of a house as they flashed by. "Is yours like that?"

"It isn't mine. My people left it to rot for about fifty years. And a bunch of Hunkies have been living in it for another fifty. From what the agent said, it now looks like the second act of *Tobacco Road*."

It did, too. The gate drooped on rusty hinges, the doorstep sagged; laths showed through the broken plaster, the cellar stairs were a trap; no bathroom; no electricity. He went through it in ominous silence: boxlike bedrooms, low-ceilinged living room, scabrous kitchen.

"The kiss of death," he said.

"It isn't. It's lovely—or could be if——"

"I know. Chintz and knock out partitions and turn the kitchen into the living room because of the fine old fireplace—which isn't there. Women are always doing that—in the stories."

"They're always doing it because it can be done. I could make this place into a dream house."

"What have you got to do with it?"

"Me? Whatever you say."

He said nothing. He went out to the sagging front entrance. She followed him. They stood there a moment in the sharp afternoon air of early April. She gave a little cry and pointed. "The view!" she said. "The barn cuts off the view!"

There across the road, staring straight back at them, was a big red barn, a huge red barn, a barn on which some farmer ancestor had spent all the time and money that might have gone into the house. It was dilapidated now, discolored with wind and weather and cow droppings; tufts of sour hay stuck out of cracks between the boards. Beyond it, to the south, you knew there was a heartbreaking vista of valley and hill and sky, but the barn blocked it almost completely so that you got only a tantalizing hint from east and west. Blix ran down the steps and down the road to the left for perhaps sixty feet. She pointed then due south, and her voice was high and excited. "It's heaven! You can even get a sliver of the Sound, like a sword, all shiny. The barn! You'll have to tear it down."

"Don't be silly," he said, strolling down the path toward her. "That's a perfectly good barn—or will be, with a little siding and a coat of paint. I'm going in and have a look at it."

"Me, too. Though if there are mice I won't stay."

"Rats, I'd say."

The door, swung open, almost fell on them and the entrance floor boards had rotted so that they had to step high and warily. He took it at a leap, leaving her to scramble up as best she could. She waited. She said plaintively, "Because I'm tall and broad-shouldered men never help me in and out of things, or up and down."

He turned back and held out his hand for hers outstretched toward him. "Itsy-bitsy dirly, eh?"

She swung herself up to his side, keeping her hand clasped in his. "Yes. I want you to feel protective toward me. I want to be treated as though I'm fragile and precious."

"Want to be kissed that way?"

"No."

"Well, I just thought I'd ask first."

He kissed her with thoroughness, intensity, and surprising expertness. She felt her bones turn liquid; she felt the muscles of his back turn solid. She opened her eyes and pushed the hair back from her forehead and started rather stumblingly to say something glib. "Sh-sh!" he whispered, as though to a dear child.

Yet five minutes later they were bickering again.

"Damned if the whole frame of this barn isn't hand-hewn and put together with wooden pegs. There isn't a nail in it. It's a museum piece. The craftsmen who made this don't exist any more."

"Move it."

"There's a foundation with stone blocks like the Pyramids."

"Use it as a walled garden right in front of the house. Blue delphiniums against the old gray stone." She took his hand and led him to the open barn door; she waved toward the panorama that now lay faintly rose-tinted in the glow from the west. "That, seen from the house, against a foreground of the garden—it would knock your eye out!"

"Spoken like a true editor of a fashion magazine. My only reason for thinking of buying this place is that this barn can house about twelve baby beef. Pasture them for about a year and a half and sell them for about ten times what you paid for them."

She stared in shocked unbelief. "You can't mean you're really thinking of leaving this barn standing here in front of us—uh—you, forever."

"Us—if you can take it."

She thought: A barn—you don't let a barn interfere with the most thrilling thing that ever came into your life. "I'll nag about it."

"Won't do you any good."

"You're going to be a terrible guy to be married to."

"You're what the insurance boys call a bad risk, yourself."

"I'll be one of those wives who say, 'I don't know why Mark acts like that when he's out in company. He's so sweet when we're alone.'"

"Oh, stop your wisecracking. You've got me. Relax." His arms were about her again. She relaxed.

Through April and May they drove up every week end. There was some maddening uncertainty about the clearance of the land title, and for a month or more they thought the sale was blocked. They brought up a kitchen table, a couple of chairs, a lamp; sometimes it was nine o'clock before they thought of dinner and the drive home. She sketched plans; they conferred for hours with the local builder who turned out to be something of an architect as well.

"A hundred acres of land and a house like this, and you've got 'em licked," Mark said grimly.

"Got who licked?"

"The world."

"You talk about the world as if it were your enemy, or a thug waiting to bop you over the head when you turn the corner. You're so busy looking for something to rise up and hit you that you never see the sky—or hardly ever."

"Yeah. I know. 'It isn't raining rain—it's raining vi-o-lets.' Look, gal, these are tough times. Most people just go stumbling down the middle of the road and let life roll over them like a truck."

"Darling, I know you've got to be practical. But you've got to be impractical, too, sometimes. Because first thing you know life is over, and you haven't seen the apple blossoms because the barn has always been in the way."

"Oh, my God! Are you back on that again? In parables!"

The apple blossoms, always late in this Connecticut high country, were swelling now. With any luck and a few sunny days, they would be out by next week. The deed had been signed, the first payment had been made, the house was theirs; they were to be married the first week in June; they planned to spend the honeymoon and all week ends at the little Deer Run Inn near by and concentrate on the remodeling of the farm.

"By the first of August we ought to be in," Blix said. "Maybe we could even camp in one of the bedrooms if they finish it first. Nobody minds getting up early in the summer. We could catch the eight o'clock into town. Sweating in an office all day doesn't matter if you've got this to come to at night."

That next week when they drove up the miracle had happened. The slopes, the orchard meadows, the valley as far as the eye could see were atoss with clouds of apple blossoms, pink and white. Waves of scent were wafted to them as they drove up the last hill toward the house. "Oh, Mark!" she cried. "Oh, Mr. Speed! Oh, sir!"

"It's just a little thing," he said modestly. "I ran it up for you during the week. I'm glad you like it."

The builder was waiting for them; his plans and sketches wanted their final approval. He pointed with the strong, spare hand of the craftsman carpenter. "This comes down, it'll give you a thirty-foot living room. . . . Three bedrooms; course, the guest room'll be small, but you don't want it too comfortable; they'll want to stay on you. . . . Gives you a good bathroom and a toilet and shower for the other room. . . . Build on here and gives you the lib'ry you wanted where the pantry was, and we can shut the kitchen part off."

Noon became afternoon. They had brought sandwiches from town; they munched as they walked and talked. Inside and outside; the shed, the fence, the barn. The barn. Below it, on the other side of it, shut out by it from the windows which would be the living room and their bedroom, the waves of apple blossoms tossed in the summer breeze.

"Now, the barn," the builder said. "I been all over it. It's a good barn; with a frame like that it'll stand you another hundred years. I'd advise a cement floor if you're really going to experiment with baby beef, and some stalls, and cut a window in the west end here. She ain't even rotted any to speak of."

Blix turned from the barn doorway where she had been standing. The two men were scraping bits of heavy wooden beams and joists with their knives for signs of decay. "Look at that view, Mr. Borglum. You can't even see it from the front of the house. Couldn't the barn be moved? Couldn't it?"

"I wouldn't advise it. Besides, the foundation's your stalls. Hay up here."

"How much would it cost to build a new one?"

Mr. Borglum poked Mark with his thumb; he waxed jovial. "Sa-ay, now we're talking! How about it, Mr. Speed? Fifteen hundred dollars—two thousand at the outside—build you the nicest little twelve-stall barn——"

Mark threw down his cigarette and stepped on it. "If we're going up back to look at that cedar stand in the north woods we'd better start. It's getting late."

Mr. Borglum knew when he was licked. "All right. You coming, Miss Carewe? It's kind of wet underfoot back there."

"No. I'll stay here. There are lots of things I want to see. I want to poke around the house. I've never been up in the attic, except for one quick look."

They were off; their backs said they were glad to be rid of her, two men walking, strong-sinewed, across the soft spring fields. She lighted a cigarette; she stood in the barn doorway a moment, looking out across the fragrant white valley to the hills beyond. It was unutterably lovely; her feeling of frustration and wrong rose like a sour cud in her throat. In that moment—for that moment only—she hated him.

The house was chilly after the sun-drenched outer air. It was the first time she had been really alone in these rooms that were to be her home for half of every year at least. She had a feeling of someone unseen in the house, and shivered a little. The attic. She didn't much relish the idea of the attic, now that she was alone. But she had said she was going to poke around up there. Mark would ask her about hidden treasure. She remembered vague objects stuck in corners up there.

The attic stair was so narrow that the walls brushed her, and she had to stoop to avoid the ceiling. In New England attics one found quaint old love letters, stacks of Currier and Ives prints, and a trunk which, opened, gave up a ghostly store of old brocades, silk wedding gowns that, cockily, always "stood alone," and a cobwebby lace wedding veil whose tragic history was revealed in the letters.

After poking around industriously, with an eye to mice, Blix was rewarded by a treasure trove of two dented nickel lamps, both soldered and both evidently discarded because of leakage; a bundle of old newspapers tied with a string, yellow but dated Danbury, Connecticut, 1934, a singularly undistinguished year; a package of morning-glory seeds; three window screens of the sliding variety whose mesh was torn to an extent which would have admitted a sizable eagle in full flight.

Disconsolately she wandered downstairs. A glance at her watch showed that she had disposed of the attic in twelve minutes. The two men would not be back for another hour at least. As though impelled by an evil force, she wandered to the front window. The red barn stared back at her malignantly with its mean little red-rimmed eyes. It squatted, an ogre, blocking the way to beauty imprisoned.

"Here I am," it grinned with its crooked, stained mouth. "I'll always be here, mocking you, thwarting you. No matter how you twist your neck and stand on tiptoe and go to the farthest window this way and that way, the lovely view is still my prisoner. Pretty soon you'll not only hate me—you'll hate the house, you'll hate the land, you'll hate——"

Abruptly she jerked away from the window. I'll have glass curtains at the windows, and a lovely chintz with cream ground and big bunches of gay flowers; nobody will ever think of looking out at the barn. But looking out when you're indoors and seeing trees and hills, that's part of the wonderful fun of living in the country. Oh, dear, I wish I'd gone to the cedar grove with the men. Perhaps she'd better go out again; the house was damp and chilly. If only she could start a brisk little fire in the living-room fireplace.

In the wall behind the place where a stove and stovepipe evidently had been, Borglum had knocked out plaster to disclose the old fireplace, boarded up. He had strictly warned them against using it until the chimney had been cleaned. How lovely it would be when the room was complete with mahogany and pickled pine and chintz and copper and flowers— salmon pinks and blues and pale lemon and burgundy and white all mixed together in an intoxicating conflagration.

Conflagration . . . conflagration . . . conflagration. She peered into the ragged hole that soon would be the very heart of the room. Old papers and bits of plaster mingled in the blackened, neglected grate. She reached in gingerly and fished up a corner of a newspaper. It was brittle as dried paste and crumbled in her fingers. Interested, she plunged her hand into the sooty recess, and her fingers encountered a firmer surface. Gingerly she brought it forth. It was an account book, evidently. As she held it between thumb and finger, she saw stubby figures scrawled in pencil. Probably the account book of the farmer who had been responsible for the walling up of the fireplace. The figures were in the back of the book. But the front pages held writing in a fine feminine hand. The ink was faded; the pages were torn and smudged. "Heh!" said Blix, aloud. "Wait a minute!"

She crossed to the window; she stood there, turning the leaves, at first with amused curiosity, then with a concentration which flexed the line of her jaw, which hunched her shoulders, which brought her breath in and out with little unconscious gasps of excitement.

October 16: Finished gathering apples this day. Very pleasant day but cold nights. Widow Abigail Trask had her youngest son aged 12 yrs died & buried yesterday.

Jan. 11: Quite unpleasant. Invited to Mrs. Enos Godfrey to quilt but did not go. Have this day been writing to Mary, Hannah & Josephine. Abel is planning to put up the barn just across the road from the house but I am trying to persuade him not to. I cannot bear to lose the look of the valley and the bit of Long Island Sound. Abel said this is childish he says he must know the stock is near and safe on winter nights and calving time.

Blix was racing the pages now; the days, the months skimmed by under her eyes.

June 12: The apple blossoms are gone or nearly. There would have been a feather of them from the house if only the barn had not been there. like looking down on perfumed clouds it must have been. I said this to

Abel he says I am fanciful because of the child coming. It is now a very growing time, clear and warm. I changed the woolen dress for the linen.

September 23: A terrible wind storm. Jeremiah Sturgis had a poor turn this day he lies in his bed and seems to be unconscious of his situation.

November 3: Limon Godfrey made me a pair of small calfskin shoes. Foggy so that I could scarcely see the red barn. I could better imagine the dip in the valley beyond.

Jan. 18: The sermon of the Rev. Wilton Burns was Luke 14-17 Come For All Things Are Now Ready. When I heard this I felt a little discomfort for all the ladies of the congregation know that I have made everything ready for the child and my time is any day now. Eliphalet's wife afflicted with tic doloroso.

Jan. 23: Low in spirits. I think if I could see out toward the distance as I sit with my sewing I should not feel so low spirited. Sometimes I have the strangest notion that the barn is grinning at me, it is the two windows and the little loft-door below it can be said to resemble a face though of course that is foolish and fanciful of me.

Feb. 1: I have such strange thoughts lately. The child is late or it may be I reckoned wrong. With the first child Miriam says this is sometimes the case. I think of terrible things, I have thought that if it were not for the cattle in the barn I would steal out at night and burn it down, I told this to Miriam she says women are fanciful at such times she has had seven she should know. Sometimes I fancy I hate Abel.

Quietly, quietly Blix closed the little book. She stood staring at nothing. Her breast rose and fell, rose and fell as though she had been running. Then she turned her head slowly as though it moved on a rusty pivot, and she stared full at the barn across the way. Her face was set and stern.

Like a woman impelled, bewitched, she went about doing what she had to do. First she walked out of the house and stared across the upper fields toward which the two men had gone a half-hour ago. There was no sign of their return. She came through the house to the kitchen. A gallon can of kerosene stood in the pantry; they had used it for the lamps during the spring days when dusk fell early in the bare little rooms. As she carried it across the yard she thought that gasoline would have been better and more thorough, but she knew no way to drain the car tank, and besides the blast might damage the house. The wind was slight as always toward the end of the day. It was from the west, too. That was perfect.

She had to be thrifty with the fuel. The barn was big. Nimbly she stepped up into the open doorway. She must work quickly. Unscrewing the spout cap she dribbled a little moist line around the edges where wall met floor; she threw a dash into the sour, blackened hay for good measure; she made a little pool in the center of the floor and the old boards soaked it in thirstily. She lifted a double armful of the dusty hay and stuffed it into bare corners and doused the last of the kerosene upon it. She lighted four cigarettes and puffed them into a good red glow; she lighted in one sputtering orange flare all the matches remaining in the paper pack in her fingers; she tossed the little brands north, east, south, west, and dropped the match packet in the center for good measure. Then she turned and ran.

It did not blaze at once. She stood, panting, on the house steps, facing the barn. Then a pinkish glow suffused the red-rimmed eyes that were leering down on her, and then the eyes themselves became red, and there was a brisk crackling. Smoke, dark and venomous, began to pour out into the fragrant June air.

"I'm sorry, Abel, to burn the barn you built with your own strong hands. But you won't ruin my life and his as you ruined hers and yours."

That's a pretty dramatic speech, she thought. I've done a bad thing, like Lennie in the Steinbeck book. No, I've done a good thing. But maybe it's going to be very bad for me—if I tell him.

It was a beautiful scarlet-and-orange pillar now. She felt it hot on her face. She heard shouts and the bleat of the little local fire engine; she saw Mark and Borglum running across the fields, and they looked small and helpless and faintly comic. Then she began to shout, too, and run around and make gestures as the Tilbury fire-engine company in its Sunday clothes came rattling up the hill.

It was no use. It was no use from the beginning. Futile squirts of water from the hand extinguishers, for there was no place for a hose attachment. Buckets, hand to hand. Dirt shoveled on. In half an hour the dry old boards were bright embers.

Mark and Borglum came toward her, their shoulders sagging, their faces streaked with soot and dirt, their eyes red-rimmed from the smoke and heat. She looked at Mark; her face was wrung with pity; she wiped his wet and grimy forehead and cheeks with her soft scented handkerchief.

"It's no use," Borglum said. "Just let her burn out, and the boys'll watch to see she doesn't spread. Good thing the ground is wet, and no dry grass."

"Yeah. Tell them to quit fighting it," Mark said. "Nothing left to fight, anyway. Which one's the chief? I'd like to—to thank him and the others."

Borglum walked toward the lean lad in shirt sleeves with his trousers rolled high. Cars were parked all about now, and neighbors and Sunday drivers stood in clumps, drawn by the fascination of flame.

Mark peeled two ten-dollar bills from his wallet. He stared at Blix. "Those kids put up a fight. . . . How long had it been burning when you first—— Oh, well, no telephone, anyway, so what's the . . . It must have been my cigarette. I thought I'd put it out. That white house down the hill has a telephone. Did you run down there, or did they see . . . ?"

Borglum and the young fire chief were coming up the slope toward them. You needn't ever tell, Blix thought. Lie for your life. She heard herself speaking as though it were someone else. "I did it. I poured kerosene on it and lighted it."

His eyes widened and seemed to deepen in his grotesquely smudged face as he stared at her. Racked between laughter and tears, she found to her astonishment that she was crying—she who so rarely wept. The tears ran down her cheeks; she did not raise her hand to wipe them away.

Borglum and the boy were on them now. Ruefully the young fire chief rubbed the back of his wrist across his grimy face. "I sure am sorry we couldn't save her for you, Mr. Speed. She went up like she was soaked in oil, almost."

Mark handed him the two ten-dollar bills. "You and the boys did a fine job," he said. "Nothing could have saved it."

The faces of the three men turned away, in masculine discomfort, from the woman's tear-ravaged face. They surveyed the glowing bed of embers that once had been a hand-hewn barn. "Well, anyway," said Borglum, the jovial, "those hills look pretty, and the apple blossoms, now the barn's gone. Like you said. The barn cut off the view so, you didn't hardly know it was there."

The lad folded the bills in his hand. "Well, say, thanks a lot, Mr. Speed. The boys'll sure be glad to get this. We'll use it for equipment." He moved off down the slope.

Borglum began to sense the silence between these two. Vaguely uneasy, he left them with a reassuring wave of the hand. "Guess if we douse her now around the edges . . ."

Mark made as if to follow him. She caught at his arm. He shook her loose. "If you were a man I'd hit you. I may, anyway."

"Please do, darling, if you want to. I wouldn't blame you. You could get into the car and go off and leave me, and I wouldn't blame you. You could even have me arrested. Mark, I couldn't help it. There was an old diary . . . But I love you, I do; and you love me." She was almost incoherent, but what she said was sound enough.

"And if I happened to wear a tie you didn't like, you'd cut my throat. That right?"

"No! No! We'll be happy in a kind of terrible way. You'll see. But I'll always burn down the barn if it cuts off the view."

"You're crazy."

"I know. So are you. If one of us was sane it wouldn't work. That's why it's going to be wonderful. Your face is all dirty. Kiss me so that mine will be dirty, too."

ABOUT THE AUTHOR

❧ AT THE AGE OF 17 EDNA FERBER BECAME A CELEBRATED AUTHOR— celebrated, that is, in the town of Appleton, Wisconsin, where her father kept a general store. In that year she was graduated from the Ryan High School, and her graduating essays so impressed the local newspaper editor that he gave her a job as a reporter at the princely salary of $3.00 a week. In 1910 she published her first short story, The Homely Heroine. The following year, after working for a Milwaukee paper, she wrote her first novel, Dawn O'Hara. Since that time, in the course of a prodigious and happy literary career, she has completed eight more novels, five plays, and more than a hundred short stories.

Kalamazoo, Michigan, is Edna Ferber's birthplace. Connecticut is her present residence. America is her home.